The
W. Somerset Maugham
Reader

The
W. Somerset Maugham Reader

Novels, Stories, Travel Writing

Edited by
Jeffrey Meyers

TAYLOR TRADE PUBLISHING
Lanham • New York • Dallas • Boulder • Toronto • Oxford

This Taylor Trade Publishing paperback edition of *The W. Somerset Maugham Reader* is an original publication. It is published by arrangement with the author.

Published by Taylor Trade Publishing
An imprint of The Rowman & Littlefield Publishing Group, Inc.
4501 Forbes Boulevard, Suite 200
Lanham, Maryland 20706

Distributed by National Book Network

Library of Congress Cataloging-in-Publication Data

Maugham, W. Somerset (William Somerset), 1874–1965.
  [Selections. 2004]
  Th W. Somerset Maugham reader : novels, stories, travel writing /
edited by Jeffrey Meyers.— 1st Tayor Trade Pub. ed.
    p. cm.
Includes bibliographical references.
  ISBN 1-58979-072-3 (pbk. : alk. paper)
  I. Meyers, Jeffrey. II. Title.
PR6025.A86A6 2003
823'.912—dc22
                                                    2003020547

To Gill Drey

CONTENTS

Introduction		ix
Chronology		xxix
1.	From *Liza of Lambeth* (novel, 1897)	I
2.	*The Hero* (novel, 1901)	37
3.	From *Mrs. Craddock* (novel, 1902)	223
4.	From *The Land of the Blessed Virgin: Sketches and Impressions in Andalusia* (travel, 1905)	273
5.	From *The Magician* (novel, 1908)	295
6.	From *Of Human Bondage* (novel, 1915)	323
7.	From *The Moon and Sixpence* (novel, 1919)	381
8.	From *The Trembling of a Leaf: Stories of the South Sea Islands* (stories, 1921)	421
9.	From *On a Chinese Screen* (travel, 1922)	529
	Bibliography	543

INTRODUCTION

Somerset Maugham lived for nearly ninety-two years, wrote seventy-eight books and kept his faithful audience from the late Victorian era to the twenty-first century. He was obsessed by his critical reputation, carefully planned the pattern of his career and gradually phased out each of his literary genres. Somerset was adept at every kind of work he ever did: as an anthologist and as a writer of novels, stories, stage and screen plays, art and travel books, autobiographies, reportage and essays; and as a doctor, linguist, secret agent, war propagandist, government adviser, art connoisseur, philanthropist and presenter of his films.

While still in medical school at St. Thomas's Hospital, Maugham sent his first novel, *Liza of Lambeth* (1897), to an English publisher. Fisher Unwin's reader, the always perceptive Edward Garnett, immediately saw the honesty and accuracy of the novel, despite its depressing conclusion, and urged him to publish this promising new author. Referring to the original title, he observed:

A Lambeth Idyll is *a very clever realistic study of factory girl and coster life.* The women; their roughness, intemperance, fits of violence, kind-heartedness, slang—all are done truthfully. Liza and her mother Mrs. Kemp are drawn with no little humour and insight. The story is a dismal one in its ending, but the temper and tone of this book is wholesome and by no means morbid. The work is *objective*, and both the atmosphere and the environment of the mean district are unexaggerated.

Liza of Lambeth, still in print after more than a hundred years, expresses not outrage but sympathy for the oppressed working class. Maugham's medical training and obstetric experience, his observation of the effects of illness, of the way women faced pain and the certain prospect of death, gave considerable power to his sharp portrayal of slum life. Liza "was a young girl of about eighteen, with dark eyes and an enormous fringe, puffed-out and curled and frizzed, covering her whole forehead from side to side, and coming down to meet her eyebrows. She was dressed in brilliant violet, with great lappets of velvet, and she had on her head an enormous black hat covered with feathers." When an Italian organ-grinder plays in the street, the audacious Liza "lifted her skirts higher, brought in new and more difficult movements into her improvisation, kicking up her legs." She's courted by the bashful young Tom, but on a Bank Holiday picnic in the country falls for the manly, married Jim Blakeston. They meet secretly, but are discovered, and she gets pregnant. In one of the great theatrical scenes in the short novel, Liza (who's constantly observed by her neighbors) is assaulted in the crowded street by Jim's wife, who—in a feral rage—spits in her face and beats her bloody:

> The blows came down heavy and rapid all over her face and head. She put up her hands to cover her face and turned her head away, while Mrs. Blakeston kept on hitting mercilessly. . . . [She] attacked Liza madly; but the girl stood up bravely, and as well as she could gave back the blows she received. The spectators grew tremendously excited. . . . They swayed about, scratching, tearing, biting, sweat and blood pouring down their faces, and their eyes fixed on one another, bloodshot and full of rage. The audience shouted and cheered and clapped their hands.

This brutal street-fight leads to Liza's miscarriage, septicemia and death.
· 	Liza is swiftly transformed from a jolly girl wearing violet stockings and turning cartwheels to a battered drab—dying, comatose, unaware of

Tom and Jim at her bedside. Jim, not an evil Victorian seducer, wants to leave his wife and marry Liza. Liza's mother has only two ambitions in life: to get as drunk as possible and to appear respectable in the eyes of her lady-friends. When she learns that Liza is dying, she shows no emotion, but insists on a proper funeral. Liza's early death saves her from the typical fate of Lambeth women: backbreaking factory work, annual childbearing, beatings by drunken husbands and premature old age.

In June 1898 the *St. Thomas's Hospital Gazette* mentioned the publication of Anderson's *Deformities of Fingers and Toes*, a textbook written by one of their own doctors. In the same issue it proudly announced that Maugham's novel "has achieved a great and well-deserved success. It deals with one aspect of Lambeth life in a powerful and perhaps lurid way: the uncompromising vigour of both plot and style will appeal strongly to all lovers of realism." Joseph Conrad, another Unwin author and friend of Garnett, noted the novel's narrow scope and its clinical point of view: "It is certainly worth reading—but whether it's worth talking about is another question. . . . There is *any amount* of good things in the story and no distinction of any kind. It will be fairly successful I believe—for it is a 'genre' picture without any atmosphere and consequently no reader can live *in* it. He just looks on—and that is just what the general reader prefers." But Conrad underrated this youthful novel, which has a vivid heroine, a compelling atmosphere and a poignant theme.

Fifty years after its first publication George Orwell, who'd described industrial slums in *The Road to Wigan Pier*, reviewed a reprint of the novel. He praised Maugham's social realism and forceful simplicity, his depiction of "slum life in the nineties—a period when vast areas of every great town were dirty, dangerous, and poverty stricken to an extent that we can now hardly imagine." In 1948 the sixteen-year-old V.S. Naipaul, who knew about London slums only from reading Dickens, published his first work, a review of *Liza of Lambeth*, in his high school magazine in Trinidad. Maugham's blend of realism and pity, his aloof and disdainful attitude towards women, appealed to the young Naipaul:

But what, I suppose, has rescued the novel from obscurity and has made it at least fit to be included in collected editions is the study of slum life. Maugham describes the slum people with a detachment that is not without humour. His novel is free from the social realism that has imposed itself on modern literature. The women, especially, are interesting. For them life is a messy monotony of motherhood and maulings. . . . The women accept blows as normal parts of their existence.

Maugham's *The Hero* (1901), a novel with a suburban setting, begins with the return of a disillusioned wounded soldier from the Boer War in South Africa (still being fought from 1899–1902, as Maugham was writing). The bitter struggle with a fierce guerrilla enemy forms the topical background to the hero's revulsion against his family's values and customs. James Parsons' arrival is announced by telegram to his eager parents and fiancée, Mary Clibborn, who expect a great deal from him. When serving as a colonel in the Indian army, his father had trapped some hostile tribes and unwisely shown them mercy, and they had massacred his men. His career ended with a dishonorable discharge; and he counts on his son—mentioned in dispatches, wounded and recommended for the Victoria Cross—to compensate for his disgrace. When James arrives home, however, he's pale and thin, strange and silent, withdrawn and alienated. He shocks the family by defending the Boers' behavior in the war and by admitting that he'd enjoyed killing men in battle. He's lost his religious belief, and feels unable to marry.

Maugham does not describe the war (vividly reported by Winston Churchill and other correspondents in the daily press) or James' specific act of bravery under fire, nor use his war experience to deepen his character. James confesses that a friend "was killed because I tried to save him" and doesn't believe he deserves the V.C. After a promising start, the novel becomes somewhat static and filled with conventional situations and characters: young hero and doting girlfriend, degraded father and self-effacing mother who are "cruel in their loving kindness."

The Hero satirizes the petty and prejudiced, stifling and snobbish society of a small Kentish village. Maugham zeroes in on the unpleasant character of Mary, James' self-righteous fiancée. She's hopelessly ignorant, yet rigidly opinionated; priggish, yet aggressively virtuous, she nurses the wounded soldiers, but makes them uncomfortable and disobeys the doctor's orders. A complete killjoy, she believes the village girls ought—for their own moral and spiritual welfare—"to be utterly miserable." James' parents, Mary's family and the vicar all pressure him to marry her. James' psychological trauma and resulting conflict becomes narrowly focused on whether he'll marry his fiancée or give himself to a widow in London. Unlike the unctuous Mary, she's a sexually experienced lover whose mere touch makes him "mad with passion." Realizing that he doesn't love Mary (and probably never did), James breaks their engagement. But when he gets enteric fever and she nurses him devotedly, he proposes again and is again accepted.

Finally, as he begins to hate her and to find her physically repellent, James decides to shoot himself rather than be forced to marry her. In another nasty twist, Mary's mother, who's been cruel to her and has become her sexual rival, convinces herself that James has shot himself because he loved *her*. Maugham scarcely develops the promising subject of the novel: the return of an alienated and traumatized hero, or the true sexual and social struggle within James: his loathing of domesticity and fear of women. The resolution is more depressing than tragic. Maugham later told his agent that "it was one of my earliest novels, it was not a success when it came out, and I don't believe it has any merit at all." But his judgment was too severe. *The Hero* is as good as *The Explorer* (1908), which has a similar theme and which he later reprinted, and is much better than his late historical novels.

Like *The Hero, Mrs. Craddock* (1902) portrays a disillusioned lover and the conflict between desire and duty. Maugham gives the subject a fresh look by switching the sex of the main character, but goes far beyond *The Hero* in treating the conflict between sexual desire and social constraints. Bertha Ley is a willful, independent young woman who gets trapped in a miserable marriage. Brought up in Europe by a rackety father, she inherits his neglected estate in Kent and falls in love with her tenant farmer, the "intensely masculine" Edward Craddock. Drawn to his farmyard odor (subtly contrasted to that of the vicar, Mr. Glover, "a somewhat feminine edition of his sister, but smelling in the most remarkable fashion of antiseptics"), Bertha aggressively courts him, and outrages her genteel neighbors by marrying him—only to realize she's made a terrible mistake. The ox-like, practical Craddock turns out to be an unresponsive lover. Bertha needs a man with intellectual interests, but he's hopelessly dense, ignorant, callous, selfish, pompous and socially pretentious. Ironically, her neighbors, unaware of his true character, praise his work on the estate and think he's a splendid husband. Bertha becomes pregnant and gives birth to a stillborn child, "naked and very small, hardly human, repulsive, yet very pitiful." The loss of her child leads to the loss of her religious faith, and in a scene that shocked contemporary readers she calls God "either impotent or cruel. . . . It's God who needs my forgiveness—not I His. . . . If God made me suffer like that it's infamous. . . . How can you imagine Him to be so stupid, so cruel?"

The novel shifts direction when Bertha leaves Craddock, goes to Italy and falls in love with her younger distant cousin, Gerald Vaudrey, who's described in a distinctly androgynous fashion: "He was quite a boy, very slight and not so tall as Bertha, with a small, girlish face. He had a tiny nose, but it was very straight, and his somewhat freckled complexion was admirable. His hair was dark and curly; he wore it long, evidently aware that it was very nice." Torn between instinct and convention, Bertha reluctantly returns to her husband, who tactfully agrees not to make any sexual demands. Like D. H. Lawrence's lonely and sexually starved Connie Chatterley, gazing at her naked self in a mirror, Bertha expresses her newly awakened passion by swimming naked in the sea: "Timidly, rapidly, she slipped off her clothes, and looking round to see that there was really no one in sight, stepped in; the wavelets about her feet made her shiver a little, and then with a splash, stretching out her arms, she ran forward, and half fell, half dived into the water. . . . It was an unknown pleasure to swim unhampered by a bathing-dress."

When Craddock suddenly dies and Bertha is finally free, she expresses Maugham's negative view of marriage: "husband and wife know nothing of one another. However ardently they love, however intimate their union, they are never one; they are scarcely more to one another than strangers." The intoxication of love is inevitably followed by bitter disappointment. But if Bertha has a right to choose for herself, she must also have the right to change her mind when that choice turns out to be wrong. Maugham punishes Bertha by making her baby die, and conveniently kills off Craddock in a riding accident. Dead babies, accidents and suicides crop up rather too often in Maugham's (as in Forster's) early novels.

Maugham not only challenged sexual conventions by arguing for Bertha's right to sexual gratification. He also dared to describe a marriage between an upper-class woman and a lower-class man and declared that sexual pleasure was essential for happiness. *Mrs. Craddock* was considered scandalous at the time, and Maugham had to take out shocking passages before Heinemann would agree to publish it. These deleted passages, restored in the 1955 edition, included Bertha's condemnation of God after her baby is stillborn and the frank expression of her adulterous sexual desire: "her very flesh cried out, and she trembled at the thought that she could give Gerald the inestimable gift of her body. . . . She did not try to hide her passion now, she clasped him to her heart. . . . Their kiss was rapture, madness; it was ecstasy beyond description, complete surrender."

Mrs. Craddock, for all its faults, is a trailblazing novel. D.H. Lawrence was influenced by the striking scene where Bertha experiences the sudden revival of her old passion as she washes her husband's dead body: "The touch of the cold flesh made her shudder voluptuously: she thought of him taking her in his strong arms, kissing her on the mouth. She wrapped him in the white shroud and surrounded him with flowers. They placed him in the coffin, and her heart stood still." A decade later, Lawrence brilliantly developed this passage in "Odour of Chrysanthemums" (1911).

The novel continued to haunt Lawrence, who took up Maugham's subject in his late masterpiece *Lady Chatterley's Lover* (1928) (Connie Chatterley's surname incorporates Bertha's). But Lawrence, who wanted to reclaim heterosexual love and place it at the center of civilization, argues against Maugham's conclusions. Maugham gave an unconvincing description of sexual passion: "Bertha, desire burning within her like a fire, had flung herself into her husband's arms, loving as the beasts love—and as the gods." Lawrence, by contrast, set out to describe the real thing, using the dialect of the gamekeeper Mellors to express the tenderness and physical responsiveness of the lovers. Like Maugham's, his novel was bowdlerized for many years. While Maugham emphasized the social contrast between the couple and the disastrous results of a high-born woman's love for a working-class man, Lawrence's great novel uses his lovers to argue for a radical change in consciousness and for the triumph of life over the destructive forces of the modern world. He goes beyond the lovers themselves to consider the rigidity of the class structure, the horrors of industrialism, the effects of war and the decayed state of English civilization. Maugham's Craddock becomes a country squire, while Lawrence's Mellors remains loyal to his background and class. In Maugham's novel the result of love is a stillborn child and sexual revulsion. Lawrence's ends with Connie's pregnancy as sexual love transcends class through the "democracy of touch."

After publishing *Liza of Lambeth,* in September 1897, and passing his medical exams the following month, Maugham had fulfilled a long-standing ambition. Establishing a dominant pattern in his life—constant travel and prolonged residence abroad—he went to live in Seville for sixteen months. Maugham had a talent for languages. He'd learned Greek and Latin at school, French in Paris, German in Heidelberg, Italian and Russian on Capri, and now studied Spanish in Seville. In his account of his first visit to Spain in *The Land of the Blessed Virgin: Sketches and Impressions in Andalusia,* published eight years later in 1905, he joyfully wrote that the country had liberated him from all imprisoning ties: "To myself Seville means ten times more than it can mean to others. I came to it after weary years in London, heartsick with much hoping, my mind dull with drudgery; and it seemed a land of freedom. There I became at last conscious of my youth."

Maugham lived on the Calle Guzmán el Bueno in the elegant Santa Cruz district, socialized with the British vice-consul, Edward Johnston, and dedicated *Orientations* (1899) to Johnston's wife. He grew a mustache, puffed Filipino cigars, strummed the guitar, wore a black, wide-brimmed Córdoba hat and swaggered down the narrow, sinuous Sierpes like a true *hidalgo.* He described the Moorish fortress, the cathedral with its famous belltower, La Giralda, the hospital and jail as well as the squalid gypsies and grotesque beggars. To extract the essence of Andalusian life, he repeatedly returned to the bullfights, though that grim spectacle filled him with loathing and horror. In those days, before the picadors' horses wore protective padding, they were frequently gored and spilled their entrails onto the hot sand.

At a time when few Englishmen visited Spain, Maugham wanted to see the very heart of the region, "that part of the country which had preserved its antique character, where railway trains were not, and the horse, the mule, the donkey were still the only means of transit. . . . I set out in the morning early, with saddle-bags fixed on either side and poncho strapped to my pommel. A loaded revolver, though of course I never had a chance to use it, made me feel pleasantly adventurous." He traveled alone and in considerable discomfort through the wild, deserted and impoverished countryside. On a journey of 150 miles, he rode northeast through Carmona and La Luisiana to Écija, and then back to Seville through Marchena and Mairena. He also traveled to Ronda, Córdoba, Granada, Jerez, Cádiz and Tangier in Morocco.

Maugham tried to interpret the Spanish character for an English audience. His main sources were Théophile Gautier's *Journey to Spain* (1845), Richard Ford's *Handbook for Travellers in Spain* (1845), Stanley Lane-Poole's *The Moors in Spain* (1893), the current Baedeker and his firsthand experience. He made generalizations which tended to reinforce clichés about the country: the Andalusian character (after nearly 800 years of Moorish occupation) is rich with Oriental strains; a realistic attitude to life is "the most conspicuous of Spanish traits"; Spain is highly traditional, a stronghold of antiquated customs, a place of somberness and gravity. The girls are beautiful in youth, often ugly in middle age. The people are lazy and vain, the food—thin soups, tough steaks, revolting sauces, disgusting innards and rancid oils—abominable.

The Spanish-American War, which finally destroyed the Spanish empire, was then being fought in Cuba. With his doctor's clinical eye Maugham described the wounded soldiers, sent home to die: "what struck me most was the deathly colour; for their faces were almost green, while round their sunken eyes were great white rings, and the white was ghastly, corpse-like." This objective writing clashed with the remnants of his ornate and stilted style, especially when he tried to describe passion. Speaking of his beloved—who may have been a young man—Maugham gushingly wrote: "It was not love I felt for you, Rosarito; I wish it had been; but now far away, in the rain, I fancy (oh no, not that I am at last in love) but perhaps that I am just faintly enamoured—of your recollection." His description of a sexual encounter with a prostitute in

Granada was much more convincing. When she took off her clothes he was shocked to find she was only thirteen and had been driven to sell herself by hunger. He paid her, but could not bring himself to have sex with her.

The paradoxical theme of the book—as in Baudelaire's "Voyage à Cythère" and Huysmans' *Against the Grain*—is that the traveler's idealistic expectations are inevitably destroyed by actual experience: "It is much better to read books of travel than to travel oneself; he really enjoys foreign lands who never goes abroad; and the man who stays at home, preserving his illusions, has certainly the best of it. How delightful is the anticipation as he looks over time-tables and books of photographs, forming delightful images of future pleasure! But the reality is full of disappointment, and the more famous the monument the bitterer the disillusion." Yet Maugham's awareness of the negative aspects of travel never stood in the way of his own obsessive journeys. He makes a neat point, but does not really subscribe to it.

D.H. Lawrence made travel writing subjective by emphasizing the author's personal experience and point of view: what he saw and what happened to him. Maugham kept his intimate feelings—his friendships, loves and longings—quite hidden. He seemed to be watching an operatic spectacle instead of actually participating in the life around him. Merimée's *Carmen* and Manet's paintings had revealed Spain's powerful influence on French culture in the nineteenth century. Gerald Brenan and Robert Graves moved to Spain after the Great War, and the Spanish Civil War aroused passionate feelings, but English writers did not really discover the country until well after World War II. Maugham anticipated this interest and—between Richard Ford's *Handbook* in 1845 and Gerald Brenan's *South from Granada* in 1957—wrote the best English travel book on Spain.

The Magician (1908), a flawed but intriguing novel, is the story of Oliver Haddo, a character based on Aleister Crowley, whom Maugham met through the painter Gerald Kelly when they were all living in Paris in 1905. The son of a rich brewer and Plymouth Brother who left him a substantial fortune, Crowley, a self-styled Satanist, claimed to be a reincarnation of the Great Beast in Revelations 11:7, "that ascendeth out of the bottomless pit [to] make war against them, and shall overcome them, and kill them." After the Great War, he settled in Sicily with a group of disciples. But rumors of drugs, orgies and magical ceremonies involving the sacrifice of infants led to his expulsion from Italy and earned his long-sought reputation for evil. He married Kelly's pretty sister Rose under strange circumstances. She was engaged to one man and involved with another, yet eloped with Crowley the day after they met. She came under his evil influence, and was the model for Margaret Daunce in *The Magician*. Nuit, his daughter by Rose, died of typhoid fever in Rangoon, Burma, at the age of two. Both Rose and his second wife, Maria Teresa, became alcoholics and were committed to insane asylums.

In *A Moveable Feast*, when Hemingway spots "the gaunt man in the cape with the tall woman [who] passed us on the sidewalk" in Paris, a friend tells him: "That's Aleister Crowley, the diabolist. He's supposed to be the wickedest man in the world." Yeats, who tangled with Crowley in mystical circles, called him " 'a person of unspeakable life,' already embroiled in homosexual scandal." Maugham told Christopher Isherwood that "he hadn't known many really evil men. The only two he could think of offhand were Aleister Crowley and Norman Douglas," who was a notorious pedophile. Maugham took an instant dislike to Crowley, though Crowley interested and amused him, and in the novel made Oliver Haddo even more sinister and ruthless. Crowley really was an accomplished big-game hunter and mountaineer, and had climbed K2, the second-highest peak in India, without using oxygen. But he was a liar and fake, and when he claimed to be starving and urgently cabled him, begging for £25, Maugham refused.

In 1907 Maugham sent the completed novel to his agent J.B. Pinker with a note that harshly concluded that it "is very dull and stupid; I wish I were an outside Broker, or [the popular novelist] Hall Caine, or something equally despicable." He also told Kelly about the difficulty of getting it into print. It was originally accepted, printed and advertised by Methuen. The head of the firm then read it, broke into a cold sweat and swore that publication of such an outrageous work would ruin Maugham as well as the publisher. Maugham thought of having it appear anonymously, but finally persuaded Heinemann to bring it out.

In *The Magician* Arthur Burdon, an established young English surgeon on a study trip to Paris, visits his fiancée, Margaret Dauncey. A vivacious and exquisitely beautiful art student, she lives with her friend Susie Boyd. Burdon, with an unusual capacity for suffering, fears that something terrible will occur to spoil their happiness. Their nemesis is the extremely tall and obese Oliver Haddo. Educated at Eton and Oxford, he speaks with fake grandiloquence, is consumed by a lust for evil knowledge and has formidable powers of magic. He makes a horse tremble by touching it, feels no pain when bitten by a snake and sets water on fire. His evil ambition is to create living beings, and he succeeds in making human blood and grotesque homunculi.

When Margaret's dog bites Haddo and he kicks it, Burdon beats and kicks him in retaliation. Haddo doesn't resist, but plots revenge. The novel describes Haddo's magic power over Margaret and the tragedy that results when—like Philip Carey in *Of Human Bondage*—she becomes mesmerized by the lover she hates: "Her contempt for him, her utter loathing, were alloyed with a feeling that aroused in her horror and dismay. She could not get the man out of her thoughts. All that he had said, all that she had seen, seemed . . . unaccountably to absorb her." In a fascinating scene Margaret, corrupted by Haddo's evil, takes "horrible delight" when Susie weeps over her frustrated love for Burdon.

Haddo casts a spell on Margaret and persuades her to marry him. But he agrees (as Crowley originally did with Rose Kelly) not to consummate the marriage because he needs a virgin for his monstrous experiments. (Burdon could deflower her to ruin her satanic value, but is too much of a gentleman to do so.) After Burdon discovers that Haddo has murdered Margaret, he kills him and burns down the house where all the evil has occurred: "as he spoke it seemed that the roof fell in, for suddenly vast flames sprang up, rising high into the still night air; and they saw that the house they had just left was blazing furiously."

The Magician's hypnotic villain comes straight out of Revenge tragedy and Gothic fiction. As in Edgar Allan Poe's stories and Mary Shelley's *Frankenstein*, there's a mad scientist, a spooky mansion, bizarre experiments, a quest for divine (or diabolical) powers, a House of Usher-like destruction (brought about by both psychological and architectural stress) as well as the heroine's split personality. "There seem to be two persons in me," Margaret tells Burdon, predicting her fate, "and my real self, the old one that you knew and loved, is growing weaker day by day,

and will soon be dead entirely." Ironically, Margaret does not seem sexually desirable to Burdon until Haddo has awakened her passion.

Though Crowley claimed "Willie's harmless as a wad of sterilized
cotton," he was wounded by Maugham's satire. He retaliated by review-
ing the novel in the London *Vanity Fair* (December 1908) under the by-
line "Oliver Haddo," pointing out Maugham's plagiarism from books on
magic and from the fantastic experiments on animals in H.G. Wells' *The
Island of Dr. Moreau* (1896). Since the books on magic were all mumbo-
jumbo and added nothing to the novel, the criticism fell flat. When
Maugham's English and American publishers were planning his *Collected
Works* in 1934, he told Nelson Doubleday that he'd been ashamed to let
The Making of a Saint, Orientations, The Hero and *The Bishop's Apron* be reissued
in their present form, and that he didn't want to spend a year revising
them. But in 1956 he rightly changed his mind about *The Magician* and
brought it out with a new preface. *The Explorer* and *The Merry-Go-Round*
were not included in his *Collected Works* until after his death. Maugham
later wished he'd practiced medicine for a while instead of writing books
that now seemed dead as mutton.

Of Human Bondage (1915)—more vivid, moving and convincing than
anything else Maugham wrote—was exactly the cathartic work that
summed up his past life and enabled him to go forward. The first version, "The Artistic Temperament of Stephen Carey," written in Seville
in the late 1890s, was rejected by the publishers and put aside for fifteen
years. In 1913 Maugham suspended his immensely successful career as
a dramatist and returned to his autobiographical novel. He did so with
a straightforward style, a keen sense of drama and a more mature point
of view.

The first half begins with the death of Philip Carey's beloved mother
after giving birth to a stillborn child; his forced move to the house of his
selfish and hypocritical uncle, the vicar of Blackstable; and the cruelties
he suffers at the King's School in Tercanbury (i.e., Canterbury), where
middle-class parents pay high fees to have their children tortured and
emotionally crippled. At school he is constantly humiliated, forced to
show the boys his clubfoot, publicly called a cripple by one master and a
"club-footed blockhead" by another. He falls in love with his classmate
Rose, a recurrent name in Maugham's fiction for attractive male or female

characters. When Philip returns after an illness, Rose brutally rejects him and calls him "a damned cripple." He endures another humiliating public examination of his clubfoot in medical school, when the surgeon remarks that Philip (the son of a doctor) has had an unsuccessful operation on his foot. Another operation, as an adult, also fails to cure his deformity.

The early part of the novel is solidly Victorian and follows the tradition of Dickens' *Great Expectations* and Butler's *The Way of All Flesh*: the drama of a gifted, sensitive and abused orphan child who overcomes disabilities and survives to adulthood. But Maugham also departs radically from this pattern by giving Philip a damning clubfoot, the symbol of his extended trial-by-degradation that forms a major motif of the novel. The book could have been called *Humiliation*.

Philip's handicap may have been suggested by several artistic and literary sources: José Ribera's vividly grotesque painting, *Boy with a Clubfoot* (1652), which Maugham often saw in the Louvre; the deformity of the equally hypersensitive Lord Byron, described by Edward Trelawny after Byron's death: "Both his feet were clubbed, and his legs withered to the knee. . . . This was a curse, chaining a proud and soaring spirit like his to the dull earth"; Charles Bovary's botched operation on the unfortunate Hippolyte's clubfoot in *Madame Bovary* (1857); and Rickie Elliott's lameness in E.M. Forster's *The Longest Journey* (1907). Philip's clubfoot stands for Maugham's stammer but, as Francis King has pointed out, it was also (as in Forster) "a metaphor for a graver disability"—his homosexuality. (Maugham once sardonically remarked that they tried to make a musical out of *Bondage*, but gave it up because the clubfoot couldn't dance.)

Philip is shy, observant, inquisitive, honest, intelligent, sharp-tongued and witty. He cheers up a bereaved Anglican clergyman by telling him that a fire has destroyed the Wesleyan chapel, and earnestly prays for a harsh winter that will kill his ailing uncle and release his inheritance. In the course of the novel he moves from idealism to disillusionment, from the love of his lost mother to love of a motherly wife. But the novel's main subject is Philip's masochistic urge, the "strange desire to torture himself . . . to do horrible, sordid things; he wanted to roll himself in gutters; his whole being yearned for beastliness; he wanted to grovel." Philip suffers from a series of degrading experiences:

not only the miseries of his clubfoot and his schooldays, but also his abject poverty, his wretched job in an accounting firm, his degrading relations with the vicious Mildred, his failed medical exams, his position as a shop-walker. He even becomes homeless and sleeps on the Thames Embankment. Philip observes the hypocrisy and absurdity of clergymen, teachers, doctors and bosses; he loses his religious faith; defies convention; longs to travel to Spain and the Far East; searches for aesthetic beauty, intellectual excitement and sexual freedom; and tries to escape the degradation of human bondage.

The Moon and Sixpence (1919) has three main settings—conventional London, Bohemian Paris and sensual Tahiti—each characterized by a different woman: the deserted wife, Amy Strickland; the abandoned mistress, Blanche Stroeve; and the faithful and obedient Ata. Maugham keeps the novel moving by frequently reversing the narrator's—and the reader's—expectations of what his characters will do. The narrator assumes that Strickland, an utterly conventional London stockbroker and family man, has run off with another woman. But when he finds him in a seedy Paris hotel he discovers that the runaway is living in squalor, not luxury, and has left his wife to dedicate himself to art. After the apparently colorless Strickland breaks free from his dull existence in London, he reveals his true self: callous, sarcastic and brutal. Maugham makes his hero less morally repulsive than Gauguin, who died of syphilis and whose mistress was fourteen, by portraying Strickland's faithful Ata as seventeen and having his hero die of leprosy.

The narrator has even more trouble understanding why the attractive Blanche ever married the buffoonish, untalented and sycophantic Dutch painter Dirk Stroeve. Only after Blanche—like Flaubert's Emma Bovary—has been deserted by her lover and scorched her throat by swallowing acid, does he learn that she had been seduced and abandoned by a Roman prince, had been turned into the street while pregnant and had tried to commit suicide. Stroeve found her, rescued her and married her—and she could never forgive his sacrificial kindness. Blanche, who at first seems so devoted to Stroeve, hates Strickland for humiliating her husband and begs Stroeve not to bring the sick painter into their home. But she abandons her devoted husband for a brief and finally fatal affair with Strickland. Stroeve willingly submits to his cruel power and allows

Strickland to take his studio, his wife and finally his home. Out of this cruel liaison Strickland creates paintings that are "a manifestation of the sexual instinct."

At the beginning of the novel the narrator declares, "to my mind the most interesting thing in art is the personality of the artist," and his quest to understand the artist drives the action. When he quotes Kant's maxim, "act so that every one of your actions is capable of being made into a universal rule," Strickland—his complete opposite in character, temperament and behavior—calls it "rotten nonsense." But the narrator—who condemns the artist's savage treatment of his family, friends and women—is deeply impressed by Strickland's complete contempt for what people think about him or his art. He grudgingly admires the disdain for convention and egomaniacal quest for freedom that have allowed Strickland to fulfill his artistic destiny, and confesses that he cannot fathom his personality. Seeking an explanation for the painter's actions, he asks himself "whether there was not in [Strickland's] soul some deep-rooted instinct of creation, which the circumstances of his life had obscured, but which grew relentlessly . . . till at last it took possession of his whole being and forced him irresistibly to action."

Stroeve immediately recognizes Strickland's genius and describes one of his paintings, which resembles Gauguin's dreamy *Nevermore* (1897, London, Courtauld Collection): "it was the picture of a woman lying on a sofa, with one arm beneath her head and the other along her body; one knee was raised, and the other leg was stretched out." The narrator, by contrast, is remarkably imperceptive about the paintings. When Strickland unexpectedly offers to show them, the narrator—who thinks "descriptions of pictures are always dull"—reflects contemporary opinion, noting that Strickland draws very badly, uses crude colors and produces ugly paintings.

Nine years after Strickland's death, the narrator travels to Tahiti in order to trace his footsteps and reconstruct his life. One friend recalls that he'd seen Strickland's final masterpiece, which the blind artist himself could no longer see; and that after his death Ata, following his instructions, had burnt his house to the ground and turned his chef d'oeuvre into smoldering embers. Though Stroeve could not bring himself to destroy a painting by the man who had driven his wife to suicide, Strickland himself, believing he had finally realized his artistic vision, had ordered the destruction of his greatest work. He thus expressed his final contempt for the opinion of the world—and his desperate alienation.

The end of the novel doesn't reconcile the conflict between artistic impulses and ordinary responsibilities. The narrator suggests that great art exempts the artist from ordinary morality and that Strickland's art has justified his despicable life, even if his defiant destruction of his best work undercuts his achievement. But Strickland's leprosy and blindness seem to punish his ruthless behavior. Having suffered no guilt about the people he's destroyed in the course of his creative life, he's doomed himself to an agonizing end. The opposition of narrator and painter suggest the conflict in Maugham's own personality: between the conventional, secure bourgeois and the ruthless creative artist who despises the norms of society.

When the novel appeared in 1919, European readers, who'd dreamed of escaping the carnage of war to an exotic paradise, responded enthusiastically. But Katherine Mansfield put her finger on the novel's weak spot when she criticized Maugham's superficial view of Strickland's creative imagination. "We are not told enough," she wrote. "We must be shown something of the workings of his mind. . . . The one outstanding quality in Strickland's nature seems to have been his contempt for life and the ways of life."

Despite its flaws, Maugham's theme made a powerful impression on two important American writers, both of whom recognized the original inspiration of the novel. Hart Crane exclaimed: "What a good job Somerset Maugham does in his *Moon and Sixpence!* Have just finished reading it at a single sitting. Pray take the time to read it if you haven't already. How far it follows the facts biographical to Gauguin, I am not able to say, but from what little I do know, it touches his case at many angles." Sherwood Anderson called it "a striking story" and told a friend that it "would help her understand him. It was based on Paul Gauguin's life; at the same time . . . it was a story he thought of writing." The theme of the artist's escape was, for artists, irresistible.

The Trembling of a Leaf (1921) was Maugham's first and best collection of short stories. "Mackintosh," the story of two incompatible men who must work together on a remote Pacific island, was strongly influenced by Conrad's "An Outpost of Progress" (1898). In Conrad's tale, after a trivial quarrel about a bit of sugar, Kayerts shoots his unarmed companion, Carlier, and is found hanging, with his tongue sticking out, when the long overdue company steamer finally arrives. In Maugham's version, Mackintosh, a Scot, hates his vulgar superior Walker, an Irishman. Walker quarrels with the natives about his obsessive desire to build a road around the island, and Mackintosh allows his revolver to be stolen by an angry Samoan. When the Samoan shoots Walker, who asks Mackintosh to forgive the murder, Mackintosh belatedly realizes that Walker was a good man. Overwhelmed by guilt and remorse, he shoots himself. Conrad expressed the dominant idea of both stories when he wrote: "contact with pure unmitigated savagery, with primitive nature and primitive man, brings sudden and profound trouble in the heart."

"The Pool," one of Maugham's most vivid and ambitious stories, contrasts the Samoan and Scottish settings, the lush heat of the tropics and the cold granite of the highland stream. The narrator, whose compassion permeates the tale, is struck by the intimate revelation of another's heart: "I held my breath, for to me there is nothing more awe-inspiring than when a man discovers to you the nakedness of his soul." Lawson falls in love with a half-caste teenage girl whom he sees swimming in a jungle pool. He marries her and expects her to behave like a European woman, but she cannot fill this role and they quarrel bitterly. Hoping to repair his marriage, he takes her to his home in Scotland, but she leaves him and returns to Samoa. He follows her and begins to drink heavily, loses his job and becomes a derelict. When he whips her for infidelity, they experience sadomasochistic pleasure: "Perhaps then she was nearer loving him than she had ever been before." In a jealous rage, Lawson pursues her to the mysterious pool (the symbol of her unfathomable tropical nature) "with the madness of those who love them that love them not." Since Lawson can't live with her and loves her too much to live without her, he drowns himself in the pool and his body is discovered by her Samoan lover. The dominant Conradian motifs are unrequited love and the degeneration of the white man in the tropics. But the story also has the power of a Greek myth, of a mortal man led to his death by a water nymph.

Maugham based the characters in his most celebrated story, "Rain," on a real-life missionary and prostitute. He'd visited Iwelei, the Red

Light district of Honolulu, and taken notes on Miss Sadie Thompson, who was on the run from the San Francisco police. He'd also observed the two characters on the ship to Pago Pago, Samoa, and in a primitive lodging house where they were all marooned during an outbreak of measles. In the story, two doctors, Macphail, a sceptical and timid Scot who'd served in the war, and Davidson, a fanatical and brave American missionary, are doubly trapped by quarantine and unremitting rain: "It did not pour, it flowed. It was like a deluge from heaven, and it rattled on the roof of corrugated iron with a steady persistence that was maddening. It seemed to have a fury of its own. And sometimes you felt that you must scream if it did not stop." The unceasing downpour resembles Davidson's self-righteous pursuit of Sadie Thompson. As in Noah's flood, rain entraps the characters and punishes them for both carnal and spiritual sin.

Davidson's obsession focuses on Sadie's overt sexuality. Their emotional struggle has an unexpected outcome when the spirited whore uses her sexual power to destroy the religious maniac who's trying to send her to prison. (Mrs. Davidson's prurient interest in the sexual depravity of the natives reveals *her* sexual repression.) After sex with Sadie, Davidson, humiliated and horrified by his own degradation, cuts his throat. Sadie then contemptuously screams: " 'You men! You filthy, dirty pigs! You're all the same, all of you. Pigs! Pigs!' Dr. Macphail gasped. He understood." Maugham had experienced this religious hypocrisy and tormenting sexual repression in his uncle's vicarage.

The fruits of Maugham's adventurous journey to China in 1919–20 were the travel book *On a Chinese Screen* (1922) and the novel *The Painted Veil* (1925). The title of his loosely structured, episodic travel book alludes to Eliot's "Prufrock" and the book offers a series of exotic images from an oriental movie, "as if a magic lantern threw the nerves in patterns on a screen." Maugham never mentions his route or indicates where he is. Though traveling with his lover Gerald Haxton, he claims to be alone. As he moves restlessly from place to place, he remains a detached and impersonal observer. He offers brief, impressionistic, sometimes satiric snapshots, with thumbnail physical descriptions of the people he meets and an ironic sting in the tail of his anecdotes. Maugham's not primarily interested in the Chinese, but in the English in China. Living in a time warp, permanent exiles with little desire to return to England, most of the old China hands don't know and don't want to know the Chinese. Their lives of quiet desperation reveal the emotional attrition and spiritual waste of the white man in the East.

Maugham memorably describes masters kicking old servants and barbers scraping the insides of eyelids; women hobbling on bound feet and newborn babies dropped down putrefying wells; cheerful and cozy opium dens (which also appealed to Graham Greene and André Malraux) and two executions by firing squad; a black pig walking across a ridge between flooded padi fields and a nameless "grey and gloomy city, shrouded in mist, [that] stands upon its rock where two great rivers meet so that it is washed on all sides but one by turbid, rushing waters." He responds to the Great Wall with a rhythmic adverbial tour de force: "Solitarily, with the indifference of nature herself, it crept up the mountain side and slipped down to the depth of the valley. Menacingly, the grim watch towers, stark and foursquare, at due intervals stood at their posts. Ruthlessly . . . it forged its dark way through a sea of rugged mountains. Fearlessly, it went on its endless journey, league upon league to the furthermost regions of Asia, in utter solitude, mysterious like the great empire it guarded. There in the mist, enormous, majestic, silent, and terrible, stood the Great Wall of China."

Maugham's exotic settings, engaging characters and riveting plots, his clear style, skillful technique and sardonic narrator, his dramatic flair and grasp of irony continue to attract a wide audience. His dominant themes—death in childbirth, unhappy marriages and covert homosexuality, the decay of the white man in the tropics and the startling difference between appearance and reality—have a perennial interest. He "never flatters his audience," wrote Richard Aldington, "never compromises with the truth as he sees it, never plays stylistic tricks and remains quite indifferent to the ins and outs of literary fashion." Maugham's books—tender and brutal, surprising and cynical—are always intelligent and entertaining. Under the sophisticated surface, they reveal in a hundred variations his essentially tragic story.

CHRONOLOGY

1874	William Somerset Maugham born on January 25 at the British Embassy in Paris.
1882	Death of his mother from tuberculosis.
1884	Death of his father, a lawyer, from cancer. Maugham sent to live with his clergyman uncle in Whitstable, Kent. Attends junior school of King's School in Canterbury.
1885–1889	King's School.
1888–1889	Spends winters convalescing from tuberculosis in Hyères, near Toulon, in south of France.
1890–1892	Lives in Heidelberg for eighteen months and attends lectures at the university.
1892–1896	Attends medical school at St. Thomas's Hospital in London.
1894–1895	Travels in Italy; summers on Capri.
1896	Spends three weeks on obstetrics ward and delivers sixty-three babies.
1897	Earns medical degrees and becomes licensed physician and surgeon. Abandons medicine for writing. *Liza of Lambeth* (novel).
1897–1899	Lives in Seville.
1898–1906	Publishes stories, novels, and plays during long struggle for literary success.

1901   *The Hero* (novel).

1902   *Mrs. Craddock* (novel).

1903   Affair with novelist Violet Hunt.

1904   *The Merry-Go-Round* (novel).

1905   Lives in Paris and Capri. Long affair with actress Sue Jones. *The Land of the Blessed Virgin* (travel).

1906   Greece and Egypt. Affair with Sasha Kropotkin.

1907   *Lady Frederick*, first theatrical success. *The Explorer* (novel).

1907–1908   Has four plays running in London: *Lady Frederick, Jack Straw, Mrs. Dot,* and *Penelope.*

1908   *The Magician* (novel).

1910   First trip to America.

1913   Begins affair with Syrie Wellcome.

1914–1915   Wartime service with Red Cross in France as interpreter, ambulance driver and medical orderly. Meets longtime lover Gerald Haxton.

1915   *Of Human Bondage* (novel). Daughter Liza born in Rome on September 1.

1915–1916   Secret agent in Geneva, Switzerland.

1916   Journey to South Seas with Haxton. Buys Gauguin's painting on glass panels in Tahiti.

1917   Marries Syrie in New Jersey on May 26. Secret agent in Petrograd from July until just before the Revolution in October. Attempts to support Alexander Kerensky's government and keep Russia in war against Germany. Enters tuberculosis sanatorium in Scotland in November.

1919   China. *The Moon and Sixpence* (novel).

1921   Hawaii, Australia, Malaya, Borneo. Almost drowns in tidal wave in Borneo. *The Circle* (play). *The Trembling of a Leaf* (stories).

1922   Burma, Siam, and Indochina. *On a Chinese Screen* (travel).

1924   New York, Mexico and Guatemala.

1925   Malaya. *The Painted Veil* (novel).

1926   Buys luxurious Villa Mauresque on Cap Ferrat in October and moves permanently to France. *The Casuarina Tree* (stories).

1927	Divorce from Syrie after a disastrous ten-year marriage. *The Constant Wife* (play).
1928	*Ashenden* (stories).
1929	Greece and Egypt.
1930	*Cakes and Ale* (novel). *The Gentleman in the Parlour* (travel).
1931	*Six Stories in the First Person Singular* (stories).
1932	Berlin. *The Narrow Corner* (novel). *For Services Rendered* (play).
1933	*Ah King* (stories).
1934	Spain.
1935	Haiti and penal colony in French Guiana. *Don Fernando* (travel).
1937	Scandinavia and Germany. *Theatre* (novel).
1938	India. First visit to Dr. Niehans' clinic in Switzerland for rejuvenation treatment through cellular therapy. *The Summing Up* (autobiography).
1939	*Christmas Holiday* (novel).
1940	Flees from Nice on British freighter in June. *France at War* (propaganda). *The Mixture as Before* (stories).
1940–1946	Spends war years in America at Yemassee, South Carolina, and Edgartown, Martha's Vineyard.
1941	*Strictly Personal* (autobiography). *Up at the Villa* (novel).
1942	*The Hour Before the Dawn* (novel).
1944	Death of Haxton. *The Razor's Edge* (novel).
1945	Works on film script of *Razor's Edge* in Hollywood.
1946	Returns to France. Alan Searle becomes his longtime lover. Establishes Somerset Maugham Award for young writers. *Then and Now* (novel).
1947	*Creatures of Circumstance* (stories).
1948	Spain. *Catalina* (novel).
1948–1951	Introduces film versions of his stories in *Quartet* (1948), *Trio* (1950) and *Encore* (1951).
1949	*A Writer's Notebook* (autobiography). Graham Sutherland paints his portrait.
1950	Morocco.
1952	Honorary doctorate from Oxford University. *The Vagrant Mood* (essays).

1953   Greece and Turkey.
1954   Companion of Honour.
1955   Death of Syrie.
1956   Egypt.
1958   *Points of View* (essays).
1959   Munich, Vienna and Venice. Japan and Singapore.
1961   Honorary Senator of Heidelberg. Companion of Literature.
1962   Sells art collection. Attacks Syrie in "Looking Back." *Purely for My Pleasure* (art).
1963   Lawsuit with Liza.
1965   Dies in Nice at almost 92 on December 15.

I

⚘

From *Liza of Lambeth*
(1897)

10

It was November. The fine weather had quite gone now, and with it much of the sweet pleasure of Jim and Liza's love. When they came out at night on the Embankment they found it cold and dreary; sometimes a light fog covered the river-banks, and made the lamps glow out dim and large; a light rain would be falling, which sent a chill into their very souls; foot passengers came along at rare intervals, holding up umbrellas, and staring straight in front of them as they hurried along in the damp and cold; a cab would pass rapidly by, splashing up the mud on each side. The benches were deserted, except, perhaps, for some poor homeless wretch who could afford no shelter, and, huddled up in a corner, with his head buried in his breast, was sleeping heavily, like a dead man. The wet mud made Liza's skirts cling about her feet, and the damp would come in and chill her legs and creep up her body, till she shivered, and for warmth pressed herself close against Jim. Sometimes they would go into the third-class waiting-rooms at Waterloo or Charing Cross and sit there, but it was not like the park or the Embankment on summer nights; they had warmth, but the heat made their wet clothes steam and smell, and the gas flared in their eyes, and they hated the people perpetually coming in and out, opening the doors and letting in a blast of cold air; they hated the noise of the guards and porters shouting out the departure of the trains, the shrill whistling of the steam-engine, the hurry and bustle and confusion. About eleven o'clock, when the trains grew less frequent, they got some quietness; but then their minds were troubled, and they felt heavy, sad and miserable.

One evening they had been sitting at Waterloo Station; it was foggy outside—a thick, yellow November fog, which filled the waiting-room, entering the lungs, and making the mouth taste nasty and the eyes smart. It was about half-past eleven, and the station was unusually quiet; a few passengers, in wraps and overcoats, were walking to and fro, waiting for the last train, and one or two porters were standing about yawning. Liza and Jim had remained for an hour in perfect silence, filled with a gloomy unhappiness, as of a great weight on their brains. Liza was sitting forward, with her elbows on her knees, resting her face on her hands.

'I wish I was straight,' she said at last, not looking up.

'Well, why won't yer come along of me altogether, an' you'll be arright then?' he answered.

'Na, that's no go; I can't do thet.' He had often asked her to live with him entirely, but she had always refused.

'You can come along of me, an' I'll tike a room in a lodgin' 'ouse in 'Olloway, an' we can live there as if we was married.'

'Wot abaht yer work?'

'I can get work over the other side as well as I can 'ere. I'm abaht sick of the wy things is goin' on.'

'So am I; but I can't leave mother.'

'She can come, too.'

'Not when I'm not married. I shouldn't like 'er ter know as I'd—as I'd gone wrong.'

'Well, I'll marry yer. Swop me bob, I wants ter badly enough.'

'Yer can't; yer married already.'

'Thet don't matter! If I give the missus so much a week aht of my screw, she'll sign a piper ter give up all clime ter me, an' then we can get spliced. One of the men as I works with done thet, an' it was arright.'

Liza shook her head.

'Na, yer can't do thet now; it's bigamy, an' the cop tikes yer, an' yer gits twelve months' 'ard for it.'

'But swop me bob, Liza, I can't go on like this. Yer knows the missus—well, there ain't no bloomin' doubt abaht it, she knows as you an' me are carryin' on, an' she mikes no bones abaht lettin' me see it.'

'She don't do thet?'

'Well, she don't exactly sy it, but she sulks an' won't speak, an' then when I says anythin' she rounds on me an' calls me all the nimes she can think of. I'd give 'er a good 'idin', but some'ow I don't like ter! She mikes the plice a 'ell ter me, an' I'm not goin' ter stand it no longer!'

'You'll 'ave ter sit it, then; yer can't chuck it.'

'Yus I can, an' I would if you'd come along of me. I don't believe you like me at all, Liza, or you'd come.'

She turned towards him and put her arms round his neck.

'Yer know I do, old cock,' she said. 'I like yer better than anyone else in the world; but I can't go awy an' leave mother.'

'Bli'me me if I see why; she's never been much ter you. She mikes yer slave awy ter pay the rent, an' all the money she earns she boozes.'

'Thet's true, she ain't been wot yer might call a good mother ter me—but some'ow she's my mother, an' I don't like ter leave 'er on 'er own, now she's old—an' she can't do much with the rheumatics. An' besides, Jim dear, it ain't only mother, but there's yer own kids, yer can't leave them.'

He thought for a while, and then said:

'You're abaht right there, Liza; I dunno if I could get on without the kids. If I could only tike them an' you too, swop me bob, I should be 'appy.'

Liza smiled sadly.

'So yer see, Jim, we're in a bloomin' 'ole, an' there ain't no way aht of it thet I can see.'

He took her on his knees, and pressing her to him, kissed her very long and very lovingly.

'Well, we must trust ter luck,' she said again, 'p'raps somethin' 'll 'appen soon, an' everythin' 'll come right in the end—when we gets four balls of worsted for a penny.'

It was past twelve, and separating, they went by different ways along the dreary, wet, deserted roads till they came to Vere Street.

The street seemed quite different to Liza from what it had been three months before. Tom, the humble adorer, had quite disappeared from her life. One day, three or four weeks after the August Bank Holiday, she saw him dawdling along the pavement, and it suddenly struck her that she had not seen him for a long time; but she had been so full of her happiness that she had been unable to think of anyone but Jim. She wondered at his absence, since before wherever she had been there was he certain to be also. She passed him, but to her astonishment he did not speak to her. She thought by some wonder he had not seen her, but she felt his gaze resting upon her. She turned back, and suddenly he dropped his eyes and looked down, walking on as if he had not seen her, but blushing furiously.

'Tom,' she said, 'why don't yer speak ter me.'

He started and blushed more than ever.

'I didn't know yer was there,' he stuttered.

'Don't tell me,' she said, 'wot's up?'

'Nothin' as I knows of,' he answered uneasily.

'I ain't offended yer, 'ave I, Tom?'

'Na, not as I knows of,' he replied, looking very unhappy.

'You don't ever come my way now,' she said.

'I didn't know as yer wanted ter see me.'

'Garn! Yer knows I likes you as well as anybody.'

'Yer likes so many people, Liza,' he said, flushing.

'What d'yer mean?' said Liza indignantly, but very red; she was afraid he knew now, and it was from him especially she would have been so glad to hide it.

'Nothin',' he answered.

'One doesn't say things like thet without any meanin', unless one's a blimed fool.'

'You're right there, Liza,' he answered. 'I am a blimed fool.' He looked at her a little reproachfully, she thought, and then he said 'Good-bye,' and turned away.

At first she was horrified that he should know of her love for Jim, but then she did not care. After all, it was nobody's business, and what did anything matter as long as she loved Jim and Jim loved her? Then she grew angry that Tom should suspect her; he could know nothing but that some of the men had seen her with Jim near Vauxhall, and it seemed mean that he should condemn her for that. Thenceforward, when she ran against Tom, she cut him; he never tried to speak to her, but as she passed him, pretending to look in front of her, she could see that he always blushed, and she fancied his eyes were very sorrowful. Then several weeks went by, and as she began to feel more and more lonely in the street she regretted the quarrel; she cried a little as she thought that she had lost his faithful gentle love and she would have much liked to be friends with him again. If he had only made some advance she would have welcomed him so cordially, but she was too proud to go to him herself and beg him to forgive her—and then how could he forgive her?

She had lost Sally too, for on her marriage Harry had made her give up the factory; he was a young man with principles worthy of a Member of Parliament, and he had said:

'A woman's plice is 'er 'ome, an' if 'er old man can't afford ter keep 'er without 'er workin' in a factory—well, all I can say is thet 'e'd better go an' git single.'

'Quite right, too,' agreed his mother-in-law; 'an' wot's more, she'll 'ave a baby ter look after soon, an' thet'll tike 'er all 'er time, an' there's no one as knows thet better than me, for I've 'ad twelve, ter sy nothin' of two stills an' one miss.'

Liza quite envied Sally her happiness, for the bride was brimming over with song and laughter; her happiness overwhelmed her.

'I am 'appy,' she said to Liza one day a few weeks after her marriage. 'You dunno wot a good sort 'Arry is. 'E's just a darlin', an' there's no mistikin' it. I don't care wot other people sy, but wot I says is, there's nothin' like marriage. Never a cross word passes his lips, an' mother 'as all 'er meals with us an' 'e says all the better. Well I'm thet 'appy I simply dunno if I'm standin' on my 'ead or on my 'eels.'

But alas! it did not last too long. Sally was not so full of joy when next Liza met her, and one day her eyes looked very much as if she had been crying.

'Wot's the matter?' asked Liza, looking at her. 'Wot 'ave yer been blubberin' abaht?'

'Me?' said Sally, getting very red. 'Oh, I've got a bit of a toothache, an'—well, I'm rather a fool like, an' it 'urt so much that I couldn't 'elp cryin'.'

Liza was not satisfied, but could get nothing further out of her. Then one day it came out. It was a Saturday night, the time when women in Vere Street weep. Liza went up into Sally's room for a few minutes on her way to the Westminster Bridge Road, where she was to meet Jim. Harry had taken the top back room, and Liza, climbing up the second flight of stairs, called out as usual,

'Wot ho, Sally!'

The door remained shut, although Liza could see that there was a light in the room; but on getting to the door she stood still, for she heard the sound of sobbing. She listened for a minute and then knocked: there was a little flurry inside, and someone called out:

"Oo's there?'

'Only me,' said Liza, opening the door. As she did so she saw Sally rapidly wipe her eyes and put her handkerchief away. Her mother was sitting by her side, evidently comforting her.

'Wot's up, Sal?' asked Liza.

'Nothin',' answered Sally, with a brave little gasp to stop the crying, turning her face downwards so that Liza should not see the tears in her eyes; but they were too strong for her, and, quickly taking out her handkerchief, she hid her face in it and began to sob broken-heartedly. Liza looked at the mother in interrogation.

'Oh, it's thet man again!' said the lady, snorting and tossing her head.

'Not 'Arry?' asked Liza, in surprise.

'Not 'Arry—'oo is it if it ain't 'Arry? The villin!'

'Wot's 'e been doin', then?' asked Liza again.

'Beatin' 'er, that's wot 'e's been doin'! Oh, the villin, 'e oughter be ashimed of 'isself 'e ought!'

'I didn't know 'e was like that!' said Liza.

'Didn't yer? I thought the 'ole street knew it by now,' said Mrs Cooper indignantly. 'Oh, 'e's a wrong 'un, 'e is.'

'It wasn't 'is fault,' put in Sally, amidst her sobs; 'it's only because 'e's 'ad a little drop too much. 'E's arright when 'e's sober.'

'A little drop too much! I should just think 'e'd 'ad, the beast! I'd give it 'im if I was a man. They're all like thet—'usbinds is all alike; they're arright when they're sober—sometimes—but when they've got the liquor in 'em, they're beasts, an' no mistike. I 'ad a 'usbind myself for five-an'-twenty years, an' I know 'em.'

'Well, mother,' sobbed Sally, 'it was all my fault. I should 'ave come 'ome earlier.'

'Na, it wasn't your fault at all. Just you look 'ere, Liza: this is wot 'e done an' call 'isself a man. Just because Sally'd gone aht to 'ave a chat with Mrs. McLeod in the next 'ouse, when she come in 'e start bangin' 'er abaht. An' me, too, wot d'yer think of that!' Mrs Cooper was quite purple with indignation.

'Yus,' she went on, 'thet's a man for yer. Of course, I wasn't goin' ter stand there an' see my daughter bein' knocked abaht; it wasn't likely—was it? An' 'e rounds on me, an' 'e 'its me with 'is fist. Look 'ere.' She pulled up her sleeves and showed two red and brawny arms. ''E's bruised my arms; I thought 'e'd broken it at fust. If I 'adn't put my arm up, 'e'd 'ave got me on the 'ead, an' 'e might 'ave killed me. An' I says to 'im, "If you touch me again, I'll go ter the police-station, thet I will!" Well, that frightened 'im a bit, an' then didn't I let 'im 'ave it! "You call yerself a man," says I, "an' you ain't fit ter clean the drains aht." You should 'ave 'eard the language 'e used. "You dirty old woman," says 'e, "you go away; you're always interferin' with me." Well, I don't like ter repeat wot 'e said, and thet's the truth. An' I says ter 'im, "I wish yer'd never married my daughter, an' if I'd known you was like this I'd 'ave died sooner than let yer."'

'Well, I didn't know 'e was like thet!' said Liza.

''E was arright at fust,' said Sally.

'Yus, they're always arright at fust! But ter think it should 'ave come to this now, when they ain't been married three months, an' the first child not born yet! I think it's disgraceful.'

Liza stayed a little while longer, helping to comfort Sally, who kept pathetically taking to herself all the blame of the dispute; and then, bidding her good night and better luck, she slid off to meet Jim.

When she reached the appointed spot he was not to be found. She waited for some time, and at last saw him come out of the neighbouring pub.

'Good night, Jim,' she said as she came up to him.

'So you've turned up, 'ave yer?' he answered roughly, turning round.

'Wot's the matter, Jim?' she asked in a frightened way, for he had never spoken to her in that manner.

'Nice thing ter keep me witin' all night for yer to come aht.'

She saw that he had been drinking, and answered humbly.

'I'm very sorry, Jim, but I went in to Sally, an' 'er bloke 'ad been knockin' 'er abaht, an' so I sat with 'er a bit.'

'Knockin' 'er abaht, 'ad 'e? and serve 'er damn well right too; an' there's many more as could do with a good 'idin'!'

Liza did not answer. He looked at her, and then suddenly said:

'Come in an' 'ave a drink.'

'Na, I'm not thirsty: I don't want a drink,' she answered.

'Come on,' he said angrily.

'Na, Jim, you've had quite enough already.'

''Oo are you talkin' ter?' he said, 'Don't come if yer don't want ter; I'll go an' 'ave one by myself.'

'Na, Jim, don't.' She caught hold of his arm.

'Yus, I shall,' he said, going towards the pub, while she held him back. 'Let me go, can't yer! Let me go!' He roughly pulled his arm away from her. As she tried to catch hold of it again, he pushed her back, and in the little scuffle caught her a blow over the face.

'Oh!' she cried, 'you did 'urt!'

He was sobered at once.

'Liza,' he said. 'I ain't 'urt yer?' She didn't answer, and he took her in his arms. 'Liza, I ain't 'urt you, 'ave I? Say I ain't 'urt yer. I'm so sorry, I beg your pardon, Liza.'

'Arright, old chap,' she said, smiling charmingly on him.

'It wasn't the blow that 'urt me much; it was the wy you was talkin'.'

'I didn't mean it, Liza.' He was so contrite, he could not humble himself enough. 'I 'ad another bloomin' row with the missus ter-night, an' then when I didn't find you 'ere, an' I kept witin' an' witin'—well, I fair downright lost my 'air. An' I 'ad two or three pints of four 'alf, an'—well, I dunno—'

'Never mind, old cock, I can stand more than thet as long as yer loves me.'

He kissed her and they were quite friends again. But the little quarrel had another effect which was worse for Liza. When she woke up next morning she noticed a slight soreness over the ridge of bone under the left eye, and on looking in the glass saw that it was black and blue and green. She bathed it, but it remained, and seemed to get more marked. She was terrified lest people should see it, and kept indoors all day; but next morning it was blacker than ever. She went to the factory with her hat over her eyes and her head bent down; she escaped observation, but on the way home she was not so lucky. The sharp eyes of some girls noticed it first.

'Wot's the matter with yer eye?' asked one of them.

'Me?' answered Liza, putting her hand up as if in ignorance. 'Nothin' thet I knows of.'

Two or three young men were standing by, and hearing the girl, looked up.

'Why, yer've got a black eye, Liza!.'

'Me? I ain't got no black eye!'

'Yus you 'ave; 'ow d'yer get it?'

'I dunno,' said Liza. 'I didn't know I 'ad one.'

'Garn! tell us another!' was the answer. 'One doesn't git a black eye without knowin' 'ow they got it.'

'Well, I did fall against the chest of drawers yesterday; I suppose I must 'ave got it then.'

'Oh yes, we believe thet, don't we?'

'I didn't know 'e was so 'andy with 'is dukes, did you, Ted?' asked one man of another.

Liza felt herself grow red to the tips of her toes.

'Who?' she asked.

'Never you mind; nobody you know.'

At that moment Jim's wife passed and looked at her with a scowl. Liza wished herself a hundred miles away, and blushed more violently than ever.

'Wot are yer blushin' abaht?' ingenuously asked one of the girls.

And they all looked from her to Mrs Blakeston and back again. Someone said: ''Ow abaht our Sunday boots on now?' And a titter went through them. Liza's nerve deserted her; she could think of nothing to say, and a sob burst from her. To hide the tears which were coming from her eyes she turned away and walked homewards. Immediately a great shout of laughter broke from the group, and she heard them positively screaming till she got into her own house.

11

A FEW days afterwards Liza was talking with Sally, who did not seem very much happier than when Liza had last seen her.

"'E ain't wot I thought 'e wos,' she said. 'I don't mind sayin' thet; but 'e 'as a lot ter put up with; I expect I'm rather tryin' sometimes, an' 'e means well. P'raps 'e'll be kinder like when the biby's born.'

'Cheer up, old gal,' answered Liza, who had seen something of the lives of many married couples; 'it won't seem so bad after yer gets used to it; it's a bit disappointin' at fust, but yer gits not ter mind it.'

After a little Sally said she must go and see about her husband's tea. She said good-bye, and then rather awkwardly:

'Say, Liza, tike care of yerself!'

'Tike care of meself—why?' asked Liza, in surprise.

'Yer know wot I mean.'

'Na, I'm darned if I do.'

'Thet there Mrs Blakeston, she's lookin' aht for you.'

'Mrs Blakeston!' Liza was startled.

'Yus; she says she's goin' ter give you somethin' if she can git 'old on yer. I should advise yer ter tike care.'

'Me?' said Liza.

Sally looked away, so as not to see the other's face.

'She says as 'ow yer've been messin' abaht with 'er old man.'

Liza didn't say anything, and Sally, repeating her good-bye, slid off.

Liza felt a chill run through her. She had several times noticed a scowl and a look of anger on Mrs Blakeston's face, and she had avoided her as much as possible; but she had no idea that the woman meant to do anything to her. She was very frightened, a cold sweat broke out over her face. If Mrs Blakeston got hold of her she would be helpless, she was so small and weak, while the other was strong and muscular. Liza wondered what she would do if she did catch her.

That night she told Jim, and tried to make a joke of it.

'I say, Jim, your missus—she says she's goin' ter give me socks if she catches me.'

'My missus! 'Ow d'yer know?'

'She's been tellin' people in the street.'

'Go' lumme,' said Jim, furious, 'if she dares ter touch a 'air of your 'ead, swop me dicky I'll give 'er sich a 'idin' as she never 'ad before! By God, give me the chanst, an' I would let 'er 'ave it; I'm bloomin' well sick of 'er sulks!' He clenched his fist as he spoke.

Liza was a coward. She could not help thinking of her enemy's threat; it got on her nerves, and she hardly dared go out for fear of meeting her; she would look nervously in front of her, quickly turning round if she saw in the distance anyone resembling Mrs Blakeston. She dreamed of her at night; she saw the big, powerful form, the heavy, frowning face, and the curiously braided brown hair; and she would wake up with a cry and find herself bathed in sweat.

It was the Saturday afternoon following this, a chill November day, with the roads sloshy, and a grey, comfortless sky that made one's spirits sink. It was about three o'clock, and Liza was coming home from work; she got into Vere Street, and was walking quickly towards her house when she saw Mrs Blakeston coming towards her. Her heart gave a great jump. Turning, she walked rapidly in the direction she had come; with a screw round of her eyes she saw that she was being followed, and therefore went straight out of Vere Street. She went right round, meaning to get into the street from the other end and, unobserved, slip into her house, which was then quite close; but she dared not risk it immediately for fear Mrs Blakeston should still be there; so she waited about for half an hour. It seemed an age. Finally, taking her courage in both hands, she turned the corner and entered Vere Street. She nearly ran into the arms of Mrs Blakeston, who was standing close to the public-house door.

Liza gave a little cry, and the woman said, with a sneer:

'Yer didn't expect ter see me, did yer?'

Liza did not answer, but tried to walk past her. Mrs Blakeston stepped forward and blocked her way.

'Yer seem ter be in a mighty fine 'urry,' she said.

'Yus, I've got ter git 'ome,' said Liza, again trying to pass.

'But supposin' I don't let yer?' remarked Mrs Blakeston, preventing her from moving.

'Why don't yer leave me alone?' Liza said. 'I ain't interferin' with you!'

'Not interferin' with me, aren't yer? I like thet!'

'Let me go by,' said Liza. 'I don't want ter talk ter you.'

'Na, I know thet,' said the other; 'but I want ter talk ter you, an' I shan't let yer go until I've said wot I wants ter sy.'

Liza looked round for help. At the beginning of the altercation the loafers about the public-house had looked up with interest, and gradually gathered round in a little circle. Passers-by had joined in, and a number of other people in the street, seeing the crowd, added themselves to it to see what was going on. Liza saw that all eyes were fixed on her, the men amused and excited, the women unsympathetic, rather virtuously indignant. Liza wanted to ask for help, but there were so many people, and they all seemed so much against her, that she had not the courage to. So, having surveyed the crowd, she turned her eyes to Mrs Blakeston, and stood in front of her, trembling a little, and very white.

'Na, 'e ain't there,' said Mrs Blakeston, sneeringly, 'so yer needn't look for 'im.'

'I dunno wot yer mean,' answered Liza, 'an' I want ter go awy. I ain't done nothin' ter you.'

'Not done nothin' ter me?' furiously repeated the woman. 'I'll tell yer wot yer've done ter me—you've robbed me of my 'usbind, you 'ave. I never 'ad a word with my 'usbind until you took 'im from me. An' now it's all you with 'im. 'E's got no time for 'is wife an' family—it's all you. An' 'is money, too. I never git a penny of it; if it weren't for the little bit I 'ad saved up in the siving-bank, me an' my children 'ud be starvin' now! An' all through you!' She shook her fist at her.

'I never 'ad any money from anyone.'

'Don' talk ter me; I know yer did. Yer dirty bitch! You oughter be ishimed of yourself tikin' a married man from 'is family, an' 'im old enough ter be yer father.'

'She's right there!' said one or two of the onlooking women. 'There can't be no good in 'er if she tikes somebody else's 'usbind.'

'I'll give it yer!' proceeded Mrs Blakeston, getting more hot and excited, brandishing her fist, and speaking in a loud voice, hoarse with rage. 'Oh, I've been tryin' ter git 'old on yer this four weeks. Why, you're a prostitute—that's wot you are!'

'I'm not!' answered Liza indignantly.

'Yus, you are,' repeated Mrs Blakeston, advancing meanacingly, so that Liza shrank back. 'An' wot's more, 'e treats yer like one. I know 'oo give yer thet black eye; thet shows what 'e thinks of yer! An' serve yer bloomin' well right if 'e'd give yer one in both eyes!'

Mrs Blakeston stood close in front of her, her heavy jaw protruded and the frown of her eyebrows dark and stern. For a moment she stood silent, contemplating Liza, while the surrounders looked on in breathless interest.

'Yer dirty little bitch, you!' she said at last. 'Tike that!' and with her open hand she gave her a sharp smack on the cheek.

Liza started back with a cry and put her hand up to her face.

'An' tike thet!' added Mrs Blakeston, repeating the blow. Then, gathering up the spittle in her mouth, she spat in Liza's face.

Liza sprang on her, and with her hands spread out like claws buried her nails in the woman's face and drew them down her cheeks. Mrs Blakeston caught hold of her hair with both hands and tugged at it as hard as she could. But they were immediately separated.

"Ere, 'old 'ard!' said some of the men. 'Fight it aht fair and square. Don't go scratchin' and maulin' like thet.'

'I'll fight 'er, I don't mind!' shouted Mrs Blakeston, tucking up her sleeves and savagely glaring at her opponent.

Liza stood in front of her, pale and trembling; as she looked at her enemy, and saw the long red marks of her nails, with blood coming from one or two of them, she shrank back.

'I don't want ter fight,' she said hoarsely.

'Na, I don't suppose yer do,' hissed the other, 'but yer'll damn well 'ave ter!'

'She's ever so much bigger than me; I've got no chanst,' added Liza tearfully.

'You should 'ave thought of thet before. Come on!' and with these words Mrs Blakeston rushed upon her. She hit her with both fists one after the other. Liza did not try to guard herself, but imitating the woman's motion, hit out with her own fists; and for a minute or two they continued thus, raining blows on one another with the same windmill motion of the arms. But Liza could not stand against the other woman's weight; the blows came down heavy and rapid all over her face and head. She put up her hands to cover her face and turned her head away, while Mrs Blakeston kept on hitting mercilessly.

'Time!' shouted some of the men—'Time!' and Mrs Blakeston stopped to rest herself.

'It don't seem 'ardly fair to set them two on tergether. Liza's got no chanst against a big woman like thet,' said a man among the crowd.

'Well, it's 'er own fault,' answered a woman; 'she didn't oughter mess about with 'er 'usbind.'

'Well, I don't think it's right,' added another man. 'She's gettin' it too much.'

'An' serve 'er right too!' said one of the women. 'She deserves all she gets an' a damn sight more inter the bargain.'

'Quite right,' put in a third; 'a woman's got no right ter tike someone's 'usbind from 'er. An' if she does she's bloomin' lucky if she gits off with a 'idin'—thet's wot I think.'

'So do I. But I wouldn't 'ave thought it of Liza. I never thought she was a wrong 'un.'

'Pretty specimen she is!' said a little dark woman, who looked like a Jewess. 'If she messed abaht with my old man, I'd stick 'er—I swear I would!'

'Now she's been carryin' on with one, she'll try an' git others—you see if she don't.'

'She'd better not come round my 'ouse; I'll soon give 'er wot for.'

Meanwhile Liza was standing at one corner of the ring, trembling all over and crying bitterly. One of her eyes was bunged up, and her hair, all dishevelled, was hanging down over her face. Two young fellows, who had constituted themselves her seconds, were standing in front of her, offering rather ironical comfort. One of them had taken the bottom corners of her apron and was fanning her with it, while the other was showing her how to stand and hold her arms.

'You stand up to 'er, Liza,' he was saying; 'there ain't no good funkin' it, you'll simply get it all the worse. You 'it 'er back. Give 'er one on the boko, like this—see; yer must show a bit of pluck, yer know.'

Liza tried to check her sobs.

'Yus, 'it 'er 'ard, that's wot yer've got ter do,' said the other. 'An' if yer find she's gettin' the better on yer, you close on 'er and catch 'old of 'er 'air and scratch 'er.'

'You've marked 'er with yer nails, Liza. By gosh, you did fly on her when she spat at yer! Thet's the way ter do the job!'

Then turning to his fellow, he said:

'D'yer remember thet fight as old Mother Cregg 'ad with another woman in the street last year?'

'Na,' he answered, 'I never saw thet.'

'It was a cawker; an' the cops come in and took 'em both off ter quod.'

Liza wished the policemen would come and take her off; she would willingly have gone to prison to escape the fiend in front of her; but no help came.

'Time's up!' shouted the referee. 'Fire away!'

'Tike care of the cops!' shouted a man.

'There's no fear abaht them,' answered somebody else.

'They always keeps out of the way when there's anythin' goin' on.'

'Fire away!'

Mrs Blakeston attached Liza madly; but the girl stood up bravely, and as well as she could gave back the blows she received. The spectators grew tremendously excited.

'Got 'im again!' they shouted. 'Give it 'er, Liza, thet's a good 'un!—'it 'er 'ard!'

'Two ter one on the old 'un!' shouted a sporting gentleman; but Liza found no backers.

'Ain't she standin' up well now she's roused?' cried someone.

'Oh, she's got some pluck in 'er, she 'as!'

'Thet's a knock-aht!' they shouted as Mrs Blakeston brought her fist down on to Liza's nose; the girl staggered back, and blood began to flow. Then, losing all fear, mad with rage, she made a rush on her enemy, and rained down blows all over her nose and eyes and mouth. The woman recoiled at the sudden violence of the onslaught, and the men cried:

'By God, the little 'un's gettin' the best of it!'

But quickly recovering herself the woman closed with Liza, and dug her nails into her flesh. Liza caught hold of her hair and pulled with all her might, and turning her teeth on Mrs Blakeston tried to bite her. And thus for a minute they swayed about, scratching, tearing, biting, sweat and blood pouring down their faces, and their eyes fixed on one another, bloodshot and full of rage. The audience shouted and cheered and clapped their hands.

'Wot the 'ell's up 'ere?'

'I sy, look there,' said some of the women in a whisper. 'It's the 'usbind!'

He stood on tiptoe and looked over the crowd.

'My Gawd,' he said, 'it's Liza!'

Then roughly pushing the people aside, he made his way through the crowd into the centre, and thrusting himself between the two women, tore them apart. He turned furiously on his wife.

'By Gawd, I'll give yer somethin' for this!'

And for a moment they all three stood silently looking at one another.

Another man had been attracted by the crowd, and he, too, pushed his way through.

'Come 'ome, Liza,' he said.

'Tom!'

He took hold of her arm, and led her through the people, who gave way to let her pass. They walked silently through the street, Tom very grave, Liza weeping bitterly.

'Oh, Tom,' she sobbed after a while, 'I couldn't 'elp it!' Then, when her tears permitted, 'I did love 'im so!'

When they got to the door she plaintively said: 'Come in,' and he followed her to her room. Here she sank on to a chair, and gave herself up to her tears.

Tom wetted the end of a towel and began wiping her face, grimy with blood and tears. She let him do it, just moaning amid her sobs:

'You are good ter me, Tom.'

'Cheer up, old gal,' he said kindly, 'it's all over now.'

After a while the excess of crying brought its cessation. She drank some water, and then taking up a broken handglass she looked at herself, saying:

'I am a sight!' and proceeded to wind up her hair. 'You 'ave been good ter me, Tom,' she repeated, her voice still broken with sobs; and as he sat down beside her she took his hand.

'Na, I ain't,' he answered; 'it's only wot anybody 'ud 'ave done.'

'Yer know, Tom,' she said, after a little silence, 'I'm so sorry I spoke cross like when I met yer in the street; you ain't spoke ter me since.'

'Oh, thet's all over now, old lidy, we needn't think of thet.'

'Oh, but I 'ave treated yer bad. I'm a regular wrong 'un, I am.'

He pressed her hand without speaking.

'I say, Tom,' she began, after another pause. 'Did yer know thet—well, you know—before ter-day?'

He blushed as he answered:

'Yus.'

She spoke very sadly and slowly.

'I thought yer did; yer seemed so cut up like when I used to meet yer. Yer did love me then, Tom, didn't yer?'

'I do now, dearie,' he answered.

'Ah, it's too lite now,' she sighed.

'D'yer know, Liza,' he said, 'I just abaht kicked the life aht of a feller 'cause 'e said you was messin' abaht with—with 'im.'

'An' yer knew I was?'

'Yus—but I wasn't goin' ter 'ave anyone say it before me.'

'They've all rounded on me except you, Tom. I'd 'ave done better if I'd tiken you when you arst me; I shouldn't be where I am now, if I 'ad.'

'Well, won't yer now? Won't yer 'ave me now?'

'Me? After wot's 'appened?'

'Oh, I don't mind abaht thet. Thet don't matter ter me if you'll marry me. I fair can't live without yer, Liza—won't yer?'

She groaned.

'Na, I can't, Tom, it wouldn't be right.'

'Why, not, if I don't mind?'

'Tom,' she said, looking down, almost whispering, 'I'm like that—you know!'

'Wot d'yer mean?'

She could scarcely utter the words—

'I think I'm in the family wy.'

He paused a moment; then spoke again.

'Well—I don't mind, if yer'll only marry me.'

'Na, I can't, Tom,' she said, bursting into tears; 'I can't, but you are so good ter me; I'd do anythin' ter mike it up ter you.'

She put her arms round his neck and slid on to his knees.

'Yer know, Tom, I couldn't marry yer now; but anythin' else—if yer wants me ter do anythin' else, I'll do it if it'll mike you 'appy.'

He did not understand, but only said:

'You're a good gal, Liza,' and bending down he kissed her gravely on the forehead.

Then with a sigh he lifted her down, and getting up left her alone. For a while she sat where he left her, but as she thought of all she had gone through her loneliness and misery overcame her, the tears welled forth, and throwing herself on the bed she buried her face in the pillows.

Jim stood looking at Liza as she went off with Tom, and his wife watched him jealously.

'It's 'er you're thinkin' abaht. Of course you'd 'ave liked ter tike 'er 'ome yerself, I know, an' leave me to shift for myself.'

'Shut up!' said Jim, angrily turning upon her.

'I shan't shut up,' she answered, raising her voice. 'Nice 'usbind you are. Go' lumme, as good as they mike 'em! Nice thing ter go an' leave yer wife and children for a thing like thet! At your age, too! You oughter be ashimed of yerself. Why, it's like messin' abaht with your own daughter!'

'By God!'—he ground his teeth with rage—'if yer don't leave me alone, I'll kick the life aht of yer!'

'There!' she said, turning to the crowd—'there, see 'ow 'e treats me! Listen ter that! I've been 'is wife for twenty years, an' yer couldn't 'ave 'ad a better wife, an' I've bore 'im nine children, yet say nothin' of a miscarriage, an' I've got another comin', an' thet's 'ow 'e treats me! Nice 'usbind, ain't it?' She looked at him scornfully, then again at the surrounders as if for their opinion.

'Well, I ain't goin' ter stay 'ere all night; get aht of the light!' He pushed aside the people who barred his way, and the one or two who growled a little at his roughness, looking at his angry face, were afraid to complain.

'Look at 'im!' said his wife. "E's afraid, 'e is. See 'im slinkin' awy like a bloomin' mongrel with 'is tail between 'is legs. Ugh!' She walked just behind him, shouting and brandishing her arms.

'Yer dirty beast, you,' she yelled, 'ter go foolin' abaht with a little girl! Ugh! I wish yer wasn't my 'usbind; I wouldn't be seen drowned with yer, if I could 'elp it. Yer mike me sick ter look at yer.'

The crowd followed them on both sides of the road, keeping at a discreet distance, but still eagerly listening.

Jim turned on her once or twice and said:

'Shut up!'

But it only made her more angry. 'I tell yer I shan't shut up. I don't care 'oo knows it, you're a ——, you are! I'm ashimed the children should 'ave such a father as you. D'yer think I didn't know wot you was up ter them nights you was awy—courtin', yus, courtin'? You're a nice man, you are!'

Jim did not answer her, but walked on. At last he turned round to the people who were following and said:

'Na then, wot d'you want 'ere? You jolly well clear, or I'll give some of you somethin'!'

They were mostly boys and women, and at his words they shrank back.

''E's afraid ter sy anythin' ter me,' jeered Mrs Blakeston. ''E's a beauty!'

Jim entered his house, and she followed him till they came up into their room. Polly was giving the children their tea. They all started up as they saw their mother with her hair and clothes in disorder, blotches of dried blood on her face, and the long scratch-marks.

'Oh, mother,' said Polly, 'wot is the matter?'

''E's the matter,' she answered, pointing to her husband. 'It's through 'im I've got all this. Look at yer father, children; e's a father to be proud of, leavin' yer ter starve an' spendin' 'is week's money on a dirty little strumper.'

Jim felt easier now he had not got so many strange eyes on him.

'Now, look 'ere,' he said, 'I'm not goin' ter stand this much longer, so just you tike care.'

'I ain't frightened of yer. I know yer'd like ter kill me, but yer'll get strung up if you do.'

'Na, I won't kill yer, but if I 'ave any more of your sauce I'll do the next thing to it.'

'Touch me if yer dare,' she said, 'I'll 'ave the law on you. An' I should-n't mind 'ow many month's 'ard you got.'

'Be quiet!' he said, and, closing his hand, gave her a heavy blow in the chest that made her stagger.

'Oh, you —!' she screamed.

She seized the poker, and in a fury of rage rushed at him.

'Would yer?' he said, catching hold of it and wrenching it from her grasp. He threw it to the end of the room and grappled with her. For a moment they swayed about from side to side, then with an effort he lifted her off her feet and threw her to the ground; but she caught hold of him and he came down on the top of her. She screamed as her head thumped down on the floor, and the children, who were standing huddled up in a corner, terrified, screamed too.

Jim caught hold of his wife's head and began beating it against the floor.

She cried out: 'You're killing me! Help! help!'

Polly in terror ran up to her father and tried to pull him off.

'Father, don't 'it 'er! Anythin' but thet—for God's sike!'

'Leave me alone,' he said, 'or I'll give you somethin' too.'

She caught hold of his arm, but Jim, still kneeling on his wife, gave Polly a backhanded blow which sent her staggering back.

'Tike that!'

Polly ran out of the room, downstairs to the first-floor front, where two men and two women were sitting at tea.

'Oh, come an' stop father!' she cried. "E's killin' mother!'

'Why, wot's 'e doin'?'

'Oh, 'e's got 'er on the floor, an' 'e's bangin' 'er 'ead. 'E's payin' 'er aht for givin' Liza Kemp a 'idin'.'

One of the women started up and said to her husband:

'Come on, John, you go an' stop it.'

'Don't you, John,' said the other man. 'When a man's givin' 'is wife socks it's best not ter interfere.'

'But 'e's killin' 'er,' repeated Polly, trembling with fright.

'Garn!' rejoined the man, 'she'll git over it; an' p'raps she deserves it, for all you know.'

John sat undecided, looking now at Polly, now at his wife, and now at the other man.

'Oh, do be quick—for God's sike!' said Polly.

At that moment a sound as of something smashing was heard upstairs, and a woman's shriek. Mrs Blakeston, in an effort to tear herself away from her husband, had knocked up against the wash-hand stand, and the whole thing had crashed down.

'Go on, John,' said the wife.

'No, I ain't goin'; I shan't do no good, an' 'e'll only round on me.'

'Well, you are a bloomin' lot of cowards, thet's all I can say,' indignantly answered the wife. 'But I ain't goin' ter see a woman murdered; I'll go an' stop 'im.'

With that she ran upstairs and threw open the door. Jim was still kneeling on his wife, hitting her furiously, while she was trying to protect her head and face with her hands.

'Leave off!' shouted the woman.

Jim looked up. ''Oo the devil are you?' he said.

'Leave off, I tell yer. Aren't yer ashimed of yerself, knockin' a woman abaht like that?' And she sprang at him, seizing his fist.

'Let go,' he said, 'or I'll give you a bit.'

'Yer'd better not touch me,' she said. 'Yer dirty coward! Why, look at 'er, she's almost senseless.'

Jim stopped and gazed at his wife. He got up and gave her a kick.

'Git up!' he said; but she remained huddled up on the floor, moaning feebly. The woman from downstairs went on her knees and took her head in her arms.

'Never mind, Mrs Blakeston. 'E's not goin' ter touch yer. 'Ere, drink this little drop of water.' Then turning to Jim, with infinite disdain: 'Yer dirty blackguard, you! If I was a man I'd give you something for this.'

Jim put on his hat and went out, slamming the door, while the woman shouted after him: 'Good riddance!'

'Lord love yer,' said Mrs Kemp, 'wot is the matter?'

She had just come in, and opening the door had started back in surprise at seeing Liza on the bed, all tears. Liza made no answer, but cried as if her heart were breaking. Mrs Kemp went up to her and tried to look at her face.

'Don't cry, dearie; tell us wot it is.'

Liza sat up and dried her eyes.

'I am so un'appy!'

'Wot 'ave yer been doin' ter yer fice? My!'

'Nothin'.'

'Garn! Yer can't 'ave got a fice like thet all by itself.'

'I 'ad a bit of a scrimmage with a woman dahn the street,' sobbed out Liza.

'She 'as give yer a doin'; an' yer all upset—an' look at yer eye! I brought in a little bit of stike for ter-morrer's dinner; you just cut a bit off an' put it over yer optic, that'll soon put it right. I always used ter do thet myself when me an' your poor father 'ad words.'

'Oh, I'm all over in a tremble, an' my 'ead, oo, my 'ead does feel bad!'

'I know wot yer want,' remarked Mrs Kemp, nodding her head, 'an' it so 'appens as I've got the very thing with me.' She pulled a medicine bottle out of her pocket, and taking out the cork smelt it. 'Thet's good stuff, none of your fire-water or your methylated spirit. I don't often in-dulge in sich things, but when I do I likes to 'ave the best.'

She handed the bottle to Liza, who took a mouthful and gave it her back; she had a drink herself, and smacked her lips.

'Thet's good stuff. 'Ave a drop more.'

'Na,' said Liza, 'I ain't used ter drinkin' spirits.'

She felt dull and miserable, and a heavy pain throbbed through her head. If she could only forget!

'Na, I know you're not, but, bless your soul, thet won' 'urt yer. It'll do you no end of good. Why, often when I've been feelin' thet done up thet I didn't know wot ter do with myself, I've just 'ad a little drop of whisky or gin—I'm not partic'ler wot spirit it is—an' it's pulled me up wonderful.'

Liza took another sip, a slightly longer one; it burnt as it went down her throat, and sent through her a feeling of comfortable warmth.

'I really do think it's doin' me good,' she said, wiping her eyes and giving a sigh of relief as the crying ceased.

'I knew it would. Tike my word for it, if people took a little drop of spirits in time, there'd be much less sickness abaht.'

They sat for a while in silence, then Mrs Kemp remarked:

'Yer know, Liza, it strikes me as 'ow we could do with a drop more. You not bein' in the 'abit of tikin' anythin' I only brought just this little drop for me; an' it ain't took us long ter finish thet up. But as you're an invalid like we'll git a little more this time; it's sure ter turn aht useful.'

'But you ain't got nothin' ter put it in.'

'Yus, I 'ave,' answered Mrs Kemp; 'there's thet bottle as they gives me at the 'orspital. Just empty the medicine aht into the pile, an' wash it aht, an' I'll tike it round to the pub myself.'

Liza, when she was left alone, began to turn things over in her mind. She did not feel so utterly unhappy as before, for the things she had gone through seemed further away.

'After all,' she said, 'it don't so much matter.'

Mrs Kemp came in.

"Ave a little drop more, Liza,' she said.

'Well, I don't mind if I do. I'll get some tumblers, shall I? There's no mistike abaht it,' she added, when she had taken a little, 'it do buck yer up.'

'You're right, Liza—you're right. An' you wanted it badly. Fancy you 'avin' a fight with a woman! Oh, I've 'ad some in my day, but then I wasn't a little bit of a thing like you is. I wish I'd been there, I wouldn't 'ave stood by an' looked on while my daughter was gettin' the worst of it; although I'm turned sixty-five, an' gettin' on for sixty-six, I'd 'ave said to 'er: "If you touch my daughter you'll 'ave me ter deal with, so just look aht!"'

She brandished her glass, and that reminding her, she refilled it and Liza's.

'Ah, Liza,' she remarked, 'you're a chip off the old block. Ter see you settin' there an' 'avin' your little drop, it mikes me feel as if I was livin' a better life. Yer used ter be rather 'ard on me, Liza, 'cause I took a little drop on Saturday nights. An', mind, I don't sy I didn't tike a little drop too much sometimes—accidents will occur even in the best regulated of families, but wot I say is this—it's good stuff, I say, an' it don't 'urt yer.'

'Buck up, old gal!' said Liza, filling the glasses, 'no 'eeltaps. I feel like a new woman now. I was thet dahn in the dumps—well, I shouldn't 'ave cared if I'd been at the bottom of the river, an' thet's the truth.'

'You don't sy so,' replied her affectionate mother.

'Yus, I do, an' I mean it too, but I don't feel like thet now. You're right, mother, when you're in trouble there's nothin' like a bit of spirits.'

'Well, if I don't know, I dunno 'oo does, for the trouble I've 'ad, it 'ud be enough to kill many women. Well, I've 'ad thirteen children, an' you can think wot thet was; everyone I 'ad I used ter sy I wouldn't 'ave no more—but one does, yer know. You'll 'ave a family some day, Liza, an' I shouldn't wonder if you didn't 'ave as many as me. We come from a very prodigal family, we do, we've all gone in ter double figures, except your Aunt Mary, who only 'ad three—but then she wasn't married, so it didn't count, like.'

They drank each other's health. Everything was getting blurred to Liza, she was losing her head.

'Yus,' went on Mrs Kemp, 'I've 'ad thirteen children an' I'm proud of it. As your poor dear father used ter sy, it shows as 'ow one's got the blood of a Briton in one. Your poor dear father, 'e was a great 'and at speakin' 'e was: 'e used ter speak at parliamentary meetin's—I really believe 'e'd 'ave been a Member of Parliament if 'e'd been alive now. Well, as I was sayin', your father 'e used ter sy, "None of your small families for me, I don't approve of them," says 'e. 'E was a man of very 'igh principles, an' by politics 'e was a Radical. "No," says 'e, when 'e got talkin', "when a man can 'ave a family risin' into double figures, it shows 'e's got the backbone of a Briton in 'im. That's the stuff as 'as built up England's nime and glory! When one thinks of the mighty British Hempire," says 'e, "on which the sun never sets from mornin' till night, one 'as ter be proud of 'isself, an' one 'as ter do one's duty in thet walk of life in which it 'as pleased Providence ter set one—an' every man's fust duty is ter get as many children as 'e bloomin' well can." Lord love yer—'e could talk, I can tell yer.'

'Drink up, mother,' said Liza. 'You're not 'alf drinkin'.' She flourished the bottle. 'I don't care a twopanny 'ang for all them blokes; I'm quite 'appy, an' I don't want anythin' else.'

'I can see you're my daughter now,' said Mrs Kemp. 'When yer used ter round on me I used ter think as 'ow if I 'adn't carried yer for nine months, it must 'ave been some mistike, an' yer wasn't my daughter at all. When you come ter think of it, a man 'e don't know if it's 'is child or somebody else's, but yer can't deceive a woman like thet. Yer couldn't palm off somebody else's kid on 'er.'

'I am beginnin' ter feel quite lively,' said Liza. 'I dunno wot it is, but I feel as if I wanted to laugh till I fairly split my sides.'

And she began to sing: 'For 'e's a jolly good feller—for 'e's a jolly good feller!'

Her dress was all disarranged; her face covered with the scars of scratches, and clots of blood had fixed under her nose; her eye had swollen up so that it was nearly closed, and red; her hair was hanging over her face and shoulders, and she laughed stupidly and leered with heavy, sodden ugliness.

'Disy, Disy! I can't afford a kerridge.
    But you'll look neat, on the seat
    Of a bicycle mide for two.'

She shouted out the tunes, beating time on the table, and her mother, grinning, with her thin, grey hair hanging dishevelled over her head, joined in with her weak, cracked voice—

'Oh, dem golden kippers, oh!'

Then Liza grew more melancholy and broke into 'Auld Lang Syne'.

'Should old acquaintance be forgot
      And never brought to mind?

   .   .   .   .

      For old lang syne'.

Finally they both grew silent, and in a little while there came a snore from Mrs Kemp; her head fell forward to her chest; Liza tumbled from her chair on to the bed, and sprawling across it fell asleep.

'Although I am drunk and bad, be you kind,
Cast a glance at this heart which is bewildered and distressed.
O God, take away from my mind my cry and my complaint.
Offer wine, and take sorrow from my remembrance.
Offer wine.'

12

ABOUT the middle of the night Liza woke; her mouth was hot and dry, and a sharp, cutting pain passed through her head as she moved. Her mother had evidently roused herself, for she was lying in bed by her side, partially undressed, with all the bedclothes rolled round her. Liza shivered in the cold night, and taking off some of her things—her boots, her skirt, and jacket—got right into bed; she tried to get some of the blanket from her mother, but as she pulled Mrs Kemp gave a growl in her sleep and drew the clothes more tightly round her. So Liza put over herself her skirt and a shawl, which was lying over the end of the bed, and tried to go to sleep.

But she could not; her head and hands were broiling hot, and she was terribly thirsty; when she lifted herself up to get a drink of water such a pang went through her head that she fell back on the bed groaning, and lay there with beating heart. And strange pains that she did not know went through her. Then a cold shiver seemed to rise in the very marrow of her bones and run down every artery and vein, freezing the blood; her skin puckered up, and drawing up her legs she lay huddled together in a heap, the shawl wrapped tightly round her, and her teeth chattering. Shivering, she whispered:

'Oh, I'm so cold, so cold. Mother, give me some clothes; I shall die of the cold. Oh, I'm freezing!'

But after a while the cold seemed to give way, and a sudden heat seized her, flushing her face, making her break out into perspiration, so that she threw everything off and loosened the things about her neck.

'Give us a drink,' she said. 'Oh, I'd give anythin' for a little drop of water!'

There was no one to hear; Mrs Kemp continued to sleep heavily, occasionally breaking out into a little snore.

Liza remained there, now shivering with cold, now panting for breath, listening to the regular, heavy breathing by her side, and in her pain she sobbed. She pulled at her pillow and said:

'Why can't I go to sleep? Why can't I sleep like 'er?'

And the darkness was awful; it was a heavy, ghastly blackness, that seemed palpable, so that it frightened her and she looked for relief at the faint light glimmering through the window from a distant street-lamp. She thought the night would never end—the minutes seemed like hours, and she wondered how she should live through till morning. And strange pains that she did not know went through her.

Still the night went on, the darkness continued, cold and horrible, and her mother breathed loudly and steadily by her side.

At last with the morning sleep came; but the sleep was almost worse than the wakefulness, for it was accompanied by ugly, disturbing dreams. Liza thought she was going through the fight with her enemy, and Mrs Blakeston grew enormous in size, and multiplied, so that every way she turned the figure confronted her. And she began running away, and she ran and ran till she found herself reckoning up an account she had puz-

zled over in the morning, and she did it backwards and forwards, up-
wards and downwards, starting here, starting there, and the figures got
mixed up with other things, and she had to begin over again, and everything jumbled up, and her head whirled, till finally, with a start, she
woke.

The darkness had given way to a cold, grey dawn, her uncovered legs
were chilled to the bone, and by her side she heard again the regular,
nasal breathing of the drunkard.

For a long while she lay where she was, feeling very sick and ill, but
better than in the night. At last her mother woke.

'Liza!' she called.

'Yus, mother,' she answered feebly.

'Git us a cup of tea, will yer?'

'I can't, mother, I'm ill.'

'Garn!' said Mrs Kemp, in surprise. Then looking at her, 'Swop me
bob, wot's up with yer? Why, yer cheeks is flushed, an' yer forehead—it
is 'ot! Wot's the matter with yer, gal?'

'I dunno,' said Liza. 'I've been thet bad all night, I thought I was goin'
ter die."

'I know wot it is,' said Mrs Kemp, shaking her head; 'the fact is, you
ain't used ter drinkin', an' of course it's upset yer. Now me, why I'm as
fresh as a disy. Tike my word, there ain't no good in teetotalism; it finds
yer aht in the end, an' it's found you aht.'

Mrs Kemp considered it a judgment of Providence. She got up and
mixed some whisky and water.

"Ere, drink this,' she said. 'When one's 'ad a drop too much at night,
there's nothin' like havin' a drop more in the mornin' ter put one right. It
just acts like magic.'

'Tike it awy,' said Liza, turning from it in disgust; 'the smell of it
gives me the sick. I'll never touch spirits again.'

'Ah, thet's wot we all says sometime in our lives, but we does, an'
wot's more we can't do withaht it. Why, me, the 'ard life I've 'ad —' It is
unnecessary to repeat Mrs Kemp's repetitions.

Liza did not get up all day. Tom came to inquire after her, and was
told she was very ill. Liza plaintively asked whether anyone else had been,
and sighed a little when her mother answered no. But she felt too ill to

think much or trouble much about anything. The fever came again as the day wore on, and the pains in her head grew worse. Her mother came to bed, and quickly went off to sleep, leaving Liza to bear her agony alone. She began to have frightful pains all over her, and she held her breath to prevent herself from crying out and waking her mother. She clutched the sheets in her agony, and at last, about six o'clock in the morning, she could bear it no longer, and in the anguish of labour screamed out, and woke her mother.

Mrs Kemp was frightened out of her wits. Going upstairs she woke the woman who lived on the floor above her. Without hesitating, the good lady put on a skirt and came down.

'She's 'ad a miss,' she said, after looking at Liza. 'Is there anyone you could send to the 'orspital?'

'Na, I dunno 'oo I could get at this hour?'

'Well, I'll git my old man ter go.'

She called her husband, and sent him off. She was a stout, middle-aged woman, rough-visaged and strong-armed. Her name was Mrs Hodges.

'It's lucky you came ter me,' she said, when she had settled down. 'I go aht nursin', yer know, so I know all abaht it.'

'Well, you surprise me,' said Mrs Kemp. 'I didn't know as Liza was thet way. She never told me nothin' abaht it.'

'D'yer know 'oo it is 'as done it?'

'Now you ask me somethin' I don't know,' replied Mrs Kemp. 'But now I come ter think of it, it must be thet there Tom. 'E's been keepin' company with Liza. 'E's a single man, so they'll be able ter get married— thet's somethin'.'

'It ain't Tom,' feebly said Liza.

'Not 'im; 'oo is it, then?'

Liza did not answer.

'Eh?' repeated the mother, ''oo is it?'

Liza lay still without speaking.

'Never mind, Mrs Kemp,' said Mrs Hodges, 'don't worry 'er now; you'll be able ter find aht all abaht it when she gits better.'

For a while the two women sat still, waiting the doctor's coming, and Liza lay gazing vacantly at the wall, panting for breath. Sometimes Jim crossed her mind, and she opened her mouth to call for him, but in her despair she restrained herself.

The doctor came.

'D'you think she's bad, doctor?' asked Mrs Hodges.

'I'm afraid she is rather,' he answered. 'I'll come in again this evening.'

'Oh, doctor,' said Mrs Kemp, as he was going, 'could yer give me somethin' for my rheumatics? I'm a martyr to rheumatism, an' these cold days I 'ardly knows wot ter do with myself. An', doctor, could you let me 'ave some beef-tea? My 'usbind's dead, an' of course I can't do no work with my daughter ill like this, an' we're very short—"

The day passed, and in the evening Mrs Hodges, who had been attending to her own domestic duties, came downstairs again. Mrs Kemp was on the bed sleeping.

'I was just 'avin' a little nap,' she said to Mrs Hodges, on waking.

''Ow is the girl?' asked that lady.

'Oh,' answered Mrs Kemp, 'my rheumatics 'as been thet bad I really 'aven't known wot ter do with myself, an' now Liza can't rub me I'm worse than ever. It is unfortunate thet she should get ill just now when I want so much attendin' ter myself, but there, it's just my luck!'

Mrs Hodges went over and looked at Liza; she was lying just as when she left in the morning, her cheeks flushed, her mouth open for breath, and tiny beads of sweat stood on her forehead.

''Ow are yer, ducky?' asked Mrs Hodges; but Liza did not answer.

'It's my belief she's unconscious,' said Mrs Kemp. 'I've been askin' 'er 'oo it was as done it, but she don't seem to 'ear wot I say. It's been a great shock ter me, Mrs 'Odges.'

'I believe you,' replied that lady, sympathetically.

'Well, when you come in and said wot it was, yer might 'ave knocked me dahn with a feather. I knew no more than the dead wot 'ad 'appened.'

'I saw at once wot it was,' said Mrs Hodges, nodding her head.

'Yus, of course, you knew. I expect you've 'ad a great deal of practice one way an' another.'

'You're right, Mrs Kemp, you're right. I've been on the job now for nearly twenty years, an' if I don't know somethin' abaht it I ought.'

'D' yer finds it pays well?'

'Well, Mrs Kemp, tike it all in all, I ain't got no grounds for complaint. I'm in the 'abit of askin' five shillings, an' I will say this, I don't think it's too much for wot I do.'

The news of Liza's illness had quickly spread, and more than once in the course of the day a neighbour had come to ask after her. There was a knock at the door now, and Mrs Hodges opened it. Tom stood on the threshold asking to come in.

'Yus, you can come,' said Mrs Kemp.

He advanced on tiptoe, so as to make no noise, and for a while stood silently looking at Liza. Mrs Hodges was by his side.

'Can I speak to 'er?' he whispered.

'She can't 'ear you.'

He groaned.

'D'yer think she'll get arright?' he asked.

Mrs Hodges shrugged her shoulders.

'I shouldn't like ter give an opinion,' she said, cautiously.

Tom bent over Liza, and, blushing. kissed her; then, without speaking further, went out of the room.

'Thet's the young man as was courtin' 'er,' said Mrs Kemp, pointing over her shoulder with her thumb.

Soon after the Doctor came.

'Wot do yer think of 'er, doctor?' said Mrs Hodges, bustling forwards authoritatively in her position of midwife and sick-nurse.

'I'm afraid she's very bad.'

'D'yer think she's goin' ter die?' she asked, dropping her voice to a whisper.

'I'm afraid so!'

As the doctor sat down by Liza's side Mrs Hodges turned round and significantly nodded to Mrs Kemp, who put her handkerchief to her eyes. Then she went outside to the little group waiting at the door.

'Wot does the doctor sy?' they asked, among them Tom.

''E says just wot I've been sayin' all along; I knew she wouldn't live.'

And Tom burst out: 'Oh, Liza!'

As she retired a woman remarked:

'Mrs 'Odges is very clever, I think.'

'Yus,' remarked another, 'she got me through my last confinement simply wonderful. If it come to choosin' between 'em I'd back Mrs 'Odges against forty doctors.'

'Ter tell yer the truth, so would I. I've never known 'er wrong yet.'

Mrs Hodges sat down beside Mrs Kemp and proceeded to comfort her.

'Why don't yer tike a little drop of brandy ter calm yer nerves, Mrs Kemp?' she said, 'you want it.'

'I was just feelin' rather faint, an' I couldn't 'elp thinkin' as 'ow twopenneth of whisky 'ud do me good.'

'Na, Mrs Kemp,' said Mrs Hodges, earnestly, putting her hand on the other's arm. 'You tike my tip—when you're queer there's nothin' like brandy for pullin' yer togither. I don't object to whisky myself, but as a medicine yer can't beat brandy.'

'Well, I won't set up myself as knowin' better than you Mrs 'Odges; I'll do wot you think right.'

Quite accidentally there was some in the room, and Mrs Kemp poured it out for herself and her friend.

'I'm not in the 'abit of tikin' anythin' when I'm aht on business,' she apologized, 'but just ter keep you company I don't mind if I do.'

'Your 'ealth, Mrs 'Odges.'

'Sime ter you, an' thank yer, Mrs Kemp.'

Liza lay still, breathing very quietly, her eyes closed. The doctor kept his fingers on her pulse.

'I've been very unfortunate of lite,' remarked Mrs Hodges, as she licked her lips, 'this mikes the second death I've 'ad in the last ten days— women, I mean, of course I don't count bibies.'

'Yer don't sy so.'

'Of course the other one—well, she was only a prostitute, so it did- n't so much matter. It ain't like another woman is it?'

'Na, you're right.'

'Still, one don't like 'em ter die, even if they are thet. One mustn't be too 'ard on 'em.'

'Strikes me you've got a very kind 'eart, Mrs 'Odges,' said Mrs Kemp.

'I 'ave thet; an' I often says if 'ud be better for my peace of mind an' my business if I 'adn't. I 'ave ter go through a lot, I do; but I can say this for myself, I always gives satisfaction, an' thet's somethin' as all lidies in my line can't say.'

They sipped their brandy for a while.

'It's a great trial ter me that this should 'ave 'appened,' said Mrs Kemp, coming to the subject that had been disturbing her for some time.

'Mine's always been a very respectable family, an' such a thing as this 'as never 'appened before. No, Mrs 'Odges, I was lawfully married in church, an' I've got my marriage lines now ter show I was, an' thet one of my daughters should 'ave gone wrong in this way—well, I can't understand it. I give 'er a good education, an' she 'ad all the comforts of a 'ome. She never wanted for nothin'; I worked myself to the bone ter keep 'er in luxury, an' then thet she should go an' disgrace me like this!'

'I understand wot yer mean, Mrs Kemp.'

'I can tell you my family was very respectable; an' my 'usband, 'e earned twenty-five shillings a week, an' was in the sime plice seventeen years; an' 'is employers sent a beautiful wreath ter put on 'is coffin; an' they tell me they never 'ad such a good workman an' sich an 'onest man before. An' me! Well, I can sy this—I've done my duty by the girl, an' she's never learnt anythin' but good from me. Of course I ain't always been in wot yer might call flourishing circumstances, but I've always set her a good example, as she could tell yer so 'erself if she wasn't speechless.'

Mrs Kemp paused for a moment's reflection.

'As they sy in the Bible,' she finished, 'it's enough ter mike one's grey 'airs go dahn into the ground in sorrer. I can show yer my marriage certificate. Of course one doesn't like ter say much, because of course she's very bad; but if she got well I should 'ave given 'er a talkin' ter.'

There was another knock.

'Do go an' see 'oo thet is; I can't, on account of my rheumatics.'

Mrs Hodges opened the door. It was Jim.

He was very white, and the blackness of his hair and beard, contrasting with the deathly pallor of his face, made him look ghastly. Mrs Hodges stepped back.

"Oo's 'e?' she said, turning to Mrs Kemp.

Jim pushed her aside and went up to the bed.

'Doctor, is she very bad?' he asked.

The doctor looked at him questioningly.

Jim whispered: 'It was me as done it. She ain't goin' ter die, is she?'

The doctor nodded.

'O God! wot shall I do? It was my fault! Wish I was dead!'

Jim took the girl's head in his hands, and the tears burst from his eyes.

'She ain't dead yet, is she?'

'She's just living,' said the doctor.

Jim bent down.

'Liza, Liza, speak ter me! Liza, say you forgive me! Oh, speak ter me!'
His voice was full of agony. The doctor spoke.

'She can't hear you.'

'Oh, she must hear me! Liza! Liza!'

He sank on his knees by the bedside.

They all remained silent: Liza lying stiller than ever, her breast
unmoved by the feeble respiration, Jim looking at her very mourn-
fully; the doctor grave, with his fingers on the pulse. the two women
looked at Jim.

'Fancy it bein' 'im!' said Mrs Kemp. 'Strike me lucky, ain't 'e a sight!'

'You 'ave got 'er insured, Mrs Kemp?' asked the mid-wife. She could
bear the silence no longer.

'Trust me fur thet!' replied the good lady. 'I've 'ad 'er insured ever
since she was born. Why, only the other dy I was sayin' ter myself thet
all thet money 'ad been wisted, but you see it wasn't; yer never know yer
luck, you see!'

'Quite right, Mrs Kemp; I'm a rare one for insurin'. It's a great thing.
I've always insured all my children.'

'The way I look on it is this,' said Mrs Kemp—'wotever yer do when
they're alive, an' we all know as children is very tryin' sometimes, you
should give them a good funeral when they dies. Thet's my motto, an' I've
always acted up to it.'

'Do you deal with Mr Stearman?' asked Mrs Hodges.

'No, Mrs 'Odges, for undertikin' give me Mr Footley every time. In
the black line 'e's fust an' the rest nowhere!'

'Well, thet's very strange now—thet's just wot I think. Mr Footley
does 'is work well, an' 'e's very reasonable. I'm a very old customer of 'is,
an' 'e lets me 'ave things as cheap as anybody.'

'Does 'e indeed! Well Mrs 'Odges if it ain't askin' too much of yer, I
should look upon it as very kind if you'd go an' mike the arrangements
for Liza.'

'Why, certainly, Mrs Kemp. I'm always willin' ter do a good turn to
anybody, if I can.'

'I want it done very respectable,' said Mrs Kemp; 'I'm not goin' ter stint for nothin' for my daughter's funeral. I like plumes, you know, although they is a bit extra.'

'Never you fear, Mrs Kemp, it shall be done as well as if it was for my own 'usbind, an' I can't say more than thet. Mr Footley thinks a deal of me, 'e does! Why, only the other dy as I was goin' inter 'is shop 'e says "Good mornin', Mrs 'Odges," "Good mornin', Mr Footley," says I. "You've jest come in the nick of time," says 'e. "This gentleman an' myself," pointin' to another gentleman as was standin' there, "we was 'avin' a bit of an argument. Now you're a very intelligent woman, Mrs 'Odges, and a good customer too." "I can say thet for myself," say I, "I gives yer all the work I can." "I believe you," says 'e. "Well," 'e says, "now which do you think? Does hoak look better than helm, or does helm look better than hoak? Hoak versus helm, thet's the question." "Well, Mr Footley," says I, "for my own private opinion, when you've got a nice brass plite in the middle, an' nice brass 'andles each end, there's nothin' like hoak." "Quite right," says 'e, "thet's wot I think; for coffins give me hoak any day, an' I 'ope," says 'e, "when the Lord sees fit ter call me to 'Imself, I shall be put in a hoak coffin myself." "Amen," says I.'

'I like hoak,' said Mrs Kemp. 'My poor 'usband 'e 'ad a hoak coffin. We did 'ave a job with 'im, I can tell yer. You know 'e 'ad dropsy, an' 'e swell up—oh, 'e did swell; 'is own mother wouldn't 'ave known 'im. Why, 'is leg swell up till it was as big round as 'is body, swop me bob, it did.'

'Did it indeed!' ejaculated Mrs Hodges.

'Yus, an' when 'e died they sent the coffin up. I didn't 'ave Mr Footley at thet time; we didn't live 'ere then, we lived in Battersea, an' all our undertikin' was done by Mr Brownin'; well, 'e sent the coffin up, an' we got my old man in, but we couldn't get the lid down, he was so swell up. Well, Mr Brownin', 'e was a great big man, thirteen stone if 'e was a ounce. Well, 'e stood on the coffin, an' a young man 'e 'ad with 'im stood on it too, an' the lid simply wouldn't go dahn; so Mr Browning', 'e said, "Jump on, missus," so I was in my widow's weeds, yer know, but we 'ad ter git it dahn, so I stood on it, an' we all jumped, an' at last we got it to, an' screwed it; but, lor', we did 'ave a job; I shall never forget it.'

Then all was silence. And a heaviness seemed to fill the air like a grey blight, cold and suffocating; and the heaviness was Death. They felt the presence in the room, and they dared not move, they dared not draw their breath. The silence was terrifying.

Suddenly a sound was heard—a loud rattle. It was from the bed and rang through the room, piercing the stillness.

The doctor opened one of Liza's eyes and touched it, then he laid on her breast the hand he had been holding, and drew the sheet over her head.

Jim turned away with a look of intense weariness on his face, and the two women began weeping silently. The darkness was sinking before the day, and a dim, grey light came through the window. The lamp spluttered out.

2

The Hero
(1901)

1

Colonel Parsons sat by the window in the dining-room to catch the last glimmer of the fading day, looking through his *Standard* to make sure that he had overlooked no part of it. Finally, with a little sigh, he folded it up, and taking off his spectacles, put them in their case.

"Have you finished the paper?" asked his wife.

"Yes, I think I've read it all. There's nothing in it."

He looked out of window at the well-kept drive that led to the house, and at the trim laurel bushes which separated the front garden from the village green. His eyes rested, with a happy smile, upon the triumphal arch which decorated the gate for the home-coming of his son, expected the next day from South Africa. Mrs. Parsons knitted diligently at a sock for her husband, working with quick and clever fingers. He watched the rapid glint of the needles.

"You'll try your eyes if you go on much longer with this light, my dear."

"Oh, I don't require to see," replied his wife, with a gentle, affectionate smile. But she stopped, rather tired, and laying the sock on the table, smoothed it out with her hand.

"I shouldn't mind if you made it a bit higher in the leg than the last pair."

"How high would you like it?"

She went to the window so that the Colonel might show the exact length he desired; and when he had made up his mind, sat down again quietly on her chair by the fireside, with hands crossed on her lap, waiting placidly for the maid to bring the lamp.

Mrs. Parsons was a tall woman of fifty-five, carrying herself with a certain diffidence, as though a little ashamed of her stature, greater than the Colonel's; it had seemed to her through life that those extra inches savoured, after a fashion, of disrespect. She knew it was her duty spiritually to look up to her husband, yet physically she was always forced to look down. And eager to prevent even the remotest suspicion of wrongdoing, she had taken care to be so submissive in her behaviour as to leave no doubt that she recognised the obligation of respectful obedience enjoined by the Bible, and confirmed by her own conscience. Mrs. Parsons was the gentlest of creatures, and the most kind-hearted; she looked upon her husband with great and unlterable affection, admiring intensely both his head and his heart. He was her type of the upright man, walking in the ways of the Lord. You saw in the placid, smooth brow of the Colonel's wife, in her calm eyes, even in the severe arrangement of the hair, parted in the middle and drawn back, that her character was frank, simple, and straightforward. She was a woman to whom evil had never offered the smallest attraction; she was merely aware of its existence theoretically. To her the only way of life had been that which led to God; the others had been non-existent. Duty had one hand only, and only one finger; and that finger had always pointed definitely in one direction. Yet Mrs. Parsons had a firm mouth, and a chin square enough to add another impression. As she sat motionless, hands crossed, watching her husband with loving eyes, you might have divined that, however kind-hearted, she was not indulgent, neither lenient to her own faults nor to those of others; perfectly unassuming, but with a sense of duty, a feeling of the absolute rightness of some deeds and of the absolute wrongness of others, which would be, even to those she loved best in the world, utterly unsparing.

"Here's a telegraph boy!" said Colonel Parsons suddenly. "Jamie can't have arrived yet!"

"Oh, Richmond!"

Mrs. Parsons sprang from her chair, and a colour brightened her pale cheeks. Her heart beat painfully, and tears of eager expectation filled her eyes.

"It's probably only from William, to say the ship is signalled," said the Colonel, to quieten her; but his own voice trembled with anxiety.

"Nothing can have happened, Richmond, can it?" said Mrs. Parsons, her cheeks blanching again at the idea.

"No, no! Of course not! How silly you are!"

The telegram was brought in by the servant. "I can't see without a light," said the Colonel.

"Oh, give it me; I can see quite well."

Mrs. Parsons took it to the window, and with trembling hand tore it open.

"*Arriving to-night; 7.25.—JAMIE.*"

Mrs. Parson looked for one moment at her husband, and then, unable to restrain herself, sank on a chair, and hiding her face with her hands, burst into tears.

"Come, come, Frances," said the Colonel, trying to smile, but half choked with his own emotion, "don't cry! You ought to laugh when you know the boy's coming home."

He patted her on the shoulder, and she took his hand, holding it for comfort. With the other, the Colonel loudly blew his nose. At last Mrs Parsons dried her eyes.

"Oh, I thank God that it's all over! He's coming home. I hope we shall never have to endure again that anxiety. It makes me tremble still when I think how we used to long for the paper to come, and dread it; how we used to look all through the list of casualties, fearing to see the boy's name."

"Well, well, it's all over now," said the Colonel cheerily, blowing his nose again. "How pleased Mary will be!"

It was characteristic of him that almost his first thought was of the pleasure this earlier arrival would cause to Mary Clibborn, the girl to whom, for five years, his son had been engaged.

"Yes," said Mrs. Parson, "but she'll be dreadfully disappointed not to be here; she's gone to the Polsons in Tunbridge Wells, and she won't be home till after supper."

"That is a pity. I'm afraid it's too late to go and meet him; it's nearly seven already."

"Oh, yes; and it's damp this evening. I don't think you ought to go out."

Then Mrs. Parsons roused herself to household matters.

"There's the supper to think of, Richmond," she said; "we've only the rest of the cold mutton, and there's not time to cook one of to-morrow's chickens."

They had invited three or four friends to dinner on the following day to celebrate the return of their son, and Mrs. Parsons had laid in for the occasion a store of solid things.

"Well, we might try and get some chops. I expect Howe is open still."

"Yes, I'll send Betty out. And we can have a blanc-mange for a sweet."

Mrs. Parsons went to give the necessary orders, and the Colonel walked up to his son's room to see, for the hundredth time, that everything was in order. They had discussed for days the question whether the young soldier should be given the best spare bedroom or that which he had used from his boyhood. It was wonderful the thought they expended in preparing everything as they fancied he would like it; no detail slipped their memory, and they arranged and rearranged so that he should find nothing altered in his absence. They attempted to satisfy in this manner the eager longing of their hearts; it made them both a little happier to know that they were actually doing something for their son. No pain in love is so hard to bear as that which comes from the impossibility of doing any service for the well-beloved, and no service is so repulsive that love cannot make it delightful and easy. They had not seen him for five years, their only child; for he had gone from Sandhurst straight to India, and thence, on the outbreak of war, to the Cape. No one knew how much the lonely parents had felt the long separation, how eagerly they awaited his letters, how often they read them.

But it was more than parental affection which caused the passionate interest they took in Jamie's career. They looked to him to restore the good name which his father had lost. Four generations of Parsons had been in the army, and had borne themselves with honour to their family and with credit to themselves. It was a fine record that Colonel Parsons inherited of brave men and good soldiers; and he, the truest, bravest, most honourable of them all, had dragged the name through the dust; had been forced from the service under a storm of obloquy, disgraced, dishonoured, ruined.

Colonel Parsons had done the greater portion of his service creditably enough. He had always put his God before the War Office, but the result had not been objectionable; he looked upon his men with fatherly affection, and the regiment, under his command, was almost a model of propriety and seemliness. His influence was invariably for good, and his subordinates knew that in him they had always a trusty friend; few men had gained more love. He was a mild, even-tempered fellow, and in no circumstance of life forgot to love his neighbour as himself; he never allowed it to slip his memory that even the lowest caste native had an immortal soul, and before God equal rights with him. Colonel Parsons was a man whose piety was so unaggressive, so good-humoured, so simple, that none could resist it; ribaldry and blasphemy were instinctively hushed in his presence, and even the most hardened ruffian was softened by his contact.

But a couple of years before he would naturally have been put on half-pay under the age limit, a little expedition was arranged against some unruly hilltribes, and Colonel Parsons was given the command. He took the enemy by surprise, finding them at the foot of the hills, and cut off, by means of flanking bodies, their retreat through the two passes behind. He placed his guns on a line of hillocks to the right, and held the tribesmen in the hollow of his hand. He could have massacred them all, but nothing was farther from his thoughts. He summoned them to surrender, and towards evening the headmen came in and agreed to give up their rifles next day; the night was cold, and dark, and stormy. The good Colonel was delighted with the success both of his stratagem and of his humanity. He had not shed a single drop of blood.

"Treat them well," he said, "and they'll treat you better."

He acted like a gentleman and a Christian; but the enemy were neither. He never dreamed that he was being completely overreached, that the natives were using the delay he had unsuspectingly granted to send over the hills urgent messages for help. Through the night armed men had been coming stealthily, silently, from all sides; and in the early morning, before dawn, his flanking parties were attacked. Colonel Parsons, rather astonished, sent them help, and thinking himself still superior in numbers to the rebellious tribesmen, attacked their main body. They wanted nothing better. Falling back slowly, they drew him into the mountain defiles until he found himself entrapped. His little force was surrounded. Five hours were passed in almost blind confusion; men were shot down like flies by an enemy they could not see; and when, by desperate fighting, they managed to cut their way out, fifty were killed and over a hundred more were wounded.

Colonel Parsons escaped with only the remnants of the fine force he had commanded, and they were nerveless, broken, almost panic-stricken. He was obliged to retreat. The Colonel was a brave man; he did what he could to prevent the march from becoming a disorderly rout. He gathered his men together, put courage into them, risked his life a dozen times; but nothing could disguise the fact that his failure was disastrous. It was a small affair and was hushed up, but the consequences were not to be forgotten. The hill-tribes, emboldened by their success, became more venturesome, more unruly. A disturbance which might have been settled without difficulty now required a large force to put it down, and ten times more lives were lost.

Colonel Parsons was required to send in his papers, and left India a broken man. . . . He came back to England, and settled in his father's house at Little Primpton. His agony continued, and looking into the future, he saw only hideous despair, unavailing regret. For months he could bear to see no one, imagining always that he was pointed out as the man whose folly had cost so many lives. When he heard people laugh he thought it was in scorn of him; when he saw compassion in their eyes he could scarcely restrain his tears. He was indeed utterly broken. He walked in his garden, away from the eyes of his fellows, up and down, continually turning over in his mind the events of that terrible week. And he could not console himself by thinking that any other course would have led to just as bad results. His error was too plain; he could put his finger exactly on the point of his failure and say, "O God! why did I do it?" And as he walked restlessly, unmindful of heat and cold, the tears ran down his thin cheeks, painful and scalding. He would not take his wife's comfort.

"You acted for the best, Richmond," she said.

"Yes, dear; I acted for the best. When I got those fellows hemmed in I could have killed them all. But I'm not a butcher; I couldn't have them shot down in cold blood. That's not war; that's murder. What should I have said to my Maker when He asked me to account for those many souls? I spared them; I imagined they'd understand; but they thought it was weakness. I couldn't know they were preparing a trap for me. And now my name is shameful. I shall never hold up my head again."

"You acted rightly in the sight of God, Richmond."

"I think and trust I acted as a Christian, Frances."

"If you have pleased God, you need not mind the opinion of man."

"Oh, it's not that they called me a fool and a coward—I could have borne that. I did what I thought was right. I thought it my duty to save the lives of my men and to spare the enemy; and the result was that ten times more lives have been lost than if I had struck boldly and mercilessly. There are widows and orphans in England who must curse me because I am the cause that their husbands are dead, and that their fathers are rotting on the hills of India. If I had acted like a savage, like a brute-beast, like a butcher, all those men would have been alive to-day. I was merciful, and I was met with treachery; I was long-suffering, and they thought me weak; I was forgiving, and they laughed at me."

Mrs. Parsons put her hand on her husband's shoulder.

"You must try to forget it, Richmond," she said "It's over, and it can't be helped now. You acted like a God-fearing man; your conscience is clear of evil intent. What is the judgment of man beside the judgment of God? If you have received insult and humiliation at the hands of man, God will repay you an hundredfold, for you acted as his servant. And I believe in you, Richmond; and I'm proud of what you did."

"I have always tried to act like a Christian and a gentleman, Frances."

At night he would continually dream of those days of confusion and mortal anxiety. He would imagine he was again making that herrible retreat, cheering his men, doing all he could to retrieve the disaster; but aware that ruin only awaited him, conscious that the most ignorant sepoy in his command thought him incapable and mad. He saw the look in the eyes of the officers under him, their bitter contempt, their anger because he forced them to retire before the enemy; and because, instead of honour and glory, they had earned only ridicule. His limbs shook and he sweated with agony as he recalled the interview with his chief: "You're only fit to be a damned missionary," and the last contemptuous words, "I shan't want you any more. You can send in your papers."

But human sorrow is like water in an earthen pot. Little by little Colonel Parsons forgot his misery; he had turned it over in his mind so often that at last he grew confused. It became then only a deep wound partly healed, scarring over; and he began to take an interest in the affairs of the life surrounding him. He could read his paper without every word stabbing him by some chance association; and there is nothing like the daily and thorough perusal of a newspaper for dulling a man's brain. He pottered about his garden gossiping with the gardener; made little alterations in the house—bricks and mortar are like an anodyne; he collected stamps; played bezique with his wife; and finally, in his mild, gentle way, found peace of mind.

But when James passed brilliantly out of Sandhurst, the thought seized him that the good name which he valued so highly might be retrieved. Colonel Parsons had shrunk from telling the youth anything of the catastrophe which had driven him from the service; but now he forced himself to give an exact account thereof. His wife sat by, listening with pain in her eyes, for she knew what torture it was to revive that half-forgotten story.

"I thought you had better hear it from me than from a stranger," the Colonel said when he had finished. "I entered the army with the reputation of my father behind me; my reputation can only harm you. Men will nudge one another and say, 'There's the son of old Parsons, who bungled the affair against the Madda Khels.' You must show them that you're of good stuff. I acted for the best, and my conscience is at ease. I think I did my duty; but if you can distinguish yourself—if you can make them forget—I think I shall die a little happier."

The commanding officer of Jamie's regiment was an old friend of the Colonel's, and wrote to him after a while to say that he thought well of the boy. He had already distinguished himself in a frontier skirmish, and presently, for gallantry in some other little expedition, his name was mentioned in despatches. Colonel Parsons regained entirely his old cheerfulness; Jamie's courage and manifest knowledge of his business made him feel that at last he could again look the world frankly in the face. Then came the Boer War; for the parents at Little Primpton and for Mary Clibborn days of fearful anxiety, of gnawing pain—all the greater because each, for the other's sake, tried to conceal it; and at last the announcement in the paper that James Parsons had been severely wounded while attempting to save the life of a brother officer, and was recommended for the Victoria Cross.

2

The Parsons sat again in their dining-room, counting the minutes which must pass before Jamie's arrival. The table was laid simply, for all their habits were simple; and the blanc-mange prepared for the morrow's festivities stood, uncompromising and stiff as a dissenting minister, in the middle of the table. I wish someone would write an invective upon that most detestable of all the national dishes, pallid, chilly, glutinous, unpleasant to look upon, insipid in the mouth. It is a preparation which seems to mark a transition stage in culture; just as the South Sea Islanders, with the advance of civilisation, forsook putrid whale for roast missionary, the great English middle classes complained that tarts and plum-puddings were too substantial, more suited to the robust digestions of a past generation. In the blanc-mange, on the other hand, they found almost an appearance of distinction; its name, at least, suggested French cookery; it was possible to the plainest cook, and it required no mastication.

"I shall have to tell Betty to make a jelly for dinner to-morrow," said Mrs. Parsons.

"Yes," replied the Colonel; and after a pause: "Don't you think we ought to let Mary know that Jamie has come back? She'd like to see him to-night."

"I've sent over already."

It was understood that James, having got his Company, would marry Mary Clibborn almost at once. His father and mother had been delighted when he announced the engagement. They had ever tried to shield him from all knowledge of evil—no easy matter when a boy has

been to a public school and to Sandhurst—holding the approved opinion that ignorance is synonymous with virtue; and they could imagine
no better safeguard for his innocence in the multi-coloured life of India
than betrothal with a pure, sweet English girl. They looked upon Mary
Clibborn already as a daughter, and she, in Jamie's absence, had been
their only solace. They loved her gentleness, her goodness, her simple
piety, and congratulated themselves on the fact that with her their son
could not fail to lead a happy and a godly life.

Mary, during those five years, had come to see them every day; her
own mother and father were rather worldly people, and she felt less happy
with them than with Colonel Parsons and his wife. The trio talked continually of the absent soldier, always reading to one another his letters.
They laughed together over his jokes, mildly, as befitted persons for
whom a sense of humour might conceivably be a Satanic snare, and trembled together at his dangers. Mary's affection was free from anything so
degrading as passion, and she felt no bashfulness in reading Jamie's love-
letters to his parents; she was too frank to suspect that there might be in
them anything for her eyes alone, and too candid to feel any delicacy.

But a lumbering fly rolled in at the gate and the good people, happy
at last, sprang to the door.

"Jamie!"

Trembling with joy, they brought him in and sat him down; they
knew no words to express their delight, and stood looking at him open-
mouthed, smiling.

"Well, here you are! We were surprised to get your telegram. When
did you land?"

When they found their tongues, it was only to say commonplace
things such as they might have spoken to a casual friend who had come
from London for the day. They were so used to controlling themselves,
that when their emotion was overpowering they were at a loss to express it.

"Would you like to go upstairs and wash your hands?"

They both accompanied him.

"You see it's all just as it was. We thought you'd like your old room.
If you want anything you can ring the bell."

They left him, and going downstairs, sat opposite one another by
the fire. The dining-room was furnished with a saddle-bag suite; and

Colonel Parsons sat in the "gentleman's chair," which had arms, while Mrs. Parsons sat in the "lady's chair," which had none; nor did either dream, under any circumstances, of using the other's seat. They were a little overcome.

"How thin he is!" said Mrs. Parsons.

"We must feed him up," answered the Colonel.

And then, till the soldier came, they remained in silence. Mrs. Parsons rang the bell for the chops as soon as he appeared, and they sat down; but James ate alone. His people were too happy to do anything but watch him.

"I have had tea made," said Mrs. Parsons, "but you can have some claret, if you prefer it."

Five years' absence had not dulled Jamie's memory of his father's wine, and he chose the tea.

"I think a strong cup of tea will do you most good," said his mother, and she poured it out for him as when he was a boy, with plenty of milk and sugar.

His tastes had never been much consulted; things had been done, in the kindest manner possible, solely for his good. James detested sweetness.

"No sugar, please, mother," he said, as she dived into the sugar-basin.

"Nonsense, Jamie," answered Mrs. Parsons, with her good-humoured, indulgent smile. "Sugar's good for you." And she put in two big lumps.

"You don't ask after Mary," said Colonel Parsons.

"How is she?" said James. "Where is she?"

"If you wait a little she'll be here."

Then Mrs. Parsons broke in.

"I don't know what we should have done without her; she's been so good and kind to us, and such a comfort. We're simply devoted to her, aren't we, Richmond?"

"She's the nicest girl I've ever seen."

"And she's so good. She works among the poor like a professional nurse. We told you that she lived with us for six months while Colonel and Mrs. Clibborn went abroad. She was never put out at anything, but was always smiling and cheerful. She has the sweetest character."

The good people thought they were delighting their son by these eulogies. He looked at them gravely.

"I'm glad you like her," he said.

Supper was finished, and Mrs. Parsons went out of the room for a moment. James took out his case and offered a cigar to his father.

"I don't smoke, Jamie," replied the Colonel.

James lit up. The old man looked at him with a start, but said nothing; he withdrew his chair a little and tried to look unconcerned. When Mrs. Parsons returned, the room was full of smoke; she gave a cry of surprise.

"James!" she said, in a tone of reproach. "Your father objects to smoking."

"It doesn't matter just this once," said the Colonel, good-humouredly.

But James threw his cigar into the fire, with a laugh.

"I quite forgot; I'm so sorry."

"You never told us you'd started smoking," observed Mrs. Parsons, almost with disapprobation.

"Would you like the windows open to let the smell out, Richmond?"

There was a ring at the door, and Mary's voice was heard.

"Has Captain Parsons arrived?"

"There she is, Jamie!" said the Colonel. "Rush out to her, my boy!"

But James contented himself with rising to his feet; he turned quite pale, and a singular expression came over his grave face.

Mary entered.

"I ran round as soon as I got your note," she said.

"Well, Jamie!"

She stopped, smiling, and a blush brightened her healthy cheeks. Her eyes glistened with happiness, and for a moment, strong as she was, Mary thought she must burst into tears.

"Aren't you going to kiss her, Jamie?" said the father. "You needn't be bashful before us."

James went up to her, and taking her hands, kissed the cheek she offered.

The impression that Mary Clibborn gave was of absolute healthiness, moral and physical. Her appearance was not distinguished, but she was well set up, with strong hands and solid feet; you knew at once that a ten-mile walk invigorated rather than tired her; her arms were muscular and energetic. She was in no way striking; a typical, country-bred girl, with a fine digestion and an excellent conscience; if not very pretty, obviously good. Her face showed a happy mingling of strength and cheerfulness; her blue eyes were guileless and frank; her hair even was rather pretty, arranged in the simplest manner; her skin was tanned by wind and weather. The elements were friendly, and she enjoyed a long walk in a gale, with the rain beating against her cheeks. She was dressed simply and without adornment, as befitted her character.

"I am sorry I wasn't at home when you arrived, Jamie," she said; "but the Polsons asked me to go and play golf at Tunbridge Wells. I went round in bogy, Colonel Parsons."

"Did you, my dear? That's very good."

The Colonel and his wife looked at her with affectionate satisfaction.

"I'm going to take off my hat."

She gave James to put in the hall her sailor hat and her rough tweed cloak. She wore a bicycling skirt and heavy, square-toed boots.

"Say you're glad to see us, Jamie!" she cried, laughing.

Her voice was rather loud, clear and strong, perhaps wanting variety of inflection. She sat by Jamie's side, and broke into a cheerful, rather humorous, account of the day's excursion.

"How silent you are, Jamie!" she cried at last.

"You haven't given me a chance to get a word in yet," he said, smiling gravely.

They all laughed, ready to be pleased at the smallest joke, and banter was the only form of humour they knew.

"Are you tired?" asked Mary, her cheerful eyes softening.

"A little."

"Well, I won't worry you to-night; but to-morrow you must be put through your paces."

"Mary will stand no nonsense," said the Colonel, laughing gently. "We all have to do as she tells us. She'll turn you round her little finger."

"Will she?" said James, glancing down at the solid boots, which the short bicycle skirt rather obtrusively exposed to view.

"Don't frighten him the moment he comes home," cried Mary. "As a matter of fact, I shan't be able to come to-morrow morning; I've got my district-visiting to do, and I don't think Jamie is strong enough to go with me yet. Does your wound hurt you still, Jamie?"

"No," he said. "I can't use my arm much, though. It'll be all right soon."

"You must tell us about the great event to-morrow," said Mary, referring to the deed which had won him the decoration. "You've put us all out by coming sooner than you were expected."

"Have I? I'm sorry."

"Didn't you notice anything when you drove in this evening?"

"No, it was quite dark."

"Good heavens! Why, we've put up a triumphal arch, and there was going to be a great celebration. All the school children were coming to welcome you."

"I'm very glad I missed it," said James, laughing. "I should have hated it."

"Oh, I don't know that you have missed it yet. We must see."

Then Mary rose to go.

"Well, at all events, we're all coming to dinner to-morrow at one."

They went to the door to let her out, and the elder couple smiled again with pleasure when James and Mary exchanged a brotherly and sisterly kiss.

At last James found himself alone in his room; he gave a sigh of relief—a sigh which was almost a groan of pain. He took out his pipe unconsciously and filled it; but then, remembering where he was, put it down. He knew his father's sensitiveness of smell. If he began to smoke there would quickly be a knock at the door, and the inquiry: "There's such a smell of burning in the house; there's nothing on fire in your room, is there, Jamie?"

He began to walk up and down, and then in exhaustion sank on a chair. He opened the window and looked into the night. He could see nothing. The sky was dark with unmoving clouds, but the fresh air blew gratefully against his face, laden with the scent of the vernal country; a light rain was falling noiselessly, and the earth seemed languid and weary, accepting the moisture with little shuddering gasps of relief.

After an event which has been long expected, there is always something in the nature of reaction. James had looked forward to this meeting, partly with terror, partly with eagerness; and now that it was over, his brain, confused and weary, would not help him to order his thoughts.

He clenched his hands, trying to force himself to think clearly; he knew he must decide upon some course at once, and a terrible indecision paralysed his ideas. He loved his people so tenderly, he was so anxious to make them happy, and yet—and yet! If he loved one better than the other it was perhaps his father, because of the pitiful weakness, because of the fragility which seemed to call for a protective gentleness. The old man had altered little in the five years. James could not remember him other than thin and bent and frail, with long wisps of silvery hair brushed over the crown to conceal his baldness, with the cheeks hollow and wrinkled, and a white moustache ineffectually concealing the weak, good-natured mouth. Ever since James could recollect his father had appeared old and worn as now; and there had always been that gentle look in the blue eyes, that manner which was almost painful in its diffidence. Colonel Parsons was a man who made people love him by a modesty which seemed to claim nothing. He was like a child compelling sympathy on account of its utter helplessness, so unsuited to the wear and tear of life that he aroused his fellows' instincts of protection.

And James knew besides what a bitter humiliation it was to his father that he had been forced to leave the service. He remembered, like a deadly, incurable pain suffered by a friend, the occasion on which the old soldier had told him the cause of his disgrace, a sweat of agony standing on his brow. The scene had eaten into Jamie's mind alongside of that other when he had first watched a man die, livid with pain, his eyes glazed and sightless. He had grown callous to such events since then.

Colonel Parsons had come to grief on account of the very kindness of heart, on account of the exquisite humanity which endeared him to the most casual acquaintance. James swore that he would do anything to save him from needless suffering. Nor did he forget his mother, for through the harder manner he saw her gentleness and tender love. He knew that he was all in the world to both of them, that in his hands lay their happiness and their misery. Their love made them feel every act of his with a force out of reason to the circumstance. He had seen in their letters, piercing through the assumed cheerfulness, a mortal anxiety when he was in danger, an anguish of mind that seemed hardly bearable. They had gone through so much for his sake; they deprived themselves of luxury, so that, in the various expenses of his regiment, he should not need to economise. All his life they had surrounded him with loving care. And what their hearts were set upon now was that he should marry Mary Clibborn quickly.

James turned from the window and put his head between his hands, swaying to and fro.

"Oh, I can't," he groaned; "I can't!"

3

In the morning, after breakfast, James went for a walk. He wanted to think out clearly what he had better do, feeling that he must make up his mind at once. Hesitation would be fatal, and yet to speak immediately seemed so cruel, so brutally callous.

Wishing to be absolutely alone, he wandered through the garden to a little wood of beech-trees, which in his boyhood had been a favourite haunt. The day was fresh and sweet after the happy rain of April, the sky so clear that it affected one like a very beautiful action.

James stood still when he came into the wood, inhaling the odour of moist soil, the voluptuous scents of our mother, the Earth, gravid with silent life. For a moment he was intoxicated by the paradise of verdure. The beech-trees rose very tall, with their delicate branches singularly black amid the young leaves of the spring, tender and vivid. They eye could not pierce the intricate greenery; it was more delicate than the summer rain, subtler than the mists of the sunset. It was a scene to drive away all thought of the sadness of life, of the bitterness. Its exquisite fresh purity made James feel pure also, and like a little child he wandered over the undulating earth, broken by the tortuous courses of the stream-lets of winter.

The ground was soft, covered with brown dead leaves, and he tried to see the rabbit rustling among them, or the hasty springing of a squir-rel. The long branches of the briar entangled his feet; and here and there, in sheltered corners, blossomed the primrose and the violet. He listened to the chant of the birds, so joyous that it seemed impossible they sang in a world of sorrow. Hidden among the leaves, aloft in the beeches, the linnet sang with full-throated melody, and the blackbird and the thrush.

In the distance a cuckoo called its mysterious note, and far away, like an echo, a fellow-bird called back.

All Nature was rejoicing in the delight of the sunshine; all Nature was rejoicing, and his heart alone was heavy as lead. He stood by a fir-tree, which rose far above the others, immensely tall, like the mast of a solitary ship; it was straight as a life without reproach, but cheerless, cold, and silent. His life, too, was without reproach, thought James—without reproach till now. . . . He had loved Mary Clibborn. But was it love, or was it merely affection, habit, esteem? She was the only girl he knew, and they had grown up together. When he came from school for his holidays, or later from Sandhurst, on leave, Mary was his constant friend, without whom he would have been miserably dull. She was masculine enough to enter into his boyish games, and even their thoughts were common. There were so few people in Little Primpton that those who lived there saw one another continually; and though Tunbridge Wells was only four miles away, the distance effectually prevented very close intimacy with its inhabitants. It was natural, then, that James should only look forward to an existence in which Mary took part; without that pleasant companionship the road seemed long and dreary. When he was appointed to a regiment in India, and his heart softened at the prospect of the first long parting from all he cared for, it was the separation from Mary that seemed hardest to bear.

"I don't know what I shall do without you, Mary," he said.

"You will forget all about us when you've been in India a month."

But her lips twitched, and he noticed that she found difficulty in speaking quite firmly. She hesitated a moment, and spoke again.

"It's different for us," she said. "Those who go forget, but those who stay—remember. We shall be always doing the same things to remind us of you. Oh, you won't forget me, Jamie?"

The last words slipped out against the girl's intention.

"Mary!" he cried.

And then he put his arms round her, and Mary rested her face on his shoulder and began to cry. He kissed her, trying to stop her tears; he pressed her to his heart. He really thought he loved her then with all his strength.

"Mary," he whispered, "Mary, do you care for me? Will you marry me?"

Then quickly he explained that it would make it so much better for both if they became engaged.

"I shan't be able to marry you for a long time; but will you wait for me, Mary?"

She began to smile through her tears.

"I would wait for you to the end of my life."

During the first two years in India the tie had been to James entirely pleasurable; and if, among the manifold experiences of his new life, he bore Mary's absence with greater equanimity than he had thought possible, he was always glad to receive her letters, with their delicate aroma of the English country; and it pleased him to think that his future was comfortably settled. The engagement was a sort of ballast, and he felt that he could compass his journey without fear and without disturbance. James did not ask himself whether his passion was very ardent, for his whole education had led him to believe that passion was hardly moral. The proper and decent basis of marriage was similarity of station, and the good, solid qualities which might be supposed endurable. From his youth, the wisdom of the world had been instilled into him through many proverbs, showing the advisability of caution, the transitoriness of beauty and desire; and, on the other hand, the lasting merit of honesty, virtue, domesticity, and good temper. . . .

But we all know that Nature is a goddess with no sense of decency, for whom the proprieties are simply non-existent; men and women in her eyes have but one point of interest, and she walks abroad, with her fashioning fingers, setting in order the only work she cares for. All the rest is subsidiary, and she is callous to suffering and to death, indifferent to the Ten Commandments and even to the code of Good Society.

James at last made the acquaintance of a certain Mrs. Pritchard-Wallace, the wife of a man in a native regiment, a little, dark-haired person, with an olive skin and big brown eyes—rather common, but excessively pretty. She was the daughter of a riding-master by a Portuguese woman from Goa, and it had been something of a scandal when Pritchard-Wallace, who was an excellent fellow, had married her against the advice of all the regimental ladies. But if those charitable persons had not ceased to look upon her with doubtful eyes, her wit and her good looks for others counterbalanced every disadvantage; and she did not fail to have a little court of subalterns and the like hanging perpetually about her skirts. At first Mrs. Wallace merely amused James. Her absolute frivolity, her cynical tongue, her light-heartedness, were a relief after the rather puritanical atmosphere in which he had passed his youth; he was astonished to hear the gay contempt which she poured upon all the things that he had held most sacred—things like the Tower of London and the British Constitution. Prejudices and cherished beliefs were dissipated before her sharp-tongued raillery; she was a woman with almost a witty way of seeing the world, with a peculiarly feminine gift for putting old things in a new, absurd light. To Mrs. Wallace, James seemed a miracle of ingenuousness, and she laughed at him continually; then she began to like him, and took him about with her, at which he was much flattered.

James had been brought up in the belief that women were fashioned of different clay from men, less gross, less earthly; he thought not only that they were pious, sweet and innocent, ignorant entirely of disagreeable things, but that it was man's first duty to protect them from all knowledge of the realities of life. To him they were an ethereal blending of milk-and-water with high principles; it had never occurred to him that they were flesh and blood, and sense, and fire and nerves—especially nerves. Most topics, of course, could not be broached in their presence; in fact, almost the only safe subject of conversation was the weather.

But Mrs. Pritchard-Wallace prided herself on frankness, which is less common in pretty women than in plain; and she had no hesitation in discussing with James matters that he had never heard discussed before. She was hugely amused at the embarrassment which made him hesitate and falter, trying to find polite ways of expressing the things which his whole training had taught him to keep rigidly to himself. Then sometimes, from pure devilry, Mrs. Wallace told stories on purpose to shock him; and revelled in his forced, polite smile, and in his strong look of disapproval.

"What a funny boy you are!" she said. "But you must take care, you know; you have all the makings of a perfect prig."

"D'you think so?"

"You must try to be less moral. The moral young man is rather funny for a change, but he palls after a time."

"If I bore you, you have only to say so, and I won't bother you again."

"And moral young men shouldn't get cross; it's very bad manners," she answered, smiling.

Before he knew what had happened, James found himself madly in love with Mrs. Wallace. But what a different passion was this, resembling not at all that pallid flame which alone he had experienced! How could he recognise the gentle mingling of friendship and of common-sense which he called love in that destroying violence which troubled his days like a fever? He dreamed of the woman at night; he seemed only to live when he was with her. The mention of her name made his heart beat, and meeting her he trembled and turned cold. By her side he found nothing to say; he was like wax in her hands, without will or strength. The touch of her fingers sent the blood rushing through his veins insanely; and understanding his condition, she took pleasure in touching him, to watch the little shiver of desire that convulsed his frame. In a very self-restrained man love works ruinously; and it burnt James now, this invisible, unconscious fire, till he was consumed utterly—till he was mad with passion. And then suddenly, at some chance word, he knew what had happened; he knew that he was in love with the wife of his good friend, Pritchard-Wallace; and he thought of Mary Clibborn.

There was no hesitation now, nor doubt; James had only been in danger because he was unaware of it. He never thought of treachery to his friend or to Mary; he was horror-stricken, hating himself. He looked over the brink of the precipice at the deadly sin, and recoiled, shuddering. He bitterly reproached himself, taking for granted that some error of his had led to the catastrophe. But his duty was obvious; he knew he must kill the sinful love, whatever pain it cost him; he must crush it as he would some noxious vermin.

James made up his mind never to see Mrs. Wallace again; and he thought that God was on his side helping him, since, with her husband, she was leaving in a month for England. He applied for leave. He could get away for a few weeks, and on his return Mrs. Wallace would be gone. He managed to avoid her for several days, but at last she came across him by chance, and he could not escape.

"I didn't know you were so fond of hide-and-seek," she said. "I think it's rather a stupid game."

"I don't understand," replied James, growing pale.

"Why have you been dodging round corners to avoid me as if I were a dun, and inventing the feeblest excuses not to come to me?"

James stood for a moment, not knowing what to answer; his knees trembled, and he sweated with the agony of his love. It was an angry, furious passion, that made him feel he could almost seize the woman by the throat and strangle her.

"Did you know that I am engaged to be married?" he asked at length.

"I've never known a sub who wasn't. It's the most objectionable of all their vicious habits. What then?" She looked at him, smiling; she knew very well the power of her dark eyes, fringed with long lashes. "Don't be silly," she added. "Come and see me, and bring her photograph, and you shall talk to me for two hours about her. Will you come?"

"It's very kind of you. I don't think I can."

"Why not? You're really very rude."

"I'm extremely busy."

"Nonsense! You must come. Don't look as if I were asking you to do something quite horrible. I shall expect you to tea."

She bound him by his word, and James was forced to go. When he showed the photograph, Mrs. Pritchard-Wallace looked at it with a curious expression. It was the work of a country photographer, awkward and ungainly, with the head stiffly poised, and the eyes hard and fixed; the general impression was ungraceful and devoid of charm. Mrs. Wallace noticed the country fashion of her clothes.

"It's extraordinary that subalterns should always get engaged to the same sort of girl."

James flushed. "It's not a very good one of her."

"They always photograph badly," murmured Mrs. Wallace.

"She's the best girl in the world. You can't think how good, and kind, and simple she is; she reminds me always of an English breeze."

"I don't like east winds myself," said Mrs. Wallace. "But I can see she has all sorts of admirable qualities."

"D'you know why I came to see you to-day?"

"Because I forced you," said Mrs. Wallace, laughing.

"I came to say good-bye; I've got a month's leave."

"Oh, but I shall be gone by the time you come back."

"I know. It is for that reason."

Mrs. Wallace looked at him quickly, hesitated, then glanced away. "Is it so bad as that?"

"Oh, don't you understand?" cried James, breaking suddenly from his reserve. "I must tell you. I shall never see you again, and it can't matter. I love you with all my heart and soul. I didn't know what love was till I met you. God help me, it was only friendship I had for Mary! This is so different. Oh, I hate myself! I can't help it; the mere touch of your hand sends me mad with passion. I daren't see you again—I'm not a blackguard. I know it's quite hopeless. And I've given my word to Mary."

The look of her eyes, the sound of her voice, sent half his fine intentions flying before the wind. He lost command over himself—but only for a moment; the old habits were strong.

"I beg your pardon! I oughtn't to have spoken. Don't be angry with me for what I've said. I couldn't help it. You thought me a fool because I ran away from you. It was all I could do. I couldn't help loving you. You understand now, don't you? I know that you will never wish to see me again, and it's better for both of us. Good-bye."

He stretched out his hand.

"I didn't know it was so bad as that," she said, looking at him with kindly eyes.

"Didn't you see me tremble when the hem of your dress touched me by accident? Didn't you hear that I couldn't speak; the words were dried up in my throat?" He sank into a chair weakly; but then immediately gathering himself together, sprang up. "Good-bye," he said. "Let me go quickly."

She gave him her hand, and then, partly in kindness, partly in malice, bent forward and kissed his lips. James gave a cry, a sob; now he lost command over himself entirely. He took her in his arms roughly, and kissed her mouth, her eyes, her hair—so passionately that Mrs. Wallace was frightened. She tried to free herself; but he only held her closer, madly kissing her lips.

"Take care," she said. "What are you doing? Let me go!" And she pushed him away.

She was a cautious woman, who never allowed flirtation to go beyond certain decorous lengths, and she was used to a milder form of philandering.

"You've disarranged my hair, you silly boy!" She went to the glass to put it in order, and when she turned back found that James had gone. "What an odd creature!" she muttered.

To Mrs. Pritchard-Wallace the affair was but an incident, such as might have been the love of Phœdra had she flourished in an age when the art of living consists in not taking things too seriously; but for Hippolitus a tragedy of one sort or another is inevitable. James was not a man of easy affections; he made the acquaintance of people with a feeling of hostility rather than with the more usual sensation of friendly curiosity. He was shy, and even with his best friends could not lessen his reserve. Some persons are able to form close intimacies with admirable facility, but James felt always between himself and his fellows a sort of barrier. He could not realise that deep and sudden sympathy was even possible, and was apt to look with mistrust upon the appearance thereof. He seemed frigid and perhaps supercilious to those with whom he came in contact; he was forced to go his way, hiding from all eyes the emotions he felt. And when at last he fell passionately in love, it meant to him ten times more than to most men; it was a sudden freedom from himself. He was like a prisoner who sees for the first time in his life the trees and the hurrying clouds, and all the various movement of the world. For a little while James had known a wonderful liberty, an ineffable bliss which coloured the whole universe with new, strange colours. But then he learnt that the happiness was only sin, and he returned voluntarily to his cold prison. . . . Till he tried to crush it, he did not know how strong was this passion; he did not realise that it had made of him a different man; it was the only thing in the world to him, beside which everything else was meaningless. He became ruthless towards himself, undergoing every torture which he fancied might cleanse him of the deadly sin.

And when Mrs. Wallace, against his will, forced herself upon his imagination, he tried to remember her vulgarity, her underbred manners, her excessive use of scent. She had merely played with him, without thinking or caring what the result to him might be. She was bent on as much enjoyment as possible without exposing herself to awkward consequences;

common scandal told him that he was not the first callow youth that she had entangled with her provoking glances and her witty tongue. The epithet by which his brother officers qualified her was expressive, though impolite. James repeated these things a hundred times: he said that Mrs. Wallace was not fit to wipe Mary's boots; he paraded before himself, like a set of unread school-books, all Mary's excellent qualities. He recalled her simple piety, her good-nature, and kindly heart; she had every attribute that a man could possibly want in his wife. And yet—and yet, when he slept he dreamed he was talking to the other; all day her voice sang in his ears, her gay smile danced before his eyes. He remembered every word she had ever said; he remembered the passionate kisses he had given her. How could he forget that ecstasy? He writhed, trying to expel the importunate image; but nothing served.

Time could not weaken the impression. Since then he had never seen Mrs. Wallace, but the thought of her was still enough to send the blood racing through his veins. He had done everything to kill the mad, hopeless passion; and always, like a rank weed, it had thriven with greater strength. James knew it was his duty to marry Mary Clibborn, and yet he felt he would rather die. As the months passed on, and he knew he must shortly see her, he was never free from a sense of terrible anxiety. Doubt came to him, and he could not drive it away. The recollection of her was dim, cold, formless; his only hope was that when he saw her love might rise up again, and kill that other passion which made him so utterly despise himself. But he had welcomed the war as a respite, and the thought came to him that its chances might easily solve the difficulty. Then followed the months of hardship and of fighting; and during these the image of Mrs. Wallace had been less persistent, so that James fancied he was regaining the freedom he longed for. And when he lay wounded and ill, his absolute weariness made him ardently look forward to seeing his people again. A hotter love sprang up for them; and the hope became stronger that reunion with Mary might awaken the dead emotion. He wished for it with all his heart.

But he had seen Mary, and he felt it hopeless; she left him cold, almost hostile. And with a mocking laugh, James heard Mrs. Wallace's words:

"Subalterns always get engaged to the same type of girl. They photograph so badly."

And now he did not know what to do. The long recalling of the past had left James more uncertain than ever. Some devil within him cried, "Wait, wait! Something may happen!" It really seemed better to let things slide a little. Perhaps—who could tell?—in a day or two the old habit might render Mary as dear to him as when last he had wandered with her in that green wood. James sighed, and looked about him. . . . The birds still sang merrily, the squirrel leaped from tree to tree; even the blades of grass stood with a certain conscious pleasure, as the light breeze rustled through them. In the midday sun all things took pleasure in their life; and all Nature appeared full of joy, coloured and various and insouciant. He alone was sad.

4

When James went home he found that the Vicar of Little Primpton and his wife had already arrived. They were both of them little, dried-up persons, with an earnest manner and no sense of humour, quite excellent in a rather unpleasant way; they resembled one another like peas, but none knew whether the likeness had grown from the propinquity of twenty years, or had been the original attraction. Deeply impressed with their sacred calling—for Mrs. Jackson would never have acknowledged that the Vicar's wife held a position inferior to the Vicar's—they argued that the whole world was God's, and they God's particular ministrants; so that it was their plain duty to concern themselves with the business of their fellows—and it must be confessed that they never shrank from this duty. They were neither well-educated, nor experienced, nor tactful; but blissfully ignorant of these defects, they shepherded their flock with little moral barks, and gave them, rather self-consciously, a good example in the difficult way to eternal life. They were eminently worthy people, who thought light-heartedness somewhat indecent. They did endless good in the most disagreeable manner possible; and in their fervour not only bore unnecessary crosses themselves, but saddled them on to everyone else, as the only certain passport to the Golden City.

The Reverend Archibald Jackson had been appointed to the living of Little Primpton while James was in India, and consequently had never seen him.

"I was telling your father," said Mrs. Jackson, on shaking hands, "that I hoped you were properly grateful for all the mercies that have been bestowed upon you."

James stared at her a little. "Were you?"

He hated the fashion these people had of discussing matters which he himself thought most private.

"Mr. Jackson was asking if you'd like a short prayer offered up next Sunday, James," said his mother.

"I shouldn't at all."

"Why not?" asked the Vicar. "I think it's your duty to thank your Maker for your safe return, and I think your parents should join in the thanksgiving."

"We're probably none of us less grateful," said James, "because we don't want to express our feelings before the united congregation."

Jamie's parents looked at him with relief, for the same thought filled their minds; but thinking it their duty to submit themselves to the spiritual direction of the Vicar and his wife, they had not thought it quite right to decline the proposal. Mrs. Jackson glanced at her husband with pained astonishment, but further argument was prevented by the arrival of Colonel and Mrs. Clibborn, and Mary.

Colonel Clibborn was a tall man, with oily black hair and fierce eyebrows, both dyed; aggressively military and reminiscent. He had been in a cavalry regiment, where he had come to the philosophic conclusion that all men are dust—except cavalrymen; and he was able to look upon Jamie's prowess—the prowess of an infantryman—from superior heights. He was a great authority upon war, and could tell anyone what were the mistakes in South Africa, and how they might have been avoided; likewise he had known in the service half the peers of the realm, and talked of them by their Christian names. He spent three weeks every season in London, and dined late, at seven o'clock, so he had every qualification for considering himself a man of fashion.

"I don't know what they'd do in Little Primpton without us," he said. "It's only us who keep it alive."

But Mrs. Clibborn missed society.

"The only people I can speak to are the Parsons," she told her husband, plaintively. "They're very good people—but only infantry, Reggie."

"Of course, they're only infantry," agreed Colonel Clibborn.

Mrs. Clibborn was a regimental beauty—of fifty, who had grown stout; but not for that ceased to use the weapons which Nature had given her against the natural enemies of the sex. In her dealings with several generations of adorers, she had acquired such a habit of languishing glances that now she used them unconsciously. Whether ordering meat from the butcher or discussing parochial matters with Mr. Jackson, Mrs. Clibborn's tone and manner were such that she might have been saying the most tender things. She had been very popular in the service, because she was the type of philandering woman who required no beating about the bush; her neighbour at the dinner-table, even if he had not seen her before, need never have hesitated to tell her with the soup that she was the handsomest creature he had ever seen, and with the *entrée* that he adored her.

On coming in, Mrs. Clibborn for a moment looked at James, quite speechless, her head on one side and her eyes screwing into the corner of the room.

"Oh, how wonderful!" she said, at last. "I suppose I mustn't call you Jamie now." She spoke very slowly, and every word sounded like a caress. Then she looked at James again in silent ecstasy. "Colonel Parsons, how proud you must be! And when I think that soon he will be my son! How thin you look, James!"

"And how well you look, dear lady!"

It was understood that everyone must make compliments to Mrs. Clibborn; otherwise she grew cross, and when she was cross she was horrid.

She smiled to show her really beautiful teeth.

"I should like to kiss you, James. May I, Mrs. Parsons?"

"Certainly," replied Jamie's mother, who didn't approve of Mrs. Clibborn at all.

She turned her cheek to James, and assumed a seraphic expression while he lightly touched it with his lips.

"I'm only an old woman," she murmured to the company in general.

She seldom made more than one remark at a time, and at the end of each assumed an appropriate attitude—coy, Madonna-like, resigned, as the circumstances might require. Mr. Jackson came forward to shake hands, and she turned her languishing glance on him.

"Oh, Mr. Jackson, how beautiful your sermon was!"

They sat down to dinner, and ate their ox-tail soup. It is terrible to think of the subtlety with which the Evil One can insinuate himself among the most pious; for soup at middle-day is one of his most dangerous wiles, and it is precisely with the simple-minded inhabitants of the country and of the suburbs that this vice is most prevalent.

James was sitting next to Mrs. Clibborn, and presently she looked at him with the melancholy smile which had always seemed to her so effective.

"We want you to tell us how you won your Victoria Cross, Jamie."

The others, eager to hear the story from the hero's lips, had been, notwithstanding, too tactful to ask; but they were willing to take advantage of Mrs. Clibborn's lack of that quality.

"We've all been looking forward to it," said the Vicar.

"I don't think there's anything to tell," replied James.

His father and mother were looking at him with happy eyes, and the Colonel nodded to Mary.

"Please, Jamie, tell us," she said. "We only saw the shortest account in the papers, and you said nothing about it in your letters."

"D'you think it's very good form of me to tell you about it?" asked James, smiling gravely.

"We're all friends here," said the Vicar.

And Colonel Clibborn added, making sheep's eyes at his wife:

"You can't refuse a lady!"

"I'm an old woman," sighed Mrs. Clibborn, with a doleful glance. "I can't expect him to do it for me."

The only clever thing Mrs. Clibborn had done in her life was to acknowledge to old age at thirty, and then she did not mean it. It had been one of her methods in flirtation, covering all excesses under a maternal aspect. She must have told hundreds of young officers that she was old enough to be their mother; and she always said it looking plaintively at the ceiling, when they squeezed her hand.

"It wasn't a very wonderful thing I did," said James, at last, "and it was completely useless."

"No fine deed is useless," said the Vicar, sententiously.

James looked at him a moment, but proceeded with his story.

"It was only that I tried to save the life of a sub who'd just joined—and didn't."

"Would you pass me the salt?" said Mrs. Clibborn.

"Mamma!" cried Mary, with a look as near irritation as her gentle nature permitted.

"Go on, Jamie, there's a good boy," said Mrs. Parsons.

And James, seeing his father's charming, pathetic look of pride, told the story to him alone. The others did not care how much they hurt him so long as they could gape in admiration, but in his father he saw the most touching sympathy.

"It was a chap called Larcher, a boy of eighteen, with fair hair and blue eyes, who looked quite absurdly young. His people live somewhere round here, near Ashford."

"Larcher, did you say?" asked Mrs. Clibborn. "I've never heard the name. It's not a county family."

"Go on, Jamie," said Mary, with some impatience.

"Well, he'd only been with us three or four weeks; but I knew him rather well. Oddly enough, he'd taken a sort of fancy to me. He was such a nice, bright boy, so enthusiastic and simple. I used to tell him that he ought to have been at school, rather than roughing it at the Cape."

Mrs. Clibborn sat with an idiotic smile on her lips, and a fixed expression of girlish innocence.

"Well, we knew we should be fighting in a day or so; and the evening before the battle young Larcher was talking to me. 'How d'you feel?' I said. He didn't answer quite so quickly as usual. 'D'you know,' he said, 'I'm so awfully afraid that I shall funk it.' 'You needn't mind that,' I said, and I laughed. 'The first time we most of us do funk it. For five minutes or so you just have to cling on to your eyelashes to prevent yourself from running away, and then you feel all right, and you think it's rather sport.' 'I've got a sort of presentiment that I shall be killed,' he said. 'Don't be an ass,' I answered. 'We've all got a presentiment that we shall be killed the first time we're under fire. If all the people were killed who had presentiments, half the army would have gone to kingdom come long ago.'"

"You should have told him to lay his trust in the hands of Him who has power to turn the bullet and to break the sword," said Mrs. Jackson.

"He wasn't that sort," replied James, drily. "I laughed at him, thinking it the better way. . . . Well, next day we did really fight. We were sent to take an unoccupied hill. Our maxim was that a hill is always unoccupied unless the enemy are actually firing from it. Of course, the place was chock full of Boers; they waited till we had come within easy range for a toy-pistol, and then fired murderously. We did all we could. We tried to storm the place, but we hadn't a chance. Men tumbled down like ninepins. I've never seen anything like it. The order was given to fire, and there was nothing to fire at but the naked rocks. We had to retire—we couldn't do anything else; and presently I found that poor Larcher had been wounded. Well, I thought he couldn't be left where he was, so I went back for him. I asked him if he could move. 'No,' he said, 'I think I'm hurt in the leg.' I knelt down and bandaged him up as well as I could. He was simply bleeding like a pig; and meanwhile brother Boer potted at us for all he was worth. 'How d'you feel?' I asked. 'Bit dicky; but comfortable. I didn't funk it, did I?' 'No, of course not, you juggins!' I said. 'Can you walk, d'you think?' 'I'll try.' I lifted him up and put my arm round him, and we got along for a bit; then he became awfully white and groaned, 'I do feel so bad, Parsons,' and then he fainted. So I had to carry him; and we went a bit farther, and then—and then I was hit in the arm. 'I say, I can't carry you now,' I said; 'for God's sake, buck up.' He opened his eyes, and I prevented him from falling. 'I think I can stand,' he said, and as he spoke a bullet got him in the neck, and his blood splashed over my face. He gave a gasp and died."

James finished, and his mother and Mary wiped the tears from their eyes. Mrs. Clibborn turned to her husband.

"Reggie, I'm sure the Larchers are not a county family."

"There was a sapper of that name whom we met at Simla once, my dear," replied the Colonel.

"I thought I'd heard it before," said Mrs. Clibborn, with an air of triumph, as though she'd found out a very difficult puzzle. "Had he a red moustache?"

"Have you heard from the young man's people, Captain Parsons?" asked Mrs. Jackson.

"I had a letter from Mrs. Larcher, the boy's mother, asking me to go over and see her."

"She must be very grateful to you, Jamie."

"Why? She has no reason to be."

"You did all you could to save him."

"It would have been better if I'd left him alone. Don't you see that if he had remained where he was he might have been alive now. He would have been taken prisoner and sent to Pretoria, but that is better than rotting on the veldt. He was killed because I tried to save him."

"There are worse things than death," said Colonel Parsons. "I have often thought that those fellows who surrendered did the braver thing. It is easy to stand and be shot down, but to hoist the white flag so as to save the lives of the men under one—that requires courage."

"It is a sort of courage which seemed not uncommon," answered James, drily. "And they had a fairly pleasant time in Pretoria. Eventually, I believe, wars will be quite bloodless; rival armies will perambulate, and whenever one side has got into a good position, the other will surrender wholesale. Campaigns will be conducted like manœuvres, and the special correspondents will decide which lot has won."

"If they were surrounded and couldn't escape, it would have been wicked not to hoist the white flag," said Mrs. Jackson.

"I daresay you know more about it than I," replied James.

But the Vicar's lady insisted:

"If you were so placed that on one hand was certain death for yourself and all your men, and on the other hand surrender, which would you chose?"

"One can never tell; and in those matters it is wiser not to boast. Certain death is an awful thing, but our fathers preferred it to surrender."

"War is horrible!" said Mary, shuddering.

"Oh, no!" cried James, shaking himself out of his despondency. "War is the most splendid thing in the world. I shall never forget those few minutes, now and then, when we got on top of the Boers and fought with them, man to man, in the old way. Ah, life seemed worth living then! One day, I remember, they'd been giving it us awfully hot all the morning, and we'd lost frightfully. At last we rushed their position, and, by Jove, we let 'em have it! How we did hate them! You should have heard the Tommies cursing as they killed! I shall never forget the exhilaration of it, the joy of thinking that we were getting our own again. By Gad, it beat cock-fighting!"

Jamie's cheeks were flushed and his eyes shone; but he had forgotten where he was, and his father's voice came to him through a mist of blood and a roar of sound.

"I have fought, too," said Colonel Parsons, looking at his son with troubled eyes—"I have fought, too, but never with anger in my heart, nor lust of vengeance. I hope I did my duty, but I never forgot that my enemy was a fellow-creature. I never felt joy at killing, but pain and grief. War is inevitable, but it is horrible, horrible! It is only the righteous cause that can excuse it; and then it must be tempered with mercy and forgiveness."

"Cause? Every cause is righteous. I can think of no war in which right has not been fairly equal on both sides; in every question there is about as much to be said on either part, and in none more than in war. Each country is necessarily convinced of the justice of its own cause."

"They can't both be right."

"Oh, yes, they can. It's generally six to one and half a dozen of the other."

"Do you mean to say that you, a military man, think the Boers were justified?" asked Colonel Clibborn, with some indignation.

James laughed.

"You must remember that if any nation but ourselves had been engaged, our sympathies would have been entirely with the sturdy peasants fighting for their independence. The two great powers in the affairs of the world are sentiment and self-interest. The Boers are the smaller, weaker nation, and they have been beaten; it is only natural that sympathy should be with them. It was with the French for the same reason, after the Franco-Prussian War. But we, who were fighting, couldn't think of sentiment; to us it was really a matter of life and death. I was interested to see how soon the English put aside their ideas of fair play and equal terms when we had had a few reverses. They forgot that one Englishman was equal to ten foreigners, and insisted on sending out as many troops as possible. I fancy you were badly panicstricken over here."

James saw that his listeners looked at him with surprise, even with consternation; and he hastened to explain.

"Of course, I don't blame them. They were quite right to send as many men as possible. The object of war is not to do glorious actions, but to win. Other things being equal, it is obviously better to be ten to one; it is less heroic, but more reasonable."

"You take from war all the honour and all the chivalry!" cried Mary. "The only excuse for war is that it brings out the noblest qualities of man—self-sacrifice, unselfishness, endurance."

"But war doesn't want any excuse," replied James, smiling gently. "Many people say that war is inhuman and absurd; many people are uncommonly silly. When they think war can be abolished, they show a phenomenal ignorance of the conditions of all development. War in one way and another is at the very root of life. War is not conducted only by fire and sword; it is in all nature, it is the condition of existence for all created things. Even the wild flowers in the meadow wage war, and they wage it more ruthlessly even than man, for with them defeat means extermination. The law of Nature is that the fit should kill the unfit. The Lord is the Lord of Hosts. The lame, and the halt, and the blind must remain behind, while the strong man goes his way rejoicing."

"How hard you are!" said Mary. "Have you no pity, James?"

"D'you know, I've got an idea that there's too much pity in the world. People seem to be losing their nerve; reality shocks them, and they live slothfully in the shoddy palaces of Sham Ideals. The sentimentalists, the cowards, and the cranks have broken the spirit of mankind. The general in battle now is afraid to strike because men may be killed. Sometimes it is worth while to lose men. When we become soldiers, we know that we cease to be human beings, and are merely the instruments for a certain work; we know that sometimes it may be part of a general's deliberate plan that we should be killed. I have no confidence in a leader who is tender-hearted. Compassion weakens his brain, and the result, too often, is disaster."

But as he spoke, James realised with a start how his father would take what he was saying. He could have torn out his tongue, he would have given anything that the words should remain unspoken. His father, in pity and in humanity, had committed just such a fatal mistake, and trying tender-heartedly to save life had brought about death and disaster. He would take the thoughtless words as a deliberate condemnation; the wound, barely closed, was torn open by his very son, and he must feel again the humiliation which had nearly killed him.

Colonel Parsons sat motionless, as though he were stunned, his eyes fixed on James with horror and pain; he looked like some hunted animal, terrorstricken, and yet surprised, wondering that man should be so cruel.

"What can I do?" thought James. "How can I make it good for him?"

The conversation was carried on by the Clibborns and by the Vicar, all happily unconscious that a tragedy was acting under their noses. James looked at his father. He wanted to show how bitterly he regretted the pain he had caused, but knew not what to say; he wanted to give a sign of his eager love, and tortured himself, knowing the impossibility of showing in any way his devotion.

Fortunately, the maid came in to announce that the school children were without, to welcome Captain Parsons; and they all rose from the table.

5

Colonel Parsons and his wife had wished no function to celebrate the home-coming of James; but gave in to the persuasions of Mary and of Mr. Dryland, the curate, who said that a public ceremony would be undoubtedly a stimulus to the moral welfare of Little Primpton. No man could escape from his obligations, and Captain Parsons owed it to his fellow-countrymen of Little Primpton to let them show their appreciation of his great deed.

The Vicar went so far as to assert that a hearty greeting to the hero would be as salutory to the parishioners as a sermon of his own, while it would awaken James, a young man and possibly thoughtless, to a proper sense of his responsibilities. But the sudden arrival of James had disturbed the arrangements, and Mr. Dryland, in some perplexity, went to see Mary.

"What are we to do, Miss Clibborn? The school children will be so disappointed."

The original plan had been to meet the hero as he drove towards Primpton House from the station, and the curate was unwilling to give it up.

"D'you think Captain Parsons would go into Tunbridge Wells and drive in at two o'clock, as if he were just arriving?"

"I'm afraid he wouldn't," replied Mary, doubtfully, "and I think he'd only laugh if I asked him. He seemed glad when he thought he had escaped the celebration."

"Did he, indeed? How true it is that real courage is always modest! But it would be an eternal disgrace to Little Primpton if we did not welcome our hero, especially now that everything is prepared. It must not be said that Little Primpton neglects to honour him whom the Empire has distinguished."

After turning over many plans, they decided that the procession should come to Primpton House at the appointed hour, when Captain Parsons would receive it from the triumphal arch at the gate. . . . When the servant announced that the function was ready to begin, an announcement emphasised by the discordant notes of the brass band, Mary hurriedly explained to James what was expected of him, and they all made for the front door.

Primpton House faced the green, and opposite the little village shops were gay with bunting; at the side, against the highroad that led to Groombridge, the church and the public-house stood together in friendly neighbourhood, decorated with Union Jacks. The whole scene, with its great chestnut-trees, and the stretch of greenery beyond, was pleasantly rural, old-fashioned and very English; and to complete it, the sun shone down comfortably like a good natured, mild old gentleman. The curate, with a fine sense of order, had arranged on the right the school-boys, nicely scrubbed and redolent of pomatum; and on the left the girls, supported by their teachers. In the middle stood the choir, the brass band, and Mr. Dryland. The village yokels were collected round in open-mouthed admiration. The little party from the house took their places under the triumphal arch, the Clibborns assuming an expression of genteel superciliousness; and as they all wore their Sunday clothes, they made quite an imposing group.

Seeing that they were ready, Mr. Dryland stepped forward, turned his back so as to command the musicians, and coughed significantly. He raised above his head his large, white clerical hand, stretching out the index-finger, and began to beat time. He bellowed aloud, and the choir, a bar or so late, followed lustily. The band joined in with a hearty braying of trumpets.

"*See, the conquering Hero comes,*
    Sound the trumpets; beat the drums."

But growing excited at the music issuing from his throat, the curate raised the other hand which held his soft felt hat, and beat time energetically with that also.

At the end of the verse the performers took a rapid breath, as though afraid of being left behind, and then galloped on, a little less evenly, until one by one they reached the highly-decorated Amen.

When the last note of the last cornet had died away on the startled air, Mr. Dryland made a sign to the head boy of the school, who thereupon advanced and waved his cap, shouting:

"Three cheers for Capting Parsons, V.C.!"

Then the curate, wiping his heated brow, turned round and cleared his throat.

"Captain Parsons," he said, in a loud voice, so that none should miss his honeyed words, "we, the inhabitants of Little Primpton, welcome you to your home. I need not say that it is with great pleasure that we have gathered together this day to offer you our congratulations on your safe return to those that love you. I need not remind you that there is no place like home. ("Hear, hear!" from the Vicar.) We are proud to think that our fellow-parishioner should have gained the coveted glory of the Victoria Cross. Little Primpton need not be ashamed now to hold up its head among the proudest cities of the Empire. You have brought honour to yourself, but you have brought honour to us also. You have shown that Englishmen know how to die; you have shown the rival nations of the Continent that the purity and the godliness of Old England still bear fruit. But I will say no more; I wished only to utter a few words to welcome you on behalf of those who cannot, perhaps, express themselves so well as I can. I will say no more. Captain Parsons, we hope that you will live long to enjoy your honour and glory, side by side with her who is to shortly become your wife. I would only assure you that your example has not been lost upon us; we all feel better, nobler, and more truly

Christian. And we say to you, now that you have overcome all dangers and tribulation, now that you have returned to the bosom of your beloved family, take her who has also given us an example of resignation, of courage, and of—and of resignation. Take her, we say, and be happy; confident in the respect, esteem, and affection of the people of Little Primpton. James Brown, who has the honour to bear the same Christian name as yourself, and is also the top boy of the Parish School, will now recite a short poem entitled 'Casabianca.'"

Mr. Dryland had wished to compose an ode especially for the occasion. It would evidently have been effective to welcome the hero, to glorify his deed, and to point the moral in a few original verses; but, unhappily, the muse was froward, which was singular, since the *élite* of Little Primpton had unimpeachable morals, ideals of the most approved character, and principles enough to build a church with; nor was an acquaintance with literature wanting. They all read the daily papers, and Mr. and Mrs. Jackson, in addition, read the *Church Times*. Mary even knew by heart whole chunks of Sir Lewis Morris, and Mr. Dryland recited Tennyson at penny readings. But when inspiration is wanting, a rhyming dictionary, for which the curate sent to London, will not help to any great extent; and finally the unanimous decision was reached to give some well-known poem apposite to the circumstance. It shows in what charming unity of spirit these simple, God-fearing people lived, and how fine was their sense of literary excellence, that without hesitation they voted in chorus for "Casabianca."

The head boy stepped forward—he had been carefully trained by Mr. Dryland—and with appropriate gestures recited the immortal verses of Felicia Hemans:

" *The boy stood on the burning deck,*
Whence all but'e'ad fled;
The flame that lit the battle's wreck,
Shone round'im o'er the dead."

When he finished, amid the discreet applause of the little party beneath the archway, Mr. Dryland again advanced.

"Polly Game, the top girl of the Parish School, will now present Miss Clibborn with a bouquet. Step forward, Polly Game."

This was a surprise arranged by the curate, and he watched with pleasure Mary's look of delighted astonishment.

Polly Game stepped forward, and made a little speech in the ingenuous words which Mr. Dryland had thought natural to her character and station.

"Please, Miss Clibborn, we, the girls of Little Primpton, wish to present you with this bouquet as a slight token of our esteem. We wish you a long life and a 'appy marriage with the choice of your 'eart."

She then handed a very stiff bunch of flowers, surrounded with frilled paper like the knuckle of a leg of mutton.

"We will now sing hymn number one hundred and thirty-seven," said Mr. Dryland.

The verses were given vigorously, while Mrs. Clibborn, with a tender smile, murmured to Mrs. Parsons that it was beautiful to see such a nice spirit among the lower classes. The strains of the brass band died away on the summer breeze, and there was a momentary pause. Then the Vicar, with a discreet cough to clear his throat, came forward.

"Captain Parsons, ladies and gentlemen, parishioners of Little Primpton, I wish to take the opportunity to say a few words."

The Vicar made an admirable speech. The sentiments were hackneyed, the observations self-evident, and the moral obvious. His phrases had the well-known ring which distinguishes the true orator. Mr. Jackson was recognised everywhere to be a fine platform speaker, but his varied excellence could not be appreciated in a summary, and he had a fine verbosity. It is sufficient to say that he concluded by asking for more cheers, which were heartily given.

James found the whole affair distasteful and ridiculous; and indeed scarcely noticed what was going on, for his thoughts were entirely occupied with his father. At first Colonel Parsons seemed too depressed to pay attention to the ceremony, and his eyes travelled every now and again to James, with that startled, unhappy expression which was horribly painful to see. But his age and weakness prevented him from feeling very intensely for more than a short while; time had brought its own good medicine, and the old man's mind was easily turned. Presently he began to smile, and the look of pride and happiness returned to his face.

But James was not satisfied. He felt he must make active reparation. When the Vicar finished, and he understood that some reply was expected, it occurred to him that he had an opportunity of salving the bitter wound he had caused. The very hatred he felt at making open allusion to his feelings made him think it a just punishment; none knew but himself how painful it was to talk in that strain to stupid, curious people.

"I thank you very much for the welcome you have all given me," he said.

His voice trembled in his nervousness, so that he could hardly command it, and he reddened. It seemed to James a frightful humiliation to have to say the things he had in mind, it made them all ugly and vulgar; he was troubled also by his inability to express what he felt. He noticed a reporter for the local newspaper rapidly taking notes.

"I have been very much touched by your kindness. Of course, I am extremely proud to have won the Victoria Cross, but I feel it is really more owing to my father than to any deed of mine. You all know my father, and you know what a brave and gallant soldier he was. It was owing to his fine example, and to his teaching, and to his constant, loving care, that I was able to do the little I did. And I should like to say that it is to him and to my mother that I owe everything. It is the thought of his unblemished and exquisite career, of the beautiful spirit which brightly coloured all his actions, that has supported me in times of difficulty. And my earnest desire has always been to prove myself worthy of my father and the name he has handed on to me. You have cheered me very kindly; now I should like to ask you for three cheers for my father."

Colonel Parsons looked at his son as he began to speak. When he realised Jamie's meaning, tears filled his eyes and streamed down his cheeks—tears of happiness and gratitude. All recollection of the affront quickly vanished, and he felt an ecstatic joy such as he had never known before. The idea came to him in his weakness: "Now I can die happy!" He was too overcome to be ashamed of his emotion, and taking out his handkerchief, quite unaffectedly wiped his eyes.

The band struck up "Rule, Britannia" and "God Save the Queen"; and in orderly fashion, as Mr. Dryland had arranged, they all marched off. The group under the triumphal arch broke up, and the Jacksons and Colonel and Mrs. Clibborn went their ways.

Mary came into the house. She took Jamie's hands, her eyes wet with tears.

"Oh, Jamie," she said, "you are good! It was charming of you to speak as you did of your father. You don't know how happy you've made him."

"I'm very glad you are pleased," he said gravely, and bending forward, put his arm round her waist and kissed her.

For a moment she leant her head against his shoulder; but with her emotion was a thing soon vanquished. She wished, above all things, to be manly, as befitted a soldier's wife. She shook herself, and withdrew from Jamie's arms.

"But I must be running off, or mamma will be angry with me. Good-bye for the present."

James went into the dining-room, where his father, exhausted by the varied agitations of the day, was seeking composure in the leading articles of the morning paper. Mrs. Parsons sat on her usual chair, knitting, and she greeted him with a loving smile. James saw that they were both pleased with his few awkward words, which still rang in his own ears as shoddy and sentimental, and he tasted, somewhat ruefully, the delight of making the kind creatures happy.

"Has Mary gone?" asked Mrs. Parsons.

"Yes. She said her mother would be angry if she stayed."

"I saw that Mrs. Clibborn was put out. I suppose because someone besides herself attracted attention. I do think she is the wickedest woman I've ever known."

"Frances, Frances!" expostulated the Colonel.

"She is, Richmond. She's a thoroughly bad woman. The way she treats Mary is simply scandalous."

"Poor girl!" said the Colonel.

"Oh, Jamie, it makes my blood boil when I think of it. Sometimes the poor thing used to come here quite upset, and simply cry as if her heart was breaking."

"But what does Mrs. Clibborn do?" asked James, surprised.

"Oh, I can't tell you! She's dreadfully unkind. She hates Mary because she's grown up, and because she sometimes attracts attention. She's always

making little cruel remarks. You only see her when she's on her good behaviour; but when she's alone with Mary, Mrs. Clibborn is simply horrible. She abuses her; she tells her she's ugly, and that she dresses badly.
How can she dress any better when Mrs. Clibborn spends all the money
on herself? I've heard her myself say to Mary: 'How stupid and clumsy
you are! I'm ashamed to take you anywhere.' And Mary's the very soul of
goodness. She teaches in the Sunday School, and she trains the choir-
boys, and she visits the poor; and yet Mrs. Clibborn complains that she's
useless. I wanted Richmond to talk to Colonel Clibborn about it."

"Mary particularly asked me not to," said Colonel Parsons. "She
preferred to bear anything rather than create unhappiness between her
father and mother."

"She's a perfect angel of goodness!" cried Mrs. Parsons, enthusiastically. "She's simply a martyr, and all the time she's as kind and affectionate to her mother as if she were the best woman in the world. She
never lets anyone say a word against her."

"Sometimes," murmured Colonel Parsons, "she used to say that her
only happiness was in the thought of you, Jamie."

"The thought of me?" said James; and then hesitatingly: "Do you
think she is very fond of me, mother?"

"Fond of you?" Mrs Parsons laughed. "She worships the very
ground you tread on. You can't imagine all you are to her."

"You'll make the boy vain," said Colonel Parsons, laughing.

"Often the only way we could comfort her was by saying that you
would come back some day and take her away from here."

"We shall have to be thinking of weddings soon, I suppose?" said
Colonel Parsons, looking at James, with a bantering smile.

James turned white. "It's rather early to think of that just yet."

"We spoke of June," said his mother.

"We must see."

"You've waited so long," said Colonel Parsons; "I'm sure you don't
want to wait any longer."

"She *will* make you a good wife, Jamie. You are lucky to have found such
a dear, sweet girl. It's a blessing to us to think that you will be so happy."

"As I was saying to Mary the other day," added Colonel Parsons,
laughing gently, "'you must begin thinking of your trousseau, my dear,'

I said. 'If I know anything of Jamie, he'll want to get married in a week. These young fellows are always impatient.'"

Mrs Parsons smiled.

"Well, it's a great secret, and Mary would be dreadfully annoyed if she thought you knew; but when we heard you were coming home, she started to order things. Her father has given her a hundred pounds to begin with."

They had no mercy, thought James. They were horribly cruel in their loving-kindness, in their affectionate interest for his welfare.

6

James had been away from England for five years; and in that time a curious change, long silently proceeding, had made itself openly felt—becoming manifest, like an insidious disease, only when every limb and every organ were infected. A new spirit had been in action, eating into the foundations of the national character; it worked through the masses of the great cities, unnerved by the three poisons of drink, the Salvation Army, and popular journalism. A mighty force of hysteria and sensationalism was created, seething, ready to burst its bonds. . . . The canker spread through the country-side; the boundaries of class and class are now so vague that quickly the whole population was affected; the current literature of the day flourished upon it; the people of England, neurotic from the stress of the last sixty years, became unstable as water. And with the petty reverses of the beginning of the war, the last barriers of shame were broken down; their arrogance was dissipated, and suddenly the English became timorous as a conquered nation, deprecating, apologetic; like frightened women, they ran to and fro, wringing their hands. Reserve, restraint, self-possession, were swept away. . . . And now we are frankly emotional; reeds tottering in the wind, our boast is that we are not even reeds that think; we cry out for idols. Who is there that will set up a golden ass that we may fall down and worship? We glory in our shame, in our swelling hearts, in our eyes heavy with tears. We want sympathy at all costs; we run about showing our bleeding vitals, asking one another whether they are not indeed a horrible sight. Englishmen now are proud of being womanish, and nothing is more manly than to weep. To be a man of feeling is better than to be a gentleman—it is certainly much easier. The halt of mind, the maim, the blind of wit, have come by their own; and the poor in spirit have inherited the earth.

James had left England when this emotional state was contemptible. Found chiefly in the dregs of the populace, it was ascribed to ignorance and to the abuse of stimulants. When he returned, it had the public conscience behind it. He could not understand the change. The persons he had known sober, equal-minded, and restrained, now seemed violently hysterical. James still shuddered, remembering the curate's allusions to his engagement; and he wondered that Mary, far from thinking them impertinent, had been vastly gratified. She seemed to take pleasure in publicly advertising her connection, in giving her private affairs to the inspection of all and sundry. The whole ceremony had been revolting; he loathed the adulation and the fulsome sentiment. His own emotions seemed vulgar now that he had been forced to display them to the gaping crowd.

But the function of the previous day had the effect also of sealing his engagement. Everyone knew of it. Jamie's name was indissolubly joined with Mary's; he could not break the tie now without exposing her to the utmost humiliation. And how could he offer her such an affront when she loved him devotedly? It was not vanity that made him think so, his mother had told him outright; and he saw it in every look of Mary's eyes, in the least inflection of her voice. James asked himself desperately why Mary should care for him. He was not good-looking; he was silent; he was not amusing; he had no particular attraction.

James was sitting in his room, and presently heard Mary's voice calling from the hall.

"Jamie! Jamie!"

He got up and came downstairs.

"Why, Jamie," said his father, "you ought to have gone to fetch Mary, instead of waiting here for her to come to you."

"You certainly ought, Jamie," said Mary, laughing; and then, looking at him, with sudden feeling: "But how seedy you look!"

James had hardly slept, troubling over his perplexity, and he looked haggard and tired.

"I'm all right," he said; "I'm not very strong yet, and I was rather exhausted yesterday."

"Mary thought you would like to go with her this morning, while she does her district visiting."

"It's a beautiful morning, Jamie; it will do you good!" cried Mary.

"I should like it very much."

They started out. Mary wore her every-day costume—a serge gown, a sailor hat, and solid, square-toed boots. She walked fast, with long steps and firm carriage. James set himself to talk, asking her insignificant questions about the people she visited. Mary answered with feeling and at length, but was interrupted by arriving at a cottage.

"You'd better not come in here," she said, blushing slightly; "although I want to take you in to some of the people. I think it will be a lesson to them."

"A lesson in what?"

"Oh, I can't tell you to your face. I don't want to make you conceited; but you can guess while you're waiting for me."

Mary's patient was about to be confined, and thinking her condition rather indecent, quite rightly, Mary had left James outside. But the good lady, since it was all in the way of nature, was not so ashamed of herself as she should have been, and insisted on coming to the door to show Miss Clibborn out.

"Take care he doesn't see you!" cried Mary in alarm, pushing her back.

"Well, there's no harm in it. I'm a married woman. You'll have to go through it yourself one day, miss."

Mary rejoined her lover, suffused in blushes, hoping he had seen nothing.

"It's very difficult to teach these people propriety. Somehow the lower classes seem to have no sense of decency."

"What's the matter?"

"Oh, nothing I can tell you," replied Mary, modestly. Then, to turn the conversation: "She asked after my young man, and was very anxious to see you."

"Was she? How did you know you had a young man?" asked James, grimly.

"Oh, everyone knows that! You can't keep secrets in Primpton. And besides, I'm not ashamed of it. Are you?"

"I haven't got a young man."

Mary laughed.

They walked on. The morning was crisp and bright, sending a healthy colour through Mary's cheeks. The blue sky and the bracing air made her feel more self-reliant, better assured than ever of her upright purpose and her candid heart. The road, firm underfoot and delightful to walk upon, stretched before them in a sinuous line. A pleasant odour came from the adjoining fields, from the farm-yards, as they passed them; the larks soared singing with happy heart, while the sparrows chirruped in the hedges. The hawthorn was bursting into leaf, all bright and green, and here and there the wild flowers were showing themselves, the buttercup and the speedwell. But while the charm of Nature made James anxious to linger, to lean on a gate and look for a while at the cows lazily grazing, Mary had too sound a constitution to find in it anything but a stimulus to renewed activity.

"We mustn't dawdle, you lazy creature!" she cried merrily. "I shall never get through my round before one o'clock if we don't put our best foot foremost."

"Can't you see them some other time?"

The limpid air softened his heart; he thought for a moment that if he could wander aimlessly with Mary, gossiping without purpose, they might end by understanding one another. The sun, the wild flowers, the inconstant breeze, might help to create a new feeling.

But Mary turned to him with grave tenderness.

"You know I'd do anything to please you, Jamie. But even for you I cannot neglect my duty."

James froze.

"Of course, you're quite right," he said. "It really doesn't matter."

They came to another cottage, and this time Mary took James in.

"It's a poor old man," she said. "I'm so sorry for him; he's always so grateful for what I do."

They found him lying in bed, writhing with pain, his head supported by a pillow.

"Oh, how uncomfortable you look!" cried Mary. "You poor thing! Who on earth arranged your pillows like that?"

"My daughter, miss."

"I must talk to her; she ought to know better."

Miss Clibborn drew away the pillows very gently, smoothed them out, and replaced them.

"I can't bear 'em like that, miss. The other is the only way I'm comfortable."

"Nonsense, John!" cried Mary, brightly. "You couldn't be comfortable with your head all on one side; you're much better as you are."

James saw the look of pain in the man's face, and ventured to expostulate.

"Don't you think you'd better put them back in the old way? He seemed much easier."

"Nonsense, Jamie. You must know that the head ought to be higher than the body."

"Please, miss, I can't bear the pillow like this."

"Oh, yes, you can. You must show more forbearance and fortitude. Remember that God sends you pain in order to try you. Think of Our Lord suffering silently on the Cross."

"You're putting him to quite unnecessary torture, Mary," said James. "He must know best how he's comfortable."

"It's only because he's obstinate. Those people are always complaining. Really, you must permit me to know more about nursing than you do, Jamie."

Jamie's face grew dark and grim, but he made no answer.

"I shall send you some soup, John," said Mary, as they went out. "You know, one can never get these people to do anything in a rational way," she added to James. "It's perfectly heartrending trying to teach them even such a natural thing as making themselves comfortable."

James was silent.

They walked a few yards farther, and passed a man in a dog-cart. Mary turned very red, staring in front of her with the fixed awkwardness of one not adept in the useful art of cutting.

"Oh," she said, with vexation, "he's going to John."

"Who is it?"

"It's Dr. Higgins—a horrid, vulgar man. He's been dreadfully rude to me, and I make a point of cutting him."

"Really?"

"Oh, he behaved scandalously. I can't bear doctors, they're so dreadfully interfering. And they seem to think no one can know anything about doctoring but themselves! He was attending one of my patients; it was a woman, and of course I knew what she wanted. She was ill and weak, and needed strengthening; so I sent her down a bottle of port. Well, Dr. Higgins came to the house, and asked to see me. He's not a gentleman, you know, and he was so rude! 'I've come to see you about Mrs. Gandy,' he said. 'I particularly ordered her not to take stimulants, and I find you've sent her down port.' 'I thought she wanted it,' I said. 'She told me that you had said she wasn't to touch anything, but I thought a little port would do her good.' Then he said, 'I wish to goodness you wouldn't interfere with what you know nothing about.' 'I should like you to remember that you're speaking to a gentlewoman,' I said. 'I don't care twopence,' he answered, in the rudest way. 'I'm not going to allow you to interfere with my patients. I took the port away, and I wish you to understand that you're not to send any more.'

"Then I confess I lost my temper. 'I suppose you took it away to drink yourself?' I said. Then what d'you think he did? He burst out laughing, and said: 'A bottle of port that cost two bob at the local grocer's! The saints preserve us!'"

James repressed a smile.

"'You impertinent man!' I said. 'You ought to be ashamed to talk to a woman like that. I shall at once send Mrs. Gandy another bottle of port, and it's no business of yours how much it cost.' 'If you do,' he said, 'and anything happens, by God, I'll have you up for manslaughter.' I rang the bell. 'Leave the house,' I said, 'and never dare come here again!' Now don't you think I was right, Jamie?"

"My dear Mary, you always are!"

James looked back at the doctor entering the cottage. It was some comfort to think that he would put the old man into a comfortable position.

"When I told papa," added Mary, "he got in a most fearful rage. He insisted on going out with a horsewhip, and said he meant to thrash Dr. Higgins. He looked for him all the morning, but couldn't find him; and then your mother and I persuaded him it was better to treat such a vulgar man with silent contempt."

James had noticed that the doctor was a burly, broad-shouldered fellow, and he could not help thinking Colonel Clibborn's resolution distinctly wise. How sad it is that in this world right is so often subordinate to brute force!

"But he's not received anywhere. We all cut him; and I get everyone I can not to employ him."

"Ah!" murmured James.

Mary's next patient was feminine, and James was again left to cool his heels in the road; but not alone, for Mr. Dryland came out of the cottage. The curate was a big, stout man, with reddish hair, and a complexion like squashed strawberries and cream; his large, heavy face, hairless except for scanty red eyebrows, gave a disconcerting impression of nakedness. His eyes were blue and his mouth small, with the expression which young ladies, eighty years back, strove to acquire by repeating the words prune and prism. He had a fat, full voice, with unctuous modulations not entirely under his control, so that sometimes, unintentionally, he would utter the most commonplace remark in a tone fitted for a benediction. Mr. Dryland was possessed by the laudable ambition to be all things to all men; and he tried, without conspicuous success, always to suit his conversation to his hearers. With old ladies he was bland; with sportsmen slangy; with yokels he was broadly humorous; and with young people aggressively juvenile. But above all, he wished to be manly, and cultivated a boisterous laugh and a joivial manner.

"I don't know if you remember me," he cried, with a ripple of fat laughter, going up to James. "I had the pleasure of addressing a few words to you yesterday in my official capacity. Miss Clibborn told me you were waiting, and I thought I would introduce myself. My name is Dryland."

"I remember quite well."

"I'm the Vicar's bottle-washer, you know," added the curate, with a guffaw. "Change for you—going round to the sick and needy of the parish—after fighting the good fight. I hear you were wounded."

"I was, rather badly."

"I wish I could have gone out and had a smack at the Boers. Nothing I should have liked better. But, of course, I'm only a parson, you know. It wouldn't have been thought the correct thing." Mr. Dryland, from his superior height, beamed down on James. "I don't know whether you remember the few words which I was privileged to address to you yesterday—"

"Perfectly," put in James.

"Impromptu, you know; but they expressed my feelings. That is one of the best things the war has done for us. It has permitted us to express our emotions more openly. I thought it a beautiful sight to see the noble tears coursing down your father's furrowed cheeks. Those few words of yours have won all our hearts. I may say that our little endeavours were nothing beside that short, unstudied speech. I hope there will be a full report in the Tunbridge Wells papers."

"I hope not!" cried James.

"You're too modest, Captain Parsons. That is what I said to Miss Clibborn yesterday; true courage is always modest. But it is our duty to see that it does not hide its light under a bushel. I hope you won't think it a liberty, but I myself gave the reporter a few notes."

"Will Miss Clibborn be long?" asked James, looking at the cottage.

"Ah, what a good woman she is, Captain Parsons. My dear sir, I assure you she's an angel of mercy."

"It's very kind of you to say so."

"Not at all! It's a pleasure. The good she does is beyond praise. She's a wonderful help in the parish. She has at heart the spiritual welfare of the people, and I may say that she is a moral force of the first magnitude."

"I'm sure that's a very delightful thing to be."

"You know I can't help thinking," laughed Mr. Dryland fatly, "that she ought to be the wife of a clergyman, rather than of a military man."

Mary came out.

"I've been telling Mrs. Gray that I don't approve of the things her daughter wears in church," she said. "I don't think it's nice for people of that class to wear such bright colours."

"I don't know what we should do in the parish without you," replied the curate, unctuously. "It's so rare to find someone who knows what is right, and isn't afraid of speaking out."

Mary said that she and James were walking home, and asked Mr. Dryland whether he would not accompany them.

"I shall be delighted, if I'm not *de trop.*"

He looked with laughing significance from one to the other.

"I wanted to talk to you about my girls," said Mary.

She had a class of village maidens, to whom she taught sewing, respect for their betters, and other useful things.

"I was just telling Captain Parsons that you were an angel of mercy, Miss Clibborn."

"I'm afraid I'm not that," replied Mary, gravely. "But I try to do my duty."

"Ah!" cried Mr. Dryland, raising his eyes so that he looked exactly like a codfish, "how few of us can say that!"

"I'm seriously distressed about my girls. They live in nasty little cottages, and eat filthy things; they pass their whole lives under the most disgusting conditions, and yet they're happy. I can't get them to see that they ought to be utterly miserable."

"Oh, I know," sighed the curate; "it makes me sad to think of it."

"Surely, if they're happy, you can want nothing better," said James, rather impatiently.

"But I do. They have no right to be happy under such circumstances. I want to make them feel their wretchedness."

"What a brutal thing to do!" cried James.

"It's the only way to improve them. I want them to see things as I see them."

"And how d'you know that you see them any more correctly than they do?"

"My dear Jamie!" cried Mary; and then as the humour of such a suggestion dawned upon her, she burst into a little shout of laughter.

"What d'you think is the good of making them dissatisfied?" asked James, grimly.

"I want to make them better, nobler, worthier; I want to make their lives more beautiful and holy."

"If you saw a man happily wearing a tinsel crown, would you go to him and say, 'My good friend, you're making a fool of yourself. Your crown isn't of real gold, and you must throw it away. I haven't a golden crown to give you instead, but you're wicked to take pleasure in that sham thing.' They're just as comfortable, after their fashion, in a hovel as you in your fine house; they enjoy the snack of fat pork they have on Sunday just as much as you enjoy your boiled chickens and blanc-manges. They're happy, and that's the chief thing."

"Happiness is not the chief thing in this world, James," said Mary, gravely.

"Isn't it? I thought it was."

"Captain Parsons is a cynic," said Mr. Dryland, with a slightly supercilious smile.

"Because I say it's idiotic to apply your standards to people who have nothing in common with you? I hate all this interfering. For God's sake let us go our way; and if we can get a little pleasure out of dross and tinsel, let us keep it."

"I want to give the poor high ideals," said Mary.

"I should have thought bread and cheese would be more useful."

"My dear Jamie," said Mary, good-naturedly, "I think you're talking of things you know nothing about."

"You must remember that Miss Clibborn has worked nobly among the poor for many years."

"My own conscience tells me I'm right," pursued Mary, "and you see Mr. Dryland agrees with me. I know you mean well, Jamie; but I don't think you quite understand the matter, and I fancy we had better change the conversation."

7

Next day Mary went into Primpton House. Colonel Parsons nodded to her as she walked up the drive, and took off his spectacles. The front door was neither locked nor bolted in that confiding neighbourhood, and Mary walked straight in.

"Well, my dear?" said the Colonel, smiling with pleasure, for he was as fond of her as of his own son.

"I thought I'd come and see you alone. Jamie's still out, isn't he? I saw him pass our house. I was standing at the window, but he didn't look up."

"I daresay he was thinking. He's grown very thoughtful now."

Mrs. Parsons came in, and her quiet face lit up, too, as she greeted Mary. She kissed her tenderly.

"Jamie's out, you know."

"Mary has come to see us," said the Colonel.

"She doesn't want us to feel neglected now that she has the boy."

"We shall never dream that you can do anything unkind, dear Mary," replied Mrs. Parsons, stroking the girl's hair. "It's natural that you should think more of him than of us."

Mary hesitated a moment.

"Don't you think Jamie has changed?"

Mrs. Parsons looked at her quickly.

"I think he has grown more silent. But he's been through so much. And then he's a man now; he was only a boy when we saw him last."

"D'you think he cares for me any more?" asked Mary, with a rapid tremor in her voice.

"Mary!"

"Of course he does! He talks of you continually," said Colonel Parsons, "and always as if he were devoted. Doesn't he, Frances?"

The old man's deep love for Mary had prevented him from seeing in Jamie's behaviour anything incongruous with that of a true lover.

"What makes you ask that question, Mary?" said Mrs. Parsons.

Her feminine tact had led her to notice a difference in Jamie's feeling towards his betrothed; but she had been unwilling to think that it amounted even to coldness. Such a change could be explained in a hundred natural ways, and might, indeed, exist merely in her own imagination.

"Oh, he's not the same as he was!" cried Mary, "I don't know what it is, but I feel it in his whole manner. Yesterday evening he barely said a word."

James had dined with the Clibborns in solemn state.

"I daresay he's not very well yet. His wound troubles him still."

"I try to put it down to that," said Mary, "but he seems to force himself to speak to me. He's not natural. I've got an awful fear that he has ceased to care for me."

She looked from Colonel Parsons to his wife, who stared at her in dismay.

"Don't be angry with me," she said; "I couldn't talk like this to anyone else, but I know you love me. I look upon you already as my father and mother. I don't want to be unkind to mamma, but I couldn't talk of it to her; she would only sneer at me. And I'm afraid it's making me rather unhappy."

"Of course, we want you to treat us as your real parents, Mary. We both love you as we love Jamie. We have always looked upon you as our daughter."

"You're so good to me!"

"Has your mother said anything to annoy you?"

Mary faltered.

"Last night, when he went away, she said she didn't think he was devoted to me."

"Oh, I knew it was your mother who'd put this in your head! She has always been jealous of you. I suppose she thinks he's in love with her."

"Mrs. Parsons!" cried Mary, in a tone of entreaty.

"I know you can't bear anything said against your mother, and it's wicked of me to vex you; but she has no right to suggest such things."

"It's not only that. It's what I feel."

"I'm sure Jamie is most fond of you," said Colonel Parsons, kindly. "You've not seen one another for five years, and you find yourselves altered. Even we feel a little strange with Jamie sometimes; don't we, Frances? What children they are, Frances!" Colonel Parsons laughed in that irresistibly sweet fashion of his. "Why, it was only the day before yesterday that Jamie came to us with a long face and asked if you cared for *him*."

"Did he?" asked Mary, with pleased surprise, anxious to believe what the Colonel suggested.

"Oh, he must see that I love him! Perhaps he finds me unresponsive. . . . How could I help caring for him? I think if he ceased to love me, I should die."

"My dearest Mary," cried Mrs. Parsons, the tears rising to her eyes, "don't talk like that! I'm sure he can't help loving you, either; you're so good and sweet. You're both of you fanciful, and he's not well. Be patient. Jamie is shy and reserved; he hasn't quite got used to us yet. He doesn't know how to show his feelings. It will all come right soon."

"Of course he loves you!" said Colonel Parsons. "Who could help it? Why, if I were a young fellow I should be mad to marry you."

"And what about me, Richmond?" asked Mrs. Parsons, smiling.

"Well, I think I should have to commit bigamy, and marry you both."

They laughed at the Colonel's mild little joke, happy to break through the cloud of doubt which oppressed them.

"You're a dear thing," said Mary, kissing the old man, "and I'm a very silly girl. It's wrong of me to give way to whims and fancies."

"You must be very brave when you're the wife of a V.C.," said the Colonel, patting her hand.

"Oh, it was a beautiful action!" cried Mary. "And he's as modest about it as though he had done nothing that any man might not do. I think there can be no sight more pleasing to God than that of a brave man risking his life to save a comrade."

"And that ought to be an assurance to you, Mary, that James will never do anything unkind or dishonourable. Trust him, and forgive his little faults of manner. I'm sure he loves you, and soon you'll get married and be completely happy."

Mary's face darkened once more.

"He's been here three days, and he's not said a word about getting married. Oh, I can't help it; I'm so frightened! I wish he'd say something—just one word to show that he really cares for me. He seems to have forgotten that we're even engaged."

Colonel Parsons looked at his wife, begging her by his glance to say something that would comfort Mary. Mrs. Parsons looked down, uncertain, ill at case.

"You don't despise me for talking like this, Mrs. Parsons?"

"Despise you, my dear! How can I, when I love you so dearly? Shall I speak to Jamie? I'm sure when he understands that he's making you unhappy, he'll be different. He has the kindest heart in the world; I've never known him do an unkind thing in his life."

"No, don't say anything to him," replied Mary. "I daresay it's all nonsense. I don't want him to be driven into making love to me."

Meanwhile James wandered thoughtfully. The country was undulating, and little hill rose after little hill, affording spacious views of the fat Kentish fields, encircled by oak trees and by chestnuts. Owned by rich landlords, each generation had done its best, and the fruitful land was tended like a garden. But it had no abandonment, no freedom; the hand of man was obvious, perpetually, in the trimness and in the careful arrangement, so that the landscape, in its formality, reminded one of those set pieces chosen by the classic painters. But the fields were fresh with the tall young grass of the new year, the buttercups flaunted them-selves gaily, careless of the pitiless night, rejoicing in the sunshine, as be-fore they had rejoiced in the enlivening rain. The pleasant raindrops still lingered on the daisies. The feathery ball of the dandelion, carried by the breeze, floated past like a symbol of the life of man—a random thing, resistless to the merest breath, with no mission but to spread its seed upon the fertile earth, so that things like unto it should spring up in the succeeding summer, and flower uncared for, and reproduce themselves, and die.

James decided finally that he must break that very evening his en-gagement with Mary. He could not put it off. Every day made his diffi-culty greater, and it was impossible any longer to avoid the discussion of their marriage, nor could he continue to treat Mary with nothing better than friendliness. He realised all her good qualities; she was frank, and honest, and simple; anxious to do right; charitable according to her light; kindness itself. James felt sincerely grateful for the affectionate tenderness which Mary showed to his father and mother. He was thankful for that and for much else, and was prepared to look upon her as a very good friend, even as a sister; but he did not love her. He could not look upon the prospect of marriage without repulsion. Nor did Mary, he said, really love him. He knew what love was—something different entirely from that pallid flame of affection and esteem, of which alone she was capable. Mary loved him for certain qualities of mind, because his station in life was decent, his manners passable, his morals beyond reproach.

"She might as well marry the Ten Commandments!" he cried impatiently.

Mary cared for him from habit, from a sense of decorum, and for the fitness of things; but that was not love. He shrugged his shoulders scornfully, looking for some word to express the mildly pleasant, unagi-tating emotion. James, who had been devoured by it, who had struggled with it as with a deadly sin, who had killed it finally while, like a serpent of evil, it clung to his throat, drinking his life's blood, James knew what love was—a fire in the veins, a divine affliction, a passion, a frenzy, a madness. The love he knew was the love of the body of flesh and blood, the love that engenders, the love that kills. At the bottom of it is sex, and sex is not ugly or immoral, for sex is the root of life. The woman is fair because man shall love her body; her lips are red and passionate that he may kiss them; her hair is beautiful that he may take it in his hands—a river of living gold.

James stopped, and the dead love rose again and tore his entrails like a beast of prey. He gasped with agony, with bitter joy. Ah, that was the true love! What did he care that the woman lacked this and that? He loved her because he loved her; he loved her for her faults. And in spite of the poignant anguish, he thanked her from the bottom of his heart, for she had taught him love. She had caused him endless pain, but she had given him the strength to bear it. She had ruined his life, perhaps, but had shown him that life was worth living. What were the agony, the torture, the despair, beside that radiant passion which made him godlike? It is only the lover who lives, and of his life every moment is intense and fervid. James felt that his most precious recollection was that ardent month, during which, at last, he had seen the world in all its dazzling movement, in its manifold colour, singing with his youth and laughing to his joy.

And he did not care that hideous names have been given to that dear passion, to that rich desire. The vulgar call it lust, and blush and hide their faces; in their folly is the shame, in their prurience the disgrace. They do not know that the appetite which shocks them is the very origin of the highest qualities of man. It is they, weaklings afraid to look life in the face, dotards and sentimentalists, who have made the body unclean. They have covered the nakedness of Aphrodite with the rags of their own impurity. They have disembowelled the great lovers of antiquity till Cleopatra serves to adorn a prudish tale and Lancelot to point a moral. Oh, Mother Nature, give us back our freedom, with its strength of sinew and its humour! For lack of it we perish in false shame, and our fig-leaves point our immodesty to all the world. Teach us that love is not a tawdry sentiment, but a fire divine in order to the procreation of children; teach us not to dishonour our bodies, for they are beautiful and

pure, and all thy works are sweet. Teach us, again, in thy merciful goodness, that man is made for woman, his body for her body, and that the
flesh cannot sin.

Teach us also not to rant too much, even in thy service; and though
we do set up for prophets and the like, let us not forget occasionally to
laugh at our very august selves.

Then, harking back, Jamie's thoughts returned to the dinner of the
previous evening at the Clibborns. He was the only guest, and when he
arrived, found Mary and the Colonel by themselves in the drawing-room.
It was an old habit of Mrs. Clibborn's not to appear till after her visitors,
thinking that so she created a greater effect. The Colonel wore a very high
collar, which made his head look like some queer flower on a long white
stalk; hair and eye-brows were freshly dyed, and glistened like the oiled
locks of a young Jewess. He was the perfect dandy, even to his bejewelled
fingers and his scented handkerchief. His manner was a happy mixture of
cordiality and condescension, by the side of which Mary's unaffected
simplicity contrasted oddly. She seemed less at home in an evening dress
than in the walking costume she vastly preferred; her free, rather masculine movements were ungainly in the silk frock, badly made and countri-
fied, while lace and ribbons suited her most awkwardly. She was out of
place, too, in that room, decorated with all the abominations of pseudo-
fashion, with draperies and tissue-paper, uncomfortable little chairs and
rickety tables. In every available place stood photographs of Mrs. Clibborn—Mrs. Clibborn sitting, standing, lying; Mrs. Clibborn full face,
three-quarter face, side face; Mrs. Clibborn in this costume or in that
costume—grave, gay, thoughtful, or smiling; Mrs. Clibborn showing her
beautiful teeth, her rounded arms, her vast shoulders; Mrs. Clibborn
dressed to the nines, and Mrs. Clibborn as undressed as she dared.

Finally, the beauty swept in with a great rustle of silk, displaying to
the full her very opulent charms. Her hair was lightly powdered, and
honestly she looked remarkably handsome.

"Don't say I've kept you waiting," she murmured. "I could never forgive myself."

James made some polite reply, and they went down to dinner. The
conversation was kept at the high level which one naturally expects from

persons fashionable enought to dine late. They discussed Literature, by which they meant the last novel but one; Art, by which they meant the Royal Academy; and Society, by which they meant their friends who kept carriages. Mrs. Clibborn said that, of course, she could not expect James to pay any attention to her, since all his thoughts must be for Mary, and then proceeded entirely to absorb him.

"You must find it very dull here," she moaned.

"I'm afraid you'll be bored to death." And she looked at Mary with her most smilingly cruel expression. "Oh, Mary, why did you put on that dreadfully dowdy frock? I've asked you over and over again to give it away, but you never pay attention to your poor mother."

"It's all right," said Mary, looking down at it, laughing and blushing a little.

Mrs. Clibborn turned again to James.

"I think it's such a mistake for women not to dress well. I'm an old woman now, but I always try to look my best. Reggie has never seen me in a dowdy gown. Have you, Reggie?"

"Any dress would become you, my love."

"Oh, Reggie, don't say that before James. He looks upon his future mother as an old woman."

Then at the end of dinner:

"Don't sit too long over your wine. I shall be so dull with nobody but Mary to amuse me."

Mrs Clibborn had been fond enough of Mary when she was a little girl, who could be petted on occasion and sent away when necessary; but as she grew up and exhibited a will of her own, she found her almost an intolerable nuisance. The girl developed a conscience, and refused indignantly to tell the little fibs which her mother occasionally suggested. She put her sense of right and wrong before Mrs. Clibborn's wishes, which that lady considered undutiful, if not entirely wicked. It seemed nothing short of an impertinence that Mary should disapprove of theatres when there was nothing to which the elder woman was more devoted. And Mrs. Clibborn felt that the girl saw through all her little tricks and artful dodges, often speaking out strongly when her mother proposed to do something particularly underhand. It was another grievance that Mary had inherited no good looks, and the faded beauty, in her vanity, was convinced that the girl spitefully observed every fresh wrinkle that appeared upon her face. But Mrs. Clibborn was also a little afraid of her daughter; such meekness and such good temper were difficult to overcome; and when she snubbed her, it was not only to chasten a proud spirit, but also to reassure herself.

When the ladies had retired, the Colonel handed James an execrable cigar.

"Now, I'm going to give you some very special port I've got," he said.

He poured out a glass with extreme care, and passed it over with evident pride. James remembered Mary's story of the doctor, and having tasted the wine, entirely sympathised with him. It was no wonder that invalids did not thrive upon it.

"Fine wine, isn't it?" said Colonel Clibborn. "Had it in my cellar for years." He shook it so as to inhale the aroma. "I got it from my old friend, the Duke of St. Olphert's. 'Reggie, my boy,' he said—'Reggie, do you want some good port?' 'Good port, Bill!' I cried—I always called him Bill, you know; his Christian name was William—'I should think I do, Billy, old boy.' 'Well,' said the Duke, 'I've got some I can let you have.'"

"He was a wine-merchant, was he?" asked James.

"Wine-merchant! My dear fellow, he was the Duke of St. Olphert's. He'd bought up the cellar of an Austrian nobleman, and he had more port than he wanted."

"And this is some of it?" asked James, gravely, holding the murky fluid to the light.

Then the Colonel stretched his legs and began to talk of the war. James, rather tired of the subject, sought to change the conversation; but Colonel Clibborn was anxious to tell one who had been through it how the thing should have been conducted; so his guest, with a mixture of astonishment and indignation, resigned himself to listen to the most pitiful inanities. He marvelled that a man should have spent his life in the service, and yet apparently be ignorant of the very elements of warfare; but having already learnt to hold his tongue, he let the Colonel talk, and was presently rewarded by a break. Something reminded the gallant cavalryman of a hoary anecdote, and he gave James that dreary round of stories which have dragged their heavy feet for thirty years from garrison to garrison. Then, naturally, he proceeded to the account of his own youthful conquests. The Colonel had evidently been a devil with the ladies, for he knew all about the forgotten ballet-dancers of the seventies, and related with gusto a number of scabrous tales.

"Ah, my boy, in my day we went the pace! I tell you in confidence, I was a deuce of a rake before I got married."

When they returned to the drawing-room, Mrs. Clibborn was ready with her langorous smile, and made James sit beside her on the sofa. In a few minutes the Colonel, as was his habit, closed his eyes, dropped his chin, and fell comfortably asleep. Mrs. Clibborn slowly turned to Mary.

"Will you try and find me my glasses, darling," she murmured. "They're either in my work-basket or on the morning-room table. And if you can't see them there, perhaps they're in your father's study. I want to read Jamie a letter."

"I'll go and look, mother."

Mary went out, and Mrs. Clibborn put her hand on Jamie's arm.

"Do you dislike me very much, Jamie?" she murmured softly.

"On the contrary!"

"I'm afraid your mother doesn't care for me."

"I'm sure she does."

"Women have never liked me. I don't know why. I can't help it if I'm not exactly—plain. I'm as God made me."

James thought that the Almightly in that case must have an unexpected familiarity with the rougepot and the powder-puff.

"Do you know that I did all I could to prevent your engagement to Mary?"

"You!" cried James, thunderstruck. "I never knew that."

"I thought I had better tell you myself. You mustn't be angry with me. It was for your own good. If I had had my way you would never have become engaged. I thought you were so much too young."

"Five years ago, d'you mean—when it first happened?"

"You were only a boy—a very nice boy, Jamie. I always liked you. I don't approve of long engagements, and I thought you'd change your mind. Most young men are a little wild; it's right that they should be."

James looked at her, wondering suddenly whether she knew or divined anything. It was impossible, she was too silly.

"You're very wise."

"Oh, don't say that!" cried Mrs. Clibborn, with a positive groan. "It sounds so middle-aged. . . . I always thought Mary was too old for you. A woman should be ten years younger than her husband."

"Tell me all about it," insisted James.

"They wouldn't listen to me. They said you had better be engaged. They thought it would benefit your morals. I was very much against it. I think boys are so much nicer when they haven't got encumbrances—or morals."

At that moment Mary came in.

"I can't find your glasses, mamma."

"Oh, it doesn't matter," replied Mrs. Clibborn, smiling softly; "I've just remembered that I sent them into Tunbridge Wells yesterday to be mended."

8

James knew he would see Mary at the tea-party which Mrs. Jackson that afternoon was giving at the Vicarage. Society in Little Primpton was exclusive, with the result that the same people met each other day after day, and the only intruders were occasional visitors of irreproachable antecedents from Tunbridge Wells. Respectability is a plant which in that fashionable watering-place has been so assiduously cultivated that it flourishes now in the open air; like the yellow gorse, it is found in every corner, thriving hardily under the most unfavourable conditions; and the keener the wind, the harder the frost, the more proudly does it hold its head. But on this particular day the gathering was confined to the immediate neighbours, and when the Parsons arrived they found, beside their hosts, only the Clibborns and the inevitable curate. There was a prolonged shaking of hands, inquiries concerning the health of all present, and observations suggested by the weather; then they sat down in a circle, and set themselves to discuss the questions of the day.

"Oh, Mr. Dryland," cried Mary, "thanks so much for that book! I am enjoying it!"

"I thought you'd like it," replied the curate, smiling blandly. "I know you share my admiration for Miss Corelli."

"Mr. Dryland has just lent me 'The Master Christian,'" Mary explained, turning to Mrs. Jackson.

"Oh, I was thinking of putting it on the list for my next book."

They had formed a club in Little Primpton of twelve persons, each buying a six-shilling book at the beginning of the year, and passing it on in return for another after a certain interval, so that at the end of twelve months all had read a dozen master-pieces of contemporary fiction.

"I thought I'd like to buy it at once," said Mr. Dryland. "I always think one ought to possess Marie Corelli's books. She's the only really great novelist we have in England now."

Mr. Dryland was a man of taste and authority, so that his literary judgments could always be relied on.

"Of course, I don't pretend to know much about the matter," said Mary, modestly. "There are more important things in life than books; but I do think she's splendid. I can't help feeling I'm wasting my time when I read most novels, but I never feel that with Marie Corelli."

"No one would think she was a woman," said the Vicar.

To which the curate answered: "*Le genie n'a pas de sexe.*"

The others, being no scholars, did not quite understand the remark, but they looked intelligent.

"I always think it's so disgraceful the way the newspapers sneer at her," said Mrs. Jackson. "And, I'm sure, merely because she's a woman."

"And because she has genius, my dear," put in the Vicar. "Some minds are so contemptibly small that they are simply crushed by greatness. It requires an eagle to look at the sun."

And the excellent people looked at one another with a certain self-satisfaction, for they had the fearless gaze of the king of birds in face of that brilliant orb.

"The critics are willing to do anything for money. Miss Corelli has said herself that there is a vile conspiracy to blacken her, and for my part I am quite prepared to believe it. They're all afraid of her because she dares to show them up."

"Besides, most of the critics are unsuccessful novelists," added Mr. Dryland, "and they are as envious as they can be."

"It makes one boil with indignation," cried Mary, "to think that people can be so utterly base. Those who revile her are not worthy to unloose the latchet of her shoes."

"It does one good to hear such whole-hearted admiration," replied the curate, beaming. "But you must remember that genius has always been persecuted. Look at Keats and Shelley. The critics abused them just as they abuse Marie Corelli. Even Shakespeare was slandered. But time has vindicated our immortal William; time will vindicate as brightly our gentle Marie."

"I wonder how many of us here could get through Hamlet without yawning!" meditatively said the Vicar.

"I see your point!" cried Mr. Dryland, opening his eyes. "While we could all read the 'Sorrows of Satan' without a break. I've read it three times, and each perusal leaves me more astounded. Miss Corelli has her revenge in her own hand; what can she care for the petty snarling of critics when the wreath of immortality is on her brow. I don't hesitate to say it, I'm not ashamed of my opinion; I consider Miss Corelli every bit as great as William Shakespeare. I've gone into the matter carefully, and if I may say so, I'm speaking of what I know something about. My deliberate opinion is that in wit, and humour, and language, she's every bit his equal."

"Her language is beautiful," said Mrs. Jackson.

"When I read her I feel just as if I were listening to hymns."

"And where, I should like to know," continued the curate, raising his voice, "can you find in a play of Shakespeare's such a gallery of portraits as in the 'Master Christian'?"

"And there is one thing you must never forget," said the Vicar, gravely, "she has a deep religious feeling which you will find in none of Shakespeare's plays. Every one of her books has a lofty moral purpose. That is the justification of fiction. The novelist has a high vocation, if he could only see it; he can inculcate submission to authority, hope, charity, obedience—in fact, all the higher virtues; he can become a handmaid of the Church. And now, when irreligion, and immorality, and scepticism are rampant, we must not despise the humblest instruments."

"How true that is!" said Mrs. Jackson.

"If all novelists were like Marie Corelli, I should willingly hold them out my hand. I think every Christian ought to read 'Barabbas.' It gives an entirely new view of Christ. It puts the incidents of the Gospel in a way that one had never dreamed. I was never so impressed in my life."

"But all her books are the same in that way!" cried Mary. "They all make me feel so much better and nobler, and more truly Christian."

"I think she's vulgar and blasphemous," murmured Mrs. Clibborn quietly, as though she were making the simplest observation.

"Mamma!" cried Mary, deeply shocked; and among the others there was a little movement of indignation and disgust.

Mrs. Clibborn was continually mortifying her daughter by this kind of illiterate gaucherie. But the most painful part of it was that the good lady always remained perfectly unconscious of having said anything incredibly silly, and continued with perfect self-assurance:

"I've never been able to finish a book of hers. I began one about electricity, which I couldn't understand, and then I tried another. I forget what it was, but there was something in it about a bed of roses, and I thought it very improper. I don't think it was a nice book for Mary to read, but girls seem to read everything now."

There was a pained hush, such as naturally occurs when someone has made a very horrible *faux pas*. They all looked at one another awkwardly; while Mary, ashamed at her mother's want of taste, kept her eyes glued to the carpet. But Mrs. Clibborn's folly was so notorious that presently anger was succeeded by contemptuous amusement, and the curate came to the rescue with a loud guffaw.

"Of course, you know your Marie Corelli by heart, Captain Parsons?"

"I'm afraid I've never read one of them."

"Not?" they all cried in surprise.

"Oh, I'll send them to you to Primpton House," said Mr. Dryland. "I have them all. Why, no one's education is complete till he's read Marie Corelli."

This was considered a very good hit at Mrs. Clibborn, and the dear people smiled at one another significantly. Even Mary could scarcely keep a straight face.

The tea then appeared, and was taken more or less silently. With the exception of the fashionable Mrs. Clibborn, they were all more used to making a sitdown meal of it, and the care of holding a cup, with a piece of cake unsteadily balanced in the saucer, prevented them from indulging in very brilliant conversational feats; they found one gymnastic exercise quite sufficient at a time. But when the tea-cups were safely restored to the table, Mrs. Jackson suggested a little music.

"Will you open the proceedings, Mary?"

The curate went up to Miss Clibborn with a bow, gallantly offering his arm to escort her to the piano. Mary had thoughtfully brought her music, and began to play a 'Song Without Words,' by Mendelssohn. She was considered a fine pianist in Little Primpton. She attacked the notes with marked resolution, keeping the loud pedal down throughout; her eyes were fixed on the music with an intense, determined air, in which you saw an eagerness to perform a social duty, and her lips moved as conscientiously she counted time. Mary played the whole piece without making a single mistake, and at the end was much applauded.

"There's nothing like classical music, is there?" cried the curate enthusiastically, as Mary stopped, rather out of breath, for she played, as she did everything else, with energy and thoroughness.

"It's the only music I really love."

"And those 'Songs Without Words' are beautiful," said Colonel Parsons, who was standing on Mary's other side.

"Mendelssohn is my favourite composer," she replied, "He's so full of soul."

"Ah, yes," murmured Mr. Dryland. "His heart seems to throb through all his music. It's strange that he should have been a Jew."

"But then Our Lord was a Jew, wasn't He?" said Mary.

"Yes, one is so apt to forget that."

Mary turned the leaves, and finding another piece which was familiar to her, set about it. It was a satisfactory thing to listen to her performance. In Mary's decided touch one felt all the strength of her character, with its simple, unaffected candour and its eminent sense of propriety. In her execution one perceived the high purpose which animated her whole conduct; it was pure and wholesome, and thoroughly English. And her piano-playing served also as a moral lesson, for none could listen without remembering that life was not an affair to be taken lightly, but a strenuous endeavour: the world was a battlefield (this one realised more particularly when Mary forgot for a page or so to take her foot off the pedal); each one of us had a mission to perform, a duty to do, a function to fulfil.

Meanwhile, James was trying to make conversation with Mrs. Clibborn.

"How well Mary plays!"

"D'you think so? I can't bear amateurs. I wish they wouldn't play."

James looked at Mrs. Clibborn quickly. It rather surprised him that she, the very silliest woman he had ever known, should say the only sensible things he had heard that day. Nor could he forget that she had done her best to prevent his engagement.

"I think you're a very wonderful woman," he said.

"Oh, Jamie!"

Mrs. Clibborn smiled and sighed, slipping forward her hand for him to take; but James was too preoccupied to notice the movement.

"I'm beginning to think you really like me," murmured Mrs. Clibborn, cooing like an amorous dove.

Then James was invited to sing, and refused.

"Please do, Jamie!" cried Mary, smiling. "For my sake. You used to sing so nicely!"

He still tried to excuse himself, but finding everyone insistent, went at last, with very bad grace, to the piano. He not only sang badly, but knew it, and was irritated that he should be forced to make a fool of himself. Mr. Dryland sang badly, but perfectly satisfied with himself, needed no pressing when his turn came. He made a speciality of old English songs, and thundered out in his most ecclesiastical manner a jovial ditty entitled, "Down Among the Dead Men."

The afternoon was concluded by an adjournment to the dining-room to play bagatelle, the most inane of games, to which the billiard-player goes with contempt, changed quickly to wrath when he cannot put the balls into absurd little holes. Mary was an adept, and took pleasure in showing James how the thing should be done. He noticed that she and the curate managed the whole affair between them, arranging partners and advising freely. Mrs. Clibborn alone refused to play, saying frankly it was too idiotic a pastime.

At last the party broke up, and in a group bade their farewells.

"I'll walk home with you, Mary, if you don't mind," said James, "and smoke a pipe."

Mary suddenly became radiant, and Colonel Parsons gave her a happy little smile and a friendly nod. . . . At last James had his opportunity. He lingered while Mary gathered together her music, and waited again to light his pipe, so that when they came out of the Vicarage gates the rest of the company were no longer in sight. The day had become overcast and sombre; on the even surface of the sky floated little ragged black clouds, like the fragments cast to the wind of some widowed, ample garment. It had grown cold, and James, accustomed to a warmer air, shivered a little. The country suddenly appeared cramped and circumscribed; in the fading light a dulness of colour came over tree and hedgerow which was singularly depressing. They walked in silence, while James looked for words. All day he had been trying to find some manner to express himself, but his mind, perplexed and weary, refused to help him. The walk to Mary's house could not take more than five minutes, and he saw the distance slipping away rapidly. If he meant to say anything it must be said at once; and his mouth was dry, he felt almost a physical inability to speak. He did not know how to prepare the way, how to approach the subject; and he was doubly tormented by the absolute necessity of breaking the silence.

But it was Mary who spoke first.

"D'you know, I've been worrying a little about you, Jamie."

"Why?"

"I'm afraid I hurt your feelings yesterday. Don't you remember, when we were visiting my patients—I think I spoke rather harshly. I didn't mean to. I'm very sorry."

"I had forgotten all about it," he said, looking at her. "I have no notion what you said to offend me."

"I'm glad of that," she answered, smiling, "but it does me good to apologise. Will you think me very silly if I say something to you?"

"Of course not!"

"Well, I want to say that if I ever do anything you don't like, or don't approve of, I wish you would tell me."

After that, how could he say immediately that he no longer loved her, and wished to be released from his engagement?

"I'm afraid you think I'm a very terrifying person," answered James.

Her words had made his announcement impossible; another day had gone, and weakly he had let it pass.

"What shall I do?" he murmured under his breath. "What a coward I am!"

They came to the door of the Clibborns' house and Mary turned to say good-bye. She bent forward, smiling and blushing, and he quickly kissed her.

In the evening, James was sitting by the fire in the dining-room, thinking of that one subject which occupied all his thoughts. Colonel Parsons and his wife were at the table, engaged upon the game of backgammon which invariably filled the interval between supper and prayers. The rattle of dice came to James indistinctly, as in a dream, and he imagined fantastically that unseen powers were playing for his life. He sat with his head between his hands, staring at the flames as though to find in them a solution to his difficulty; but mockingly they spoke only of Mrs. Wallace and the caress of her limpid eyes. He turned away with a gesture of impatience. The game was just finished, and Mrs. Parsons, catching the expression on his face, asked:

"What are you thinking of, Jamie?"

"I?" he answered, looking up quickly, as though afraid that his secret had been divined. "Nothing!"

Mrs. Parsons put the backgammon board away, making up her mind to speak, for she too suffered from a shyness which made the subjects she had nearest at heart precisely those that she could least bear to talk about.

"When do you think of getting married, Jamie?"

James started.

"Why, you asked me that yesterday." He tried to make a joke of it. "Upon my word, you're very anxious to get rid of me."

"I wonder if it's occurred to you that you're making Mary a little un-happy?"

James stood up and leaned against the mantelpiece, his face upon his hand.

"I should be sorry to do that, mother."

"You've been home four days, and you've not said a word to show you love her."

"I'm afraid I'm not very demonstrative."

"That's what I said!" cried the Colonel, triumphantly.

"Can't you try to say a word or two to prove you care for her, Jamie? She is so fond of you," continued his mother. "I don't want to interfere with your private concerns, but I think it's only thoughtlessness on your part; and I'm sure you don't wish to make Mary miserable. Poor thing, she's so unhappy at home; she yearns for a little affection. . . . Won't you say something to her about your marriage?"

"Has she asked you to speak to me?" inquired James.

"No, dear. You know that she would never do anything of the kind. She would hate to think that I had said anything."

James paused a moment.

"I will speak to her to-morrow, mother."

"That's right!" said the Colonel, cheerfully. "I know she's going to be in all the morning. Colonel and Mrs. Clibborn are going into Tunbridge Wells."

"It will be a good opportunity."

9

In the morning Mrs. Parsons was in the hall, arranging flowers, when James passed through to get his hat.

"Are you going to see Mary now?"

"Yes, mother."

"That's a good boy."

She did not notice that her son's usual gravity was intensified, or that his very lips were pallid, and his eyes careworn and lustreless.

It was raining. The young fresh leaves, in the colourless day, had lost their verdure, and the massive shapes of the elm trees were obscured in the mist. The sky had so melancholy a tone that it seemed a work of man—a lifeless hue of infinite sorrow, dreary and cheerless.

James arrived at the Clibborns' house.

"Miss Mary is in the drawing-room," he was told by a servant, who smiled on him, the accepted lover, with obtrusive friendliness.

He went in and found her seated at the piano, industriously playing scales. She wore the weather beaten straw hat without which she never seemed comfortable.

"Oh, I'm glad you've come," she said. "I'm alone in the house, and I was taking the opportunity to have a good practice." She turned round on the music-stool, and ran one hand chromatically up the piano, smiling the while with pleasure at Jamie's visit.

"Would you like to go for a walk?" she asked. "I don't mind the rain a bit."

"I would rather stay here, if you don't mind."

James sat down and began playing with a paper-knife. Still he did not know how to express himself. He was torn asunder by rival emotions; he felt absolutely bound to speak, and yet could not bear the thought of the agony he must cause. He was very tender-hearted; he had never in his life consciously given pain to any living creature, and would far rather have inflicted hurt upon himself.

"I've been wanting to have a long talk with you alone ever since I came back."

"Have you? Why didn't you tell me?"

"Because what I want to say is very difficult, Mary; and I'm afraid it must be very—distressing to both of us."

"What do you mean?"

Mary suddenly became grave. James glanced at her, and hesitated; but there was no room for hesitation now. Somehow he must get to the end of what he had to say, attempting only to be as gentle as possible. He stood up and leant against the mantelpiece, still toying with the paper-knife; Mary also changed her seat, and took a chair by the table.

"Do you know that we've been engaged for over five years now, Mary?"

"Yes."

She looked at him steadily, and he dropped his eyes.

"I want to thank you for all you've done for my sake, Mary. I know how good you have been to my people; it was very kind of you. I cannot think how they would have got along without you."

"I love them as I love my own father and mother, Jamie. I tried to act towards them as though I was indeed their daughter."

He was silent for a while.

"We were both very young when we became engaged," he said at last.

He looked up quickly, but she did not answer. She stared with frightened eyes, as if already she understood. It was harder even than he thought. James asked himself desperately whether he could not stop there, taking back what he had said. The cup was too bitter! But what was the alternative? He could not go on pretending one thing when he felt another; he could not live a constant, horrible lie. He felt there was only one course open to him. Like a man with an ill that must be fatal unless instantly treated, he was bound to undergo everything, however great the torture.

"And it's a very bad return I'm making you for all your kindness. You have done everything for me, Mary. You've waited for me patiently and lovingly; you've sacrificed yourself in every way; and I'm afraid I must make you very unhappy— Oh, don't think I'm not grateful to you; I can never thank you sufficiently."

He wished Mary would say something to help him, but she kept silent. She merely dropped her eyes, and now her face seemed quite expressionless.

"I have asked myself day and night what I ought to do, and I can see no way clear before me. I've tried to say this to you before, but I've funked it. You think I'm brave—I'm not; I'm a pitiful coward! Sometimes I can only loathe and despise myself. I want to do my duty, but I can't tell what my duty is. If I only knew for sure which way I ought to take, I should have strength to take it; but it is all so uncertain."

James gave Mary a look of supplication, but she did not see it; her glance was still riveted to the ground.

"I think it's better to tell you the whole truth, Mary; I'm afraid I'm speaking awfully priggishly. I feel I'm acting like a cad, and yet I don't know how else to act. God help me!"

"I've known almost from the beginning that you no longer cared for me," said Mary quietly, her face showing no expression, her voice hushed till it was only a whisper.

"Forgive me, Mary; I've tried to love you. Oh, how humiliating that must sound! I hardly know what I'm saying. Try to understand me. If my words are harsh and ugly, it's because I don't know how to express myself. But I must tell you the whole truth. The chief thing is that I should be honest with you. It's the only return I can make for all you've done for me."

Mary bent her head a little lower, and heavy tears rolled down her cheeks.

"Oh, Mary, don't cry!" said James, his voice breaking; and he stepped forward, with outstretched arms, as though to comfort her.

"I'm sorry," she said; "I didn't mean to."

She took out her handkerchief and dried her eyes, trying to smile. Her courageous self-command was like a stab in Jamie's heart.

"I am an absolute cad!" he said, hoarsely.

Mary made no gesture; she sat perfectly still, rigid, not seeking to hide her emotion, but merely to master it. One could see the effort she made.

"I'm awfully sorry, Mary! Please forgive me—I don't ask you to release me. All I want to do is to explain exactly what I feel, and then leave you to decide."

"Are you—are you in love with anyone else?"

"No!"

The smile of Mrs. Wallace flashed scornfully across his mind, but he set his teeth. He hated and despised her; he would not love her.

"Is there anything in me that you don't like which I might be able to correct?"

Her humility was more than he could bear.

"No, no, no!" he cried. "I can never make you understand. You must think me simply brutal. You have all that a man could wish for. I know how kind you are, and how good you are. I think you have every quality which a good woman should have. I respect you entirely; I can never help feeling for you the most intense gratitude and affection."

In his own ears the words he spoke rang hollow, awkward, even impertinent. He could say nothing which did not seem hideously supercilious; and yet he wanted to abase himself. He knew that Mary's humiliation must be very, very bitter.

"I'm afraid that I am distressing you frightfully, and I don't see how I can make things easier."

"Oh, I knew you didn't love me! I felt it. D'you think I could talk to you for five minutes without seeing the constraint in your manner? They told me I was foolish and fanciful, but I knew better."

"I must have caused you very great unhappiness?"

Mary did not answer, and James looked at her with pity and remorse. At last he broke out passionately:

"I can't command my love! It's not a thing I have at my beck and call. If it were, do you think I should give you this pain? Love is outside all calculation. You think love can be tamed, and led about on a chain like a dog. You think it's a gentle sentiment that one can subject to considerations of propriety and decorum, and God knows what. Oh, you don't know! Love is a madness that seizes one and shakes one like a leaf in the wind. I can't counterfeit love; I can't pretend to have it. I can't command the nerves of my body."

"Do you think I don't know what love is, James? How little you know me."

James sank on a chair and hid his face.

"We none of us understand one another. We're all alike, and yet so different. I don't even know myself. Don't think I'm a prig when I say that I've tried with all my might to love you. I would have given worlds to feel as I felt five years ago. But I can't. God help me! . . . Oh, you must hate and despise me, Mary!"

"I, my dear?" she shook her head sadly. "I shall never do that. I want you to speak frankly. It is much better that we should try to understand one another."

"That is what I felt. I did not think it honest to marry you with a lie in my heart. I don't know whether we can ever be happy; but our only chance is to speak the whole truth."

Mary looked helplessly at him, cowed by her grief.

"I knew it was coming. Every day I dreaded it."

The pain in her eyes was more than James could bear; it was cruel to make her suffer so much. He could not do it. He felt an intense pity, and the idea came to him that there might be a middle way, which would lessen the difficulty. He hesitated a moment, and then, looking down, spoke in a low voice:

"I am anxious to do my duty, Mary. I have promised to marry you. I do not wish to break my word. I don't ask you to release me. Will you take what I can offer? I will be a good husband to you. I will do all I can to make you happy. I can give you affection and confidence—friendship; but I can't give you love. It is much better that I should tell you than that you should find out painfully by yourself—perhaps when it is too late."

"You came to ask me to release you. Why do you hesitate now? Do you think I shall refuse?"

James was silent.

"You cannot think that I will accept a compromise. Do you suppose that because I am a woman I am not made of flesh and blood? You said you wished to be frank."

"I had not thought of the other way till just now."

"Do you imagine that it softens the blow? How could I live with you as your wife, and yet not your wife? What are affection and esteem to me without love? You must think me a very poor creature, James, when you want to make me a sort of legal housekeeper."

"I'm sorry. I didn't think you would look upon it as an impertinence. I didn't mean to say anything offensive. It struck me as a possible way out of the difficulty. You would, at all events, be happier than you are here."

"It is you who despise me now!"

"Mary!"

"I can bear pain. It's not the first humiliation I have suffered. It is very simple, and there's no reason why we should make a fuss about it. You thought you loved me, and you asked me to marry you. I don't know whether you ever really loved me; you certainly don't now, and you wish me to release you. You know that I cannot and will not refuse."

"I see no way out of it, Mary," he said, hoarsely. "I wish to God I did! It's frightfully cruel to you."

"I can bear it. I don't blame you. It's not your fault. God will give me strength." Mary thought of her mother's cruel sympathy. Her parents would have to be told that James had cast her aside like a plaything he was tired of. "God will give me strength."

"I'm so sorry, Mary," cried James, kneeling by her side. "You'll have to suffer dreadfully; and I can't think how to make it any better for you."

"There is no way. We must tell them the whole truth, and let them say what they will."

"Would you like me to go away from Primpton?"

"Why?"

"It might make it easier for you."

"Nothing can make it easier. I can face it out. And I don't want you to run away and hide yourself as if you had done something to be ashamed of. And your people want you. Oh, Jamie, you will be as gentle with them as you can, won't you? I'm afraid it will—disappoint them very much. They had set their hearts upon our marriage. I'm afraid they'll feel it a good deal. But it can't be helped. Anything is better than a loveless marriage."

James was profoundly touched that at the time of her own bitter grief, Mary could think of the pain of others.

"I wish I had your courage, Mary. I've never seen such strength."

"It's well that I have some qualities. I haven't the power to make you love me, and I deserve something to make up."

"Oh, Mary, don't speak like that! I do love you! There's no one for whom I have a purer, more sincere affection. Why won't you take me with what I can offer? I promise that you will never regret it. You know exactly what I am now—weak, but anxious to do right. Why shouldn't we be married? Perhaps things may change. Who can tell what time may bring about?"

"It's impossible. You ask me to do more than I can. And I know very well that you only make the offer out charity. Even from you I cannot accept charity."

"My earnest wish is to make you happy."

"And I know you would sacrifice yourself willingly for that; but I can sacrifice myself, too. You think that if we got married love might arise; but it wouldn't. You would feel perpetually that I was a reproach to you; you would hate me."

"I should never do that."

"How can you tell? We are the same age now, but each year I should seem older. At forty I should be an old woman, and you would still be a young man. Only the deepest love can make that difference endurable; but the love would be all on my side—if I had any then. I should probably have grown bitter and ill-humoured. Ah, no, Jamie, you know it is utterly impracticable. You know it as well as I do. Let us part altogether. I give you back your word. It is not your fault that you do not love me. I don't blame you. One gets over everything in this world eventually. All I ask you is not to trouble too much about me; I shan't die of it."

She stretched out her hand, and he took it, his eyes all blurred, unable to speak.

"And I thank you," she continued, "for having come to me frankly and openly, and told me everything. It is still something that you have confidence in me. You need never fear that I shall feel bitter towards you. I can see that you have suffered—perhaps more than you have made me suffer. Good-bye!"

"Is there nothing I can do, Mary?"

"Nothing," she said, trying to smile, "except not to worry."

"Good-bye," he said. "And don't think too ill of me."

She could not trust herself to answer. She stood perfectly quiet till he had gone out of the room; then with a moan sank to the floor and hid her face, bursting into tears. She had restrained herself too long; the composure became intolerable. She could have screamed, as though suffering some physical pain that destroyed all self-control. The heavy sobs rent her chest, and she did not attempt to stop them. She was heart-broken.

"Oh, how could he!" she groaned. "How could he!"

Her vision of happiness was utterly gone. In James she had placed the joy of her life; in him had found strength to bear every displeasure. Mary had no thought in which he did not take part; her whole future was inextricably mingled with his. But now the years to come, which had seemed so bright and sunny, turned suddenly grey as the melancholy sky without. She saw her life at Little Primpton, continuing as in the past years, monotonous and dull—a dreary round of little duties, of little vexations, of little pleasures.

"Oh, God help me!" she cried.

And lifting herself painfully to her knees, she prayed for strength to bear the woeful burden, for courage to endure it steadfastly, for resignation to believe that it was God's will.

10

James felt no relief. He had looked forward to a sensation of freedom such as a man might feel when he had escaped from some tyrannous servitude, and was at liberty again to breathe the buoyant air of heaven.

He imagined that his depression would vanish like an evil spirit exorcised so soon as ever he got from Mary his release; but instead it sat more heavily upon him. Unconvinced even yet that he had acted rightly, he went over the conversation word for word. It seemed singularly ineffectual. Wishing to show Mary that he did not break with her from caprice or frivolous reason, but with sorrowful reluctance, and full knowledge of her suffering, he had succeeded only in being futile and commonplace.

He walked slowly towards Primpton House. He had before him the announcement to his mother and father; and he tried to order his thoughts.

Mrs. Parsons, her household work finished, was knitting the inevitable socks; while the Colonel sat at the table, putting new stamps into his album. He chattered delightedly over his treasures, getting up now and then gravely to ask his wife some question or to point out a surcharge; she, good woman, showed interest by appropriate rejoinders.

"There's no one in Tunbridge Wells who has such a fine collection as I have."

"General Newsmith showed me his the other day, but it's not nearly so good as yours, Richmond."

"I'm glad of that. I suppose his Mauritius are fine?" replied the Colonel, with some envy, for the general had lived several years on the island.

"They're fair," said Mrs. Parsons, reassuringly; "but not so good as one would expect."

"It takes a clever man to get together a good collection of stamps, although I shouldn't say it."

They looked up when James entered.

"I've just been putting in those Free States you brought me, Jamie. They look very well."

The Colonel leant back to view them, with the satisfied look with which he might have examined an old master.

"It was very thoughtful of Jamie to bring them," said Mrs. Parsons.

"Ah, I knew he wouldn't forget his old father. Don't you remember, Frances, I said to you, 'I'll be bound the boy will bring some stamps with him.' They'll be valuable in a year or two. That's what I always say with regard to postage stamps; you can't waste your money. Now jewellery, for instance, gets old-fashioned, and china breaks; but you run no risk with stamps. When I buy stamps, I really feel that I'm as good as investing my money in consols."

"Well, how's Mary this morning?"

"I've been having a long talk with her."

"Settled the day yet?" asked the Colonel, with a knowing little laugh. "No!"

"Upon my word, Frances, I think we shall have to settle it for them. Things weren't like this when we were young. Why, Jamie, your mother and I got married six weeks after I was introduced to her at a croquet party."

"We were married in haste, Richmond," said Mrs. Parsons, laughing.

"Well, we've taken a long time to repent of it, my dear. It's over thirty years."

"I fancy it's too late now."

The Colonel took her hand and patted it.

"If you get such a good wife as I have, Jamie, I don't think you'll have reason to complain. Will he, my dear?"

"It's not for me to say, Richmond," replied Mrs. Parsons, smiling contentedly.

"Do you want me to get married very much, father?"

"Of course I do. I've set my heart upon it. I want to see what the new generations of Parsons are like before I die."

"Listen, Richmond, Jamie has something to tell us."

Mrs. Parsons had been looking at her son, and was struck at last by the agony of his expression.

"What is it, Jamie?" she asked.

"I'm afraid you'll be dreadfully disappointed. I'm so sorry—Mary and I are no longer engaged to be married."

For a minute there was silence in the room. The old Colonel looked helplessly from wife to son.

"What does he mean, Frances?" he said at last.

Mrs. Parsons did not answer, and he turned to James.

"You're not in earnest, Jamie? You're joking with us?"

James went over to his father, as the weaker of the two, and put his arm round his shoulders.

"I'm awfully sorry to have to grieve you, father. It's quite true—worse luck! It was impossible for me to marry Mary."

"D'you mean that you've broken your engagement with her after she's waited five years for you?" said Mrs. Parsons.

"I couldn't do anything else. I found I no longer loved her. We should both have been unhappy if we had married."

The Colonel recovered himself slowly, he turned round and looked at his son.

"Jamie, Jamie, what have you done?"

"Oh, you can say nothing that I've not said to myself. D'you think it's a step I should have taken lightly? I feel nothing towards Mary but friendship. I don't love her."

"But—" the Colonel stopped, and then a light shone in his face, and he began to laugh. "Oh, it's only a lovers' quarrel, Frances. They've had a little tiff, and they say they'll never speak to one another again. I warrant they're both heartily sorry already, and before night they'll be engaged as fast as ever."

James, by a look, implored his mother to speak. She understood, and shook her head sadly.

"No, Richmond, I'm afraid it's not that. It's serious."

"But Mary loves him, Frances."

"I know," said James. "That's the tragedy of it. If I could only persuade myself that she didn't care for me, it would be all right."

Colonel Parsons sank into his chair, suddenly collapsing. He seemed smaller than ever, wizened and frail; the wisp of white hair that concealed his baldness fell forward grotesquely. His face assumed again that expression, which was almost habitual of anxious fear.

"Oh, father, don't look like that! I can't help it! Don't make it harder for me than possible. You talk to him, mother. Explain that it's not my fault. There was nothing else I could do."

Colonel Parsons sat silent, with his head bent down, but Mrs. Parsons asked:

"What did you say to Mary this morning?"

"I told her exactly what I felt."

"You said you didn't love her?"

"I had to."

"Poor thing!"

They all remained for a while without speaking, each one thinking his painful thoughts.

"Richmond," said Mrs. Parsons at last, "we mustn't blame the boy. It's not his fault. He can't help it if he doesn't love her."

"You wouldn't have me marry her without love, father?"

The question was answered by Mrs. Parsons.

"No; if you don't love her, you mustn't marry her. But what's to be done, I don't know. Poor thing, poor thing, how unhappy she must be!"

James sat with his face in his hands, utterly wretched, beginning already to see the great circle of confusion that he had caused. Mrs. Parsons looked at him and looked at her husband. Presently she went up to James.

"Jamie, will you leave us for a little? Your father and I would like to talk it over alone."

"Yes, mother."

James got up, and putting her hands on his shoulders, she kissed him.

When James had gone, Mrs. Parsons looked compassionately at her husband; he glanced up, and catching her eye, tried to smile. But it was a poor attempt, and it finished with a sigh.

"What's to be done, Richmond?"

Colonel Parsons shook his head without answering.

"I ought to have warned you that something might happen. I saw there was a difference in Jamie's feelings, but I fancied it would pass over. I believed it was only strangeness. Mary is so fond of him, I thought he would soon love her as much as ever."

"But it's not honourable what he's done, Frances," said the old man at last, his voice trembling with emotion. "It's not honourable."

"He can't help it if he doesn't love her."

"It's his duty to marry her. She's waited five years; she's given him the best of her youth—and he jilts her. He can't, Frances; he must behave like a gentleman."

The tears fell down Mrs. Parsons' careworn cheeks—the slow, sparse tears of the woman who has endured much sorrow.

"Don't let us judge him, Richmond. We're so ignorant of the world. You and I are old-fashioned."

"There are no fashions in honesty."

"Let us send for William. Perhaps he'll be able to advise us."

William was Major Forsyth, the brother of Mrs. Parsons. He was a bachelor, living in London, and considered by his relatives a typical man of the world.

"He'll be able to talk to the boy better than we can."

"Very well, let us send for him."

They were both overcome by the catastrophe, but as yet hardly grasped the full extent of it. All their hopes had been centred on this marriage; all their plans for the future had been in it so intricately woven that they could not realise the total overthrow. They felt as a man might feel who was crippled by a sudden accident, and yet still pictured his life as though he had free use of his limbs. . . . Mrs. Parsons wrote a telegram, and gave it to the maid. The servant went out of the room, but as she did so, stepped back and announced:

"Miss Clibborn, ma'am."

"Mary!"

The girl came in, and lifted the veil which she had put on to hide her pallor and her eyes, red and heavy with weeping.

"I thought I'd better come round and see you quietly," she said. "I suppose you've heard?"

"Mary, Mary!"

Mrs. Parsons took her in her arms, kissing her tenderly. Mary pretended to laugh, and hastily dried the tears which came to her eyes.

"You've been crying, Mrs. Parsons. You mustn't do that. . . . Let us sit down and talk sensibly."

She took the Colonel's hand, and gently pressed it.

"Is it true, Mary?" he asked. "I can't believe it."

"Yes, it's quite true. We've decided that we don't wish to marry one another. I want to ask you not to think badly of Jamie. He's very—cut up about it. He's not to blame."

"We're thinking of you, my dear."

"Oh, I shall be all right. I can bear it."

"It's not honourable what he's done, Mary," said the Colonel.

"Oh, don't say that, please! That is why I came round to you quickly. I want you to think that Jamie did what he considered right. For my sake, don't think ill of him. He can't help it if he doesn't love me. I'm not very attractive; he must have known in India girls far nicer than I. How could I hope to keep him all these years? I was a fool to expect it."

"I am so sorry, Mary!" cried Mrs. Parsons. "We've looked forward to your marriage with all our hearts. You know Jamie's been a good son to us; he's never given us any worry. We did want him to marry you. We're so fond of you, and we know how really good you are. We felt that whatever happened after that—if we died—Jamie would be safe and happy."

"It can't be helped. Things never turn out in this world as one wants them. Don't be too distressed about it, and, above all things, don't let Jamie see that you think he hasn't acted—as he might have done."

"How can you think of him now, when your heart must be almost breaking?"

"You see, I've thought of him for years," answered Mary, smiling sadly. "I can't help it now. Oh, I don't want him to suffer! His worrying can do no good. I should like him to be completely happy."

Colonel Parsons sighed.

"He's my son, and he's behaved dishonourably."

"Don't say that. It's not fair to him. He did not ask me for his release. But I couldn't marry him when I knew he no longer cared for me."

"He might have learned to love you, Mary," said Mrs. Parsons.

"No, no! I could see, as he pressed me to marry him nothwithstanding, he was hoping with all his might that I would refuse. He would have hated me. No; it's the end. We have separated for ever, and I will do my best to get over it."

They fell into silence, and presently Mary got up.

"I must go home now, and tell mamma."

"She'll probably have hysterics," said Mrs. Parsons, with a little sniff of contempt.

"No, she'll be delighted," returned Mary. "I know her so well."

"Oh, how much you will have to suffer, dearest!"

"It'll do me good. I was too happy."

"Don't you think you could wait a little before telling anyone else?" asked the Colonel. "Major Forsyth is coming down. He may be able to arrange it; he's a man of the world."

"Can he make Jamie love me? Ah, no, it's no good waiting. Let me get it over quickly while I have the courage. And it helps me to think I have something to do. It only means a few sneers and a little false sympathy."

"A great deal of real sympathy."

"People are always rather glad when some unhappiness befalls their friends! Oh, I didn't mean that! I don't want to be bitter. Don't think badly of me either. I shall be different to-morrow."

"We can never think of you without the sincerest, fondest love."

At that moment James, who did not know that Mary was there, came into the room. He started when he saw her and turned red; but Mary, with a woman's self-possession, braced herself together.

"Oh, Jamie, I've just been having a little chat with your people."

"I'm sorry I interrupted you," he answered, awkwardly. "I didn't know you were here."

"You need not avoid me because we've broken off our engagement. At all events, you have no reason to be afraid of me now. Good-bye! I'm just going home."

She went out, and James looked uncertainly at his parents. His father did not speak, staring at the ground, but Mrs. Parsons said:

"Mary has been asking us not to be angry with you, Jamie. She says it's not your fault."

"It's very kind of her."

"Oh, how could you? How could you?"

11

Not till luncheon was nearly finished did Mary brace herself for the further ordeal, and in a steady, unmoved voice tell Colonel and Mrs. Clibborn what had happened. The faded beauty merely smiled, and lifted her eyes to the chandelier with the expression that had melted the hearts of a thousand and one impressionable subalterns.

"I knew it," she murmured; "I knew it! You can't deceive a woman and a mother."

But the Colonel for a moment was speechless. His face grew red, and his dyed eyebrows stood up in a fury of indignation.

"Impossible!" he spluttered at last.

"You'd better drink a little water, Reggie dear," said his wife. "You look as if you were going to have a fit."

"I won't have it," he shouted, bringing his fist down on the table so that the cheese-plates clattered and the biscuits danced a rapid jig. "I'll make him marry you. He forgets he has me to deal with! I disapproved of the match from the beginning, didn't I, Clara? I said I would never allow my daughter to marry beneath her."

"Papa!"

"Don't talk to me, Mary! Do you mean to deny that James Parsons is infantry, or that his father was infantry before him? But he shall marry you now. By George! he shall marry you if I have to lead him to the altar by the scruff of his neck!"

Neglecting his cheese, the Colonel sprang to his feet and walked to and fro, vehemently giving his opinion of James, his father, and all his ancestors; of the regiments to which they had belonged, and all else that was theirs. He traced their origin from a pork butcher's shop, and prophesied their end, ignominiously, in hell. Every now and then he assured Mary that she need have no fear; the rascal should marry her, or die a violent death.

"But there's nothing more to be said now, papa. We've agreed quite amicably to separate. All I want you to do is to treat him as if nothing had happened."

"I'll horsewhip him," said Colonel Clibborn. "He's insulted you, and I'll make him beg your pardon on his bended knees. Clara, where's my horsewhip?"

"Papa, do be reasonable!"

"I am reasonable, Mary," roared the gallant soldier, becoming a rich purple. "I know my duty, thank God! and I'm going to do it. When a man insults my daughter, it's my duty, as a gentleman and an officer, to give him a jolly good thrashing. When that twopenny sawbones of a doctor was rude to you, I licked him within an inch of his life. I kicked him till he begged for mercy; and if more men had the courage to take the law into their own hands, there'd be fewer damned blackguards in the world."

As a matter of fact, the Colonel had neither thrashed nor kicked the doctor, but it pleased him to think he had. Moralists teach us that the intention is praiseworthy, rather than the brutal act; consequently, there could be no objection if the fearless cavalryman took credit for things which he had thought of doing, but, from circumstances beyond his control, had not actually done.

Mary felt no great alarm at her father's horrid threats, for she knew him well, but still was doubtful about her mother.

"You will treat James as you did before, won't you, mamma?"

Mrs. Clibborn smiled, a portly seraph.

"My dear, I trust I am a gentlewoman."

"He shall never darken my doors again!" cried the Colonel. "I tell you, Clara, keep him out of my way. If I meet him I won't be responsible for my actions; I shall knock him down."

"Reggie dear, you'll have such dreadful indigestion if you don't calm down. You know it always upsets you to get excited immediately after meals."

"It's disgraceful! I suppose he forgets all those half-crowns I gave him when he was a boy, and the cigars, and the port wine he's had since. I opened a special bottle for him only the night before last. I'll never sit down to dinner with him again—don't ask me to, Clara. . . . It's the confounded impertinence of it which gets over me. But he shall marry you, my dear; or I'll know the reason why."

"You can't have him up for breach of promise, Reggie," cooed Mrs. Clibborn.

"A gentleman takes the law in his own hands in these matters. Ah, it's a pity the good old days have gone when they settled such things with cold steel!"

And the Colonel, to emphasise his words, flung himself into the appropriate attitude, throwing his left hand up behind his head, and lunging fiercely with the right.

"Go and look for my *pince-nez*, my dear," said Mrs. Clibborn, turning to Mary. "I think they're in my work-basket or in your father's study."

Mary was glad to leave the room, about which the Colonel stamped in an ever-increasing rage, pausing now and then to take a mouthful of bread and cheese. The request for the glasses was Mrs. Clibborn's usual way of getting rid of Mary, a typical subterfuge of a woman who never, except by chance, put anything straightforwardly. . . . When the door was closed, the buxom lady clasped her hands, and cried:

"Reginald! Reginald! I have a confession to make."

"What's the matter with you?" said the Colonel, stopping short.

"I am to blame for this, Reginald." Mrs. Clibborn threw her head on one side, and looked at the ceiling as the only substitute for heaven. "James Parsons has jilted Mary—on my account."

"What the devil have you been doing now?"

"Oh, forgive me, Reginald!" she cried, sliding off the chair and falling heavily on her knees. "It's not my fault: he loves me."

"Fiddlesticks!" said her husband angrily, walking on again.

"It isn't, Reginald. How unjust you are to me!"

The facile tears began to flow down Mrs. Clibborn's well-powdered cheeks.

"I know he loves me. You can't deceive a woman and a mother."

"You're double his age!"

"These boys always fall in love with women older than themselves; I've noticed it so often. And he's almost told me in so many words, though I'm sure I've given him no encouragement."

"Fiddlesticks, Clara!"

"You wouldn't believe me when I told you that poor Algy Turner loved me, and he killed himself."

"Nothing of the kind; he died of cholera."

"Reginald," retorted Mrs. Clibborn, with asperity, "his death was most mysterious. None of the doctors understood it. If he didn't poison himself, he died of a broken heart. And I think you're very unkind to me."

With some difficulty, being a heavy woman, she lifted herself from the floor; and by the time she was safely on her feet, Mrs. Clibborn was blowing and puffing like a grampus.

The Colonel, whose mind had wandered to other things, suddenly bethought himself that he had a duty to perform.

"Where's my horsewhip, Clara? I command you to give it me."

"Reginald, if you have the smallest remnant of affection for me, you will not hurt this unfortunate young man. Remember that Algy Turner killed himself. You can't blame him for not wanting to marry poor Mary. My dear, she has absolutely no figure. And men are so susceptible to those things."

The Colonel stalked out of the room, and Mrs. Clibborn sat down to meditate.

"I thought my day for such things was past," she murmured. "I knew it all along. The way he looked at me was enough—we women have such quick perceptions! Poor boy, how he must suffer!"

She promised herself that no harsh word of hers should drive James into the early grave where lay the love-lorn Algy Turner. And she sighed, thinking what a curse it was to possess that fatal gift of beauty!

When Little Primpton heard the news, Little Primpton was agitated. Certainly it was distressed, and even virtuously indignant, but at the same time completely unable to divest itself of that little flutter of excitement which was so rare, yet so enchanting, a variation from the monotony of its daily course. The well-informed walked with a lighter step, and held their heads more jauntily, for life had suddenly acquired a novel interest. With something new to talk about, something fresh to think over, with a legitimate object of sympathy and resentment, the torpid blood raced through their veins as might that of statesmen during some crisis in national affairs. Let us thank God, who has made our neighbours frail, and in His infinite mercy caused husband and wife to quarrel; Tom, Dick, and Harry to fall more or less discreditably in love; this dear friend of ours to lose his money, and that her reputation. In all humility, let us be grateful for the scandal which falls at our feet like ripe fruit, for the Divorce Court and for the newspapers that, with a witty semblance of horror, report for us the spicy details. If at certain intervals propriety obliges us to confess that we are miserable sinners, has not the Lord sought to comfort us in the recollection that we are not half so bad as most people?

Mr. Dryland went to the Vicarage to enter certificates in the parish books. The Vicar was in his study, and gave his curate the keys of the iron safe.

"Sophie Bunch came last night to put up her banns," he said.

"She's going to marry out of the parish, isn't she?"

"Yes, a Tunbridge Wells man."

The curate carefully blotted the entries he had made, and returned the heavy books to their place.

"Will you come into the dining-room, Dryland?" said the Vicar, with a certain solemnity. "Mrs Jackson would like to speak to you."

"Certainly."

Mrs. Jackson was reading the *Church Times*. Her thin, sharp face wore an expression of strong disapproval; her tightly-closed mouth, her sharp nose, even the angular lines of her body, signified clearly that her moral sense was outraged. She put her hand quickly to her massive fringe to see that it was straight, and rose to shake hands with Mr. Dryland. His heavy red face assumed at once a grave look; his moral sense was outraged, too.

"Isn't this dreadful news, Mr. Dryland?"

"Oh, very sad! Very sad!"

In both their voices, hidden below an intense sobriety, there was discernible a slight ring of exultation.

"The moment I saw him I felt he would give trouble," said Mrs. Jackson, shaking her head. "I told you, Archibald, that I didn't like the look of him."

"I'm bound to say you did," admitted her lord and master.

"Mary Clibborn is much too good for him," added Mrs. Jackson, decisively. "She's a saint."

"The fact is, that he's suffering from a swollen head," remarked the curate, who used slang as a proof of manliness.

"There, Archibald!" cried the lady, triumphantly. "What did I tell you?"

"Mrs. Jackson thought he was conceited."

"I don't think it; I'm sure of it. He's odiously conceited. All the time I was talking to him I felt he considered himself superior to me. No niceminded man would have refused our offer to say a short prayer on his behalf during morning service."

"Those army men always have a very good opinion of themselves," said Mr. Dryland, taking advantage of his seat opposite a looking-glass to arrange his hair.

He spoke in such a round, full voice that his shortest words carried a sort of polysyllabic weight.

"I can't see what he has done to be so proud of," said Mrs. Jackson. "Anyone would have done the same in his position. I'm sure it's no more heroic than what clergymen do every day of their lives, without making the least fuss about it."

"They say that true courage is always modest," answered Mr. Dryland.

The remark was not very apposite, but sounded damaging.

"I didn't like the way he had when he came to tea here—as if he were dreadfully bored. I'm sure he's not so clever as all that."

"No clever man would act in an ungentlemanly way," said the curate, and then smiled, for he thought he had unconsciously made an epigram.

"I couldn't express in words what I feel with regard to his treatment of Mary!" cried Mrs. Jackson; and then proceeded to do so—and in many, to boot.

They had all been a little oppressed by the greatness which, much against his will, they had thrust upon the unfortunate James. They had set him on a pedestal, and then were disconcerted because he towered above their heads, and the halo with which they had surrounded him dazzled their eyes. They had wished to make a lion of James, and his modest resistance wounded their self-esteem; it was a relief to learn that he was not worth making a lion of. Halo and pedestal were quickly demolished, for the golden idol had feet of clay, and his late adorers were ready to reproach him because he had not accepted with proper humility the gifts he did not want. Their little vanities were comforted by the assurance that, far from being a hero, James was, in fact, distinctly inferior to themselves. For there is no superiority like moral superiority. A man who stands akimbo on the top of the Ten Commandments need bow the knee to no earthly potentate.

Little Primpton was conscious of its virtue, and did not hesitate to condemn.

"He has lowered himself dreadfully."

"Yes, it's very sad. It only shows how necessary it is to preserve a meek and contrite spirit in prosperity. Pride always goes before a fall."

The Jacksons and Mr. Dryland discussed the various accounts which had reached them. Mary and Mrs. Parsons were determinedly silent, but

Mrs. Clibborn was loquacious, and it needed little artifice to extract the whole story from Colonel Parsons.

"One thing is unfortunately certain," said Mrs. Jackson, with a sort of pious vindictiveness, "Captain Parsons has behaved abominably, and it's our duty to do something."

"Colonel Clibborn threatens to horsewhip him."

"It would do him good," cried Mrs. Jackson; "and I should like to be there to see it!"

They paused a moment to gloat over the imaginary scene of Jamie's chastisement.

"He's a wicked man. Fancy throwing the poor girl over when she's waited five years. I think he ought to be made to marry her."

"I'm bound to say that no gentleman would have acted like that," said the Vicar.

"I wanted Archibald to go and speak seriously to Captain Parsons. He ought to know what we think of him, and it's obviously our duty to tell him."

"His parents are very much distressed. One can see that, although they say so little."

"It's not enough to be distressed. They ought to have the strength of mind to insist upon his marrying Mary Clibborn. But they stick up for everything he does. They think he's perfect. I'm sure it's not respectful to God to worship a human being as they do their son."

"They certainly have a very exaggerated opinion of him," assented Mr. Dryland.

"And I should like to know why. He's not goodlooking."

"Very ordinary," agreed Mr. Dryland, with a rapid glance at the convenient mirror. "I don't think his appearance is manly."

Whatever the curate's defects of person—and he flattered himself that he was modest enough to know his bad points—no one, he fancied, could deny him manliness. It is possible that he was not deceived. Put him in a bowler-hat and a bell-bottomed coat, and few could have distinguished him from a cabdriver.

"I don't see anything particular in his eyes or hair," pursued Mrs. Jackson.

"His features are fairly regular. But that always strikes me as insipid in a man."

"And he's not a good conversationalist."

"I'm bound to confess I've never heard him say anything clever," remarked the Vicar.

"No," smiled the curate; "one could hardly call him a brilliant epigrammatist."

"I don't think he's well informed."

"Oh, well, you know, one doesn't expect knowledge from army men," said the curate, with a contemptuous smile and a shrug of the shoulders. "I must say I was rather amused when he confessed he hadn't read Marie Corelli."

"I can hardly believe that. I think it was only pose."

"I'm sorry to say that my experience of young officers is that there are absolutely no bounds to their ignorance."

They had satisfactorily stripped James of every quality, mental and physical, which could have made him attractive in Mary's eyes; and the curate's next remark was quite natural.

"I'm afraid it sounds a conceited thing to say, but I can't help asking myself what Miss Clibborn saw in him."

"Love is blind," replied Mrs. Jackson. "She could have done much better for herself."

They paused to consider the vagaries of the tender passion, and the matches which Mary might have made, had she been so inclined.

"Archibald," said Mrs. Jackson at last, with the decision characteristic of her, "I've made up my mind. As vicar of the parish, you must go to Captain Parsons."

"I, my dear?"

"Yes, Archibald. You must insist upon him fulfilling his engagement with Mary. Say that you are shocked and grieved; and ask him if his own conscience does not tell him that he has done wrong."

"I'm not sure that he'd listen to reason," nervously remarked the Vicar.

"It's your duty to try, Archibald. We're so afraid of being called busybodies that even when we ought to step in we hesitate. No motives of delicacy should stop one when a wicked action is to be prevented. It's often the clergy's duty to interfere with other people's affairs. For my part, I will never shrink from doing my duty. People may call me a busybody if they like; hard words break no bones."

"Captain Parsons is very reserved. He might think it an impertinence if I went to him."

"How could he? Isn't it our business if he breaks his word with a parishioner of ours? If you don't talk to him, I shall. So there, Archibald!"

"Why don't you, Mrs. Jackson?"

"Nothing would please me better. I should thoroughly enjoy giving him a piece of my mind. It would do him good to be told frankly that he's not quite so great as he thinks himself. I will never shrink from doing my duty."

"My dear," remonstrated the Vicar, "if you really think I ought to speak—"

"Perhaps Mrs. Jackson would do better. A women can say many things that a man can't."

This was a grateful suggestion to the Vicar, who could not rid himself of the discomforting thought that James, incensed and hot-tempered, might use the strength of his arms—or legs—in lieu of argument. Mr. Jackson would have affronted horrid tortures for his faith, but shrank timidly before the least suspicion of ridicule. His wife was braver, or less imaginative.

"Very well, I'll go," she said. "It's true he might be rude to Archibald, and he couldn't be rude to a lady. And what's more, I shall go at once."

Mrs. Jackson kept her hat on a peg in the hall, and was quickly ready. She put on her black kid gloves; determination sat upon her mouth, and Christian virtue rested between her brows. Setting out with a brisk step, the conviction was obvious in every movement that duty called, and to that clarion note Maria Jackson would never turn a deaf ear. She went like a Hebrew prophet, conscious that the voice of the Lord was in her.

12

James was wandering in the garden of Primpton House while Mrs. Jackson thither went her way. Since the termination of his engagement with Mary three days back, the subject had not been broached between him and his parents; but he divined their thoughts. He knew that they awaited the arrival of his uncle, Major Forsyth, to set the matter right. They did not seek to reconcile themselves with the idea that the break was final; it seemed too monstrous a thing to be true. James smiled, with bitter amusement, at their simple trust in the man of the world who was due that day.

Major Forsyth was fifty-three, a haunter of military clubs, a busy sluggard, who set his pride in appearing dissipated, and yet led the blameless life of a clergyman's daughter; preserving a spotless virtue, nothing pleased him more than to be thought a rake. He had been on half-pay for many years, and blamed the War Office on that account rather than his own incompetence. Ever since retiring he had told people that advancement, in these degenerate days, was impossible without influence: he was, indeed, one of those men to whom powerful friends offer the only chance of success; and possessing none, inveighed constantly against the corrupt officialism of those in authority. But to his Jeremiads upon the decay of the public services he added a keen interest in the world of fashion; it is always well that a man should have varied activities; it widens his horizon, and gives him a greater usefulness. If his attention had been limited to red-tape, Major Forsyth, even in his own circle, might have been thought a little one-sided; but his knowledge of etiquette and tailors effectually prevented the reproach. He was pleased to consider himself in society; he read assiduously those papers which give detailed accounts of the goings-on in the "hupper succles," and could give you with considerable accuracy the whereabouts of titled people. If he had a weakness, it was by his manner of speaking to insinuate that he knew certain noble persons whom, as a matter of fact, he had never set eyes on; he would not have told a direct lie on the subject, but his conscience permitted him a slight equivocation. Major Forsyth was well up in all the gossip of the clubs, and if he could not call himself a man of the world, he had not the least notion who could. But for all that, he had the strictest principles; he was true brother to Mrs. Parsons, and though he concealed the fact like something disreputable, regularly went to church on Sunday mornings. There was also a certain straitness in his income which confined him to the paths shared by the needy and the pure at heart.

Major Forsyth had found no difficulty in imposing upon his sister and her husband.

"Of course, William is rather rackety," they said. "It's a pity he hasn't a wife to steady him; but he has a good heart."

For them Major Forsyth had the double advantage of a wiliness gained in the turmoil of the world and an upright character. They scarcely knew how in the present juncture he could help, but had no doubt that from the boundless store of his worldly wisdom he would invent a solution to their difficulty.

James had found his uncle out when he was quite a boy, and seeing his absurdity, had treated him ever since with good-natured ridicule.

"I wonder what they think he can say?" he asked himself.

James was profoundly grieved at the unhappiness which bowed his father down. His parents had looked forward with such ecstatic pleasure to his arrival, and what sorrow had he not brought them!

"I wish I'd never come back," he muttered.

He thought of the flowing, undulating plains of the Orange Country, and the blue sky, with its sense of infinite freedom. In that trim Kentish landscape he felt hemmed in; when the clouds were low it seemed scarcely possible to breathe; and he suffered from the constraint of his father and mother, who treated him formally, as though he had become a stranger. There was always between them and him that painful topic which for the time was carefully shunned. They did not mention Mary's name, and the care they took to avoid it was more painful than would have been an open reference. They sat silent and sad, trying to appear natural, and dismally failing; their embarrassed manner was such as they might have adopted had he committed some crime, the mention of which for his sake must never be made, but whose recollection perpetually haunted them. In every action was the belief that James must be suffering from remorse, and that it was their duty not to make his burden heavier. James knew that his father was convinced that he had acted dishonourably, and he—what did he himself think?

James asked himself a hundred times a day whether he had acted well or ill; and though he forced himself to answer that he had done the only possible thing, deep down in his heart was a terrible, a perfectly maddening uncertainty. He tried to crush it, and would not listen, for his intelligence told him clearly it was absurd; but it was stronger than intelligence, an incorporeal shape through which passed harmlessly the sword-cuts of his reason. It was a little devil curled up in his heart, mut-tering to all his arguments, "Are you sure?"

Sometimes he was nearly distracted, and then the demon laughed, so that the mocking shrillness rang in his ears:

"Are you sure, my friend—are you sure? And where, pray, is the ho-nour which only a while ago you thought so much of?"

James walked to and fro restlessly, impatient, angry with himself and with all the world.

But then on the breath of the wind, on the perfume of the roses, yel-low and red, came suddenly the irresistible recollection of Mrs. Wallace. Why should he not think of her now? He was free; he could do her no harm; he would never see her again. The thought of her was the only sunshine in his life; he was tired of denying himself every pleasure. Why should he continue the pretence that he no longer loved her? It was, in-deed, a consolation to think that the long absence had not dulled his passion; the strength of it was its justification. It was useless to fight against it, for it was part of his very soul; he might as well have fought against the beating of his heart. And if it was torture to remember those old days in India, he delighted in it; it was a pain more exquisite than the suffocating odours of tropical flowers, a voluptuous agony such as might feel the fakir lacerating his flesh in a divine possession. . . . Every little occurrence was clear, as if it had taken place but a day before.

James repeated to himself the conversations they had had, of no consequence, the idle gossip of a stray half-hour; but each word was op-ulent in the charming smile, in the caressing glance of her eyes. He was able to imagine Mrs. Wallace quite close to him, wearing the things that he had seen her wear, and with her movements he noticed the excessive scent she used. He wondered whether she had overcome that failing, whether she still affected the artificiality which was so adorable a relief from the grimness of manner which he had thought the natural way of women.

If her cheeks were not altogether innocent of rouge or her eyebrows of pencil, what did he care; he delighted in her very faults; he would not have her different in the very slightest detail; everything was part of that complex, elusive fascination. And James thought of the skin which had the even softness of fine velvet, and the little hands. He called himself a fool for his shyness. What could have been the harm if he had taken those hands and kissed them? Now, in imagination, he pressed his lips passionately on the warm palms. He liked the barbaric touch in the many rings which bedecked her fingers.

"Why do you wear so many rings?" he asked. "Your hands are too fine."

He would never have ventured the question, but now there was no danger. Her answer came with a little, good-humoured laugh; she stretched out her fingers, looking complacently at the brilliant gems.

"I like to be gaudy. I should like to be encrusted with jewels. I want to wear bracelets to my elbow and diamond spangles on my arms; and jewelled belts, and jewels in my hair, and on my neck. I should like to flash from head to foot with exotic stones."

Then she looked at him with amusement.

"Of course, you think it's vulgar. What do I care? You all of you think it's vulgar to be different from other people. I want to be unique."

"You want everybody to look at you?"

"Of course I do! Is it sinful? Oh, I get so impatient with all of you, with your good taste and your delicacy, and your insupportable dulness. When you admire a woman, you think it impertinent to tell her she's beautiful; when you have good looks, you carry yourselves as though you were ashamed."

And in a bold moment he replied:

"Yet you would give your soul to have no drop of foreign blood in your veins!"

"I?" she cried, her eyes flashing with scorn. "I'm proud of my Eastern blood. It's not blood I have in my veins, it's fire—a fire of gold. It's because of it that I have no prejudices, and know how to enjoy my life."

James smiled, and did not answer.

"You don't believe me?" she asked."

"No!"

"Well, perhaps I should like to be quite English. I should feel more comfortable in my scorn of these regimental ladies if I thought they could find no reason to look down on me."

"I don't think they look down on you."

"Oh, don't they? They despise and loathe me."

"When you were ill, they did all they could for you."

"Foolish creature! Don't you know that to do good to your enemy is the very best way of showing your contempt."

And so James could go on, questioning, replying, putting little jests into her mouth, or half-cynical repartees. Sometimes he spoke aloud, and then Mrs. Wallace's voice sounded in his ears, clear and rich and passionate, as though she were really standing in the flesh beside him. But always he finished by taking her in his arms and kissing her lips and her closed eyes, the lids transparent like the finest alabaster. He knew no pleasure greater than to place his hands on that lustrous hair. What could it matter now? He was not bound to Mary; he could do no harm to Mrs. Wallace, ten thousand miles away.

But Colonel Parsons broke into the charming dream. Bent and weary, he came across the lawn to find his son. The wan, pathetic figure brought back to James all the present bitterness. He sighed, and advanced to meet him.

"You're very reckless to come out without a hat, father. I'll fetch you one, shall I?"

"No, I'm not going to stay." The Colonel could summon up no answering smile to his boy's kind words. "I only came to tell you that Mrs. Jackson is in the drawing-room, and would like to see you."

"What does she want?"

"She'll explain herself. She has asked to see you alone."

Jamie's face darkened, as some notion of Mrs. Jackson's object dawned upon him.

"I don't know what she can have to talk to me about alone."

"Please listen to her, Jamie. She's a very clever woman, and you can't fail to benefit by her advice."

The Colonel never had an unfriendly word to say of anyone, and even for Mrs. Jackson's unwarrantable interferences could always find a good-natured justification. He was one of those deprecatory men who, in every difference of opinion, are convinced that they are certainly in the wrong. He would have borne with the most cheerful submission any rebuke of his own conduct, and been, indeed, vastly grateful to the Vicar's wife for pointing out his error.

James found Mrs. Jackson sitting bolt upright on a straight-backed chair, convinced, such was her admirable sense of propriety, that a lounging attitude was incompatible with the performance of a duty. She held her hands on her lap, gently clasped; and her tight lips expressed as plainly as possible her conviction that though the way of righteousness was hard, she, thank God! had strength to walk it.

"How d'you do, Mrs. Jackson?"

"Good morning," she replied, with a stiff bow.

James, though there was no fire, went over to the mantelpiece and leant against it, waiting for the lady to speak.

"Captain Parsons, I have a very painful duty to perform."

Those were her words, but it must have been a dense person who failed to perceive that Mrs. Jackson found her duty anything but painful. There was just that hard resonance in her voice that an inquisitor might have in condemning to the stake a Jew to whom he owed much money.

"I suppose you will call me a busybody?"

"Oh, I'm sure you would never interfere with what does not concern you," replied James, slowly.

"Certainly not!" said Mrs. Jackson. "I come here because my conscience tells me to. What I wish to talk to you about concerns us all."

"Shall I call my people? I'm sure they'd be interested."

"I asked to see you alone, Captain Parsons," answered Mrs. Jackson, frigidly. "And it was for your sake. When one has to tell a person home-truths, he generally prefers that there should be no audience."

"So you're going to tell me some home-truths, Mrs. Jackson?" said James, with a laugh. "You must think me very good-natured. How long have I had the pleasure of your acquaintance?"

Mrs. Jackson's grimness did not relax.

"One learns a good deal about people in a week."

"D'you think so? I have an idea that ten years is a short time to get to know them. You must be very quick."

"Actions often speak."

"Actions are the most lying things in the world. They are due mostly to adventitious circumstances which have nothing to do with the character of the agent. I would never judge a man by his actions."

"I didn't come here to discuss abstract things with you, Captain Parsons."

"Why not? The abstract is so much more entertaining than the concrete. It affords opportunities for generalisation, which is the salt of conversation."

"I'm a very busy woman," retorted Mrs. Jackson sharply, thinking that James was not treating her with proper seriousness. He was not so easy to tackle as she had imagined.

"It's very good of you, then, to spare time to come and have a little chat with me," said James.

"I did not come for that purpose, Captain Parsons."

"Oh, I forgot—home-truths, wasn't it? I was thinking of Shakespeare and the musical glasses!"

"Would you kindly remember that I am a clergyman's wife, Captain Parsons? I daresay you are not used to the society of such."

"Pardon me, I even know an archdeacon quite well. He has a great gift of humour; a man wants it when he wears a silk apron."

"Captain Parsons," said Mrs. Jackson, sternly, "there are some things over which it is unbecoming to jest. I wish to be as gentle as possible with you, but I may remind you that flippancy is not the best course for you to pursue."

James looked at her with a good-tempered stare.

"Upon my word," he said to himself, "I never knew I was so patient."

"I can't beat about the bush any longer," continued the Vicar's lady; "I have a very painful duty to perform."

"That quite excuses you hesitation."

"You must guess why I have asked to see you alone."

"I haven't the least idea."

"Does your conscience say nothing to you?"

"My conscience is very well-bred. It never says unpleasant things."

"Then I'm sincerely sorry for you."

James smiled.

"Oh, my good woman," he thought, "if you only knew what a troublesome spirit I carry about with me!"

But Mrs. Jackson saw only hardness of heart in the grave face; she never dreamed that behind those quiet eyes was a turmoil of discordant passions, tearing, rending, burning.

"I'm sorry for you," she repeated. "I think it's very sad, very sad indeed, that you should stand there and boast of the sluggishness of your conscience. Conscience is the voice of God, Captain Parsons; if it does not speak to you, it behoves others to speak in its place."

"And supposing I knew what you wanted to say, do you think I should like to hear?"

"I'm afraid not."

"Then don't you think discretion points to silence?"

"No, Captain Parsons. There are some things which one is morally bound to say, however distasteful they may be."

"The easiest way to get through life is to say pleasant things on all possible occasions."

"That is not my way, and that is not the right way."

"I think it rash to conclude that a course is right merely because it is difficult. Likewise an uncivil speech is not necessarily a true one."

"I repeat that I did not come here to bandy words with you."

"My dear Mrs. Jackson, I have been wondering why you did not come to the point at once."

"You have been wilfully interrupting me."

"I'm so sorry. I thought I had been making a series of rather entertaining observations."

"Captain Parsons, what does your conscience say to you about Mary Clibborn?"

James looked at Mrs. Jackson very coolly, and she never imagined with what difficulty he was repressing himself.

"I thought you said your subject was of national concern. Upon my word, I thought you proposed to hold a thanksgiving service in Little Primpton Church for the success of the British arms."

"Well, you know different now," retorted Mrs. Jackson, with distinct asperity. "I look upon your treatment of Mary Clibborn as a matter which concerns us all."

"Then, as politely as possible, I must beg to differ from you. I really cannot permit you to discuss my private concerns. You have, doubtless, much evil to say of me; say it behind my back."

"I presumed that you were a gentleman, Captain Parsons."

"You certainly presumed."

"And I should be obliged if you would treat me like a lady."

James smiled. He saw that it was folly to grow angry.

"We'll do our best to be civil to one another, Mrs. Jackson. But I don't think you must talk of what really is not your business."

"D'you think you can act shamefully and then slink away as soon as you are brought to book? Do you know what you've done to Mary Clibborn?"

"Whatever I've done, you may be sure that I have not acted rashly. Really, nothing you can say will make the slightest difference. Don't you think we had better bring our conversation to an end?"

James made a movement towards the door.

"Your father and mother wish me to speak with you, Colonel Parsons," said Mrs. Jackson. "And they wish you to listen to what I have to say."

James paused. "Very well."

He sat down and waited. Mrs. Jackson felt unaccountably nervous; it had never occurred to her that a mere soldier could be so hard to deal with, and it was she who hesitated now. Jamie's stern eyes made her feel singularly like a culprit; but she cleared her throat and straightened herself.

"It's very sad," she said, "to find how much we've been mistaken in you, Captain Parsons. When we were making all sorts of preparations to welcome you, we never thought that you would repay us like this. It grieves me to have to tell you that you have done a very wicked thing. I was hoping that your conscience would have something to say to you, but unhappily I was mistaken. You induced Mary to become engaged to you; you kept her waiting for years; you wrote constantly, pretending to love her, deceiving her odiously; you let her waste the best part of her life, and then, without excuse and without reason, you calmly say that you're sick of her, and won't marry her. I think it is horrible, and brutal, and most ungentlemanly. Even a common man wouldn't have behaved in that way. Of course, it doesn't matter to you, but it means the ruin of Mary's whole life. How can she get a husband now when she's wasted her best years? You've spoilt all her chances. You've thrown a slur upon her which people will never forget. You're a cruel, wicked man, and however you won the Victoria Cross I don't know; I'm sure you don't deserve it."

Mrs. Jackson stopped.

"Is that all?" asked James, quietly.

"It's quite enough."

"Quite! In that case, I think we may finish our little interview."

"Have you nothing to say?" asked Mrs. Jackson indignantly, realising that she had not triumphed after all.

"I? Nothing."

Mrs. Jackson was perplexed, and still those disconcerting eyes were fixed upon her; she angrily resented their polite contempt.

"Well, I think it's disgraceful!" she cried. "You must be utterly shameless!"

"My dear lady, you asked me to listen to you, and I have. If you thought I was going to argue, I'm afraid you were mistaken. But since you have been very frank with me, you can hardly mind if I am equally frank with you. I absolutely object to the way in which not only you, but all the persons who took part in that ridiculous function the other day, talk of my private concerns. I am a perfect stranger to you, and you have no business to speak to me of my engagement with Miss Clibborn or the rupture of it. Finally, I would remark that I consider your particular interference a very gross piece of impertinence. I am sorry to have to speak so directly, but apparently nothing but the very plainest language can have any effect upon you."

Then Mrs. Jackson lost her temper.

"Captain Parsons, I am considerably older than you, and you have no right to speak to me like that. You forget that I am a lady; and if I didn't know your father and mother, I should say that you were no gentleman. And you forget also that I come here on the part of God. You are certainly no Christian. You've been very rude to me, indeed."

"I didn't mean to be," replied James, smiling.

"If I'd known you would be so rude to a lady, I should have sent Archibald to speak with you."

"Perhaps it's fortunate you didn't. I might have kicked him."

"Captain Parsons, he's a minister of the gospel."

"Surely it is possible to be that without being a malicious busybody."

"You're heartless and vain! You're odiously conceited."

"I should have thought it a proof of modesty that for half an hour I have listened to you with some respect and with great attention."

"I must say in my heart I'm glad that Providence has stepped in and prevented Mary from marrying you. You are a bad man. And I leave you now to the mercies of your own conscience; I am a Christian woman, thank Heaven! and I forgive you. But I sincerely hope that God will see fit to punish you for your wickedness."

Mrs. Jackson bounced to the door, which James very politely opened.

"Oh, don't trouble!" she said, with a sarcastic shake of the head. "I can find my way out alone, and I shan't steal the umbrellas."

13

Major Forsyth arrived in time for tea, red-faced, dapper, and immaculate. He wore a check suit, very new and very pronounced, with a beautiful line down each trouser-leg; and his collar and his tie were of the latest mode. His scanty hair was carefully parted in the middle, and his moustache bristled with a martial ardour. He had lately bought a fine set of artificial teeth, which, with pardonable pride, he constantly exhibited to the admiration of all and sundry. Major Forsyth's consuming desire was to appear juvenile; he affected slang, and carried himself with a youthful jauntiness. He vowed he felt a mere boy, and flattered himself that on his good days, with the light behind him, he might pass for five-and-thirty.

"A woman," he repeated—"a woman is as old as she looks; but a man is as old as he feels!"

The dandiness which in a crammer's pup—most overdressed of all the human race—would merely have aroused a smile, looked oddly with the Major's wrinkled skin and his old eyes. There was something almost uncanny in the exaggerated boyishness; he reminded one of some figure in a dance of death, of a living skeleton, hollow-eyed, strutting gaily by the side of a gallant youth.

It was not difficult to impose upon the Parsons, and Major Forsyth had gained over them a complete ascendancy. They took his opinion on every possible matter, accepting whatever he said with gratified respect.

He was a man of the world, and well acquainted with the goings-on of society. They had an idea that he disappointed duchesses to come down to Little Primpton, and always felt that it was a condescension on his part to put up with their simple manners. They altered their hours; luncheon was served at the middle of the day, and dinner in the evening.

Mrs. Parsons put on a Sabbath garment of black silk to receive her brother, and round her neck a lace fichu. When he arrived with Colonel Parsons from the station, she went into the hall to meet him.

"Well, William, have you had a pleasant journey?"

"Oh, yes, yes! I came down with the prettiest woman I've seen for many a long day. I made eyes at her all the way, but she wouldn't look at me."

"William, William!" expostulated Mrs. Parsons, smiling.

"You see he hasn't improved since we saw him last, Frances," laughed the Colonel, leading the way into the drawing-room.

"No harm in looking at a pretty woman, you know. I'm a bachelor still, thank the Lord! That reminds me of a funny story I heard at the club."

"Oh, we're rather frightened of your stories, William," said Mrs. Parsons.

"Yes, you're very risky sometimes," assented the Colonel, good-humouredly shaking his head.

Major Forsyth was anecdotal, as is only decent in an old bachelor, and he made a speciality of stories which he thought wicked, but which, as a matter of fact, would not have brought a blush to any cheek less innocent than that of Colonel Parsons.

"There's no harm in a little spice," said Uncle William. "And you're a married woman, Frances."

He told an absolutely pointless story of how a man had helped a young woman across the street, and seen her ankle in the process. He told it with immense gusto, laughing and repeating the point at least six times.

"William, William!" laughed Colonel Parsons, heartily. "You should keep those things for the smoking-room."

"What d'you think of it, Frances?" asked the gallant Major, still hugely enjoying the joke.

Mrs. Parsons blushed a little, and for decency's sake prevented herself from smiling; she felt rather wicked.

"I don't want to hear any more of your tales, William."

"Ha, ha!" laughed Uncle William, "I knew you'd like it. And that one I told you in the fly, Richmond—you know, about the petticoat."

"Sh-sh!" said the Colonel, smiling. "You can't tell that to a lady."

"P'r'aps I'd better not. But it's a good story, though."

They both laughed.

"I think it's dreadful the things you men talk about as soon as you're alone," said Mrs. Parsons.

The two God-fearing old soldiers laughed again, admitting their wickedness.

"One must talk about something," said Uncle William. "And upon my word, I don't know anything better to talk about than the fair sex."

Soon James appeared, and shook hands with his uncle.

"You're looking younger than ever, Uncle William. You make me feel quite old."

"Oh, I never age, bless you! Why, I was talking to my old friend, Lady Green, the other day—she was a Miss Lake, you know—and she said to me: 'Upon my word, Major Forsyth, you're wonderful. I believe you've found the secret of perpetual youth.' 'The fact is,' I said, 'I never let myself grow old. If you once give way to it, you're done.' 'How do you manage it?' she said. 'Madam,' I answered, 'it's the simplest thing in the world. I keep regular hours, and I wear flannel next to my skin.'"

"Come, come, Uncle William," said James, with a smile. "You didn't mention your underlinen to a lady!"

"Upon my word, I'm telling you exactly what I said."

"You're very free in your conversation."

"Well, you know, I find the women expect it from me. Of course, I never go beyond the line."

Then Major Forsyth talked of the fashions, and of his clothes, of the scandal of the day, and the ancestry of the persons concerned, of the war.

"You can say what you like," he remarked, "but my opinion is that Roberts is vastly overrated. I met at the club the other day a man whose first cousin has served under Roberts in India—his first cousin, mind you, so it's good authority—and this chap told me, in strict confidence, of course, that his first cousin had no opinion of Roberts. That's what a man says who has actually served under him."

"It is certainly conclusive," said James. "I wonder your friend's first cousin didn't go to the War Office and protest against Bobs being sent out."

"What's the good of going to the War Office? They're all corrupt and incompetent there. If I had my way, I'd make a clean sweep of them. Talking of red-tape, I'll just give you an instance. Now, this is a fact. It was told me by the brother-in-law of the uncle of the man it happened to."

Major Forsyth told his story at great length, finishing up with the assertion that if the army wasn't going to the dogs, he didn't know what going to the dogs meant.

James, meanwhile, catching the glances which passed between his mother and Colonel Parsons, understood that they were thinking of the great subject upon which Uncle William was to be consulted. Half scornfully he gave them their opportunity.

"I'm going for a stroll," he said, "through Groombridge. I shan't be back till dinner-time."

"How lucky!" remarked Colonel Parsons naively, when James had gone. "We wanted to talk with you privately, William. You're a man of the world."

"I think there's not much that I don't know," replied the Major, shooting his linen.

"Tell him, Frances."

Mrs. Parsons, accustomed to the part of spokes-woman, gave her tale, interrupted now and again by a long whistle with which the Major signified his shrewdness, or by an energetic nod which meant that the difficulty was nothing to him.

"You're quite right," he said at last; "one has to look upon these things from the point of view of the man of the world."

"We knew you'd be able to help us," said Colonel Parsons.

"Of course! I shall settle the whole thing in five minutes. You leave it to me."

"I told you he would, Frances," cried the Colonel, with a happy smile. "You think that James ought to marry the girl, don't you?"

"Certainly. Whatever his feelings are, he must act as a gentleman and an officer. Just you let me talk it over with him. He has great respect for all I say; I've noticed that already."

Mrs. Parsons looked at her brother doubtfully.

"We haven't known what to do," she murmured. "We've prayed for guidance, haven't we, Richmond? We're anxious not to be hard on the boy, but we must be just."

"Leave it to me," repeated Uncle William. "I'm a man of the world, and I'm thoroughly at home in matters of this sort."

According to the little plan which, in his subtlety, Major Forsyth had suggested, Mrs. Parsons, soon after dinner, fetched the backgammon board.

"Shall we have our usual game, Richmond?"

Colonel Parsons looked significantly at his brother-in-law.

"If William doesn't mind?"

"No, no, of course not! I'll have a little chat with Jamie."

The players sat down at the corner of the table, and rather nervously began to set out the men. James stood by the window, silent as ever, looking at the day that was a-dying, with a milk-blue sky and tenuous clouds, copper and gold. Major Forsyth took a chair opposite him, and pulled his moustache.

"Well, Jamie, my boy, what is all this nonsense I hear about you and Mary Clibborn?"

Colonel Parsons started at the expected question, and stole a hurried look at his son. His wife noisily shook the dice-box and threw the dice on the board.

"Nine!" she said.

James turned to look at his uncle, noting a little contemptuously the change of his costume, and its extravagant juvenility.

"A lot of stuff and nonsense, isn't it?"

"D'you think so?" asked James, wearily. "We've been taking it very seriously."

"You're a set of old fogies down here. You want a man of the world to set things right."

"Ah, well, you're a man of the world, Uncle William," replied James, smiling.

The dice-box rattled obtrusively as Colonel Parsons and his wife played on with elaborate unconcern of the conversation.

"A gentleman doesn't jilt a girl when he's been engaged to her for five years."

James squared himself to answer Major Forsyth. The interview with Mrs. Jackson in the morning had left him extremely irritated. He was resolved to say now all he had to say and have done with it, hoping that a complete explanation would relieve the tension between his people and himself.

"It is with the greatest sorrow that I broke off my engagement with Mary Clibborn. It seemed to me the only honest thing to do since I no longer loved her. I can imagine nothing in the world so horrible as a loveless marriage."

"Of course, it's unfortunate; but the first thing is to keep one's word."

"No," answered James, "that is prejudice. There are many more important things."

Colonel Parsons stopped the pretence of his game.

"Do you know that Mary is breaking her heart?" he asked in a low voice.

"I'm afraid she's suffering very much. I don't see how I can help it."

"Leave this to me, Richmond," interrupted the Major, impatiently. "You'll make a mess of it."

But Colonel Parsons took no notice.

"She looked forward with all her heart to marrying you. She's very unhappy at home, and her only consolation was the hope that you would soon take her away."

"Am I managing this or are you, Richmond? I'm a man of the world."

"If I married a woman I did not care for because she was rich, you would say I had dishonoured myself. The discredit would not be in her wealth, but in my lack of love."

"That's not the same thing," replied Major Forsyth. "You gave your word, and now you take it back."

"I promised to do a thing over which I had no control. When I was a boy, before I had seen anything of the world, before I had ever known a woman besides my mother, I promised to love Mary Clibborn all my life. Oh, it was cruel to let me be engaged to her! You blame me; don't you think all of you are a little to blame as well?"

"What could we have done?"

"Why didn't you tell me not to be hasty? Why didn't you say that I was too young to become engaged?"

"We thought it would steady you."

"But a young man doesn't want to be steadied. Let him see life and taste all it has to offer. It is wicked to put fetters on his wrists before ever he has seen anything worth taking. What is the virtue that exists only because temptation is impossible!"

"I can't understand you, Jamie," said Mrs. Parsons, sadly. "You talk so differently from when you were a boy."

"Did you expect me to remain all my life an ignorant child? You've never given me any freedom. You've hemmed me in with every imaginable barrier. You've put me on a leading-string, and thanked God that I did not stray."

"We tried to bring you up like a good man, and a true Christian."

"If I'm not a hopeless prig, it's only by miracle."

"James, that's not the way to talk to your mother," said Major Forsyth.

"Oh, mother, I'm sorry; I don't want to be unkind to you. But we must talk things out freely; we've lived in a hot-house too long."

"I don't know what you mean. You became engaged to Mary of your own free will; we did nothing to hinder it, nothing to bring it about. But I confess we were heartily thankful, thinking that no influence could be better for you than the love of a pure, sweet English girl."

"It would have been kinder and wiser if you had forbidden it."

"We could not have taken the responsibility of crossing your affections."

"Mrs. Clibborn did."

"Could you expect us to be guided by her?"

"She was the only one who showed the least common sense."

"How you have changed, Jamie!"

"I would have obeyed you if you had told me I was too young to become engaged. After all, you are more responsible than I am. I was a child. It was cruel to let me bind myself."

"I never thought you would speak to us like that."

"All that's ancient history," said Major Forsyth, with what he flattered himself was a very good assumption of jocularity. It was his idea to treat the matter lightly, as a man of the world naturally would. But his interruption was unnoticed.

"We acted for the best. You know that we have always had your interests at heart."

James did not speak, for his only answer would have been bitter. Throughout, they had been unwilling to let him live his own life, but desirous rather that he should live theirs. They loved him tyrannically, on the condition that he should conform to all their prejudices. Though full of affectionate kindness, they wished him always to dance to their piping—a marionette of which they pulled the strings.

"What would you have me do?"

"Keep your word, James," answered his father.

"I can't, I can't! I don't understand how you can wish me to marry Mary Clibborn when I don't love her. *That* seems to me dishonourable."

"It would be nothing worse than a *mariage de convenance*," said Uncle William. "Many people marry in that sort of way, and are perfectly happy."

"I couldn't," said James. "That seems to me nothing better than prostitution. It is no worse for a street-walker to sell her body to any that care to buy."

"James, remember your mother is present."

"For God's sake, let us speak plainly. You must know what life is. One can do no good by shutting one's eyes to everything that doesn't square with a shoddy, false ideal. On one side I must break my word, on the other I must prostitute myself. There is no middle way. You live here surrounded by all sorts of impossible ways of looking at life. How can your outlook be sane when it is founded on a sham morality? You think the body is indecent and ugly, and that the flesh is shameful. Oh, you don't understand. I'm sick of this prudery which throws its own hideousness over all it sees. The soul and the body are one, indissoluble. Soul is body, and body is soul. Love is the God-like instinct of procreation. You think sexual attraction is something to be ignored, and in its place you put a bloodless sentimentality—the vulgar rhetoric of a penny novelette. If I marry a woman, it is that she may be the mother of children. Passion is the only reason for marriage; unless it exists, marriage is ugly and beastly. It's worse than beastly; the beasts of the field are clean. Don't you understand why I can't marry Mary Clibborn?"

"What you call love, James," said Colonel Parsons, "is what I call lust."

"I well believe it," replied James, bitterly.

"Love is something higher and purer."

"I know nothing purer than the body, nothing higher than the divine instincts of nature."

"But that sort of love doesn't last, my dear," said Mrs. Parsons, gently. "In a very little while it is exhausted, and then you look for something different in your wife. You look for friendship and companionship, confidence, consolation in your sorrows, sympathy with your success. Beside all that, the sexual love sinks into nothing."

"It may be. The passion arises for the purposes of nature, and dies away when those purposes are fulfilled. It seems to me that the recollection of it must be the surest and tenderest tie between husband and wife; and there remains for them, then, the fruit of their love, the children whom it is their blessed duty to rear till they are of fit age to go into the world and continue the endless cycle."

There was a pause, while Major Forsyth racked his brain for some apposite remark; but the conversation had run out of his depth.

Colonel Parsons at last got up and put his hands on Jamie's shoulders.

"And can't you bring yourself to marry that poor girl, when you think of the terrible unhappiness she suffers?"

James shook his head.

"You were willing to sacrifice your life for a mere stranger, and cannot you sacrifice yourself for Mary, who has loved you long and tenderly, and unselfishly?"

"I would willingly risk my life if she were in danger. But you ask more."

Colonel Parsons was silent for a little, looking into his son's eyes. Then he spoke with trembling voice.

"I think you love me, James. I've always tried to be a good father to you; and God knows I've done all I could to make you happy. If I did wrong in letting you become engaged, I beg your pardon. No; let me go on." This he said in answer to Jamie's movement of affectionate protest. "I don't say it to reproach you, but your mother and I have denied ourselves in all we could so that you should be happy and comfortable. It's been a pleasure to us, for we love you with all our hearts. You know what happened to me when I left the army. I told you years ago of the awful disgrace I suffered. I could never have lived except for my trust in God and my trust in you. I looked to you to regain the honour which I had lost. Ah! you don't know how anxiously I watched you, and the joy with which I said to myself, 'There is a good and honourable man.' And now you want to stain that honour. Oh, James, James! I'm old, and I can't live long. If you love me, if you think you have cause for gratitude to me, do this one little thing I ask you! For my sake, my dear, keep your word to Mary Clibborn."

"You're asking me to do something immoral, father."

Then Colonel Parsons helplessly dropped his hands from Jamie's shoulders, and turned to the others, his eyes full of tears.

"I don't understand what he means!" he groaned.

He sank on a chair and hid his face.

14

Major Forsyth was not at all discouraged by the issue of his intervention.

"Now I see how the land lies," he said, "it's all plain sailing. Reconnoitre first, and then wire in."

He bravely attacked James next day, when they were smoking in the garden after breakfast. Uncle William smoked nothing but gold-tipped cigarettes, which excited his nephew's open scorn.

"I've been thinking about what you said yesterday, James," he began.

"For Heaven's sake, Uncle William, don't talk about it any more. I'm heartily sick of the whole thing. I've made up my mind, and I really shall not alter it for anything you may say."

Major Forsyth changed the conversation with what might have been described as a strategic movement to the rear. He said that Jamie's answer told him all he wished to know, and he was content now to leave the seeds which he had sown to spring up of their own accord.

"I'm perfectly satisfied," he told his sister, complacently. "You'll see that it'll all come right now."

Meanwhile, Mary conducted herself admirably. She neither avoided James nor sought him, but when chance brought them together, was perfectly natural. Her affection had never been demonstrative, and now there was in her manner but little change. She talked frankly, as though nothing had passed between them, with no suspicion of reproach in her tone. She was, indeed, far more at ease than James. He could not hide the effort it was to make conversation, nor the nervous discomfort which in her presence he felt. He watched her furtively, asking himself whether she still suffered. But Mary's face betrayed few of her emotions; tanned by exposure to all weathers, her robust colour remained unaltered; and it was only in her eyes that James fancied he saw a difference. They had just that perplexed, sorrowful expression which a dog has, unjustly beaten. James, imaginative and conscience-stricken, tortured himself by reading in their brown softness all manner of dreadful anguish. He watched them, unlit by the smile which played upon the lips, looking at him against their will, with a pitiful longing. He exaggerated the pain he saw till it became an obsession, intolerable and ruthless; if Mary desired revenge, she need not have been dissatisfied. But that apparently was the last thing she thought of. He was grateful to hear of her anger with Mrs. Jackson, whose sympathy had expressed itself in round abuse of him. His mother repeated the words.

"I will never listen to a word against Captain Parsons, Mrs. Jackson. Whatever he did, he had a perfect right to do. He's incapable of acting otherwise than as an honourable gentleman."

But if Mary's conduct aroused the admiration of all that knew her, it rendered James still more blameworthy.

The hero-worship was conveniently forgotten, and none strove to conceal the dislike, even the contempt, which he felt for the fallen idol. James had outraged the moral sense of the community; his name could not be mentioned without indignation; everything he did was wrong, even his very real modesty was explained as overweening conceit.

And curiously enough, James was profoundly distressed by the general disapproval. A silent, shy man, he was unreasonably sensitive to the opinion of his fellows; and though he told himself that they were stupid, ignorant, and narrow, their hostility nevertheless made him miserable. Even though he condemned them, he was anxious that they should like him. He refused to pander to their prejudices, and was too proud to be conciliatory; yet felt bitterly wounded when he had excited their aversion. Now he set to tormenting himself because he had despised the adulation of Little Primpton, and could not equally despise its censure.

Sunday came, and the good people of Little Primpton trooped to church. Mrs Clibborn turned round and smiled at James when he took his seat, but the Colonel sat rigid, showing by the stiffness of his backbone that his indignation was supreme.

The service proceeded, and in due course Mr. Jackson mounted the pulpit steps. He delivered his text: "*The fear of the Lord is to hate evil: pride, and arrogancy, and the evil way, and the froward mouth, do I hate.*"

The Vicar of Little Primpton was an earnest man, and he devoted much care to the composition of his sermons. He was used to expound twice a Sunday the more obvious parts of Holy Scripture, making in twenty minutes or half an hour, for the benefit of the vulgar, a number of trite reflections; and it must be confessed that he had great facility for explaining at decorous length texts which were plain to the meanest intelligence.

But having a fair acquaintance with the thought of others, Mr. Jackson flattered himself that he was a thinker; and on suitable occasions attacked from his village pulpit the scarlet weed of heresy, expounding to an intelligent congregation of yokels and small boys the manifold difficulties of the Athanasian Creed. He was at his best in pouring vials of contempt upon the false creed of atheists, Romanists, Dissenters, and men of science. The theory of Evolution excited his bitterest scorn, and he would set up, like a row of nine-pins, the hypotheses of the greatest philosophers of the century, triumphantly to knock them down by the force of his own fearless intellect. His congregation were inattentive, and convinced beyond the need of argument, so they remained pious members of the Church of England.

But this particular sermon, after mature consideration, the Vicar had made up his mind to devote to a matter of more pressing interest. He repeated the text. Mrs. Jackson, who knew what was coming, caught the curate's eye, and looked significantly at James. The homily, in fact, was directed against him; his were the pride, the arrogancy, and the evil way. He was blissfully unconscious of these faults, and for a minute or two the application missed him; but the Vicar of Little Primpton, intent upon what he honestly thought his duty, meant that there should be no mistake. He crossed his t's and dotted his i's, with the scrupulous accuracy of the scandal-monger telling a malicious story about some person whom charitably he does not name, yet wishes everyone to identify.

Colonel Parsons started when suddenly the drift of the sermon dawned upon him, and then bowed his head with shame. His wife looked straight in front of her, two flaming sports upon her pale cheeks Mary, in the next pew, dared not move, hardly dared breathe; her heart sank with dismay, and she feared she would faint.

"How he must be suffering!" she muttered.

They all felt for James intensely; the form of Mr. Jackson, hooded and surpliced, had acquired a new authority, and his solemn invective was sulphurous with the fire of Hell. They wondered how James could bear it.

"He hasn't deserved this," thought Mrs. Parsons.

But the Colonel bent his head still lower, accepting for his son the reproof, taking part of it himself. The humiliation seemed merited, and the only thing to do was to bear it meekly. James alone appeared unconcerned; the rapid glances at him saw no change in his calm, indifferent face. His eyes were closed, and one might have thought him asleep. Mr. Jackson noted the attitude, and attributed it to a wicked obstinacy, For the repentant sinner, acknowledging his fault, he would have had entire forgiveness; but James showed no contrition. Stiff-necked and sin-hardened, he required a further chastisement.

"Courage, what is courage?" asked the preacher.

"There is nothing more easy than to do a brave deed when the blood is hot. But to conduct one's life simply, modestly, with a meek spirit and a Christlike submission, that is ten timess more difficult. Courage, unaccompanied by moral worth, is the quality of a brute-beast."

He showed how much more creditable were the artless virtues of honesty and truthfulness; how better it was to keep one's word, to be kind-hearted and dutiful. Becoming more pointed, he mentioned the case which had caused them so much sorrow, warning the delinquent against conceit and self-assurance.

"Pride goeth before a fall," he said. "And he that is mighty shall be abased."

They walked home silently, Colonel Parsons and his wife with downcast eyes, feeling that everyone was looking at them. Their hearts were too full for them to speak to one another, and they dared say nothing to James. But Major Forsyth had no scruples of delicacy; he attacked his nephew the moment they sat down to dinner.

"Well, James, what did you think of the sermon? Feel a bit sore?"

"Why should I?"

"I fancy it was addressed pretty directly to you."

"So I imagine," replied James, good-humouredly smiling. "I thought it singularly impertinent, but otherwise uninteresting."

"Mr. Jackson doesn't think much of you," said Uncle William, with a laugh, ignoring his sister's look, which implored him to be silent.

"I can bear that with equanimity. I never set up for a very wonderful person."

"He was wrong to make little of your attempt to save young Larcher," said Mrs. Parsons, gently.

"Why?" asked James. "He was partly right. Physical courage is more or less accidental. In battle one takes one's chance. One soon gets used to shells flying about; they're not so dangerous as they look, and after a while one forgets all about them. Now and then one gets hit, and then it's too late to be nervous."

"But you went back—into the very jaws of death—to save that boy."

"I've never been able to understand why. It didn't occur to me that I might get killed; it seemed the natural thing to do. It wasn't really brave, because I never realised that there was danger."

In the afternoon James received a note from Mrs. Clibborn, asking him to call upon her. Mary and her father were out walking, she said, so there would be no one to disturb them, and they could have a pleasant little chat. The invitation was a climax to Jamie's many vexations, and he laughed grimly at the prospect of that very foolish lady's indignation. Still, he felt bound to go. It was, after a fashion, a point of honour with him to avoid none of the annoyances which his act had brought upon him. It was partly in order to face every infliction that he insisted on remaining at Little Primpton.

"Why haven't you been to see me, James?" Mrs. Clibborn murmured, with a surprisingly tender smile.

"I thought you wouldn't wish me to."

"James!"

She sighed and cast up her eyes to heaven.

"I always liked you. I shall never feel differently towards you."

"It's very kind of you to say so," replied James, somewhat relieved.

"You must come and see me often. It'll comfort you."

"I'm afraid you and Colonel Clibborn must be very angry with me?"

"I could never be angry with you, James. . . . Poor Reginald, he doesn't understand! But you can't deceive a woman." Mrs. Clibborn put her hand on Jamie's arm and gazed into his eyes. "I want you to tell me something. Do you love anyone else?"

James looked at her quickly and hesitated.

"If you had asked me the other day, I should have denied it with all my might. But now—I don't know."

Mrs. Clibborn smiled.

"I thought so," she said. "You can tell *me*, you know."

She was convinced that James adored her, but wanted to hear him say so. It is notorious that to a handsome woman even the admiration of a crossing-sweeper is welcome.

"Oh, it's no good any longer trying to conceal it from myself!" cried James, forgetting almost to whom he was speaking. "I'm sorry about Mary; no one knows how much. But I do love someone else, and I love her with all my heart and soul; and I shall never get over it now."

"I knew it," sighed Mrs. Clibborn, complacently, "I knew it!" Then looking coyly at him: "Tell me about her."

"I can't. I know my love is idiotic and impossible; but I can't help it. It's fate."

"You're in love with a married woman, James."

"How d'you know?"

"My poor boy, d'you think you can deceive me! And is it not the wife of an officer?"

"Yes."

"A very old friend of yours?"

"It's just that which makes it so terrible."

"I knew it."

"Oh, Mrs. Clibborn, I swear you're the only woman here who's got two ounces of gumption. If they'd only listened to you five years ago, we might all have been saved this awful wretchedness."

He could not understand that Mrs. Clibborn, whose affectations were manifest, whose folly was notorious, should alone have guessed his secret. He was tired of perpetually concealing his thoughts.

"I wish I could tell you everything!" he cried.

"Don't! You'd only regret it. And I know all you can tell me."

"You can't think how hard I've struggled. When I found I loved her, I nearly killed myself trying to kill my love. But it's no good. It's stronger than I am."

"And nothing can ever come of it, you know," said Mrs. Clibborn.

"Oh, I know! Of course, I know! I'm not a cad. The only thing is to live on and suffer."

"I'm so sorry for you."

Mrs. Clibborn thought that even poor Algy Turner, who had killed himself for love of her, had not been so desperately hit.

"It's very kind of you to listen to me," said James. "I have nobody to speak to, and sometimes I feel I shall go mad."

"You're such a nice boy, James. What a pity it is you didn't go into the cavalry!"

James scarcely heard; he stared at the floor, brooding sorrowfully.

"Fate is against me," he muttered.

"If things had only happened a little differently. Poor Reggie!"

Mrs. Clibborn was thinking that if she were a widow, she could never have resisted the unhappy young man's pleading.

James got up to go.

"It's no good," he said; "talking makes it no better. I must go on trying to crush it. And the worst of it is, I don't want to crush it; I love my love. Though it embitters my whole life, I would rather die than lose it. Good-bye, Mrs. Clibborn. Thank you for being so kind. You can't imagine what good it does me to receive a little sympathy."

"I know. You're not the first who has told me that he is miserable. I think it's fate, too."

James looked at her, perplexed, not understanding what she meant. With her sharp, feminine intuition, Mrs. Clibborn read in his eyes the hopeless yearning of his heart, and for a moment her rigid virtue faltered.

"I can't be hard on you, Jamie," she said, with that effective, sad smile of hers. "I don't want you to go away from here quite wretched."

"What can you do to ease the bitter aching of my heart?"

Mrs. Clibborn, quickly looking at the window, noticed that she could not possibly be seen by anyone outside. She stretched out her hand.

"Jamie, if you like you may kiss me."

She offered her powdered cheek, and James, rather astonished, pressed it with his lips.

"I will always be a mother to you. You can depend on me whatever happens. . . . Now go away, there's a good boy."

She watched him as he walked down the garden, and then sighed deeply, wiping away a tear from the corner of her eyes.

"Poor boy!" she murmured.

Mary was surprised, when she came home, to find her mother quite affectionate and tender. Mrs. Clibborn, indeed, intoxicated with her triumph, could afford to be gracious to a fallen rival.

15

A few days later Mary was surprised to receive a little note from Mr. Dryland:

"MY DEAR MISS CLIBBORN, — With some trepidation I take up my pen to address you on a matter which, to me at least, is of the very greatest importance. We have so many sympathies in common that my meaning will hardly escape you. I daresay you will find my diffidence ridiculous, but, under the circumstances, I think it is not unpardonable. It will be no news to you when I confess that I am an exceptionally shy man, and that must be my excuse in sending you this letter. In short, I wish to ask you to grant me a brief interview; we have so few opportunities of seeing one another in private that I can find no occasion of saying to you what I wish. Indeed, for a long period my duty has made it necessary for me to crush my inclination. Now, however, that things have taken a different turn, I venture, as I said, to ask you to give me a few minutes' conversation.—I am, my dear Miss Clibborn, your very sincere, THOMAS DRYLAND."

"P.S.—I open this letter to say that I have just met your father on the Green, who tells me that he and Mrs. Clibborn are going into Tunbridge Wells this afternoon. Unless, therefore, I hear from you to the contrary, I shall (D.V.) present myself at your house at 3 P.M."

"What can he want to see me about?" exclaimed Mary, the truth occurring to her only to be chased away as a piece of egregious vanity. It was more reasonable to suppose that Mr. Dryland had on hand some charitable scheme in which he desired her to take part.

"Anyhow," she thought philosophically, "I suppose I shall know when he comes."

At one and the same moment the church clock struck three, and Mr. Dryland rang the Clibborns' bell.

He came into the dining-room in his best coat, his honest red face shining with soap, and with a consciousness that he was about to perform an heroic deed.

"This is kind of you, Miss Clibborn! Do you know, I feared the servant was going to say you were 'not at home.'"

"Oh, I never let her say that when I'm in. Mamma doesn't think it wrong, but one can't deny that it's an untruth."

"What a beautiful character you have!" cried the curate, with enthusiasm.

"I'm afraid I haven't really; but I like to be truthful."

"Were you surprised to receive my letter?"

"I'm afraid I didn't understand it."

"I was under the impression that I expressed myself with considerable perspicacity," remarked the curate, with a genial smile.

"I don't pretend to be clever."

"Oh, but you are, Miss Clibborn. There's no denying it."

"I wish I thought so."

"You're so modest. I have always thought that your mental powers were very considerable indeed. I can assure you it has been a great blessing to me to find someone here who was capable of taking an intelligent interest in Art and Literature. In these little country places one misses intellectual society so much."

"I'm not ashamed to say that I've learnt a lot from you, Mr. Dryland."

"No, that is impossible. All I lay claim to is that I was fortunate enough to be able to lend you the works of Ruskin and Marie Corelli."

"That reminds me that I must return you the 'Master Christian.'"

"Please don't hurry over it. I think it's a book worth pondering over; quite unlike the average trashy novel."

"I haven't had much time for reading lately."

"Ah, Miss Clibborn, I understand! I'm afraid you've been very much upset. I wanted to tell you how sorry I was; but I felt it would be perhaps indelicate."

"It is very kind of you to think of me."

"Besides, I must confess that I cannot bring myself to be very sorry. It's an ill wind that blows nobody good."

"I'm afraid I don't understand what you mean, Mr. Dryland."

"Miss Clibborn, I have come here to-day to converse with you on a matter which I venture to think of some importance. At least, it is to me. I will not beat about the bush. In these matters it is always best, I believe, to come straight to the point." The curate cleared his throat, and assumed his best clerical manner. "Miss Clibborn, I have the honour to solemnly ask you for your hand."

"Oh!"

Mary blushed scarlet, and her heart went pit-a-pat in the most alarming fashion.

"I think I should tell you that I am thirty-three years of age. I have some private means, small, but sufficient, with my income and economy, to support a wife. My father was for over a quarter of a century vicar of Easterham."

Mary by this time had recovered herself.

"I feel very much honoured by your proposal, Mr. Dryland. And no one can be more convinced than I of my unworthiness. But I'm afraid I must refuse."

"I don't press for an immediate answer, Miss Clibborn. I know at first blush it must surprise you that I should come forward with an offer so soon after the rupture of your engagement with Captain Parsons. But if you examine the matter closely, you will see that it is less surprising than it seems. While you were engaged to Captain Parsons it was my duty to stifle my feelings; but now I cannot. Indeed, I have not the right to conceal from you that for a long time they have been of the tenderest description."

"I feel very much flattered."

"Not at all," reassuringly answered Mr. Dryland.

"I can honestly say that you are deserving of the very highest—er—admiration and esteem. Miss Clibborn, I have loved you in secret almost ever since I came to the parish. The moment I saw you I felt an affinity between us. Our tastes are so similar; we both understand Art and Literature. When you played to me the divine melodies of Mendelssohn, when I read to you the melodious verses of Lord Tennyson, I felt that my happiness in life would be a union with you."

"I'm afraid I can never be unfaithful to my old love."

"Perhaps I'm a little previous?"

"No; time can make no possible difference. I'm very grateful to you."

"You have no need to be. I have always tried to do my duty, and while you were engaged to another, I allowed not even a sigh to escape my lips. But now I venture to think that the circumstances are altered. I know I am not a gallant officer, I have done no doughty deeds, and the Victoria Cross does not adorn my bosom. I am comparatively poor; but I can offer an honest heart and a very sincere and respectful love. Oh, Miss Clibborn, cannot you give me hope that as time wears on you will be able to look upon my suit with favour?"

"I'm afraid my answer must be final."

"I hope to be soon appointed to a living, and I looked forward ardently to the life of usefulness and of Christian fellowship which we might have lived together. You are an angel of mercy, Miss Clibborn. I cannot help thinking that you are eminently suitable for the position which I make so bold as to offer you."

"I won't deny that nothing could attract me more than to be the wife of a clergyman. One has such influence for good, such power of improving one's fellow-men. But I love Captain Parsons. Even if he has ceased to care for me, I could never look upon him with other feelings."

"Even though it touches me to the quick, Miss Clibborn," said the curate, earnestly, "I respect and admire you for your sentiments. You are wonderful. I wonder if you'd allow me to make a little confession?" The curate hesitated and reddened. "The fact is, I have written a few verses comparing you to Penelope, which, if you will allow me, I should very much like to send you."

"I should like to see them very much," said Mary, blushing a little and smiling.

"Of course, I'm not a poet, I'm too busy for that; but they are the outpouring of an honest, loving heart."

"I'm sure," said Mary, encouragingly, "that it's better to be sincere and upright than to be the greatest poet in the world."

"It's very kind of you to say so. I should like to ask one question, Miss Clibborn. Have you any objection to me personally?"

"Oh, no!" cried Mary. "How can you suggest such a thing? I have the highest respect and esteem for you, Mr. Dryland. I can never forget the great compliment you have paid me. I shall always think of you as the best friend I have."

"Can you say nothing more to me than that?" asked the curate, despondently.

Mary stretched out her hand. "I will be a sister to you."

"Oh, Miss Clibborn, how sad it is to think that your affections should be unrequited. Why am I not Captain Parsons? Miss Clibborn, can you give me no hope?"

"I should not be acting rightly towards you if I did not tell you at once that so long as Captain Parsons lives, my love for him can never alter."

"I wish I were a soldier!" murmured Mr. Dryland.

"Oh, it's not that. I think there's nothing so noble as a clergyman. If it is any consolation to you, I may confess that if I had never known Captain Parsons, things might have gone differently."

"Well, I suppose I had better go away now. I must try to bear my disappointment."

Mary gave him her hand, and, bending down with the utmost gallantry, the curate kissed it; then, taking up his low, clerical hat, hurriedly left her.

Mrs. Jackson was a woman of singular penetration, so that it was not strange if she quickly discovered what had happened. Mr. Dryland was taking tea at the Vicarage, whither, with characteristic manliness, he had gone to face his disappointment. Not for him was the solitary moping, nor the privacy of a bedchamber; his robust courage sent him rather into the field of battle, or what was under the circumstances the only equivalent, Mrs. Jackson's drawing-room.

But even he could not conceal the torments of unsuccessful love. He stirred his tea moodily, and his usual appetite for plum-cake had quite deserted him.

"What's the matter with you, Mr. Dryland?" asked the Vicar's wife, with those sharp eyes which could see into the best hidden family secret.

Mr. Dryland started at the question. "Nothing!"

"You're very funny this afternoon."

"I've had a great disappointment."

"Oh!" replied Mrs. Jackson, in a tone which half-a-dozen marks of interrogation could inadequately express.

"It's nothing. Life is not all beer and skittles. Ha! ha!"

"Did you say you'd been calling on Mary Clibborn this afternoon?"

Mr. Dryland blushed, and to cover his confusion filled his mouth with a large piece of cake.

"Yes," he said, as soon as he could. "I paid her a little call."

"Mr. Dryland, you can't deceive me. You've proposed to Mary Clibborn."

He swallowed his food with a gulp. "It's quite true."

"And she's refused you?"

"Yes!"

"Mr. Dryland, it was a noble thing to do. I must tell Archibald."

"Oh, please don't, Mrs. Jackson! I don't want it to get about."

"Oh, but I shall. We can't let you hide your light under a bushel. Fancy you proposing to that poor, dear girl! But it's just what I should have expected of you. That's what I always say. The clergy are constantly doing the most beautiful actions that no one hears anything about. You ought to receive a moral Victoria Cross. I'm sure you deserve it far more than that wicked and misguided young man."

"I don't think I ought to take any credit for what I've done," modestly remonstrated the curate.

"It was a beautiful action. You don't know how much it means to that poor, jilted girl."

"It's true my indignation was aroused at the heartless conduct of Captain Parsons; but I have long loved her, Mrs. Jackson."

"I knew it; I knew it! When I saw you together I said to Archibald: 'What a good pair they'd make!' I'm sure you deserve her far more than that worthless creature."

"I wish she thought so."

"I'll go and speak to her myself. I think she ought to accept you. You've behaved like a knight errant, Mr. Dryland. You're a true Christian saint."

"Oh, Mrs. Jackson, you embarrass me!"

The news spread like wild-fire, and with it the opinion that the curate had vastly distinguished himself. Neither pagan hero nor Christian martyr could have acted more becomingly. The consideration which had once been Jamie's was bodily transferred to Mr. Dryland. He was the man of the hour, and the contemplation of his gallant deed made everyone feel nobler, purer. The curate accepted with quiet satisfaction the homage that was laid at his feet, modestly denying that he had done anything out of the way. With James, all unconscious of what had happened, he was mildly patronising; with Mary, tender, respectful, subdued. If he had been an archbishop, he could not have behaved with greater delicacy, manliness, and decorum.

"I don't care what anyone says," cried Mrs. Jackson, "I think he's worth ten Captain Parsons! He's so modest and gentlemanly. Why, Captain Parsons simply used to look bored when one told him he was brave."

"He's a conceited creature!"

But in Primpton House the proposal was met with consternation.

"Suppose she accepted him?" said Colonel Parsons, anxiously.

"She'd never do that."

Major Forsyth suggested that James should be told, in the belief that his jealousy would be excited.

"I'll tell him," said Mrs. Parsons.

She waited till she was alone with her son, and then, without stopping her needlework, said suddenly:

"James, have you heard that Mr. Dryland has proposed to Mary?"

He looked up nonchalantly. "Has she accepted him?"

"James!" cried his mother, indignantly, "how can you ask such a question? Have you no respect for her? You must know that for nothing in the world would she be faithless to you."

"I should like her to marry the curate. I think it would be a very suitable match."

"You need not insult her, James."

16

The tension between James and his parents became not less, but greater. That barrier which, almost from the beginning, they had watched with pain rise up between them now seemed indestructible, and all their efforts only made it more obvious and more stable. It was like some tropical plant which, for being cut down, grew ever with greater luxuriance. And there was a mischievous devil present at all their conversations that made them misunderstand one another as completely as though they spoke in different tongues. Notwithstanding their love, they were like strangers together; they could look at nothing from the same point of view.

The Parsons had lived their whole lives in an artificial state. Ill-educated as most of their contemporaries in that particular class, they had just enough knowledge to render them dogmatic and intolerant. It requires a good deal of information to discover one's own ignorance, but to the consciousness of this the good people had never arrived. They felt they knew as much as necessary, and naturally on the most debatable questions were most assured. Their standpoint was inconceivably narrow. They had the best intentions in the world of doing their duty, but what their duty was they accepted on trust, frivolously. They walked round and round in a narrow circle, hemmed in by false ideals and by ugly prejudices, putting for the love of God unnecessary obstacles in their path and convinced that theirs was the only possible way, while all others led to damnation. They had never worked out an idea for themselves, never done a single deed on their own account, but invariably acted and thought according to the rule of their caste. They were not living creatures, but dogmatic machines.

James, going into the world, quickly realised that he had been brought up to a state of things which did not exist. He was like a sailor who has put out to sea in an ornamental boat, and finds that his sail is useless, the ropes not made to work, and the rudder immovable. The long, buoyant wind of the world blew away like thistle-down the conventions which had seemed so secure a foundation. But he discovered in himself a wonderful curiosity, an eagerness for adventure which led him boldly to affront every peril; and the unknown lands of the intellect are every bit as dangerously fascinating as are those of sober fact. He read omnivorously, saw many and varied things; the universe was spread out before him like an enthralling play. Knowledge is like the root of a tree, attaching man by its tendrils to the life about him. James found in existence new beauties, new interests, new complexities; and he gained a lighter heart and, above all, an exquisite sense of freedom. At length he

looked back with something like horror at that old life in which the fetters of ignorance had weighed so terribly upon him.

On his return to Little Primpton, he found his people as he had left
them, doing the same things, repeating at every well-known juncture the
same trite observations. Their ingenuousness affected him as a negro,
civilised and educated, on visiting after many years his native tribe, might
be affected by their nose-rings and yellow ochre. James was astounded
that they should ignore matters which he fancied common knowledge,
and at the same time accept beliefs that he had thought completely dead.
He was willing enough to shrug his shoulders and humour their prejudices, but they had made of them a rule of life which governed every action with an iron tyranny. It was in accordance with all these outworn
conventions that they conducted the daily round. And presently James
found that his father and mother were striving to draw him back into the
prison. Unconsciously, even with the greatest tenderness, they sought to
place upon his neck again that irksome yoke which he had so difficultly
thrown off.

If James had learnt anything, it was at all hazards to think for himself, accepting nothing on authority, questioning, doubting; it was to
look upon life with a critical eye, trying to understand it, and to receive
no ready-made explanations. Above all, he had learnt that every question
has two sides. Now this was precisely what Colonel Parsons and his wife
could never acknowledge; for them one view was certainly right, and the
other as certainly wrong. There was no middle way. To doubt what they
believed could only be ascribed to arrant folly or to wickedness. Sometimes James was thrown into a blind rage by the complacency with which
from the depths of his nescience his father dogmatised. No man could
have been more unassuming than he, and yet on just the points which
were most uncertain his attitude was almost inconceivably arrogant.

And James was horrified at the pettiness and the prejudice which he
found in his home. Reading no books, for they thought it waste of time
to read, the minds of his father and mother had sunk into such a narrow sluggishness that they could interest themselves only in trivialities.
Their thoughts were occupied by their neighbours and the humdrum details of the life about them. Flattering themselves on their ideals and
their high principles, they vegetated in stupid sloth and in a less than animal vacuity. Every topic of conversation above the most commonplace

they found dull or incomprehensible. James learned that he had to talk to them almost as if they were children, and the tedium of those endless days was intolerable.

Occasionally he was exasperated that he could not avoid the discussions which his father, with a weak man's obstinacy, forced upon him. Some unhappy, baneful power seemed to drive Colonel Parsons to widen the rift, the existence of which caused him such exquisite pain; his natural kindliness was obscured by an uncontrollable irritaion. One day he was reading the paper.

"I see we've had another unfortunate reverse," he said, looking up.

"Oh!"

"I suppose you're delighted, Jamie?"

"I'm very sorry. Why should I be otherwise?"

"You always stick up for the enemies of your country." Turning to his brother-in-law, he explained: "James says that if he'd been a Cape Dutchman he'd have fought against us."

"Well, he deserves to be court-martialled for saying so!" cried Major Forsyth.

"I don't think he means to be taken seriously," said his mother.

"Oh, yes, I do." It constantly annoyed James that when he said anything that that was not quite an obvious truism, they should think he was speaking merely for effect. "Why, my dear mother, if you'd been a Boer woman you'd have potted at us from behind a haystack with the best of them."

"The Boers are robbers and brigands."

"That's just what they say we are."

"But we're right."

"And they're equally convinced that they are."

"God can't be on both sides, James."

"The odd thing is the certainty with which both sides claim His exclusive protection."

"I should think it wicked to doubt that God is with us in a righteous war," said Mrs. Parsons.

"If the Boers weren't deceived by that old villain Kruger, they'd never have fought us."

"The Boers are strange people," replied James. "They actually prefer their independence to all the privileges and advantages of subjection. . . .

The wonderful thing to me is that people should really think Mr. Kruger a hypocrite. A ruler who didn't honestly believe in himself and in his mission would never have had such influence. If a man wants power he must have self-faith; but then he may be narrow, intolerant, and vicious. His fellows will be like wax in his hands."

"If Kruger had been honest, he wouldn't have put up with bribery and corruption."

"The last thing I expect is consistency in an animal of such contrary instincts as man."

"Every true Englishman, I'm thankful to say, thinks him a scoundrel and a blackguard."

"In a hundred years he will probably think him a patriot and a hero. In that time the sentimental view will be the only one of interest; and the sentimental view will put the Transvaal in the same category as Poland."

"You're nothing better than a pro-Boer, James."

"I'm nothing of the kind; but seeing how conflicting was current opinion, I took some trouble to find for myself a justification of the war. I couldn't help wondering why I went and killed people to whom I was personally quite indifferent."

"I hope because it was your duty as an officer of Her Majesty the Queen."

"Not exactly. I came to the conclusion that I killed people because I liked it. The fighting instinct is in my blood, and I'm never so happy as when I'm shooting things. Killing tigers is very good sport, but it's not in it with killing men. That is my justification, so far as I personally am concerned. As a member of society, I wage war for a different reason. War is the natural instinct of all creatures; not only do progress and civilisation arise from it, but it is the very condition of existence. Men, beasts, and plants are all in the same position: unless they fight incessantly they're wiped out; there's no sitting on one side and looking on. . . . When a state wants a neighbour's land, it has a perfect right to take it—if it can. Success is its justification. We English wanted the Transvaal for our greater numbers, for our trade, for the continuance of our power; that was our right to take it. The only thing that seems to me undignified is the rather pitiful set of excuses we made up."

"If those are your ideas, I think they are utterly ignoble."

"I believe they're scientific."

"D'you think men go to war for scientific reasons?"

"No, of course not; they don't realise them. The great majority are incapable of abstract ideas, but fortunately they're emotional and sentimental; and the pill can be gilded with high falutin. It's for them that the Union Jack and the honour of Old England are dragged through every newspaper and brandished in every music hall. It's for them that all these atrocities are invented—most of them bunkum.

"Men are only savages with a thin veneer of civilisation, which is rather easily rubbed off, and then they act just like Red Indians; but as a general rule they're well enough behaved. The Boer isn't a bad sort, and the Englishman isn't a bad sort; but there's not room for both of them on the earth, and one of them has to go."

"My father fought for duty and honour's sake, and so fought his father before him."

"Men have always fought really for the same reasons—for self-protection and gain; but perhaps they have not seen quite so clearly as now the truth behind all their big words. The world and mankind haven't altered suddenly in the last few years."

Afterwards, when Colonel Parsons and his wife were alone together, and she saw that he was brooding over his son's words, she laid her hand on his shoulder, and said:

"Don't worry, Richmond; it'll come right in the end, if we trust and pray."

"I don't know what to make of him," he returned, sadly shaking his head. "It's not our boy, Frances; he couldn't be callous and unscrupulous, and—dishonourable. God forgive me for saying it!"

"Don't be hard on him, Richmond. I daresay he doesn't mean all he says. And remember that he's been very ill. He's not himself yet."

The Colonel sighed bitterly.

"When we looked forward so anxiously to his return, we didn't know that he would be like this."

James had gone out. He wandered along the silent roads, taking in large breaths of the fresh air, for his home affected him like a hot-house. The atmosphere was close and heavy, so that he could neither think freely nor see things in any reasonable light. He felt sometimes as though a weight were placed upon his head, that pressed him down, and pressed him down till he seemed almost forced to his knees.

He blamed himself for his lack of moderation. Why, remembering ever his father's unhappiness and his infirmities, could he not humour him? He was an old man, weak and frail; it should not have been so difficult to use restraint towards him. James knew he had left them in Primpton House distressed and angry; but the only way to please them was to surrender his whole personality, giving up to their bidding all his thoughts and all his actions. They wished to exercise over him the most intolerable of all tyrannies, the tyranny of love. It was a heavy return they demanded for their affection if he must abandon his freedom, body and soul; he earnestly wished to make them happy, but that was too hard a price to pay. And then, with sudden rage, James asked himself why they should be so self-sufficiently certain that they were right. What an outrageous assumption it was that age must be infallible! Their idea of filial duty was that he should accept their authority, not because they were wise, but because they were old. When he was a child they had insisted on the utmost submission, and now they expected the same submission—to their prejudice, intolerance, and lack of knowledge. They had almost ridiculously that calm, quiet, well-satisfied assurance which a king by right divine might have in the certainty that he could do no wrong.

And James, with bitter, painful scorn, thought of that frightful blunder which had forced Colonel Parsons to leave the service. At first his belief in his father had been such that James could not conceive the possibility even that he had acted wrongly; the mere fact that his father had chosen a certain course was proof of its being right and proper, and the shame lay with his chief, who had used him ill. But when he examined the affair and thought over it, the truth became only too clear; it came to him like a blow, and for a while he was overcome with shame. The fact was evident—alas! only too evident—his father was incapable of command. James was simply astounded; he tried not to hear the cruel words that buzzed in his ears, but he could not help it—imbecility, crass idiocy, madness. It was worse than madness, the folly of it was almost criminal; he thought now that his father had escaped very easily.

James hastened his step, trying to rid himself of the irritating thoughts. He walked along the fat and fertile Kentish fields, by the neat iron railing with which they were enclosed. All about him was visible the care of man. Nothing was left wild. The trees were lopped into proper shape, cut down where their presence seemed inelegant, planted to complete the symmetry of a group. Nature herself was under the power of the formal influence, and flourished with a certain rigidity and decorum. After a while the impression became singularly irksome; it seemed to emphasise man's lack of freedom, reminding one of the iron conventions with which he is inevitably bound. In the sun, the valley, all green and wooded, was pleasantly cool; but when the clouds rolled up from the west heavily, brushing the surrounding hills, the aspect was so circumscribed that James could have cried out as with physical pain. The primness of the scene then was insufferable; the sombre, well-ordered elms, the meadows so carefully kept, seemed the garden of some great voluptuous prison, and the air was close with servitude.

James panted for breath. He thought of the vast distances of South Africa, bush and prairie stretching illimitably, and above, the blue sky, vaster still. There, at least, one could breathe freely, and stretch one's limbs.

"Why did I ever come back?" he cried.

The blood went thrilling through his veins at the mere thought of those days in which every minute had been intensely worth living. Then, indeed, was no restraint or pettiness; then men were hard and firm and strong. By comparison, people in England appeared so pitifully weak, vain, paltry, insignificant. What were the privations and the hardships beside the sense of mastery, the happy adventure, and the carelessness of life?

But the grey clouds hung over the valley, pregnant with rain. It gave him a singular feeling of discomfort to see them laden with water, and yet painfully holding it up.

"I can't stay in this place," he muttered. "I shall go mad."

A sudden desire for flight seized him. The clouds sank lower and lower, till he imagined he must bend his head to avoid them. If he could only get away for a little, he might regain his calm. At least, absence, he thought bitterly, was the only way to restore the old affection between him and his father.

He went home, and announced that he was going to London.

17

After the quiet of Little Primpton, the hurry and the noise of Victoria were a singular relief to James. Waiting for his luggage, he watched the various movements of the scene—the trollies pushed along with warning cries, the porters lifting heavy packages on to the bellied roof of hansoms, the people running to and fro, the crowd of cabs; and driving out, he was exhilarated by the confusion in the station yard, and the intense life, half gay, half sordid, of the Wilton Road. He took a room in Jermyn Street, according to Major Forsyth's recommendation, and walked to his club. James had been out of London so long that he came back with the emotions of a stranger; common scenes, the glitter of shops, the turmoil of the Circus, affected him with pleased surprise, and with a child's amusement he paused to stare at the advertisements on a hoarding. He looked forward to seeing old friends, and on his way down Piccadilly even expected to meet one or two of them sauntering along.

As a matter of form, James asked at his club whether there were any letters for him.

"I don't think so, sir," said the porter, but turned to the pigeon-holes and took out a bundle. He looked them over, and then handed one to James.

"Hulloa, who's this from?"

Suddenly something gripped his heart; he felt the blood rush to his cheeks, and a cold tremor ran through all his limbs. He recognised the handwriting of Mrs. Pritchard-Wallace, and there was a penny stamp on the envelope. She was in England. The letter had been posted in London.

He turned away and walked towards a table that stood near the window of the hall. A thousand recollections surged across his memory tumultuously; the paper was scented (how characteristic that was of her, and in what bad taste!); he saw at once her smile and the look of her eyes. He had a mad desire passionately to kiss the letter; a load of weariness fell from his heart; he felt insanely happy, as though angry storm-clouds had been torn asunder, and the sun in its golden majesty shone calmly upon the earth. . . . Then, with sudden impulse, he tore the unopened letter into a dozen pieces and threw them away. He straightened himself, and walked into the smoking-room.

James looked round and saw nobody he knew, quietly took a magazine from the table, and sat down; but the blood-vessels in his brain throbbed so violently that he thought something horrible would happen to him. He heard the regular, quick beating, like the implacable hammering of gnomes upon some hidden, distant anvil.

"She's in London," he repeated.

When had the letter been posted? At least, he might have looked at the mark on the envelope. Was it a year ago? Was it lately? The letter did not look as though it had been lying about the club for many months. Had it not still the odour of those dreadful Parma violets? She must have seen in the paper his return from Africa, wounded and ill. And what did she say? Did she merely write a few cold words of congratulation or—more?

It was terrible that after three years the mere sight of her handwriting should have power to throw him into this state of eager, passionate anguish. He was seized with the old panic, the terrified perception of his surrender, of his utter weakness, which made flight the only possible resistance. That was why he had destroyed the letter unread. When Mrs. Wallace was many thousand miles away there had been no danger in confessing that he loved her; but now it was different. What did she say in the letter? Had she in some feminine, mysterious fashion discovered his secret? Did she ask him to go and see her? James remembered one of their conversations.

"Oh, I love going to London!" she had cried, opening her arms with the charming, exotic gesticulation which distinguished her from all other women. "I enjoy myself awfully."

"What do you do?"

"Everything. And I write to poor Dick three times a week, and tell him all I haven't done."

"I can't bear the grass-widow," said James.

"Poor boy, you can't bear anything that's amusing! I never knew anyone with such an ideal of woman as you have—a gloomy mixture of frumpishness and angularity."

James did not answer.

"Don't you wish we were in London now?" she went on. "You and I together? I really believe I should have to take you about. You're as innocent as a babe."

"D'you think so?" said James, rather hurt.

"Now, if we were in town, on our own, what would you do?"

"Oh, I don't know. I suppose make a little party and dine some-where, and go to the Savoy to see the 'Mikado.'"

Mrs. Wallace laughed.

"I know. A party of four—yourself and me, and two maiden aunts. And we should be very prim, and talk about the weather, and go in a growler for propriety's sake. I know that sort of evening. And after the maiden aunts had seen me safely home, I should simply howl from bore-dom. My dear boy, I'm respectable enough here. When I'm on my own, I want to go on the loose. Now, I'll tell you what I want to do if ever we are in town together. Will you promise to do it?"

"If I possibly can."

"All right! Well, you shall fetch me in the fastest hansom you can find, and remember to tell the driver to go as quick as ever he dare. We'll dine alone, please, at the most expensive restaurant in London! You'll en-gage a table in the middle of the room, and you must see that the peo-ple all round us are very smart and very shady. It always makes me feel so virtuous to look at disreputable women! Do I shock you?"

"Not more than usual."

"How absurd you are! Then we'll go to the Empire. And after that we'll go somewhere else, and have supper where the people are still smarter and still shadier; and then we'll go to Covent Garden Ball. Oh, you don't know how I long to go on the rampage sometimes! I get so tired of propriety."

"And what will P. W. say to all this?"

"Oh, I'll write and tell him that I spent the evening with some of his poor relations, and give eight pages of corroborative evidence."

James thought of Pritchard-Wallace, gentlest and best-humoured of men. He was a great big fellow, with a heavy moustache and kind eyes; always ready to stand by anyone in difficulties, always ready with com-fort or with cheery advice; whoever wanted help went to him as though it were the most natural thing in the world. And it was touching to see the doglike devotion to his wife; he had such confidence in her that he never noticed her numerous flirtations. Pritchard-Wallace thought him-self rather a dull stick, and he wanted her to amuse herself. So brilliant a creature could not be expected to find sufficient entertainment in a quiet man of easy-going habits.

"Go your own way, my girl," he said; "I know you're all right. And so long as you keep a place for me in the bottom of your heart, you can do whatever you like."

"Of course, I don't care two straws for anyone but you, silly old thing!"

And she pulled his moustache and kissed his lips; and he went off on his business, his heart swelling with gratitude, because Providence had given him the enduring love of so beautiful and enchanting a little woman.

"P. W. is worth ten of you," James told her indignantly one day, when he had been witness to some audacious deception.

"Well, he doesn't think so. And that's the chief thing."

James dared not see her. It was obviously best to have destroyed the letter. After all, it was probably nothing more than a curt, formal congratulation, and its coldness would nearly have broken his heart. He feared also lest in his never-ceasing thought he had crystallised his beloved into something quite different from reality. His imagination was very active, and its constant play upon those few recollections might easily have added many a false delight. To meet Mrs. Wallace would only bring perhaps a painful disillusion; and of that James was terrified, for without this passion which occupied his whole soul he would be now singularly alone in the world. It was a fantastic, charming figure that he had made for himself, and he could worship it without danger and without reproach. Was it not better to preserve his dream from the sullen irruption of fact? But why would that perfume come perpetually entangling itself with his memory? It gave the image new substance; and when he closed his eyes, the woman seemed so near that he could feel against his face the fragrance of her breath.

He dined alone, and spent the hours that followed in reading. By some chance he was able to find no one he knew, and he felt rather bored. He went to bed with a headache, feeling already the dreariness of London without friends.

Next morning James wandered in the Park, fresh and delightful with the rhododendrons; but the people he saw hurt him by their almost aggressive happiness—vivacious, cheerful, and careless, they were all evidently of opinion that no reasonable creature could complain with the best of all possible worlds. The girls that hurried past on ponies, or on bicycles up and down the well-kept road, gave him an impression of light-heartedness which was fascinating, yet made his own solitude more intolerable. Their cheeks glowed with healthiness in the summer air, and their gestures, their laughter, were charmingly animated. He noticed the smile which a slender Amazon gave to a man who raised his hat, and read suddenly in their eyes a happy, successful tenderness. Once, galloping towards him, he saw a woman who resembled Mrs. Wallace, and his heart stood still. He had an intense longing to behold her just once more, unseen of her; but he was mistaken. The rider approached and passed, and it was no one he knew.

Then, tired and sore at heart, James went back to his club. The day passed monotonously, and the day after he was seized by the peculiar discomfort of the lonely sojourner in great cities. The thronging, busy crowd added to his solitariness. When he saw acquaintances address one another in the club, or walk along the streets in conversation, he could hardly bear his own friendlessness; the interests of all these people seemed so fixed and circumscribed, their lives were already so full, that they could only look upon a new-comer with hostility. He would have felt less lonely on a desert island than in the multitudinous city, surrounded by hurrying strangers. He scarcely knew how he managed to drag through the day, tired of the eternal smoking-room, tired of wandering about. The lodgings which Major Forsyth had recommended were like barracks; a tall, narrow house, in which James had a room at the top, looking on to a blank wall. They were dreadfully cheerless. And as James climbed the endless stairs he felt an irritation at the joyous laughter that came from other rooms. Behind those closed, forbidding doors people were happy and light of heart; only he was alone, and must remain perpetually imprisoned within himself. He went to the theatre, but here again, half insanely, he felt a barrier between himself and the rest of the audience. For him the piece offered no illusions; he could only see painted actors strutting affectedly in unnatural costumes; the scenery was mere painted cloth, and the dialogue senseless inanity. With all his might James wished that he were again in Africa, with work to do and danger to encounter. There the solitude was never lonely, and the nights were blue and silent, rich with the countless stars.

He had been in London a week. One day, towards evening, while he walked down Piccadilly, looking aimlessly at the people and asking himself what their inmost thoughts could be, he felt a hand on his shoulder, and a cheery voice called out his name.

"I knew it was you, Parsons! Where the devil have you sprung from?"

He turned round and saw a man he had known in India. Jamie's solitude and boredom had made him almost effusive.

"By Jove, I am glad to see you!" he said, wringing the fellow's hand. "Come and have a drink. I've seen no one for days, and I'm dying to have some one to talk to."

"I think I can manage it. I've got a train to catch at eight; I'm just off to Scotland."

Jamie's face fell.

"I was going to ask you to dine with me."

"I'm awfully sorry! I'm afraid I can't."

They talked of one thing and another, till Jamie's friend said he must go immediately; they shook hands.

"Oh, by the way," said the man, suddenly remembering, "I saw a pal of yours the other day, who's clamouring for you."

"For me?"

James reddened, knowing at once, instinctively, that it could only be one person.

"D'you remember Mrs. Pritchard-Wallace? She's in London. I saw her at a party, and she asked me if I knew anything about you. She's staying in Half Moon Street, at 201. You'd better go and see her. Good-bye! I must simply bolt."

He left James hurriedly, and did not notice the effect of his few words. . . . She still thought of him, she asked for him, she wished him to go to her. The gods in their mercy had sent him the address; with beating heart and joyful step, James immediately set out. The throng in his way vanished, and he felt himself walking along some roadway of ethereal fire, straight to his passionate love—a roadway miraculously fashioned for his feet, leading only to her. Every thought left him but that the woman he adored was waiting, waiting, ready to welcome him with that exquisite smile, with the hands which were like the caresses of Aphrodite, turned to visible flesh. But he stopped short.

"What's the good?" he cried, bitterly.

Before him the sun was setting like a vision of love, colouring with softness and with quiet the manifold life of the city. James looked at it, his heart swelling with sadness; for with it seemed to die his short joy, and the shadows lengthening were like the sad facts of reality which crept into his soul one by one silently.

"I won't go," he cried; "I daren't! Oh, God help me, and give me strength!"

He turned into the Green Park, where lovers sat entwined upon the benches, and in the pleasant warmth the idlers and the weary slept upon the grass. James sank heavily upon a seat, and gave himself over to his wretchedness.

The night fell, and the lamps upon Piccadilly were lit, and in the increasing silence the roar of London sounded more intensely. From the darkness, as if it were the scene of a play, James watched the cabs and 'buses pass rapidly in the light, the endless procession of people like disembodied souls drifting aimlessly before the wind. It was a comfort and a relief to sit there unseen, under cover of the night. He observed the turmoil with a new, disinterested curiosity, feeling strangely as if he were no longer among the living. He found himself surprised that they thought it worth while to hurry and to trouble. The couples on the benches remained in silent ecstasy; and sometimes a dark figure slouched past, sorrowful and mysterious.

At last James went out, surprised to find it was so late. The theatres had disgorged their crowds, and Piccadilly was thronged, gay, vivacious, and insouciant. For a moment there was a certain luxury about its vice; the harlot gained the pompousness of a Roman courtesan, and the vulgar debauchee had for a little while the rich, corrupt decadence of art and splendour.

James turned into Half Moon Street, which now was all deserted and silent, and walked slowly, with anguish tearing at his heart, towards the house in which lodged Mrs. Wallace. One window was still lit, and he wondered whether it was hers; it would have been an exquisite pleasure if he could but have seen her form pass the drawn blind. Ah, he could not have mistaken it! Presently the light was put out, and the whole house was in darkness. He waited on, for no reason—pleased to be near her. He waited half the night, till he was so tired he could scarcely drag himself home.

In the morning James was ill and tired, and disillusioned; his head ached so that he could hardly bear the pain, and in all his limbs he felt a strange and heavy lassitude. He wondered why he had troubled himself about the woman who cared nothing—nothing whatever for him. He repeated about her the bitter, scornful things he had said so often. He fancied he had suddenly grown indifferent.

"I shall go back to Primpton," he said; "London is too horrible."

18

The lassitude and the headache explained themselves, for the day after Jamie's arrival at Little Primpton he fell ill, and the doctor announced that he had enteric fever. He explained that it was not uncommon for persons to develop the disease after their return from the Cape. In their distress, the first thought of Mrs. Parsons and the Colonel was to send for Mary; they knew her to be quick and resourceful.

"Dr. Radley says we must have a nurse down. Jamie is never to be left alone, and I couldn't manage by myself."

Mary hesitated and reddened:

"Oh, I wish Jamie would let me nurse him! You and I could do everything much better than a strange woman. D'you think he'd mind?"

Mrs. Parsons looked at her doubtfully.

"It's very kind of you, Mary. I'm afraid he's not treated you so as to deserve that. And it would exhaust you dreadfully."

"I'm very strong; I should like it so much. Won't you ask Jamie? He can only refuse."

"Very well."

Mrs. Parsons went up to her son, by whom sat the Colonel, looking at him wistfully. James lay on his back, breathing quickly, dull, listless, and apathetic. Every now and then his dark dry lips contracted as the unceasing pain of his head became suddenly almost insufferable.

"Jamie, dear," said Mrs. Parsons, "Dr. Radley says you must have a second nurse, and we thought of getting one from Tunbridge Wells. Would you mind if Mary came instead?"

James opened his eyes, bright and unnatural, and the dilated pupils gave them a strangely piercing expression.

"Does she want to?"

"It would make her very happy."

"Does she know that enteric is horrid to nurse?"

"For your sake she will do everything willingly."

"Then let her." He smiled faintly. "It's an ill wind that blows nobody good. That's what the curate said."

He had sufficient strength to smile to Mary when she came up, and to stretch out his hand.

"It's very good of you, Mary."

"Nonsense!" she said, cheerily. "You mustn't talk. And you must do whatever I tell you, and let yourself be treated like a little boy."

For days James remained in the same condition, with aching head, his face livid in its pallor, except for the bright, the terrifying flush of the cheeks; and the lips were dark with the sickly darkness of death. He lay on his back continually, apathetic and listless, his eyes closed. Now and again he opened them, and their vacant brilliancy was almost unearthly. He seemed to see horrible things, impossible to prevent, staring in front of him with the ghastly intensity of the blind.

Meanwhile, Mrs. Parsons and Mary nursed him devotedly. Mary was quite splendid. In her loving quickness she forestalled all Jamie's wants, so that they were satisfied almost before he had realised them. She was always bright and good-tempered and fresh; she performed with constant cheerfulness the little revolting services which the disease necessitates; nothing was too difficult, or too harassing, or too unpleasant for her to do. She sacrificed herself with delight, taking upon her shoulders the major part of the work, leaving James only when Mrs. Parsons forced her to rest. She sat up night after night uncomplainingly; having sent for her clothes, and, notwithstanding Mrs. Clibborn's protests, taken up her abode altogether at Primpton House.

Mrs. Clibborn said it was a most improper proceeding; that a trained nurse would be more capable, and the Parsons could well afford it; and also that it was indelicate for Mary to force herself upon James when he was too ill to defend himself.

"I don't know what we should do without you, Mary," said Colonel Parsons, with tears in his eyes. "If we save him it will be your doing."

"Of course we shall save him! All I ask you is to say nothing of what I've done. It's been a pleasure to me to serve him, and I don't deserve, and I don't want, gratitude."

But it became more than doubtful whether it would be possible to save James, weakened by his wound and by the privations of the campaign. The disease grew worse. He was constantly delirious, and his prostration extreme. His cheeks sank in, and he seemed to have lost all power of holding himself together; he lay low down in the bed, as if he had given up trying to save himself. His face became dusky, so that it was terrifying to look upon.

The doctor could no longer conceal his anxiety, and at last Mrs. Parsons, alone with him, insisted upon knowing the truth.

"Is there any chance?" she asked, tremulously. "I would much rather know the worst."

"I'm afraid very, very little."

Mrs. Parsons shook hands silently with Dr. Radley and returned to the sick room, where Mary and the Colonel were sitting at the bedside. "Well?"

Mrs. Parsons bent her head, and the silent tears rolled down her cheeks. The others understood only too well.

"The Lord's will be done," whispered the father. "Blessed be the name of the Lord!"

They looked at James with aching hearts. All their bitterness had long gone, and they loved him again with the old devotion of past time.

"D'you think I was hard on him, dear?" said the Colonel.

Mary took his hand and held it affectionately.

"Don't worry about that," she said. "I'm sure he never felt any bitterness towards you."

James now was comatose. But sometimes a reflex movement would pass through him, a sort of quiver, which seemed horribly as though the soul were parting from his body; and feebly he clutched at the bed-clothes.

"Was it for this that he was saved from war and pestilence?" muttered the Colonel, hopelessly.

But the Fates love nothing better than to mock the poor little creatures whose destinies ceaselessly they weave, refusing the wretched heart's desire till long waiting has made it listless, and giving with both hands only when the gift entails destruction. . . . James did not die; the passionate love of those three persons who watched him day by day and night by night seemed to have exorcised the might of Death. He grew a little better; his vigorous frame battled for life with all the force of that unknown mysterious power which cements into existence the myriad wandering atoms. He was listless, indifferent to the issue; but the will to live fought for him, and he grew better. Quickly he was out of danger.

His father and Mary and Mrs. Parsons looked at one another almost with surprise, hardly daring to believe that they had saved him. They had suffered so much, all three of them, that they hesitated to trust their good fortune, superstitiously fearing that if they congratulated themselves too soon, some dreadful thing would happen to plunge back their beloved into deadly danger. But at last he was able to get up, to sit in the garden, now luxuriant with the ripe foliage of August; and they felt the load of anxiety gradually lift itself from their shoulders. They ventured again to laugh, and to talk of little trivial things, and of the future. They no longer had that panic terror when they looked at him, pale and weak and emaciated.

Then again the old couple thanked Mary for what she had done; and one day, in secret, went off to Tunbridge Wells to buy a little present as a proof of their gratitude. Colonel Parsons suggested a bracelet, but his wife was sure that Mary would prefer something useful; so they brought back with them a very elaborate and expensive writing-case, which with a few shy words they presented to her. Mary, poor thing, was overcome with pleasure.

"It's awfully good of you," she said. "I've done nothing that I wouldn't have done for any of the cottagers."

"We know it was you who saved him. You—you snatched him from the very jaws of Death."

Mary paused, and held out her hand.

"Will you promise me one thing?"

"What is it?" asked Colonel Parsons, unwilling to give his word rashly.

"Well, promise that you will never tell James that he owes anything to me. I couldn't bear him to think I had forced myself on him so as to have a sort of claim. Please promise me that."

"I should never be able to keep it!" cried the Colonel.

"I think she's right, Richmond. We'll promise, Mary. Besides, James can't help knowing."

The hopes of the dear people were reviving, and they began to look upon Jamie's illness, piously, as a blessing of Providence in disguise. While Mrs. Parsons was about her household work in the morning, the Colonel would sometimes come in, rubbing his hands gleefully.

"I've been watching them from the kitchen garden," he said.

James lay on a long chair, in a sheltered, shady place, and Mary sat beside him, reading aloud or knitting.

"Oh, you shouldn't have done that, Richmond," said his wife, with an indulgent smile, "it's very cruel."

"I couldn't help it, my dear. They're sitting there together just like a pair of turtle-doves."

"Are they talking or reading?"

"She's reading to him, and he's looking at her. He never takes his eyes off her."

Mrs. Parsons sighed with a happy sadness.

"God is very good to us, Richmond."

James was surprised to find how happily he could spend his days with Mary. He was carried into the garden as soon as he got up, and remained there most of the day. Mary, as ever, was untiring in her devotion, thoughtful, anxious to obey his smallest whim. . . . He saw very soon the thoughts which were springing up again in the minds of his father and mother, intercepting the little significant glances which passed between them when Mary went away on some errand and he told her not to be long, when they exchanged gentle chaff, or she arranged the cushions under his head. The neighbours had asked to visit him, but this he resolutely declined, and appealed to Mary for protection.

"I'm quite happy alone here with you, and if anyone else comes I swear I'll fall ill again."

And with a little flush of pleasure and a smile, Mary answered that she would tell them all he was very grateful for their sympathy, but didn't feel strong enough to see them.

"I don't feel a bit grateful, really," he said.

"Then you ought to."

Her manner was much gentler now that James was ill, and her rigid moral sense relaxed a little in favour of his weakness. Mary's common sense became less aggressive, and if she was practical and unimaginative as ever, she was less afraid than before of giving way to him. She became almost tolerant, allowing him little petulances and little evasions—petty weaknesses which in complete health she would have felt it her duty not to compromise with. She treated him like a child, with whom it was possible to be indulgent without a surrender of principle; he could still claim to be spoiled and petted, and made much of.

And James found that he could look forward with something like satisfaction to the condition of things which was evolving. He did not doubt that if he proposed to Mary again, she would accept him, and all their difficulties would be at an end. After all, why not? He was deeply touched by the loving, ceaseless care she had taken of him; indeed, no words from his father were needed to make him realise what she had gone through. She was kindness itself, tender, considerate, cheerful; he felt an utter prig to hesitate. And now that he had got used to her again, James was really very fond of Mary. In his physical weakness, her strength was peculiarly comforting. He could rely upon her entirely, and trust her; he admired her rectitude and her truthfulness. She reminded him of a granite cross standing alone in a desolate Scotch island, steadfast to wind and weather, unyielding even to time, erect and stern, and yet somehow pathetic in its solemn loneliness.

Was it a lot of nonsense that he had thought about the immaculacy of the flesh? The world in general found his theories ridiculous or obscene. The world might be right. After all, the majority is not necessarily wrong. Jamie's illness interfered like a blank space between his present self and the old one, with its strenuous ideals of a purity of body which vulgar persons knew nothing of. Weak and ill, dependent upon the strength of others, his former opinions seemed singularly uncertain. How much more easy and comfortable was it to fall back upon the ideas of all and sundry? One cannot help being a little conscience-stricken sometimes when one thinks differently from others. That is why society holds together; conscience is its most efficient policeman. But when one shares common opinions, the whole authority of civilisation backs one up, and the reward is an ineffable self-complacency. It is the easiest thing possible to wallow in the prejudices of all the world, and the most eminently satisfactory. For nineteen hundred years we have learnt that the body is shameful, a pitfall and a snare to the soul. It is to be hoped we have one, for our bodies, since we began worrying about our souls, leave much to be desired. The common idea is that the flesh is beastly, the spirit divine; and it sounds reasonable enough. If it means little, one need not care, for the world has turned eternally to one senseless formula after another. All one can be sure about is that in the things of this world there is no absolute certainty.

James, in his prostration, felt only indifference; and his old strenuousness, with its tragic despair, seemed not a little ridiculous. His eagerness to keep clean from what he thought prostitution was melodramatic and silly, his idea of purity mere foolishness. If the body was excrement, as from his youth he had been taught, what could it matter how one used it! Did anything matter, when a few years would see the flesh he had thought divine corrupt and worm-eaten? James was willing now to float along the stream, sociably, with his fellows, and had no doubt that he would soon find a set of high-sounding phrases to justify his degradation. What importance could his actions have, who was an obscure unit in an ephemeral race? It was much better to cease troubling, and let things come as they would. People were obviously right when they said that Mary must be an excellent helpmate. How often had he not told himself that she would be all that a wife should—kind, helpful, trustworthy. Was it not enough?

And his marriage would give such pleasure to his father and mother, such happiness to Mary. If he could make a little return for all her goodness, was he not bound to do so? He smiled with bitter scorn at his dead, lofty ideals. The workaday world was not fit for them; it was much safer and easier to conform oneself to its terrestrial standard. And the amusing part of it was that these new opinions which seemed to him a falling away, to others meant precisely the reverse. They thought it purer and more ethereal that a man should marry because a woman would be a housekeeper of good character than because the divine instincts of Nature irresistibly propelled him.

James shrugged his shoulders, and turned to look at Mary, who was coming towards him with letters in her hand.

"Three letters for you, Jamie!"

"Whom are they from?"

"Look." She handed him one.

"That's a bill, I bet," he said. "Open it and see."

She opened and read out an account for boots.

"Throw it away."

Mary opened her eyes.

"It must be paid, Jamie."

"Of course it must; but not for a long time yet. Let him send it in a few times more. Now the next one."

He looked at the envelope, and did not recognise the handwriting.

"You can open that, too."

It was from the Larchers, repeating their invitation to go and see them.

"I wonder if they're still worrying about the death of their boy?"

"Oh, well! it's six months ago, isn't it?" replied Mary.

"I suppose in that time one gets over most griefs. I must go over some day. Now the third."

He reddened slightly, recognising again the handwring of Mrs. Wallace. But this time it affected him very little; he was too weak to care, and he felt almost indifferent.

"Shall I open it?" said Mary.

James hesitated.

"No," he said; "tear it up." And then in reply to her astonishment, he added, smiling: "It's all right, I'm not off my head. Tear it up, and don't ask questions, there's a dear!"

"Of course, I'll tear it up if you want me to," said Mary, looking rather perplexed.

"Now, go to the hedge and throw the pieces in the field."

She did so, and sat down again.

"Shall I read to you?"

"No, I'm sick of the 'Antiquary.' Why the goodness they can't talk English like rational human beings, Heaven only knows!"

"Well, we must finish it now we've begun."

"D'you think something dreadful will happen to us if we don't?"

"If one begins a book I think one should finish it, however dull it is. One is sure to get some good out of it."

"My dear, you're a perfect monster of conscientousness."

"Well, if you don't want me to read, I shall go on with my knitting."

"I don't want you to knit either. I want you to talk to me."

Mary looked almost charming in the subdued light of the sun as it broke through the leaves, giving a softness of expression and a richness of colour that James had never seen in her before. And the summer frock she wore made her more girlish and irresponsible than usual.

"You've been very, very good to me all this time, Mary," said James, suddenly.

Mary flushed. "I?"

"I can never thank you enough."

"Nonsense! Your father has been telling you a lot of rubbish, and he promised he wouldn't."

"No, he's said nothing. Did you make him promise? That was very nice, and just like you."

"I was afraid he'd say more than he ought."

"D'you think I haven't been able to see for myself? I owe my life to you."

"You owe it to God, Jamie."

He smiled, and took her hand.

"I'm very, very grateful!"

"It's been a pleasure to nurse you, Jamie. I never knew you'd make such a good patient."

"And for all you've done, I've made you wretched and miserable. Can you ever forgive me?"

"There's nothing to forgive, dear. You know I always think of you as a brother."

"Ah, that's what you told the curate!" cried James, laughing.

Mary reddened.

"How d'you know?"

"He told Mrs. Jackson, and she told father."

"You're not angry with me?"

"I think you might have made it second cousin," said James, with a smile.

Mary did not answer, but tried to withdraw her hand. He held it fast.

"Mary, I've treated you vilely. If you don't hate me, it's only because you're a perfect angel."

Mary looked down, blushing deep red.

"I can never hate you," she whispered.

"Oh, Mary, can you forgive me? Can you forget? It sounds almost impertinent to ask you again—Will you marry me, Mary?"

She withdrew her hand.

"It's very kind of you, Jamie. You're only asking me out of gratitude, because I've helped a little to look after you. But I want no gratitude; it was all pleasure. And I'm only too glad that you're getting well."

"I'm perfectly in earnest, Mary. I wouldn't ask you merely from gratitude. I know I have humiliated you dreadfully, and I have done my best to kill the love you had for me. But I really honestly love you now—with all my heart. If you still care for me a little, I beseech you not to dismiss me."

"If I still care for you!" cried Mary, hoarsely. "Oh, my God!"

"Mary, forgive me! I want you to marry me."

She looked at him distractedly, the fire burning through her heart. He took both her hands and drew her towards him.

"Mary, say yes."

She sank helplessly to her knees beside him.

"It would make me very happy," she murmured, with touching humility.

Then he bent forward and kissed her tenderly.

"Let's go and tell them," he said. "They'll be so pleased."

Mary, smiling and joyful, helped him to his feet, and supporting him as best she could, they went towards the house.

Colonel Parsons was sitting in the dining-room, twirling his old Panama in a great state of excitement; he had interrupted his wife at her accounts, and she was looking at him good-humouredly over her spectacles.

"I'm sure something's happening," he said. "I went out to take Jamie his beef-tea, and he was holding Mary's hand. I coughed as loud as I could, but they took no notice at all. So I thought I'd better not disturb them."

"Here they come," said Mrs. Parsons.

"Mother," said James, "Mary has something to tell you."

"I haven't anyting of the sort!" cried Mary, blushing and laughing. "Jamie has something to tell you."

"Well, the fact is, I've asked Mary to marry me and she's said she would."

19

James was vastly relieved. His people's obvious delight, Mary's quiet happiness, were very grateful to him, and if he laughed at himself a little for feeling so virtuous, he could not help thoroughly enjoying the pleasure he had given. He was willing to acknowledge now that his conscience had been uneasy after the rupture of his engagement: although he had assured himself so vehemently that reason was upon his side, the common disapproval, and the influence of all his bringing-up, had affected him in his own despite.

"When shall we get married, Mary?" he asked, when the four of them were sitting together in the garden.

"Quickly!" cried Colonel Parsons.

"Well, shall we say in a month, or six weeks?"

"D'you think you'll be strong enough?" replied Mary, looking affectionately at him. And then, blushing a little: "I can get ready very soon."

The night before, she had gone home and taken out the trousseau which with tears had been put away. She smoothed out the things, unfolded them, and carefully folded them up. Never in her life had she possessed such dainty linen. Mary cried a while with pleasure to think that she could begin again to collect her little store. No one knew what agony it had been to write to the shops at Tunbridge Wells countermanding her orders, and now she looked forward with quiet delight to buying all that remained to get.

Finally, it was decided that the wedding should take place at the beginning of October. Mrs. Parsons wrote to her brother, who answered that he had expected the event all along, being certain that his conversation with James would eventually bear fruit. He was happy to be able to congratulate himself on the issue of his diplomacy; it was wonderful how easily all difficulties were settled, if one took them from the point of view of a man of the world. Mrs. Jackson likewise flattered herself that the renewed engagement was due to her intervention.

"I saw he was paying attention to what I said," she told her husband. "I knew all he wanted was a good, straight talking to."

"I am sorry for poor Dryland," said the Vicar.

"Yes, I think we ought to do our best to console him. Don't you think he might go away for a month, Archibald?"

Mr. Dryland came to tea, and the Vicar's wife surrounded him with little attentions. She put an extra lump of sugar in his tea, and cut him even a larger piece of seed-cake than usual.

"Of course you've heard, Mr. Dryland?" she said, solemnly.

"Are you referring to Miss Clibborn's engagement to Captain Parsons?" he asked, with a gloomy face. "Bad news travels fast."

"You have all our sympathies. We did everything we could for you."

"I can't deny that it's a great blow to me. I confess I thought that time and patience on my part might induce Miss Clibborn to change her mind. But if she's happy, I cannot complain. I must bear my misfortune with resignation."

"But will she be happy?" asked Mrs. Jackson, with foreboding in her voice.

"I sincerely hope so. Anyhow, I think it my duty to go to Captain Parsons and offer him my congratulations."

"Will you do that, Mr. Dryland?" cried Mrs. Jackson. "That is noble of you!"

"If you'd like to take your holiday now, Dryland," said the Vicar, "I daresay we can manage it."

"Oh, no, thanks; I'm not the man to desert from the field of battle."

Mrs. Jackson sighed.

"Things never come right in this world. That's what I always say; the clergy are continually doing deeds of heroism which the world never hears anything about."

The curate went to Primpton House and inquired whether he might see Captain Parsons.

"I'll go and ask if he's well enough," answered the Colonel, with his admirable respect for the cloth.

"Do you think he wants to talk to me about my soul?" asked James, smiling.

"I don't know; but I think you'd better see him."

"Very well."

Mr. Dryland came forward and shook hands with James in an ecclesiastical and suave manner, trying to be dignified, as behoved a rejected lover in the presence of his rival, and at the same time cordial, as befitted a Christian who could bear no malice.

"Captain Parsons, you will not be unaware that I asked Miss Clibborn to be my wife?"

"The fact was fairly generally known in the village," replied James, trying to restrain a smile.

Mr. Dryland blushed.

"I was annoyed at the publicity which the circumstance obtained. The worst of these little places is that people will talk."

"It was a very noble deed," said James gravely, repeating the common opinion.

"Not at all," answered the curate, with characteristic modesty. "But since it was not to be, since Miss Clibborn's choice has fallen on you, I think it my duty to inform you of my hearty goodwill. I wish, in short, to offer you again my sincerest congratulations."

"I'm sure that's very kind of you."

Two days, later Mrs. Jackson called on a similar errand.

She tripped up to James and frankly held out her hand, neatly encased as ever in a shining black kid glove.

"Captain Parsons, let us shake hands, and let bygones be bygones. You have taken my advice, and if, in the heat of the moment, we both said things which we regret, after all, we're only human."

"Surely, Mrs. Jackson, I was moderation itself?—even when you told me I should infallibly go to Hell."

"You were extremely irritating," said the Vicar's lady, smiling, "but I forgive you. After all, you paid more attention to what I said than I expected you would."

"It must be very satisfactory for you to think that."

"You know I have no ill-feeling towards you at all. I gave you a piece of my mind because I thought it was my duty. If you think I stepped over the limits of—moderation, I am willing and ready to apologise."

"What a funny woman you are!" said James, looking at her with a good-humoured, but rather astonished smile.

"I'm sure I don't know what makes you think so," she answered, bridling a little.

"It never occured to me that you honestly thought you were acting rightly when you came and gave me a piece of your mind, as you call it. I thought your motives were simply malicious and uncharitable."

"I have a very high ideal of my duties as a clergyman's wife."

"The human animal is very odd."

"I don't look upon myself as an animal, Captain Parsons."

James smiled.

"I wonder why we all torture ourselves so unnecessarily. It really seems as if the chief use we made of our reason was to inflict as much pain upon ourselves and upon one another as we possibly could."

"I'm sure I don't know what you mean, Captain Parsons."

"When you do anything, are you ever tormented by a doubt whether you are doing right or wrong?"

"Never," she answered, firmly. "There is always a right way and a wrong way, and, I'm thankful to say, God has given me sufficient intelligence to know which is which; and obviously I choose the right way."

"What a comfortable idea! I can never help thinking that every right way is partly wrong, and every wrong way partly right. There's always so much to be said on both sides; to me it's very hard to know which is which."

"Only a very weak man could think like that."

"Possibly! I have long since ceased to flatter myself on my strength of mind. I find it is chiefly a characteristic of unintelligent persons."

It was Mary's way to take herself seriously. It flattered her to think that she was not blind to Jamie's faults; she loved him none the less on their account, but determined to correct them. He had an unusual way of looking at things, and an occasional flippancy in his conversation, both of which she hoped in time to eradicate. With patience, gentleness, and dignity a woman can do a great deal with a man.

One of Mary's friends had a husband with a bad habit of swearing, which was cured in a very simple manner. Whenever he swore, his wife swore too. For instance, he would say: "That's a damned bad job;" and his wife answered, smiling: "Yes, damned bad." He was rather surprised, but quickly ceased to employ objectionable words. Story does not relate whether he also got out of the habit of loving his wife; but that, doubtless, is a minor detail. Mary always looked upon her friend as a pattern.

"James is not really cynical," she told herself. "He says things, not because he means them, but because he likes to startle people."

It was inconceivable that James should not think on all subjects as she had been brought up to do, and the least originality struck her naturally as a sort of pose. But on account of his illness Mary allowed him a certain latitude, and when he said anything she did not approve of, instead of arguing the point, merely smiled indulgently and changed the subject. There was plenty of time before her, and when James became her husband she would have abundant opportunity of raising him to that exalted level upon which she was so comfortably settled. The influence of a simple Christian woman could not fail to have effect; at bottom James was as good as gold, and she was clever enough to guide him insensibly along the right path.

James, perceiving this, scarcely knew whether to be incensed or amused. Sometimes he could see the humour in Mary's ingenuous conceit, and in the dogmatic assurance with which she uttered the most astounding opinions; but at others, when she waved aside superciliously a remark that did not square with her prejudices, or complacently denied a statement because she had never heard it before, he was irritated beyond all endurance. And it was nothing very outrageous he said, but merely some commonplace of science which all the world had accepted for twenty years. Mary, however, entrenched herself behind the impenetrable rock of her self-sufficiency.

"I'm not clever enough to argue with you," she said; "but I know I'm right, and I'm quite satisfied."

Generally she merely smiled.

"What nonsense you talk, Jamie! You don't really believe what you say."

"But, my dear Mary, it's a solemn fact. There's no possibility of doubting it. It's a truism."

Then with admirable self-command, remembering that James was still an invalid, she would pat his hand and say:

"Well, it doesn't matter. Of course, you're much cleverer than I am. It must be almost time for your beef-tea."

James sank back, baffled. Mary's ignorance was an impenetrable cuirass; she would not try to understand, she could not even realise that she might possibly be mistaken. Quite seriously she thought that what she ignored could be hardly worth knowing. People talk of the advance of education; there may be a little among the lower classes, but it is inconceivable that the English gentry can ever have been more illiterate than they are now. Throughout the country, in the comfortable villa or in the stately mansion, you will find as much prejudice and superstition in the drawing-room as in the kitchen; and you will find the masters less receptive of new ideas than their servants; and into the bargain, presumptuously satisfied with their own nescience.

James saw that the only way to deal with Mary and with his people was to give in to all their prejudices. He let them talk, and held his tongue. He shut himself off from them, recognising that there was, and could be, no bond between them. They were strangers to him; their ways of looking at every detail of life were different from his; they had not an interest, not a thought, in common.... The preparations for the marriage went on.

One day Mary decided that it was her duty to speak with James about his religion. Some of his remarks had made her a little uneasy, and he was quite strong enough now to be seriously dealt with.

"Tell me, Jamie," she said, in reply to an observation which she was pleased to consider flippant, "you do believe in God, don't you?"

But James had learnt his lesson well.

"My dear, that seems to me a private affair of my own."

"Are you ashamed to say?" she asked, gravely.

"No; but I don't see the advantage of discussing the matter."

"I think you ought to tell me as I'm going to be your wife. I shouldn't like you to be an atheist."

"Atheism is exploded, Mary. Only very ignorant persons are certain of what they cannot possibly know."

"Then I don't see why you should be afraid to tell me."

"I'm not; only I think you have no right to ask. We both think that in marriage each should leave the other perfect freedom. I used to imagine the ideal was that married folk should not have a thought, nor an idea apart; but that is all rot. The best thing is evidently for each to go his own way, and respect the privacy of the other. Complete trust entails complete liberty."

"I think that is certainly the noblest way of looking at marriage."

"You may be quite sure I shall not intrude upon your privacy, Mary."

"I'm sorry I asked you any question. I suppose it's no business of mine."

James returned to his book; he had fallen into the habit again of reading incessantly, finding therein his only release from the daily affairs of life; but when Mary left him, he let his novel drop and began to think. He was bitterly amused at what he had said. The parrot words which he had so often heard on Mary's lips sounded strangely on his own. He understood now why the view of matrimony had become prevalent that it was an institution in which two casual persons lived together, for the support of one and the material comfort of the other. Without love it was the most natural thing that husband and wife should seek all manner of protection from each other; with love none was needed. It harmonised well with the paradox that a marriage of passion was rather indecent, while lukewarm affection and paltry motives of convenience were elevating and noble.

Poor Mary! James knew that she loved him with all her soul, such as it was (a delicate conscience and a collection of principles are not enough to make a great lover), and again he acknowledged to himself that he could give her only friendship. It had been but an ephemeral tenderness which drew him to her for the second time, due to weakness of body and to gratitude. If he ever thought it was love, he knew by now that he had been mistaken. Still, what did it matter? He supposed they would get along very well—as well as most people; better even than if they adored one another; for passion is not conducive to an even life. Fortunately she was cold and reserved, little given to demonstrative affection; she made few demands upon him, and occupied with her work in the parish and the collection of her trousseau, was content that he should remain with his books.

The day fixed upon for the marriage came nearer.

But at last James was seized with a wild revolt. His father was sitting by him.

"Mary's wedding-dress is nearly ready," he said, suddenly.

"So soon?" cried James, his heart sinking.

"She's afraid that something may happen at the last moment, and it won't be finished in time."

"What could happen?"

"Oh, I mean something at the dressmaker's!"

"Is that all? I imagine there's little danger."

There was a pause, broken again by the Colonel.

"I'm so glad you're going to be happily married, Jamie."

His son did not answer.

"But man is never satisfied. I used to think that when I got you spliced, I should have nothing else to wish for; but now I'm beginning to want little grandsons to rock upon my knees."

Jamie's face grew dark.

"We should never be able to afford children."

"But they come if one wants them or not, and I shall be able to increase your allowance a little, you know. I don't want you to go short of anything."

James said nothing, but he thought: "If I had children by her, I should hate them." And then with sudden dismay, losing all the artificial indifference of the last week, he rebelled passionately against his fate. "Oh, I hate and loathe her!"

He felt he could no longer continue the pretence he had been making—for it was all pretence. The effort to be loving and affectionate was torture, so that all his nerves seemed to vibrate with exasperation. Sometimes he had to clench his hands in order to keep himself under restraint. He was acting all the time. James asked himself what madness blinded Mary that she did not see? He remembered how easily speech had come in the old days when they were boy and girl together; they could pass hours side by side, without a thought of time, talking of little insignificant things, silent often, and always happy. But now he racked his brain for topics of conversation, and the slightest pause seemed irksome and unnatural. He was sometimes bored to death, savagely, cruelly; so that he was obliged to leave Mary for fear that he would say bitter and horrible things. Without his books he would have gone mad. She must be blind not to see. Then he thought of their married life. How long would it last? The years stretched themselves out endlessly, passing one after another in dreary monotony. Could they possibly be happy? Sooner or later Mary would learn how little he cared for her, and what agony must she suffer then! But it was inevitable. Now, whatever happened, he could not draw back; it was too late for explanations. Would love come? He felt it impossible; he felt, rather, that the physical repulsion which vainly he tried to crush would increase till he abhorred the very sight of his wife.

Passionately he cried out against Fate because he had escaped death so often. The gods played with him as a cat plays with a mouse. He had been through dangers innumerable; twice he had lain on the very threshold of eternal night, and twice he had been snatched back. Far rather would he have died the soldier's death, gallantly, than live on to this humiliation and despair. A friendly bullet could have saved him many difficulties and much unhappiness. And why had he recovered from the fever? What an irony it was that Mary should claim gratitude for doing him the greatest possible disservice!

"I can't help it," he cried; "I loathe her!"

The strain upon him was becoming intolerable. James felt that he could not much longer conceal the anguish which was destroying him. But what was to be done? Nothing! Nothing! Nothing!

James held his head in his hands, cursing his pitiful weakness. Why did he not realise, in his convalescence, that it was but a passing emotion which endeared Mary to him? He had been so anxious to love her, so eager to give happiness to all concerned, that he had welcomed the least sign of affection; but he knew what love was, and there could be no excuse. He should have had the courage to resist his gratitude.

"Why should I sacrifice myself?" he cried. "My life is as valuable as theirs. Why should it be always I from whom sacrifice is demanded?"

But it was no use rebelling. Mary's claims were too strong, and if he lived he must satisfy them. Yet some respite he could not do without; away from Primpton he might regain his calm. James hated London, but even that would be better than the horrible oppression, the constraint he was forced to put upon himself.

He walked up and down the garden for a few minutes to calm down, and went in to his mother. He spoke as naturally as he could.

"Father tells me that Mary's wedding-dress is nearly ready."

"Yes; it's a little early. But it's well to be on the safe side."

"It's just occurred to me that I can hardly be married in rags. I think I had better go up to town for a few days to get some things."

"Must you do that?"

"I think so. And there's a lot I want to do."

"Oh, well, I daresay Mary won't mind, if you don't stay too long. But you must take care not to tire yourself."

20

On his second visit to London, James was more fortunate, for immediately he got inside his club he found an old friend, a man named Barker, late adjutant of his regiment. Barker had a great deal to tell James of mutual acquaintance, and the pair dined together, going afterwards to a music-hall. James felt in better spirits than for some time past, and his good humour carried him well into the following day. In the afternoon, while he was reading a paper, Barker came up to him.

"I say, old chap," he said, "I quite forgot to tell you yesterday. You remember Mrs. Wallace, don't you—Pritchard, of that ilk? She's in town, and in a passion with you. She says she's written to you twice, and you've taken no notice."

"Really? I thought nobody was in town now."

"She is; I forget why. She told me a long story, but I didn't listen, as I knew it would be mostly fibs. She's probably up to some mischief. Let's go round to her place and have tea, shall we?"

"I hardly think I can," replied James, reddening. "I've got an engagement at four."

"Rot—come on! She's just as stunning as ever. By Gad, you should have seen her in her weeds!"

"In her weeds! What the devil do you mean?"

"Didn't you know? P. W. was bowled over at the beginning of the war—after Colenso, I think."

"By God!—I didn't know. I never saw!"

"Oh, well, I didn't know till I came home.... Let's stroll along, shall we? She's looking out for number two; but she wants money, so there's no danger for us!"

James rose mechanically, and putting on his hat, accompanied Barker, all unwitting of the thunderblow that his words had been.... Mrs. Wallace was at home. James went upstairs, forgetting everything but that the woman he loved was free—free! His heart beat so that he could scarcely breathe; he was afraid of betraying his agitation, and had to make a deliberate effort to contain himself.

Mrs. Wallace gave a little cry of surprise on seeing James.... She had not changed. The black gown she wore, fashionable, but slightly fantastic, set off the dazzling olive clearness of her skin and the rich colour of her hair. James turned pale with the passion that consumed him; he could hardly speak.

"You wretch!" she cried, her eyes sparkling, "I've written to you twice—once to congratulate you, and then to ask you to come and see me—and you took not the least notice."

"Barker has just told me you wrote. I am so sorry."

"Oh, well, I thought you might not receive the letters. I'll forgive you."

She wore Indian anklets on her wrists and a barbaric chain about her neck, so that even in the London lodging-house she preserved a mysterious Oriental charm. In her movements there was a sinuous feline grace which was delightful, and yet rather terrifying. One fancied that she was not quite human, but some cruel animal turned into the likeness of a woman. Vague stories floated through the mind of Lamia, and the unhappy end of her lovers.

The three of them began to talk, chattering of the old days in India, of the war. Mrs. Wallace bemoaned her fate in having to stay in town when all smart people had left. Barker told stories. James did not know how he joined in the flippant conversation; he wondered at his self-command in saying insignificant things, in laughing heartily, when his whole soul was in a turmoil. At length the adjutant went away, and James was left alone with Mrs. Wallace.

"D'you wish me to go?" he asked. "You can turn me out if you do."

"Oh, I should—without hesitation," she retorted, laughing; "but I'm bored to death, and I want you to amuse me."

Strangely enough, James felt that the long absence had created no barrier between them. Thinking of Mrs. Wallace incessantly, sometimes against his will, sometimes with a fierce delight, holding with her imaginary conversations, he felt, on the contrary, that he knew her far more intimately than he had ever done. There seemed to be a link between them, as though something had passed which prevented them from ever again becoming strangers. James felt he had her confidence, and he was able to talk frankly as before, in his timidity, he had never ventured. He treated her with the loving friendliness with which he had been used to treat the imaginary creature of his dreams.

"You haven't changed a bit," he said, looking at her.

"Did you expect me to be haggard and wrinkled? I never let myself grow old. One only needs strength of mind to keep young indefinitely."

"I'm surprised, because you're so exactly as I've thought of you."

"Have you thought of me often?"

The fire flashed to Jamie's eyes, and it was on his lips to break out passionately, telling her how he had lived constantly with her recollection, how she had been meat and drink to him, life, and breath, and soul; but he restrained himself.

"Sometimes," he answered, smiling.

Mrs. Wallace smiled, too.

"I seem to remember that you vowed once to think of me always."

"One vows all sorts of things." He hoped she could not hear the trembling in his voice.

"You're very cool, friend Jim—and much less shy than you used to be. You were a perfect monster of bashfulness, and your conscience was a most alarming animal. It used to frighten me out of my wits; I hope you keep it now under lock and key, like the beasts in the Zoo."

James was telling himself that it was folly to remain, that he must go at once and never return. The recollection of Mary came back to him, in the straw hat and the soiled serge dress, sitting in the dining-room with his father and mother; she had brought her knitting so as not to waste a minute; and while they talked of him, her needles clicked rapidly to and fro. Mrs. Wallace was lying in a long chair, coiled up in a serpentine, characteristic attitude; every movement wafted to him the oppressive perfume she wore; the smile on her lips, the caress of her eyes, were maddening. He loved her more even than he had imagined; his love was a fury, blind and destroying. He repeated to himself that he must fly, but the heaviness in his limbs chained him to her side; he had no will, no strength; he was a reed, bending to every word she spoke and to every look. Her fascination was not human, the calm, voluptuous look of her eyes was too cruel; and she was poised like a serpent about to spring.

At last, however, James was obliged to take his leave.

"I've stayed an unconscionable time."

"Have you? I've not noticed it."

Did she care for him? He took her hand to say good-bye and the pressure sent the blood racing through his veins. He remembered vividly the passionate embrace of their last farewell. He thought then that he should never see her again, and it was Fate which had carried him to her feet. Oh, how he longed now to take her in his arms and to cover her soft mouth with his kisses!

"What are you doing this evening?" she said.

"Nothing."

"Would you like to take me to the Carlton? You remember you promised."

"Oh, that is good of you! Of course I should like it!"

At last he could not hide the fire in his heart, and the simple words were said so vehemently that Mrs. Wallace looked up in surprise. She withdrew the hand which he was still holding.

"Very well. You may fetch me at a quarter to eight."

After taking Mrs. Wallace home, James paced the streets for an hour in a turmoil of wild excitement. They had dined at the Carlton expensively, as was her wish, and then, driving to the Empire, James had taken a box. Through the evening he had scarcely known how to maintain his calm, how to prevent himself from telling her all that was in his heart. After the misery he had gone through, he snatched at happiness with eager grasp, determined to enjoy to the full every single moment of it. He threw all scruples to the wind. He was sick and tired of holding himself in; he had checked himself too long, and now, at all hazards, must let himself go. Bridle and curb now were of no avail. He neither could nor would suppress his passion, though it devoured him like a raging fire. He thought his conscientiousness absurd. Why could he not, like other men, take the brief joy of life? Why could he not gather the roses without caring whether they would quickly fade? "Let me eat, drink, and be merry," he cried, "for to-morrow I die!"

It was Wednesday, and on the Saturday he had promised to return to Little Primpton. But he put aside all thought of that, except as an incentive to make the most of his time. He had wrestled with temptation and been overcome, and he gloried in his defeat. He would make no further effort to stifle his love. His strength had finally deserted him, and he had no will to protect himself; he would give himself over entirely to his passion, and the future might bring what it would.

"I'm a fool to torment myself!" he cried. "After all, what does anything matter but love?"

Mrs. Wallace was engaged for the afternoon of the next day, but she had invited him to dine with her.

"They feed you abominably at my place," she said, "but I'll do my best. And we shall be able to talk."

Until then he would not live; and all sorts of wild, mad thoughts ran through his head.

"Is there a greater fool on earth than the virtuous prig?" he muttered, savagely.

He could not sleep, but tossed from side to side, thinking ever of the soft hands and the red lips that he so ardently wished to kiss. In the morning he sent to Half Moon Street a huge basket of flowers.

"It was good of you," said Mrs. Wallace, when he arrived, pointing to the roses scattered through the room. She wore three in her hair, trailing behind one ear in an exotic, charming fashion.

"It's only you who could think of wearing them like that."

"Do they make me look very barbaric?" She was flattered by the admiration in his eyes. "You certainly have improved since I saw you last."

"Now, shall we stay here or go somewhere?" she asked after dinner, when they were smoking cigarettes.

"Let us stay here."

Mrs. Wallace began talking the old nonsense which, in days past, had delighted James; it enchanted him to hear her say, in the tone of voice he knew so well, just those things which he had a thousand times repeated to himself. He looked at her with a happy smile, his eyes fixed upon her, taking in every movement.

"I don't believe you're listening to a word I'm saying!" she cried at last. "Why don't you answer?"

"Go on. I like to see you talk. It's long since I've had the chance."

"You spoke yesterday as though you hadn't missed me much."

"I didn't mean it. You knew I didn't mean it."

She smiled mockingly.

"I thought it doubtful. If it had been true, you could hardly have said anything so impolite."

"I've thought of you always. That's why I feel I know you so much better now. I don't change. What I felt once, I feel always."

"I wonder what you mean by that?"

"I mean that I love you as passionately as when last I saw you. Oh, I love you ten times more!"

"And the girl with the bun and the strenuous look? You were engaged when I knew you last."

James was silent for a moment.

"I'm going to be married to her on the 10th of October," he said finally, in an expressionless voice.

"You don't say that as if you were wildly enthusiastic."

"Why did you remind me?" cried James. "I was so happy. Oh, I hate her!"

"Then why on earth are you marrying her?"

"I can't help it; I must. You've brought it all back. How could you be so cruel! When I came back from the Cape, I broke the engagement off. I made her utterly miserable, and I took all the pleasure out of my poor father's life. I knew I'd done right; I knew that unless I loved her it was madness to marry; I felt even that it was unclean. Oh, you don't know how I've argued it all out with myself time after time! I was anxious to do right, and I felt such a cad. I can't escape from my bringing-up. You can't imagine what are the chains that bind us in England. We're wrapped from our infancy in the swaddling-clothes of prejudice, ignorance, and false ideas; and when we grow up, though we know they're all absurd and horrible, we can't escape from them; they've become part of our very flesh. Then I grew ill—I nearly died; and Mary nursed me devotedly. I

don't know what came over me, I felt so ill and weak. I was grateful
to her. The old self seized me again, and I was ashamed of what I'd
done. I wanted to make them all happy. I asked her again to marry me,
and she said she would. I thought I could love her, but I can't—I can't,
God help me!"

Jamie's passion was growing uncontrollable. He walked up and down
the room, and then threw himself heavily on a chair.

"Oh, I know it was weakness! I used to pride myself on my strength
of mind, but I'm weak. I'm weaker than a woman. I'm a poor reed—vacillating, uncertain, purposeless. I don't know my own mind. I haven't the
courage to act according to my convictions. I'm afraid to give pain. They
all think I'm brave, but I'm simply a pitiful coward. . . .

"I feel that Mary has entrapped me, and I hate her. I know she has
good qualities—heaps of them—but I can't see them. I only know
that the mere touch of her hand curdles my blood. She excites absolute physical repulsion in me; I can't help it. I know it's madness to
marry her, but I can't do anything else. I daren't inflict a second time
the humiliation and misery upon her, or the unhappiness upon my
people."

Mrs. Wallace now was serious.

"And do you really care for anyone else?"

He turned savagely upon her.

"You know I do. You know I love you with all my heart and soul.
You know I've loved you passionately from the first day I saw you. Did-
n't you feel, even when we were separated, that my love was inextin-
guishable? Didn't you feel it always with you? Oh, my dear, my dear you
must have known that death was too weak to touch my love! I tried to
crush it, because neither you nor I was free. Your husband was my friend.
I couldn't do anything blackguardly. I ran away from you. What a fool
you must have thought me! And now I know that at last we were both
free, I might have made you love me. I had my chance of happiness at
last; what I'd longed for, cursing myself for treachery, had come to pass.
But I never knew. In my weakness I surrendered my freedom. O God!
what shall I do?"

He hid his face in his hands and groaned with agony. Mrs. Wallace
was silent for a while.

"I don't know if it will be any consolation for you" she said at last; "you're sure to know sooner or later, and I may as well tell you now. I'm engaged to be married."

"What!" cried James, springing up. "It's not true; it's not true!"

"Why not? Of course it's true!"

"You can't—oh, my dearest, be kind to me!"

"Don't be silly, there's a good boy! You're going to be married yourself in a month, and you really can't expect me to remain single because you fancy you care for me. I shouldn't have told you, only I thought it would make things easier for you."

"You never cared two straws for me! I knew that. You needn't throw it in my face."

"After all, I was a married woman."

"I wonder how much you minded when you heard your husband was lying dead on the veldt?"

"My dear boy, he wasn't; he died of fever at Durban—quite comfortably, in a bed."

"Were you sorry?"

"Of course I was! He was extremely satisfactory—and not at all exacting."

James did not know why he asked the questions; they came to his lips unbidden. He was sick at heart, angry, contemptuous.

"I'm going to marry a Mr. Bryant—but, of course, not immediately," she went on, occupied with her own thoughts, and pleased to talk of them.

"What is he?"

"Nothing! He's a landed proprietor." She said this with a certain pride.

James looked at her scornfully; his love all through had been mingled with contrary elements; and trying to subdue it, he had often insisted upon the woman's vulgarity, and lack of taste, and snobbishness. He thought bitterly now that the daughter of the Portuguese and of the riding-master had done very well for herself.

"Really, I think you're awfully unreasonable," she said. "You might make yourself pleasant."

"I can't," he said, gravely. "Let me go away. You don't know what I've felt for you. In my madness, I fancied that you must realise my love; I thought even that you might care for me a little in return."

"You're quite the nicest boy I've ever known. I like you immensely."

"But you like the landed proprietor better. You're very wise. He can marry you. Good-bye!"

"I don't want you to think I'm horrid," she said, going up to him and taking his arm. It was an instinct with her to caress people and make them fond of her. "After all, it's not my fault."

"Have I blamed you? I'm sorry; I had no right to."

"What are you going to do?"

"I don't know—I can always shoot myself if things get unendurable. Thank God, there's always that refuge!"

"Oh, I hope you won't do anything silly!"

"It would be unlike me," James murmured, grimly. "I'm so dreadfully prosaic and matter-of-fact. Good-bye!"

Mrs. Wallace was really sorry for James, and she took his hand affectionately. She always thought it cost so little to be amiable.

"We may never meet again," she said; "but we shall still be friends, Jim."

"Are you going to say that you'll be a sister to me, as Mary told the curate?"

"Won't you kiss me before you go?"

James shook his head, not trusting himself to answer. The light in his life had all gone; the ray of sunshine was hidden; the heavy clouds had closed in, and all the rest was darkness. But he tried to smile at Mrs. Wallace as he touched her hand; he hardly dared look at her again, knowing from old experience how every incident and every detail of her person would rise tormentingly before his recollection. But at last he pulled himself together.

"I'm sorry I've made a fool of myself," he said, quietly. "I hope you'll be very happy. Please forget all I've said to you. It was only nonsense. Good-bye! I'll send you a bit of my wedding-cake."

21

James was again in Little Primpton, ill at ease and unhappy. The scene with Mrs. Wallace had broken his spirit, and he was listless now, indifferent to what happened; the world had lost its colour and the sun its light. In his quieter moments he had known that it was impossible for her to care anything about him; he understood her character fairly well, and realised that he had been only a toy, a pastime to a woman who needed admiration as the breath of her nostrils. But notwithstanding, some inner voice had whispered constantly that his love could not be altogether in vain; it seemed strong enough to travel the infinite distance to her heart and awaken at least a kindly feeling. He was humble, and wanted very little. Sometimes he had even felt sure that he was loved. The truth rent his heart, and filled it with bitterness; the woman who was his whole being had forgotten him, and the woman who loved him he hated.... He tried to read, striving to forget; but his trouble overpowered him, and he could think of nothing but the future, dreadful and inevitable. The days passed slowly, monotonously; and as each night came he shuddered at the thought that time was flying. He was drifting on without hope, tortured and uncertain.

"Oh, I'm so weak," he cried; "I'm so weak!"

He knew very well what he should do if he were strong of will. A firm man in his place would cut the knot brutally—a letter to Mary, a letter to his people, and flight. After all, why should he sacrifice his life for the sake of others? The catastrophe was only party his fault; it was unreasonable that he alone should suffer.

If his Colonel came to hear of the circumstance, and disapproving, questioned him, he could send in his papers. James was bored intensely by the dull routine of regimental life in time of peace; it was a question of performing day after day the same rather unnecessary duties, seeing the same people, listening to the same chatter, the same jokes, the same chaff. And added to the incurable dullness of the mess was the irksome feeling of being merely an overgrown schoolboy at the beck and call of every incompetent and foolish senior. Life was too short to waste in such solemn trifling, masquerading in a ridiculous costume which had to be left at home when any work was to be done. But he was young, with the world before him; there were many careers free to the man who had no fear of death. Africa opened her dusky arms to the adventurer, ruthless and desperate; the world was so large and manifold, there was ample scope for all his longing. If there were difficulties, he could overcome them; perils would add salt to the attempt, freedom would be like strong wine. Ah, that was what he desired, freedom—freedom to feel that he was his own master; that he was not enchained by the love and hate of others, by the ties of convention and of habit. Every bond was tedious. He had nothing to lose, and everything to win. But just those ties which every man may divide of his own free will are the most oppressive; they are unfelt, unseen, till suddenly they burn the wrists like fetters of fire, and the poor wretch who wears them has no power to help himself.

James knew he had not strength for this fearless disregard of others; he dared not face the pain he would cause. He was acting like a fool; his kindness was only cowardly. But to be cruel required more courage than he possessed. If he went away, his anguish would never cease; his vivid imagination would keep before his mind's eye the humiliation of Mary, the unhappiness of his people. He pictured the consternation and the horror when they discovered what he had done. At first they would refuse to believe that he was capable of acting in so blackguardly a way; they would think it a joke, or that he was mad. And then the shame when they realised the truth! How could he make such a return for all the affection and the gentleness he had received? His father, whom he loved devotedly, would be utterly crushed.

"It would kill him," muttered James.

And then he thought of his poor mother, affectionate and kind, but capable of hating him if he acted contrary to her code of honour. Her immaculate virtue made her very hard; she exacted the highest from herself, and demanded no less from others. James remembered in his boyhood how she punished his petty crimes by refusing to speak to him, going about in cold and angry silence; he had never forgotten the icy indignation of her face when once she had caught him lying. Oh, these good people, how pitiless they can be!

He would never have courage to confront the unknown dangers of a new life, unloved, unknown, unfriended. He was too merciful; his heart bled at the pain of others, he was constantly afraid of soiling his hands. It required a more unscrupulous man than he to cut all ties, and push out into the world with no weapons but intelligence and a ruthless heart. Above all, he dreaded his remorse. He knew that he would brood over what he had done till it attained the proportions of a monomania; his conscience would never give him peace. So long as he lived, the claims of

Mary would call to him, and in the furthermost parts of the earth he would see her silent agony. James knew himself too well.

And the only solution was that which, in a moment of passionate bitterness, had come thoughtlessly to his lips:

"I can always shoot myself."

"I hope you won't do anything silly," Mrs. Wallace had answered.

It would be silly. After all, one has only one life. But sometimes one has to do silly things.

The whim seized James to visit the Larchers, and one day he set out for Ashford, near which they lived. . . . He was very modest about his attempt to save their boy, and told himself that such courage as it required was purely instinctive. He had gone back without realising in the least that there was any danger. Seeing young Larcher wounded and helpless, it had seemed the obvious thing to get him to a place of safety. In the heat of action fellows were constantly doing reckless things. Everyone had a sort of idea that he, at least, would not be hit; and James, by no means oppressed with his own heroism, knew that courageous deeds without number were performed and passed unseen. It was a mere chance that the incident in which he took part was noticed.

Again, he had from the beginning an absolute conviction that his interference was nothing less than disastrous. Probably the Boer sharpshooters would have let alone the wounded man, and afterwards their doctors would have picked him up and properly attended to him.

James could not forget that it was in his very arms that Larcher had been killed, and he repeated: "If I had minded my own business, he might have been alive to this day." It occurred to him also that with his experience he was much more useful than the callow, ignorant boy, so that to risk his more valuable life to save the other's, from the point of view of the general good, was foolish rather than praiseworthy. But it appealed to his sense of irony to receive the honour which he was so little conscious of deserving.

The Larchers had been anxious to meet James, and he was curious to know what they were like. There was at the back of his mind also a desire to see how they conducted themselves, whether they were still prostrate with grief or reconciled to the inevitable. Reggie had been an only son—just as he was. James sent no message, but arrived unexpectedly, and found that they lived some way from the station, in a new, red-brick villa. As he walked to the front door, he saw people playing tennis at the side of the house.

He asked if Mrs. Larcher was at home, and, being shown into the drawing-room the lady came to him from the tennis-lawn. He explained who he was.

"Of course, I know quite well," she said. "I saw your portrait in the illustrated papers."

She shook hands cordially, but James fancied she tried to conceal a slight look of annoyance. He saw his visit was inopportune.

"We're having a little tennis-party," she said. "It seems a pity to waste the fine weather, doesn't it?"

A shout of laughter came from the lawn, and a number of voices were heard talking loudly. Mrs. Larcher glanced towards them uneasily; she felt that James would expect them to be deeply mourning for the dead son, and it was a little incongruous that on his first visit he should find the whole family so boisterously gay.

"Shall we go out to them?" said Mrs. Larcher. "We're just going to have tea, and I'm sure you must be dying for some. If you'd let us know you were coming we should have sent to meet you."

James had divined that if he came at a fixed hour they would all have tuned their minds to a certain key, and he would see nothing of their natural state.

They went to the lawn, and James was introduced to a pair of buxom, healthy-looking girls, panting a little after their violent exercise. They were dressed in white, in a rather masculine fashion, and the only sign of mourning was the black tie that each wore in a sailor's knot. They shook hands vigorously (it was a family trait), and then seemed at a loss for conversation; James, as was his way, did not help them, and they plunged at last into a discussion about the weather and the dustiness of the road from Ashford to their house.

Presently a loose-limbed young man strolled up, and was presented to James. He appeared on friendly terms with the two girls, who called him Bobbikins.

"How long have you been back?" he asked. "I was out in the Imperial Yeomanry—only I got fever and had to come home."

James stiffened himself a little, with the instinctive dislike of the regular for the volunteer.

"Oh, yes! Did you go as a trooper?"

"Yes; and pretty rough it was, I can tell you."

He began to talk of his experience in a resonant voice, apparently well-pleased with himself, while the red-faced girls looked at him admiringly. James wondered whether the youth intended to marry them both.

The conversation was broken by the appearance of Mr. Larcher, a rosy-cheeked and be-whiskered man, dapper and suave. He had been picking flowers, and handed a bouquet to one of his guests. James fancied he was a prosperous merchant, who had retired and set up as a country gentleman; but if he was the least polished of the family, he was also the most simple. He greeted the visitor very heartily, and offered to take him over his new conservatory.

"My husband takes everyone to the new conservatory," said Mrs. Larcher, laughing apologetically.

"It's the biggest round Ashford," explained the worthy man.

James, thinking he wished to talk of his son, consented, and as they walked away, Mr. Larcher pointed out his fruit trees, his pigeons. He was a fancier, said he, and attended to the birds entirely himself; then in the conservatory, made James admire his orchids and the luxuriance of his maidenhair.

"I suppose these sort of things grow in the open air at the Cape?" he asked.

"I believe everything grows there."

Of his son he said absolutely nothing, and presently they rejoined the others. The Larchers were evidently estimable persons, healthy-minded and normal, but a little common. James asked himself why they had invited him if they wished to hear nothing of their boy's tragic death. Could they be so anxious to forget him that every reference was distasteful? He wondered how Reggie had managed to grow up so simple, frank, and charming amid these surroundings. There was a certain pretentiousness about his people which caused them to escape complete vulgarity only by a hair's-breadth. But they appeared anxious to make much of James, and in his absence had explained who he was to the remaining visitors, and these beheld him now with an awe which the hero found rather comic.

Mrs. Larcher invited him to play tennis, and when he declined seemed hardly to know what to do with him. Once when her younger daughter laughed more loudly than usual at the very pointed chaff of the Imperial Yeoman, she slightly frowned at her, with a scarcely perceptible but significant glance in Jamie's direction. To her relief, however, the conversation became general, and James found himself talking with Miss Larcher of the cricket week at Canterbury.

After all, he could not be surprised at the family's general happiness. Six months had passed since Reggie's death, and they could not remain in perpetual mourning. It was very natural that the living should forget the dead, otherwise life would be too horrible; and it was possibly only the Larchers' nature to laugh and to talk more loudly than most people. James saw that it was a united, affectionate household, homely and kind, cursed with no particular depth of feeling; and if they had not resigned themselves to the boy's death, they were doing their best to forget that he had ever lived. It was obviously the best thing, and it would be cruel—too cruel—to expect people never to regain their cheerfulness.

"I think I must be off," said James, after a while; "the trains run so awkwardly to Tunbridge Wells."

They made polite efforts to detain him, but James fancied they were not sorry for him to go.

"You must come and see us another day when we're alone," said Mrs. Larcher. "We want to have a long talk with you."

"It's very kind of you to ask me," he replied, not committing himself.

Mrs. Larcher accompanied him back to the drawing-room, followed by her husband.

"I thought you might like a photograph of Reggie," she said.

This was her first mention of the dead son, and her voice neither shook nor had in it any unwonted expression.

"I should like it very much."

It was on Jamie's tongue to say how fond he had been of the boy, and how he regretted his sad end; but he restrained himself, thinking if the wounds of grief were closed, it was cruel and unnecessary to reopen them.

Mrs. Larcher found the photograph and gave it to James. Her husband stood by, saying nothing.

"I think that's the best we have of him."

She shook hands, and then evidently nerved herself to say something further.

"We're very grateful to you, Captain Parsons, for what you did. And we're glad they gave you the Victoria Cross."

"I suppose you didn't bring it to-day?" inquired Mr. Larcher.

"I'm afraid not."

They showed him out of the front door.

"Mind you come and see us again. But let us know beforehand, if you possibly can."

Shortly afterwards James received from the Larchers a golden cigarette-case, with a Victoria Cross in diamonds on one side and an inscription on the other. It was much too magnificent for use, evidently expensive, and not in very good taste.

"I wonder whether they take that as equal in value to their son?" said James.

Mary was rather dazzled.

"Isn't it beautiful!" she cried. "Of course, it's too valuable to use; but it'll do to put in our drawing-room."

"Don't you think it should be kept under a glass case?" asked James, with his grave smile.

"It'll get so dirty if we leave it out, won't it?" replied Mary, seriously.

"I wish there were no inscription. It won't fetch so much if we get hard-up and have to pop our jewels."

"Oh, James," cried Mary, shocked, "you surely wouldn't do a thing like that!"

James was pleased to have seen the Larchers. It satisfied and relieved him to know that human sorrow was not beyond human endurance: as the greatest of their gifts, the gods have vouchsafed to man a happy forgetfulness.

In six months the boy's family were able to give parties, to laugh and jest as if they had suffered no loss at all; and the thought of this cleared his way a little. If the worst came to the worst—and that desperate step of which he had spoken seemed his only refuge—he could take it with less apprehension. Pain to those he loved was inevitable, but it would not last very long; and his death would trouble them far less than his dishonour.

Time was pressing, and James still hesitated, hoping distractedly for some unforeseen occurrence that would at least delay the marriage. The House of Death was dark and terrible, and he could not walk rashly to its dreadful gates: something would surely happen! He wanted time to think—time to see whether there was really no escape. How horrible it was that one could know nothing for certain: He was torn and rent by his indecision.

Major Forsyth had been put off by several duchesses, and was driven to spend a few economical weeks at Little Primpton; he announced that since Jamie's wedding was so near he would stay till it was over. Finding also that his nephew had not thought of a best man, he offered himself; he had acted as such many times—at the most genteel functions; and with a pleasant confusion of metaphor, assured James that he knew the ropes right down to the ground.

"Three weeks to-day, my boy!" he said heartily to James one morning, on coming down to breakfast.

"Is it?" replied James.

"Getting excited?"

"Wildly!"

"Upon my word, Jamie, you're the coolest lover I've ever seen. Why, I've hardly known how to keep in some of the fellows I've been best man to."

"I'm feeling a bit seedy to-day, Uncle William."

James thanked his stars that ill-health was deemed sufficient excuse for all his moodiness. Mary spared him the rounds among her sick and needy, whom, notwithstanding the approaching event, she would on no account neglect. She told Uncle William he was not to worry her lover, but leave him quietly with his books; and no one interfered when he took long, solitary walks in the country. Jamie's reading now was a pretence; his brain was too confused, he was too harassed and uncertain to understand a word; and he spent his time face to face with the eternal problem, trying to see a way out, when before him was an impassable wall, still hoping blindly that something would happen, some catastrophe which should finish at once all his perplexities, and everything else besides.

22

In solitary walks James had found his only consolation. He knew even in that populous district unfrequented parts where he could wander without fear of interruption. Among the trees and the flowers, in the broad meadows, he forgot himself; and, his senses sharpened by long absence, he learnt for the first time the exquisite charm of English country. He loved the spring, with its yellow, countless buttercups, spread over the green fields like a cloth of gold, whereon might fitly walk the angels of Messer Perugino. The colours were so delicate that one could not believe it possible for paints and paintbrush to reproduce them; the atmosphere visibly surrounded things, softening their out lines. Sometimes from a hill higher than the rest James looked down at the plain, bathed in golden sunlight. The fields of corn, the fields of clover, the roads and the rivulets, formed themselves in that flood of light into an harmonious pattern, luminous and ethereal. A pleasant reverie filled his mind, unanalysable, a waking dream of half-voluptuous sensation.

On the other side of the common, James knew a wood of tall fir trees, dark and ragged, their sombre green veiled in a silvery mist, as though, like a chill vapour, the hoar-frost of a hundred winters still lingered among their branches. At the edge of the hill, up which they climbed in serried hundreds, stood here and there an oak tree, just bursting into leaf, clothed with its new-born verdure, like the bride of the young god, Spring. And the everlasting youth of the oak trees contrasted wonderfully with the undying age of the firs. Then later, in the height of the summer, James found the pine wood cool and silent, fitting his humour. It was like the forest of life, the grey and sombre labybrinth where wandered the poet of Hell and Death. The tall trees rose straight and slender, like the barren masts of sailing ships; the gentle aromatic odour, the light subdued; the purple mist, so faint as to be scarcely discernible, a mere tinge of warmth in the day—all gave him an exquisite sense of rest. Here he could forget his trouble, and give himself over to the love which seemed his real life; here the recollection of Mrs. Wallace gained flesh and blood, seeming so real that he almost stretched out his arms to seize her. . . . His footfall on the brown needles was noiseless, and the tread was soft and easy; the odours filled him like an Eastern drug with drowsy intoxication.

But all that now was gone. When, unbidden, the well-known laugh rang again in his ears, or he felt on his hands the touch of the slender fingers, James turned away with a gesture of distaste. Now Mrs. Wallace brought him only bitterness, and he tortured himself insanely trying to forget her. . . . With tenfold force the sensation returned which had so terribly oppressed him before his illness; he felt that Nature had become intolerably monotonous; the circumscribed, prim country was horrible. On every inch of it the hand of man was apparent. It was a prison, and his hands and feet were chained with heavy iron. . . . The dark, immovable clouds were piled upon one another in giant massess—so distinct and sharply cut, so rounded, that one almost saw the impressure of the fingers of some Titanic sculptor; and they hung low down, overwhelming, so that James could scarcely breathe. The sombre elms were too well-ordered, the meadows too carefully tended. All round, the hills were dark and drear; and that very fertility, that fat Kentish luxuriance, added to the oppression. It was a task impossible to escape from that iron circle. All power of flight abandoned him. Oh! he loathed it!

The past centuries of people, living in a certain way, with certain standards, influenced by certain emotions, were too strong for him. James was like a foolish bird—a bird born in a cage, without power to attain its freedom. His lust for a free life was futile; he acknowledged with cruel self-contempt that he was weaker than a woman—ineffectual. He could not lead the life of his little circle, purposeless and untrue; and yet he had not power to lead a life of his own. Uncertain, vacillating, torn between the old and the new, his reason led him; his conscience drew him back. But the ties of his birth and ancestry were too strong; he had not the energy even of the poor tramp, who carries with him his whole fortune, and leaves in the lap of the gods the uncertain future. James envied with all his heart the beggar boy, wandering homeless and penniless, but free. He, at least, had not these inhuman fetters which it was death to suffer and death to cast off; he, indeed, could make the world his servant. Freedom, freedom! If one were only unconscious of captivity, what would it matter? It is the knowledge that kills. And James walked again by the neat, iron railing which enclosed the fields, his head aching with the rigidity and decorum, wishing vainly for just one piece of barren, unkept land to remind him that all the world was not a prison.

Already the autumn had come. The rich, mouldering colours were like an air melancholy with the approach of inevitable death; but in those passionate tints, in the red and gold of the apples, in the many tones of the first-fallen leaves, there was still something which forbade one to forget that in the death and decay of Nature there was always the beginning of other life. Yet to James the autumn heralded death, with no consoling afterthought. He had nothing to live for since he knew that Mrs. Wallace could never love him. His love for her had borne him up and sustained him; but now it was hateful and despicable. After all, his life was his own to do what he liked with; the love of others had no right to claim his self-respect. If he had duties to them, he had duties to himself also; and more vehemently than ever James felt that such a union as was before him could only be a degradation. He repeated with new emotion that marriage without love was prostitution. If death was the only way in which he could keep clean that body ignorantly despised, why, he was not afraid of death! He had seen it too often for the thought to excite alarm. It was but a common, mechanical process, quickly finished, and not more painful than could be borne. The flesh is all which is certainly immortal; the dissolution of consciousness is the signal of new birth. Out of corruption springs fresh life, like the roses from a Roman tomb; and the body, one with the earth, pursues the eternal round.

But one day James told himself impatiently that all these thoughts were mad and foolish; he could only have them because he was still out of health. Life, after all, was the most precious thing in the world. It was absurd to throw it away like a broken toy. He rebelled against the fate which seemed forcing itself upon him. He determined to make the effort and, come what might, break the hateful bonds. It only required a little courage, a little strength of mind. If others suffered, he had suffered too. The sacrifice they demanded was too great. . . . But when he returned to Primpton House, the inevitability of it all forced itself once again upon him. He shrugged his shoulders despairingly; it was no good.

The whole atmosphere oppressed him so that he felt powerless; some hidden influence surrounded James, sucking from his blood, as it were, all manliness, dulling his brain. He became a mere puppet, acting in accordance to principles that were not his own, automatic, will-less. His father sat, as ever, in the dining-room by the fire, for only in the warmest weather could he do without artificial heat, and he read the pa-per, sometimes aloud, making little comments. His mother, at the table, on a stiffbacked chair, was knitting—everlastingly knitting. Outwardly there was in them a placid content, and a gentleness which made them seem pliant as wax; but really they were iron. James knew at last how piti-less was their love, how inhumanly cruel their intolerance; and of the two his father seemed more implacable, more horribly relentless. His mother's anger was bearable, but the Colonel's very weakness was a deadly weapon. His despair, his dumb sorrow, his entire dependence on the forbearance of others, were more tyrannical than the most despotic power. James was indeed a bird beating himself against the imprisoning cage; and its bars were loving-kindness and trust, tears, silent distress, bitter disillusion, and old age.

"Where's Mary?" asked James.

"She's in the garden, walking with Uncle William."

"How well they get on together," said the Colonel, smiling.

James looked at his father, and thought he had never seen him so old and feeble. His hands were almost transparent; his thin white hair, his bowed shoulders, gave an impression of utter weakness.

"Are you very glad the wedding is so near, father?" asked James, plac-ing his hand gently on the old man's shoulder.

"I should think I was."

"You want to get rid of me so badly?"

"'A man shall leave his father and his mother, and shall cleave unto his wife; and they shall be one flesh.' We shall have to do without you."

"I wonder whether you are fonder of Mary than of me?"

The Colonel did not answer, but Mrs. Parsons laughed.

"My impression is that your father has grown so devoted to Mary that he hardly thinks you worthy of her."

"Really? And yet you want me to marry her, don't you, daddy?"

"It's the wish of my heart."

"Were you very wretched when our engagement was broken off?"

"Don't talk of it! Now it's all settled, Jamie, I can tell you that I'd sooner see you dead at my feet than that you should break your word to Mary."

James laughed.

"And you, mother?" he asked, lightly.

She did not answer, but looked at him earnestly.

"What, you too? Would you rather see me dead than not married to Mary? What a bloodthirsty pair you are!"

James, laughing, spoke so gaily, it never dawned on them that his words meant more than was obvious; and yet he felt that they, loving but implacable, had signed his death-warrant. With smiling faces they had thrown open the portals of that House, and he, smiling, was ready to enter.

Mary at that moment came in, followed by Uncle William.

"Well, Jamie, there you are!" she cried, in that hard, metallic voice which to James betrayed so obviously the meanness of her spirit and her self-complacency. "Where on earth have you been?"

She stood by the table, straight, uncompromising, self-reliant; by her immaculate virtue, by the strength of her narrow will, she completely domineered the others. She felt herself capable of managing them all, and, in fact, had been giving Uncle William a friendly little lecture upon some action of which she disapproved. Mary had left off her summer things and wore again the plain serge skirt, and because it was rainy, the battered straw hat of the preceding winter. She was using up her old things, and having got all possible wear out of them, intended on the day before her marriage generously to distribute them among the poor.

"Is my face very red?" she asked. "There's a lot of wind to-day."

To James she had never seemed more unfeminine; that physical repulsion which at first had terrified him now was grown into an ungovernable hate. Everything Mary did irritated and exasperated him; he wondered she did not see the hatred in his eyes as he looked at her, answering her question.

"Oh, no," he said to himself, "I would rather shoot myself than marry you!"

His dislike was unreasonable, but he could not help it, and the devotion of his parents made him detest her all the more; he could not imagine what they saw in her. With hostile glance he watched her movements as she took off her hat and arranged her hair, grimly drawn back and excessively neat; she fetched her knitting from Mrs. Parsons's workbasket and sat down. All her actions had in them an insufferable air of patronage, and she seemed more than usually pleased with herself. James had an insane desire to hurt her, to ruffle that self-satisfaction; and he wanted to say something that should wound her to the quick. And all the time he laughed and jested as though he were in the highest spirits.

"And what were you doing this morning, Mary?" asked Colonel Parsons.

"Oh, I biked in to Tunbridge Wells with Mr. Dryland to play golf. He plays a rattling good game."

"Did he beat you?"

"Well, no," she answered, modestly. "It so happened that I beat him. But he took his thrashing remarkably well—some men get so angry when they're beaten by a girl."

"The curate has many virtues," said James.

"He was talking about you, Jamie. He said he thought you disliked him; but I told him I was certain you didn't. He's really such a good man, one can't help liking him. He said he'd like to teach you golf."

"And is he going to?"

"Certainly not. I mean to do that myself."

"There are many things you want to teach me, Mary. You'll have your hands full."

"Oh, by the way, father told me to remind you and Uncle William that you were shooting with him the day after to-morrow. You're to fetch him at ten."

"I hadn't forgotten," replied James. "Uncle William, we shall have to clean our guns tomorrow."

James had come to a decision at last, and meant to waste no time; indeed, there was none to waste. And to remind him how near was the date fixed for the wedding were the preparations almost complete. One or two presents had already arrive. With all his heart he thanked his father and mother for having made the way easier for him. He thought what he was about to do the kindest thing both to them and to Mary. Under no circumstances could he marry her; that would be adding a greater lie to those which he had already been forced into, and the misery was more than he could bear. But his death was the only other way of satisfying her undoubted claims. He had little doubt that in six months he would be as well forgotten as poor Reggie Larcher, and he did not care; he was sick of the whole business, and wanted the quiet of death. His love for Mrs. Wallace would never give him peace upon earth; it was utterly futile, and yet unconquerable.

James saw his opportunity in Colonel Clibborn's invitation to shoot; he was most anxious to make the affair seem accidental, and that, in cleaning his gun, was easy. He had been wounded before and knew that the pain was not very great. He had, therefore, nothing to fear.

Now at last he regained his spirits. He did not read or walk, but spent the day talking with his father; he wished the last impression he would leave to be as charming as possible, and took great pains to appear at his best.

He slept well that night, and in the morning dressed himself with unusual care. At Primpton House they breakfasted at eight, and afterwards James smoked his pipe, reading the newspaper. He was a little astonished at his calm, for doubt no longer assailed him, and the indecision which paralysed all his faculties had disappeared.

"It is the beginning of my freedom," he thought. All human interests had abandoned him, except a vague sensation of amusement. He saw the humour of the comedy he was acting, and dispassionately approved himself, because he did not give way to histrionics.

"Well, Uncle William," he said, at last, "what d'you say to setting to work on our guns?"

"I'm always ready for everything," said Major Forsyth.

"Come on, then."

They went into what they called the harness-room, and James began carefully to clean his gun.

"I think I'll take my coat off," he said; "I can work better without."

The gun had not been used for several months, and James had a good deal to do. He leant over and rubbed a little rust off the lock.

"Upon my word," said Uncle William, "I've never seen anyone handle a gun so carelessly as you. D'you call yourself a soldier?"

"I am a bit slack," replied James, laughing. "People are always telling me that."

"Well, take care, for goodness' sake! It may be loaded."

"Oh, no, there's no danger. It's not loaded, and besides, it's locked."

"Still, you oughtn't to hold it like that."

"It would be rather comic if I killed myself accidentally. I wonder what Mary would say?"

"Well, you've escaped death so often by the skin of your teeth, I think you're pretty safe from everything but old age."

Presently James turned to his uncle.

"I say, this is rotten oil. I wish we could get some fresh."

"I was just thinking that."

"Well, you're a pal of the cook. Go and ask her for some, there's a good chap."

"She'll do anything for me," said Major Forsyth, with a self-satisfied smile. It was his opinion that no woman, countess or scullery-maid, could resist his fascination; and taking the cup, he trotted off.

James immediately went to the coupboard and took out a cartridge. He slipped it in, rested the butt on the ground, pointed the barrel to his heart, and—fired!

Epilogue

A letter from Mrs. Clibborn to General Sir Charles Clow, K.C.B., 8 Gladhorn Terrace, Bath:

"DEAR CHARLES,—I am so glad to hear you are settled in your new house in Bath, and it is *most* kind to ask us down. I am devoted to Bath; one meets such *nice* people there, and all one's friends whom one knew centuries ago. It is such a comfort to see how fearfully old they're looking! I don't know whether we can manage to accept your kind invitation, but I must say I should be glad of a change after the truly *awful* things that have happened here. I have been dreadfully upset all the winter, and have had several touches of rheumatism, which is a thing I never suffered from before.

"I wrote and told you of the sudden and *mysterious* death of poor James Parsons, a fortnight before he was going to marry my dear Mary. He shot himself accidentally while cleaning a gun—that is to say, every one *thinks* it was an accident. But I am certain it was nothing of the kind. Ever since the dreadful thing happened—six months ago—it has been on my conscience, and I assure you that the whole time I have not slept a wink. My sufferings have been *horrible!* You will be surprised at the change in me; I am beginning to look like an *old* woman. I tell you this in strict confidence. *I believe he committed suicide.* He confessed that he loved me, Charles. Of course, I told him I was old enough to be his mother; but love is blind. When I think of the tragic end of poor Algy Turner, who poisoned himself in India for my sake, I don't know how I shall ever forgive myself. I never gave James the least encouragement, and when he said that he loved me, I was so taken aback that I *nearly fainted*. I am convinced that he shot himself rather than marry a woman he did not love, and what is more, *my* daughter. You can imagine my feelings! I have taken care not to breathe a word of this to Reginald, whose gout is making him more irritable every day, or to anyone else. So no one suspects the truth.

"But I shall never get over it. I could not bear to think of poor Algy Turner, and now I have on my head as well the blood of James Parsons. They were dear boys, both of them. I think I am the only one who is really sorry for him. If it had been my son who was killed I should either have gone *raving mad* or had hysterics for a week; but Mrs. Parsons merely said: 'The Lord has given, and the Lord has taken away. Blessed be the name of the Lord.' I cannot help thinking it was rather profane, and *most* unfeeling. *I* was dreadfully upset, and Mary had to sit up with me for several nights. I don't believe Mary really loved him. I hate to say anything against my own daughter, but I feel bound to tell the truth, and my private opinion is that she loved *herself* better. She loved her constancy and the good opinion of Little Primpton; the fuss the Parsons have made of her I'm sure is very bad for anyone. It can't be good for a girl to be given way to so much; and I never really liked the Parsons. They're very good people, of course; but only infantry!

"I am happy to say that poor Jamie's death was almost instantaneous. When they found him he said: 'It was an accident; I didn't know the gun was loaded.' (*Most improbable*, I think. It's wonderful how they've all been taken in; but then they didn't know his secret!) A few minutes later, just before he died, he said: 'Tell Mary she's to marry the curate.'

"If my betrothed had died, *nothing* would have induced me to marry anybody else. I would have remained an *old maid*. But so few people have any really nice feeling! Mr. Dryland, the curate, had already proposed to Mary, and she had refused him. He is a pleasant-spoken young man, with a rather fine presence—not *my* ideal at all; but that, of course, doesn't matter! Well, a month after the funeral, Mary told me that he had asked her again, and she had declined. I think it was very bad taste on his part, but Mary said she thought it *most noble.*

"It appears that Colonel and Mrs. Parsons both pressed her very much to accept the curate. They said it was Jamie's dying wish, and that his last thought had been for her happiness. There is no doubt that Mr. Dryland is an excellent young man, but if the Parsons had *really* loved their son, they would never have advised Mary to get married. I think it was most *heartless.*

"Well, a few days ago, Mr. Dryland came and told us that he had been appointed vicar of Stone Fairley, in Kent. I went to see Mrs. Jackson, the wife of our Vicar, and she looked it out in the clergy list. The stipend is $300 a year, and I am told that there is a good house. Of course, it's not very much, but better than nothing. This morning Mr. Dryland called and asked for a private interview with Mary. He said he must, of course, leave Little Primpton, and his vicarage would sadly want a mistress; and finally, for the third time, *begged* her on his *bended knees* to marry her. He had previously been to the Parsons, and the Colonel sent for Mary, and told her that he hoped she would not refuse Mr. Dryland for their sake, and that they thought it was her duty to marry. The result is that Mary accepted him, and is to be married very quietly by special license in a month. The widow of the late incumbent of Stone Fairley moves out in six weeks, so this will give them time for a fortnight's honeymoon before settling down. They think of spending it in Paris.

"I think, on the whole, it is as good a match as poor Mary could *expect to make.* The stipend is paid by the Ecclesiastical Commissioners, which, of course, is much safer than glebe. She is no longer a young girl, and I think it was her last chance. Although she is my own daughter, I cannot help confessing that she is not the sort of girl that wears well; she has always been plain—(no one would think she was my daughter)—and as time goes on, she will grow *plainer.* When I was eighteen my mother's maid used to say: 'Why, miss, there's many a married woman of thirty who would be proud to have your bust.' But our poor, *dear* Mary has *no figure.* She will do excellently for the wife of a country vicar. She's so fond of giving people advice, and of looking after the poor, and it won't matter that she's dowdy. She has no idea of dressing herself, although I've always done my best for her.

"Mr. Dryland is, of course, in the seventh heaven of delight. He has gone into Tunbridge Wells to get a ring, and as an engagement present has just sent round a complete edition of the works of Mr. Hall Caine. He is evidently *generous*. I think they will suit one another very well, and I am glad to get my only daughter married. She was always rather a tie on Reginald and me. We are so devoted to one another that a third person has often seemed a little in the way. Although you would not believe it, and we have been married for nearly thirty years, nothing gives us more happiness than to sit holding one another's hands. I have always been sentimental, and I am not ashamed to own it. Reggie is sometimes afraid that I shall get an attack of my rheumatism when we sit out together at night; but I always take care to wrap myself up well, and I invariably make him put a muffler on.

"Give my kindest regards to your wife, and tell her I hope to see her soon.—Yours very sincerely,

"CLARA DE TULLEVILLE CLIBBORN."

3

⤜

From *Mrs. Craddock*
(1902)

11

But Edward was certainly not an ardent lover. Bertha could not tell when first she had noticed his unresponsiveness to her passionate outbursts; at the beginning she had known nothing but that she loved her husband with all her heart, and her ardour had lit up his slightly pallid attachment till it seemed to glow as fiercely as her own. Yet, little by little, she seemed to see very small return for the wealth of affection that she lavished upon him. The causes of her dissatisfaction were scarcely explicable, a slight motion of withdrawal, an indifference to her feelings—little nothings that had seemed almost comic. Bertha at first likened Edward to the Hippolytus of Phaedra; he was untamed and wild, the kisses of women frightened him, his phlegm, disguised as rustic savagery, pleased her, and she said her passion should thaw the icicles in his heart. But soon she ceased to consider his passiveness amusing, sometimes she upbraided him, and often, when alone, she wept.

"I wonder if you realize what pain you cause me at times," said Bertha.

"Oh, I don't think I do anything of the kind."

"You don't see it. When I come up and kiss you it's the most natural thing in the world for you to push me away, as if—almost as if you couldn't bear me."

"Nonsense," he replied.

To himself Edward was the same now as when they were first married.

"Of course after four months of married life you can't expect a man to be the same as on his honeymoon. One can't always be making love and canoodling. Everything in its proper time and season."

After the day's work he liked to read his *Standard* in peace, so when Bertha came up to him he put her gently aside.

"Leave me alone for a bit, there's a good girl," he said.

"Oh, you don't love me," she cried then, feeling as if her heart would break.

He did not look up from his paper or make reply: he was in the middle of a leading article.

"Why don't you answer?" she cried.

"Because you're talking nonsense."

He was the best-humoured of men, and Bertha's bad temper never disturbed his equilibrium. He knew that women felt a little irritable at times, but if a man gave 'em plenty of rope they'd calm down after a bit.

"Women are like chickens," he told a friend. "Give 'em a good run, properly closed in with stout wire-netting so that they can't get into mischief, and when they cluck and cackle just sit tight and take no notice."

Marriage had made no great difference in Edward's life. He had always been a man of regular habits, and these he continued to cultivate. Of course he was more comfortable.

"There's no denying it, a fellow wants a woman to look after him," he told Dr Ramsay, whom he sometimes met on the latter's rounds. "Before I was married I used to find my shirts worn out in no time, but now when I see a cuff getting a bit groggy I just give it to the missus, and she makes it as good as new."

"There's a good deal of extra work, isn't there, now you've taken on the Home Farm?"

"Oh, bless you, I enjoy it. Fact is, I can't get enough work to do. And it seems to me that if you want to make farming pay nowadays you must do it on a big scale."

All day Edward was occupied, if not on the farms, then with business at Blackstable, Tercanbury or Faversley.

"I don't approve of idleness," he said. "They always say the devil finds work for idle hands to do, and upon my word I think there's a lot of truth in it."

Miss Glover, to whom this sentiment was addressed, naturally approved, and when Edward immediately afterwards went out, leaving her with Bertha, she said: "What a good fellow your husband is! You don't mind my saying so, do you?"

"Not if it pleases you," said Bertha, drily.

"I hear praise of him from every side. Of course Charles has the highest opinion of him."

Bertha did not answer, and Miss Glover added: "You can't think how glad I am that you're so happy."

Bertha smiled: "You've got such a kind heart, Fanny."

The conversation dragged, and after five minutes of heavy silence Miss Glover rose to go. When the door was closed upon her Bertha sank back in her chair, thinking. This was one of her unhappy days: Eddie had walked into Blackstable, and she had wished to accompany him.

"I don't think you'd better come with me," he said. "I'm in rather a hurry and I shall walk fast."

"I can walk fast too," she said, her face clouding over.

"No, you can't. I know what you call walking fast. If you like you can come and meet me on the way back."

"Oh, you do everything you can to hurt me. It looks as if you welcomed an opportunity of being cruel."

"How unreasonable you are, Bertha! Can't you see that I'm in a hurry, and I haven't got time to saunter along and chatter about the buttercups?"

"Well, let's drive in."

"That's impossible. The mare isn't well and the pony had a hard day yesterday; he must rest today."

"It's simply because you don't want me to come. It's always the same, day after day. You invent anything to get rid of me, you push me away even when I want to kiss you."

She burst into tears, knowing that what she said was unjust, but feeling notwithstanding extremely ill-used. Edward smiled with irritating good-temper.

"You'll be sorry for what you've said when you've calmed down, and then you'll want me to forgive you."

She looked up, flushing: "You think I'm a child and a fool."

"No I just think you're out of sorts today."

Then he went out whistling, and she heard him give an order to the gardener in his usual manner, as cheerful as if nothing had happened. Bertha knew that he had already forgotten the little scene; nothing affected his good humour—she might weep, she might tear her heart out (metaphorically) and bang it on the floor. Edward would not be perturbed; he would still be placid, good-tempered and forbearing. Hard words, he said, broke nobody's bones. "Women are like chickens, when they cluck and cackle sit tight and take no notice."

On his return Edward appeared not to see that his wife was out of temper. His spirits were always equable, and he was an observant person; she answered him in monosyllables, but he chattered away, delighted at having driven a good bargain with a man in Blackstable. Bertha longed for him to remark upon her condition, so that she might burst into reproaches, but Edward was hopelessly dense—or else he saw and was unwilling to give her an opportunity to speak. Bertha, almost for the first time, was seriously angry with her husband, and it frightened her: suddenly Edward seemed an enemy, and she wished to inflict some hurt upon him. She did not understand herself. What was going to happen next? Why wouldn't he say something so that she might pour forth her woes and then be reconciled? The day wore on and she preserved a sullen silence; her heart was beginning to ache terribly. The night came, and still Edward made no sign; she looked about for a chance of beginning the quarrel, but nothing offered. They went to bed, and, turning her back on him, Bertha pretended to go to sleep; she did not give him the kiss, the never-ending kiss of lovers, that they always exchanged at night. Surely he would notice it, surely he would ask what troubled her, and then she could at last bring him to his knees. But he said nothing, he was dog-tired after a hard day's work, and without a word went to sleep. In five minutes Bertha heard his heavy, regular breathing.

Then she broke down; she could never sleep without saying good night to him, without the kiss of his lips.

"He's stronger than I," she said, "because he doesn't love me."

Bertha sobbed silently; she couldn't bear to be angry with her husband. She would submit to anything rather than pass the night in wrath and the next day as unhappily as this. She was entirely humbled. At last, unable any longer to bear the agony, she awoke him.

"Eddie, you've not said good night to me."

"By Jove, I forgot all about it," he answered sleepily.

Bertha stifled a sob.

"Hulloa, what's the matter? You're not crying just because I forgot to kiss you? I was awfully fagged, you know."

He really had noticed nothing. While she was passing through utter distress he had been as happily self-satisfied as usual. But the momentary recurrence of Bertha's anger was quickly stifled. She could not afford now to be proud.

"You're not angry with me?" she said. "I can't sleep unless you kiss me."

"Silly girl!" he whispered.

"You do love me, don't you?"

"Yes."

He kissed her as she loved to be kissed, and in the delight of it her anger was entirely forgotten.

"I can't live unless you love me." She nestled against his bosom, sobbing. "Oh, I wish I could make you understand how I love you. We're friends again now, aren't we?"

"We haven't been ever otherwise."

Bertha gave a sigh of relief, and lay in his arms completely happy. A minute more and Edward's breathing told her that he had already fallen asleep; she dared not move for fear of waking him.

The summer brought Bertha new pleasures, and she set herself to enjoy the pastoral life that she had looked forward to. The elms of Court Leys now were dark with leaves, and the heavy, close-fitting verdure gave quite a stately look to the house. The elm is the most respectable of trees, over-pompous if anything, but perfectly well-bred, and the shade it casts is no ordinary shade, but solid and self-assured as befits the estate of a county family. The fallen trunk had been removed, and in the autumn young trees were to be placed in the vacant spaces. Edward had set himself with a will to put the place to rights. The spring had seen a new coat of paint on Court Leys, so that it looked as spick and span as the suburban mansion of a stockbroker; the beds, which for years had been neglected, now were trim with the abominations of carpet bedding; squares of red geraniums contrasted with circles of yellow calceolarias; the overgrown boxwood was cut down to a just height; the hawthorn hedge was doomed, and Edward had arranged to enclose the grounds with a wooden palisade and laurel bushes. The drive was decorated with several loads of gravel, so that it became a thing of pride to the successor of an ancient and lackadaisical race. Craddock had not reigned in their stead a fortnight before the grimy sheep were expelled from the lawns on either side of the avenue, and since then the grass had been industriously mown and rolled. Now a tennis-court had been marked out, which, as Edward said, made things look homely. Finally, the iron gates were gorgeous in black and gold, as suited the entrance to a gentleman's mansion, and the renovated lodge proved to all and sundry that Court Leys was in the hands of a man who knew what was what and delighted in the proprieties.

Though Bertha abhorred all innovations, she had meekly accepted Edward's improvements; they formed an inexhaustible topic of conversation, and his enthusiasm delighted her.

"By Jove," he said, rubbing his hands, "the changes will make your aunt simply jump, won't they?"

"They will indeed," said Bertha, smiling, but with a shudder at the prospect of Miss Ley's sarcastic praise.

"She'll hardly recognize the place; the house looks as good as new, and the grounds might have been laid out only half a dozen years ago. Give me five years more, and even you won't know your old home."

Miss Ley had at last accepted one of the invitations that Edward had insisted should be showered upon her, and wrote to say she was coming down for a week. Edward was, of course, much pleased; as he said, he wanted to be friends with everybody, and it didn't seem natural that Bertha's only relative should make a point of avoiding them.

"It looks as if she didn't approve of our marriage, and it makes people talk."

He met the good lady at the station, and, somewhat to her dismay, greeted her with effusion.

"Ah, here you are at last!" he bellowed in his jovial way. "We thought you were never coming. Here, porter!"

He raised his voice so that the platform shook and rumbled. He seized both Miss Ley's hands, and the terrifying thought flashed through her head that he would kiss her before the assembled multitude. Six people.

"He's cultivating the airs of the country squire," she thought. "I wish he wouldn't."

He took the innumerable bags with which she travelled and scattered them among the attendants. He even tried to induce her to take his arm to the dog-cart, but this honour she stoutly refused.

"Now, will you come round to this side, and I'll help you up. Your luggage will come on afterwards with the pony."

He was managing everything in a self-confident and masterful fashion. Miss Ley noticed that marriage had dispelled the shyness that had been in him rather an attractive feature. He was becoming bluff and hearty. Also he was filling out; prosperity and a consciousness of his greater importance had broadened his back and straightened his shoulders; he was quite three inches more round the chest than when she had first known him, and his waist had proportionately increased.

"If he goes on developing in this way," she thought, "the good man will be colossal by the time he's forty."

"Of course, Aunt Polly," he said, boldly dropping the respectful *Miss Ley* that hitherto he had invariably used, though his new relative was not a woman whom most men would have ventured to treat familiarly, "of course, it's all rot about your leaving us in a week; you must stay a couple of months at least."

"It's very good of you, dear Edward," replied Miss Ley drily. "But I have other engagements."

"Then you must break them. I can't have people leave my house immediately they come."

Miss Ley raised her eyebrows and smiled. Was it his house already? Dear me!

"My dear Edward," she answered, "I never stay anywhere longer than two days—the first day I talk to people, the second I let them talk to me and the third I go. I stay a week at hotels so as to go *en pension* and get my washing properly aired."

"You're treating us like a hotel," said Edward, laughing.

"It's a great compliment; in private houses one gets so abominably waited on."

"Ah, well, we'll say no more about it. But I shall have your boxes taken to the box-room, and I keep the key of it."

Miss Ley gave the short dry laugh that denoted that the remark of the person she was with had not amused her, but something in her own mind. They arrived at Court Leys.

"D'you see all the differences since you were last here?" asked Edward jovially.

Miss Ley looked round and pursed her lips.

"It's charming," she said.

"I knew it would make you sit up," he cried, laughing.

Bertha received her aunt in the hall, and embraced her with the grave decorum that had always characterized their relations.

"How clever you are, Bertha," said Miss Ley. "You manage to preserve your beautiful figure."

Then she set herself solemnly to investigate the connubial bliss of the youthful couple.

12

The passion to analyse the casual fellow-creature was the most absorbing vice that Miss Ley possessed, and no ties of relationship or affection prevented her from exercising her talents in this direction. She observed Bertha and Edward during luncheon. Bertha was talkative, chattering with a vivacity that seemed suspicious about the neighbours—Mrs Branderton's new bonnets and new hair, Miss Glover's good works and Mr Glover's visit to London. Edward was silent, except when he pressed Miss Ley to take a second helping. He ate largely, and the maiden lady noticed the enormous mouthfuls he took and the heartiness with which he drank his beer. Of course she drew conclusions; and she drew further conclusions when, having devoured half a pound of cheese and taken a last drink of all, he pushed back his chair with a sort of low roar reminding one of a beast of prey gorged with food, and said:

"Ah, well, I suppose I must set about my work. There's no rest for the weary."

He pulled a new briarwood pipe out of his pocket, filled and lit it.

"I feel better now. Well, good-bye, I shall be in to tea."

Conclusions buzzed about Miss Ley like midges on a summer's day. She drew them all the afternoon and again at dinner. Bertha was effusive too, unusually so; and Miss Ley asked herself a dozen times if this stream of chatter, these peals of laughter, proceeded from a light heart or from a base desire to deceive a middle-aged and inquiring aunt. After dinner, Edward, telling her that, of course she was one of the family, so he hoped she did not wish him to stand on ceremony, began reading the paper. When Bertha at Miss Ley's request played the piano, good manners made him put it aside, and he yawned a dozen times in a quarter of an hour.

"I mustn't play any more," said Bertha, "or Eddie will go to sleep. Won't you, darling?"

"I shouldn't wonder," he replied, laughing. "The fact is that the things Bertha plays when we've got company give me the fair hump."

"Edward only consents to listen when I play 'The Blue Bells of Scotland' or 'Yankee Doodle'."

Bertha made the remark, smiling good-naturedly at her husband, but Miss Ley drew conclusions.

"I don't mind confessing that I can't stand all this foreign music. What I say to Bertha is, Why can't you play English stuff?"

"If you must play at all," interposed his wife.

"After all's said and done, 'The Blue Bells of Scotland' has got a tune about it that a fellow can get his teeth into."

"You see, there's the difference," said Bertha, strumming a few bars of 'Rule, Britannia,' "it sets mine on edge."

"Well, I'm patriotic," retorted Edward. "I like the good, honest, homely English airs. I like 'em because they're English. I'm not ashamed to say that for me the best piece of music that's ever been written is 'God Save the Queen'."

"Which was written by a German, dear Edward," said Miss Ley, smiling.

"That's as it may be," said Edward, unabashed, "but the sentiment's English, and that's all I care about."

"Hear! Hear!" cried Bertha. "I believe Edward has aspirations towards a political career. I know I shall finish up as the wife of the local M.P."

"I'm patriotic," said Edward, "and I'm not ashamed to confess it."

"Rule, Britannia," sang Bertha, "Britannia rules the waves, Britons never, never shall be slaves. Ta-ra-boom-de-ay! Ta-ra-ra-boom-de-ay!"

"It's the same everywhere now," proceeded the orator. "We're chock full of foreigners and their goods. I think it's scandalous. English music isn't good enough for you; you get it from France and Germany. Where do you get your butter from? Brittany! Where d'you get your meat from? New Zealand!" This he said with great scron, and Bertha punctuated it with a resounding chord. "And as far as the butter goes, it isn't butter—it's margarine. Where does your bread come from? America. Your vegetables from Jersey."

"Your fish from the sea," interposed Bertha.

"And so it is all along the line; the British farmer hasn't got a chance."

To this speech Bertha played a burlesque accompaniment that would have irritated a more sensitive man than Craddock; but he merely laughed good-naturedly.

"Bertha won't take these things seriously," he said, passing his hand affectionately over her hair.

She suddenly stopped playing, and his good humour, joined with the loving gesture, filled her with remorse. Her eyes filled with tears.

"You are a dear good thing," she faltered, "and I'm utterly horrid."

"Now don't talk stuff before Aunt Polly. You know she'll laugh at us."

"Oh, I don't care," said Bertha, smiling happily. She stood up and linked her arm with his. "Eddie's the best-tempered person in the world; he's perfectly wonderful."

"He must be indeed," said Miss Ley, "if you have preserved your faith in him after six months of marriage."

But the maiden lady had stored so many observations, her impressions were so multitudinous, that she felt an urgent need to retire to the privacy of her bed-chamber and sort them. She kissed Bertha and held out her hand to Edward.

"Oh, if you kiss Bertha, you must kiss me too," said he, bending forward with a laugh.

"Upon my word!" said Miss Ley, somewhat taken aback, then, as he was evidently insisting, she embraced him on the cheek. She positively blushed.

The upshot of Miss Ley's investigation was that once again the hymeneal path had not been found strewn with roses; and the notion crossed her head, as she laid it on the pillow, that Dr Ramsay would certainly come and crow over her; it was not in masculine human nature, she thought, to miss an opportunity of exulting over a vanquished foe.

"He'll vow that I was the direct cause of the marriage. The dear man, he'll be so pleased with my discomfiture that I shall never hear the last of it. He's sure to call tomorrow."

Indeed the news of Miss Ley's arrival had been by Edward industriously spread abroad, and promptly Mrs Ramsay put on her blue velvet calling dress and in the doctor's brougham drove with him to Court Leys. The Ramsays found Miss Glover and the Vicar of Leanham already in possession of the field. Mr Glover looked thinner and older than when Miss Ley had last seen him; he was more weary, meek and brow-beaten. Miss Glover never altered.

"The parish?" said the parson, in answer to Miss Ley's polite inquiry, "I'm afraid it's in a bad way. The dissenters have got a new chapel, you know; and they say the Salvation Army is going to set up 'barracks,' as they call them. It's a great pity the Government doesn't step in; after all, we are established by law, and the law ought to protect us from encroachment."

"You don't believe in liberty of conscience?" asked Miss Ley.

"My dear Miss Ley," said the vicar in his tired voice, "everything has its limits. I should have thought there was in the Established Church enough liberty of conscience for anyone."

"Things are becoming dreadful in Leanham," said Miss Glover. "Practically all the tradesmen go to chapel now, and it makes it so difficult for us."

"Yes," replied the vicar with a weary sigh, "and as if we hadn't enough to put up with, I hear that Walker has ceased coming to church."

"Oh, dear! oh, dear!" said Miss Glover.

"Walker, the baker?" asked Edward.

"Yes, and now the only baker in Leanham who goes to church is Andrews."

"Well, we can't possibly deal with him, Charles," said Miss Glover. "His bread is too bad."

"My dear, we must," groaned her brother. "It would be against all my principles to deal with a tradesman who goes to chapel. You must tell Walker to send his book in, unless he will give an assurance that he'll come to church regularly."

"But Andrews's bread always gives you indigestion, Charles," cried Miss Glover.

"I must put up with it. If none of our martyrdoms were more serious than that we should have no cause to complain."

"Well, it's quite easy to get your bread from Tercanbury," said Mrs Ramsay, who was severely practical.

Both Mr and Miss Glover threw up their hands in dismay.

"Then Andrews would go to chapel too. The only thing that keeps them at church, I'm sorry to say, is the vicarage custom, or the hope of getting it."

Presently Miss Ley found herself alone with the parson's sister.

"You must be very glad to see Bertha again, Miss Ley."

"Now she's going to crow," thought the good lady. "Of course I am," she said aloud.

"And it must be such a relief to you to see how well it's all turned out."

Miss Ley looked sharply at Miss Glover, but saw no trace of irony.

"Oh, I think it's beautiful to see a married couple so thoroughly happy. It really makes me feel a better woman when I come here and see how those two worship one another."

"Of course the poor thing's a perfect idiot," thought Miss Ley.

"Yes, it's very satisfactory," she said, drily.

She glanced round for Dr Ramsay, looking forward, notwithstanding that she was on the losing side, to the tussle she foresaw. She had the instinct of the fighting woman, and even though defeat was inevitable, never avoided an encounter. The doctor approached.

"Well, Miss Ley, so you have come back to us. We're all delighted to see you."

"How cordial these people are," thought Miss Ley, rather crossly, thinking Dr Ramsay's remark preliminary to coarse banter or reproach. "Shall we take a turn in the garden? I'm sure you wish to quarrel with me."

"There's nothing I should like better. To walk in the garden, I mean; of course no one could quarrel with so charming a lady as yourself."

"He would never be so polite if he did not mean afterwards to be very rude," thought Miss Ley. "I'm glad you like the garden."

"Craddock has improved it so wonderfully. It's a perfect pleasure to look at all he's done."

This Miss Ley considered a gibe, and she looked for a repartee, but, finding none, was silent: Miss Ley was a wise woman. They walked a few steps without a word, and then Dr Ramsay suddenly burst out:

"Well, Miss Ley, you were right after all."

She stopped and looked at the speaker. He seemed quite serious.

"Yes," he said, "I don't mind acknowledging it. I was wrong. It's a great triumph for you, isn't it?"

He looked at her and shook with good-tempered laughter.

"Is he making fun of me?" Miss Ley asked herself, with something not very far removed from dismay; this was the first occasion upon which she had been unable to understand, not only the good doctor, but his inmost thoughts as well. "So you think the estate has been improved?"

"I can't make out how the man's done so much in so short a time. Why, just look at it!"

Miss Ley pursed her lips. "Even in its most dilapidated days, Court Leys looked gentlemanly; now all this," she glanced round with upturned nose, "might be the country mansion of a porkbutcher."

"My dear Miss Ley, you must pardon my saying so, but the place wasn't even respectable."

"But it is now; that is my complaint. My dear doctor, in the old days the passer-by could see that the owners of Court Leys were decent people; that they could not make both ends meet was a detail; it was possibly because they burnt one end too rapidly, which is the sign of a rather delicate mind,"—Miss Ley was mixing her metaphors—"And he moralized accordingly. For a gentleman there are only two decorous states, absolute poverty or overpowering wealth; the middle condition is vulgar. Now the passer-by sees thrift and careful management, the ends meet, but they do it aggressively, as if it were something to be proud of. Pennies are looked at before they are spent; and, good Heavens, the Leys serve to point a moral and adorn a tale. The Leys who gambled and squandered their sustenance, who bought diamonds when they hadn't got bread, and pawned the diamonds to give the king a garden-party, now form the heading of a copy-book and the ideal of a market-gardener."

Miss Ley had the characteristics of the true phrase-maker, for so long as her period was well rounded off she did not mind how much nonsense it contained. Coming to the end of her tirade, she looked at the doctor for the signs of disapproval which she thought her right; but he merely laughed.

"I see you want to rub it in," he said.

"What on earth does the creature mean?" Miss Ley asked herself.

"I confess I did believe things would turn out badly," the doctor proceeded. "And I couldn't help thinking he'd be tempted to play ducks and drakes with the whole property. Well, I don't mind frankly acknowledging that Bertha couldn't have chosen a better husband; he's a thoroughly good fellow, no one realized what he had in him, and there's no knowing how far he'll go."

A man would have expressed Miss Ley's feeling with a little whistle, but that lady merely raised her eyebrows. Then Dr Ramsay shared the opinion of Miss Glover?

"And what precisely is the opinion of the county?" she asked. "Of that odious Mrs Branderton, of Mrs Ryle (she has no right to the *Mayston* at all), of the Hancocks and the rest?"

"Edward Craddock has won golden opinions all round. Everyone likes him and thinks well of him. He's not conceited—he never had an ounce of conceit and he's not a bit changed. No, I assure you, although I'm not so fond as all that of confessing I was wrong, he's the right man in the right place. It's extraordinary how people look up to him and respect him already. I give you my word for it, Bertha has reason to congratulate herself; a girl doesn't pick up a husband like that every day of the week."

Miss Ley smiled; it was a great relief to find that she really was no more foolish than most people (so she modestly put it), for a doubt on the subject had for a short while given her some uneasiness.

"So everyone thinks they're as happy as turtle-doves?"

"Why, so they are," cried the doctor. "Surely you don't think otherwise?"

Miss Ley never considered it a duty to dispel the error of her fellow-creatures, and whenever she had a little piece of knowledge, vastly preferred keeping it to herself.

"I?" she answered. "I make a point of thinking with the majority; it's the only way to get a reputation for wisdom." But Miss Ley, after all, was only human. "Which do you think is the predominant partner?" she asked, smiling drily.

"The man, as he should be," gruffly replied the doctor.

"Do you think he has more brains?"

"Ah, you're a feminist," said Dr Ramsay, with great scorn.

"My dear doctor, my gloves are sixes, and perceive my shoes."

She put out for the old gentleman's inspection a very pointed, high-heeled shoe, displaying at the same time the elaborate openwork of a silk stocking.

"Do you intend me to take that as an acknowledgment of the superiority of man?"

"Heavens, how argumentative you are!" Miss Ley laughed, for she was getting into her own particular element. "I knew you wished to quarrel with me. Do you really want my opinion?"

"Yes."

"Well, it seems to me that if you take the very clever woman and set her beside an ordinary man, you prove nothing. That is how we women mostly argue. We place George Eliot (who, by the way, had nothing of the woman but petticoats, and those not always) beside plain John Smith and ask tragically if such a woman can be considered inferior to such a man. But that's silly. The question I've been asking myself for the last five-and-twenty years is whether the average fool of a woman is a greater fool than the average fool of a man."

"And the answer?"

"Well, upon my word, I don't think there's much to choose between them."

"Then you haven't really an opinion on the subject at all?" cried the doctor.

"That is why I give it to you," said Miss Ley.

"H'm!" grunted Dr Ramsay. "And how does that apply to the Craddocks?"

"It doesn't apply to them. I don't think Bertha is a fool."

"She couldn't be, having had the discretion to be born your niece, eh?"

"Why, doctor, you are growing quite pert," answered Miss Ley, with a smile.

They had finished the tour of the garden, and Mrs Ramsay was seen in the drawing-room bidding Bertha good-bye.

"Now, seriously, Miss Ley," said the doctor, "they're quite happy, aren't they? Everyone thinks so."

"Everyone is always right," said Miss Ley.

"And what is your opinion?"

"Good Heavens, what an insistent man it is! Well, Dr Ramsay, all I would suggest is that for Bertha, you know, the book of life is written throughout in italics; for Edward it is all in the big round hand of the copy-book heading. Don't you think it will make the reading of the book somewhat difficult?"

13

Rural pastimes had been one of the pleasures to which Bertha had chiefly looked forward, and with the summer Edward began to teach her the noble game of lawn tennis.

In the long evenings, when Craddock had finished his work and changed into the flannels that suited him so well, they played set after set. He prided himself upon his skill in this pursuit, and naturally found it trying to play with a beginner; but on the whole he was very patient, hoping that eventually Bertha would acquire sufficient skill to give him a good game. She did not find the sport so exhilarating as she had expected; it was difficult and she was slow at learning. However, to be doing something with her husband sufficiently amused her; she liked him to correct her mistakes, to show her this stroke and that, she admired his good-nature and inexhaustible spirits; with him she would have found endless entertainment even in such dull games as Beggar-my-Neighbour and Bagatelle. And now she looked for fine days so that their amusement might not be hindered. Those evenings were always pleasant; but the greatest delight for Bertha was to lie on the long chair by the lawn when the game was over and enjoy her fatigue, gossiping of the little nothings that love made absorbingly interesting.

Miss Ley had been persuaded to prolong her stay; she had vowed to go at the end of her week, but Edward, in his high-handed fashion, had ordered the key of the box-room to be given him, and refused to surrender it.

"Oh, no," he said, "I can't make people come here, but I can prevent them from going away. In this house everyone has to do as I tell them. Isn't that so, Bertha?"

"If you say it, my dear," replied his wife.

Miss Ley gracefully acceded to her nephew's desire, which was the more easy since the house was comfortable; she had really no pressing engagements and her mind was set upon making further examination into the married life of her relatives. It would have been weakness, unworthy of her, to maintain her intention for consistence' sake. Why, for days and days, were Edward and Bertha the happiest lovers, and then suddenly why did Bertha behave almost brutally towards her husband, while he remained invariably good-tempered and amiable? The obvious reason was that some little quarrel had arisen, such as, since Adam and Eve, has troubled every married couple in the world; but the obvious reason was that which Miss Ley was least likely to credit. She never saw anything in the way of a disagreement; Bertha acceded to all her husband's proposals; and with such docility on the one hand, such good humour on the other, what on earth could form a bone of contention?

Miss Ley had discovered that when the green leaves of life are turning red and golden with approaching autumn more pleasure can be obtained by a judicious mingling in simplicity of the gifts of nature and the resources of civilization; she was satisfied to come in the evenings to the tennis lawn and sit on a comfortable chair, shaded by trees and protected by a red parasol from the rays of the setting sun. She was not a woman to find distraction in needle-work, and brought with her, therefore, a volume of Montaigne, who was her favourite writer. She read a page and then lifted her sharp eyes to the players. Edward was certainly very handsome; he looked very clean; he was one of those men who carry the morning tub stamped on every line of their faces. You felt that Pears'

Soap was as essential to him as his belief in the Conservative Party, Derby Day and the Depression of Agriculture.

As Bertha often said, his energy was superabundant; notwithstanding his increasing size he was most agile; he was perpetually doing unnecessary feats of strength, such as jumping and hopping over the net, and holding chairs with outstretched arm.

"If health and a good digestion are all that is necessary in a husband, Bertha certainly ought to be the most contented woman alive."

Miss Ley never believed so implicitly in her own theories that she was prevented from laughing at them; she had an impartial mind, and saw the two sides of a question clearly enough to find little to choose between them; consequently she was able and willing to argue with equal force from either point of view.

The set was finished, and Bertha threw herself on a chair, panting.

"Find the balls, there's a dear," she cried.

Edward went off on the search, and Bertha looked at him with a delighted smile.

"He is such a good-tempered person," she said to Miss Ley. "Sometimes he makes me feel positively ashamed."

"He has all the virtues. Dr Ramsay, Miss Glover, even Mrs Branderton have been drumming his praise into my ears."

"Yes, they all like him. Arthur Branderton is always here, asking his advice about something or other. He's a dear good thing."

"Who? Arthur Branderton?"

"No, of course not. Eddie."

Bertha took off her hat and stretched herself more comfortably in the long chair; her hair was somewhat disarranged, and the rich locks wandered about her forehead and the nape of her neck in a way that would have distracted any minor poet under seventy. Miss Ley looked at her niece's fine profile, and wondered again at the complexion made of the softest colours in the setting sun. Her eyes now were liquid with love, languourous with the shade of long lashes, and her full, sensual mouth was half-open with a smile.

"Is my hair very untidy?" asked Bertha, catching Miss Ley's look and its meaning.

"No, I think it suits you when it is not done too severely."

"Edward hates it; he likes me to be trim. And of course I don't care how I look as long as he's pleased. Don't you think he's very good-looking?"

Then, without waiting for an answer, she asked a second question.

"Do you think me a great fool for being so much in love, Aunt Polly?"

"My dear, it's surely the proper behaviour with one's lord and master."

Bertha's smile became a little sad as she replied:

"Edward seems to think it unusual." She followed him with her eyes, picking up the balls one by one, hunting among bushes; she was in the mood for confidences that afternoon. "You don't know how different everything has been since I fell in love. The world is fuller. It's the only state worth living in." Edward advanced with the eight balls on his racket. "Come here and be kissed, Eddie," she cried.

"Not if I know it," he replied, laughing. "Bertha's a perfect terror. She wants me to spend my whole life in kissing her. Don't you think it's unreasonable, Aunt Polly? My motto is: everything in its place and season."

"One kiss in the morning," said Bertha, "one kiss at night will do to keep your wife quiet, and the rest of the time you can attend to your work and read your paper."

Again Bertha smiled charmingly, but Miss Ley saw no amusement in her eyes.

"Well, one can have too much of a good thing," said Edward, balancing his racket on the tip of his nose.

"Even of proverbial philosophy," remarked Bertha.

A few days later, his guest having definitely announced that she must go, Edward proposed a tennis-party as a parting honour. Miss Ley would gladly have escaped an afternoon of small-talk with the notabilities of Leanham, but Edward was determined to pay his aunt every attention, and his inner consciousness assured him that at least a small party was necessary to the occasion. They came, Mr and Miss Glover, the Brandertons, Mr Atthill Bacot, the great politician (of the district), and the Hancocks. But Mr Atthill Bacot was more than political, he was gallant; he devoted himself to the entertainment of Miss Ley. He discussed with her the sins of the Government and the incapacity of the army.

"More men, more guns," he said. "An elementary education in common sense for the officers, and the rudiments of grammar if there's time."

"Good Heavens, Mr Bacot, you mustn't say such things. I thought you were a Conservative."

"Madam, I stood for the constituency in '85. I may say that if a Conservative member could have got in, I should have. But there are limits. Even the staunch Conservative will turn. Now look at General Hancock."

"Please don't talk so loud," said Miss Ley with alarm; for Mr Bacot had instinctively adopted his platform manner, and his voice could be heard through the whole garden.

"Look at General Hancock, I say," he repeated, taking no notice of the interruption. "Is that the sort of man whom you would wish to have the handling of ten thousand of your sons?"

"Oh, but be fair," cried Miss Ley, laughing, "they're not all such fools as poor General Hancock."

"I give you my word, madam, I think they are. As far as I can make out, when a man has shown himself incapable of doing anything else they make him a general, just to encourage the others. I understand the reason. It's a great thing, of course, for parents sending their sons into the army to be able to say: 'Well, he may be a fool, but there's no reason why he shouldn't become a general.'"

"You wouldn't rob us of our generals," said Miss Ley, "they're so useful at tea-parties."

Mr Bacot was about to make a heated retort, when Edward called to him: "We want you to make up a set at tennis. Will you play with Miss Hancock against my wife and the General? Come on, Bertha."

"Oh, no, I mean to sit out, Eddie," said Bertha quickly. She saw that Edward was putting all the bad players into one set, so that they might be got rid of. "I'm not going to play."

"You must, or you'll disarrange the next lot," said her husband. "It's all settled; Miss Glover and I are going to take on Miss Jane Hancock and Arthur Branderton."

Bertha looked at him with eyes flashing angrily; of course he did not notice her vexation. he preferred playing with Miss Glover. The parson's sister played well, and for a good game he would never hesitate to sacrifice his wife's feelings. Didn't he know that she cared nothing for the game, but merely for the pleasure of playing with him? Only Miss Glover and young Branderton were within earshot, and in his jovial, pleasant manner, Edward laughingly said:

"Bertha's such a duffer. Of course she's only just beginning. You don't mind playing with the General, do you, dear?"

Arthur Branderton laughed, and Bertha smiled at the sally, but she flushed.

"I'm not going to play at all; I must see to the tea, and I daresay some more people will be coming in presently."

"Oh, I forgot that," said Edward. "No, perhaps you oughtn't to." And then, putting his wife out of his thoughts and linking his arm with young Branderton's, he sauntered off: "Come along, old chap, we must find someone else to make up the pat-ball set."

Edward had such a charming, frank manner, one could not help liking him. Bertha watched the two men go, and turned very white.

"I must just go into the house a moment," she said to Miss Glover. "Go and entertain Mrs Branderton, there's a dear."

And precipitately she fled. She ran to her bedroom and, flinging herself on the bed, burst into a flood of tears. To her the humiliation seemed dreadful. She wondered how Eddie, whom she loved above all else in the world, could treat her so cruelly. What had she done? He knew—ah, yes, he knew well enough the happiness he could cause her—and he went out of his way to be brutal. She wept bitterly, and jealousy of Miss Glover (Miss Glover, of all people!) stabbed her to the heart with sudden pain.

"He doesn't love me," she moaned, her tears redubling.

Presently there was a knock at the door.

"Who is it?" she cried.

The handle was turned and Miss Glover came in, red-faced with nervousness.

"Forgive me for coming in, Bertha. But I thought you seemed unwell. Can't I do something for you?"

"Oh, I'm all right," said Bertha, drying her tears. "Only the heat upset me, and I've got a headache."

"Shall I send Edward up to you?" asked Miss Glover, compassionately.

"What do I want with Edward?" replied Bertha, petulantly. "I shall be all right in five minutes; I often have attacks like this."

"I'm sure he didn't mean to say anything unkind. He's kindness itself, I know."

Bertha flushed: "What on earth d'you mean, Fanny? Who didn't say anything unkind?"

"I thought you were hurt by Edward's saying you were a duffer and a beginner."

"Oh, my dear, you must think me a fool," Bertha laughed hysterically. "It's quite true that I'm a duffer. I tell you it's only the weather. Why, if my feelings were hurt each time Eddie said a thing like that I should lead a miserable life."

"I wish you'd let me send him up to you," said Miss Glover, unconvinced.

"Good Heavens, why? See, I'm all right now." She washed her eyes and passed the powder-puff over her face. "My dear, it was only the sun."

With an effort she braced herself, and burst into a laugh joyful enough almost to deceive the vicar's sister.

"Now, we must go down, or Mrs Branderton will complain more than ever of my bad manners."

She put her arm round Miss Glover's waist and ran her down the stairs, to the mingled terror and amazement of that good lady. For the rest of the afternoon, though her eyes never rested on Edward, she was perfectly-charming, in the highest spirits, chattering incessantly, and laughing; everyone noticed her high spirits and commented upon her happiness.

"It does one good to see a couple like that," said General Hancock. "Just as happy as the day is long."

But the little scene had not escaped Miss Ley's sharp eyes, and she noticed with agony that Miss Glover had gone to Bertha; she could not stop her, being at the moment in the toils of Mrs Branderton.

"Oh, these good people are too offcious. Why can't she leave the girl alone to have it out with herself?"

But the explanation of everything now flashed across Miss Ley.

"What a fool I am!" she thought, and she was able to cogitate quite clearly while exchanging honeyed impertinences with Mrs Branderton. "I noticed it the first day I saw them together. How could I ever forget?"

She shrugged her shoulders and murmured the maxim of La Rochefoucauld:

"*Entre deux amants il y a toujours un qui aime et un qui se laisse aimer.*"

And to this she added another, in the same language, which, knowing no original, she ventured to claim as her own; it seemed to summarize the situation.

"*Celui qui aime a toujours tort.*"

14

Bertha and Miss Ley passed a troubled night, while Edward, of course, after much exercise and a hearty dinner slept the sleep of the just and of the pure at heart. Bertha was nursing her wrath; she had with difficulty brought herself to kiss her husband before, according to his habit, he turned his back upon her and began to snore. She had never felt so angry; she could hardly bear his touch, and withdrew as far from him as possible. Miss Ley, with her knowledge of the difficulties in store for the couple, asked herself if she could do anything. But what could she do? They were reading the book of life in their separate ways, one in italics, the other in the big round letters of the copy-book; and how could she help them to find a common character? Of course the first year of married life is difficult, and the weariness of the flesh adds to the inevitable disillusionment. Every marriage has its moments of despair. The great danger is in the onlooker, who may pay them too much attention, and by stepping in render the difficulty permanent. Miss Ley's cogitations brought her not unnaturally to the course that most suited her temperament; she concluded that far and away the best plan was to attempt nothing and let things right themselves as best they could. She did not postpone her departure but according to arrangement went on the following day.

"Well, you see," said Edward, bidding her good-bye, "I told you that I should make you stay longer than a week."

"You're a wonderful person, Edward," said Miss Ley, drily. "I have never doubted it for an instant."

He was pleased, seeing no irony in the compliment. Miss Ley took leave of Bertha with a suspicion of awkward tenderness that was quite unusual; she hated to show her feelings, and found it difficult, yet wanted to tell Bertha that if she were ever in difficulties she would always find in her an old friend and a true one. All she said was:

"If you want to do any shopping in London, I can always put you up, you know. And for the matter of that, I don't see why you shouldn't come and stay a month or so with me—if Edward can spare you. It will be a change."

When Miss Ley drove off with him to the station, Bertha felt suddenly a terrible loneliness. Her aunt had been a barrier between herself and her husband, coming opportunely just when, after the first months of mad passion, she was beginning to see herself linked to a man she did not know. A third person in the house had been a restraint, and the moments alone with her husband had gained a sweetness by their comparative rarity. She looked forward already to the future with something like terror. Her love for Edward was a bitter heart-ache. Oh, yes, she loved him well, she loved him passionately; but he—he was fond of her in his placid, calm way; it made her furious to think of it.

The weather was rainy, and for two days there was no question of tennis. On the third, however, the sun came out, and the lawn was soon dry. Edward had driven over to Tercanbury, but returned towards the evening.

"Hulloa!" he said, "you haven't got your tennis things on. You'd better hurry up."

This was the opportunity for which Bertha had been looking. She was tired of always giving way, of humbling herself; she wanted an explanation.

"You're very good," she said, "but I don't want to play tennis with you any more."

"Why on earth not?"

She burst out furiouly: "Because I'm sick and tired of being made a convenience by you. I'm too proud to be treated like that. Oh, don't look as if you didn't understand. You play with me because you've got no one else to play with. Isn't that so? That is how you are always with me. You prefer the company of the veriest fool in the world to mine. You seem to do everything you can to show your contempt for me."

"Why, what have I done now?"

"Oh, of course, you forget. You never dream that you are making me frightfully unhappy. Do you think I like to be treated before people as a sort of poor idiot that you can laugh and sneer at?"

Edward had never seen his wife so angry, and this time he was forced to pay her attention. She stood before him, at the end of her speech, with her teeth clenched, her cheeks flaming.

"It's about the other day, I suppose. I saw at the time you were in a passion."

"And didn't care two straws," she cried. "You knew I wanted to play with you, but what was that to you so long as you had a good game."

"You're too silly," he said, with a laugh. "We couldn't play together the whole afternoon when we had a lot of people here. They laugh at us as it is for being so devoted to one another."

"If only they knew how little you cared for me!"

"I might have managed a set with you later on, if you hadn't sulked and refused to play at all."

"Why didn't you suggest it? I should have been so pleased. I'm satisfied with the smallest crumbs you let fall for me. But it would never have occurred to you; I know you better than that. You're absolutely selfish."

"Come, come, Bertha," he cried, good-humouredly. "That's a thing I've not been accused of before. No one has ever called me selfish."

"Oh, no. They think you charming. They think because you're cheerful and even-tempered, because you're hail-fellow-well-met with everyone you meet, that you've got such a nice character. If they knew you as well as I do they'd understand it was merely because you're perfectly indifferent to them. You treat people as if they were your bosom friends, and then, five minutes after they've gone, you've forgotten all about them. And the worst of it is that I'm no more to you than anybody else."

"Oh, come, I don't think you can really find such awful things wrong with me."

"I've never known you sacrifice your slightest whim to gratify my most earnest desire."

"You can't expect me to do things that I think unreasonable."

"If you loved me you'd not always be asking if the things I want are reasonable. I didn't think of reason when I married you."

Edward made no answer, which naturally added to Bertha's irritation. She was arranging flowers for the table, and broke off the stalks savagely. Edward after a pause went to the door.

"Where are you going?" she asked.

"Since you won't play, I'm just going to do a few serves for practice."

"Why don't you send for Miss Glover to come and play with you?"

A new idea suddenly came to him (they came at sufficiently rare intervals not to spoil his equanimity), but the absurdity of it made him laugh: "Surely you're not jealous of her, Bertha?"

"I?" began Bertha with tremendous scorn, and then, changing her mind: "You preferred to play with her than to play with me."

He wisely ignored part of the charge: "Look at her and look at yourself. Do you think I could prefer her to you?"

"I think you're fool enough."

The words slipped out of Bertha's mouth almost before she knew she had said them, and the bitter, scornful tone added to their violence. They rather frightened her, and going very white, she turned to look at her husband.

"Oh, I didn't mean to say that, Eddie."

Fearing now that she had really wounded him, Bertha was entirely sorry; she would have given anything for the words to be unsaid. Was he very angry? Edward was turning over the pages of a book, looking at it listlessly. She went up to him gently.

"I haven't offended you, have I, Eddie? I didn't mean to say that."

She put her arm in his; he didn't answer.

"Don't be angry with me," she faltered again, and then, breaking down, buried her face in his bosom. "I didn't mean what I said. I lost command over myself. You don't know how you humiliated me the other day. I haven't been able to sleep at night, thinking of it. Kiss me."

He turned his face away, but she would not let him go; at last she found his lips.

"Say you're not angry with me."

"I'm not angry with you," he said, smiling.

"Oh, I want your love so much, Eddie," she murmured. "Now more than ever. I'm going to have a child." Then, in reply to his astonished exclamation: "I wasn't certain till today. Oh, Eddie, I'm so glad. I think it's what I wanted to make me happy."

"I'm glad too," he said.

"But you will be kind to me, Eddie, and not mind if I'm fretful and bad-tempered? You know I can't help it, and I'm always sorry afterwards."

He kissed her as passionately as his cold nature allowed, and peace returned to Bertha's tormented heart.

Bertha had intended as long as possible to make a secret of her news; it was a comfort in her distress and a bulwark against her increasing disillusionment. The knowledge that she was at last with child came as a great joy and as an even greater relief. She was unable to reconcile herself to the discovery, seen as yet dimly, that Edward's cold temperament could not satisfy her burning desires. Love to her was a fire, a flame that absorbed the rest of life; love to him was a convenient and necessary institution of Providence, a matter about which there was as little need for excitement as about the ordering of a suit of clothes. Bertha's passion for a while had masked her husband's want of ardour, and she would not see that his temperament was to blame. She accused him of not loving her, and asked herself distractedly how to gain his affection. Her pride found cause for humiliation in the circumstance that her own love was so much greater than his. For six months she had loved him blindly; and now, opening her eyes, she refused to look upon the naked fact, but insisted on seeing only what she wished.

But the truth, elbowing itself through the crowd of her illusions, tormented her. A cold fear seized her that Edward neither loved her nor had ever loved her, and she wavered uncertainly between the old passionate devotion and a new equally passionate hatred. She told herself that she could not do things by halves; she must love or detest, but in either case fiercely. And now the child made up for everything. Now it did not matter if Edward loved her or not; it no longer gave her terrible pain to realize how foolish had been her hopes, how quickly her ideal had been shattered; she felt that the infantine hands of her son were already breaking, one by one, the links that bound her to her husband. When she guessed her pregnancy, she gave a cry, not only of joy and pride, but also of exultation in her approaching freedom.

But when the suspicion was changed into a certainty, and Bertha knew finally that she would bear a child, her feelings veered round. Her emotions were always as unstable as the light winds of April. An extreme weakness made her long for the support and sympathy of her husband; she could not help telling him. In the hateful dispute of that very day she had forced herself to say bitter things, but all the time she wished him to take her in his arms, saying he loved her. It wanted so little to rekindle her dying affection, she wanted his help and she could not live without his love.

The weeks went on, and Bertha was touched to see a change in Edward's behaviour, more noticeable after his past indifference. He looked upon her now as an invalid, and, as such, entitled to consideration. He was really kind-hearted, and during this time did everything for his wife that did not involve a sacrifice of his own convenience. When the doctor suggested some dainty to tempt her apetite, Edward was delighted to ride over to Tercanbury to fetch it, and in her presence he trod more softly and spoke in a gentler voice. After a while he used to insist on carrying her up and downstairs, and though Dr Ramsay assured them it was a quite unnecessary proceeding, Bertha would not allow Edward to give it up. It amused her to feel a little child in his strong arms, and she loved to nestle against his breast. Then with the winter, when it was too cold to drive out, Bertha would lie for long hours on a couch by the window, looking at the line of elm trees, now leafless again and melancholy, and watch the heavy clouds that drove over from the sea; her heart was full of peace.

One day of the new year she was sitting as usual at her window when Edward came prancing up the drive on horseback. He stopped in front of her and waved his whip.

"What d'you think of my new horse?" he cried.

At that moment the animal began to cavort, and backed almost into a flower-bed.

"Quiet, old fellow," cried Edward. "Now then, don't make a fuss, quiet!"

The horse stood on its hind legs and laid its ears back viciously. Presently Edward dismounted and led him up to Bertha.

"Isn't he a stunner? Just look at him."

He passed his hand down the beast's forelegs and stroked its sleek coat.

"I only gave thirty-five guineas for him," he remarked. "I must just take him round to the stable, and then I'll come in."

In a few minutes Edward joined his wife. The riding-clothes suited him well, and in his top-boots he looked more than ever the fox-hunting country squire, which had always been his ideal. He was in high spirits over the new purchase.

"It's the beast that threw Arthur Branderton when we were out last week. Arthur's limping about now with a sprained ankle and a smashed collar-bone. He says the horse is the greatest devil he's ever ridden; he's frightened to try him again."

Edward laughed scornfully.

"But you haven't bought him?" asked Bertha, with alarm.

"Of course I have," said Edward; "I couldn't miss a chance like that. Why, he's a perfect beauty—only he's got a temper, like we all have."

"But is he dangerous?"

"A bit. That's why I got him cheap. Arthur gave a hundred guineas for him, and he told me I could have him for seventy. 'No,' I said, 'I'll give you thirty-five—and take the risk of breaking my neck.' Well, he just had to accept my offer. The horse has got a bad name in the county, and he wouldn't get anyone to buy him in a hurry. A man has to get up early if he wants to do me over a gee."

By this time Bertha was frightened out of her wits.

"But, Eddie, you're not going to ride him? Supposing something should happen? Oh, I wish you hadn't bought him."

"He's all right," said Craddock. "If anyone can ride him, I can—and, by Jove, I'm going to risk it. Why, if I bought him and then didn't use him, I'd never hear the last of it."

"To please me, Eddie, don't. What does it matter what people say? I'm so frightened. And now, of all times, you might do something to please me. It isn't often I ask you to do me a favour."

"Well, when you ask for something reasonable, I always try my best to do it; but really, after I've paid thirty-five guineas for a horse, I can't cut him up for cat's-meat."

"That means you'll always do anything for me as long as it doesn't interfere with your own likes and dislikes."

"Ah, well, we're all like that, aren't we? Come, come, don't be nasty about it, Bertha." He pinched her cheek good-naturedly. Women, we all know, would like the moon if they could get it; and the fact that they can't doesn't prevent them from persistently asking for it. Edward sat down beside his wife, holding her hand. "Now, tell us what you've been up to today. Has anyone been?"

Bertha sighed deeply: she had absolutely no influence over her husband. Neither prayers nor tears would stop him from doing a thing he had set his mind on. However much she argued, he always managed to make her seem in the wrong, and then went his way rejoicing. But she had her child now.

"Thank God for that!" she murmured.

15

Craddock went out on his new horse, and returned triumphant.

"He was as quiet as a lamb," he said. "I could ride him with my arms tied behind my back; and as to jumping—he takes a five-barred gate in his stride."

Bertha was rather angry with him for having caused her such terror, angry with herself also for troubling so much.

"And it was rather lucky I had him today. Old Lord Philip Dirk was there, and he asked Branderton who I was. 'You tell him,' says he, 'that it isn't often I've seen a man ride as well as he does.' You should see Branderton; he isn't half glad at having let me take the beast for thirty-five guineas. And Mr Molson came up to me and said: 'I knew that horse would get into your hands before long, you're the only man in this part who can ride it; but if it don't break your neck, you'll be lucky'."

He recounted with satisfaction the compliments paid to him.

"We had a good run today. And how are you, dear? Feeling comfy? Oh, I forgot to tell you: you know Rodgers, the hunts-man? Well, he said to me: 'That's a mighty fine hack you've got there, governor; but he takes some riding.' 'I know he does,' I said, 'but I flatter myself I know a thing or two more than most horses.' They all thought I should get rolled over before the day was out, but I just went slick at everything, just to show I wasn't frightened."

Then he gave details of the affair, and he had as great a passion for the meticulous as a German historian; he was one of those men who take infinite pains over trifles, flattering themselves that they never do things by halves. Bertha had a headache, and her husband bored her; she thought herself a great fool to be so concerned about his safety.

As the months wore on Miss Glover became dreadfully solicitous. The parson's sister looked upon birth as a mysteriously heart-fluttering business which, however, modesty required decent people to ignore. She treated her friend in an absurdly self-conscious manner, and blushed like a peony when Bertha, with the frankness usual in her, referred to the coming event. The greatest torment of Miss Glover's life was that, as lady of the vicarage, she had to manage the Maternity Bag, an institution to provide the infants of the needy with articles of raiment and their mothers with flannel petticoats. Miss Glover could never without much blushing ask the necessary questions of the recipients of her charity: and feeling that the whole thing ought not to be discussed at all, when she did so kept her eyes averted. Her manner caused great indignation among the virtuous poor.

"Well," said one good lady, "I'd rather not 'ave her bag at all than be treated like that. Why, she treats you as if—well, as if you wasn't married."

"Yes," said another, "that's just what I complain of. I promise you I 'ad 'alf a mind to take me marriage lines out of me pocket an' show 'er. It ain't nothin' to be ashamed about. Nice thing it would be after 'aving sixteen if I was bashful."

But of course the more unpleasant a duty was, the more zealously Miss Glover performed it; she felt it right to visit Bertha with frequency, and manfully bore the young wife's persistence in referring to an unpleasant subject. She carried her herosim to the pitch of knitting socks for the forthcoming baby, although to do so made her heart palpitate uncomfortably, and when she was surprised at the work by her brother her cheeks burned like two fires.

"Now, Bertha dear," she said one day, pulling herself together and straightening her back as she always did when she was mortifying her flesh, "now, Bertha dear, I want to talk to you seriously."

Bertha smiled: "Oh, don't, Fanny, you know how uncomfortable it makes you."

"I must," answered the good creature gravely. "I know you'll think me ridiculous; but it's my duty."

"I shan't think anything of the kind," said Bertha, touched by her friend's humility.

"Well, you talk a great deal of—of what's going to happen." Miss Glover blushed. "But I'm not sure if you are really prepared for it."

"Oh, is that all?" cried Bertha. "The nurse will be here in a fortnight, and Dr Ramsay says she's a most reliable woman."

"I wasn't thinking of earthly preparations," said Miss Glover. "I was thinking of the other. Are you quite sure you're approaching the—the *thing* in the right spirit?"

"What do you want me to do?" asked Bertha.

"It isn't what I want you to do. It's what you ought to do. I'm no-body. But have you thought at all of the spiritual side of it?"

Bertha gave a sigh that was chiefly voluptuous.

"I've thought that I'm going to have a son that's mine and Eddie's, and I'm awfully thankful."

"Wouldn't you like me to read the Bible to you sometimes?"

"Good Heavens, you talk as if I were going to die."

"One can never tell, dear Bertha," replied Miss Glover, gloomily. "I think you ought to be prepared. In the midst of life we are in death, and one can never tell what may happen."

Bertha looked at her a trifle anxiously. She had been forcing herself of late to be cheerful, and had found it necessary to stifle a recurring presentiment of evil fortune. The vicar's sister never realized that she was doing everything possible to make Bertha thoroughly unhappy.

"I brought my own Bible with me," she said. "Do you mind if I read you a chapter?"

"I should like it," said Bertha, and a cold shiver went through her.

"Have you got any preference for some particular part?" asked Miss Glover, on extracting the book from a little black bag that she always carried.

On Bertha's answer that she had no preference, she suggested open-ing the Bible at random and reading on from the first line that crossed her eyes.

"Charles doesn't quite approve of it," she said. "He thinks it smacks of superstition. But I can't help doing it, and the early Protestants con-stantly did the same."

Miss Glover, having opened the book with closed eyes, began to read: "The sons of Pharez; Hezron, and Hamul. And the sons of Zerah; Zimri, and Ethan, and Heman, and Calcol, and Dara: five of them in all." Miss Glover cleared her throat: "And the sons of Ethan: Azariah. The sons also of Hezron, that were born unto him; Jerahmeel, and Ram, and Chelubai. And Ram begat Amminadab; and Amminadab begat Nahshon, prince of the children of Judah."

She had fallen upon the genealogical table at the beginning of the Book of Chronicles. The chapter was very long, and consisted entirely of names, uncouth and difficult to pronounce; but Miss Glover shirked not one of them. With grave and rather high-pitched delivery, modelled upon her brother's, she read out the endless list. Bertha looked at her in amazement, but Miss Glover went steadily on.

"That's the end of the chapter," she said at last. "Would you like me to read you another one?"

"Yes, I should like it very much; but I don't think the part you've hit on is quite to the point."

"My dear, I don't want to reprove you—that's not my duty—but all the Bible is to the point."

And as the time of her delivery approached, Bertha quite lost her courage, and was often seized by a panic fear; suddenly, without obvious cause, her heart sank, and she asked herself frantically how she could possibly get through her confinement. She thought she was going to die, and wondered what would happen if she did. What would Edward do without her? The tears came to her eyes thinking of his bitter grief; but her lips trembled with pity for herself when the suspicion came to her that he would not be heart-broken; he was not a man to feel either grief or joy very poignantly. He would not weep; at the most his gaiety for a couple of days would be obscured, and then he would go about as before. She imagined him relishing the sympathy of his friends. In six months he would almost have forgotten her, and such memory as remained would not be extraordinarily pleasing. He would marry again, she thought bitterly; Edward loathed solitude, and next time doubtless he would choose a different sort of woman, one less remote than she from his ideal. Edward cared nothing for appearance, and Bertha imagined her successor plain as Miss Hancock or dowdy as Miss Glover; and the irony of it lay in the knowledge that either of those two would make a wife more suitable than she to his character, answering better to his conception of a helpmate.

Bertha fancied that Edward would willingly have given her beauty for some solid advantage, such as a knowledge of dress-making; her taste, her arts and accomplishments were nothing to him, and her impulsive passion was a positive defect. Handsome is as handsome does, said he; he was a plain, simple man, and he wanted a plain, simple wife.

She wondered if her death would really cause him much sorrow. Bertha's will gave him everything of which she was possessed, and he would spend it with a second wife. She was seized with insane jealousy.

"No, I won't die," she cried between her teeth. "I won't!"

But one day, while Edward was out hunting, her morbid thoughts took another turn; supposing he should die! The thought was unendurable, but the very horror of it fascinated her; she could not drive away the scenes which, with strange distinctness, her imagination set before her. She was sitting at the piano and heard suddenly a horse stop at the front door—Edward was back. But the bell rang. Why should Edward ring? There was a murmur of voices without, and then Arthur Branderton came in. In her mind's eye she saw every detail most clearly. He was in his hunting things! Something had happened, and, knowing what it was, Bertha was yet able to realize her terrified wonder as one possibility and another rushed through her brain. He was uneasy; he had something to tell, but dared not say it; she looked at him, horror-stricken, and a faintness came over her so that she could hardly stand.

Bertha's heart beat fast; she told herself it was absurd to allow her imagination to run away with her; but while she was arguing with herself the pictures went on developing themselves in her mind: she seemed to be assisting at a ghastly play in which she was the principal actor.

And what would she do when the fact was finally told her that Edward was dead? She would faint or cry out.

"There's been an accident," said Branderton. "Your husband is rather hurt."

Bertha put her hands to her eyes, the agony was dreadful.

"You musn't upset yourself," he went on, trying to break it to her.

Then, rapidly passing over the intermediate details, she found herself with her husband. He was dead, lying on the floor, and she pictured him to herself; she knew exactly how he would look; sometimes he slept so soundly, so quietly, that she was nervous, and put her ear to his heart to hear if it was beating. Now he was dead. Despair suddenly swept down upon her, overpoweringly. Bertha tried again to shake off her fancies, she even went to the piano and played a few notes; but the morbid attraction was too strong for her, and the scene went on. Now that he was dead he could not repulse her passion; now he was helpless and she kissed him with all her love; she passed her hands through his hair, and stroked his face (he had hated this in life), she kissed his lips and his closed eyes.

The imagined grief was so poignant that Bertha burst into tears. She remained with the body, refusing to be separated from it, and Bertha buried her face in cushions so that nothing might disturb her illusion; she had ceased trying to drive it away. Ah, she loved him passionately, she had always loved him and could not live without him. She knew that she would shortly die—and she had been afraid of death. Ah, now it was welcome! She kissed his hands—he could not prevent her now—and with a little shudder opened one of his eyes; it was glassy, expressionless, immobile. She burst into tears and, clinging to him, sobbed in love and anguish. She would let no one touch him but herself; it was a relief to perform the last offices for him who had been her whole life. She did not know that her love was so great.

She undressed the body and washed it; she washed the limbs one by one and sponged them; then very gently dried them with a towel. The touch of the cold flesh made her shudder voluptuously: she thought of him taking her in his strong arms, kissing her on the mouth. She wrapped him in the white shroud and surrounded him with flowers. They placed him in the coffin, and her heart stood still. She could not leave him, she passed with him all day and all night, looking ever at the quiet, restful face. Dr Ramsay came and Miss Glover came, urging her to go away, but she refused. What was the care of her own health now? She had only wanted to live for him. The coffin was closed, and she saw the faces of the undertakers; she had seen her husband's face for the last time, her beloved; her heart was like a stone, and she clutched at her breast in the pain of the oppression.

Hurriedly now the pictures thronged upon her, the drive to the churchyard, the service, the coffin covered with flowers and finally the graveside. They tried to keep her at home. What cared she for the silly, the abominable convention that sought to prevent her from going to the funeral? Was it not her husband, the only light of her life, whom they were burying? They could not realize the horror of it, the utter despair. And distinctly, by the dimness of the winter day, in the drawing-room of Court Leys, Bertha saw the lowering of the coffin, heard the rattle of earth thrown upon it.

What would her life be afterwards? She would try to live, she would surround herself with Edward's things, so that his memory might be always with her. The loneliness of life was appalling. Court Leys was empty and bare. She saw the endless succession of grey days; the seasons brought no change, and continually the clouds hung heavily above her; the trees were always leafless, and it was desolate. She could not imagine that travel would bring solace; the whole of life was blank, and what to her now were the pictures and churches, the blue skies of Italy? Her only happiness was to weep.

Then distractedly Bertha thought she would kill herself; her life was impossible to endure. No life at all, the blankness of the grave was preferable to the pangs gnawing continually at her heart. It would be so easy to finish, with a little morphia to close the book of trouble; despair would give her courage, and the prick of the needle was the only pain. But her vision became dim, and she had to make an effort to retain it. Her thoughts, growing less coherent, travelled back to previous incidents, to the scene at the grave and to the voluptuous pleasure of washing the body.

It was all so vivid that the entrance of Edward came upon her as a surprise. But the relief was almost too great for words, it was the awakening from a horrible nightmare. When he came forward to kiss her, she flung her arms round his neck and pressed him passionately to her heart.

"Oh, thank God!" she cried.

"Hulloa, what's up now?"

"I don't know what's been the matter with me. I've been so miserable, Eddie. I thought you were dead."

"You've been crying."

"It was so awful, I couldn't get the idea out of my head. Oh, I should die also."

Bertha could hardly realize that her husband was by her side in the flesh, alive and well.

"Would you be sorry if *I* died?" she asked him.

"But you're not going to do anything of the sort," he said, cheerily.

"Sometimes I'm so frightened, I don't believe I'll get over it."

He laughed at her, and his joyous tones were peculiarly comforting. She made him sit by her side, and held his strong hands, the hands that to her were the visible signs of his powerful manhood. She stroked them and kissed the palms. She was quite broken with the past emotions; her limbs trembled and her eyes glistened with tears.

16

The nurse arrived, bringing new apprehensions. She was an old woman who for twenty years had brought the neighbouring gentry into the world, and she had a copious store of ghastly anecdotes. In her mouth the terrors of birth were innumerable, and she told her stories with a cumulative art that was appalling. Of course, in her own mind she acted for the best. Bertha was nervous, and the nurse could imagine no better way of reassuring her than to give detailed accounts of patients who for days had been at death's door, given up by all the doctors, and yet had finally recovered and lived happily ever afterwards.

Bertha's quick invention magnified the coming anguish till, for thinking of it, she could hardly sleep at night. The impossibility of even conceiving it rendered it more formidable; she saw before her a long, long agony and then death. She could not bear Eddie to be out of her sight.

"Why, of course you'll get over it," he said. "I promise you it's nothing to make a fuss about."

He had bred animals for years, and was quite used to the process that supplied him with veal, mutton and beef for the local butchers. It was a ridiculous fuss that human beings made over a natural and ordinary phenomenon.

"Why, Dinah, the Irish terrier I used to have, had litters as regular as clockwork, and she was running about ten minutes afterwards."

Bertha lay with her face to the wall, holding Edward's fingers with a feverish hand.

"Oh, I'm so afraid of the pain. I feel certain that I shan't get over it—it's awful. I wish I hadn't got to go through it."

Then as the days passed she looked upon Dr Ramsay as her very stay.

"You won't hurt me," she begged. "I can't bear pain a bit. You'll give me chloroform all the time, won't you?"

"Good Heavens," cried the doctor, "one would think no one had ever had a baby before you."

"Oh, don't laugh at me. Can't you see how frightened I am?"

She asked the nurse how long her agony must last. She lay in bed, white, with terror-filled eyes, her lips set and a little vertical line between the brows.

"I shall never get through it," she whispered. "I have a presentiment that I shall die."

"I never knew a woman yet," said Dr Ramsay, "who hadn't a presentiment that she would die, even if she had nothing worse than a finger-ache the matter with her."

"Oh, you can laugh," said Bertha. "I've got to go through it."

And the thought recurred persistently that she would die.

Another day passed, and the nurse said the doctor must be immediately sent for. Bertha had made Edward promise to remain with her all the time.

"I think I shall have courage if I can hold your hand," she said.

"Nonsense," said Dr Ramsay, when Edward told him this. "I'm not going to have a man meddling about."

"I thought not," said Edward, "but I just promised to keep her quiet."

"If you'll keep yourself quiet," answered the doctor, "that's all I shall expect."

"Oh, you needn't fear about me. I know all about these things. Why, my dear doctor, I've brought a good sight more living things into the world than you have, I bet."

Edward was an eminently sensible man, whom any woman might admire. He was neither hysterical nor nervous; calm, self-possessed and unimaginative, he was the ideal person for an emergency.

"There's no good my knocking about the house all the afternoon," he said. "I should only mope, and if I'm wanted I can always be sent for."

He left word that he was going to Bewlie's Farm to see a cow that was sick. He was anxious about her.

"She's the best milker I've ever had. I don't know what I should do if something went wrong with her. She gives her so many pints a day as regular as possible. She's brought in over and over again the money I gave for her."

He walked along with the free-and-easy stride that Bertha so much admired, glancing now and then at the fields that bordered the highway. He stopped to examine the beans of a rival farmer.

"That soil's no good," he said, shaking his head. "It don't pay to grow beans on a patch like that."

Then, arriving at Bewlie's Farm, he called for the labourer in charge of the sick cow.

"Well, how's she going?"

"She ain't no better, squire."

"Bad job! Has Thompson been to see her today?"

Thompson was the vet.

"'E can't make nothin' of it. 'E thinks it's a habscess she's got, but I don't put much faith in Mister Thompson: 'is father was a labourer same as me, only 'e didn't 'ave to do with farming, bein' a bricklayer; and wot 'is son can know about cattle I don't know."

"Well, let's go and look at her," said Edward.

He strode over to the barn, followed by the labourer. The poor beast was standing in one corner, looking even more meditative than is usual with cows, hanging her head and humping her back; she looked profoundly pessimistic.

"I should have thought Thompson could do something," said Edward.

"'E says the butcher's the only thing for 'er," said the other, with great contempt.

Edward snorted indignantly. "Butcher indeed! I'd like to butcher him if I got the chance."

He went into the farmhouse, which for years had been his home, but he was a practical, sensible fellow, and it brought him no memories, no particular emotion.

"Well, Mrs Jones," he said to the tenant's wife, "how's yourself?"

"Middlin', sir. And 'ow are you and Mrs Craddock?"

"I'm all right. The missus is having a baby, you know."

He spoke in the jovial, careless way that endeared him to all and sundry.

"Bless my soul, is she indeed, sir? And I knew you when you was a boy. When d'you expect it?"

"I expect it every minute. Why, for all I know I may be a happy father when I get back to tea."

"Oh, I didn't know it was so soon as all that."

"Well, it was about time, Mrs Jones. We've been married sixteen months, and chance it."

"Ah, well, sir, it's a thing as 'appens to everybody. I 'ope she's takin' it well."

"As well as can be expected, you know. Of course she's very fanciful. Women are full of ideas; I never saw anything like 'em. Now as I was saying to Dr Ramsay only today, a bitch'll have half a dozen pups and be running about before you can say Jack Robinson. What I want to know is, why aren't women the same? All this fuss and bother; it's enough to turn a man's hair grey."

"You take it pretty cool, governor," said Farmer Jones, who had known Edward in the days of his poverty.

"Me?" cried Edward, laughing. "I know all about this sort of thing, you see. Why, look at all the calves I've had; and, mind you, I've not had an accident with a cow above twice all the time I've gone in for breeding. But I'd better be going to see how the missues is getting on. Good afternoon to you, Mrs Jones."

"Now what I like about the squire," said Mrs Jones, "is that there's no 'aughtiness in 'im. 'E ain't too proud to take a cup of tea with you, although 'e is the squire now."

"'E's the best squire we've 'ad for thirty years," said Farmer Jones. "And as you say, my dear, there's not a drop of 'aughtiness in 'im—which is more than you can say for his missus."

"Oh, well, she's young-like," replied his wife. "They do say as 'ow 'e's the master, and I daresay 'e 'll teach 'er better."

"Trust 'im for makin' 'is wife buckle under; 'e's not a man to stand nonsense from anybody."

Edward swung along the road, whirling his stick round, whistling and talking to the dogs that accompanied him. He was of a hopeful disposition, and did not think it would be necessary to slaughter his best cow. He didn't believe in the vet half so much as in himself, and his private opinion was that she would recover. He walked up the avenue of Court Leys, looking at the young elms he had planted to fill up the gaps; they were pretty healthy on the whole, and he was pleased with his success. He entered, and as he was hanging up his hat a piercing scream reached his ears.

"Hulloa!" he said, "things are beginning to get a bit lively."

He went up to the bedroom and knocked at the door. Dr Ramsay opened it, but with his burly frame barred the passage.

"Oh, don't be afraid," said Edward. "I don't want to come in. I know when I'm best out of the way. How is she getting on?"

"Well, I'm afraid it won't be such an easy job as I thought," whispered the doctor. "But there's no reason to get alarmed. It's only a bit slow."

"I shall be downstairs if you want me for anything."

"She was asking for you a good deal just now, but Nurse told her it would upset you if you were there; so then she said: 'Don't let him come. I'll bear it alone.'"

"Oh, that's all right. In a time like this the husband is much better out of the way, I think."

Dr Ramsay shut the door upon him. "Sensible chap that!" he said. "I like him better and better. Why, most men would be fussing about and getting hysterical and Lord knows what."

"Was that Eddie?" asked Bertha, her voice trembling with recent agony.

"Yes, he came to see how you were."

"Oh, the darling!" she groaned. "He isn't very much upset, is he? Don't tell him I'm very bad. It'll make him wretched. I'll bear it alone."

Edward, downstairs, told himself it was no use getting into a state, which was quite true, and taking the most comfortable chair in the room, settled down to read his paper. Before dinner he went upstairs to make more inquiries. Dr Ramsay came out saying he had given Bertha opium and for a while she was quiet.

"It's lucky you did it just at dinner-time," said Edward, with a laugh. "We'll be able to have a snack together."

They sat down and began to eat; they rivalled one another in their appetites, and the doctor, liking Edward more and more said it did him good to see a man who could eat well. But before they had reached the pudding a message came from the nurse to say that Bertha was awake, and Dr Ramsay regretfully left the table. Edward went on eating steadily. At last, with the happy sigh of a man conscious of virtue and a distended stomach, he lit his pipe and again settling himself in the armchair in a little while began to nod. The evening was long and he felt bored.

"It ought to be all over by now," he said. "I wonder if I need stay up."

Dr Ramsay was looking worried when Edward went up to him a third time.

"I'm afraid it's a difficult case," he said. "It's most unfortunate. She's been suffering a good deal, poor thing."

"Well, is there anything I can do?" asked Edward.

"No, except to keep calm and not make a fuss."

"Oh, I shan't do that, you needn't fear. I will say that for myself, I have got nerve."

"You're splendid," said Dr Ramsay. "I tell you I like to see a man keep his head so well through a job like this."

"Well, what I came to ask you was, is there any good in my sitting up? Of course I'll do it if anything can be done; but if not I may as well go to bed."

"Yes, I think you'd much better. I'll call you if you're wanted. I think you might come in and say a word or two to Bertha; it will encourage her."

Edward entered. Bertha was lying with staring, terrified eyes, eyes that seemed to have lately seen entirely new things; they shone glassily. Her face was whiter than ever, the blood had fled from her lips, and the cheeks were sunken: she looked as if she were dying. She greeted Edward with the faintest smile.

"How are you, little woman?" he asked.

His presence seemed to call her back to life, and a faint colour lit up her cheeks.

"I'm all right," she groaned, making an effort. "You musn't worry yourself, dear."

"Been having a bad time?"

"No," she said, bravely. "I've not really suffered much. There's nothing for you to upset yourself about."

He went out, and she called Dr Ramsay.

"You haven't told him what I've gone through, have you? I don't want him to know."

"No, that's all right. I've told him to go to bed."

"Oh, I'm glad. He can't bear not to get his proper night's rest. How long d'you think it will last? Already I feel as if I'd been tortured for ever, and it seems endless."

"Oh, it'll soon be over now, I hope."

"I'm sure I'm going to die," she whispered. "I feel that life is being gradually drawn out of me. I shouldn't mind if it weren't for Eddie. He'll be so cut up."

"What nonsense!" said the nurse. "You all say you're going to die. You'll be all right in a couple of hours."

"D'you think it will last a couple of hours longer? I can't stand it. Oh, doctor, don't let me suffer any more."

Edward went to bed quietly and soon was fast asleep. But his slumbers were somewhat troubled; generally he enjoyed the heavy, dreamless sleep of the man who has no nerves and takes plenty of exercise; tonight he dreamt. He dreamt not only that one cow was sick, but that all his cattle had fallen ill: the cows stood about with gloomy eyes and humpbacks, surly and dangerous, evidently with their livers totally deranged; the oxen were "blown" and lay on their backs with legs kicking feebly in the air, and swollen to double their normal size.

"You must send them all to the butcher's," said the vet. "There's nothing to be done with them."

"Good Lord deliver us," said Edward. "I shan't get four bob a stone for them."

But his dream was disturbed by a knock at the door, and Edward awoke to find Dr Ramsay shaking him.

"Wake up, man. Get up and dress quickly."

"What's the matter?" cried Edward, jumping out of bed and seizing his clothes. "What's the time?"

"It's half-past four. I want you to go into Tercanbury for Dr Spencer. Bertha is very bad."

"All right, I'll bring him back with me."

Edward rapidly dressed.

"I'll go round and wake up the man to put the horse in."

"No, I'll do that myself; it'll take me half the time."

He methodically laced his boots.

"Bertha is in no immediate danger. But I must have a consultation. I still hope we shall bring her through it."

"By Jove," said Edward, "I didn't know it was so bad as that."

"You need not get alarmed yet. The great thing is for you to keep calm and bring Spencer along as quickly as possible. It's not hopeless yet."

Edward with all his wits about him, was soon ready, and with equal rapidity set to harnessing the horse. He carefully lit the lamps as the proverb "more haste less speed' passed through his mind. In two minutes he was on the main road, and whipped up the horse. He went with a quick, steady trot through the silent night.

Dr Ramsay, returning to the sick-room, thought what a splendid object a man was who could be relied upon to do anything, who never lost his head or got excited. His admiration for Edward was growing by leaps and bounds.

17

Edward Craddock was a strong man and unimaginative. Driving through the night to Tercanbury he did not give way to distressing thoughts, but easily kept his anxiety within proper bounds, and gave his whole attention to conducting the horse. He kept his eyes on the road in front of him. The horse stepped out with swift, regular stride, rapidly passing the milestones. Edward rang Dr Spencer up and gave him the note he carried. The doctor presently came down, an undersized man with a squeaky voice and a gesticulative manner. He looked upon Edward with suspicion.

"I suppose you're the husband?" he said, as they clattered down the street. "Would you like me to drive? I daresay you're rather upset."

"No, and don't want to be," answered Edward with a laugh. He looked down a little upon people who lived in towns, and never trusted a man who was less than six feet high and burly in proportion.

"I'm rather nervous of anxious husbands who drive me at break-neck pace in the middle of the night," said the doctor. "The ditches have an almost irresistible attraction for them."

"Well, I'm not nervous, doctor, so it doesn't matter twopence if you are."

When they reached the open country, Edward set the horse going at its fastest; he was amused at the doctor's desire to drive. Absurd little man!

"Are you holding on tight?" he asked, with good-natured scorn.

"I can see you can drive," said the doctor.

"It is not the first time I've had reins in my hands," replied Edward modestly. "Here we are."

He showed the specialist to the bedroom and asked whether Dr Ramsay required him further.

"No, I don't want you just now; but you'd better stay up to be ready, if anything happens. I'm afraid Bertha is very bad indeed. You must be prepared for everything."

Edward retired to the next room and sat down. He was genuinely disturbed, but even now he could not realize that Bertha was dying; his mind was sluggish and he was unable to imagine the future. A more emotional man would have been white with fear, his heart beating painfully, and his nerves quivering with a hundred anticipated terrors. He would have been quite useless, while Edward was fit for any emergency; he could have been trusted to drive another ten miles in search of some appliance, and with perfect steadiness to help in any necessary operation.

"You know," he said to Dr Ramsay, "I don't want to get in your way; but if I should be any use in the room you can trust me not to get flurried."

"I don't think there's anything you can do; the nurse is very trustworthy and capable."

"Women," said Edward, "get so excited; they always make fools of themselves if they possibly can."

But the night air had made Craddock sleepy, and after half an hour in the chair, trying to read a book, he dozed off. Presently, however, he awoke, and the first light of day filled the room with a grey coldness. He looked at his watch.

"By Jove, it's a long job," he said.

There was a knock at the door, and the nurse came in.

"Will you please come?"

Dr Ramsay met him in the passage.

"Thank God, it's over. She's had a terrible time."

"Is she all right?"

"I think she's in no danger now, but I'm sorry to say we couldn't save the child."

A pang went through Edward's heart. "Is it dead?"

"It was still-born. I was afraid it was hopeless. You'd better go to Bertha now, she wants you. She doesn't know about the child."

Bertha was lying in an attitude of extreme exhaustion: she lay on her back, with arms stretched in utter weakness by her sides. Her face was grey with past anguish, her eyes now were dull and lifeless, half closed, and her jaw hung almost as hangs the jaw of a dead man. She tried to form a smile as she saw Edward, but in her feebleness the lips scarcely moved.

"Don't try to speak, dear," said the nurse, seeing that Bertha was attempting words.

Edward bent down and kissed her; the faintest blush coloured her cheeks, and then she began to cry; the tears stealthily glided down her cheeks.

"Come nearer to me, Eddie," she whispered.

He knelt down beside her, suddenly touched. He took her hand, and the contact had a vivifying effect; she drew a long breath and her lips formed a weary, weary smile.

"Thank God, it's over," she groaned. "Oh, Eddie darling, you can't think what I've gone through. It hurt so awfully."

"Well, it's all over now," said Edward.

"And you've been worrying too, Eddie. It encouraged me to think that you shared my trouble. You must go to sleep now. It was good of you to drive to Tercanbury for me."

"You musn't talk," said Dr Ramsay, coming back into the room after seeing the specialist sent off.

"I'm better now," said Bertha, "since I've seen Eddie."

"Well, you must go to sleep."

"You've not told me yet if it's a boy or a girl; tell me, Eddie, you know."

Edward looked uneasily at the doctor.

"It's a boy," said Dr Ramsay.

"I knew it would be," she murmured. An expression of ecstatic pleasure came into her face, chasing away the greyness of death. "I'm so glad. Have you seen it, Eddie?"

"Not yet."

"It's our child, isn't it? It's worth going through the pain to have a baby. I'm so happy."

"You must go to sleep now."

"I'm not a bit sleepy, and I want to see my son."

"No, you can't see him now," said Dr Ramsay, "he's asleep, and you mustn't disturb him."

"Oh, I should like to see him—just for one minute. You needn't wake him."

"You shall see him after you've been asleep," said the doctor soothingly. "It'll excite you too much."

"Well, you go and see him, Eddie, and kiss him; and then I'll go to sleep."

She seemed so anxious that at least its father should see his child that the nurse led Edward into the next room. On a chest of drawers was lying something covered with a towel. This the nurse lifted, and Edward saw his child; it was naked and very small, hardly human, repulsive, yet very pitiful. The eyes were closed, the eyes that had never opened. Edward looked at it for a minute.

"I promised I'd kiss it," he whispered.

He bent down and touched with his lips the cold forehead; the nurse drew the towel over the body and they went back to Bertha.

"Is he sleeping?" she asked.

"Yes."

"Did you kiss him?"

"Yes."

Bertha smiled: "Fancy your kissing my baby before me."

But the soporific that Dr Ramsay had administered was taking its effect, and almost immediately Bertha fell into a happy sleep.

"Let's take a turn in the garden," said Dr Ramsay, "I think I ought to be here when she wakes."

The air was fresh, scented with the spring flowers and the odour of the earth. Both men inspired it with relief after the close atmosphere of the sick-room. Dr Ramsay put his arm in Edward's.

"Cheer up, my boy," he said. "You've borne it all magnificently. I've never seen a man go through a night like this better than you; and upon my word you're as fresh as paint this morning."

"Oh, I'm all right," said Edward. "What's to be done about—about the baby?"

"I think she'll be able to bear it better after she's had a sleep. I really didn't dare say it was still-born; I thought the shock would be too much for her."

They went in and washed and ate, then waited for Bertha to wake. At last the nurse called them.

"You poor things," cried Bertha as they entered the room. "Have you had no sleep at all? I feel quite well now, and I want my baby. Nurse says it's sleeping and I can't have it, but I will. I want it to sleep with me, I want to look at my son."

Edward and the nurse looked at Dr Ramsay, who for once was disconcerted.

"I don't think you'd better have him today, Bertha," he said. "It would upset you."

"Oh, but I must have my baby. Nurse, bring him to me at once."

Edward knelt down again by the bedside and took her hands. "Now, Bertha, you musn't be alarmed, but the baby's not well and—"

"What d'you mean?"

Bertha suddenly sprang up in bed.

"Lie down. Lie down," cried both Dr Ramsay and the nurse, forcing her back on the pillow.

"What's the matter with him, doctor?" she cried, in sudden terror.

"It's as Edward says, he's not well."

"Oh, he isn't going to die—after all I've gone through."

She looked from one to the other.

"Oh, tell me, don't keep me in suspense. I can bear it, whatever it is."

Dr Ramsay touched Edward, encouraging him.

"You must prepare yourself for bad news, darling. You know—"

"He isn't dead?" she shrieked.

"I'm awfully sorry, dear. He was still-born."

"Oh, God!" groaned Bertha.

It was a cry of despair. And then she burst into passionate weeping. Her sobs were terrible, unbridled, it was her life that she was weeping away, her hope of happiness, all her desires and dreams. Her heart seemed breaking. She put her hands to her eyes in agony.

"Then I went through it all for nothing? Oh, Eddie, you don't know the frightful pain of it. All night I thought I should die. I would have given anything to be put out of my suffering. And it was all useless."

She sobbed uncontrollably. She was crushed by the recollection of what she had gone through and its futility.

"Oh, I wish I could die."

The tears were in Edward's eyes, and he kissed her hands.

"Don't give way, darling," he said, searching in vain for words to console her. His voice faltered and broke.

"Oh, Eddie," she said, "you're suffering just as much as I am. I forgot. Let me see him now."

Dr Ramsay made a sign to the nurse, and she fetched the dead child. She carried it to the bedside, and uncovering its head showed the face to Bertha. She looked a moment, and then asked:

"Let me see the whole body."

The nurse removed the cloth, and Bertha looked again. She said nothing, but finally turned away, and the nurse withdrew.

Bertha's tears now had ceased, but her mouth was set to a hopeless woe.

"Oh, I loved him already so much," she murmured.

Edward bent over: "Don't grieve, darling."

She put her arms round his neck as she had delighted to do.

"Oh, Eddie, love me with all your heart. I want your love so badly."

4

✐

From *The Land of the Blessed Virgin: Sketches and Impressions in Andalusia* (1905)

26

On Horseback

I had a desire to see something of the very heart of Andalusia, of that part of the country which had preserved its antique character, where railway trains were not, and the horse, the mule, the donkey were still the only means of transit. After much scrutiny of local maps and conversation with horse-dealers and others, I determined from Seville to go circuitously to Écija, and thence return by another route as best I could. The district I meant to traverse in olden times was notorious for its brigands; even thirty years ago the prosperous tradesmen, voyaging on his mule from town to town, was liable to be seized by unromantic outlaws and detained till his friends forwarded ransom, while ears and fingers were playfully sent to prove identity. In Southern Spain brigandage necessarily flourished, for not only were the country-folk in collusion with the bandits, but the very magistrates united with them to share the profits of lawless undertakings. Drastic measures were needful to put down the evil, and in a truly Spanish way drastic measures were employed. The Civil Guard, whose duty it was to see to the safety of the country side, had no confidence in the justice of Madrid, whither captured highwaymen were sent for trial; once there, for a few hundred dollars, the most murderous ruffian could prove his babe-like innocence, forthwith return to the scene of his former exploits and begin

273

again. So they hit upon an expedient. The Civil Guards set out for the capital with their prisoner handcuffed between them; but, curiously enough, in every single case the brigand had scarcely marched a couple of miles before he incautiously tried to escape, whereupon he was, of course, promptly shot through the back. People noticed two things: first, that the clothes of the dead man were often singed, as if he had not escaped very far before he was shot down; that only proved his guardians' zeal. But the other was stranger: the two Civil Guards, when after a couple of hours they returned to the town, as though by a mysterious premonition they had known the bandit would make some rash attempt, invariably had waiting for them an excellent hot dinner.

The only robber of importance who avoided such violent death was the chief of a celebrated band who, when captured, signed a declaration that he had not the remotest idea of escaping, and insisted on taking with him to Madrid his solicitor and a witness. He reached the capital alive, and having settled his little affairs with benevolent judges, turned to a different means of livelihood, and eventually, it is said, occupied a responsible post in the Government. It is satisfactory to think that his felonious talents were not in after-life entirely wasted.

It was the beginning of March when I started. According to the old proverb, the dog was already seeking the shade: *En Marzo busca la sombra el perro*; the chilly Spaniard, loosening the folds of his capa, acknowledged that at midday in the sun it was almost warm. The winter rains appeared to have ceased; the sky over Seville was cloudless, not with the intense azure of midsummer, but with a blue that seemed mixed with silver. And in the sun the brown water of the Guadalquivir glittered like the scales on a fish's back, or like the burnished gold of old Moorish pottery.

I set out in the morning early, with saddle-bags fixed on either side and poncho strapped to my pommel. A loaded revolver, though of course I never had a chance to use it, made me feel pleasantly adventurous. I walked cautiously over the slippery cobbles of the streets, disturbing the silence with the clatter of my horse's shoes. Now and then a mule or a donkey trotted by, with panniers full of vegetables, of charcoal or of bread, between which on the beast's neck sat perched a man in a short blouse. I came to the old rampart of the town, now a promenade; and at the gate groups of idlers, with cigarettes between their lips, stood talking.

An hospitable friend had offered lodging for the night and food; after which, my ideas of the probable accommodation being vague, I expected to sleep upon straw, for victuals depending on the wayside inns. I arrived at the *Campo de la Cruz,* a tiny chapel which marks the same distance from the Cathedral as Jesus Christ walked to the Cross; it is the final boundary of Seville.

Immediately afterwards I left the high-road, striking across country to Carmona. The land was already wild; on either side of the bridle-path were great wastes of sand covered only by palmetto. The air was cool and fresh, like the air of English country in June when it has rained through the night; and Aguador, snorting with pleasure, cantered over the uneven ground, nimbly avoiding holes and deep ruts with the sure-footedness of his Arab blood. An Andalusian horse cares nothing for the ground on which he goes, though it be hard and unyielding as iron; and he clambers up and down steep, rocky precipices as happily as he trots along a cinder-path.

I passed a shepherd in a ragged cloak and a broad-brimmed hat, holding a crook. He stared at me, his flock of brown sheep clustered about him as I scampered by, and his dog rushed after, barking.

"*Vaya Usted con Dios!*"

I came to little woods of pine-trees, with long, thin trunks, and the foliage spreading umbrella-wise; round them circled innumerable hawks, whose nests I saw among the branches. Two ravens crossed my path, their wings heavily flapping.

The great charm of the Andalusian country is that you seize romance, as it were, in the act. In northern lands it is only by a mental effort that you can realise the picturesque value of the life that surrounds you; and, for my part, I can perceive it only by putting it mentally in black and white, and reading it as though between the covers of a book. Once, I remember, in Brittany, in a distant corner of that rock-bound coast, I sat at midnight in a fisherman's cottage playing cards by the light of two tallow candles. Next door, with only a wall between us, a very old sailor lay dying in the great cupboard-bed which had belonged to his fathers before him; and he fought for life with the remains of that strenuous vigour with which in other years he had battled against the storms of the Atlantic. In the stillness of the night, the waves, with the murmur of a lullaby, washed gently upon the shingle, and the stars shone down from a clear sky. I looked at the yellow light on the faces of the players, gathered in that desolate spot from the four corners of the earth, and cried out: "By Jove, this is romance!" I had never before caught that impression in the very making, and I was delighted with my good fortune.

The answer came quickly from the American: "Don't talk bosh! It's your deal."

But for all that it was romance, seized fugitively, and life at that moment threw itself into a decorative pattern fit to be remembered. It is the same effect which you get more constantly in Spain, so that the commonest things are transfigured into beauty. For in the cactus and the aloe and the broad fields of grain, in the mules with their wide panniers and the peasants, in the shepherds' huts and the straggling farm-houses, the romantic is there, needing no subtlety to be discovered; and the least imaginative may feel a certain thrill when he understands that the life he leads is not without its aesthetic meaning.

I rode for a long way in complete solitude, through many miles of this sandy desert. Then the country changed, and olive-groves in endless succession followed one another, the trees with curiously decorative effect were planted in long, even lines. The earth was a vivid red, contrasting with the blue sky and the sombre olives, gnarled and fantastically twisted, like evil spirits metamorphosed: in places they had sown corn, and the young green enhanced the shrill diversity of colour. With its clear, brilliant outlines and its lack of shadow, the scene reminded one of a prim pattern, such as in Jane Austen's day young gentlewomen worked in worsted. Sometimes I saw women among the trees, perched like monkeys on the branches, or standing below with large baskets; they were extraordinarily quaint in the trousers which modesty bade them wear for the concealment of their limbs when olive-picking. The costume was so masculine, their faces so red and weather-beaten, that the yellow handkerchief on their heads was really the only means of distinguishing their sex.

But the path became more precipitous, hewn from the sandstone, and so polished by the numberless shoes of donkeys and of mules that I hardly dared walk upon it; and suddenly I saw Carmona in front of me—quite close.

27
By the Road—I

The approach to Carmona is a very broad, white street, much too wide for
the cottages which line it, deserted; and the young trees planted on either
side are too small to give shade. The sun beat down with a fierce glare and
the dust rose in clouds as I passed. Presently I came to a great Moorish
gateway, a dark mass of stone, battlemented, with a lofty horseshoe arch.
People were gathered about it in many-coloured groups, I found it was a
holiday in Carmona, and the animation was unwonted; in a corner stood
the hut of the *Consumo*, and the men advanced to examine my saddle-bags.
I passed through, into the town, looking right and left for a *parador*, an
hostelry whereat to leave my horse. I bargained for the price of food and
saw Aguador comfortably stalled; then made my way to the Nekropolis
where lived my host. There are many churches in Carmona, and into one
of these I entered; it had nothing of great interest, but to a certain degree
it was rich, rich in its gilded woodwork and in the brocade that adorned
the pillars; and I felt that these Spanish churches lent a certain dignity to
life: for all the careless flippancy of Andalusia they still remained to strike
a nobler note. I forgot willingly that the land was priest-ridden and super-
stitious, so that a Spaniard could tell me bitterly that there were but two
professions open to his countrymen, the priesthood and the bull-ring. It
was pleasant to rest in that cool and fragrant darkness.

My host was an archaeologist, and we ate surrounded by broken earth-
enware, fragmentary mosaics, and grinning skulls. It was curious afterwards to wander in the graveyard which, with indefatigable zeal, he had
excavated, among the tombs of forgotten races, letting oneself down to
explore the subterranean cells. The paths he had made in the giant cemetery were lined with a vast number of square sandstone boxes which contained human ashes; and now, when the lid was lifted, a green lizard or
a scoropion darted out. From the hill I saw stretched before me the great
valley of the Guadalquivir: with the squares of olive and of ploughed
field, and the various greens of the corn, it was like a vast, multicoloured
carpet. But later, with the sunset, black clouds arose, splendidly piled
upon one another; and the twilight air was chill and grey. A certain
sternness came over the olive-groves, and they might well have served as

a reproves to the facile Andaluz; for their cold passionless green seemed to offer a waring to his folly.

At night my host left me to sleep in the village, and I lay in bed alone in the little house among the tombs; it was very silent. The wind sprang up and blew about me, whistling through the windows, whistling weirdly; and I felt as though the multitudes that had been buried in that old cemetery filled the air with their serried numbers, a vast, silent congregation waiting motionless for they knew not what. I recalled a gruesome fact that my friend had told me; not far from there, in tombs that he had disinterred the skeletons lay huddled spasmodically, with broken skulls and a great stone by the side; for when a man, he said, lay sick unto death, his people took him, and placed him in his grave, and with the stone killed him.

In the morning I set out again. It was five-and-thirty miles to Ecija, but a new high road stretched from place to place and I expected easy riding. Carmona stands on the top of a precipitous hill, round which winds the beginning of the road; below, after many *zigzags*, I saw its continuation, a straight white line reaching as far as I could see. In Andalusia, till a few years ago, there were practically no high roads, and even now they are few and bad. The chief communication from town to town is usually an uneven track, which none attempts to keep up, with deep ruts, and palmetto growing on either side, and occasional pools of water. A day's rain makes it a quagmire, impassable for anything beside the sure-footed mule.

I went on, meeting now and then a string of asses, their panniers filled with stones or with wood for Carmona: the drivers sat on the rump of the hind-most animal, for that is the only comfortable way to ride a donkey. A peasant trotted briskly by on his mule, his wife behind him with her arms about his waist. I saw a row of ploughs in a field; to each were attached two oxen, and they went along heavily, one behind the other in regular line. By the side of every pair a man walked bearing a long goad, and one of them sang a *Malagueña*, its monotonous notes rising and falling slowly. From time to time I passed a white farm, a little way from the road, invitingly cool in the heat; the sun began to beat down fiercely. The inevitable storks were perched on a chimney, by their big nest; and when they flew in front of me, with their broad white wings and their red legs against the blue sky, they gave a quaint impression of a Japanese screen.

A farmhouse such as this seems to me always a type of the Spanish impenetrability. I have been over many of them, and know the manner of their rooms and the furniture, the round of duties there performed and how the day is portioned out; but the real life of the inhabitants escapes me. My knowledge is merely external. I am conscious that it is the same of the Andalusians generally, and am dismayed because I know practically nothing more after a good many years than I learnt in the first months of my acquaintance with them. Below the superficial similarity with the rest of Europe which of late they have acquired, there is a difference which makes it impossible to get at the bottom of their hearts. They have no openness as have the French and the Italians, with whom a good deal of intimacy is possible even to an Englishman, but on the contrary an Eastern reserve which continually baffles me. I cannot realise their thoughts nor their outlook. I feel always below the grace of their behaviour the instinctive, primeval hatred of the stranger.

Gradually the cultivation ceased, and I saw no further sign of human beings. I returned to the desert of the previous day, but the land was more dreary. The little groves of pine-trees had disappeared, there were no olives, no cornfields, not even the aloe nor the wilder cactus; but on either side as far as the horizon, desert wastes, littered with stones and with rough boulders, grown over only by palmetto. For many miles I went, dismounting now and then to stretch my legs and sauntering a while with the reins over my shoulder. Towards mid-day I rested by the wayside and let Aguador eat what grass he could.

Presently, continuing my journey, I caught sight of a little hovel, where the fir-branch over the door told me wine was to be obtained. I fastened my horse to a ring in the wall, and, going in, found an aged crone who gave me a glass of that thin white wine, produce of the last year's vintage, which is called *Vino de la Hoja*, wine of the leaf; she looked at me incuriously as though she saw so many people and they were so much alike that none repaid particular scrutiny. I tried to talk with her, for it seemed a curious life that she must lead, alone in that hut many miles from the nearest hamlet, with never a house in sight; but she was taciturn and eyed me now with something like suspicion. I asked for food, but with a sullen frown she answered that she had none to spare. I inquired the distance to Luisiana, a village on the way to Ecija where I had proposed to lunch, and shrugging her shoulders, she replied: "How should I know!" I was about to go when I heard a great clattering, and a horseman galloped up. He dismounted and walked in, a fine example of the Andalusian countryman, handsome and tall, well-shaved, with close-cropped hair. He wore elaborately decorated gaiters, the usual short, close-fitting jacket, and a broad-brimmed hat; in his belt were a knife and a revolver, and slung across his back a long gun. He would have made an admirable brigand of comic-opera; but was in point of fact a farmer riding, as he told me, to see his *novia*, or lady-love, at a neighbouring farm.

I found him more communicative and in the politest fashion we discussed the weather and the crops. He had been in Seville.

"*Maravilla!*" he cried, waving his fine, strong hands. "What a marvel! But I cannot bear the town-folk. What thieves and liars!"

"Town-folk should stick to the towns," muttered the old woman, looking at me somewhat pointedly.

The remark drew the farmer's attention more closely to me.

"And what are you doing here?" he asked.

"Riding to Ecija."

"Ah, you're a commercial traveller," he cried, with fine scorn. "You foreigners bleed the country of all its money. You and the government!"

"Rogues and vagabonds!" muttered the old woman.

Nothwithsanding, the farmer with much condescension accepted one of my cigars, and made me drink with him a glass of *aguardiente*.

We went off together. The mare he rode was really magnificent, rather large, holding her head beautifully, with a tail that almost swept the ground. She carried as if it were nothing the heavy Spanish saddle, covered with a white sheep-skin, its high triangular pommel of polished wood. Our ways, however, quickly diverged. I inquired again how far it was to the nearest village.

"Eh!" said the farmer, with a vague gesture. "Two leagues. Three leagues. *Quien Sabe?* Who knows? *Adios!*"

He put the spurs to his mare and galloped down a bridle-track. I, whom no fair maiden awaited, trotted on soberly.

28
By the Road—II

The endless desert grew rocky and less sandy, the colours duller. Even the palmetto found scanty sustenance, and huge boulders, strewn as though some vast torrent had passed through the plain, alone broke the desolate flatness. The dusty road pursued its way, invariably straight, neither turning to one side nor to the other, but continually in front of me, a long white line.

Finally in the distance I saw a group of white buildings and a cluster of trees. I thought it was Luisiana, but Luisiana, they had said, was a populous hamlet, and here were only two or three houses and not a soul. I rode up and found among the trees a tall white church, and a pool of murky water, further back, a low, new edifice, which was evidently a monastery, and a *posada*. Presently a Franciscan monk in his brown cowl came out of the church, and he told me that Luisiana was a full league off, but that food could be obtained at the neighbouring inn.

The *posada* was merely a long barn, with an open roof of wood, on one side of which were half a dozen mangers and in a corner two mules. Against another wall were rough benches for travellers to sleep on. I dismounted and walked to the huge fireplace at one end, where I saw three very old women seated like witches round a *brasero*, the great brass dish of burning cinders. With true Spanish stolidity they did not rise as I approached, but waited for me to speak, looking at me indifferently. I asked whether I could have anything to eat.

"Fried eggs."

"Anything else?"

The hostess, a tall creature, haggard and grim, shrugged her shoulders. Her jaws were toothless, and when she spoke it was difficult to understand. I tied Aguador to a manger and took off his saddle. The old women stirred themselves at last, and one brought a portion of chopped straw and a little barley. Another with the bellows below on the cinders, and the third, taking the eggs from a basket, fried them on the *brasero*. Besides, they gave me coarse brown bread and red wine, which was coarser still; for dessert the hostess went to the door and from a neighbouring tree plucked oranges.

When I had finished—it was not a very substantial meal—I drew my chair to the *brasero* and handed round my cigarette-case. The old women helped themselves, and a smile of thanks made the face of my gaunt hostess somewhat less repellent. We smoked a while in silence.

"Are you all alone here?" I asked, at length.

The hostess made a movement of her head towards the country. "My son is out shooting," she said, "and two others are in Cuba, fighting the rebels."

"God protect them!" muttered another.

"All our sons go to Cuba now," said the first.

"Oh, I don't blame the Cubans, but the government."

An angry light filled her eyes, and she lifted her clenched hand, cursing the rulers at Madrid who took her children. "They're robbers and fools. Why can't they let Cuba go? It isn't worth the money we pay in taxes."

She spoke so vehemently, mumbling the words between her toothless gums, that I could scarcely make them out.

"In Madrid they don't care if the country goes to rack and ruin so long as they fill their purses. Listen." She put one hand on my arm. "My boy came back with fever and dysentery. He was ill for months—at death's door—and I nursed him day and night. And almost before he could walk they sent him out again to that accursed country."

The tears rolled heavily down her wrinkled cheeks.

Luisiana is a curious place. It was a colony formed by Charles III of Spain with Germans whom he brought to people the desolate land; and I fancied the Teuton ancestry was apparent in the smaller civility of the inhabitants. They looked sullenly as I passed, and none gave the friendly Andalusian greeting. I saw a woman hanging clothes on the line outside her house; she had blue eyes and flaxen hair, a healthy red face, and a solidity of build which proved the purity of her northern blood. The houses, too, had a certain exotic quaintness; notwithstanding the universal whitewash of the South, there was about them still a northern character. They were prim and regularly built, with little plots of garden; the fences and the shutters were bright green. I almost expected to see German words on the post-office and on the tobacco-shop, and the grandiloquent Spanish seemed out of place; I thought the Spanish clothes of the men sat upon them uneasily.

The day was drawing to a close and I pushed on to reach Ecija before night, but Aguador was tired and I was obliged mostly to walk. Now the highway turned and twisted among little hills and it was a strange relief to leave the dead level of the plains: on each side the land was barren and desolate, and in the distance were dark mountains. The sky had clouded over, and the evening was grey and very cold; the solitude was awful. At last I overtook a pedlar plodding along by his donkey, the panniers filled to overflowing with china and glass, which he was taking to sell in Ecija. He wished to talk, but he was going too slowly, and I left him. I had hills to climb now, and at the top of each expected to see the town, but every time was disappointed. The traces of man surrounded me at last; again I rode among olive-groves and cornfields; the highway now was bordered with straggling aloes and with hedges of cactus.

At last! I reached the brink of another hill, and then, absolutely at my feet, so that I could have thrown a stone on its roofs, lay Ecija with its numberless steeples.

29
Écija

The central square, where are the government offices, the taverns, and a little inn, is a charming place, quiet and lackadaisical, its pale browns and greys very restful in the twilight, and harmonious. The houses with their queer windows and their balconies of wrought iron are built upon arcades which give a pleasant feeling of intimacy: in summer, cool and dark, they must be the promenade of all the gossips and the loungers. One can imagine the uneventful life, the monotonous round of existence: and yet the Andalusian blood runs in the people's veins. To my writer's fantasy Ecija seemed a fit background for some tragic story of passion or of crime.

I dined, unromantically enough, with a pair of commercial travellers, a post-office clerk, and two stout, elderly men who appeared to be retired officers. Spanish victuals are terrible and strange; food is even more an affair of birth than religion, since a man may change his faith, but

hardly his manner of eating: the stomach used to roast meat and York-
shire pudding rebels against Eastern cookery, and a Christian may sooner
become a Buddhist than a beef-eater a guzzler of olla podrida. The
Spaniards without weariness eat the same dinner day after day, year in,
year out; it is always the same white, thin, oily soup; a dish of haricot
beans and maize swimming in a revolting sauce; a nameless *entrée* fried in
oil—Andalusians have a passion for other animals' insides; a thin steak,
tough as leather and grilled to utter dryness; raisins and oranges. You rise
from table feeling that you have been soaked in rancid oil.

My table-companions were disposed to be sociable. The travellers
desired to know whether I was there to sell anything, and one drew from
his pocket, for my inspection, a case of watch-chains. The officers surmised that I had come from Gibraltar to spy the land, and to terrify me,
spoke of the invincible strength of the Spanish forces.

"Are you aware," said the elder, whose adiposity prevented his outward appearance from corresponding with his warlike heart, "Are you
aware that in the course of history our army has never once been de-
feated, and our fleet but twice?"

He mentioned the catastrophes, but I had never heard of them: and
Trafalgar was certainly not included. I hazarded a discreet inquiry,
whereupon, with much emphasis, both explained how on that occasion
the Spanish had soundly thrashed old Nelson, although he had discom-
fited the French.

"It is odd," I observed, "that British historians should be so inaccurate."

"It is discreditable," retorted my acquaintance, with a certain severity.

"How long did the English take to conquer the Soudan?" remarked
the other, somewhat aggressively picking his teeth. "Twenty years? We
conquered Morocco in three months."

"And the Moors are devils," said the commercial traveller. "I know,
because I once went to Tangiers for my firm."

After dinner I wandered about the streets, past the great old houses
of the nobles in the *Calle de los Caballeros*, empty now and dilapidated, for
every gentleman that can put a penny in his pocket goes to Madrid to
spend it; down to the river which flowed swiftly between high banks. Below the bridge two Moorish mills, irregular masses of blackness, stood
finely against the night. Near at hand they were still working at a forge,

and I watched the flying sparks as the smith hammered a horseshoe; the workers were like silhouettes in front of the leaping flames.

At many windows, to my envy, couples were philandering; the night was cold and Corydon stood huddled in his cape. But the murmuring as I passed was like the flow of a rapid brook, and I imagined, I am sure, far more passionate and romantic speeches than ever the lovers made. I might have uttered them to the moon, but I should have felt ridiculous, and it was more practical to jot them down afterwards in a note-book. In some of the surrounding villages they have so far preserved the Moorish style as to have no windows within reach of the ground, and lovers then must take advantage of the aperture at the bottom of the door made for the domestic cat's particular convenience. Stretched full length on the ground, on opposite sides of the impenetrable barrier, they can still whisper amorous commonplaces to one another. But imagine the confusion of a polite Spaniard, on a dark night, stumbling over a recumbent swain:

"My dear sir, I beg your pardon. I had no idea . . ."

In old days the disturbance would have been sufficient cause for a duel, but now manners are more peaceful: the gallant, turning a little, removes his hat and politely answers:

"It is of no consequence. *Vaya Usted con Dios!*"

"Good-night!"

The intruder passes and the beau endeavours passionately to catch sight of his mistress' black eyes.

Next day was Sunday, and I walked by the river till I found a plot of grass sheltered from the wind by a bristly hedge of cactus. I lay down in the sun, lazily watching two oxen that ploughed a neighbouring field.

I felt it my duty in the morning to buy a chap-book relating the adventures of the famous brigands who were called the Seven Children of Ecija: and this, somewhat sleepily, I began to read. It required a byronic stomach, for the very first chapter led me to a monastery where mass proceeded in memory of some victim of undiscovered crime. Seven handsome men appeared, most splendidly arrayed, but armed to the teeth; each one was every inch a brigand, pitiless yet great of heart, saturnine yet gentlemanly; and their peculiarity was that though six were killed one day seven would invariably be seen the next. The most gorgeously apparelled of them all, entering the sacristy, flung a purse of gold to the Superior, while a scalding tear coursed down his sunburnt cheek; and this he dried with a noble gesture and a richly embroidered handkerchief! In a whirlwind of romantic properties I read of a wicked miser who refused to support his brother's widow, of the widow herself (brought at birth to a gardener in the dead of night by a mysterious mulatto), and of this lady's lovely offspring. My own feelings can never be harrowed on behalf of a widow with a marriageable daughter, but I am aware that habitual readers of romance, like ostriches, will swallow anything. I was hurried to a subterranean chamber where the Seven Children, in still more elaborate garments, performed various dark deeds, smoked expensive Havanas, and seated on silken cushions, partook (like Freemasons) of a succulent cold collation.

The sun shone down with comfortable warmth, and I stretched my legs. My pipe was out and I refilled it. A meditative snail crawled up and observed me with flattering interest.

I grew somewhat confused. A stolen will was of course inevitable, and so were prison dungeons; but the characters had an irritating trick of revealing at critical moments that they were long-lost relatives. It must have been a tedious age when poor relations were never safely buried. However, youth and beauty were at last triumphant and villainy confounded, virtue was crowned with orange blossom and vice died a miserable death. Rejoicing in duty performed I went to sleep.

30
Wind and Storm

But next morning the sky was dark with clouds; people looked up dubiously when I asked the way and distance to Marchena, prophesying rain. Fetching my horse, the owner of the stable robbed me with peculiar callousness, for he had bound my hands the day before, when I went to see how Aguador was treated, by giving me with most courteous ceremony a glass of *aguardiente*; and his urbanity was then so captivating that now I lacked assurance to protest. I paid the scandalous overcharge with a good grace, finding some solace in the reflection that he was at least a picturesque blackguard, tall and spare, grey-headed, with fine features sharpened by age to the strongest lines; for I am always grateful to the dishonest when they add a certain aesthetic charm to their crooked ways. There is a proverb which says that in Ecija every man is a thief and every woman—no better than she should be: I was not disinclined to believe it.

I set out, guided by a sign-post, and the good road seemed to promise an easy day. They had told me that the distance was only six leagues, and I expected to arrive before luncheon. Aguador, fresh after his day's rest, broke into a canter when I put him on the green plot, which the old Spanish law orders to be left for cattle by the side of the highway. But after three miles, without warning, the road suddenly stopped. I found myself in an olive-grove, with only a narrow path in front of me. It looked doubtful, but there was no one in sight and I wandered on, trusting to luck.

Presently, in a clearing, I caught sight of three men on donkeys, walking slowly one after the other, and I galloped after to ask my way. The beasts were laden with undressed skins which they were taking to Fuentes, and each man squatted crosslegged on the top of his load. The hindermost turned right round when I asked my question and sat unconcernedly with his back to the donkey's head. He looked about him vaguely as though expecting the information I sought to be written on the trunk of an olive-tree, and scratched his head.

"Well," he said, "I should think it was a matter of seven leagues, but it will rain before you get there."

"This is the right way, isn't it?"

"It may be. If it doesn't lead to Marchena it must lead somewhere else."

There was a philosophic ring about the answer which made up for the uncertainty. The skinner was a fat, good-humoured creature, like all Spaniards intensely curious; and to prepare the way for inquires, offered a cigarette.

"But why do you come to Ecija by so roundabout a way as Carmona, and why should you return to Seville by such a route as Marchena?"

His opinion was evidently that the shortest way between two places was also the best. He received my explanation with incredulity and asked, more insistently, why I went to Ecija on horseback when I might go by train to Madrid.

"For pleasure," said I.

"My good sir, you must have come on some errand."

"Oh, yes," I answered, hoping to satisfy him, "on the search for emotion."

At this he bellowed with laughter and turned round to tell his fellows.

"*Usted es muy guason*," he said at length, which may be translated: "You're a mighty funny fellow."

I expressed my pleasure at having provided the skinners with amusement and bidding them farewell, trotted on.

I went for a long time among the interminable olives, grey and sad beneath the sullen clouds, and at last the rain began to fall. I saw a farm not very far away and cantered up to ask for shelter. An old woman and a labourer came to the door and looked at me very doubtfully; they said it was not a *posada*, but my soft words turned their hearts and they allowed me to come in. The rain poured down in heavy, oblique lines.

The labourer took Aguador to the stable and I went into the parlour, a long, low, airy chamber like the refectory of a monastery, with windows reaching to the ground. Two girls were sitting round the brasero, sewing; they offered me a chair by their side, and as the rain fell steadily we began to talk. The old woman discreetly remained away. They asked me about my journey, and as is the Spanish mode, about my country, myself, and my belongings. It was a regular volley of questions I had to answer, but they sounded pleasanter in the mouth of a pretty girl than in that of an obese old skinner; and the rippling laughter which greeted my replies made me feel quite witty. When they smiled they showed the whitest teeth. Then came my turn for questioning. The girl on my right, prettier than her sister, was very Spanish, with black, expressive eyes, an olive skin, and a bunch of violets in her abundant hair. I asked whether she had a *novio*, or lover; and the question set her laughing immoderately. What was her name? "Soledad—Solitude."

I looked somewhat anxiously at the weather, I feared the shower would cease, and in a minute, alas! the rain passed away; and I was forced to notice it, for the sun-rays came dancing through the window, importunately, making patterns of light upon the floor. I had no further excuse to stay, and said good-bye; but I begged for the bunch of violets in Soledad's dark hair and she gave it with a pretty smile. I plunged again into the endless oliver-groves.

It was a little strange, the momentary irruption into other people's lives, the friendly gossip with persons of a different tongue and country, whom I had never seen before, whom I should never see again; and were I not strictly truthful I might here lighten my narrative by the invention of a charming and romantic adventure. But if chance brings us often for a moment into other existences, it takes us out with equal suddenness so that we scarcely know whether they were real or mere imaginings of an idle hour: the Fates have a passion for the unfinished sketch and seldom trouble to unravel the threads which they have so laboriously entangled. The little scene brought another to my mind. When I was "on accident duty" at St. Thomas's Hospital a man brought his son with a broken leg; it was hard luck on the little chap, for he was seated peacefully on the ground when another boy, climbing a wall, fell on him and did the damage. When I returned him, duly bandaged, to his father's arms, the child bent forward and put out his lips for a kiss, saying good-night with babyish pronunciation. The father and the attendant nurse laughed, and I, being young, was confused and blushed profusely. They went away and somehow or other I never saw them again. I wonder if the pretty child, (he must be eight or ten now,) remembers kissing a very weary medical student, who had not slept much for several days, and was dead tired. Probably he has quite forgotten that he ever broke his leg. And I suppose no recollection remains with the pretty girl in the farm of a foreigner riding mysteriously through the olive-groves, to whom she gave shelter and a bunch of violets.

I came at last to the end of the trees and found then that a mighty wind had risen, which blew straight in my teeth. It was hard work to ride against it, but I saw a white town in the distance, on a hill; and made for it, rejoicing in the prospect. Presently I met some men shooting, and to make sure, asked whether the houses I saw really were Marchena.

"Oh no," said one. "You've come quite out of the way. That is Fuentes. Marchena is over there, beyond the hill."

My heart sank, for I was growing very hungry, and I asked whether I could not get shelter at Fuentes. They shrugged their shoulders and advised me to go to Marchena, which had a small inn. I went on for several hours, battling against the wind, bent down in order to expose myself as little as possible, over a huge expanse of pasture land, a desert of green. I reached the crest of the hill, but there was no sign of Marchena, unless that was a tower which I saw very far away, its summit just rising above the horizon.

I was ravenous. My saddle-bags contained spaces for a bottle and for food; and I cursed my folly in stuffing them with such useless refinements of civilisation as hair-brushes and soap. It is possible that one could allay the pangs of hunger with soap; but under no imaginable circumstances with hair-brushes.

It was a tower in the distance, but it seemed to grow neither nearer nor larger; the wind blew without pity, and miserably Aguador tramped on. I no longer felt very hungry, but dreadfully bored. In that waste of greenery the only living things beside myself were a troop of swallows that had accompanied me for miles. They flew close to the ground, in front of me, circling round; and the wind was so high that they could scarcely advance against it.

I remembered the skinner's question, why I rode through the country when I could go by train. I thought of the *Cheshire Cheese* in Fleet Street, where persons more fortunate than I had that day eaten hearty luncheons. I imagined to myself a well-grilled steak with boiled potatoes, and a pint of old ale, Stilton! The smoke rose to my nostrils.

But at last, the Saints be praised! I found a real bridle-path, signs of civilisation, ploughed fields; and I came in sight of Marchena perched on a hilltop, surrounded by its walls. When I arrived the sun was setting finely behind the town.

31
Two Villages

Marchena was all white, and on the cold windy eve I spent there, deserted of inhabitants. Quite rarely a man sidled past wrapped to the eyes in his cloak, or a woman with a black shawl over her head. I saw in the town nothing characteristic but the wicker-work frame in front of each window, so that people within could not possibly be seen; it was evidently a Moorish survival. At night men came into the eating-room of the inn, ate their dinner silently, and muffing themselves, quickly went out; the cold seemed to have killed all life in them. I slept in a little windowless cellar, on a straw bed which was somewhat verminous.

But next morning, as I looked back, the view of Marchena was charming. It stood on the crest of a green hill, surrounded by old battlements, and the sun shone down upon it. The wind had fallen, and in the early hour the air was pleasant and balmy. There was no road whatever, not even a bridletrack this time, and I made straight for Seville. I proposed to rest my horse and lunch at Mairena. On one side was a great plain of young corn stretching to the horizon, and on the other, with the same mantle of green, little hills, round which I slowly wound. The sun gave all manner of varied tints to the verdure—sometimes it was all emerald and gold, and at others it was like dark green velvet.

But the clouds in the direction of Seville were very black, and coming nearer I saw that it rained upon the hills. The water fell on the earth like a transparent sheet of grey. Soon I felt an occasional drop, and I put on my *poncho*.

The rain began in earnest, no northern drizzle, but a streaming downpour that soaked me to the skin. The path became marsh-like, and Aguador splashed along at a walk; it was impossible to go faster. The rain pelted down, blinding me. Then, oddly enough, for the occasion hardly warranted such high-flown thoughts, I felt suddenly the utter helplessness of man: I had never before realised with such completeness his insignificance beside the might of Nature; alone, with not a soul in sight, I felt strangely powerless. The plain flaunted itself insolently in face of my distress, and the hills raised their heads with a scornful pride; they met the rain as equals, but me it crushed; I felt as though it would beat me down into the mire. I fell into a passion with the elements, and was seized with a desire to strike out. But the white sheet of water was senseless and impalpable, and I relieved myself by raging inwardly at the fools who complain of civilisation and of railway-trains; they have never walked for hours foot-deep in mud, terrified lest their horse should slip, with the rain falling as though it would never cease.

The path led me to a river; there was a ford, but the water was very high, and rushed and foamed like a torrent. Ignorant of the depth and mistrustful, I trotted up-stream a little, seeking shallower parts; but none could be seen, and it was no use to look for a bridge. I was bound to cross, and I had to risk it: my only consolation was that even if Aguador could not stand, I was already so wet that I could hardly get wetter. The good horse required some persuasion before he would enter; the water rushed and bubbled and rapidly became deeper; he stopped and tried to turn back, but I urged him on. My feet went under water, and soon it was up to my knees; then, absurdly, it struck me as rather funny, and I began to laugh; I could not help thinking how foolish I should look and feel on arriving at the other side, if I had to swim for it. But immediately it grew shallower; all my adventures tailed off thus unheroically just when they began to grow exciting, and in a minute I was on comparatively dry land.

I went on, still with no view of Mairena; but I was coming nearer. I met a group of women walking with their petticoats over their heads. I passed a labourer sheltered behind a hedge, while his oxen stood in a field, looking miserably at the rain. Still it fell, still it fell!

And when I reached Mairena it was the most cheerless place I had come across on my journey, merely a poverty-stricken hamlet that did not even boast a bad inn. I was directed from place to place before I could find a stable; I was soaked to the skin, and there seemed no shelter. At last I discovered a wretched wine-shop; but the woman who kept it said there was no fire and no food. Then I grew very cross. I explained with heat that I had money; it is true I was bedraggled and disreputable, but when I showed some coins, to prove that I could pay for what I bought, she asked unwillingly what I required. I ordered a *brasero*, and dried my clothes as best I could by the burning cinders. I ate a scanty meal of eggs, and comforted myself with the thin wine of the leaf, sufficiently alcoholic to be exhilarating, and finally, with *aguardiente* regained my equilibrium.

But the elements were against me. The rain had ceased while I lunched, but no sooner had I left Mairena than it began again, and Seville was sixteen miles away. It poured steadily. I tramped up the hills, covered with nut-trees; I wound down into valleys; the way seemed interminable. I tramped on. At last from the brow of a hill I saw in the distance the Giralda and the clustering houses of Seville, but all grey in the wet; above it heavy clouds were lowering. On and on!

The day was declining, and Seville now was almost hidden in the mist, but I reached a road. I came to the first tavern of the environs; after a while to the first houses, then the road gave way to slippery cobbles, and I was in Seville. The Saints be praised!

5

☙

From *The Magician*
(1908)

3

"Here is somebody I don't know," said Susie.

"But I do, at least, by sight," answered Burdon. He leaned over to Dr Porhoët who was sitting opposite, quietly eating his dinner and enjoying the nonsense which everyone talked. "Is not that your magician?"

"Oliver Haddo," said Dr Porhoët, with a little nod of amusement.

The new arrival stood at the end of the room with all eyes upon him. He threw himself into an attitude of command and remained for a moment perfectly still.

"You look as if you were posing, Haddo," said Warren huskily.

"He couldn't help doing that if he tried," laughed Clayson.

Oliver Haddo slowly turned his glance to the painter.

"I grieve to see, O most excellent Warren, that the ripe juice of the *aperitif* has glazed your sparkling eye."

"Do you mean to say I'm drunk, sir?"

"In one gross, but expressive, word, drunk."

The painter grotesquely flung himself back in his chair as though he had been struck a blow, and Haddo looked steadily at Clayson.

"How often have I explained to you, O Clayson, that your deplorable lack of education precludes you from the brilliancy to which you aspire?"

For an instant Oliver Haddo resumed his effective pose; and Susie, smiling, looked at him. He was a man of great size, two or three inches more than six feet high; but the most noticeable thing about him was a vast obesity. His paunch was of imposing dimensions. His face was large and fleshy. He had thrown himself into the arrogant attitude of Velasquez's portrait of Del Borro in the Museum of Berlin; and his countenance bore of set purpose the same contemptuous smile. He advanced and shook hands with Dr Porhoët.

"Hail, brother wizard! I greet in you, if not a master, at least a student not unworthy my esteem."

Susie was convulsed with laughter at his pompousness, and he turned to her with the utmost gravity.

"Madam, your laughter is more soft in mine ears than the singing of Bulbul in a Persian garden."

Dr Porhoët interposed with introductions. The magician bowed solemnly as he was in turn made known to Susie Boyd, and Margaret, and Arthur Burdon. He held out his hand to the grim Irish painter.

"Well, my O'Brien, have you been mixing as usual the waters of bitterness with the thin claret of Bordeaux?"

"Why don't you sit down and eat your dinner?" returned the other, gruffly.

"Ah, my dear fellow, I wish I could drive the fact into this head of yours that rudeness is not synonymous with wit. I shall not have lived in vain if I teach you in time to realize that the rapier of irony is more effective an instrument than the bludgeon of insolence."

O'Brien reddened with anger, but could not at once find a retort, and Haddo passed on to that faded, harmless youth who sat next to Margaret.

"Do my eyes deceive me, or is this the Jagson whose name in its inanity is so appropriate to the bearer? I am eager to know if you still devote upon the ungrateful arts talents which were more profitably employed upon haberdashery."

The unlucky creature, thus brutally attacked, blushed feebly without answering, and Haddo went on to the Frenchman, Meyer as more worthy of his mocking.

"I'm afraid my entrance interrupted you in a discourse. Was it the celebrated harangue on the greatness of Michelangelo, or was it the searching analysis of the art of Wagner?"

"We were just going," said Meyer, getting up with a frown.

"I am desolated to lose the pearls of wisdom that habitually fall from your cultivated lips," returned Haddo, as he politely withdrew Madame Meyer's chair.

He sat down with a smile.

"I saw the place was crowded, and with Napoleonic instinct decided that I could only make room by insulting somebody. It is cause for congratulation that my gibes, which Raggles, a foolish youth, mistakes for wit, have caused the disappearance of a person who lives in open sin; thereby vacating two seats, and allowing me to eat a humble meal with ample room for my elbows."

Marie brought him the bill of fare, and he looked at it gravely.

"I will have a vanilla ice, O well-beloved, and a wing of a tender chicken, a fried sole, and some excellent peasoup."

"*Bien, un potage, une sole,* one chicken, and an ice."

"But why should you serve them in that order rather than in the order I gave you?"

Marie and the two Frenchwomen who were still in the room broke into exclamations at this extravagance, but Oliver Haddo waved his fat hand.

"I shall start with the ice, O Marie, to cool the passion with which your eyes inflame me, and then without hesitation I will devour the wing of a chicken in order to sustain myself against your smile. I shall then proceed to a fresh sole, and with the pea-soup I will finish a not unsustaining meal."

Having succeeded in capturing the attention of everyone in the room, Oliver Haddo proceeded to eat these dishes in the order he had named. Margaret and Burdon watched him with scornful eyes, but Susie, who was not revolted by the vanity which sought to attract notice, looked at him curiously. He was clearly not old, though his corpulence added to his apparent age. His features were good, his ears small, and his nose delicately shaped. He had big teeth, but they were white and even. His mouth was large, with heavy moist lips. He had the neck of a bullock. His dark, curling hair had retreated from the forehead and temples in such a way as to give his clean-shaven face a disconcerting nudity. The baldness of his crown was vaguely like a tonsure. He had the look of a very wicked, sensual priest. Margaret, stealing a glance at him as he ate, on a sudden violently shuddered; he affected her with an uncontrollable dislike. He lifted his eyes slowly, and she looked away, blushing as though she had been taken in some indiscretion. These eyes were the most curious thing about him. They were not large, but an exceedingly pale blue, and they looked at you in a way that was singularly embarrassing. At first Susie could not discover in what precisely their peculiarity lay, but in a moment she found out: the eyes of most persons converge when they look at you, but Oliver Haddo's, naturally or by a habit he had acquired for effect, remained parallel. It gave the impression that he looked straight through you and saw the wall beyond. It was uncanny. But another strange thing about him was the impossibility of telling whether he was serious. There was a mockery in that queer glance, a sardonic smile upon the mouth, which made you hesitate how to take his outrageous utterances. It was irritating to be uncertain whether, while you were laughing at him, he was not really enjoying an elaborate joke at your expense.

His presence cast an unusual chill upon the party. The French members got up and left. Warren reeled out with O'Brien, whose uncouth sarcasms were no match for Haddo's bitter gibes. Raggles put on his coat with the scarlet lining and went out with the tall Jagson, who smarted still under Haddo's insolence. The American sculptor paid his bill silently. When he was at the door, Haddo stopped him.

"You have modelled lions at the Jardin des Plantes, my dear Clayson. Have you ever hunted them on their native plains?"

"No, I haven't."

Clayson did not know why Haddo asked the question, but he bristled with incipient wrath.

"Then you have not seen the jackal, gnawing at a dead antelope, scamper away in terror when the King of Beasts stalked down to make his meal."

Clayson slammed the door behind him. Haddo was left with Margaret, and Arthur Burdon, Dr Porhoët, and Susie. He smiled quietly.

"By the way, are you a lion-hunter?" asked Susie flippantly.

He turned on her his straight uncanny glance.

"I have no equal with big game. I have shot more lions than any man alive. I think Jules Gérard, whom the French of the nineteenth century called *Le Tueur de Lions*, may have been fit to compare with me, but I can call to mind no other."

This statement, made with the greatest calm, caused a moment of silence. Margaret stared at him with amazement.

"You suffer from no false modesty," said Arthur Burdon.

"False modesty is a sign of ill-breeding, from which my birth amply protects me."

Dr Porhoët looked up with a smile of irony.

"I wish Mr Haddo would take this opportunity to disclose to us the mystery of his birth and family. I have a suspicion that, like the immortal Cagliostro, he was born of unknown but noble parents, and educated secretly in Eastern palaces."

"In my origin I am more to be compared with Denis Zachaire or with Raymond Lully. My ancestor, George Haddo, came to Scotland in the suite of Anne of Denmark, and when James I, her consort, ascended the English throne, he was granted the estates in Staffordshire which I still possess. My family has formed alliances with the most noble blood of England, and the Merestons, the Parnabys, the Hollingtons, have been proud to give their daughters to my house."

"Those are facts which can be verified in works of reference," said Arthur dryly.

"They can," said Oliver.

"And the Eastern palaces in which your youth was spent, and the black slaves who waited on you, and the bearded sheikhs who imparted to you secret knowledge?" cried Dr Porhoët.

"I was educated at Eton, and I left Oxford in 1896."

"Would you mind telling me at what college you were?" said Arthur.

"I was at the House."

"Then you must have been there with Frank Hurrell."

"Now assistant physician at St Luke's Hospital. He was one of my most intimate friends."

"I'll write and ask him about you."

"I'm dying to know what you did with all the lions you slaughtered," said Susie Boyd.

The man's effrontery did not exasperate her as it obviously exasperated Margaret and Arthur. He amused her, and she was anxious to make him talk.

"They decorate the floors of Skene, which is the name of my place in Staffordshire." He paused for a moment to light a cigar. "I am the only man alive who has killed three lions with three successive shots."

"I should have thought you could have demolished them by the effects of your oratory," said Arthur.

Oliver leaned back and placed his two large hands on the table.

"Burkhardt, a German with whom I was shooting, was down with fever and could not stir from his bed. I was awakened one night by the uneasiness of my oxen, and I heard the roaring of lions close at hand. I took my carbine and came out of my tent. There was only the meagre light of the moon. I walked alone, for I knew natives could be of no use to me. Presently I came upon the carcass of an antelope, half-consumed, and I made up my mind to wait for the return of the lions. I hid myself among the boulders twenty paces from the prey. All about me was the immensity of Africa and the silence. I waited, motionless, hour after hour, till the dawn was nearly at hand. At last three lions appeared over a rock. I had noticed, the day before, spoor of a lion and two females."

"May I ask how you could distinguish the sex?" asked Arthur, incredulously.

"The prints of a lion's fore feet are disproportionately larger than those of the hind feet. The fore feet and hind feet of the lioness are nearly the same size."

"Pray go on," said Susie.

"They came into full view, and in the dim light, as they stood chest on, they appeared as huge as the strange beasts of the Arabian tales. I aimed at the lioness which stood nearest to me and fired. Without a sound, like a bullock felled at one blow, she dropped. The lion gave vent to a sonorous roar. Hastily I slipped another cartridge in my rifle. Then I became conscious that he had seen me. He lowered his head, and his crest was erect. His lifted tail was twitching, his lips were drawn back from the red gums, and I saw his great white fangs. Living fire flashed from his eyes, and he growled incessantly. Then he advanced a few steps, his head held low; and his eyes were fixed on mine with a look of rage. Suddenly he jerked up his tail, and when a lion does this he charges. I got a quick sight on his chest and fired. He reared up on his hind legs, roaring loudly and clawing at the air, and fell back dead. One lioness remained, and through the smoke I saw her spring to her feet and rush towards me. Escape was impossible, for behind me were high boulders that I could not climb. She came on with hoarse, coughing grunts, and with desperate courage I fired my remaining barrel. I missed her clean. I took one step backwards in the hope of getting a cartridge into my rifle, and fell, scarcely two lengths in front of the furious beast. She missed me. I owed my safety to that fall. And then suddenly I found that she had collapsed. I had hit her after all. My bullet went clean through her heart, but the spring had carried her forwards. When I scrambled to my feet I found that she was dying. I walked back to my camp and ate a capital breakfast."

Oliver Haddo's story was received with astonished silence. No one could assert that it was untrue, but he told it with a grandiloquence that carried no conviction. Arthur would have wagered a considerable sum that there was no word of truth in it. He had never met a person of this kind before, and could not understand what pleasure there might be in the elaborate invention of improbable adventures.

"You are evidently very brave," he said.

"To follow a wounded lion into thick cover is probably the most dangerous proceeding in the world," said Haddo calmly. "It calls for the utmost coolness and for iron nerve."

The answer had an odd effect on Arthur. He gave Haddo a rapid glance, and was seized suddenly with uncontrollable laughter. He leaned back in his chair and roared. His hilarity affected the others, and they broke into peal upon peal of laughter. Oliver watched them gravely. He seemed neither disconcerted nor surprised. When Arthur recovered himself, he found Haddo's singular eyes fixed on him.

"Your laughter reminds me of the crackling of thorns under a pot," he said.

Haddo looked round at the others. Though his gaze preserved its fixity, his lips broke into a queer, sardonic smile.

"It must be plain even to the feeblest intelligence that a man can only command the elementary spirits if he is without fear. A capricious mind can never rule the sylphs, nor a fickle disposition the undines."

Arthur stared at him with amazement. He did not know what on earth the man was talking about. Haddo paid no heed.

"But if the adept is active, pliant, and strong, the whole world will be at his command. He will pass through the storm and no rain shall fall upon his head. The wind will not displace a single fold of his garment. He will go through fire and not be burned."

Dr Porhoët ventured upon an explanation of these cryptic utterances.

"These ladies are unacquainted with the mysterious beings of whom you speak, *cher ami*. They should know that during the Middle Ages imagination peopled the four elements with intelligences, normally unseen, some of which were friendly to man and others hostile. They were thought to be powerful and conscious of their power, though at the same time they were profoundly aware that they possessed no soul. Their life depended upon the continuance of some natural object, and hence for them there could be no immortality. They must return eventually to the abyss of unending night, and the darkness of death afflicted them always. But it was thought that in the same manner as man by his union with God had won a spark of divinity, so might the sylphs, gnomes, undines, and salamanders by an alliance with man partake of his immortality. And many of their women, whose beauty was more than human, gained a human soul by loving one of the race of men. But the reverse occurred also, and often a love-sick youth lost his immortality because he left the haunts of his kind to dwell with the fair, soulless denizens of the running streams or of the forest airs."

"I didn't know that you spoke figuratively," said Arthur to Oliver Haddo.

The other shrugged his shoulders.

"What else is the world than a figure? Life itself is but a symbol. You must be a wise man if you can tell us what is reality."

"When you begin to talk of magic and mysticism I confess that I am out of my depth."

"Yet magic is no more than the art of employing consciously invisible means to produce visible effects. Will, love, and imagination are magic powers that everyone possesses; and whoever knows how to develop them to their fullest extent is a magician. Magic has but one dogma, namely, that the seen is the measure of the unseen."

"Will you tell us what the powers are that the adept possesses?"

"They are enumerated in a Hebrew manuscript of the sixteenth century, which is in my possession. The privileges of him who holds in his right hand the Keys of Solomon and in his left the Branch of the Blossoming Almond are twenty-one. He beholds God face to face without dying, and converses intimately with the Seven Genii who command the celestial army. He is superior to every affliction and to every fear. He reigns with all heaven and is served by all hell. He holds the secret of the resurrection of the dead, and the key of immortality."

"If you possess even these you have evidently the most varied attainments," said Arthur ironically.

"Everyone can make game of the unknown," retorted Haddo, with a shrug of his massive shoulders.

Arthur did not answer. He looked at Haddo curiously. He asked himself whether he believed seriously these preposterous things, or whether he was amusing himself in an elephantine way at their expense. His manner was earnest, but there was an odd expression about the mouth, a hard twinkle of the eyes, which seemed to belie it. Susie was vastly entertained. It diverted her enormously to hear occult matters discussed with apparent gravity in this prosaic tavern. Dr Porhoët broke the silence.

"Arago, after whom has been named a neighouring boulevard, declared that doubt was a proof of modesty, which has rarely interfered with the progress of science. But one cannot say the same of incredulity, and he that uses the word impossible outside of pure mathematics is lacking in prudence. It should be remembered that Lactantius proclaimed belief in the existence of antipodes inane, and Saint Augustine of Hippo added that in any case there could be no question of inhabited lands."

"That sounds as if you were not quite sceptical, dear doctor," said Miss Boyd.

"In my youth I believed nothing, for science had taught me to distrust even the evidence of my five sense," he replied, with a shrug of the shoulders. "But I have seen many things in the East which are inexplicable by the known processes of science. Mr Haddo has given you one definition of magic, and I will give you another. It may be described merely as the intelligent utilization of forces which are unknown, contemned, or misunderstood of the vulgar. The young man who settles in the East sneers at the ideas of magic which surround him, but I know not what there is in the atmosphere that saps his unbelief. When he has sojourned for some years among Orientals, he comes insensibly to share the opinion of many sensible men that perhaps there is something in it after all."

Arthur Burdon made a gesture of impatience.

"I cannot imagine that, however much I lived in Eastern countries, I could believe anything that had the whole weight of science against it. If there were a word of truth in anything Haddo says, we should be unable to form any reasonable theory of the universe."

"For a scientific man you argue with singular fatuity," said Haddo icily, and his manner had an offensiveness which was intensely irritating. "You should be aware that science, dealing only with the general, leaves out of consideration the individual cases that contradict the enormous majority. Occasionally the heart is on the right side of the body, but you would not on that account ever put your stethoscope in any other than the usual spot. It is possible that under certain conditions the law of gravity does not apply, yet you will conduct your life under the conviction that it does so invariably. Now, there are some of us who choose to deal only with these exceptions to the common run. The dull man who plays at Monte Carlo puts his money on the colours, and generally black or red turns up; but now and then zero appears, and he loses. But we, who have backed zero all the time, win many times our stake. Here and there you will find men whose imagination raises them above the humdrum of mankind. They are willing to lose their all if only they have chance of a great prize. Is it nothing not only to know the future, as did the prophets of old, but by making it to force the very gates of the unknown?"

Suddenly the bantering gravity with which he spoke fell away from him. A singular light came into his eyes, and his voice was hoarse. Now at last they saw that he was serious.

"What should you know of that lust for great secrets which consumes me to the bottom of my soul!"

"Anyhow, I'm perfectly delighted to meet a magician," cried Susie gaily.

"Ah, call me not that," he said, with a flourish of his fat hands, regaining immediately his portentous flippancy. "I would be known rather as the Brother of the Shadow."

"I should have thought you could be only a very distant relation of anything so unsubstantial," said Arthur, with a laugh.

Oliver's face turned red with furious anger. His strange blue eyes grew cold with hatred, and he thrust out his scarlet lips till he had the ruthless expression of a Nero. The gibe at his obesity had caught him on the raw. Susie feared that he would make so insulting a reply that a quarrel must ensure.

"Well, really, if we want to go to the fair we must start," she said quickly. "And Marie is dying to be rid of us."

They got up, and clattered down the stairs into the street.

16

Arthur would not leave the little village of Venning. Neither Susie nor the doctor could get him to make any decision. None of them spoke of the night which they had spent in the woods of Skene; but it coloured all their thoughts, and they were not free for a single moment from the ghastly memory of it. They seemed still to hear the sound of that passionate weeping. Arthur was moody. When he was with them, he spoke little; he opposed a stubborn resistance to their efforts at diverting his mind. He spent long hours by himself, in the country, and they had no idea what he did. Susie was terribly anxious. He had lost his balance so completely that she was prepared for any rashness. She divined that his hatred of Haddo was no longer within the bounds of reason. The desire for vengeance filled him entirely, so that he was capable of any violence.

Several days went by.

At last, in concert with Dr Porhoët, she determined to make one more attempt. It was late at night, and they sat with open windows in the sitting-room of the inn. There was a singular oppressiveness in the air which suggested that a thunderstorm was at hand. Susie prayed for it; for she ascribed to the peculiar heat of the last few days much of Arthur's sullen irritability.

"Arthur, you *must* tell us what you are going to do," she said. "It is useless to stay here. We are all so ill and nervous that we cannot consider anything rationally. We want you to come away with us tomorrow."

"You can go if you choose," he said. "I shall remain till that man is dead."

"It is madness to talk like that. You can do nothing. You are only making yourself worse by staying here."

"I have quite made up my mind."

"The law can offer you no help, and what else can you do?"

She asked the question, meaning if possible to get from him some hint of his intentions; but the grimness of his answer, though it only confirmed her vague suspicions, startled her.

"If I can do nothing else, I shall shoot him like a dog."

She could think of nothing to say, and for a while they remained in silence. Then he got up.

"I think I should prefer it if you went," he said. "You can only hamper me."

"I shall stay here as long as you do."

"Why?"

"Because if you do anything, I shall be compromised. I may be arrested. I think the fear of that may restrain you."

He looked at her steadily. She met his eyes with a calmness which showed that she meant exactly what she said, and he turned uneasily away. A silence even greater than before fell upon them. They did not move. It was so still in the room that it might have been empty. The breathlessness of the air increased, so that it was horribly oppressive. Suddenly there was a loud rattle of thunder, and a flash of lightning tore across the heavy clouds. Susie thanked Heaven for the storm which would give presently a welcome freshness. She felt excessively ill at ease, and it was a relief to ascribe her sensation to a state of the atmosphere. Again the thunder rolled. It was so loud that it seemed to be immediately above their heads. And the wind rose suddenly and swept with a long moan through the trees that surrounded the house. It was a sound so human that it might have come from the souls of dead men suffering hopeless torments of regret.

The lamp went out, so suddenly that Susie was vaguely frightened. It gave one flicker, and they were in total darkness. It seemed as though someone had leaned over the chimney and blown it out. The night was very black, and they could not see the window which opened on to the country. The darkness was so peculiar that for a moment no one stirred.

Then Susie heard Dr Porhoët slip his hand across the table to find matches, but it seemed that they were not there. Again a loud peal of thunder startled them, but the rain would not fall. They panted for fresh air. On a sudden Susie's heart gave a bound, and she sprang up.

"There's someone in the room."

The words were no sooner out of her mouth than she heard Arthur fling himself upon the intruder. She knew at once, with the certainty of an intuition, that it was Haddo. But how had he come in? What did he want? She tried to cry out, but no sound came from her throat. Dr Porhoët seemed bound to his chair. He did not move. He made no sound. She knew that an awful struggle was proceeding. It was a struggle to the death between two men who hated one another, but the most terrible part of it was that nothing was heard. They were perfectly noiseless. She tried to do something, but she could not stir. And Arthur's heart exulted, for his enemy was in his grasp, under his hands, and he would not let him go while life was in him. He clenched his teeth and tightened his straining muscles. Susie heard his laboured breathing, but she only heard the breathing of one man. She wondered in abject terror what that could mean. They struggled silently, hand to hand, and Arthur knew that his strength was greater. He had made up his mind what to do and directed all his energy to a definite end. His enemy was extraordinarily powerful, but Arthur appeared to create some strength from the sheer force of his will. It seemed for hours that they struggled. He could not bear him down.

Suddenly, he knew that the other was frightened and sought to escape from him. Arthur tightened his grasp; for nothing in the world now would he ever loosen his hold. He took a deep, quick breath, and then put out all his strength in a tremendous effort. They swayed from side to side. Arthur felt as if his muscles were being torn from the bones, he could not continue for more than a moment longer; but the agony that flashed across his mind at the thought of failure braced him to a sudden angry jerk. All at once Haddo collapsed, and they fell heavily to the ground. Arthur was breathing more quickly now. He thought that if he could keep on for one instant longer, he would be safe. He threw all his weight on the form that rolled beneath him, and bore down furiously on the man's arm. He twisted it sharply, with all his might, and felt it give way. He gave a low cry of triumph; the arm was broken. And now his enemy was seized with panic; he struggled madly, he wanted only to get away from those long hands that were killing him. They seemed to be of iron. Arthur seized the huge bullock throat and dug his fingers into it, and they sunk into the heavy rolls of fat; and he flung the whole weight of his body into them. He exulted, for he knew that his enemy was in his power at last; he was strangling him, strangling the life out of him. He wanted light so that he might see the horror of that vast face, and the deadly fear, and the staring eyes. And still he pressed with those iron hands. And now the movements were strangely convulsive. His victim writhed in the agony of death. His struggles were desperate, but the avenging hands held him as in a vice. And then the movements grew spasmodic, and then they grew weaker. Still the hands pressed upon the gigantic throat, and Arthur forgot everything. He was mad with rage and fury and hate and sorrow. He thought of Margaret's anguish and of her fiendish torture, and he wished the man had ten lives so that he might take them one by one. And at last all was still, and that vast mass of flesh was motionless, and he knew that his enemy was dead. He loosened his grasp and slipped one hand over the heart. It would never beat again. The man was stone dead. Arthur got up and straightened himself. The darkness was intense still, and he could see nothing. Susie heard him, and at length she was able to speak.

"Arthur what have you done?"

"I've killed him," he said hoarsely.

"O God, what shall we do?"

Arthur began to laugh aloud, hysterically, and in the darkness his hilarity was terrifying.

"For God's sake let us have some light."

"I've found the matches," said Dr Porhoët.

He seemed to awake suddenly from his long stupor. He struck one, and it would not light. He struck another, and Susie took off the globe and the chimney as he kindled the wick. Then he held up the lamp, and they saw Arthur looking at them. His face was ghastly. The sweat ran off his forehead in great beads, and his eyes were bloodshot. He trembled in every limb. Then Dr Porhoët advanced with the lamp and held it forward. They looked down on the floor for the man who lay there dead. Susie gave a sudden cry of horror.

There was no one there.

Arthur stepped back in terrified surprise. There was no one in the room, living or dead, but the three friends. The ground sank under

Susie's feet, she felt horribly ill, and she fainted. When she awoke, seeming difficultly to emerge from an eternal night, Arthur was holding down her head.

"Bend down," he said. "Bend down."

All that had happened came back to her, and she burst into tears. Her self-control deserted her, and, clinging to him for protection, she sobbed as though her heart would break. She was shaking from head to foot. The strangeness of this last horror had overcome her, and she could have shrieked with fright.

"It's all right," he said. "You need not be afraid."

"Oh, what does it mean?"

"You must pluck up courage. We're going now to Skene."

She sprang to her feet, as though to get away from him; her heart beat wildly.

"No, I can't; I'm frightened."

"We must see what it means. We have no time to lose, or the morning will be upon us before we get back."

Then she sought to prevent him.

"Oh, for God's sake, don't go, Arthur. Something awful may await you there. Don't risk your life."

"There is no danger. I tell you the man is dead."

"If anything happened to you . . ."

She stopped, trying to restrain her sobs; she dared not go on. But he seemed to know what was in her mind.

"I will take no risks, because of you. I know that whether I live or die is not a—matter of indifference to you."

She looked up and saw that his eyes were fixed upon her gravely. She reddened. A curious feeling came into her heart.

"I will go with you wherever you choose," she said humbly.

"Come, then."

They stepped out into the night. And now, without rain, the storm had passed away, and the stars were shining. They walked quickly. Arthur went in front of them. Dr Porhoët and Susie followed him, side by side, and they had to hasten their steps in order not to be left behind. It seemed to them that the horror of the night was passed, and there was a fragrancy in the air which was wonderfully refreshing. The sky was beautiful. And at last they came to Skene. Arthur led them again to the opening in the palisade, and he took Susie's hand. Presently they stood in the place from which a few days before they had seen the house. As then, it stood in massive blackness against the night and, as then, the attic windows shone out with brilliant lights. Susie started, for she had expected that the whole place would be in darkness.

"There is no danger, I promise you," said Arthur gently. "We are going to find out the meaning of all this mystery."

He began to walk towards the house.

"Have you a weapon of some sort?" asked the doctor.

Arthur handed him a revolver.

"Take this. It will reassure you, but you will have no need of it. I bought it the other day when—I had other plans."

Susie gave a little shudder. They reached the drive and walked to the great portico which adorned the facade of the house. Arthur tried the handle, but it would not open.

"Will you wait here?" he said. "I can get through one of the windows, and I will let you in."

He left them. They stood quietly there, with anxious hearts; they could not guess what they would see. They were afraid that something would happen to Arthur, and Susie regretted that she had not insisted on going with him. Suddenly she remembered that awful moment when the light of the lamp had been thrown where all expected to see a body, and there was nothing.

"What do you think it meant?" she cried suddenly. "What is the explanation?"

"Perhaps we shall see now," answered the doctor.

Arthur still lingered, and she could not imagine what had become of him. All sorts of horrible fancies passed through her mind, and she dreaded she knew not what. At last they heard a footstep inside the house, and the door was opened.

"I was convinced that nobody slept here, but I was obliged to make sure. I had some difficulty in getting in."

Susie hesitated to enter. She did not know what horrors awaited her, and the darkness was terrifying.

"I cannot see," she said.

"I've brought a torch," said Arthur.

He pressed a button, and a narrow ray of bright light was cast upon the floor. Dr Porhoët and Susie went in. Arthur carefully closed the door, and flashed the light of his torch all round them. They stood in a large hall, the floor of which was scattered with the skins of lions that Haddo on his celebrated expedition had killed in Africa. There were perhaps a dozen, and their number gave a wild, barbaric note. A great oak staircase led to the upper floors.

"We must go through all the rooms," said Arthur.

He did not expect to find Haddo till they came to the lighted attics, but it seemed needful nevertheless to pass right through the house on their way. A flash of his torch had shown him that the walls of the hall were decorated with all manner of armour, ancient swords of Eastern handiwork, barbaric weapons from central Africa, savage implements of medieval warfare; and an idea came to him. He took down a huge battle-axe and swung it in his hand.

"Now come."

Silently, holding their breath as though they feared to wake the dead, they went into the first room. They saw it difficultly with their scant light, since the thin shaft of brilliancy, emphasising acutely the surrounding darkness, revealed it only piece by piece. It was a large room, evidently unused, for the furniture was covered with holland, and there was a mustiness about it which suggested that the windows were seldom opened. As in many old houses, the rooms led not from a passage but into one another, and they walked through many till they came back into the hall. They had all a desolate, uninhabited air. Their sombreness was increased by the oak with which they were panelled. There was panelling in the hall too, and on the stairs that led broadly to the top of the house. As they ascended, Arthur stopped for one moment and passed his hand over the polished wood.

"It would burn like tinder," he said.

They went through the rooms on the first floor, and they were as empty and as cheerless. Presently they came to that which had been Margaret's. In a bowl were dead flowers. Her brushes were still on the toilet table. But it was a gloomy chamber, with its dark oak, and so comfortless that Susie shuddered. Arthur stood for a time and looked at it, but he said nothing. They found themselves again on the stairs and they went to the second storey. But here they seemed to be at the top of the house.

"How does one get up to the attics?" said Arthur, looking about him with surprise.

He paused for a while to think. Then he nodded his head.

"There must be some steps leading out of one of the rooms."

They went on. And now the ceilings were much lower, with heavy beams, and there was no furniture at all. The emptiness seemed to make everything more terrifying. They felt that they were on the threshold of a great mystery, and Susie's heart began to beat fast. Arthur conducted his examination with the greatest method; he walked round each room carefully, looking for a door that might lead to a staircase; but there was no sign of one.

"What will you do if you can't find the way up?" asked Susie.

"I shall find the way up," he answered.

They came to the staircase once more and had discovered nothing. They looked at one another helplessly.

"It's quite clear there is a way," said Arthur, with impatience.

"There must be something in the nature of a hidden door some-where or other."

He leaned against the balustrade and meditated. The light of his lantern threw a narrow ray upon the opposite wall.

"I feel certain it must be in one of the rooms at the end of the house. That seems the most natural place to put a means of ascent to the attics."

They went back, and again he examined the panelling of a small room that had outside walls on three sides of it. It was the only room that did not lead into another.

"It must be here," he said.

Presently he gave a little laugh, for he saw that a small door was concealed by the woodwork. He pressed it where he thought there might be a spring, and it flew open. Their torch showed them a narrow wooden staircase. They walked up and found themselves in front of a door. Arthur tried it, but it was locked. He smiled grimly.

"Will you get back a little," he said.

He lifted his axe and swung it down upon the latch. The handle was shattered, but the lock did not yield. He shook his head. As he paused for a moment, and there was a complete silence, Susie distinctly heard a slight noise. She put her hand on Arthur's arm to call his attention to it, and with strained ears they listened. There was something alive on the other side of the door. They heard its curious sound: it was not that of a human voice, it was not the crying of an animal, it was extraordinary.

It was the sort of gibber, hoarse and rapid, and it filled them with an icy terror because it was so weird and so unnatural.

"Come away, Arthur," said Susie. "Come away."

"There's some living thing in there," he answered.

He did not know why the sound horrified him. The sweat broke out on his forehead.

"Something awful will happen to us," whispered Susie, shaking with uncontrollable fear.

"The only thing is to break the door down."

The horrid gibbering was drowned by the noise he made. Quickly, without pausing, he began to hack at the oak door with all his might. In rapid succession his heavy blows rained down, and the sound echoed through the empty house. There was a crash, and the door swung back. They had been so long in almost total darkness that they were blinded for an instant by the dazzling light. And then instinctively they started back, for, as the door opened, a wave of heat came out upon them so that they could hardly breathe. The place was like an oven.

They entered. It was lit by enormous lamps, the light of which was increased by reflectors, and warmed by a great furnace. They could not understand why so intense a heat was necessary. The narrow windows were closed. Dr Porhoët caught sight of a thermometer and was astounded at the temperature it indicated. The room was used evidently as a laboratory. On broad tables were test-tubes, basins and baths of white porcelain, measuring-glasses, and utensils of all sorts; but the surprising thing was the great scale upon which everything was. Neither Arthur nor Dr Porhoët had ever seen such gigantic measures nor such large test-tubes. There were rows of bottles, like those in the dispensary of a hospital, each containing great quanties of a different chemical. The three friends stood in silence. The emptiness of the room contrasted so oddly with its appearance of being in immediate use that it was uncanny. Susie felt that he who worked there was in the midst of his labours, and might return at any moment; he could have only gone for an instant into another chamber in order to see the progress of some experiment. It was quite silent. Whatever had made those vague, unearthly noises was hushed by their approach.

The door was closed between this room and the next. Arthur opened it, and they found themselves in a long, low attic, ceiled with great rafters, as brilliantly lit and as hot as the first. Here too were broad tables laden with retorts, instruments for heating, huge test-tubes, and all manner of vessels. The furnace that warmed it gave a steady heat. Arthur's gaze travelled slowly from table to table, and he wondered what Haddo's experiments had really been. The air was heavy with an extraordinary odour: it was not musty, like that of the closed rooms through which they had passed, but singularly pungent, disagreeable and sickly. He asked himself what it could spring from. Then his eyes fell upon a huge receptacle that stood on the table nearest to the furneace. It was covered with a white cloth. He took it off. The vessel was about four feet high, round, and shaped somewhat like a washing tub, but it was made of glass more than an inch thick. In it a spherical mass, a little larger than a football, of a peculiar, livid colour. The surface was smooth, but rather coarsely grained, and over it ran a dense system of blood-vessels. It reminded, the two medical men of those huge tumours which are preserved in spirit in hospital museums. Susie looked at it with an incomprehensible disgust. Suddenly she gave a cry.

"Good God, it's moving!"

Arthur put his hand on her arm quickly to quieten her and bent down with irresistible curiosity. They saw that it was a mass of flesh unlike that of any human being; and it pulsated regularly. The movement was quite distinct, up and down, like the delicate heaving of a woman's breast when she is asleep. Arthur touched the thing with one finger and it shrank slightly.

"Its quite warm," he said.

He turned it over, and it remained in the position in which he had placed it, as if there were neither top nor bottom to it. But they could see now, irregularly placed on one side, a few short hairs. They were just like human hairs.

"Is it alive?" whispered Susie, struck with horror and amazement.

"Yes!"

Arthur seemed fascinated. He could not take his eyes off the loathsome thing. He watched it slowly heave with even motion.

"What can it mean?" he asked.

He looked at Dr Porhoët with pale startled face. A thought was coming to him, but a thought so unnatural, extravagant, and terrible that he pushed it from him with a movement of both hands, as though it were a material thing. Then all three turned around abruptly with a start, for they heard again the wild gibbering which had first shocked their ears. In the wonder of this revolting object they had forgotten all the rest. The sound seemed extraordinarily near, and Susie drew back instinctively, for it appeared to come from her very side.

"There's nothing here," said Arthur. "It must be in the next room."

"Oh, Arthur, let us go," cried Susie. "I'm afraid to see what may be in store for us. It is nothing to us, and what we see may poison our sleep for ever."

She looked appealingly at Dr Porhoët. He was white and anxious. The heat of that place had made the sweat break out on his forehead.

"I have seen enough. I want to see no more," he said.

"Then you may go, both of you," answered Arthur. "I do not wish to force you to see anything. But I shall go on. Whatever it is, I wish to find out."

"But Haddo? Supposing he is there, waiting? Perhaps you are only walking into a trap that he has set for you."

"I am convinced that Haddo is dead."

Again that unintelligible jargon, unhuman and shrill, fell upon their ears, and Arthur stepped forward. Susie did not hesitate. She was prepared to follow him anywhere. He opened the door, and there was a sudden quiet. Whatever made those sounds was there. It was a larger room than any on the others and much higher, for it ran along the whole front of the house. The powerful lamps showed every corner of it at once, but, above, the beams of the open ceiling were dark with shadow.

And here the nauseous odour, which had struck them before, was so overpowering that for a while they could not go in. It was indescribably foul. Even Arthur thought it would make him sick, and he looked at the windows to see if it was possible to open them; but it seemed they were hermetically closed. The extreme warmth made the air more overpowering.

There were four furnaces here, and they were all alight. In order to give out more heat and to burn slowly, the fronts of them were open, and one could see that they were filled with glowing coke.

The room was furnished no differently from the others, but to the various instruments for chemical operations on a large scale were added all manner of electrical appliances. Several books were lying about, and one had been left open face downwards on the edge of a table. But what immediately attracted their atention was a row of those large glass vessels like that which they had seen in the adjoining room. Each was covered with a white cloth. They hesitated a moment, for they knew that here they were face to face with the great enigma. At last Arthur pulled away the cloth from one. None of them spoke. They stared with astonished eyes. For here, too, was a strange mass of flesh, almost as large as a new-born child, but there was in it the beginnings of something ghastly human. It was shaped vaguely like an infant, but the legs were joined together so that it looked like a mummy rolled up in its coverings. There were neither feet nor knees. The trunk was formless, but there was a curious thickening on each side; it was as if a modeller had meant to make a figure with the arms loosely bent, but had left the work unfinished so that they were still one with the body. There was something that resembled a human head, covered with long golden hair, but it was horrible; it was an uncouth mass, without eyes or nose or mouth. The colour was a kind of sickly pink, and it was almost transparent. There was a very slight movement in it, rhythmical and slow. It was living too.

Then quickly Arthur removed the covering from all the other jars but one; and in a flash of the eyes they saw abominations so awful that Susie had to clench her fists in order not to scream. There was one monstrous thing in which the limbs approached nearly to the human. It was extraordinarily heaped up, with fat tiny arms, little bloated legs, and an absurd squat body, so that it looked like a Chinese mandarin in porcelain. In another the trunk was almost like that of a human child, except that it was patched strangely with red and grey. But the terror of it was that at the neck it branched hideously, and there were two distinct heads, monstrously large, but duly provided with all their features. The features were a caricature of humanity so shameful that one could hardly bear to look. And as the light fell on it, the eyes of each head opened slowly. They had no pigment in them, but were pink, like the eyes of white rabbits; and they stared for a moment with an odd, unseeing glance. Then they were shut again, and what was curiously terrifying was that the movements were not quite simultaneous; the eyelids of one head fell slowly just before those of the other. And in another place was a ghastly monster in which it seemed that two bodies had been dreadfully entangled with one another. It was a creature of nightmare, with four arms and four legs, and this one actually moved. With a peculiar motion it crawled along the bottom of the great receptacle in which it was kept, towards the three persons who looked at it. It seemed to wonder what they did. Susie started back with fright, as it raised itself on its four legs and tried to reach up to them.

Susie turned away and hid her face. She could not look at those ghastly counterfeits of humanity. She was terrified and ashamed.

"Do you understand what this means?" said Dr Porhoët to Arthur, in an awed voice. "It means that he has discovered the secret of life."

"Was it for these vile monstrosities that Margaret was sacrificed in all her loveliness?"

The two men looked at one another with sad, wondering eyes.

"Don't you remember that he talked of the manufacture of human beings? It's these misshapen things that he's succeeding in producing," said the doctor.

"There is one more that we haven't seen," said Arthur.

He pointed to the covering which still hid the largest of the vases. He had a feeling that it contained the most fearful of all these monsters; and it was not without an effort that he drew the cloth away. But no sooner had he done this than something sprang up, so that instinctively he started back, and it began to gibber in piercing tones. These were the unearthly sounds that they had heard. It was not a voice, it was a kind of raucous crying, hoarse yet shrill, uneven like the barking of a dog, and appalling. The sounds came forth in rapid succession, angrily, as though the being that uttered them sought to express itself in furious words. It was mad with passion and beat against the glass walls of its prison with clenched fists. For the hands were human hands, and the body, though much larger, was of the shape of a new-born child. The creature must have stood about four feet high. The head was horribly misshapen. The skull was enormous, smooth and distended like that of a hydrocephalic, and the forehead protruded over the face hideously. The features were almost unformed, preternaturally small under the great, overhanging brow; and they had an expression of fiendish malignity.

The tiny, misshapen countenance writhed with convulsive fury, and from the mouth poured out a foaming spume. It raised its voice higher and higher, shrieking senseless gibberish in its rage. Then it began to hurl its whole body madly against the glass walls and to beat its head. It appeared to have a sudden incomprehensible hatred for the three strangers. It was trying to fly at them. The toothless gums moved spasmodically, and it threw its face into horrible grimaces. That nameless, loathsome abortion was the nearest that Oliver Haddo had come to the human form.

"Come away," said Arthur. "We must not look at this."

He quickly flung the covering over the jar.

"Yes, for God's sake let us go," said Susie.

"We haven't done yet," answered Arthur. "We haven't found the author of all this."

He looked at the room in which they were, but there was no door except that by which they had entered. Then he uttered a startled cry, and stepping forward fell on his knee.

On the other side of the long tables heaped up with instruments, hidden so that at first they had not seen him, Oliver Haddo lay on the floor, dead. His blue eyes were staring wide, and they seemed larger than they had ever been. They kept still the expression of terror which they had worn in the moment of his agony, and his heavy face was distorted with deadly fear. It was purple and dark, and the eyes were injected with blood.

"He died of suffocation," whispered Dr Porhoët.

Arthur pointed to the neck. There could be seen on it distinctly the marks of the avenging fingers that had strangled the life out of him. It was impossible to hesitate.

"I told you that I had killed him," said Arthur.

Then he remembered something more. He took hold of the right arm. He was convinced that it had been broken during that desperate struggle in the darkness. He felt it carefully and listened. He heard plainly the two parts of the bone rub against one another. The dead man's arm was broken just in the place where he had broken it. Arthur stood up. He took one last look at his enemy. That vast mass of flesh lay heaped up on the floor in horrible disorder.

"Now that you have seen, will you come away?" said Susie, interrupting him.

The words seemed to bring him suddenly to himself.

"Yes, we must go quickly."

They turned away and with hurried steps walked through those bright attics till they came to the stairs.

"Now go down and wait for me at the door," said Arthur. "I will follow you immediately."

"What are you going to do?" asked Susie.

"Never mind. Do as I tell you. I have not finished here yet."

They went down the great oak staircase and waited in the hall. They wondered what Arthur was about. Presently he came running down.

"Be quick!" he cried. "We have no time to lose."

"What have you done, Arthur?"

"There's no time to tell you now."

He hurried them out and slammed the door behind him. He took Susie's hand.

"Now we must run. Come."

She did not know what his haste signified, but her heart beat furiously. He dragged her along. Dr Porhoët hurried on behind them. Arthur plunged into the wood. He would not leave them time to breathe.

"You must be quick," he said.

At last they came to the opening in the fence, and he helped them to get through. Then he carefully replaced the wooden paling and, taking Susie's arm began to walk rapidly towards their inn.

"I'm frightfully tired," she said. "I simply can't go so fast."

"You must. Presently you can rest as long as you like."

They walked very quickly for a while. Now and then Arthur looked back. The night was still quite dark, and the stars shone out in their myriads. At last he slackened their pace.

"Now you can go more slowly," he said.

Susie saw the smiling glance that he gave her. His eyes were full of tenderness. He put his arm affectionately round her shoulders to support her.

"I'm afraid you're quite exhausted, poor thing," he said. "I'm sorry to have had to hustle you so much."

"It doesn't matter at all."

She leaned against him comfortably. With that protecting arm about her, she felt capable of any fatigue. Dr Porhoët stopped.

"You must really let me roll myself a cigarette," he said.

"You may do whatever you like," answered Arthur.

There was a different ring in his voice now, and it was soft with a good-humour that they had not heard in it for many months. He appeared singularly relieved. Susie was ready to forget the terrible past and give herself over to the happiness that seemed at last in store for her. They began to saunter slowly on. And now they could take pleasure in the exquisite night. The air was very suave, odorous with the heather that was all about them, and there was an enchanting peace in that scene which wonderfully soothed their weariness. It was dark still, but they knew the dawn was at hand, and Susie rejoiced in the approaching day. In the east the azure of the night began to thin away into pale amethyst, and the trees seemed gradually to stand out from the darkness in a ghostly beauty. Suddenly birds began to sing all around them in a splendid chorus. From their feet a lark sprang up with a rustle of wings and, mounting proudly upon the air, chanted blithe canticles to greet the morning. They stood upon a little hill.

"Let us wait here and see the sun rise," said Susie.

"As you will."

They stood all three of them, and Susie took in deep, joyful breaths of the sweet air of dawn. The whole land, spread at her feet, was clothed in the purple dimness that heralds day, and she exulted in its beauty. But she noticed that Arthur, unlike herself and Dr Porhoët, did not look toward the east. His eyes were fixed steadily upon the place from which they had come. What did he look for in the darkness of the west? She turned round, and a cry broke from her lips, for the shadows there were lurid with a deep red glow.

"It looks like a fire," she said.

"It is. Skene is burning like tinder."

And as he spoke it seemed that the roof fell in, for suddenly vast flames sprang up, rising high into the still night air; and they saw that the house they had just left was blazing furiously. It was a magnificent sight from the distant hill on which they stood to watch the fire as it soared and sank, as it shot scarlet tongues along like strange Titanic monsters, as it raged from room to room. Skene was burning. It was beyond the reach of human help. In a little while there would be no trace of all those crimes and all those horrors. Now it was one mass of flame. It looked like some primeval furnace, where the gods might work unheard-of miracles.

"Arthur, what have you done?" asked Susie, in a tone that was hardly audible.

He did not answer directly. He put his arm about her shoulder again, so that she was obliged to turn round.

"Look, the sun is rising."

In the east, a long ray of light climbed up the sky, and the sun, yellow and round, appeared upon the face of the earth.

6

@

From *Of Human Bondage*
(1915)

10

The Careys made up their minds to send Philip to King's School at Tercanbury. The neighbouring clergy sent their sons there. It was united by long tradition to the Cathedral: its headmaster was an honorary Canon, and a past headmaster was the Archdeacon. Boys were encouraged there to aspire to Holy Orders, and the education was such as might prepare an honest lad to spend his life in God's service. A preparatory school was attached to it, and to this it was arranged that Philip should go. Mr Carey took him into Tercanbury one Thursday afternoon towards the end of September. All day Philip had been excited and rather frightened. He knew little of school life but what he had read in the stories of *The Boy's Own Paper*. He had also read *Eric, or Little by Little*.

When they got out of the train at Tercanbury, Philip felt sick with apprehension, and during the drive in to the town sat pale and silent. The high brick wall in front of the school gave it the look of a prison. There was a little door in it, which opened on their ringing; and a clumsy, untidy man came out and fetched Philip's tin trunk and his play-box. They were shown into the drawing-room; it was filled with massive, ugly furniture, and the chairs of the suite were placed round the walls with a forbidding rigidity. They waited for the headmaster.

"What's Mr Watson like?" asked Philip, after a while.

"You'll see for yourself."

There was another pause. Mr Carey wondered why the headmaster did not come. Presently Philip made an effort and spoke again.

"Tell him I've got a club-foot," he said.

Before Mr Carey could speak the door burst open and Mr Watson swept into the room. To Philip he seemed gigantic. He was a man of over six feet high, and broad, with enormous hands and a great red beard; he talked loudly in a jovial manner; but his aggressive cheerfulness struck terror in Philip's heart. He shook hands with Mr Carey, and then took Philip's small hand in his.

"Well, young fellow, are you glad to come to school?" he shouted.

Philip reddened and found no word to answer.

"How old are you?"

"Nine," said Philip.

"You must say sir," said his uncle.

"I expect you've got a good lot to learn," the headmaster bellowed cheerily.

To give the boy confidence he began to tickle him with rough fingers. Philip, feeling shy and uncomfortable, squirmed under his touch.

"I've put him in the small dormitory for the present. . . . You'll like that, won't you?" he added to Philip. "Only eight of you in there. You won't feel so strange."

Then the door opened, and Mrs Watson came in. She was a dark woman with black hair, neatly parted in the middle. She had curiously thick lips and a small round nose. Her eyes were large and black. There was a singular coldness in her appearance. She seldom spoke and smiled more seldom still. Her husband introduced Mr Carey to her, and then gave Philip a friendly push towards her.

"This is a new boy, Helen. His name's Carey."

Without a word she shook hands with Philip and then sat down, not speaking, while the headmaster asked Mr Carey how much Philip knew and what books he had been working with. The Vicar of Blackstable was a little embarrassed by Mr Watson's boisterous heartiness, and in a moment or two got up.

"I think I'd better leave Philip with you now."

"That's all right," said Mr Watson. "He'll be safe with me. He'll get on like a house on fire. Won't you, young fellow?"

Without waiting for an answer from Philip the big man burst into a great bellow of laughter. Mr Carey kissed Philip on the forehead and went away.

"Come along, young fellow," shouted Mr Watson. "I'll show you the school-room."

He swept out of the drawing-room with giant strides, and Philip hurriedly limped behind him. He was taken into a long, bare room with two tables that ran along its whole length; on each side of them were wooden forms.

"Nobody much here yet," said Mr Watson. "I'll just show you the play-ground, and then I'll leave you to shift for yourself."

Mr Watson led the way. Philip found himself in a large play-ground with high brick walls on three sides of it. On the fourth side was an iron railing through which you saw a vast lawn and beyond this some of the buildings of King's School. One small boy was wandering disconsolately, kicking up the gravel as he walked.

"Hulloa, Venning," shouted Mr Watson. "When did you turn up?"

The small boy came forward and shook hands.

"Here's a new boy. He's older and bigger than you, so don't you bully him."

The headmaster glared amicably at the two children, filling them with fear by the roar of his voice, and then with a guffaw left them.

"What's your name?"

"Carey."

"What's your father?"

"He's dead."

"Oh! Does your mother wash?"

"My mother's dead, too."

Philip thought this answer would cause the boy a certain awkwardness, but Venning was not to be turned from his facetiousness for so little.

"Well, did she wash?" he went on.

"Yes," said Philip indignantly.

"She was a washerwoman then?"

"No, she wasn't."

"Then she didn't wash."

The little boy crowed with delight at the success of his dialectic. Then he caught sight of Philip's feet.

"What's the matter with your foot?"

Philip instinctively tried to withdraw it from sight. He hid it behind the one which was whole.

"I've got a club-foot," he answered.

"How did you get it?"

"I've always had it."

"Let's have a look."

"No."

"Don't then."

The little boy accompanied the words with a sharp kick on Philip's shin, which Philip did not expect and thus could not guard against. The pain was so great that it made him gasp, but greater than the pain was the surprise. He did not know why Venning kicked him. He had not the presence of mind to give him a black eye. Besides, the boy was smaller than he, and he had read in *The Boy's Own Paper* that it was a mean thing to hit anyone smaller than yourself. While Philip was nursing his shin a third boy appeared, and his tormentor left him. In a little while he noticed that the pair were talking about him, and he felt they were looking at his feet. He grew hot and uncomfortable.

But others arrived, a dozen together, and then more, and they began to talk about their doings during the holidays, where they had been, and what wonderful cricket they had played. A few new boys appeared, and with these presently Philip found himself talking. He was shy and nervous. He was anxious to make himself pleasant, but he could not think of anything to say. He was asked a great many questions and answered them all quite willingly. One boy asked him whether he could play cricket.

"No," answered Philip. "I've got a club-foot."

The boy looked down quickly and reddened. Philip saw that he felt he had asked an unseemly question. He was too shy to apologise and looked at Philip awkwardly.

11

Next morning when the clanging of a bell awoke Philip he looked round his cubicle in astonishment. Then a voice sang out, and he remembered where he was.

"Are you awake, Singer?"

The partitions of the cubicle were of polished pitch-pine, and there was a green curtain in front. In those days there was little thought of ventilation, and the windows were closed except when the dormitory was aired in the morning.

Philip got up and knelt down to say his prayers. It was a cold morning, and he shivered a little; but he had been taught by his uncle that his prayers were more acceptable to God if he said them in his nightshirt than if he waited till he was dressed. This did not surprise him, for he was beginning to realise that he was the creature of a God who appreciated the discomfort of his worshippers. Then he washed. There were two baths for the fifty boarders, and each boy had a bath once a week. The rest of his washing was done in a small basin on a wash-stand, which, with the bed and a chair, made up the furniture of each cubicle. The boys chatted gaily while they dressed. Philip was all ears. Then another bell sounded, and they ran downstairs. They took their seats on the forms on each side of the two long tables in the school-room; and Mr Watson, followed by his wife and the servants, came in and sat down. Mr Watson read prayers in an impressive manner, and the supplications thundered out in his loud voice as though they were threats personally addressed to each boy. Philip listened with anxiety. Then Mr Watson read a chapter from the Bible, and the servants trooped out. In a moment the untidy youth brought in two large pots of tea and on a second journey immense dishes of bread and butter.

Philip had a squeamish appetite, and the thick slabs of poor butter on the bread turned his stomach, but he saw other boys scraping it off and followed their example. They all had potted meats and such like, which they had brought in their play-boxes; and some had 'extras,' eggs or bacon, upon which Mr Watson made a profit. When he had asked Mr Carey whether Philip was to have these, Mr Carey replied that he did not think boys should be spoilt. Mr Watson quite agreed with him—he considered nothing was better than bread and butter for growing lads—but some parents, unduly pampering their offspring, insisted on it.

Philip noticed that 'extras' gave boys a certain consideration and made up his mind, when he wrote to Aunt Louisa, to ask for them.

After breakfast the boys wandered out into the play-ground. Here the day-boys were gradually assembling. They were sons of the local clergy, of the officers at the Depot, and of such manufacturers of men of business as the old town possessed. Presently a bell rang, and they all trooped into school. This consisted of a large, long room at opposite ends of which two under-masters conducted the second and third forms, and of a smaller one, leading out of it, used by Mr Watson, who taught the first form. To attach the preparatory to the senior school these three classes were known officially, on speech days and in reports, as upper, middle, and lower second. Philip was put in the last. The master, a red-faced man with a pleasant voice, was called Rice; he had a jolly manner with boys, and the time passed quickly. Philip was surprised when it was a quarter to eleven and they were let out for ten minutes' rest.

The whole school rushed noisily into the play-ground. The new boys were told to go into the middle, while the others stationed themselves along opposite walls. They began to play *Pig in the Middle*. The old boys ran from wall to wall while the new boys tried to catch them: when one was seized and the mystic words said—one, two, three, and a pig for me—he became a prisoner and, turning sides, helped to catch those who were still free. Philip saw a boy running past and tried to catch him, but his limp gave him no chance; and the runners, taking their opportunity, made straight for the ground he covered. Then one of them had the brilliant idea of imitating Philip's clumsy run. Other boys saw it and began to laugh; then the all copied the first; and they ran round Philip, limping grotesquely, screaming in their treble voices with shrill laughter. They lost their heads with the delight of their new amusement, and choked with helpless merriment. One of them tripped Philip up and he fell, heavily as he always fell, and cut his knee. They laughed all the louder when he got up. A boy pushed him from behind, and he would have fallen again if another had not caught him. The game was forgotten in the entertainment of Philip's deformity. One of them invented an odd, rolling limp that struck the rest as supremely ridiculous, and several of the boys lay down on the ground and rolled about in laughter: Philip was completely scared. He could not make out why they were laughing at him. His heart beat so that he could hardly breathe, and he was more frightened than he had ever been in his life. He stood still stupidly while the boys ran round him, mimicking and laughing; they shouted to him to try and catch them; but he did not move. He did not want them to see him run any more. He was using all his strength to prevent himself from crying.

Suddenly the bell rang, and they all trooped back to school. Philip's knee was bleeding, and he was dusty and dishevelled. For some minutes Mr Rice could not control his form. They were excited still by the strange novelty, and Philip saw one or two of them furtively looking down at his feet. He tucked them under the bench.

In the afternoon they went up to play football, but Mr Watson stopped Philip on the way out after dinner.

"I suppose you can't play football, Carey?" he asked him. Philip blushed self-consciously.

"No, sir."

"Very well. You'd better go up to the field. You can walk as far as that, can't you?"

Philip had no idea where the field was, but he answered all the same.

"Yes, sir."

The boys went in charge of Mr Rice, who glanced at Philip and; seeing he had not changed, asked why he was not going to play.

"Mr Watson said I needn't, sir," said Philip.

"Why?"

There were boys all round him, looking at him curiously, and a feeling of shame came over Philip. He looked down without answering. Other gave the reply.

"He's got a club-foot, sir."

"Oh, I see."

Mr Rice was quite young; he had only taken his degree a year before; and he was suddenly embarrassed. His instinct was to beg the boy's pardon, but he was too shy to do so. He made his voice gruff and loud.

"Now then, you boys, what are you waiting about for? Get on with you."

Some of them had already started and those that were left now set off, in groups of two or three.

"You'd better come along with me, Carey," said the master. "You don't know the way, do you?"

Philip guessed the kindness, and a sob came to his throat.

"I can't go very fast, sir."

"Then I'll go very slow," said the master, with a smile.

Philip's heart went out to the red-faced, commonplace young man who said a gentle word to him. He suddenly felt less unhappy.

But at night when they went up to bed and were undressing, the boy who was called Singer came out of his cubicle and put his head in Philip's.

"I say, let's look at your foot," he said.

"No," answered Philip.

He jumped into bed quickly.

"Don't say no to me," said Singer. "Come on, Mason."

The boy in the next cubicle was looking round the corner, and at the words he slipped in. They made for Philip and tried to tear the bed-clothes off him, but he held them tightly.

"Why can't you leave me alone?" he cried.

Singer seized a brush and with the back of it beat Philip's hands clenched on the blanket. Philip cried out.

"Why don't you show us your foot quietly?"

"I won't."

In desperation Philip clenched his fist and hit the boy who tormented him, but he was at a disadvantage, and the boy seized his arm. He began to turn it.

"Oh, don't, don't," said Philip. "You'll break my arm."

"Stop still then and put out your foot."

Philip gave a sob and a gasp. The boy gave the arm another wrench. The pain was unendurable.

"All right. I'll do it," said Philip.

He put out his foot. Singer still kept his hand on Philip's wrist. He looked curiously at the deformity.

"Isn't it beastly?" said Mason.

Another came in and looked too.

"Ugh," he said, in disgust.

"My word, it is rum," said Singer, making a face. "Is it hard?"

He touched it with the tip of his forefinger, cautiously, as though it were something that had a life of its own. Suddenly they heard Mr Watson's heavy tread on the stairs. They threw the clothes back on Philip and dashed like rabbits into their cubicles. Mr Watson came into the dormitory. Raising himself on tiptoe he could see over the rod that bore the green curtain, and he looked into two or three of the cubicles. The little boys were safely in bed. He put out the light and went out.

Singer called out to Philip, but he did not answer. He had got his teeth in the pillow so that his sobbing should be inaudible. He was not crying for the pain they had caused him, nor for the humiliation he had suffered when they looked at his foot, but with rage at himself because, unable to stand the torture, he had put out his foot of his own accord.

And then he felt the misery of his life. It seemed to his childish mind that this unhappiness must go on for ever. For no particular reason he remembered that cold morning when Emma had taken him out of bed and put him beside his mother. He had not thought of it once since it happened, but now he seemed to feel the warmth of his mother's body against his and her arms around him, Suddenly it seemed to him that his life was a dream, his mother's death, and the life at the vicarage, and these two wretched days at school, and he would awake in the morning and be back again at home. His tears dried as he thought of it. He was too unhappy, it must be nothing but a dream, and his mother was alive, and Emma would come up presently and go to bed. He fell asleep.

But when he awoke next morning it was to the clanging of a bell, and the first thing his eyes saw was the green curtain of his cubicle.

12

As time went on Philip's deformity ceased to interest. It was accepted like one boy's red hair and another's unreasonable corpulence. But meanwhile he had grown horribly sensitive. He never ran if he could help it, because he knew it made his limp more conspicuous, and he adopted a peculiar walk. He stood still as much as he could, with his club-foot behind the other, so that it should not attract notice, and he was constantly on the look out for any reference to it. Because he could not join in the games which other boys played, their life remained strange to him; he only interested himself from the outside in their doings; and it seemed to him that there was a barrier between them and him. Sometimes they seemed to think that it was his fault if he could not play football, and he was unable to make them understand. He was left a good deal to himself. He had been inclined to talkativeness, but gradually he became silent. He began to think of the difference between himself and others.

The biggest boy in his dormitory, Singer, took a dislike to him, and Philip, small for his age, had to put up with a good deal of hard treatment. About half-way through the term a mania ran through the school for a game called Nibs. It was a game for two, played on a table or a form with steel pens. You had to push your nib with the fingernail so as to get the point of it over your opponent's, while he manœuvred to prevent this and to get the point of his nib over the back of yours; when this result was achieved you breathed on the ball of your thumb, pressed it hard on the two nibs, and if you were able then to lift them without dropping either, both nibs became yours. Soon nothing was seen but boys playing this game, and the more skilful acquired vast stores of nibs. But in a little while Mr Watson made up his mind that it was a form of gambling, forbade the game, and confiscated all the nibs in the boys' possession. Philip had been very adroit, and it was with a heavy heart that he gave up his winnings; but his fingers itched to play still, and a few days later, on his way to the football field, he went into a shop and bought a pennyworth of J pens. He carried them loose in his pocket and enjoyed feeling them. Presently Singer found out that he had them. Singer had given up his nibs too, but he had kept back a very large one, called a Jumbo, which was almost unconquerable, and he could not resist the opportunity of getting Philip's Js out of him. Though Philip knew that he was at a disadvantage with his small nibs, he had an adventurous disposition and was willing to take the risk; besides, he was aware that Singer would not allow him to refuse. He had not played for a week and sat down to the game now with a thrill of excitement. He lost two of his small nibs quickly, and Singer was jubilant, but the third time by some chance the Jumbo slipped round and Philip was able to push his J across it. He crowed with triumph. At that moment Mr Watson came in.

"What are you doing?" he asked.

He looked from Singer to Philip, but neither answered.

"Don't you know that I've forbidden you to play that idiotic game?"

Philip's heart beat fast. He knew what was coming and was dreadfully frightened, but in his fright there was a certain exultation. He had never been swished. Of course it would hurt, but it was something to boast about afterwards.

"Come into my study."

The headmaster turned, and they followed him side by side. Singer whispered to Philip:

"We're in for it."

Mr Watson pointed to Singer.

"Bend over," he said.

Philip, very white, saw the boy quiver at each stroke, and after the third he heard him cry out. Three more followed.

"That'll do. Get up."

Singer stood up. The tears were streaming down his face. Philip stepped forward. Mr Watson looked at him for a moment.

"I'm not going to cane you. You're a new boy. And I can't hit a cripple. Go away, both of you, and don't be naughty again."

When they got back into the school-room a group of boys, who had learned in some mysterious way what was happening, were waiting for them. They set upon Singer at once with eager questions. Singer faced them, his face red with the pain and marks of tears still on his cheeks. he pointed with his head at Philip, who was standing a little behind him.

"He got off because he's a cripple," he said angrily.

Philip stood silent and flushed. He felt that they looked at him with contempt.

"How many did you get?" one boy asked Singer.

But he did not answer. He was angry because he had been hurt.

"Don't ask me to play Nibs with you again," he said to Philip. "It's jolly nice for you. You don't risk anything."

"I didn't ask you."

"Didn't you!"

He quickly put out his foot and tripped Philip up. Philip was always rather unsteady on his feet, and he fell heavily to the ground.

"Cripple," said Singer.

For the rest of the term he tormented Philip cruelly, and, though Philip tried to keep out of his way, the school was so small that it was impossible; he tried being friendly and jolly with him; he abased himself so far as to buy him a knife; but though Singer took the knife he was not placated. Once or twice, driven beyond endurance, he hit and kicked the bigger boy, but Singer was so much stronger that Philip was helpless, and he was always forced after more or less torture to beg his pardon. It was that which rankled with Philip: he could not bear the humiliation of apologies, which were wrung from him by pain greater than he could bear. And what made it worse was that there seemed no end to his wretchedness; Singer was only eleven and would not go to the upper school till he was thirteen. Philip realized that he must live two years with a tormentor from whom there was no escape. He was only happy while he was working and when he got into bed. And often there recurred to him then that queer feeling that his life with all its misery was nothing but a dream, and that he would awake in the morning in his own little bed in London.

13

Two years passed, and Philip was nearly twelve. He was in the first form, within two or three places of the top, and after Christmas when several boys would be leaving for the senior school he would be head boy. He had already quite a collection of prizes, worthless books on bad paper, but in gorgeous bindings decorated with the arms of the school: his position had freed him from bullying, and he was not unhappy. His fellows forgave him his success because of his deformity.

"After all, it's jolly easy for him to get prizes," they said, "there's nothing he can do but swot."

He had lost his early terror of Mr Watson. He had grown used to the loud voice, and when the headmaster's heavy hand was laid on his shoulder Philip discerned vaguely the intention of a caress. He had the good memory which is more useful for scholastic achievements than mental power, and he knew Mr Watson expected him to leave the preparatory school with a scholarship.

But he had grown very self-conscious. The new-born child does not realise that his body is more a part of himself than surrounding objects, and will play with his toes without any feeling that they belong to him more than the rattle by his side; and it is only by degrees, through pain, that he understands the fact of the body. And experiences of the same kind are necessary for the individual to become conscious of himself; but here there is the difference that, although everyone becomes equally conscious of his body as a separate and complete organism, everyone does not become equally conscious of himself as a complete and separate personality. The feeling of apartness from others comes to most with puberty, but it is not always developed to such a degree as to make the difference between the individual and his fellows noticeable to the individual. It is such as he, as little conscious of himself as the bee in a hive, who are the lucky in life, for they have the best chance of happiness: their activities are shared by all, and their pleasures are only pleasures because they are enjoyed in common; you will see them on Whit-Monday dancing on Hampstead Heath, shouting at a football match, or from club windows in Pall Mall cheering a royal procession. It is because of them that man has been called a social animal.

Philip passed from the innocence of childhood to bitter consciousness of himself by the ridicule which his club-foot had excited. The circumstances of his case were so peculiar that he could not apply to them the ready-made rules which acted well enough in ordinary affairs, and he was forced to think for himself. The many books he had read filled his mind with ideas which, because he only half understood them, gave more scope to his imagination. Beneath his painful shyness something was growing up within him, and obscurely he realised his personality. But at times it gave him odd surprises; he did things, he knew not why, and afterwards when he thought of them found himself all at sea.

There was a boy called Luard between whom and Philip a friendship had arisen, and one day, when they were playing together in the schoolroom, Luard began to perform some trick with an ebony pen-holder of Philip's.

"Don't play the giddy ox," said Philip. "You'll only break it."

"I shan't."

But no sooner were the words out of the boy's mouth than the pen-holder snapped in two. Luard looked at Philip with dismay.

"Oh, I say, I'm awfully sorry."

The tears rolled down Philip's cheeks, but he did not answer.

"I say, what's the matter?" said Luard, with surprise. "I'll get you another one exactly the same."

"It's not about the pen-holder I care," said Philip, in a trembling
voice, "only it was given me by my mater, just before she died."

"I say, I'm awfully sorry, Carey."

"It doesn't matter. It wasn't your fault."

Philip took the two pieces of the pen-holder and looked at them.
He tried to restrain his sobs. He felt utterly miserable. And yet he
could not tell why, for he knew quite well that he had bought the pen-
holder during his last holidays at Blackstable for one and twopence.
He did not know in the least what had made him invent that pathetic
story, but he was quite as unhappy as though it had been true. The pious atmosphere of the vicarage and the religious tone of the school
had made Philip's conscience very sensitive; he absorbed insensibly the
feeling about him that the Tempter was ever on the watch to gain his
immortal soul; and though he was not more truthful than most boys
he never told a lie without suffering from remorse. When he thought
over this incident he was very much distressed, and made up his mind
that he must go to Luard and tell him that the story was an invention.
Though he dreaded humiliation more than anything in the world, he
hugged himself for two or three days at the thought of the agonising
joy of humiliating himself to the Glory of God. But he never got any
further. He satisfied his conscience by the more comfortable method
of expressing his repentance only to the Almighty. But he could not
understand why he should have been so genuinely affected by the story
he was making up. The tears that flowed down his grubby cheeks were
real tears. Then by some accident of association there occurred to him
that scene when Emma had told him of his mother's death, and,
though he could not speak for crying, he had insisted on going in to
say good-bye to the Misses Watkin so that they might see his grief and
pity him.

14

Then a wave of religiosity passed through the school. Bad language was
no longer heard, and the little nastinesses of small boys were looked

upon with hostility; the bigger boys, like the lords temporal of the Middle Ages, used the strength of their arms to persuade those weaker than themselves to virtuous courses.

Philip, his restless mind avid for new things, became very devout. He heard soon that it was possible to join Bible League, and wrote to London for particulars. These consisted in a form to be filled up with the applicant's name, age, and school; a solemn declaration to be signed that he would read a set portion of Holy Scripture every night for a year; and a request for half a crown; this, it was explained, was demanded partly to prove the earnestness of the applicant's desire to become a member of the League, and partly to cover clerical expenses. Philip duly sent the papers and the money, and in return received a calendar worth about a penny, on which was set down the appointed passage to be read each day, and a sheet of paper on one side of which was a picture of the Good Shepherd and a lamb, and on the other, decoratively framed in red lines, a short prayer which had to be said before beginning to read.

Every evening he undressed as quickly as possible in order to have time for his task before the gas was put out. He read industriously, as he read always, without criticism, stories of cruelty, deceit, ingratitude, dishonesty, and low cunning. Actions which would have excited his horror in the life about him, in the reading passed through his mind without comment, because they were committed under direct inspiration of God. The method of the League was to alternate a book of the Old Testament with a book of the New, and one night Philip came across these words of Jesus Christ:

> *If ye have faith, and doubt not, ye shall not only do this which is done to the fig-tree, but also if ye shall say unto this mountain, Be thou removed, and be thou cast into the sea; it shall be done.*
>
> *And all this, whatsoever ye shall ask in prayer, believing, ye shall receive.*

They made no particular impression on him, but it happened that two or three days later, being Sunday, the Canon in residence chose them for the text of his sermon. Even if Philip had wanted to hear this it would have been impossible, for the boys of King's School sit in the choir, and the pulpit stands at the corner of the transept so that the preacher's back is almost turned to them. The distance also is so great that it needs a man with a fine voice and a knowledge of elocution to make himself heard in the choir: and according to long usage the Canons of Tercanbury are chosen for their learning rather than for any qualities which might be of use in a cathedral church. But the words of the text, perhaps because he had read them so short a while before, came clearly enough to Philip's ears, and they seemed on a sudden to have a personal application. He thought about them through most of the sermon, and that night, on getting into bed, he turned over the pages of the Gospel and found once more the passage. Though he believed implicitly everything he saw in print, he had learned already that in the Bible things that said one thing quite clearly often mysteriously meant another. There was no one he liked to ask at school, so he kept the question he had in mind till the Christmas holidays, and then one day he made an opportunity. It was after supper and prayers were just finished. Mrs Carey was counting the eggs that Mary Ann had brought in as usual and writing on each one the date. Philip stood at the table and pretended to turn listlessly the pages of the Bible.

"I say, Uncle William, this passage here, does it really mean that?"

He put his finger against it as though he had come across it accidentally.

Mr Carey looked up over his spectacles. He was holding *The Blackstable Times* in fornt of the fire. It had come in that evening damp from the press, and the Vicar always aired it for ten minutes before he began to read.

"What passage is that?" he asked.

"Why, this about if you have faith you can remove mountains."

"If it says so in the Bible it is so, Philip," said Mrs Carey gently, taking up the plate-basket.

Philip looked at his uncle for an answer.

"It's a matter of faith."

"D'you mean to say that if you really believed you could move mountains you could?"

"By the grace of God," said the Vicar.

"Now, say good-night to your uncle, Philip," said Aunt Louisa. "You're not wanting to move a mountain tonight, are you?"

Philip allowed himself to be kissed on the forehead by his uncle and preceded Mrs Carey upstairs. He had got the information he wanted. His little room was icy, and he shivered when he put on his nightgown. But he always felt that his prayers were more pleasing to God when he said them under conditions of discomfort. The coldness of his hands and feet were an offering to the Almighty. And tonight he sank on his knees, buried his face in his hands, and prayed to God with all his might that He would make his club-foot whole. It was a very small thing beside the moving of mountains. He knew that God could do it if He wished, and his own faith was complete. Next morning, finishing his prayers with the same request, he fixed a date for the miracle.

"Oh, God, in Thy loving mercy and goodness, if it be Thy will, please make my foot all right on the night before I go back to school."

He was glad to get his petition into a formula, and he repeated it later in the dining-room during the short pause which the Vicar always made after prayers, before he rose from his knees. He said it again in the evening and again, shivering in his nightshirt, before he got into bed. And he believed. For once he looked forward with eagerness to the end of the holidays. He laughed to himself as he thought of his uncle's astonishment when he ran down the stairs three at a time; and after breakfast he and Aunt Louisa would have to hurry out and buy a new pair of boots. At school they would be astounded.

"Hulloa, Carey, what have you done with your foot?"

"Oh, it's all right now," he would answer casually, as though it were the most natural thing in the world.

He would be able to play football. His heart leaped as he saw himself running, running, faster than any of the other boys. At the end of the Easter term there were the sports, and he would be able to go in for the races; he rather fancied himself over the hurdles. It would be splendid to be like everyone else, not to be stared at curiously by new boys who did not know about his deformity, nor at the baths in summer to need incredible precautions, while he was undressing, before he could hide his foot in the water.

He prayed with all the power of his soul. No doubts assailed him. He was confident in the word of God. And the night before he was to go back to school he went up to bed tremulous with excitement. There was snow on the ground, and Aunt Louisa had allowed herself the un-accustomed luxury of a fire in her bedroom; but in Philip's little room it was so cold that his fingers were numb, and he had great difficulty in undoing his collar. His teeth chattered. The idea came to him that he must do something more than usual to attract the attention of God, and he turned back the rug which was in front of his bed so that he could kneel on the bare boards; and then it struck him that his nightshirt was a softness that might displease his Maker, so he took it off and said his prayers naked. When he got into bed he was so cold that for some time he could not sleep, but when he did, it was so soundly that Mary Ann had to shake him when she brought in his hot water next morning. She talked to him while she drew the curtains, but he did not answer; he had remembered at once that this was the morning for the miracle. His heart was filled with joy and gratitude. His first instinct was to put down his hand and feel the foot which was whole now, but to do this seemed to doubt the goodness of God. He knew that his foot was well. But at last he made up his mind, and with the toes of his right foot he just touched his left. Then he passed his hand over it.

He limped downstairs just as Mary Ann was going into the dining-room for prayers, and then he sat down to breakfast.

"You're very quiet this morning, Philip," said Aunt Louisa presently.

"He's thinking of the good breakfast he'll have at school to-morrow," said the Vicar.

When Philip answered, it was in a way that always irritated his un-cle, with something that had nothing to do with the matter in hand. He called it a bad habit of wool-gathering.

"Supposing you'd asked God to do something," said Philip, "and re-ally believed it was going to happen, like moving a mountain, I mean, and you had faith, and it didn't happen, what would it mean?"

"What a funny boy you are!" said Aunt Louisa. "You asked about moving mountains two ar three weeks ago."

"It would just mean that you hadn't got faith," answered Uncle William.

Philip accepted the explanation. If God had not cured him, it was because he did not really believe. And yet he did not see how he could believe more than he did. But perhaps he had not given God enough time. He had only asked Him for nineteen days. In a day or two he began his prayer again, and this time he fixed upon Easter. That was the day of His Son's glorious resurrection, and God in His happiness might be mercifully inclined. But now Philip added other means of attaining his desire: he began to wish, when he saw a new moon or a dappled horse, and he looked out for shooting stars; during exeat they had a chicken at the vicarage, and he broke the lucky bone with Aunt Louisa and wished again, each time that his foot might be made whole. He was appealing unconsciously to gods older to his race than the God of Israel. And he bombarded the Almighty with his prayer, at odd times of the day, whenever it occurred to him, in identical words always, for it seemed to him important to make his request in the same terms. But presently the feeling came to him that this time also his faith would not be great enough. He could not resist the doubt that assailed him. He made his own experience into a general rule.

"I suppose no one ever has faith enough," he said.

It was like the salt which his nurse used to tell him about: you could catch any bird by putting salt on his tail; and once he had taken a little bag of it into Kensington Gardens. But he could never get near enough to put the salt on a bird's tail. Before Easter he had given up the struggle. He felt a dull resentment against his uncle for taking him in. The text which spoke of the moving of mountains was just one of those that said one thing and meant another. He thought his uncle had been playing a practical joke on him.

15

The King's School at Tercanbury, to which Philip went when he was thirteen, prided itself on its antiquity. It traced its origin to an abbey school, founded before the Conquest, where the rudiments of learning were taught by Augustine monks; and, like many another establishment of this sort, on the destruction of the monasteries it had been reorganised by the officers of King Henry VIII and thus acquired its name. Since then, pursuing its modest course, it had given to the sons of the local gentry and of the professional people of Kent an education sufficient to their needs. One or two men of letters, beginning with a poet, than whom only Shakespeare had a more splendid genius, and ending with a writer of prose whose view of life has affected profoundly the generation of which Philip was a member, had gone forth from its gates to achieve fame; it had produced one or two eminent lawyers, but eminent lawyers are common, and one or two soldiers of distinction; but during the three centuries since its separation from the monastic order it had trained especially men of the church, bishops, deans, canons, and above all country clergymen: there were boys in the school whose fathers, grandfathers, great-grandfathers, had been educated there and had all been rectors of parishes in the diocese of Tercanbury; and they came to it with their minds made up already to be ordained. But there were signs notwithstanding that even there changes were coming; for a few, repeating what they had heard at home, said that the Church was no longer what it used to be. It wasn't so much the money; but the class of people who went in for it weren't the same; and two or three boys knew curates whose fathers were tradesmen: they'd rather go out to the Colonies (in those days the Colonies were still the last hope of those who could get nothing to do in England) than be a curate under some chap who wasn't a gentleman. At King's School, as at Blackstable Vicarage, a tradesman was anyone who was not lucky enough to own land (and here a fine distinction was made between the gentleman farmer and the landowner), or did not follow one of the four professions to which it was possible for a gentleman to belong. Among the day-boys, of whom there were about a hundred and fifty, sons of the local gentry and of the men stationed at the dépôt, those whose fathers were engaged in business were made to feel the degradation of their state.

The masters had no patience with modern ideas of education, which they read of sometimes in *The Times* or *The Guardian*, and hoped fervently that King's School would remain true to its old traditions. The dead languages were taught with such thoroughness that an old boy seldom thought of Homer or Virgil in after life without a qualm of boredom; and though in the common room at dinner one or two bolder spirits suggested that mathematics were of increasing importance, the general feeling was that they were a less noble study than the classics. Neither German nor chemistry was taught, and French only by the form-masters;

they could keep order better than a foreigner, and, since they knew the grammar as well as any Frenchman, it seemed unimportant that none of them could have got a cup of coffee in the restaurant at Boulogne unless the waiter had known a little English. Geography was taught chiefly by making boys draw maps, and this was a favourite occupation, especially when the country dealt with was mountainous: it was possible to waste a great deal of time in drawing the Andes or the Apennines. The masters, graduates of Oxford or Cambridge, were ordained and unmarried; if by chance they wished to marry they could only do so by accepting one of the smaller livings at the disposal of the Chapter; but for many years none of them had cared to leave the refined society of Tercanbury, which owing to the cavalry dépôt had a martial as well as an ecclesiastical tone, for the monotony of life in a country rectory; and they were now all men of middle age.

The headmaster, on the other hand, was obliged to be married, and he conducted the school till age began to tell upon him. When he retired he was rewarded with a much better living than any of the undermasters could hope for, and an honorary Canonry.

But a year before Philip entered the school a great change had come over it. It had been obvious for some time that Dr Fleming, who had been headmaster for the quarter of a century, was become too deaf to continue his work to the greater glory of God; and when one of the livings on the outskirts of the city fell vacant, with a stipend of six hundred a year, the Chapter offered it to him in such a manner as to imply that they thought it high time for him to retire. He could nurse his ailments comfortably on such an income. Two or three curates who had hoped for preferment told their wives it was scandalous to give a parish that needed a young, strong, and energetic man to an old fellow who knew nothing of parochial work, and had feathered his nest already; but the mutterings of the unbeneficed clergy do not reach the ears of a cathedral Chapter. And as for the parishioners they had nothing to say in the matter, and therefore nobody asked for their opinion. The Wesleyans and the Baptists both had chapels in the village.

When Dr Fleming was thus disposed of it became necessary to find a successor. It was contrary to the traditions of the school that one of the lower-masters should be chosen. The common-room was unanimous in desiring the election of Mr Watson, headmaster of the preparatory school; he could hardly be described as already a master of King's School, they had all known him for twenty years, and there was no danger that he would make a nuisance of himself. But the Chapter sprang a surprise on them. It chose a man called Perkins. At first nobody knew who Perkins was, and the name favourably impressed no one; but before the shock of it had passed away, it was realised that Perkins was the son of Perkins the linendraper. Dr Fleming informed the masters just before dinner, and his manner showed his consternation. Such of them as were dining in, ate their meal almost in silence, and no reference was made to the matter till the servants had left the room. Then they set to. The names of those present on this occasion are unimportant, but they had been known to generations of school-boys as Sighs, Tar, Winks, Squirts, and Pat.

They all knew Tom Perkins. The first thing about him was that he was not a gentleman. They remembered him quite well. He was a small, dark boy, with untidy black hair and large eyes. He looked like a gipsy. He had come to the school as a day-boy, with the best scholarship on their endowment, so that his education had cost him nothing. Of course he was brilliant. At every Speech-Day he was loaded with prizes. He was their show-boy, and they remembered now bitterly their fear that he would try to get some scholarship at one of the larger public schools and so pass out of their hands. Dr Fleming had gone to the linendraper his father—they all remembered the shop, Perkins and Cooper, in St. Catherine's Street—and said he hoped Tom would remain with them till he went to Oxford. The school was Perkins and Cooper's best customer, and Mr Perkins was only too glad to give the required assurance. Tom Perkins continued to triumph, he was the finest classical scholar that Dr Fleming remembered, and on leaving the school took with him the most valuable scholarship they had to offer. He got another at Magdalen and settled down to a brilliant career at the University. The school magazine recorded the distinctions he achieved year after year, and when he got his double first Dr Fleming himself wrote a few words of eulogy on the front page. It was with greater satisfaction that they welcomed his success, since Perkins and Cooper had fallen upon evil days: Cooper drank like a fish, and just before Tom Perkins took his degree the linendrapers filed their petition in bankruptcy.

In due course Tom Perkins took Holy Orders and entered upon the profession for which he was so admirably suited. He had been an assistant master at Wellington and then at Rugby.

But there was quite a difference between welcoming his success at other schools and serving under his leadership in their own. Tar had frequently given him lines, and Squirts had boxed his ears. They could not imagine how the Chapter had made such a mistake. No one could be expected to forget that he was the son of a bankrupt linendraper, and the alcoholism of Cooper seemed to increase the disgrace. It was understood that the Dean had supported his candidature with zeal, so the Dean would probably ask him to dinner; but would the pleasant little dinners in the precincts ever be the same when Tom Perkins sat at the table? And what about the dépôt? He really could not expect officers and gentlemen to receive him as one of themselves. It would do the school incalculable harm. Parents would be dissatisfied, and no one could be surprised if there were wholesale withdrawals. And then the indignity of calling him Mr Perkins! The masters thought by way of protest of sending in their resignations in a body, but the uneasy fear that they would be accepted with equanimity restrained them.

"The only thing is to prepare ourselves for changes," said Sighs, who had conducted the fifth form for five and twenty years with unparalleled incompetence.

And when they saw him they were not reassured. Dr Fleming invited them to meet him at luncheon. He was now a man of thirty-two, tall and lean, but with the same wild and unkempt look they remembered on him as a boy. His clothes, ill-made and shabby, were put on untidily. His hair was as black and as long as ever, and he had plainly never learned to brush it; it fell over his forehead with every gesture, and he had a quick movement of the hand with which he pushed it back from his eyes. He had a black moustache and a beard which came high up on his face almost to the cheek-bones. He talked to the masters quite easily, as though he had parted from them a week or two before; he was evidently delighted to see them. He seemed unconscious of the strangeness of the position and appeared not to notice any oddness in being addressed as Mr Perkins.

When he bade them good-bye, one of the masters, for something to say, remarked that he was allowing himself plenty of time to catch his train.

"I want to go round and have a look at the shop," he answered cheerfully.

There was a distinct embarrassment. They wondered that he could be so tactless, and to make it worse Dr Fleming had not heard what he said. His wife shouted it in his ear.

"He wants to go round and look at his father's old shop."

Only Tom Perkins was unconscious of the humiliation which the whole party felt. He turned to Mrs Fleming.

"Who's got it now, d'you know?"

She could hardly answer. She was very angry.

"It's still a linendraper's," she said bitterly. "Grove is the name. We don't deal there any more."

"I wonder if he'd let me go over the house."

"I expect he would if you explain who you are."

It was not till the end of dinner that evening that any reference was made in the common-room to the subject that was in all their minds. Then it was Sighs who asked:

"Well, what did you think of our new head?"

They thought of the conversation at luncheon. It was hardly a conversation; it was a monologue. Perkins had talked incessantly. He talked very quickly, with a flow of easy words and in a deep, resonant voice. He had a short, odd little laugh which showed his white teeth. They had followed him with difficulty, for his mind darted from subject to subject with a connection they did not always catch. He talked of pedagogics, and this was natural enough; but he had much to say of modern theories in Germany which they had never heard of and received with misgiving. He talked of the classics, but he had been to Greece, and he discoursed on archæology; he had once spent a winter digging; they could not see how that helped a man to teach boys to pass examinations. He talked of politics. It sounded odd to them to hear him compare Lord Beaconsfield with Alcibiades. He talked of Mr Gladstone and Home Rule. They realised that he was a Liberal. Their hearts sank. He talked of German philosophy and of French fiction. They could not think a man profound whose interests were so diverse.

It was Winks who summed up the general impression and put it into a form they all felt conclusively damning. Winks was the master of the upper third, a weak-kneed man with drooping eyelids. He was too tall for his strength, and his movements were slow and languid. He gave an impression of lassitude, and his nickname was eminently appropriate.

"He's very enthusiastic," said Winks.

Enthusiasm was ill-bred. Enthusiasm was ungentlemanly. They thought of the Salvation Army with its braying trumpets and its drums. Enthusiasm meant change. They had gooseflesh when they thought of all the pleasant old habits which stood in imminent danger. They hardly dared to look forward to the future.

"He looks more of a gipsy than ever," said one, after a pause.

"I wonder if the Dean and Chapter knew that he was a Radical when they elected him," another observed bitterly.

But conversation halted. They were too much disturbed for words.

When Tar and Sighs were walking together to the Chapter House on Speech-Day a week later, Tar, who had a bitter tongue, remarked to his colleague:

"Well, we've seen a good many Speech-Days here, haven't we? I wonder if we shall see another."

Sighs was more melancholy even than usual.

"If anything worth having comes along in the way of a living I don't mind when I retire."

16

A year passed, and when Philip came to the school the old masters were all in their places; but a good many changes had taken place notwithstanding their stubborn resistance, none the less formidable because it was concealed under an apparent desire to fall in with the new head's ideas. Though the form-masters still taught French to the lower school, another master had come, with a degree of doctor of philology from the University of Heidelberg and a record of three years spent in a French lycée, to teach French to the upper forms and German to anyone who cared to take it up instead of Greek. Another master was engaged to teach mathematics more systematically than had been found necessary hitherto. Neither of these was ordained. This was a real revolution, and when the pair arrived the older masters received them with distrust. A laboratory had been fitted up, army classes were instituted; they all said the character of the school was changing. And heaven only knew what further projects Mr Perkins turned in that untidy head of his. The school was small as public schools go, there were not more than two hundred boarders; and it was difficult for it to grow larger, for it was huddled up against the Cathedral; the precincts, with the exception of a house in which some of the masters lodged, were occupied by the cathedral clergy; and there was no more room for building. But Mr Perkins devised an elaborate scheme by which he might obtain sufficient space to make the school double its present size. He wanted to attract boys from London. He thought it would be good for them to be thrown in contact with the Kentish lads, and it would sharpen the country wits of these.

"It's against all our traditions," said Sighs, when Mr Perkins made the suggestion to him. "We've rather gone out of our way to avoid the contamination of boys from London."

"Oh, what nonsense!" said Mr Perkins.

No one had ever told the form-master before that he talked nonsense, and he was meditating an acid reply, in which perhaps he might insert a veiled reference to hosiery, when Mr Perkins in his impetuous way attacked him outrageously.

"That house in the Precincts—if you'd only marry I'd get the Chapter to put another couple of stories on, and we'd make dormitories and studies, and your wife could help you."

The elderly clergyman gasped. Why should he marry? He was fifty-seven, a man couldn't marry at fifty-seven. He couldn't start looking after a house at his time of life. He didn't want to marry. If the choice lay between that and the country living he would much sooner resign. All he wanted now was peace and quietness.

"I'm not thinking of marrying," he said.

Mr Perkins looked at him with his dark, bright eyes, and if there was a twinkle in them poor Sighs never saw it.

"What a pity! Couldn't you marry to oblige me? It would help me a great deal with the Dean and Chapter when I suggest rebuilding your house."

But Mr Perkins' most unpopular innovation was his system of taking occasionally another man's form. He asked it as a favour, but after all it was a favour which could not be refused, and as Tar, otherwise Mr Turner, said, it was undignified for all parties. He gave no warning, but after morning prayers would say to one of the masters:

"I wonder if you'd mind taking the Sixth today at eleven. We'll change over, shall we?"

They did not know whether this was usual at other schools, but certainly it had never been done at Tercanbury. The results were curious. Mr Turner, who was the first victim, broke the news to his form that the headmaster would take them for Latin that day, and on the pretence that they might like to ask him a question or two so that they should not make perfect fools of themselves, spent the last quarter of an hour of the history lesson in construing for them the passage of Livy which had been set for the day; but when he rejoined his class and looked at the paper on which Mr Perkins had written the marks, a surprise awaited him; for the two boys at the top of the form seemed to have done very ill, while others who had never distinguished themselves before were given full marks. When he asked Eldridge, his cleverest boy, what was the meaning of this the answer came sullenly:

"Mr Perkins never gave us any construing to do. He asked me what I knew about General Gordon."

Mr Turner looked at him in astonishment. The boys evidently felt they had been hardly used, and he could not help agreeing with their silent dissatisfaction. He could not see either what General Gordon had to do with Livy. He hazarded an enquiry afterwards.

"Eldridge was dreadfully put out because you asked him what he knew about General Gordon," he said to the headmaster, with an attempt at a chuckle.

Mr Perkins laughed.

"I saw they'd got to the agrarian laws of Caius Gracchus, and I wondered if they knew anything about the agrarian troubles in Ireland. But all they knew about Ireland was that Dublin was on the Liffey. So I wondered if they'd ever heard of General Gordon."

Then the horrid fact was disclosed that the new head had a mania for general information. He had doubts about the utility of examinations on subjects which had been crammed for the occasion. He wanted common sense.

Sighs grew more worried every month; he could not get the thought out of his head that Mr Perkins would ask him to fix a day for his marriage; and he hated the attitude the head adopted towards classical literature. There was no doubt that he was a fine scholar, and he was engaged on a work which was quite in the right tradition: he was writing a treatise on the trees in Latin literature; but he talked of it flippantly, as though it were a pastime of no great importance, like billiards, which engaged his leisure but was not to be considered with seriousness. And Squirts, the master of the middle-third, grew more ill-tempered every day.

It was in his form that Philip was put on entering the school. The Rev. B. B. Gordon was a man by nature ill-suited to be a schoolmaster: he was impatient and choleric. With no one to call him to account, with only small boys to face him, he had long lost all power of self-control. He began his work in a rage and ended it in a passion. He was a man of middle height and of a corpulent figure; he had sandy hair, worn very short and now growing gray, and a small bristly moustache. His large face, with indistinct features and small blue eyes, was naturally red, but during his frequent attacks of anger it grew dark and purple. His nails were bitten to the quick, for while some trembling boy was construing he would sit at his desk shaking with the fury that consumed him, and gnaw his fingers. Stories, perhaps exaggerated, were told of his violence, and two years before there had been some excitement in the school when it was heard that one father was threatening a prosecution: he had boxed the ears of a boy named Walters with a book so violently that his hearing was affected and the boy had to be taken away from the school. The boy's father lived in Tercanbury, and there had been much indignation in the city, the local paper had referred to the matter; but Mr Walters was only a brewer, so the sympathy was divided. The rest of the boys, for reasons best known to themselves, though they loathed the master, took his side in the affair, and, to show their indignation that the school's business had been dealt with outside, made things as uncomfortable as they could for Walters' younger brother, who still remained. But Mr Gordon had only escaped the country living by the skin of his teeth, and he had never hit a boy since. The right the masters possessed to cane boys on the hand was taken away from them, and Squirts could no longer emphasize his anger by beating his desk with the cane. He never did more now than take a boy by the shoulders and shake him. He still made a naughty or refractory lad stand with one arm stretched out for anything from ten minutes to half an hour, and he was as violent as before with his tongue.

No master could have been more unfitted to teach things to so shy a boy as Philip. He had come to the school with fewer terrors than he had when first he went to Mr Watson's. He knew a good many boys who had been with him at the preparatory school. He felt more grown-up, and instinctively realised that among the larger numbers his deformity would be less noticeable. But from the first day Mr Gordon struck terror in his heart; and the master, quick to discern the boys who were frightened of him, seemed on that account to take a peculiar dislike to him. Philip had enjoyed his work, but now he began to look upon the hours passed in school with horror. Rather than risk an answer which might be wrong and excite a storm of abuse from the master, he would sit stupidly silent, and when it came towards his turn to stand up and construe he grew sick and white with apprehension. His happy moments were those when Mr Perkins took the form. He was able to gratify the passion for general knowledge which beset the headmaster; he had read all sorts of strange books beyond his years, and often Mr Perkins, when a question was going round the room, would stop at Philip with a smile that filled the boy with rapture, and say:

"Now, Carey, you tell them."

The good marks he got on these occasions increased Mr Gordon's indignation. One day it came to Philip's turn to translate, and the master sat there glaring at him and furiously biting his thumb. He was in a ferocious mood. Philip began to speak in a low voice.

"Don't mumble," shouted the master.

Something seemed to stick in Philip's throat.

"Go on. Go on. Go on."

Each time the words were screamed more loudly. The effect was to drive all he knew out of Philip's head, and he looked at the printed page vacantly. Mr Gordon began to breathe heavily.

"If you don't know why don't you say so? Do you know it or not? Did you hear all this construed last time or not? Why don't you speak? Speak, you blockhead, speak!"

The master seized the arms of his chair and grasped them as though to prevent himself from falling upon Philip. They knew that in past days he often used to seize boys by the throat till they almost choked. The veins in his forehead stood out and his face grew dark and threatening. He was a man insane.

Philip had known the passage perfectly the day before, but now he could remember nothing.

"I don't know it," he gasped.

"Why don't you know it? Let's take the words one by one. We'll soon see if you don't know it."

Philip stood silent, very white, trembling a little, with his head bent down on the book. The master's breathing grew almost stertorous.

"The headmaster says you're clever. I don't know how he sees it. General information." He laughed savagely. "I don't know what they put you in this form for. Blockhead."

He was pleased with the word, and he repeated it at the top of his voice.

"Blockhead! Blockhead! Club-footed blockhead!"

That relieved him a little. He saw Philip redden suddenly. He told him to fetch the Black Book. Philip put down his Cæsar and went silently out. The Black Book was a sombre volume in which the names of boys were written with their misdeeds, and when a name was down three times it meant a caning. Philip went to the headmaster's house and knocked at his study-door. Mr Perkins was seated at his table.

"May I have the Black Book, please, sir."

"There it is," answered Mr Perkins, indicating its place by a nod of his head. "What have you been doing that you shouldn't?"

"I don't know, sir."

Mr Perkins gave him a quick look, but without answering went on with his work. Philip took the book and went out. When the hour was up, a few minutes later, he brought it back.

"Let me have a look at it," said the headmaster. "I see Mr Gordon has black-booked you for 'gross impertinence.' What was it?"

"I don't know, sir. Mr Gordon said I was a club-footed blockhead."

Mr Perkins looked at him again. He wondered whether there was sarcasm behind the boy's reply, but he was still much too shaken. His

face was white and his eyes had a look of terrified distress. Mr
Perkins got up and put the book down. As he did so he took up some
photographs.

"A friend of mine sent me some pictures of Athens this morning,"
he said casually. "Look here, there's the Acropolis."

He began explaining to Philip what he saw. The ruin grew vivid with
his words. He showed him the theatre of Dionysus and explained in
what order the people sat, and how beyond they could see the blue
Aegean. And then suddenly he said:

"I remember Mr Gordon used to call me a gipsy counter jumper
when I was in his form."

And before Philip, his mind fixed on the photographs, had time to
gather the meaning of the remark, Mr Perkins was showing him a picture of Salamis, and with his finger, a finger of which the nail had a little black edge to it, was pointing out how the Greek ships were placed
and how the Persian.

17

Philip passed the next two years with comfortable monotony. He was
not bullied more than other boys of his size; and his deformity, with-
drawing him from games, acquired for him an insignificance for which
he was grateful. He was not popular, and he was very lonely. He spent a
couple of terms with Winks in the Upper Third. Winks, with his weary
manner and his drooping eyelids, looked infinitely bored. He did his
duty, but he did it with an abstracted mind. He was kind, gentle, and
foolish. He had a great belief in the honour of boys; he felt that the first
thing to make them truthful was not to let it enter your head for a moment that it was possible for them to lie. "Ask much," he quoted, "and
much shall be given to you." Life was easy in the Upper Third. You knew
exactly what lines would come to your turn to construe, and with the
crib that passed from hand to hand you could find out all you wanted in
two minutes; you could hold a Latin Grammar open on your knees while
questions were passing round; and Winks never noticed anything odd in
the fact that the same incredible mistake was to be found in a dozen different exercises. He had no great faith in examinations, for he noticed

that boys never did so well in them as in form: it was disappointing, but not significant. In due course they were moved up, having learned little but a cheerful effrontery in the distortion of truth, which was possibly of greater service to them in after life than an ability to read Latin at sight.

Then they fell into the hands of Tar. His name was Turner; he was the most vivacious of the old masters, a short man with an immense belly, a black beard turning now to gray, and a swarthy skin. In his clerical dress there was indeed something in him to suggest the tar-barrel; and though on principle he gave five hundred lines to any boy on whose lips he overheard his nickname, at dinner-parties in the precincts he often made little jokes about it. He was the most worldly of the masters; he dined out more frequently than any of the others, and the society he kept was not so exclusively clerical. The boys looked upon him as rather a dog. He left off his clerical attire during the holidays and had been seen in Switzerland in gay tweeds. He liked a bottle of wine and good dinner, and having once been seen at the Café Royal with a lady who was very probably a near relation, was thenceforward supposed by generations of school-boys to indulge in orgies the circumstantial details of which pointed to an unbounded belief in human depravity.

Mr Turner reckoned that it took him a term to lick boys into shape after they had been in the Upper Third; and now and then he let fall a sly hint, which showed that he knew perfectly what went on in his colleague's form. He took it good-humouredly. He looked upon boys as young ruffians who were more apt to be truthful if it was quite certain a lie would be found out, whose sense of honour was peculiar to themselves and did not apply to dealings with masters, and who were least likely to be troublesome when they learned that it did not pay. He was proud of his form and as eager at fifty-five that it should do better in examinations than any of the others as he had been when he first came to the school. He had the choler of the obese, easily roused and as easily calmed, and his boys soon discovered that there was much kindliness beneath the invective with which he constantly assailed them. He had no patience with fools, but was willing to take much trouble with boys whom he suspected of concealing intelligence behind their wilfulness. He was fond of inviting them to tea; and, though vowing they never got

a look in with him at the cakes and muffins, for it was the fashion to believe that his corpulence pointed to a voracious appetite, and his voracious appetite to tapeworms, they accepted his invitations with real
pleasure.

Philip was now more comfortable, for space was so limited that
there were only studies for boys in the upper school, and till then he had
lived in the great hall in which they all ate and in which the lower forms
did preparation in a promiscuity which was vaguely distasteful to him.
Now and then it made him restless to be with people and he wanted urgently to be alone. He set out for solitary walks into the country. There
was a little stream, with pollards on both sides of it, that ran through
green fields, and it made him happy, he knew not why, to wander along
its banks. When he was tired he lay face-downward on the grass and
watched the eager scurrying of minnows and of tadpoles. It gave him a
peculiar satisfaction to saunter round the precincts. On the green in the
middle they practised at nets in the summer, but during the rest of the
year it was quiet: boys used to wander round sometimes arm in arm, or
a studious fellow with abstracted gaze walked slowly, repeating to himself something he had to learn by heart. There was a colony of rooks in
the great elms, and they filled the air with melancholy cries. Along one
side lay the Cathedral with its great central tower, and Philip, who knew
as yet nothing of beauty, felt when he looked at it a troubling delight
which he could not understand. When he had a study (it was a little
square room looking on a slum, and four boys shared it), he bought a
photograph of that view of the Cathedral, and pinned it up over his
desk. And he found himself taking a new interest in what he saw from
the window of the Fourth Form room. It looked on to old lawns, carefully tended, and fine trees with foliage dense and rich. It gave him an
odd feeling in his heart, and he did not know if it was pain or pleasure.
It was the first dawn of the æsthetic emotion. It accompanied other
changes. His voice broke. It was no longer quite under his control, and
queer sounds issued from his throat.

Then he began to go to the classes which were held in the headmaster's study, immediately after tea, to prepare boys for confirmation.
Philip's piety had not stood the test of time, and he had long since given
up his nightly reading of the Bible; but now, under the influence of Mr

Perkins, with this new condition of the body which made him so rest-less, his old feelings revived, and he reproached himself bitterly for his backsliding. The fires of Hell burned fiercely before his mind's eye. If he had died during that time when he was little better than an infidel he would have been lost; he believed implicitly in pain everlasting, he be-lieved in it much more than in eternal happiness; and he shuddered at the dangers he had run.

Since the day on which Mr Perkins had spoken kindly to him, when he was smarting under the particular form of abuse which he could least bear, Philip had conceived for his headmaster a dog-like adoration. He racked his brains vainly for some way to please him. He treasured the smallest word of commendation which by chance fell from his lips. And when he came to the quiet little meetings in his house he was prepared to surrender himself en-tirely. He kept his eyes fixed on Mr Perkins' shining eyes, and sat with mouth half open, his head a little thrown forward so as to miss no word. The ordinariness of the surroundings made the matters they dealt with ex-traordinarily moving. And often the master, seized himself by the wonder of his subject, would push back the book in front of him, and with his hands clasped together over his heart, as though to still the beating, would talk of the mysteries of their religion. Sometimes Philip did not under-stand, but he did not want to understand, he felt vaguely that it was enough to feel. It seemed to him then that the headmaster, with his black, straggling hair and his pale face, was like those prophets of Israel who feared not to take kings to task; and when he thought of the Redeemer he saw Him only with the same dark eyes and those wan cheeks.

Mr Perkins took this part of his work with great seriousness. There was never here any of that flashing humour which made the other mas-ters suspect him of flippancy. Finding time for everything in his busy day, he was able at certain intervals to take separately for a quarter of an hour or twenty minutes the boys whom he was preparing for confirmation. He wanted to make them feel that this was the first consciously serious step in their lives; he tried to grope into the depths of their souls; he wanted to instil in them his own vehement devotion. In Philip, notwithstanding his shyness, he felt the possibility of a passion equal to his own. The boy's temperament seemed to him essentially religious. One day he broke off suddenly from the subject on which he had been talking.

"Have you thought at all what you're going to be when you grow up?" he asked.

"My uncle wants me to be ordained," said Philip.

"And you?"

Philip looked away. He was ashamed to answer that he felt himself unworthy.

"I don't know any life that's so full of happiness as ours. I wish I could make you feel what a wonderful privilege it is. One can serve God in every walk, but we stand nearer to Him. I don't want to influence you, but if you made up your mind—oh, at once—you couldn't help feeling that joy and relief which never desert one again."

Philip did not answer, but the headmaster read in his eyes that he realised already something of what he tried to indicate

"If you go on as you are now you'll find yourself head of the school one of these days, and you ought to be pretty safe for a scholarship when you leave. Have you got anything of your own?"

"My uncle says I shall have a hundred a year when I'm twenty-one."

"You'll be rich. I had nothing."

The headmaster hesitated a moment, and then, idly drawing lines with a pencil on the blotting paper in front of him went on.

"I'm afraid your choice of professions will be rather limited. You naturally couldn't go in for anything that required physical activity."

Philip reddened to the roots of his hair, as he always did when any reference was made to his club-foot. Mr Perkins looked at him gravely.

"I wonder if you're not oversensitive about your misfortune? Has it ever struck you to thank God for it?"

Philip looked up quickly. His lips tightened. He remembered how for months, trusting in what they told him, he had implored God to heal him as He had healed the Leper and made the Blind to see.

"As long as you accept it rebelliously it can only cause you shame. But if you looked upon it as a cross that was given you to bear only because your shoulders were strong enough to bear it, a sign of God's favour, then it would be a source of happiness to you instead of misery."

He saw that the boy hated to discuss the matter and he let him go.

But Philip thought over all that the headmaster had said, and presently, his mind taken up entirely with the ceremony that was before

him, a mystical rapture seized him. His spirit seemed to free itself from
the bonds of the flesh and he seemed to be living a new life. He aspired
to perfection with all the passion that was in him. He wanted to surrender himself entirely to the service of God, and he made up his mind definitely that he would be ordained. When the great day arrived, his soul
deeply moved by all the preparation, by the books he had studied and
above all by the overwhelming influence of the head, he could hardly
contain himself for fear and joy. One thought had tormented him. He
knew that he would have to walk alone through the chancel, and he
dreaded showing his limp thus obviously, not only to the whole school,
who were attending the service, but also to the strangers, people from the
city or parents who had come to see their sons confirmed. But when the
time came he felt suddenly that he could accept the humiliation joyfully;
and as he limped up the chancel, very small and insignificant beneath the
lofty vaulting of the Cathedral, he offered consciously his deformity as
a sacrifice to the God who loved him.

18

But Philip could not live long in the rarefied air of the hilltops. What
had happened to him when first he was seized by the religious emotion
happened to him now. Because he felt so keenly the beauty of faith, because the desire for self-sacrifice burned in his heart with such a gem-like
glow, his strength seemed inadequate to his ambition. He was tired out
by the violence of his passion. His soul was filled on a sudden with a
singular aridity. He began to forget the presence of God which had
seemed so surrounding; and his religious exercises, still very punctually
performed, grew merely formal. At first he blamed himself for this
falling away, and the fear of hellfire urged him to renewed vehemence;
but the passion was dead, and gradually other interests distracted his
thoughts.

Philip had few friends. His habit of reading isolated him: it became
such a need that after being in company for some time he grew tired and
restless; he was vain of the wider knowledge he had acquired from the
perusal of so many books, his mind was alert, and he had not the skill
to hide his contempt for his companions' stupidity. They complained

that he was conceited; and, since he excelled only in matters which to them were unimportant, they asked satirically what he had to be conceited about. He was developing a sense of humour, and found that he had a knack of saying bitter things, which caught people on the raw; he said them because they amused him, hardly realising how much they hurt, and was much offended when he found that his victims regarded him with active dislike. The humiliations he suffered when first he went to school had caused in him a shrinking from his fellows which he could never entirely overcome; he remained shy and silent. But though he did everything to alienate the sympathy of other boys he longed with all his heart for the popularity which to some was so easily accorded. These from his distance he admired extravagantly; and though he was inclined to be more sarcastic with them than with others, though he made little jokes at their expense, he would have given anything to change places with them. Indeed he would gladly have changed places with the dullest boy in the school who was whole of limb. He took to a singular habit. He would imagine that he was some boy whom he had a particular fancy for; he would throw his soul, as it were, into the other's body, talk with his voice and laugh with his heart; he would imagine himself doing all the things the other did. It was so vivid that he seemed for a moment really to be no longer himself. In this way he enjoyed many intervals of fantastic happiness.

At the beginning of the Christmas term which followed on his confirmation Philip found himself moved into another study. One of the boys who shared it was called Rose. He was in the same form as Philip, and Philip had always looked upon him with envious admiration. He was not good-looking; though his large hands and big bones suggested that he would be a tall man, he was clumsily made; but his eyes were charming, and when he laughed (he was constantly laughing) his face wrinkled all round them in a jolly way. He was neither clever nor stupid, but good enough at his work and better at games. He was a favourite with masters and boys, and he in his turn liked everyone.

When Philip was put in the study he could not help seeing that the others, who had been together for three terms, welcomed him coldly. It made him nervous to feel himself an intruder; but he had learned to hide his feelings, and they found him quiet and unobtrusive. With Rose, because he was as little able as anyone else to resist his charm, Philip was even more than usually shy and abrupt; and whether on account of this, unconsciously bent upon exerting the fascination he knew was his only by the results, or whether from sheer kindness of heart, it was Rose who first took Philip into the circle. One day, quite suddenly, he asked Philip if he would walk to the football field with him. Philip flushed.

"I can't walk fast enough for you," he said.

"Rot. Come on."

And just before they were setting out some boy put his head in the study-door and asked Rose to go with him.

"I can't," he answered. "I've already promised Carey."

"Don't bother about me," said Philip quickly. "I shan't mind."

"Rot," said Rose.

He looked at Philip with those good-natured eyes of his and laughed. Philip felt a curious tremor in his heart.

In a little while, their friendship growing with boyish rapidity, the pair were inseparable. Other fellows wondered at the sudden intimacy, and Rose was asked what he saw in Philip.

"Oh, I don't know," he answered. "He's not half a bad chap really."

Soon they grew accustomed to the two walking into chapel arm in arm or strolling round the precincts in conversation; wherever one was the other could be found also, and, as though acknowledging his proprietorship, boys who wanted Rose would leave messages with Carey. Philip at first was reserved. He would not let himself yield entirely to the proud joy that filled him; but presently his distrust of the fates gave way before a wild happiness. He thought Rose the most wonderful fellow he had ever seen. His books now were insignificant; he could not bother about them when there was something infinitely more important to occupy him. Rose's friends used to come in to tea in the study sometimes or sit about when there was nothing better to do—Rose liked a crowd and the chance of a rag—and they found that Philip was quite a decent fellow. Philip was happy.

When the last day of term came he and Rose arranged by which train they should come back, so that they might meet at the station and have tea in the town before returning to school. Philip went home with a heavy heart. He thought of Rose all through the holidays, and his fancy was active with the things they would do together next term. He was bored at the vicarage, and when on the last day his uncle put him the usual question in the usual facetious tone:

"Well, are you glad to be going back to school?"

Philip answered joyfully:

"Rather."

In order to be sure of meeting Rose at the station he took an earlier train than he usually did, and he waited about the platform for an hour. When the train came in from Faversham, where he knew Rose had to change, he ran along it excitedly. But Rose was not there. He got a porter to tell him when another train was due, and he waited; but again he was disappointed; and he was cold and hungry, so he walked, through side-streets and slums, by a short cut to the school. He found Rose in the study, with his feet on the chimney-piece, talking eighteen to the dozen with half a dozen boys who were sitting on whatever there was to sit on. He shook hands with Philip enthusiastically, but Philip's face fell, for he realised that Rose had forgotten all about their appointment.

"I say, why are you so late?" said Rose. "I thought you were never coming."

"You were at the station at half-past four," said another boy. "I saw you when I came."

Philip blushed a little. He did not want Rose to know that he had been such a fool as to wait for him.

"I had to see about a friend of my people's," he invented readily. "I was asked to see her off."

But his disappointment made him a little sulky. He sat in silence, and when spoken to answered in monosyllables. He was making up his mind to have it out with Rose when they were alone. But when the others had gone Rose at once came over and sat on the arm of the chair in which Philip was lounging.

"I say, I'm jolly glad we're in the same study this term. Ripping, isn't it?"

He seemed so genuinely pleased to see Philip that Philip's annoyance vanished. They began as if they had not been separated for five minutes to talk eagerly of the thousand things that interested them.

19

At first Philip had been too grateful for Rose's friendship to make any demands on him. He took things as they came and enjoyed life. But presently he began to resent Rose's universal amiability; he wanted a more exclusive attachment, and he claimed as a right what before he had accepted as a favour. He watched jealously Rose's companionship with others; and though he knew it was unreasonable could not help sometimes saying bitter things to him. If Rose spent an hour playing the fool in another study, Philip would receive him when he returned to his own with a sullen frown. He would sulk for a day, and he suffered more because Rose either did not notice his ill-humour or deliberately ignored it. Not seldom Philip, knowing all the time how stupid he was, would force a quarrel, and they would not speak to one another for a couple of days. But Philip could not bear to be angry with him long, and even when convinced that he was in the right, would apologise humbly. Then for a week they would be as great friends as ever. But the best was over, and Philip could see that Rose often walked with him merely from old habit or from fear of his anger; they had not so much to say to one another as at first, and Rose was often bored. Philip felt that his lameness began to irritate him.

Towards the end of the term two or three boys caught scarlet fever, and there was much talk of sending them all home in order to escape an epidemic; but the sufferers were isolated, and since no more were attacked it was supposed that the outbreak was stopped. One of the stricken was Philip. He remained in hospital through the Easter holidays, and at the beginning of the summer term was sent home to the vicarage to get a little fresh air. The Vicar, notwithstanding medical assurance that the boy was no longer infectious, received him with suspicion; he thought it very inconsiderate of the doctor to suggest that his nephew's convalescence should be spent by the seaside, and consented to have him in the house only because there was nowhere else he could go.

Philip went back to shcool at half-term. He had forgotten the quarrels he had had with Rose, but remembered only that he was his greatest friend. He knew that he had been silly. He made up his mind to be more reasonable. During his illness Rose had sent him in a couple of little notes, and he had ended each with the words: "Hurry up and come back." Philip thought Rose must be looking forward as much to his return as he was himself to seeing Rose.

He found that owing to the death from scarlet fever of one of the boys in the Sixth there had been some shifting in the studies and Rose was no longer in his. It was a bitter disappointment. But as soon as he arrived he burst into Rose's study. Rose was sitting at his desk, working with a boy called Hunter, and turned round crossly as Philip came in.

"Who the devil's that?" he cried. And then, seeing Philip "Oh, it's you."

Philip stopped in embarrassment.

"I thought I'd come in and see how you were."

"We were just working."

Hunter broke into the conversation.

"When did you get back?"

"Five minutes ago."

They sat and looked at him as though he was disturbing them. They evidently expected him to go quickly. Philip reddened.

"I'll be off. You might look in when you've done," he said to Rose.

"All right."

Philip closed the door behind him and limped back to his own study. He felt frightfully hurt. Rose, far from seeming glad to see him, had looked almost put out. They might never have been more than acquaintances. Though he waited in his study, not leaving it for a moment in case just then Rose should come, his friend never appeared; and next morning when he went into prayers he saw Rose and Hunter swinging along arm in arm. What he could not see for himself others told him. He had forgotten that three months is a long time in a school-boy's life, and though he had passed them in solitude Rose had lived in the world. Hunter had stepped into the vacant place. Philip found that Rose was quietly avoiding him. But he was not the boy to accept a situation without putting it into words; he waited till he was sure Rose was alone in his study and went in.

"May I come in?" he asked.

Rose looked at him with an embarrassment that made him angry with Philip.

"Yes, if you want to."

"It's very kind of you," said Philip sarcastically.

"What d'you want?"

"I say, why have you been so rotten since I came back?"

"Oh, don't be an ass," said Rose.

"I don't know what you see in Hunter."

"That's my business."

Philip looked down. He could not bring himself to say what was in his heart. He was afraid of humiliating himself. Rose got up.

"I've got to go to the Gym," he said.

When he was at the door Philip forced himself to speak.

"I say, Rose, don't be a perfect beast."

"Oh, go to hell."

Rose slammed the door behind him and left Philip alone. Philip shivered with rage. He went back to his study and turned the conversation over in his mind. He hated Rose now, he wanted to hurt him, he thought of biting things he might have said to him. He brooded over the end to their friendship and fancied that others were talking of it. In his sensitiveness he saw sneers and wonderings in other fellows' manner when they were not bothering their heads with him at all. He imagined to himself what they were saying.

"After all, it wasn't likely to last long. I wonder he ever stuck Carey at all. Blighter!"

To show his indifference he struck up a violent friendship with a boy called Sharp whom he hated and despised. He was a London boy, with a loutish air, a heavy fellow with the beginnings of a moustache on his lip and bushy eyebrows that joined one another across the bridge of his nose. He had soft hands and manners too suave for his years. He spoke with the suspicion of a cockney accent. He was one of those boys who are too slack to play games, and he exercised great ingenuity in making excuses to avoid such as were compulsory. He was regarded by boys and masters with a vague dislike, and it was from arrogance that Philip now sought his society. Sharp in a couple of terms was going to Germany for a year. He hated school, which he looked upon as an indignity to be endured till he was old enough to go out into the world. London was all he cared for, and he had many stories to tell of his doings there during the holidays. From his conversation—he spoke in a soft, deep-toned voice—there emerged the vague rumour of the London streets by night. Philip listened to him at once fascinated and repelled. With his vivid fancy he seemed to see the surging throng round the pit-door of the-atres, and the glitter of cheap restaurants, bars where men, half drunk, sat on high stools talking with barmaids; and under the street lamps the mysterious passing of dark crowds bent upon pleasure. Sharp lent him cheap novels from Holywell Row, which Philip read in his cubicle with a sort of wonderful fear.

Once Rose tried to effect a reconciliation. He was a good-natured fellow, who did not like having enemies.

"I say, Carey, why are you being such a silly ass? It doesn't do you any good cutting me and all that."

"I don't know what you mean," answered Philip.

"Well, I don't see why you shouldn't talk."

"You bore me," said Philip.

"Please yourself."

Rose shrugged his shoulders and left him. Philip was very white, as he always became when he was moved, and his heart beat violently. When Rose went away he felt suddenly sick with misery. He did not know why he had answered in that fashion. He would have given anything to be friends with Rose. He hated to have quarrelled with him, and now that he saw he had given him pain he was very sorry. But at the moment he had not been master of himself. It seemed that some devil had seized him, forcing him to say bitter things against his will, even though at the time he wanted to shake hands with Rose and meet him more than half-way. The desire to wound had been too strong for him. He had wanted to revenge himself for the pain and the humiliation he had endured. It was pride: it was folly too, for he knew that Rose would not care at all, while he would suffer bitterly. The thought came to him that he would go to Rose, and say:

"I say, I'm sorry I was such a beast. I couldn't help it. Let's make it up."

But he knew he would never be able to do it. He was afraid that Rose would sneer at him. He was angry with himself, and when Sharp came in a little while afterwards he seized upon the first opportunity to quar-rel with him. Philip had a fiendish instinct for discovering other people's raw spots, and was able to say things that rankled because they were true. But Sharp had the last word.

"I heard Rose talking about you to Mellor just now," he said. "Mellor said: why didn't you kick him? It would teach him manners. And Rose said: I didn't like to. Damned cripple."

Philip suddenly became scarlet. He could not answer, for there was a lump in his throat that almost choked him.

20

Philip was moved into the Sixth, but he hated school now with all his heart, and, having lost his ambition, cared nothing whether he did ill or well. He awoke in the morning with a sinking heart because he must go through another day of drudgery. He was tired of having to do things because he was told; and the restrictions irked him, not because they were unreasonable, but because they were restrictions. He yearned for freedom. He was weary of repeating things that he knew already and of the hammering away, for the sake of a thickwitted fellow, at something that he understood from the beginning.

With Mr Perkins you could work or not as you chose. He was at once eager and abstracted. The Sixth Form room was in a part of the old abbey which had been restored, and it had Gothic window: Philip tried to cheat his boredom by drawing this over and over again; and sometimes out of his head he drew the great tower of the Cathedral or the gateway that led into the precincts. He had a knack for drawing. Aunt Louisa during her youth had painted in water colours, and she had several albums filled with sketches of churches, old bridges, and picturesque cottages. They were often shown at the vicarage tea-parties. She had once given Philip a paint-box as a Christmas present, and he had started by copying her pictures. He copied them better than anyone could have expected, and presently he did little pictures of his own. Mrs Carey encouraged him. It was a good way to keep him out of mischief, and later on his sketches would be useful for bazaars. Two or three of them had been framed and hung in his bedroom.

But one day, at the end of the morning's work, Mr Perkins stopped him as he was lounging out of the form-room.

"I want to speak to you, Carey."

Philip waited. Mr Perkins ran his lean fingers through his beard and looked at Philip. He seemed to be thinking over what he wanted to say.

"What's the matter with you, Carey?" he said abruptly.

Philip, flushing, looked at him quickly. But knowing him well by now, without answering, he waited for him to go on.

"I've been dissatisfied with you lately. You've been slack and inattentive. You seem to take no interest in your work. It's been slovenly and bad."

"I'm very sorry, sir," said Philip.

"Is that all you have to say for yourself?"

Philip looked down sulkily. How could he answer that he was bored to death?

"You know, this term you'll go down instead of up. I shan't give you a very good report."

Philip wondered what he would say if he knew how the report was treated. It arrived at breakfast. Mr Carey glanced at it indifferently, and passed it over to Philip.

"There's your report. You'd better see what it says," he remarked, as he ran his fingers through the wrapper of a catalogue of second-hand books.

Philip read it.

"Is it good?" asked Aunt Louisa.

"Not so good as I deserve," answered Philip, with a smile, giving it to her.

"I'll read it afterwards when I've got my spectacles," she said.

But after breakfast Mary Ann came in to say the butcher was there, and she generally forgot.

Mr Perkins went on.

"I'm disappointed with you. And I can't understand. I know you can do things if you want to, but you don't seem to want to any more. I was going to make you a monitor next term, but I think I'd better wait a bit."

Philip flushed. He did not like the thought of being passed over. He tightened his lips.

"And there's something else. You must begin thinking of your scholarship now. You won't get anything unless you start working very seriously."

Philip was irritated by the lecture. He was angry with the headmaster, and angry with himself.

"I don't think I'm going up to Oxford," he said.

"Why not? I thought your idea was to be ordained."

"I've changed my mind."

"Why?"

Philip did not answer. Mr Perkins, holding himself oddly as he always did, like a figure in one of Perugino's pictures, drew his fingers thoughtfully through his beard. He looked at Philip as though he were trying to understand and then abruptly told him he might go.

Apparently he was not satisfied, for one evening, a week later, when Philip had to go into his study with some papers, he resumed the conversation; but this time he adopted a different method: he spoke to Philip not as a schoolmaster with a boy but as one human being with another. He did not seem to care now that Philip's work was poor, that he ran small chance against keen rivals of carrying off the scholarship necessary for him to go to Oxford: the important matter was his changed intention about his life afterwards. Mr Perkins set himself to revive his eagerness to be ordained. With infinite skill he worked on his feelings, and this was easier since he was himself genuinely moved. Philip's change of mind caused him bitter distress, and he really thought he was throwing away his chance of happiness in life for he knew not what. His voice was very persuasive. And Philip, easily moved by the emotion of others, very emotional himself notwithstanding a placid exterior—his face, partly by nature but also from the habit of all these years at school, seldom except by his quick flushing showed what he felt—Philip was deeply touched by what the master said. He was very grateful to him for the interest he showed, and he was conscience-stricken by the grief which he felt his behaviour caused him. It was subtly flattering to know that with the whole school to think about Mr Perkins should trouble with him, but at the same time something else in him, like another person standing at his elbow, clung desperately to two words.

"I won't. I won't. I won't."

He felt himself slipping. He was powerless against the weakness that seemed to well up in him; it was like the water that rises up in an empty bottle held over a full basin; and he set his teeth, saying the words over and over to himself.

"I won't. I won't. I won't."

At last Mr Perkins put his hand on Philip's shoulder.

"I don't want to influence you," he said. "You must decide for yourself. Pray to Almighty God for help and guidance."

When Philip came out of the headmaster's house there was a light rain falling. He went under the archway that led to the precincts, there was not a soul there, and the rooks were silent in the elms. He walked round slowly. He felt hot, and the rain did him good. He thought over all that Mr Perkins had said calmly now that he was withdrawn from the fervour of his personality, and he was thankful he had not given way.

In the darkness he could but vaguely see the great mass of the Cathedral: he hated it now because of the irksomeness of the long services which he was forced to attend. The anthem was interminable, and you had to stand drearily while it was being sung; you could not hear the droning sermon, and your body twitched because you had to sit still when you wanted to move about. Then Philip thought of the two services every Sunday at Blackstable. The church was bare and cold, and there was a smell all about one of pomade and starched clothes. The curate preached once and his uncle preached once. As he grew up he had learned to know his uncle; Philip was downright and intolerant, and he could not understand that a man might sincerely say things as a clergyman which he never acted up to as a man. The deception outraged him. His uncle was a weak and selfish man, whose chief desire it was to be saved trouble.

Mr Perkins had spoken to him of the beauty of a life dedicated to the service of God. Philip knew what sort of lives the clergy led in the corner of East Anglia which was his home. There was the Vicar of Whitestone, a parish a little way from Blackstable: he was a bachelor and to give himself something to do had lately taken up farming: the local paper constantly reported the cases he had in the county court against this one and that, labourers he would not pay their wages to or tradesmen whom he accused of cheating him; scandal said he starved his cows, and there was much talk about some general action which should be taken against him. Then there was the Vicar of Ferne, a bearded, fine figure of a man: his wife had been forced to leave him because of his cruelty, and she had filled the neighbourhood with stories of his immorality. The Vicar of Surle, a tiny hamlet by the sea, was to be seen every evening in the public house a stone's throw from his vicarage; and the churchwardens had been to Mr Carey to ask his advice. There was not a soul for any of them to talk to except small farmers or fishermen; there were long winter evenings when the wind blew, whistling drearily through the leafless trees, and all around they saw nothing but the bare monotony of ploughed fields; and there was poverty, and there was lack of any work that seemed to matter; every kink in their characters had free play; there was nothing to restrain them; they grew narrow and eccentric: Philip knew all this, but in his young intolerance he did not offer it as an excuse. He shivered at the thought of leading such a life; he wanted to get out into the world.

21

Mr Perkins soon saw that his words had had no effect on Philip, and for the rest of the term ignored him. He wrote a report which was vitriolic. When it arrived and Aunt Louisa asked Philip what it was like, he answered cheerfully:

"Rotten."

"Is it?" said the Vicar. "I must look at it again."

"Do you think there's any use in my staying on at Tercanbury? I should have thought it would be better if I went to Germany for a bit."

"What has put that in your head?" said Aunt Louisa.

"Don't you think it's rather a good idea?"

Sharp had already left King's School and had written to Philip from Hanover. He was really starting life, and it made Philip more restless to think of it. He felt he could not bear another year of restraint.

"But then you wouldn't get a scholarship."

"I haven't a chance of getting one anyhow. And besides, don't know that I particularly want to go to Oxford."

"But if you're going to be ordained, Philip?" Aunt Louisa exclaimed in dismay.

"I've given up that idea long ago."

Mrs Carey looked at him with startled eyes, and then, used to self-restraint, she poured out another cup of tea for his uncle. They did not speak. In a moment Philip saw tears slowly falling down her cheeks. His heart was suddenly wrung because he caused her pain. In her tight black dress, made by the dressmaker down the street, with her wrinkled face and pale tired eyes, her gray hair still done in the frivolous ringlets of her youth, she was a ridiculous but strangely pathetic figure. Philip saw it for the first time.

Afterwards, when the Vicar was shut up in his study with the curate, he put his arms round her waist.

"I say, I'm sorry you're upset, Aunt Louisa," he said. "But it's no good my being ordained if I haven't a real vocation, is it?"

"I'm so disappointed, Philip," she moaned. "I'd set my heart on it. I thought you could be your uncle's curate, and then when our time came—after all, we can't last for ever, can we?—you might have taken his place."

Philip shivered. He was seized with panic. His heart beat like a pigeon in a trap beating with its wings. His aunt wept softly, her head upon his shoulder.

"I wish you'd persuade Uncle William to let me leave Tercanbury. I'm so sick of it."

But the Vicar of Blackstable did not easily alter any arrangements he had made, and it had always been intended that Philip should stay at King's School till he was eighteen, and should then go to Oxford. At all events he would not hear of Philip leaving then, for no notice had been given and the term's fee would have to be paid in any case.

"Then will you give notice for me to leave at Christmas?" said Philip, at the end of a long and often bitter conversation.

"I'll write to Mr Perkins about it and see what he says."

"Oh, I wish to goodness I were twenty-one. It is awful to be at somebody else's beck and call."

"Philip, you shouldn't speak to your uncle like that," said Mrs Carey gently.

"But don't you see that Perkins will want me to stay? He gets so much a head for every chap in the school."

"Why don't you want to go to Oxford?"

"What's the good if I'm not going into the Church?"

"You can't go into the Church; you're in the Church already," said the Vicar.

"Ordained then," replied Philip impatiently.

"What are you going to be, Philip?" asked Mrs Carey.

"I don't know. I've not made up my mind. But whatever I am, it'll be useful to know foreign languages. I shall get far more out of a year in Germany than by staying on at that hole."

He would not say that he felt Oxford would be little better than a continuation of his life at school. He wished immensely to be his own master. Besides he would be known to a certain extent among old schoolfellows, and he wanted to get away from them all. He felt that his life at school had been a failure. He wanted to start fresh.

It happened that his desire to go to Germany fell in with certain ideas which had been of late discussed at Blackstable. Sometimes friends came to stay with the doctor and brought news of the world outside; and the visitors spending August by the sea had their own way of looking at things. The Vicar had heard that there were people who did not think the old-fashioned education so useful nowadays as it had been in the past, and modern languages were gaining an importance which they had not had in his own youth. His own mind was divided, for a younger brother of his had been sent to Germany when he failed in some examination, thus creating precedent, but since he had there died of typhoid it was impossible to look upon the experiment as other than dangerous. The result of innumerable conversations was that Philip should go back to Tercanbury for another term, and then should leave. With this agreement Philip was not dissatisfied. But when he had been back a few days the headmaster spoke to him.

"I've had a letter from your uncle. It appears you want go to Germany, and he asks me what I think about it."

Philip was astounded. He was furious with his guardian for going back on his word.

"I thought it was settled, sir," he said.

"Far from it. I've written to say I think it the greatest mistake to take you away."

Philip immediately sat down and wrote a violent letter to his uncle. He did not measure his language. He was so angry that he could not get to sleep till quite late that night, and he woke in the early morning and began brooding over the way they had treated him. He waited impatiently for an answer. In two or three days it came. It was a mild, pained letter from Aunt Louisa, saying that he should not write such things to his uncle, who was very much distressed. He was unkind and unchristian. He must know they were only trying to do their best for him, and they were so much older than he that they must be better judges of what was good for him. Philip clenched his hands. He had heard that statement so often, and he could not see why it was true; they did not know the conditions as he did, why should they accept it as self-evident that their greater age gave them greater wisdom? The letter ended with the information that Mr Carey had withdrawn the notice he had given.

Philip nursed his wrath till the next half-holiday. They had them on Tuesdays and Thursdays, since on Saturday afternoons they had to go to a service in the Cathedral. He stopped behind when the rest of the Sixth went out.

"May I go to Blackstable this afternoon, please, sir?" he asked.

"No," said the headmaster briefly.

"I wanted to see my uncle about something very important."

"Didn't you hear me say no?"

Philip did not answer. He went out. He felt almost sick with humiliation, the humiliation of having to ask and the humiliation of the curt refusal. He hated the headmaster now. Philip writhed under that despotism which never vouchsafed a reason for the most tyrannous act. He was too angry to care what he did, and after dinner walked down to the station, by the back ways he knew so well, just in time to catch the train to Blackstable. He walked into the vicarage and found his uncle and aunt sitting in the dining-room.

"Hulloa, where have you sprung from?" said the Vicar.

It was very clear that he was not pleased to see him. He looked a little uneasy.

"I thought I'd come and see you about my leaving. I want to know what you mean by promising me one thing when I was here, and doing something different a week after."

He was a little frightened at his own boldness, but he had made up his mind exactly what words to use, and, though his heart beat violently, he forced himself to say them.

"Have you got leave to come here this afternoon?"

"No. I asked Perkins and he refused. If you like to write and tell him I've been here you can get me into a really fine old row."

Mrs Carey sat knitting with trembling hands. She was unused to scenes and they agitated her extremely.

"It would serve you right if I told him," said Mr Carey.

"If you like to be a perfect sneak you can. After writing to Perkins as you did you're quite capable of it."

It was foolish of Philip to say that, because it gave the Vicar exactly the opportunity he wanted.

"I'm not going to sit still while you say impertinent things to me," he said with dignity.

He got up and walked quickly out of the room into his study. Philip heard him shut the door and lock it.

"Oh, I wish to God I were twenty-one. It is awful to be tied down like this."

Aunt Louisa began to cry quietly.

"Oh, Philip, you oughtn't to have spoken to your uncle like that. Do please go and tell him you're sorry."

"I'm not in the least sorry. He's taking a mean advantage. Of course it's just waste of money keeping me on at school, but what does he care? It's not his money. It was cruel to put me under the guardianship of people who know nothing about things."

"Philip."

Philip in his voluble anger stopped suddenly at the sound of her voice. It was heart-broken. He had not realised what bitter things he was saying.

"Philip, how can you be so unkind? You know we are only trying to do our best for you, and we know that we have no experience; it isn't as if we'd had any children of our own: that's why we consulted Mr Perkins." Her voice broke. "I've tried to be like a mother to you. I've loved you as if you were my own son."

She was so small and frail, there was something so pathetic in her old-maidish air, that Philip was touched. A great lump came suddenly in his throat and his eyes filled with tears.

"I'm so sorry," he said. "I didn't mean to be beastly."

He knelt down beside her and took her in his arms, and kissed her wet, withered cheeks. She sobbed bitterly, and he seemed to feel on a sudden the pity of that wasted life. She had never surrendered herself before to such a display of emotion.

"I know I've not been what I wanted to be to you, Philip, but I didn't know how. It's been just as dreadful for me to have no children as for you to have no mother."

Philip forgot his anger and his own concerns, but thought only of consoling her, with broken words and clumsy little caresses. Then the clock struck, and he had to bolt off at once to catch the only train that would get him back to Tercanbury in time for call-over. As he sat in the corner of the railway carriage he saw that he had done nothing. He was angry with himself for his weakness. It was despicable to have allowed himself to be turned from his purpose by the pompous airs of the Vicar and the tears of his aunt. But as the result of he knew not what conversation between the couple another letter was written to the headmaster. Mr Perkins read it with an impatient shrug of the shoulders. He showed it to Philip. It ran:

Dear Mr Perkins,

Forgive me for troubling you again about my ward, but both his Aunt and I have been uneasy about him. He seems very anxious to leave school, and his Aunt thinks he is unhappy. It is very difficult for us to know what to do as we are not his parents. He does not seem to think he is doing very well and he feels it is wasting his money to stay on. I should be very much obliged if you would have a talk to him, and if he is still of the same mind perhaps it would be better if he left at Christmas as I originally intended.

Yours very truly,

William Carey.

Philip gave him back the letter. He felt a thrill of pride in his triumph. He had got his own way, and he was satisfied. His will had gained a victory over the wills of others.

"It's not much good my spending half an hour writing to your uncle if he changes his mind the next letter he gets from you," said the headmaster irritably.

Philip said nothing, and his face was perfectly placid; but he could not prevent the twinkle in his eyes. Mr Perkins noticed it and broke into a little laugh.

"You've rather scored, haven't you?" he said.

Then Philip smiled outright. He could not conceal his exultation.

"Is it true that you're very anxious to leave?"

"Yes, sir."

"Are you unhappy here?"

Philip blushed. He hated instinctively any attempt to get into the depths of his feelings.

"Oh, I don't know, sir."

Mr Perkins, slowly dragging his fingers through his beared, looked at him thoughtfully. He seemed to speak almost to himself.

"Of course schools are made for the average. The holes are all round, and whatever shape the pegs are they must wedge in somehow. One hasn't time to bother about anything but the average." Then suddenly he addressed himself to Philip: "Look here, I've got a suggestion to make to you. It's getting on towards the end of the term now. Another term won't kill you, and if you want to go to Germany you'd better go after Easter than after Christmas. It'll be much pleasanter in the spring than in midwinter. If at the end of the next term you still want to go I'll make no objection. What d'you say to that?"

"Thank you very much, sir."

Philip was so glad to have gained the last three months that he did not mind the extra term. The school seemed less of a prison when he knew that before Easter he would be free from it for ever. His heart danced within him. That evening in chapel he looked round at the boys, standing according to their forms, each in his due place, and he chuckled with satisfaction at the thought that soon he would never see them again. It made him regard them almost with a friendly feeling. His eyes rested on Rose. Rose took his position as a monitor very seriously: he had quite an idea of being a good influence in the school; it was his turn to read the lesson that evening, and he read it very well. Philip smiled when he thought that he would be rid of him for ever, and it would not matter in six months whether Rose was tall and straight-limbed; and where would the importance be that he was a monitor and captain of the eleven? Philip looked at the masters in their gowns. Gordon was dead, he had died of apoplexy two years before, but all the rest were there. Philip knew now what a poor lot they were, except Turner perhaps, there was

something of a man in him; and he writhed at the thought of the subjection in which they had held him. In six months they would not matter either. Their praise would mean nothing to him, and he would shrug
his shoulders at their censure.

Philip had learned not to express his emotions by outward signs, and
shyness still tormented him, but he had often very high spirits; and then,
though he limped about demurely, silent and reserved, it seemed to be
hallooing in his heart. He seemed to himself to walk more lightly. All
sorts of ideas danced through his head, fancies chased one another so furiously that he could not catch them; but their coming and their going
filled him with exhilaration. Now, being happy, he was able to work, and
during the remaining weeks of the term set himself to make up for his
long neglect. His brain worked easily, and he took a keen pleasure in the
activity of his intellect. He did very well in the examinations that closed
the term. Mr Perkins made only one remark: he was talking to him about
an essay he had written, and, after the usual criticisms, said:

"So you've made up your mind to stop playing the fool for a bit,
have you?"

He smiled at him with his shining teeth, and Philip, looking down,
gave an embarrassed smile.

The half dozen boys who expected to divide between them the various prizes which were given at the end of the summer term had ceased
to look upon Philip as a serious rival, but now they began to regard him
with some uneasiness. He told no one that he was leaving at Easter and
so was in no sense a competitor, but left them to their anxieties. He
knew that Rose flattered himself on his French, for he had spent two or
three holidays in France; and he expected to get the Dean's Prize for English essay; Philip got a good deal of satisfaction in watching his dismay
when he saw how much better Philip was doing in these subjects than
himself. Another fellow, Norton, could not go to Oxford unless he got
one of the scholarships at the disposal of the school. He asked Philip if
he was going in for them.

"Have you any objection?" asked Philip.

It entertained him to think that he held someone else's future in his
hand. There was something romantic in getting these various rewards actually in his grasp, and then leaving them to others because he disdained

them. At last the breaking-up day came, and he went to Mr Perkins to bid him good-bye.

"You don't mean to say you really want to leave?"

Philip's face fell at the headmaster's evident surprise.

"You said you wouldn't put any objection in the way, sir," he answered.

"I thought it was only a whim that I'd better humour. I know you're obstinate and headstrong. What on earth d'you want to leave for now? You've only got another term in any case. You can get the Magdalen scholarship easily; you'll get half the prizes we've got to give."

Philip looked at him sullenly. He felt that he had been tricked; but he had the promise, and Perkins would have to stand by it.

"You'll have a very pleasant time at Oxford. You needn't decide at once what you're going to do afterwards. I wonder if you realise how delightful the life is up there for anyone who has brains."

"I've made all my arrangements now to go to Germany, sir," said Philip.

"Are they arrangements that couldn't possibly be altered?" asked Mr Perkins, with his quizzical smile. "I shall be very sorry to lose you. In schools the rather stupid boys who work always do better than the clever boy who's idle, but when the clever boy works—why then, he does what you've done this term."

Philip flushed darkly. He was unused to compliments, and no one had ever told him he was clever. The headmaster put his hand on Philip's shoulder.

"You know, driving things into the heads of thick-witted boys is dull work, but when now and then you have the chance of teaching a boy who comes half-way towards you, who understands almost before you've got the words out of your mouth, why, then teaching is the most exhilarating thing in the world."

Philip was melted by kindness; it had never occurred to him that it mattered really to Mr Perkins whether he went or stayed. He was touched and immensely flattered. It would be pleasant to end up his school-days with glory and then go to Oxford: in a flash there appeared before him the life which he had heard described from boys who came back to play in the O. K. S. match or in letters from the University read out in one of the studies. But he was ashamed; he would look such a fool in his own eyes if he gave in now; his uncle would chuckle at the success of the headmaster's ruse. It was rather a come-down from the dramatic surrender of all these prizes which were in his reach, because he disdained to take them, to the plain, ordinary winning of them. It only required a little more persuasion, just enough to save his self-respect, and Philip would have done anything that Mr Perkins wished; but his face showed nothing of his conflicting emotions. It was placid and sullen.

"I think I'd rather go, sir," he said.

Mr Perkins, like many men who manage things by their personal influence, grew a little impatient when his power was not immediately manifest. He had a great deal of work to do, and could not waste more time on a boy who seemed to him insanely obstinate.

"Very well, I promised to let you if you really wanted it, and I keep my promise. When do you go to Germany?"

Philip's heart beat violently. The battle was won, and he did not know whether he had not rather lost it.

"At the beginning of May, sir," he answered.

"Well, you must come and see us when you get back."

He held out his hand. If he had given him one more chance Philip would have changed his mind, but he seemed to look upon the matter as settled. Philip walked out of the house. His school-days were over, and he was free; but the wild exultation to which he had looked forward at that moment was not there. He walked round the precincts slowly, and a profound depression seized him. He wished now that he had not been foolish. He did not want to go, but he knew he could never bring himself to go to the headmaster and tell him he would stay. That was a humiliation he could never put upon himself. He wondered whether he had done right. He was dissatisfied with himself and with all his circumstances. He asked himself dully whether whenever you got your way you wished afterwards that you hadn't.

7

*

From *The Moon and Sixpence*
(1919)

It is here that I purposed to end my book. My first idea was to begin it with the account of Strickland's last years in Tahiti and with his horrible death, and then to go back and relate what I knew of his beginnings. This I meant to do, not from wilfulness, but because I wished to leave Strickland setting out with I know not what fancies in his lonely soul for the unknown islands which fired his imagination. I liked the picture of him starting at the age of forty-seven, when most men have already settled comfortably in a groove, for a new world. I saw him, the sea gray under the mistral and foam-flecked, watching the vanishing coast of France, which he was destined never to see again; and I thought there was something gallant in his bearing and dauntless in his soul. I wished so to end on a note of hope. It seemed to emphasise the unconquerable spirit of man. But I could not manage it. Somehow I could not get into my story, and after trying once or twice I had to give it up; I started from the beginning in the usual way, and made up my mind I could only tell what I knew of Strickland's life in the order in which I learnt the facts.

Those that I have now are fragmentary. I am in the position of a biologist who from a single bone must reconstruct not only the appearance of an extinct animal, but its habits. Strickland made no particular impression on the people who came in contact with him in Tahiti. To them he was no more than a beach-comber in constant need of money, remarkable only for the peculiarity that he painted pictures which seemed to them absurd; and it was not till he had been dead for some years and agents came from the dealers in Paris and Berlin to look for any pictures which might still remain on the island, that they had any idea that among them had dwelt a man of consequence. They remembered then that they could have bought for a song canvases which now were worth large sums, and they could not forgive themselves for the opportunity which had escaped them. There was a Jewish trader called Cohen, who had come by one of Strickland's pictures in a singular way. He was a little old Frenchman, with soft kind eyes and a pleasant smile, half trader and half seaman, who owned a cutter in which he wandered boldly among the Paumotus and the Marquesas, taking out trade goods and bringing back copra, shell, and pearls. I went to see him because I was told he had a large black pearl which he was willing to sell cheaply, and when I discovered that it was beyond my means I began to talk to him about Strickland. He had known him well.

"You see, I was interested in him because he was a painter," he told me. "We don't get many painters in the islands, and I was sorry for him because he was such a bad one. I gave him his first job. I had a plantation on the peninsula, and I wanted a white overseer. You never get any work out of the natives unless you have a white man over them. I said to him: 'You'll have plenty of time for painting, and you can earn a bit of money.' I knew he was starving, but I offered him good wages."

"I can't imagine that he was a very satisfactory overseer," I said, smiling.

"I made allowances. I have always had a sympathy for artists. It is in our blood, you know. But he only remained a few months. When he had enough money to buy paints and canvases he left me. The place had got hold of him by then, and he wanted to get away into the bush. But I continued to see him now and then. He would turn up in Papeete every few months and stay a little while; he'd get money out of someone or other and then disappear again. It was on one of these visits that he came to me and asked for the loan of two hundred francs. He looked as if he hadn't had a meal for a week, and I hadn't the heart to refuse him. Of course, I never expected to see my money again. Well, a year later he came to see me once more, and he brought a picture with him. He did not mention the money he owed me, but he said: 'Here is a picture of your plantation that I've painted for you.' I looked at it. I did not know what to say, but of course I thanked him, and when he had gone away I showed it to my wife."

"What was it like?" I asked.

"Do not ask me. I could not make head or tail of it. I never saw such a thing in my life. 'What shall we do with it?' I said to my wife. 'We can never hang it up,' she said. 'People would laugh at us.' So she took it into an attic and put it away with all sorts of rubbish, for my wife can never throw anything away. It is her mania. Then, imagine to yourself, just before the war my brother wrote to me from Paris, and said: 'Do you know anything about an English painter who lived in Tahiti? It appears that he was a genius, and his pictures fetch large prices. See if you, can lay your hands on anything and send it to me. There's money to be made.' So I said to my wife: 'What about that picture that Strickland gave me? Is it possible that it is still in the attic?' 'Without doubt,' she answered, 'for you know that I never throw anything away. It is my mania.' We went up to the attic, and there, among I know not what rubbish that had been gathered during the thirty years we have inhabited that house, was the picture. I looked at it again, and I said: 'Who would have thought that the overseer of my plantation on the peninsula, to whom I lent two hundred francs, had genius? Do you see anything in the picture?' 'No,' she said, 'it does not resemble the plantation and I have never seen cocoanuts with blue leaves; but they are mad in Paris, and it may be that your brother will be able to sell it for the two hundred francs you lent Strickland.' Well, we packed it up and we sent it to my brother. And at last I received a letter from him. What do you think he said? 'I received your picture,' he said, 'and I confess I thought it was a joke that you had played on me. I would not have given the cost of postage for the picture. I was half afraid to show it to the gentleman who had spoken to me about it. Imagine my surprise when he said it was a masterpiece, and offered me thirty thousand francs. I dare say he would have paid more, but frankly I was so taken aback that I lost my head; I accepted the offer before I was able to collect myself.' "

Then Monsieur Cohen said an admirable thing.

"I wish that poor Strickland had been still alive. I wonder what he would have said when I gave him twenty-nine thousand eight hundred francs for his picture."

49

I lived at the Hotel de la Fleur, and Mrs. Johnson, the proprietress, had a sad story to tell of lost opportunity. After Strickland's death certain of his effects were sold by auction in the market-place at Papeete, and she went to it herself because there was among the truck an American stove she wanted. She paid twenty-seven francs for it.

"There were a dozen pictures," she told me, "but they were un-framed, and nobody wanted them. Some of them sold for as much as ten francs, but mostly they went for five or six. Just think, if I had bought them I should be a rich woman now."

But Tiaré Johnson would never under any circumstances have been rich. She could not keep money. The daughter of a native and an English sea-captain settled in Tahiti, when I knew her she was a woman of fifty, who looked older, and of enormous proportions. Tall and extremely stout, she would have been of imposing presence if the great good-nature of her face had not made it impossible for her to express anything but kindliness. Her arms were like legs of mutton, her breasts like giant cab-bages; her face, broad and fleshy, gave you an impression of almost inde-cent nakedness, and vast chin succeeded to vast chin. I do not know how many of them there were. They fell away voluminously into the capa-ciousness of her bosom. She was dressed usually in a pink Mother Hub-bard, and she wore all day long a large straw hat. But when she let down her hair, which she did now and then, for she was vain of it, you saw that it was long and dark and curly; and her eyes had remained young and vi-vacious. Her laughter was the most catching I ever heard; it would begin, a low peal in her throat, and would grow louder and louder till her whole vast body shook. She loved three things—a joke, a glass of wine, and a handsome man. To have known her is a privilege.

She was the best cook on the island, and she adored good food. From morning till night you saw her sitting on a low chair in the kitchen, surrounded by a Chinese cook and two or three native girls, giving her orders, chatting sociably with all and sundry, and tasting the savoury messes she devised. When she wished to do honour to a friend she cooked the dinner with her own hands. Hospitality was a passion with her, and there was no one on the island who need go without a dinner when there was anything to eat at the Hotel de la Fleur. She never turned her customers out of her house because they did not pay their bills. She always hoped they would pay when they could. There was one man there who had fallen on adversity, and to him she had given board and lodging for several months. When the Chinese laundryman refused to wash for him without payment she had sent his things to be washed with hers. She could not allow the poor fellow to go about in a dirty shirt, she said, and since he was a man, and men must smoke, she gave him a franc a day for cigarettes. She used him with the same affability as those of her clients who paid their bills once a week.

Age and obesity had made her inapt for love, but she took a keen interest in the amatory affairs of the young. She looked upon venery as the natural occupation for men and women, and was ever ready with precept and example from her own wide experience.

"I was not fifteen when my father found that I had a lover," she said. "He was third mate on the *Tropic Bird*. A good-looking boy."

She sighed a little. They say a woman always remembers her first lover with affection; but perhaps she does not always remember him.

"My father was a sensible man."

"What did he do?" I asked.

"He thrashed me within an inch of my life, and then he made me marry Captain Johnson. I did not mind. He was older, of course, but he was good-looking too."

Tiaré—her father had called her by the name of the white, scented flower which, they tell you, if you have once smelt, will always draw you back to Tahiti in the end, however far you may have roamed—Tiaré remembered Strickland very well.

"He used to come here sometimes, and I used to see him walking about Papeete. I was sorry for him, he was so thin, and he never had any money. When I heard he was in town, I used to send a boy to find him and make him come to dinner with me. I got him a job once or twice, but he couldn't stick to anything. After a little while he wanted to get back to the bush, and one morning he would be gone."

Strickland reached Tahiti about six months after he left Marseilles. He worked his passage on a sailing vessel that was making the trip from Auckland to San Francisco, and he arrived with a box of paints, an easel, and a dozen canvases. He had a few pounds in his pocket, for he had found work in Sydney, and he took a small room in a native house outside the town. I think the moment he reached Tahiti he felt himself at home. Tiaré told me that he said to her once:

"I'd been scrubbing the deck, and all at once a chap said to me: 'Why, there it is.' And I looked up and I saw the outline of the island. I knew right away that there was the place I'd been looking for all my life. Then we came near, and I seemed to recognise it. Sometimes when I walk about it all seems familiar. I could swear I've lived here before."

"Sometimes it takes them like that," said Tiaré. "I've known men come on shore for a few hours while their ship was taking in cargo, and never go back. And I've known men who came here to be in an office for a year, and they cursed the place, and when they went away they took their dying oath they'd hang themselves before they came back again, and in six months you'd see them land once more, and they'd tell you they couldn't live anywhere else."

50

I have an idea that some men are born out of their due place. Accident has cast them amid certain surroundings, but they have always a nostalgia for a home they know not. They are strangers in their birthplace, and the leafy lanes they have known from childhood or the populous streets in which they have played, remain but a place of passage. They may spend their whole lives aliens among their kindred and remain aloof among the only scenes they have ever known. Perhaps it is this sense of strangeness that sends men far and wide in the search for something permanent, to which they may attach themselves. Perhaps some deep-rooted atavism urges the wanderer back to lands which his ancestors left in the dim beginnings of history. Sometimes a man hits upon a place to which he mysteriously feels that he belongs. Here is the home he sought, and he will settle amid scenes that he has never seen before, among men he has never known, as though they were familiar to him from his birth. Here at last he finds rest.

I told Tiaré the story of a man I had known at St. Thomas's Hospital. He was a Jew named Abraham, a blond, rather stout young man, shy and very unassuming; but he had remarkable gifts. He entered the hospital with a scholarship, and during the five years of the curriculum gained every prize that was open to him. He was made house-physician and house-surgeon. His brilliance was allowed by all. Finally he was elected to a position on the staff, and his career was assured. So far as human things can be predicted, it was certain that he would rise to the greatest heights of his profession. Honours and wealth awaited him. Before he entered upon his new duties he wished to take a holiday, and, having no private means, he went as surgeon on a tramp steamer to the Levant. It did not generally carry a doctor, but one of the senior surgeons at the hospital knew a director of the line, and Abraham was taken as a favour.

In a few weeks the authorities received his resignation of the coveted position on the staff. It created profound astonishment, and wild rumours were current. Whenever a man does anything unexpected, his fellows ascribe it to the most discreditable motives. But there was a man ready to step into Abraham's shoes, and Abraham was forgotten. Nothing more was heard of him. He vanished.

It was perhaps ten years later that one morning on board ship, about to land at Alexandria, I was bidden to line up with the other passengers for the doctor's examination. The doctor was a stout man in shabby clothes, and when he took off his hat I noticed that he was very bald. I had an idea that I had seen him before. Suddenly I remembered.

"Abraham," I said.

He turned to me with a puzzled look, and then, recognising me, seized my hand. After expressions of surprise on either side, hearing that I meant to spend the night in Alexandria, he asked me to dine with him at the English Club. When we met again I declared my astonishment at finding him there. It was a very modest position that he occupied, and there was about him an air of straitened circumstance. Then he told me his story. When he set out on his holiday in the Mediterranean he had every intention of returning to London and his appointment at St. Thomas's. One morning the tramp docked at Alexandria, and from the deck he looked at the city, white in the sunlight, and the crowd on the wharf; he saw the natives in their shabby gabardines, the blacks from the Soudan, the noisy throng of Greeks and Italians, the grave Turks in tarbooshes, the sunshine and the blue sky; and something happened to him. He could not describe it. It was like a thunder-clap, he said, and then, dissatisfied with this, he said it was like a revelation. Something seemed to twist his heart, and suddenly he felt an exultation, a sense of wonderful freedom. He felt himself at home, and he made up his mind there and then, in a minute, that he would live the rest of his life in Alexandria. He had no great difficulty in leaving the ship, and in twenty-four hours, with all his belongings, he was on shore.

"The Captain must have thought you as mad as a hatter," I smiled.

"I didn't care what anybody thought. It wasn't I that acted, but something stronger within me. I thought I would go to a little Greek hotel, while I looked about, and I felt I knew where to find one. And do you know, I walked straight there, and when I saw it, I recognised it at once."

"Had you been to Alexandria before?"

"No; I'd never been out of England in my life."

Presently he entered the Government service, and there he had been ever since.

"Have you never regretted it?"

"Never, not for a minute. I earn just enough to live upon, and I'm satisfied. I ask nothing more than to remain as I am till I die. I've had a wonderful life."

I left Alexandria next day, and I forgot about Abraham till a little while ago, when I was dining with another old friend in the profession, Alec Carmichael, who was in England on short leave. I ran across him in the street and congratulated him on the knighthood with which his eminent services during the war had been rewarded. We arranged to spend an evening together for old time's sake, and when I agreed to dine with him, he proposed that he should ask nobody else, so that we could chat without interruption. He had a beautiful old house in Queen Anne Street, and being a man of taste he had furnished it admirably. On the walls of the dining-room I saw a charming Bellotto, and there was a pair of Zoffanys that I envied. When his wife, a tall, lovely creature in cloth of gold, had left us, I remarked laughingly on the change in his present circumstances from those when we had both been medical students. We had looked upon it then as an extravagance to dine in a shabby Italian restaurant in the Westminster Bridge Road. Now Alec Carmichael was on the staff of half a dozen hospitals. I should think he earned ten thousand a year, and his knighthood was but the first of the honours which must inevitably fall to his lot.

"I've done pretty well," he said, "but the strange thing is that I owe it all to one piece of luck."

"What do you mean by that?"

"Well, do you remember Abraham? He was the man who had the future. When we were students he beat me all along the line. He got the prizes and the scholarships that I went in for. I always played second fiddle to him. If he'd kept on he'd be in the position I'm in now. That man had a genius for surgery. No one had a look in with him. When he was appointed Registrar at Thomas's I hadn't a chance of getting on the staff. I should have had to become a G.P., and you know what likelihood there is for a G.P. ever to get out of the common rut. But Abraham fell out, and I got the job. That gave me my opportunity."

"I dare say that's true."

"It was just luck. I suppose there was some kink in Abraham. Poor devil, he's gone to the dogs altogether. He's got some twopenny-halfpenny job in the medical at Alexandria—sanitary officer or something like that. I'm told he lives with an ugly old Greek woman and has half a dozen scrofulous kids. The fact is, I suppose, that it's not enough to have brains. The thing that counts is character. Abraham hadn't got character."

Character? I should have thought it needed a good deal of character to throw up a career after half an hour's meditation, because you saw in another way of living a more intense significance. And it required still more character never to regret the sudden step. But I said nothing, and Alec Carmichael proceeded reflectively:

"Of course it would be hypocritical for me to pretend that I regret what Abraham did. After all, I've scored by it." He puffed luxuriously at the long Corona he was smoking. "But if I weren't personally concerned I should be sorry at the waste. It seems a rotten thing that a man should make such a hash of life."

I wondered if Abraham really had made a hash of life. Is to do what you most want, to live under the conditions that please you, in peace with yourself, to make a hash of life; and is it success to be an eminent surgeon with ten thousand a year and a beautiful wife? I suppose it depends on

what meaning you attach to life, the claim which you acknowledge to society, and the claim of the individual. But again I held my tongue, for
who am I to argue with a knight?

51

Tiaré, when I told her this story, praised my prudence, and for a few
minutes we worked in silence, for we were shelling peas. Then her eyes,
always alert for the affairs of her kitchen, fell on some action of the Chinese cook which aroused her violent disapproval. She turned on him
with a torrent of abuse. The Chink was not backward to defend himself,
and a very lively quarrel ensued. They spoke in the native language, of
which I had learnt but half a dozen words, and it sounded as though the
world would shortly come to an end; but presently peace was restored
and Tiaré gave the cook a cigarette. They both smoked comfortably.

"Do you know, it was I who found him his wife?" said Tiaré suddenly, with a smile that spread all over her immense face.

"The cook?"

"No, Strickland."

"But he had one already."

"That is what he said, but I told him she was in England, and England is at the other end of the world."

"True," I replied.

"He would come to Papeete every two or three months, when he
wanted paints or tobacco or money, and then he would wander about
like a lost dog. I was sorry for him. I had a girl here then called Ata to
do the rooms; she was some sort of a relation of mine, and her father
and mother were dead, so I had her to live with me. Strickland used to
come here now and then to have a square meal or to play chess with one
of the boys. I noticed that she looked at him when he came, and I asked
her if she liked him. She said she liked him well enough. You know what
these girls are; they're always pleased to go with a white man."

"Was she a native?" I asked.

"Yes; she hadn't a drop of white blood in her. Well, after I'd talked
to her I sent for Strickland, and I said to him: 'Strickland, it's time for

you to settle down. A man of your age shouldn't go playing about with the girls down at the front. They're bad lots, and you'll come to no good with them. You've got no money, and you can never keep a job for more than a month or two. No one will employ you now. You say you can always live in the bush with one or other of the natives, and they're glad to have you because you're a white man, but it's not decent for a white man. Now, listen to me, Strickland.'"

Tiaré mingled French with English in her conversation, for she used both languages with equal facility. She spoke them with a singing accent which was not unpleasing. You felt that a bird would speak in these tones if it could speak English.

"'Now, what do you say to marrying Ata? She's a good girl and she's only seventeen. She's never been promiscuous like some of these girls—a captain or a first mate, yes, but she's never been touched by a native. *Elle se respecte, vois-tu.* The purser of the *Oahu* told me last journey that he hadn't met a nicer girl in the islands. It's time she settled down too, and besides, the captains and the first mates like a change now and then. I don't keep my girls too long. She has a bit of property down by Taravao, just before you come to the peninsula, and with copra at the price it is now you could live quite comfortably. There's a house, and you'd have all the time you wanted for your painting. What do you say to it?'"

Tiaré paused to take breath.

"It was then he told me of his wife in England. 'My poor Strickland,' I said to him, 'they've all got a wife somewhere; that is generally why they come to the islands. Ata is a sensible girl, and she doesn't expect any ceremony before the Mayor. She's a Protestant, and you know they don't look upon these things like the Catholics.'"

"Then he said: 'But what does Ata say to it?' 'It appears that she has a *beguin* for you,' I said. 'She's willing if you are. Shall I call her?' He chuckled in a funny, dry way he had, and I called her. She knew what I was talking about, the hussy, and I saw her out of the corner of my eyes listening with all her ears, while she pretended to iron a blouse that she had been washing for me. She came. She was laughing, but I could see that she was a little shy, and Strickland looked at her without speaking."

"Was she pretty?" I asked.

"Not bad. But you must have seen pictures of her. He painted her over and over again, sometimes with a pareo on and sometimes with nothing at all. Yes, she was pretty enough. And she knew how to cook. I taught her myself. I saw Strickland was thinking of it, so I said to him: 'I've given her good wages and she's saved them, and the captains and the first mates she's known have given her a little something now and then. She's saved several hundred francs.'"

He pulled his great red beard and smiled.

"'Well, Ata,' he said, 'do you fancy me for a husband?'"

"She did not say anything, but just giggled."

"'But I tell you, my poor Strickland, the girl has a *béguin* for you,'" I said.

"'I shall beat you,' he said, looking at her."

"'How else should I know you loved me,' she answered."

Tiaré broke off her narrative and addressed herself to me reflectively.

"My first husband, Captain Johnson, used to thrash me regularly. He was a man. He was handsome, six foot three, and when he was drunk there was no holding him. I would be black and blue all over for days at a time. Oh, I cried when he died. I thought I should never get over it. But it wasn't till I married George Rainey that I knew what I'd lost. You can never tell what a man is like till you live with him. I've never been so deceived in a man as I was in George Rainey. He was a fine, upstanding fellow too. He was nearly as tall as Captain Johnson, and he looked strong enough. But it was all on the surface. He never drank. He never raised his hand to me. He might have been a missionary. I made love with the officers of every ship that touched the island, and George Rainey never saw anything. At last I was disgusted with him, and I got a divorce. What was the good of a husband like that? It's a terrible thing the way some men treat women."

I condoled with Tiaré, and remarked feelingly that men were deceivers ever, then asked her to go on with her story of Strickland.

"'Well,' I said to him, 'there's no hurry about it. Take your time and think it over. Ata has a very nice room in the annexe. Live with her for a month, and see how you like her. You can have your meals here. And at the end of a month, if you decide you want to marry her, you can just go and settle down on her property.'"

"Well, he agreed to that. Ata continued to do the housework, and I gave him his meals as I said I would. I taught Ata to make one or two dishes I knew he was fond of. He did not paint much. He wandered about the hills and bathed in the stream. And he sat about the front looking at the lagoon, and at sunset he would go down and look at Murea. He used to go fishing on the reef. He loved to moon about the harbour talking to the natives. He was a nice, quiet fellow. And every evening after dinner he would go down to the annexe with Ata. I saw he was longing to get away to the bush, and at the end of the month I asked him what he intended to do. He said if Ata was willing to go, he was willing to go with her. So I gave them a wedding dinner. I cooked it with my own hands. I gave them a pea soup and lobster *à la portugaise*, and a curry, and a cocoa-nut salad—you've never had one of my cocoa-nut salads, have you? I must make you one before you go—and then I made them an ice. We had all the champagne we could drink and liqueurs to follow. Oh, I'd made up my mind to do things well. And afterwards we danced in the drawing-room. I was not so fat, then, and I always loved dancing."

The drawing-room at the Hotel de la Fleur was a small room, with a cottage piano, and a suite of mahogany furniture, covered in stamped velvet, neatly arranged around the walls. On round tables were photograph albums, and on the walls enlarged photographs of Tiaré and her first husband, Captain Johnson. Still, though Tiaré was old and fat, on occasion we rolled back the Brussels carpet, brought in the maids and one or two friends of Tiaré's, and danced, though now to the wheezy music of a gramaphone. On the verandah the air was scented with the heavy perfume of the Tiaré, and overhead the Southern Cross shone in a cloudless sky.

Tiaré smiled indulgently as she remembered the gaiety of a time long passed.

"We kept it up till three, and when we went to bed I don't think anyone was very sober. I had told them they could have my trap to take them as far as the road went, because after that they had a long walk. Ata's property was right away in a fold of the mountain. They started at dawn, and the boy I sent with them didn't come back till next day.

"Yes, that's how Strickland was married."

52

I suppose the next three years were the happiest of Strickland's life. Ata's house stood about eight kilometres from the road that runs round the island, and you went to it along a winding pathway shaded by the luxuriant trees of the tropics. It was a bungalow of unpainted wood, consisting of two small rooms, and outside was a small shed that served as a kitchen. There was no furniture except the mats they used as beds, and a rocking-chair, which stood on the verandah. Bananas with their great ragged leaves, like the tattered habiliments of an empress in adversity, grew close up to the house. There was a tree just behind which bore alligator pears, and all about were the cocoa-nuts which gave the land its revenue. Ata's father had planted crotons round his property, and they grew in coloured profusion, gay and brilliant; they fenced the land with flame. A mango grew in front of the house, and at the edge of the clearing were two flamboyants, twin trees, that challenged the gold of the cocoa-nuts with their scarlet flowers.

Here Strickland lived, coming seldom to Papeete, on the produce of the land. There was a little stream that ran not far away, in which he bathed, and down this on occasion would come a shoal of fish. Then the natives would assemble with spears, and with much shouting would transfix the great startled things as they hurried down to the sea. Sometimes Strickland would go down to the reef, and come back with a basket of small, coloured fish that Ata would fry in cocoa-nut oil, or with a lobster; and sometimes she would make a savoury dish of the great land-crabs that scuttled away under your feet. Up the mountain were wild-orange trees, and now and then Ata would go with two or three women from the village and return laden with the green, sweet, luscious fruit. Then the cocoa-nuts would be ripe for picking, and her cousins (like all the natives, Ata had a host of relatives) would swarm up the trees and throw down the big ripe nuts. They split them open and put them in the sun to dry. Then they cut out the copra and put it into sacks, and the women would carry it down to the trader at the village by the lagoon, and he would give in exchange for it rice and soap and tinned meat and a little money. Sometimes there would be a feast in the neighbourhood, and a pig would be killed. Then they would go and eat themselves sick, and dance, and sing hymns.

But the house was a long way from the village, and the Tahitians are lazy. They love to travel and they love to gossip, but they do not care to walk, and for weeks at a time Strickland and Ata lived alone. He painted and he read, and in the evening, when it was dark, they sat together on the verandah, smoking and looking at the night. Then Ata had a baby, and the old woman who came up to help her through her trouble stayed on. Presently the granddaughter of the old woman came to stay with her, and then a youth appeared—no one quite knew where from or to whom he belonged—but he settled down with them in a happy-go-lucky way, and they all lived together.

53

"*Tenez, voilà le Capitaine Brunot*," said Tiaré, one day when I was fitting together what she could tell me of Strickland. "He knew Strickland well; he visited him at his house."

I saw a middle-aged Frenchman with a big black beard, streaked with gray, a sunburned face, and large, shining eyes. He was dressed in a neat suit of ducks. I had noticed him at luncheon, and Ah Lin, the Chinese boy, told me he had come from the Paumotus on the boat that had that day arrived. Tiaré introduced me to him, and he handed me his card, a large card on which was printed *René Brunot*, and underneath, *Capitaine au Long Cours*. We were sitting on a little verandah outside the kitchen, and Tiaré was cutting out a dress that she was making for one of the girls about the house. He sat down with us.

"Yes; I knew Strickland well," he said. "I am very fond of chess, and he was always glad of a game. I come to Tahiti three or four times a year for my business, and when he was at Papeete he would come here and we would play. When he married"—Captain Brunot smiled and shrugged his shoulders—"*enfin*, when he went to live with the girl that Tiaré gave him, he asked me to go and see him. I was one of the guests at the wedding feast." He looked at Tiaré, and they both laughed. "He did not come much to Papeete after that, and about a year later it chanced that I had to go to that part of the island for I forget what business, and when I had finished it I said to myself: '*Voyons*, why should I not go and

see that poor Strickland?' I asked one or two natives if they knew anything about him, and I discovered that he lived not more than five kilometres from where I was. So I went. I shall never forget the impression
my visit made on me. I live on an atoll, a low island, it is a strip of land
surrounding a lagoon, and its beauty is the beauty of the sea and sky and
the varied colour of the lagoon, and the grace of the cocoa-nut trees; but
the place where Strickland lived had the beauty of the Garden of Eden.
Ah, I wish I could make you see the enchantment of that spot, a corner
hidden away from all the world, with the blue sky overhead and the rich,
luxuriant trees. It was a feast of colour. And it was fragrant and cool.
Words cannot describe that paradise. And here he lived, unmindful of
the world and by the world forgotten. I suppose to European eyes it
would have seemed astonishingly sordid. The house was dilapidated and
none too clean. Three or four natives were lying on the verandah. You
know how natives love to herd together. There was a young man lying full
length, smoking a cigarette, and he wore nothing but a *pareo*."

The *pareo* is a long strip of trade cotton, red or blue, stamped with
a white pattern. It is worn round the waist and hangs to the knees.

"A girl of fifteen, perhaps, was plaiting pandanus-leaf to make a hat,
and an old woman was sitting on her haunches smoking a pipe. Then I saw
Ata. She was suckling a new-born child, and another child, stark naked, was
playing at her feet. When she saw me she called out to Strickland, and he
came to the door. He, too, wore nothing but a pareo. He was an extraordinary figure, with his red beard and matted hair, and his great hairy chest.
His feet were horny and scarred, so that I knew he went always barefoot.
He had gone native with a vengeance. He seemed pleased to see me, and
told Ata to kill a chicken for our dinner. He took me into the house to show
me the picture he was at work on when I came in. In one corner of the
room was the bed, and in the middle was an easel with the canvas upon it.
Because I was sorry for him, I had bought a couple of his pictures for small
sums, and I had sent others to friends of mine in France. And though I had
bought them out of compassion, after living with them I began to like
them. Indeed, I found a strange beauty in them. Everyone thought I was
mad, but it turns out that I was right. I was his first admirer in the islands."

He smiled maliciously at Tiaré, and with lamentations she told us
again the story of how at the sale of Strickland's effects she had neg-

lected the pictures, but bought an American stove for twenty-seven francs.

"Have you the pictures still?" I asked.

"Yes; I am keeping them till my daughter is of marriageable age, and then I shall sell them. They will be her *dot*."

Then he went on with the account of his visit to Strickland.

"I shall never forget the evening I spent with him. I had not intended to stay more than an hour, but he insisted that I should spend the night. I hesitated, for I confess I did not much like the look of the mats on which he proposed that I should sleep; but I shrugged my shoulders. When I was building my house in the Paumotus I had slept out for weeks on a harder bed than that, with nothing to shelter me but wild shrubs; and as for vermin, my tough skin should be proof against their malice.

"We went down to the stream to bathe while Ata was preparing the dinner, and after we had eaten it we sat on the verandah. We smoked and chatted. The young man had a concertina, and he played the tunes popular on the music-halls a dozen years before. They sounded strangely in the tropical night thousands of miles from civilisation. I asked Strickland if it did not irk him to live in that promiscuity. No, he said; he liked to have his models under his hand. Presently, after loud yawning, the natives went away to sleep, and Strickland and I were left alone. I cannot describe to you the intense silence of the night. On my island in the Paumotus there is never at night the complete stillness that there was here. There is the rustle of the myriad animals on the beach, all the little shelled things that crawl about ceaselessly, and there is the noisy scurrying of the land-crabs. Now and then in the lagoon you hear the leaping of a fish, and sometimes a hurried noisy splashing as a brown shark sends all the other fish scampering for their lives. And above all, ceaseless like time, is the dull roar of the breakers on the reef. But here there was not a sound, and the air was scented with the white flowers of the night. It was a night so beautiful that your soul seemed hardly able to bear the prison of the body. You felt that it was ready to be wafted away on the immaterial air, and death bore all the aspect of a beloved friend."

Tiaré sighed.

"Ah, I wish I were fifteen again."

Then she caught sight of a cat trying to get at a dish of prawns on the kitchen table, and with a dexterous gesture and a lively volley of abuse flung a book at its scampering tail.

"I asked him if he was happy with Ata.

"'She leaves me alone,' he said. 'She cooks my food and looks after her babies. She does what I tell her. She gives me what I want from a woman.'"

"'And do you never regret Europe? Do you not yearn sometimes for the light of the streets in Paris or London, the companionship of your friends, and equals, *que sais-je?* for theatres and newspapers, and the rumble of omnibuses on the cobbled pavements?'"

"For a long time he was silent. Then he said:

'I shall stay here till I die.'"

"'But are you never bored or lonely?'" I asked.

"He chuckled."

"'*Mon pauvre ami*,' he said. 'It is evident that you do not know what it is to be an artist.'"

Capitaine Brunot turned to me with a gentle smile, and there was a wonderful look in his dark, kind eyes.

"He did me an injustice, for I too know what it is to have dreams. I have my visions too. In my way I also am an artist."

We were all silent for a while, and Tiaré fished out of her capacious pocket a handful of cigarettes. She handed one to each of us, and we all three smoked. At last she said:

"Since *ce monsieur* is interested in Strickland, why do you not take him to see Dr. Coutras? He can tell him something about his illness and death."

"*Volontiers*," said the Captain, looking at me.

I thanked him, and he looked at his watch.

"It is past six o'clock. We should find him at home if you care to come now."

I got up without further ado, and we walked along the road that led to the doctor's house. He lived out of the town, but the Hotel de la Fleur was on the edge of it, and we were quickly in the country. The broad road was shaded by pepper-trees, and on each side were the plantations, cocoa-nut and vanilla. The pirate birds were screeching among the leaves of the palms. We came to a stone bridge over a shallow river, and we stopped for a few minutes to see the native boys bathing. They chased one another with shrill cries and laughter, and their bodies, brown and wet, gleamed in the sunlight.

54

As we walked along I reflected on a circumstance which all that I had lately heard about Strickland forced on my attention. Here, on this remote island, he seemed to have aroused none of the detestation with which he was regarded at home, but compassion rather; and his vagaries were accepted with tolerance. To these people, native and European, he was a queer fish, but they were used to queer fish, and they took him for granted; the world was full of odd persons, who did odd things; and perhaps they knew that a man is not what he wants to be, but what he must be. In England and France he was the square peg in the round hole, but here the holes were any sort of shape, and no sort of peg was quite amiss. I do not think he was any gentler here, less selfish or less brutal, but the circumstances were more favourable. If he had spent his life amid these surroundings he might have passed for no worse a man than another. He received here what he neither expected nor wanted among his own people—sympathy.

I tried to tell Captain Brunot something of the astonishment with which this filled me, and for a little while he did not answer.

"It is not strange that I, at all events, should have had sympathy for him," he said at last, "for, though perhaps neither of us knew it, we were both aiming at the same thing."

"What on earth can it be that two people so dissimilar as you and Strickland could aim at?" I asked, smiling.

"Beauty."

"A large order," I murmured.

"Do you know how men can be so obsessed by love that they are deaf and blind to everything else in the world? They are as little their own masters as the slaves chained to the benches of a galley. The passion that held Strickland in bondage was no less tyrannical than love."

"How strange that you should say that!" I answered. "For long ago I had the idea that he was possessed of a devil."

"And the passion that held Strickland was a passion to create beauty. It gave him no peace. It urged him hither and thither. He was eternally a pilgrim, haunted by a divine nostalgia, and the demon within him was ruthless. There are men whose desire for truth is so great that to attain it they will shatter the very foundation of their world. Of such was Strickland, only beauty with him took the place of truth. I could only feel for him a profound compassion."

"That is strange also. A man whom he had deeply wronged told me that he felt a great pity for him." I was silent for a moment. "I wonder if there you have found the explanation of a character which has always seemed to me inexplicable. How did you hit on it?"

He turned to me with a smile.

"Did I not tell you that I, too, in my way was an artist? I realised in myself the same desire as animated him. But whereas his medium was paint, mine has been life."

Then Captain Brunot told me a story which I must repeat, since, if only by way of contrast, it adds something to my impression of Strickland. It has also to my mind a beauty of its own.

Captain Brunot was a Breton, and had been in the French Navy. He left it on his marriage, and settled down on a small property he had near Quimper to live for the rest of his days in peace; but the failure of an attorney left him suddenly penniless, and neither he nor his wife was willing to live in penury where they had enjoyed consideration. During his seafaring days he had cruised the South Seas, and he determined now to seek his fortune there. He spent some months in Papeete to make his plans and gain experience; then, on money borrowed from a friend in France, he bought an island in the Paumotus. It was a ring of land round a deep lagoon, uninhabited, and covered only with scrub and wild guava. With the intrepid woman who was his wife, and a few natives, he landed there, and set about building a house, and clearing the scrub so that he could plant cocoa-nuts. That was twenty years before, and now what had been a barren island was a garden.

"It was hard and anxious work at first, and we worked strenuously, both of us. Every day I was up at dawn, clearing, planting, working on my house, and at night when I threw myself on my bed it was to sleep like a log till morning. My wife worked as hard as I did. Then children were born to us, first a son and then a daughter. My wife and I have taught them all they know. We had a piano sent out from France, and she has taught them to play and to speak English, and I have taught them Latin and mathematics, and we read history together. They can sail a boat. They can swim as well as the natives. There is nothing about the land of which they are ignorant. Our trees have prospered, and there is shell on my reef. I have come to Tahiti now to buy a schooner. I can get enough shell to make it worth while to fish for it, and, who knows? I may find pearls. I have made something where there was nothing. I too have made beauty. Ah, you do not know what it is to look at those tall, healthy trees and think that every one I planted myself."

"Let me ask you the question that you asked Strickland. Do you never regret France and your old home in Brittany?"

"Some day, when my daughter is married and my son has a wife and is able to take my place on the island, we shall go back and finish our days in the old house in which I was born."

"You will look back on a happy life," I said.

"*Evidemment*, it is not exciting on my island, and we are very far from the world—imagine, it takes me four days to come to Tahiti—but we are happy there. It is given to few men to attempt a work and to achieve it. Our life is simple and innocent. We are untouched by ambition, and what pride we have, is due only to our contemplation of the work of our hands. Malice cannot touch us, nor envy attack. Ah, *mon cher monsieur*, they talk of the blessedness of labour, and it is a meaningless phrase, but to me it has the most intense significance. I am a happy man."

"I am sure you deserve to be," I smiled.

"I wish I could think so. I do not know how I have deserved to have a wife who was the perfect friend and helpmate, the perfect mistress and the perfect mother."

I reflected for a while on the life that the Captain suggested to my imagination.

"It is obvious that to lead such an existence and make so great a success of it, you must both have needed a strong will and a determined character."

"Perhaps; but without one other factor we could have achieved nothing."

"And what was that?"

He stopped, somewhat dramatically, and stretched out his arm.

"Belief in God. Without that we should have been lost."

Then we arrived at the house of Dr. Coutras.

55

Dr. Coutras was an old Frenchman of great stature and exceeding bulk. His body was shaped like a huge duck's egg; and his eyes, sharp, blue, and good-natured, rested now and then with self-satisfaction on his enormous paunch. His complexion was florid and his hair white. He was a man to attract immediate sympathy. He received us in a room that might have been in a house in a provincial town in France, and the one or two Polynesian curios had an odd look. He took my hand in both of his—they were huge—and gave me a hearty look, in which, however, was great shrewdness. When he shook hands with Capitaine Brunot he enquired politely after *Madame et les enfants.* For some minutes there was an exchange of courtesies and some local gossip about the island, the prospects of copra and the vanilla crop; then we came to the object of my visit.

I shall not tell what Dr. Coutras related to me in his words, but in my own, for I cannot hope to give at second hand any impression of his vivacious delivery. He had a deep, resonant voice, fitted to his massive frame, and a keen sense of the dramatic. To listen to him was, as the phrase goes, as good as a play; and much better than most.

It appears that Dr. Coutras had gone one day to Taravao in order to see an old chiefess who was ill, and he gave a vivid picture of the obese old lady, lying in a huge bed, smoking cigarettes, and surrounded by a crowd of dark-skinned retainers. When he had seen her he was taken into another room and given dinner—raw fish, fried bananas, and chicken—*que sais-je*, the typical dinner of the *indigène*—and while he was eating it he saw a young girl being driven away from the door in tears. He thought nothing of it, but when he went out to get into his trap and drive home, he saw her again, standing a little way off; she looked at him with a woebegone air, and tears streamed down her cheeks. He asked someone what was wrong with her, and was told that she had come down from the hills to ask him to visit a white man who was sick. They had told her that the doctor could not be disturbed. He called her, and himself asked what she wanted. She told him that Ata had sent her, she who used to be at the Hotel de la Fleur, and that the Red One was ill. She thrust into his hand a crumpled piece of newspaper, and when he opened it he found in it a hundred-franc note.

"Who is the Red One?" he asked of one of the bystanders.

He was told that that was what they called the Englishman, a painter, who lived with Ata up in the valley seven kilometres from where they were. He recognised Strickland by the description. But it was necessary to walk. It was impossible for him to go; that was why they had sent the girl away.

"I confess," said the doctor, turning to me, "that I hesitated. I did not relish fourteen kilometres over a bad pathway, and there was no chance that I could get back to Papeete that night. Besides, Strickland was not sympathetic to me. He was an idle, useless scoundrel, who preferred to live with a native woman rather than work for his living like the rest of us. *Mon Dieu*, how was I to know that one day the world would come to the conclusion that he had genius? I asked the girl if he was not well enough to have come down to see me. I asked her what she thought was the matter with him. She would not answer. I pressed her, angrily perhaps, but she looked down on the ground and began to cry. Then I shrugged my shoulders; after all, perhaps it was my duty to go, and in a very bad temper I bade her lead the way."

His temper was certainly no better when he arrived, perspiring freely and thirsty. Ata was on the look-out for him, and came a little way along the path to meet him.

"Before I see anyone give me something to drink or I shall die of thirst," he cried out. "*Pour l'amour de Dieu*, get me a cocoa-nut."

She called out, and a boy came running along. He swarmed up a tree, and presently threw down a ripe nut. Ata pierced a hole in it, and the doctor took a long, refreshing draught. Then he rolled himself a cigarette and felt in a better humour.

"Now, where is the Red One?" he asked.

"He is in the house, painting. I have not told him you were coming. Go in and see him."

"But what does he complain of? If he is well enough to paint, he is well enough to have come down to Taravao and save me this confounded walk. I presume my time is no less valuable than his."

Ata did not speak, but with the boy followed him to the house. The girl who had brought him was by this time sitting on the verandah, and here was lying an old woman, with her back to the wall, making native cigarettes. Ata pointed to the door. The doctor, wondering irritably why they behaved so strangely, entered, and there found Strickland cleaning his palette. There was a picture on the easel. Strickland, clad only in a *pareo*, was standing with his back to the door, but he turned round when he heard the sound of boots. He gave the doctor a look of vexation. He was surprised to see him, and resented the intrusion. But the doctor gave a gasp, he was rooted to the floor, and he stared with all his eyes. This was not what he expected. He was seized with horror.

"You enter without ceremony," said Strickland. "What can I do for you?"

The doctor recovered himself, but it required quite an effort for him to find his voice. All his irritation was gone, and he felt—*eh bien, oui, je ne le nie pas*—he felt an overwhelming pity.

"I am Dr. Coutras. I was down at Taravao to see the chiefess, and Ata sent for me to see you."

"She's a damned fool. I have had a few aches and pains lately and a little fever, but that's nothing; it will pass off. Next time anyone went to Papeete I was going to send for some quinine."

"Look at yourself in the glass."

Strickland gave him a glance, smiled, and went over to a cheap mirror in a little wooden frame, that hung on the wall.

"Well?"

"Do you not see a strange change in your face? Do you not see the thickening of your features and a look—how shall I describe it?—the books call it lion-faced. *Mon pauvre ami*, must I tell you that you have a terrible disease?"

"I?"

"When you look at yourself in the glass you see the typical appearance of the leper."

"You are jesting," said Strickland.

"I wish to God I were."

"Do you intend to tell me that I have leprosy?"

"Unfortunately, there can be no doubt of it."

Dr. Coutras had delivered sentence of death on many men, and he could never overcome the horror with which it filled him. He felt always the furious hatred that must seize a man condemned when he compared himself with the doctor, sane and healthy, who had the inestimable privilege of life. Strickland looked at him in silence. Nothing of emotion could be seen on his face, disfigured already by the loathsome disease.

"Do they know?" he asked at last, pointing to the persons on the verandah, now sitting in unusual, unaccountable silence.

"These natives know the signs so well," said the doctor. "They were afraid to tell you."

Strickland stepped to the door and looked out. There must have been something terrible in his face, for suddenly they all burst out into loud cries and lamentation. They lifted up their voices and they wept. Strickland did not speak. After looking at them for a moment, he came back into the room.

"How long do you think I can last?"

"Who knows? Sometimes the disease continues for twenty years. It is a mercy when it runs its course quickly."

Strickland went to his easel and looked reflectively at the picture that stood on it.

"You have had a long journey. It is fitting that the bearer of important tidings should be rewarded. Take this picture. It means nothing to you now, but it may be that one day you will be glad to have it."

Dr. Coutras protested that he needed no payment for his journey; he had already given back to Ata the hundred-franc note, but Strickland insisted that he should take the picture. Then together they went out on the verandah. The natives were sobbing violently.

"Be quiet, woman. Dry thy tears," said Strickland, addressing Ata. "There is no great harm. I shall leave thee very soon."

"They are not going to take thee away?" she cried.

At that time there was no rigid sequestration on the islands, and lepers, if they chose, were allowed to go free.

"I shall go up into the mountain," said Strickland.

Then Ata stood up and faced him.

"Let the others go if they choose, but I will not leave thee. Thou art my man and I am thy woman. If thou leavest me I shall hang myself on the tree that is behind the house. I swear it by God."

There was something immensely forcible in the way she spoke. She was no longer the meek, soft native girl, but a determined woman. She was extraordinarily transformed.

"Why shouldst thou stay with me? Thou canst go back to Papeete, and thou will soon find another white man. The old woman can take care of thy children, and Tiaré will be glad to have thee back."

"Thou art my man and I am thy woman. Whither thou goest I will go, too."

For a moment Strickland's fortitude was shaken, and a tear filled each of his eyes and trickled slowly down his cheeks. Then he gave the sardonic smile which was usual with him.

"Women are strange little beasts," he said to Dr. Coutras. "You can treat them like dogs, you can beat them till your arm aches, and still they love you." He shrugged his shoulders. "Of course, it is one of the most absurd illusions of Christianity that they have souls."

"What is it that thou art saying to the doctor?" asked Ata suspiciously. "Thou wilt not go?"

"If it please thee I will stay, poor child."

Ata flung herself on her knees before him, and clasped his legs with her arms and kissed them. Strickland looked at Dr. Coutras with a faint smile.

"In the end they get you, and you are helpless in their hands. White or brown, they are all the same."

Dr. Coutras felt that it was absurd to offer expressions of regret in so terrible a disaster, and he took his leave. Strickland told Tane, the boy, to lead him to the village. Dr. Coutras paused for a moment, and then he addressed himself to me.

"I did not like him, I have told you he was not sympathetic to me, but as I walked slowly down to Taravao I could not prevent an unwilling admiration for the stoical courage which enabled him to bear perhaps the most dreadful of human afflictions. When Tané left me I told him I would send some medicine that might be of service; but my hope was small that Strickland would consent to take it, and even smaller that, if he did, it would do him good. I gave the boy a message for Ata that I would come whenever she sent for me. Life is hard, and Nature takes sometimes a terrible delight in torturing her children. It was with a heavy heart that I drove back to my comfortable home in Papeete."

For a long time none of us spoke.

"But Ata did not send for me," the doctor went on, at last, "and it chanced that I did not go to that part of the island for a long time. I had no news of Strickland. Once or twice I heard that Ata had been to Papeete to buy painting materials, but I did not happen to see her. More than two years passed before I went to Taravao again, and then it was once more to see the old chiefess. I asked them whether they had heard anything of Strickland. By now it was known everywhere that he had leprosy. First Tané, the boy, had left the house, and then, a little time afterwards, the old woman and her grandchild. Strickland and Ata were left alone with their babies. No one went near the plantation, for, as you know, the natives have a very lively horror of the disease, and in the old days when it was discovered the sufferer was killed; but sometimes, when the village boys were scrambling about the hills, they would catch sight of the white man, with his great red beard, wandering about. They fled in terror. Sometimes Ata would come down to the village at night and arouse the trader, so that he might sell her various things of which she stood in need. She knew that the natives looked upon her with the same horrified aversion as they looked upon Strickland, and she kept out of their way. Once some women, venturing nearer than usual to the plantation, saw her washing clothes in the brook, and they threw stones at her. After that the trader was told to give her the message that if she used the brook again men would come and burn down her house."

"Brutes," I said.

"*Mais non, mon cher monsieur*, men are always the same. Fear makes them cruel. . . . I decided to see Strickland, and when I had finished with the chiefess asked for a boy to show me the way. But none would accompany me, and I was forced to find it alone."

When Dr. Coutras arrived at the plantation he was seized with a feeling of uneasiness. Though he was hot from walking, he shivered. There was something hostile in the air which made him hesitate, and he felt that invisible forces barred his way. Unseen hands seemed to draw him back. No one would go near now to gather the cocoa-nuts, and they lay rotting on the ground. Everywhere was desolation. The bush was encroaching, and it looked as though very soon the primeval forest would regain possession of that strip of land which had been snatched from it at the cost of so much labour. He had the sensation that here was the abode of pain. As he approached the house he was struck by the unearthly silence, and at first he thought it was deserted. Then he saw Ata. She was sitting on her haunches in the lean-to that served her as kitchen, watching some mess cooking in a pot. Near her a small boy was playing silently in the dirt. She did not smile when she saw him.

"I have come to see Strickland," he said.

"I will go and tell him."

She went to the house, ascended the few steps that led to the verandah, and entered. Dr. Coutras followed her, but waited outside in obedience to her gesture. As she opened the door he smelt the sickly sweet smell which makes the neighbourhood of the leper nauseous. He heard her speak, and then he heard Strickland's answer, but he did not recognise the voice. It had become hoarse and indistinct. Dr. Coutras raised his eyebrows. He judged that the disease had already attacked the vocal cords. Then Ata came out again.

"He will not see you. You must go away."

Dr. Coutras insisted, but she would not let him pass. Dr. Coutras shrugged his shoulders, and after a moment's reflection turned away. She walked with him. He felt that she too wanted to be rid of him.

"Is there nothing I can do at all?" he asked.

"You can send him some paints," she said. "There is nothing else he wants."

"Can he paint still?"

"He is painting the walls of the house."

"This is a terrible life for you, my poor child."

Then at last she smiled, and there was in her eyes a look of superhuman love. Dr. Coutras was startled by it, and amazed. And he was awed. He found nothing to say.

"He is my man," she said.

"Where is your other child?" he asked. "When I was here last you had two."

"Yes; it died. We buried it under the mango."

When Ata had gone with him a little way she said she must turn back. Dr. Coutras surmised she was afraid to go farther in case she met any of the people from the village. He told her again that if she wanted him she had only to send and he would come at once.

56

Then two years more went by, or perhaps three, for time passes imperceptibly in Tahiti, and it is hard to keep count of it; but at last a message was brought to Dr. Coutras that Strickland was dying. Ata had waylaid the cart that took the mail into Papeete, and besought the man who drove it to go at once to the doctor. But the doctor was out when the summons came, and it was evening when he received it. It was impossible to start at so late an hour, and so it was not till next day soon after dawn that he set out. He arrived at Taravao, and for the last time tramped the seven kilometres that led to Ata's house. The path was overgrown, and it was clear that for years now it had remained all but untrodden. It was not easy to find the way. Sometimes he had to stumble along the bed of the stream, and sometimes he had to push through shrubs, dense and thorny; often he was obliged to climb over rocks in order to avoid the hornet-nests that hung on the trees over his head. The silence was intense.

It was with a sigh of relief that at last he came upon the little unpainted house, extraordinarily bedraggled now, and unkempt; but here too was the same intolerable silence. He walked up, and a little boy, playing unconcernedly in the sunshine, started at his approach and fled quickly away: to him the stranger was the enemy. Dr. Coutras had a sense that the child was stealthily watching him from behind a tree. The door was wide open. He called out, but no one answered. He stepped in. He knocked at a door, but again there was no answer. He turned the handle and entered. The stench that assailed him turned him horribly sick. He put his handkerchief to his nose and forced himself to go in. The light was dim, and after the brilliant sunshine for a while he could see nothing. Then he gave a start. He could not make out where he was. He seemed on a sudden to have entered a magic world. He had a vague impression of a great primeval forest and of naked people walking beneath the trees. Then he saw that there were paintings on the walls.

"*Mon Dieu*, I hope the sun hasn't affected me," he muttered.

A slight movement attracted his attention, and he saw that Ata was lying on the floor, sobbing quietly.

"Ata," he called. "Ata."

She took no notice. Again the beastly stench almost made him faint, and he lit a cheroot. His eyes grew accustomed to the darkness, and now he was seized by an overwhelming sensation as he stared at the painted walls. He knew nothing of pictures, but there was something about these that extraordinarily affected him. From floor to ceiling the walls were covered with a strange and elaborate composition. It was indescribably wonderful and mysterious. It took his breath away. It filled him with an emotion which he could not understand or analyse. He felt the awe and the delight which a man might feel who watched the beginning of a world. It was tremendous, sensual, passionate; and yet there was something horrible there, too, something which made him afraid. It was the work of a man who had delved into the hidden depths of nature and had discovered secrets which were beautiful and fearful too. It was the work of a man who knew things which it is unholy for men to know. There was something primeval there and terrible. It was not human. It brought to his mind vague recollections of black magic. It was beautiful and obscene.

"*Mon Dieu*, this is genius."

The words were wrung from him, and he did not know he had spoken.

Then his eyes fell on the bed of mats in the corner, and he went up, and he saw the dreadful, mutilated, ghastly object which had been Strickland. He was dead. Dr. Coutras made an effort of will and bent over that battered horror. Then he started violently, and terror blazed in his heart, for he felt that someone was behind him. It was Ata. He had not heard her get up. She was standing at his elbow, looking at what he looked at.

"Good Heavens, my nerves are all distraught," he said. "You nearly frightened me out of my wits."

He looked again at the poor dead thing that had been man, and then he started back in dismay.

"But he was blind."

"Yes; he had been blind for nearly a year."

57

At that moment we were interrupted by the appearance of Madame Coutras, who had been paying visits. She came in, like a ship in full sail, an imposing creature, tall and stout, with an ample bust and an obesity girthed in alarmingly by straight-fronted corsets. She had a bold hooked nose and three chins. She held herself upright. She had not yielded for an instant to the enervating charm of the tropics, but contrariwise was more active, more worldly, more decided than anyone in a temperate clime would have thought it possible to be. She was evidently a copious talker, and now poured forth a breathless stream of anecdote and comment. She made the conversation we had just had seem far away and unreal.

Presently Dr. Coutras turned to me.

"I still have in my *bureau* the picture that Strickland gave me," he said. "Would you like to see it?"

"Willingly."

We got up, and he led me on to the verandah which surrounded his house. We paused to look at the gay flowers that rioted in his garden.

"For a long time I could not get out of my head the recollection of the extraordinary decoration with which Strickland had covered the walls of his house," he said reflectively.

I had been thinking of it, too. It seemed to me that here Strickland had finally put the whole expression of himself. Working silently, knowing that it was his last chance, I fancied that here he must have said all that he knew of life and all that he divined. And I fancied that perhaps here he had at last found peace. The demon which possessed him was exorcised at last, and with the completion of the work, for which all his life had been a painful preparation, rest descended on his remote and tortured soul. He was willing to die, for he had fulfilled his purpose.

"What was the subject?" I asked.

"I scarcely know. It was strange and fantastic. It was a vision of the beginnings of the world, the Garden of Eden, with Adam and Eve—*que sais-je?*—it was a hymn to the beauty of the human form, male and female, and the praise of Nature, sublime, indifferent, lovely, and cruel. It gave you an awful sense of the infinity of space and of the endlessness of time. Because he painted the trees I see about me every day, the cocoa-nuts, the banyans, the flamboyants, the alligator-pears, I have seen them ever since differently, as though there were in them a spirit and a mystery which I am ever on the point of seizing and which for ever escapes me. The colours were the colours familiar to me, and yet they were different. They had a significance which was all their own. And those nude men and women. They were of the earth, and yet apart from it. They seemed to possess something of the clay of which they were created, and at the same time something divine. You saw man in the nakedness of his primeval instincts, and you were afraid, for you saw yourself."

Dr. Coutras shrugged his shoulders and smiled.

"You will laugh at me. I am a materialist, and I am a gross, fat man—Falstaff, eh?—the lyrical mode does not become me. I make myself ridiculous. But I have never seen painting which made so deep an impression upon me. *Tenez*, I had just the same feeling as when I went to the Sistine Chapel in Rome. There too I was awed by the greatness of the man who had painted that ceiling. It was genius, and it was stupendous and overwhelming. I felt small and insignificant. But you are prepared for the greatness of Michael Angelo. Nothing had prepared me for the immense surprise of these pictures in a native hut, far away from civilisation, in a fold of the mountain above Taravao. And Michael Angelo is sane and healthy. Those great works of his have the calm of the sublime; but here, notwithstanding beauty, was something troubling. I do not know what it was. It made me uneasy. It gave me the impression you get when you are sitting next door to a room that you know is empty, but in which, you know not why, you have a dreadful consciousness that notwithstanding there is someone. You scold yourself; you know it is only your nerves—and yet, and yet . . . In a little while it is impossible to resist the terror that seizes you, and you are helpless in the clutch of an unseen horror. Yes; I confess I was not altogether sorry when I heard that those strange masterpieces had been destroyed."

"Destroyed?" I cried.

"*Mais oui*; did you not know?"

"How should I know? It is true I had never heard of this work; but I thought perhaps it had fallen into the hands of a private owner. Even now there is no certain list of Strickland's paintings."

"When he grew blind he would sit hour after hour in those two rooms that he had painted, looking at his works with sightless eyes, and seeing, perhaps, more than he had ever seen in his life before. Ata told me that he never complained of his fate, he never lost courage. To the end his mind remained serene and undisturbed. But he made her promise that when she had buried him—did I tell you that I dug his grave with my own hands, for none of the natives would approach the infected house, and we buried him, she and I, sewn up in three *pareos* joined together, under the mango-tree—he made her promise that she would set fire to the house and not leave it till it was burned to the ground and not a stick remained."

I did not speak for a while, for I was thinking. Then I said:

"He remained the same to the end, then."

"Do you understand? I must tell you that I thought it my duty to dissuade her."

"Even after what you have just said?"

"Yes; for I knew that here was a work of genius, and I did not think we had the right to deprive the world of it. But Ata would not listen to me. She had promised. I would not stay to witness the barbarous deed, and it was only afterwards that I heard what she had done. She poured paraffin on the dry floors and on the pandanus-mats, and then she set fire. In a little while nothing remained but smouldering embers, and a great masterpiece existed no longer."

"I think Strickland knew it was a masterpiece. He had achieved what he wanted. His life was complete. He had made a world and saw that it was good. Then, in pride and contempt, he destroyed it."

"But I must show you my picture," said Dr. Coutras, moving on.

"What happened to Ata and the child?"

"They went to the Marquesas. She had relations there. I have heard that the boy works on one of Cameron's schooners. They say he is very like his father in appearance."

At the door that led from the verandah to the doctor's consulting-room, he paused and smiled.

"It is a fruit-piece. You would think it not a very suitable picture for a doctor's consulting-room, but my wife will not have it in the drawing-room. She says it is frankly obscene."

"A fruit-piece!" I exclaimed in surprise.

We entered the room, and my eyes fell at once on the picture. I looked at it for a long time.

It was a pile of mangoes, bananas, oranges, and I know not what; and at first sight it was an innocent picture enough. It would have been passed in an exhibition of the Post-Impressionists by a careless person as an excellent but not very remarkable example of the school; but perhaps afterwards it would come back to his recollection, and he would wonder why. I do not think then he could ever entirely forget it.

The colours were so strange that words can hardly tell what a troubling emotion they gave. They were sombre blues, opaque like a delicately carved bowl in lapis lazuli, and yet with a quivering lustre that suggested the palpitation of mysterious life; there were purples, horrible like raw and putrid flesh, and yet with a glowing, sensual passion that called up vague memories of the Roman Empire of Heliogabalus; there were reds, shrill like the berries of holly—one thought of Christmas in England, and the snow, the good cheer, and the pleasure of children—and yet by some magic softened till they had the swooning tenderness of a dove's breast; there were deep yellows that died with an unnatural passion into a green as fragrant as the spring and as pure as the sparkling water of a mountain brook. Who can tell what anguished fancy made these fruits? They belonged to a Polynesian garden of the Hesperides. There was something strangely alive in them, as though they were created in a stage of the earth's dark history when things were not irrevocably fixed to their forms. They were extravagantly luxurious. They were heavy with tropical odours. They seemed to possess a sombre passion of their own. It was enchanted fruit, to taste which might open the gateway to God knows what secrets of the soul and to mysterious palaces of the imagination. They were sullen with unawaited dangers, and to eat them might turn a man to beast or god. All that was healthy and natural, all that clung to happy relationships and the simple joys of simple men, shrunk from them in dismay; and yet a fearful attraction was in them, and, like the fruit on the Tree of the Knowledge of Good and Evil they were terrible with the possibilities of the Unknown.

At last I turned away. I felt that Strickland had kept his secret to the grave.

"*Voyons, René, mon ami*," came the loud, cheerful voice of Madame Coutras, "what are you doing all this time? Here are the *aperitifs*. Ask *Monsieur* if he will not drink a little glass of Quinquina Dubonnet."

"*Volontiers*, Madame," I said, going out on to the verandah.

The spell was broken.

58

The time came for my departure from Tahiti. According to the gracious custom of the island, presents were given me by the persons with whom I had been thrown in contact—baskets made of the leaves of the cocoa-nut tree, mats of pandanus, fans; and Tiaré gave me three little pearls and three jars of guava jelly made with her own plump hands. When the mail-boat, stopping for twenty-four hours on its way from Wellington to San Francisco, blew the whistle that warned the passengers to get on board, Tiaré clasped me to her vast bosom, so that I seemed to sink into a billowy sea, and pressed her red lips to mine. Tears glistened in her eyes. And when we steamed slowly out of the lagoon, making our way gingerly through the opening in the reef, and then steered for the open sea, a certain melancholy fell upon me. The breeze was laden still with the pleasant odours of the land. Tahiti is very far away, and I knew that I should never see it again. A chapter of my life was closed, and I felt a little nearer to inevitable death.

Not much more than a month later I was in London; and after I had arranged certain matters which claimed my immediate attention, thinking Mrs. Strickland might like to hear what I knew of her husband's last years, I wrote to her. I had not seen her since long before the war, and I had to look out her address in the telephone-book. She made an appointment, and I went to the trim little house on Campden Hill which she now inhabited. She was by this time a woman of hard on sixty, but she bore her years well, and no one would have taken her for more than fifty. Her face, thin and not much lined, was of the sort that ages gracefully, so that you thought in youth she must have been a much handsomer woman than in fact she was. Her hair, not yet very gray, was becomingly arranged, and her black gown was modish. I remembered having heard that her sister, Mrs. MacAndrew, outliving her husband but a couple of years, had left money to Mrs. Strickland; and by the look of the house and the trim maid who opened the door I judged that it was a sum adequate to keep the widow in modest comfort.

When I was ushered into the drawing-room I found that Mrs. Strickland had a visitor, and when I discovered who he was, I guessed that I had been asked to come at just that time not without intention. The caller was Mr. Van Busche Taylor, an American, and Mrs. Strickland gave me particulars with a charming smile of apology to him.

"You know, we English are so dreadfully ignorant. You must forgive me if it's necessary to explain." Then she turned to me. "Mr. Van Busche Taylor is the distinguished American critic. If you haven't read his book your education has been shamefully neglected, and you must repair the omission at once. He's writing something about dear Charlie, and he's come to ask me if I can help him."

Mr. Van Busche Taylor was a very thin man with a large, bald head, bony and shining; and under the great dome of his skull his face, yellow, with deep lines in it, looked very small. He was quiet and exceedingly polite. He spoke with the accent of New England, and there was about his demeanour a bloodless frigidity which made me ask myself why on earth he was busying himself with Charles Strickland. I had been slightly tickled at the gentleness which Mrs. Strickland put into her mention of her husband's name, and while the pair conversed I took stock of the room in which we sat. Mrs. Strickland had moved with the times. Gone were the Morris papers and gone the severe cretonnes, gone were the Arundel prints that had adorned the walls of her drawing-room in Ashley Gardens; the room blazed with fantastic colour, and I wondered if she knew that those varied hues, which fashion had imposed upon her, were due to the dreams of a poor painter in a South Sea island. She gave me the answer herself.

"What wonderful cushions you have," said Mr. Van Busche Taylor.

"Do you like them?" she said, smiling. "Bakst, you know."

And yet on the walls were coloured reproductions of several of Strickland's best pictures, due to the enterprise of a publisher in Berlin.

"You're looking at my pictures," she said, following my eyes. "Of course, the originals are out of my reach, but it's a comfort to have these. The publisher sent them to me himself. They're a great consolation to me."

"They must be very pleasant to live with," said Mr. Van Busche Taylor.

"Yes; they're so essentially decorative."

"That is one of my profoundest convictions," said Mr. Van Busche Taylor. "Great art is always decorative."

Their eyes rested on a nude woman suckling a baby, while a girl was kneeling by their side holding out a flower to the indifferent child. Looking over them was a wrinkled, scraggy hag. It was Strickland's version of the Holy Family. I suspected that for the figures had sat his household above Taravao, and the woman and the baby were Ata and his first son. I asked myself if Mrs. Strickland had any inkling of the facts.

The conversation proceeded, and I marvelled at the tact with which Mr. Van Busche Taylor avoided all subjects that might have been in the least embarrassing, and at the ingenuity with which Mrs. Strickland, without saying a word that was untrue, insinuated that her relations with her husband had always been perfect. At last Mr. Van Busche Taylor rose to go. Holding his hostess' hand, he made her a graceful, though perhaps too elaborate, speech of thanks, and left us.

"I hope he didn't bore you," she said, when the door closed behind him. "Of course it's a nuisance sometimes, but I feel it's only right to give people any information I can about Charlie. There's a certain responsibility about having been the wife of a genius."

She looked at me with those pleasant eyes of hers, which had remained as candid and as sympathetic as they had been more than twenty years before. I wondered if she was making a fool of me.

"Of course you've given up your business," I said.

"Oh, yes," she answered airily. "I ran it more by way of a hobby than for any other reason, and my children persuaded me to sell it. They thought I was overtaxing my strength."

I saw that Mrs. Strickland had forgotten that she had ever done anything so disgraceful as to work for her living. She had the true instinct of the nice woman that it is only really decent for her to live on other people's money.

"They're here now," she said. "I thought they'd like to hear what you had to say about their father. You remember Robert, don't you? I'm glad to say he's been recommended for the Military Cross."

She went to the door and called them. There entered a tall man in khaki, with the parson's collar, handsome in a somewhat heavy fashion, but with the frank eyes that I remembered in him as a boy. He was followed by his sister. She must have been the same age as was her mother when first I knew her, and she was very like her. She too gave one the impression that as a girl she must have been prettier than indeed she was.

"I suppose you don't remember them in the least," said Mrs. Strickland, proud and smiling. "My daughter is now Mrs. Ronaldson. Her husband's a Major in the Gunners."

"He's by way of being a pukka soldier, you know," said Mrs. Ronaldson gaily. "That's why he's only a Major."

I remembered my anticipation long ago that she would marry a soldier. It was inevitable. She had all the graces of the soldier's wife. She was civil and affable, but she could hardly conceal her intimate conviction that she was not quite as others were. Robert was breezy.

"It's a bit of luck that I should be in London when you turned up," he said. "I've only got three days' leave."

"He's dying to get back," said his mother.

"Well, I don't mind confessing it, I have a rattling good time at the front. I've made a lot of good pals. It's a first-rate life. Of course war's terrible, and all that sort of thing; but it does bring out the best qualities in a man, there's no denying that."

Then I told them what I had learned about Charles Strickland in Tahiti. I thought it unnecessary to say anything of Ata and her boy, but for the rest I was as accurate as I could be. When I had narrated his lamentable death I ceased. For a minute or two we were all silent. Then Robert Strickland struck a match and lit a cigarette.

"The mills of God grind slowly, but they grind exceeding small," he said, somewhat impressively.

Mrs. Strickland and Mrs. Ronaldson looked down with a slightly pious expression which indicated, I felt sure, that they thought the quotation was from Holy Writ. Indeed, I was unconvinced that Robert Strickland did not share their illusion. I do not know why I suddenly thought of Strickland's son by Ata. They had told me he was a merry, light-hearted youth. I saw him, with my mind's eye, on the schooner on which he worked, wearing nothing but a pair of dungarees; and at night, when the boat sailed along easily before a light breeze, and the sailors were gathered on the upper deck, while the captain and the supercargo lolled in deck-chairs, smoking their pipes, I saw him dance with another lad, dance wildly, to the wheezy music of the concertina. Above was the blue sky, and the stars, and all about the desert of the Pacific Ocean.

A quotation from the Bible came to my lips, but I held my tongue, for I know that clergymen think it a little blasphemous when the laity poach upon their preserves. My Uncle Henry, for twenty-seven years Vicar of Whitstable, was on these occasions in the habit of saying that the devil could always quote scripture to his purpose. He remembered the days when you could get thirteen Royal Natives for a shilling.

8

ᕗ

From *The Trembling of a Leaf: Stories of the South Sea Islands* (1921)

"Mackintosh" (1920)

He splashed about for a few minutes in the sea; it was too shallow to swim in and for fear of sharks he could not go out of his depth; then he got out and went into the bath-house for a shower. The coldness of the fresh water was grateful after the heavy stickiness of the salt Pacific, so warm, though it was only just after seven, that to bathe in it did not brace you but rather increased your languor; and when he had dried himself, slipping into a bath-gown, he called out to the Chinese cook that he would be ready for breakfast in five minutes. He walked barefoot across the patch of coarse grass which Walker, the administrator, proudly thought was a lawn, to his own quarters and dressed. This did not take long, for he put on nothing but a shirt and a pair of duck trousers and then went over to his chief's house on the other side of the compound. The two men had their meals together, but the Chinese cook told him that Walker had set out on horseback at five and would not be back for another hour.

Mackintosh had slept badly and he looked with distaste at the paw-paw and the eggs and bacon which were set before him. The mosquitoes had been maddening that night; they flew about the net under which he slept in such numbers that their humming, pitiless and menacing, had the effect of a note, infinitely drawn out, played on a distant organ, and whenever he dozed off he awoke with a start in the belief that one had found its way inside his curtains. It was so hot that he lay naked. He turned from side to side. And gradually the dull roar of the breakers on the reef, so unceasing and so regular that generally you did not hear it, grew distinct on his consciousness, its rhythm hammered on his tired nerves and he held himself with clenched hands in the effort to bear it. The thought that nothing could stop that sound, for it would continue to all eternity, was almost impossible to bear, and, as though his strength were a match for the ruthless forces of nature, he had an insane impulse to do some violent thing. He felt he must cling to his self-control or he would go mad. And now, looking out of the window at the lagoon and the strip of foam which marked the reef, he shuddered with hatred of the brilliant scene. The cloudless sky was like an inverted bowl that hemmed it in. He lit his pipe and turned over the pile of Auckland papers that had come over from Apia a few days before. The newest of them was three weeks old. They gave an impression of incredible dullness.

Then he went into the office. It was a large, bare room with two desks in it and a bench along one side. A number of natives were seated on this, and a couple of women. They gossiped while they waited for the administrator, and when Mackintosh came in they greeted him.

"*Talofa li.*"

He returned their greeting and sat down at his desk. He began to write, working on a report which the governor of Samoa had been clamouring for and which Walker, with his usual dilatoriness, had neglected to prepare. Mackintosh as he made his notes reflected vindictively that Walker was late with his report because he was so illiterate that he had an invincible distaste for anything to do with pens and paper; and now when it was at last ready, concise and neatly official, he would accept his subordinate's work without a word of appreciation, with a sneer rather or a gibe, and send it on to his own superior as though it were his own composition. He could not have written a word of it. Mackintosh thought with rage that if his chief pencilled in some insertion it would be childish in expression and faulty in language. If he remonstrated or sought to put his meaning into an intelligible phrase, Walker would fly into a passion and cry:

"What the hell do I care about grammar? That's what I want to say and that's how I want to say it."

At last Walker came in. The natives surrounded him as he entered, trying to get his immediate attention, but he turned on them roughly and told them to sit down and hold their tongues. He threatened that if they were not quiet he would have them all turned out and see none of them that day. He nodded to Mackintosh.

"Hulloa, Mac; up at last? I don't know how you can waste the best part of the day in bed. You ought to have been up before dawn like me. Lazy beggar."

He threw himself heavily into his chair and wiped his face with a large bandana.

"By heaven, I've got a thirst."

He turned to the policeman who stood at the door, a picturesque figure in his white jacket and *lava-lava*, the loin cloth of the Samoan, and told him to bring *kava*. The *kava* bowl stood on the floor in the corner of the room, and the policeman filled a half coconut shell and brought it to Walker. He poured a few drops on the ground, murmured the customary words to the company, and drank with relish. Then he told the policeman to serve the waiting natives, and the shell was handed to each one in order of importance and emptied with the same ceremonies.

Then he set about the day's work. He was a little man, considerably less than of middle height, and enormously stout; he had a large, fleshy face, clean-shaven, with the cheeks hanging on each side in great dewlaps, and three vast chins; his small features were all dissolved in fat; and, but for a crescent of white hair at the back of his head, he was completely bald. He reminded you of Mr. Pickwick. He was grotesque, a figure of fun, and yet, strangely enough, not without dignity. His blue eyes, behind large gold-rimmed spectacles, were shrewd and vivacious, and there was a great deal of determination in his face. He was sixty, but his native vitality triumphed over advancing years. Notwithstanding his corpulence his movements were quick, and he walked with a heavy, resolute tread as though he sought to impress his weight upon the earth. He spoke in a loud, gruff voice.

It was two years now since Mackintosh had been appointed Walker's assistant. Walker, who had been for a quarter of a century administrator of Talua, one of the larger islands in the Samoan group, was a man known in person or by report through the length and breadth of the

South Seas; and it was with lively curiosity that Mackintosh looked forward to his first meeting with him. For one reason or another he stayed a couple of weeks at Apia before he took up his post and both at Chaplin's hotel and at the English club he heard innumerable stories about the administrator. He thought now with irony of his interest in them. Since then he had heard them a hundred times from Walker himself. Walker knew that he was a character, and, proud of his reputation, deliberately acted up to it. He was jealous of his "legend" and anxious that you should know the exact details of any of the celebrated stories that were told of him. He was ludicrously angry with anyone who had told them to the stranger incorrectly.

There was a rough cordiality about Walker which Mackintosh at first found not unattractive, and Walker, glad to have a listener to whom all he said was fresh, gave of his best. He was good-humoured, hearty, and considerate. To Mackintosh, who had lived the sheltered life of a government official in London till at the age of thirty-four an attack of pneumonia, leaving him with the threat of tuberculosis, had forced him to seek a post in the Pacific, Walker's existence seemed extraordinarily romantic. The adventure with which he started on his conquest of circumstance was typical of the man. He ran away to sea when he was fifteen and for over a year was employed in shovelling coal on a collier. He was an undersized boy and both men and mates were kind to him, but the captain for some reason conceived a savage dislike of him. He used the lad cruelly so that, beaten and kicked, he often could not sleep for the pain that racked his limbs. He loathed the captain with all his soul. Then he was given a tip for some race and managed to borrow twenty-five pounds from a friend he had picked up in Belfast. He put it on the horse, an outsider, at long odds. He had no means of repaying the money if he lost, but it never occurred to him that he could lose. He felt himself in luck. The horse won and he found himself with something over a thousand pounds in hard cash. Now his chance had come. He found out who was the best solicitor in the town—the collier lay then somewhere on the Irish coast—went to him, and, telling him that he heard the ship was for sale, asked him to arrange the purchase for him. The solicitor was amused at his small client, he was only sixteen and did not look so old, and, moved perhaps by sympathy, promised not only to arrange the matter for him but to see that he made a good bargain. After a little while Walker found himself the owner of the ship. He went back to her and had what he described as the most glorious moment of his life when he gave the skipper notice and told him that he must get off *his* ship in half an hour. He made the mate captain and sailed on the collier for another nine months, at the end of which he sold her at a profit.

He came out to the islands at the age of twenty-six as a planter. He was one of the few white men settled in Talua at the time of the German occupation and had then already some influence with the natives. The Germans made him administrator, a position which he occupied for twenty years, and when the island was seized by the British he was confirmed in his post. He ruled the island despotically, but with complete success. The prestige of this success was another reason for the interest that Mackintosh took in him.

But the two men were not made to get on. Mackintosh was an ugly man, with ungainly gestures, a tall thin fellow, with a narrow chest and bowed shoulders. He had sallow, sunken cheeks, and his eyes were large and sombre. He was a great reader, and when his books arrived and were unpacked Walker came over to his quarters and looked at them. Then he turned to Mackintosh with a coarse laugh.

"What in Hell have you brought all this muck for?" he asked.

Mackintosh flushed darkly.

"I'm sorry you think it muck. I brought my books because I want to read them."

"When you said you'd got a lot of books coming I thought there'd be something for me to read. Haven't you got any detective stories?"

"Detective stories don't interest me."

"You're a damned fool then."

"I'm content that you should think so."

Every mail brought Walker a mass of periodical literature, papers from New Zealand and magazines from America, and it exasperated him that Mackintosh showed his contempt for these ephemeral publications. He had no patience with the books that absorbed Mackintosh's leisure and thought it only a pose that he read Gibbon's *Decline and Fall* or Burton's *Anatomy of Melancholy*. And since he had never learned to put any restraint

on his tongue, he expressed his opinion of his assistant freely. Mackintosh began to see the real man, and under the boisterous good-humour
he discerned a vulgar cunning which was hateful; he was vain and dom-
ineering, and it was strange that he had notwithstanding a shyness which
made him dislike people who were not quite of his kidney. He judged
others, naively, by their language, and if it was free from the oaths and
the obscenity which made up the greater part of his own conversation,
he looked upon them with suspicion. In the evening the two men played
piquet. He played badly but vaingloriously, crowing over his opponent
when he won and losing his temper when he lost. On rare occasions a
couple of planters or traders would drive over to play bridge, and then
Walker showed himself in what Mackintosh considered a characteristic
light. He played regardless of his partner, calling up in his desire to play
the hand, and argued interminably, beating down opposition by the
loudness of his voice. He constantly revoked, and when he did so said
with an ingratiating whine: "Oh, you wouldn't count it against an old
man who can hardly see." Did he know that his opponents thought it
as well to keep on the right side of him and hesitated to insist on the
rigour of the game? Mackintosh watched him with an icy contempt.
When the game was over, while they smoked their pipes and drank
whisky, they would begin telling stories. Walker told with gusto the
story of his marriage. He had got so drunk at the wedding feast that
the bride had fled and he had never seen her since. He had had numberless adventures, commonplace and sordid, with the women of the
island and he described them with a pride in his own prowess which
was an offence to Mackintosh's fastidious ears. He was a gross, sensual
old man. He thought Mackintosh a poor fellow because he would not
share his promiscuous amours and remained sober when the company
was drunk.

He despised him also for the orderliness with which he did his official work. Mackintosh liked to do everything just so. His desk was always tidy, his papers were always neatly docketed, he could put his hand
on any document that was needed, and he had at his fingers' ends all the
regulations that were required for the business of their adminstration.

"Fudge, fudge," said Walker. "I've run this island for twenty years
without red tape, and I don't want it now."

"Does it make it any easier for you that when you want a letter you have to hunt half an hour for it?" answered Mackintosh.

"You're nothing but a damned official. But you're not a bad fellow: when you've been out here a year or two you'll be all right. What's wrong about you is that you won't drink. You wouldn't be a bad sort if you got soused once a week."

The curious thing was that Walker remained perfectly unconscious of the dislike for him which every month increased in the breast of his subordinate. Although he laughed at him, as he grew accustomed to him, he began almost to like him. He had a certain tolerance for the peculiarities of others, and he accepted Mackintosh as a queer fish. Perhaps he liked him, unconsciously, because he could chaff him. His humour consisted of coarse banter and he wanted a butt. Mackintosh's exactness, his morality, his sobriety, were all fruitful subjects; his Scot's name gave an opportunity for the usual jokes about Scotland; he enjoyed himself thoroughly when two or three men were there and he could make them all laugh at the expense of Mackintosh. He would say ridiculous things about him to the natives, and Mackintosh, his knowledge of Samoan still imperfect, would see their unrestrained mirth when Walker had made an obscene reference to him. He smiled good-humouredly.

"I'll say this for you, Mac," Walker would say in his gruff loud voice, "you can take a joke."

"Was it a joke?" smiled Mackintosh. "I didn't know."

"Scots wha hae!" shouted Walker, with a bellow of laughter.

"There's only one way to make a Scotchman see a joke and that's by a surgical operation."

Walker little knew that there was nothing Mackintosh could stand less than chaff. He would wake in the night, the breathless night of the rainy season, and brood sullenly over the gibe that Walker had uttered carelessly days before. It rankled. His heart swelled with rage, and he pictured to himself ways in which he might get even with the bully. He had tried answering him, but Walker had a gift of repartee, coarse and obvious, which gave him an advantage. The dullness of his intellect made him impervious to a delicate shaft. His self-satisfaction made it impossible to wound him. His loud voice, his bellow of laughter, were weapons against which Mackintosh had nothing to counter, and he learned that the wisest thing was

From *The Trembling of a Leaf*

never to betray his irritation. He learned to control himself. But his hatred grew till it was a monomania. He watched Walker with an insane vigilance. He fed his own self-esteem by every instance of meanness on Walker's part, by every exhibition of childish vanity, of cunning and of vulgarity. Walker ate greedily, noisily, filthily, and Mackintosh watched him with satisfaction. He took note of the foolish things he said and of his mistakes in grammar. He knew that Walker held him in small esteem, and he found a bitter satisfaction in his chief's opinion of him; it increased his own contempt for the narrow, complacent old man. And it gave him a singular pleasure to know that Walker was entirely unconscious of the hatred he felt for him. He was a fool who liked popularity, and he blandly fancied that everyone admired him. Once Mackintosh had overheard Walker speaking of him.

"He'll be all right when I've licked him into shape," he said. "He's a good dog and he loves his master."

Mackintosh silently, without a movement of his long, sallow face, laughed long and heartily.

But his hatred was not blind; on the contrary, it was peculiarly clear-sighted, and he judged Walker's capabilities with precision. He ruled his small kingdom with efficiency. He was just and honest. With opportunities to make money he was a poorer man than when he was first appointed to his post, and his only support for his old age was the pension which he expected when at last he retired from official life. His pride was that with an assistant and a half-caste clerk he was able to administer the island more competently than Upolu, the island of which Apia is the chief town, was administered with its army of functionaries. He had a few native policemn to sustain his authority, but he made no use of them. He governed by bluff and his Irish humour.

"They insisted on building a jail for me," he said. "What the devil do I want a jail for? I'm not going to put the natives in prison. If they do wrong I know how to deal with them."

One of his quarrels with the higher authorities at Apia was that he claimed entire jurisdiction over the natives of his island. Whatever their crimes he would not give them up to courts competent to deal with them, and several times an angry correspondence had passed between him and the Governor at Upolu. For he looked upon the natives as his children. And that was the amazing thing about this coarse, vulgar, selfish man; he loved the island on which he had lived so long with passion, and he had for the natives a strange rough tenderness which was quite wonderful.

He loved to ride about the island on his old grey mare and he was never tired of its beauty. Sauntering along the grassy roads among the coconut trees he would stop every now and then to admire the loveliness of the scene. Now and then he would come upon a native village and stop while the head man brought him a bowl of kava. He would look at the little group of bell-shaped huts with their high thatched roofs, like beehives, and a smile would spread over his fat face. His eyes rested happily on the spreading green of the breadfruit trees.

"By George, it's like the garden of Eden."

Sometimes his rides took him along the coast and through the trees he had a glimpse of the wide sea, empty, with never a sail to disturb the loneliness; sometimes he climbed a hill so that a great stretch of country, with little villages nestling among the tall trees, was spread out before him like the kingdom of the world, and he would sit there for an hour in an ecstasy of delight. But he had no words to express his feelings and to relieve them would utter an obscene jest; it was as though his emotion was so violent that he needed vulgarity to break the tension.

Mackintosh observed this sentiment with an icy disdain. Walker had always been a heavy drinker, he was proud of his capacity to see men half his age under the table when he spent a night in Apia, and he had the sentimentality of the toper. He could cry over the stories he read in his magazines and yet would refuse a loan to some trader in difficulties whom he had known for twenty years. He was close with his money. Once Mackintosh said to him:

"No one could accuse you of giving money away."

He took it as a compliment. His enthusiasm for nature was but the drivelling sensibility of the drunkard. Nor had Mackintosh any sympathy for his chief's feelings towards the natives. He loved them because they were in his power, as a selfish man loves his dog, and his mentality was on a level with theirs. Their humour was obscene and he was never at a loss for the lewd remark. He understood them and they understood him. He was proud of his influence over them. He looked upon them as his children and he mixed himself in all their affairs. But he was very jealous of his authority; if he ruled them with a rod of iron, brooking no contradiction, he would not suffer any of the white men on the island to take advantage of them. He watched the missionaries suspiciously and, if they did anything of which he disapproved was able to make life so unendurable to them that if he could not get them removed they were glad to go of their own accord. His power over the natives was so great that on his word they would refuse labour and food to their pastor. On the other hand he showed the traders no favour. He took care that they should not cheat the natives; he saw that they got a fair reward for their work and their copra and that the traders made no extravagant profit on the wares they sold them. He was merciless to a bargain that he thought unfair. Sometimes the traders would complain at Apia that they did not get fair opportunities. They suffered for it. Walker then hesitated at no calumny, at no outrageous lie, to get even with them, and they found that if they wanted not only to live at peace, but to exist at all, they had to accept the situation on his own terms. More than once the store of a trader obnoxious to him had been burned down, and there was only the appositeness of the event to show that the administrator had instigated it. Once a Swedish half-caste, ruined by the burning, had gone to him and roundly accused him of arson. Walker laughed in his face.

"You dirty dog. Your mother was a native and you try to cheat the natives. If your rotten old store is burned down it's a judgment of Providence; that's what it is, a judgment of Providence. Get out."

And as the man was hustled out by two native policemen the administrator laughed fatly.

"A judgment of Providence."

And now Mackintosh watched him enter upon the day's work. He began with the sick, for Walker added doctoring to his other activities, and he had a small room behind the office full of drugs. An elderly man came forward, a man with a crop of curly grey hair, in a blue *lava-lava*, elaborately tatooed, with the skin of his body wrinkled like a wine-skin.

"What have you come for?" Walker asked him abruptly.

In a whining voice the man said that he could not eat without vomiting and that he had pains here and pains there.

"Go to the missionaries," said Walker. "You know that I only cure children."

"I have been to the missionaries and they do me no good."

"Then go home and prepare yourself to die. Have you lived so long and still want to go on living? You're a fool."

The man broke into querulous expostulation, but Walker, pointing to a woman with a sick child in her arms, told her to bring it to his desk. He asked her questions and looked at the child.

"I will give you medicine," he said. He turned to the halfcaste clerk. "Go into the dispensary and bring me some calomel pills."

He made the child swallow one there and then and gave another to the mother.

"Take the child away and keep it warm. Tomorrow it will be dead or better."

He learned back in his chair and lit his pipe.

"Wonderful stuff, calomel. I've saved more lives with it than all the hospital doctors at Apia put together."

Walker was very proud of his skill, and with the dogmatism of ignorance had no patience with the members of the medical profession.

"The sort of case I like," he said, "is the one that all the doctors have given up as hopeless. When the doctors have said they can't cure you, I say to them, 'come to me.' Did I ever tell you about the fellow who had a cancer?"

"Frequently," said Mackintosh.

"I got him right in three months."

"You've never told me about the people you haven't cured."

He finished this part of the work and went on to the rest. It was a queer medley. There was a woman who could not get on with her husband and a man who complained that his wife had run away from him.

"Lucky dog," said Walker. "Most men wish their wives would too."

There was a long complicated quarrel about the ownership of a few yards of land. There was a dispute about the sharing out of a catch of fish. There was a complaint against a white trader because he had given short measure. Walker listened attentively to every case, made up his mind quickly, and gave his decision. Then he would listen to nothing more; if the complainant went on he was hustled out of the office by a policeman. Mackintosh listened to it all with sullen irritation. On the whole, perhaps, it might be admitted that rough justice was done, but it exasperated the assistant that his chief trusted his instinct rather than the evidence. He would not listen to reason. He browbeat the witnesses and when they did not see what he wished them to called them thieves and liars.

He left to the last a group of men who were sitting in the corner of the room. He had deliberately ignored them. The party consisted of an old chief, a tall, dignified man with short, white hair, in a new *lava-lava*, bearing a huge fly wisp as a badge of office, his son, and half a dozen of the important men of the village. Walker had had a feud with them and had beaten them. As was characteristic of him he meant now to rub in his victory, and because he had them down to profit by their helplessness. The facts were peculiar. Walker had a passion for building roads. When he had come to Talua there were but a few tracks here and there, but in course of time he had cut roads through the country, joining the villages together, and it was to this that a great part of the island's prosperity was due. Whereas in the old days it had been impossible to get the produce of the land, copra chiefly, down to the coast where it could be put on schooners or motor launches and so taken to Apia, now transport was easy and simple. His ambition was to make a road right round the island and a great part of it was already built.

"In two years I shall have done it, and then I can die or they can fire me, I don't care."

His roads were the joy of his heart and he made excursions constantly to see that they were kept in order. They were simple enough, wide tracks, grass covered, cut through the scrub or through the plantations; but trees had to be rooted out, rocks dug up or blasted, and here and there levelling had been necessary. He was proud that he had surmounted by his own skill such difficulties as they presented. He rejoiced in his disposition of them so that they were not only convenient, but showed off the beauties of the island which his soul loved. When he spoke of his roads he was almost a poet. They meandered through those lovely scenes, and Walker had taken care that here and there they should run in a straight line, giving you a green vista through the tall trees, and here and there should turn and curve so that the heart was rested by the diversity. It was amazing that this coarse and sensual man should exercise so subtle an ingenuity to get the effects which his fancy suggested to him. He had used in making his roads all the fantastic skill of a Japanese gardener. He received a grant from headquarters for the work but took a curious pride in using but a small part of it, and the year before had spent only a hundred pounds of the thousand assigned to him.

"What do they want money for?" he boomed. "They'll only spend it on all kinds of muck they don't want; what the missionaries leave them, that is to say."

For no particular reason, except perhaps pride in the economy of his administration and the desire to contrast his efficiency with the wasteful methods of the authorities at Apia, he got the natives to do the work he wanted for wages that were almost nominal. It was owing to this that he had lately had difficulty with the village whose chief men now were come to see him. The chief's son had been in Upolu for a year and on coming back had told his people of the large sums that were paid at Apia for the public works. In long, idle talks he had inflamed their hearts with the desire for gain. He held out to them visions of vast wealth and they thought of the whisky they could buy—it was dear, since there was a law that it must not be sold to natives, and so it cost them double what the white man had to pay for it—they thought of the great sandal-wood boxes in which they kept their treasures, and the scented soap and potted salmon, the luxuries for which the Kanaka will sell his soul; so that when the administrator sent for them and told them he wanted a road made from their village to a certain point along the coast and offered them twenty pounds, they asked him a hundred. The chief's son was called Manuma. he was a tall, handsome fellow, copper-coloured, with his fuzzy hair dyed red with lime, a wreath of red berries round his neck, and behind his ear a flower like a scarlet flame against his brown face. The upper part of his body was naked, but to show that he was no longer a savage, since he had lived in Apia, he wore a pair of dungarees instead of a *lava-lava*. He told them that if they held together the administrator would be obliged to accept their terms. His heart was set on building the road and when he found they would not work for less, he would give them what they asked. But they must not move; whatever he said they must not abate their claim; they had asked a hundred and that they must keep to. When they mentioned the figure, Walker burst into a shout of his long, deep-voiced laughter. He told them not to make fools of themselves, but to set about the work at once. Because he was in a good humour that day he promised to give them a feast when the road was finished. But when he found that no attempt was made to start work, he went to the village and asked the men what silly game they were playing. Manuma had coached them well. They were quite calm, they did not attempt to argue—and argument is a passion with the Kanaka—they merely shrugged their shoulders: they would do it for a hundred pounds, and if he would not give them that they would do no work. He could please himself. They did not care. Then Walker flew into a passion. He was ugly then. His short fat neck swelled ominously, his red face grew purple, he foamed at the mouth. He set upon the natives with invective. He knew well how to wound and how to humiliate. He was terrifying. The older men grew pale and uneasy. They hesitated. If it had not been for Manuma, with his knowledge of the great world, and their dread of his ridicule, they would have yielded. It was Manuma who answered Walker.

"Pay us a hundred pounds and we will work."

Walker, shaking his fist at him, called him every name he could think of. He riddled him with scorn. Manuma sat still and smiled. There may have been more bravado than confidence in his smile, but he had to make a good show before the others. He repeated his words.

"Pay us a hundred pounds and we will work."

They thought that Walker would spring on him. It would not have been the first time that he had thrashed a native with his own hands; they knew his strength, and though Walker was three times the age of the young man and six inches shorter they did not doubt that he was more than a match for Manuma. No one had ever thought of resisting the savage onslaught of the administrator. But Walker said nothing. He chuckled.

"I am not going to waste my time with a pack of fools," he said. "Talk it over again. You know what I have offered. If you do not start in a week, take care."

He turned round and walked out of the chief's hut. He untied his old mare and it was typical of the relations between him and the natives that one of the elder men hung on to the off stirrup while Walker from a convenient boulder hoisted himself heavily into the saddle.

That same night when Walker, according to his habit, was strolling along the road that ran past his house, he heard something whizz past him and with a thud strike a tree. Something had been thrown at him. He ducked instinctively. With a shout, "Who's that"? he ran towards the place from which the missile had come and he heard the sound of a man escaping through the bush. He knew it was hopeless to pursue in the darkness, and besides he was soon out of breath, so he stopped and made his way back to the road. He looked about for what had been thrown, but could find nothing. It was quite dark. He went quickly back to the house and called Mackintosh and the Chinese boy.

"One of those devils has thrown something at me. Come along and let's find out what it was."

He told the boy to bring a lantern and the three of them made their way back to the place. They hunted about the ground, but could not find what they sought. Suddenly the boy gave a guttural cry. They turned to look. He held up the lantern, and there, sinister in the light that cut the surrounding darkness, was a long knife sticking into the trunk of a co-conut tree. It had been thrown with such force that it required quite an effort to pull it out.

"By George, if he hadn't missed me I'd have been in a nice state."

Walker handled the knife. It was one of those knives, made in imitation of the sailor knives brought to the islands a hundred years before by the first white men, used to divide the coconuts in two so that the copra might be dried. It was a murderous weapon, and the blade, twelve inches long, was very sharp. Walker chuckled softly.

"The devil, the impudent devil."

He had no doubt it was Manuma who had flung the knife. He had escaped death by three inches. He was not angry. On the contrary, he was in high spirits; the adventure exhilarated him, and when they got back to the house, calling for drinks, he rubbed his hands gleefully.

"I'll make them pay for this!"

His little eyes twinkled. He blew himself out like a turkeycock, and for the second time within half an hour insisted on telling Mackintosh every detail of the affair. Then he asked him to play piquet, and while they played he boasted of his intentions. Mackintosh listened with tightened lips.

"But why should you grind them down like this?" he asked. "Twenty pounds is precious little for the work you want them to do."

"They ought to be precious thankful I give them anything."

"Hang it all, it's not your own money. The government allots you a reasonable sum. They won't complain if you spend it."

"They're a bunch of fools at Apia."

Mackintosh saw that Walker's motive was merely vanity. He shrugged his shoulders.

"It won't do you much good to score off the fellows at Apia at the cost of your life."

"Bless you, they wouldn't hurt me, these people. They couldn't do without me. They worship me. Manuma is a fool. He only threw that knife to frighten me."

The next day Walker rode over again to the village. It was called Matautu. He did not get off his horse. When he reached the chief's house he saw that the men were sitting round the floor in a circle, talking, and he gussed they were discussing again the question of the road. The Samoan huts are formed in this way: Trunks of slender trees are placed in a circle at intervals of perhaps five or six feet; a tall tree is set in the middle and from this downwards slopes the thatched roof. Venetian blinds of coconut leaves can be pulled down at night or when it is raining. Ordinarily the hut is open all round so that the breeze can blow through freely. Walker rode to the edge of the hut and called out to the chief.

"Oh, there, Tangatu, your son left his knife in a tree last night. I have brought it back to you."

He flung it down on the ground in the midst of the circle, and with a low burst of laughter ambled off.

On Monday he went out to see if they had started work. There was no sign of it. He rode through the village. The inhabitants were about their ordinary avocations. Some were weaving mats of the pandanus leaf, one old man was busy with a *kava* bowl, the children were playing, the women went about their household chores. Walker, a smile on his lips, came to the chief's house.

"*Talofa-li,*" said the chief.

"*Talofa,*" answered Walker.

Manuma was making a net. He sat with a cigarette between his lips and looked up at Walker with a smile of triumph.

"You have decided that you will not make the road?"

The chief answered.

"Not unless you pay us one hundred pounds."

"You will regret it." He turned to Manuma. "And you, my lad, I shouldn't wonder if your back was very sore before you're much older."

He rode away chuckling. He left the natives vaguely uneasy.

They feared the fat sinful old man, and neither the missionaries abuse of him nor the scorn which Manuma had learnt in Apia made them forget that he had a devilish cunning and that no man had ever braved him without in the long run suffering for it. They found out within twenty-four hours what scheme he had devised. It was characteristic. For next morning a great band of men, women, and children came into the village and the chief men said that they had made a bargain with Walker to build the road. He had offered them twenty pounds and they had accepted. Now the cunning lay in this, that the Polynesians have rules of hospitality which have all the force of laws; an etiquette of absolute rigidity made it necessary for the people of the village not only to give lodging to the strangers, but to provide them with food and drink as long as they wished to stay. The inhabitants of Matautu were outwitted. Every morning the workers went out in a joyous band, cut down trees, blasted rocks, levelled here and there and then in the evening tramped back again, and ate and drank, ate heartily, danced, sang hymns, and enjoyed life. For them it was a picnic. But soon their hosts began to wear long faces; the strangers had enormous appetites, and the plantains and the breadfruit vanished before their rapacity; the alligator-pear trees, whose fruit sent to Apia might sell for good money, were stripped bare. Ruin stared them in the face. And then they found that the strangers were working very slowly. Had they received a hint from Walker that they might take their time? At this rate by the time the road was finished there would not be a scrap of food in the village. And worse than this, they were a laughing-stock; when one or other of them went to some distant hamlet on an errand he found that the story had got there before him, and he was met with derisive laughter. There is nothing the Kanaka can endure less than ridicule. It was not long before much angry talk passed

among the sufferers. Manuma was not longer a hero; he had to put up
with a good deal of plain speaking, and one day what Walker had suggested came to pass: a heated argument turned into a quarrel and half a
dozen of the young men set upon the chief's son and gave him such a
beating that for a week he lay bruised and sore on the pandanus mats.
He turned from side to side and could find no ease. Every day or two
the administrator rode over on his old mare and watched the progress of
the road. He was not a man to resist the temptation of taunting the
fallen foe, and he missed no opportunity to rub into the shamed inhabitants of Matautu the bitterness of their humiliation. He broke their
spirit. And one morning, putting their pride in their pockets, a figure of
speech, since pockets they had not, they all set out with the strangers and
started working on the road. It was urgent to get it done quickly if they
wanted to save any food at all, and the whole village joined in. But they
worked silently, with rage and mortification in their hearts, and even the
children toiled in silence. The women wept as they carried away bundles
of brushwood. When Walker saw them he laughed so much that he almost rolled out of his saddle. The news spread quickly and tickled the
people of the island to death. This was the greatest joke of all, the
crowning triumph of that cunning old white man whom no Kanaka had
ever been able to circumvent; and they came from distant villages, with
their wives and children, to look at the foolish folk who had refused
twenty pounds to make the road and now were forced to work for nothing. But the harder they worked the more easily went the guests. Why
should they hurry, when they were getting good food for nothing and
the longer they took about the job the better the joke became? At last
the wretched villagers could stand it no longer, and they were come this
morning to beg the administrator to send the strangers back to their own
homes. If he would do this they promised to finish the road themselves
for nothing. For him it was a victory complete and unqualified. They
were humbled. A look of arrogant complacence spread over his large,
naked face, and he seemed to swell in his chair like a great bullfrog. There
was something sinister in his appearance, so that Mackintosh shivered
with disgust. Then in his booming tones he began to speak.

"Is it for my good that I make the road? What benefit do you think
I get out of it? It is for you, so that you can walk in comfort and carry

your copra in comfort. I offered to pay you for your work, though it was for your own sake the work was done. I offered to pay you generously. Now you must pay. I will send the people of Manua back to their homes if you will finish the road and pay the twenty pounds that I have to pay them."

There was an outcry. They sought to reason with him. They told him they had not the money. But to everything they said he replied with brutal gibes. Then the clock struck.

"Dinner time," he said. "Turn them all out."

He raised himself heavily from his chair and walked out of the room. When Mackintosh followed him he found him already seated at table, a napkin tied round his neck, holding his knife and fork in readiness for the meal the Chinese cook was about to bring. He was in high spirits.

"I did 'em down fine," he said, as Mackintosh sat down. "I shan't have much trouble with the roads after this."

"I suppose you were joking," said Mackintosh icily.

"What do you mean by that?"

"You're not really going to make them pay twenty pounds?"

"You bet your life I am."

"I'm not sure you've got any right to."

"Ain't you? I guess I've got the right to do any damned thing I like on this island."

"I think you've bullied them quite enough."

Walker laughed fatly. He did not care what Mackintosh thought.

"When I want your opinion I'll ask for it."

Mackintosh grew very white. He knew by bitter experience that he could do nothing but keep silence, and the violent effort at self-control made him sick and faint. He could not eat the food that was before him and with disgust he watched Walker shovel meat into his vast mouth. He was a dirty feeder, and to sit at table with him needed a strong stomach. Mackintosh shuddered. A tremendous desire seized him to humiliate that gross and cruel man; he would give anything in the world to see him in the dust, suffering as much as he had made others suffer. He had never loathed the bully with such loathing as now.

The day wore on. Mackintosh tried to sleep after dinner, but the passion in his heart preventd him; he tried to read, but the letters swam before his eyes. The sun beat down pitilessly, and he longed for rain; but he knew that rain would bring no coolness; it would only make it hotter and more steamy. He was a native of Aberdeen and his heart yearned suddenly for the icy winds that whistled through the granite streets of that city. Here he was a prisoner, imprisoned not only by that placid sea, but by his hatred for that horrible old man. He pressed his hands to his aching head. He would like to kill him. But he pulled himself together. He must do something to distract his mind, and since he could not read he thought he would set his private papers in order. It was a job which he had long meant to do and which he had constantly put off. He unlocked the drawer of his desk and took out a handful of letters. He caught sight of his revolver. An impulse, no sooner realized than set aside, to put a bullet through his head and so escape from the intolerable bondage of life flashed through his mind. He noticed that in the damp air the revolver was slightly rusted, and he got an oil rag and began to clean it. It was while he was thus occupied that he grew aware of someone slinking round the door. He looked up and called:

"Who is there?"

There was a moment's pause, then Manuma showed himself.

"What do you want?"

The chief's son stood for a moment, sullen and silent, and when he spoke it was with a strangled voice.

"We can't pay twenty pounds. We haven't the money."

"What am I to do?" said Mackintosh. "You heard what Mr. Walker said."

Manuma began to plead, half in Samoan and half in English.

It was a sing-song whine, with the quavering intonations of a begger, and it filled Mackintosh with disgust. It outraged him that the man should let himself be so crushed. He was a pitiful object.

"I can do nothing," said Mackintosh irritably. "You know that Mr. Walker is master here."

Manuma was silent again. He still stood in the doorway.

"I am sick," he said at last. "Give me some medicine."

"What is the matter with you?"

"I do not know. I am sick. I have pains in my body."

"Don't stand there," said Mackintosh sharply. "Come in and let me look at you."

Manuma entered the little room and stood before the desk.

"I have pains here and here."

He put his hands to his loins and his face assumed an expression of pain. Suddenly Mackintosh grew conscious that the boy's eyes were resting on the revolver which he had laid on the desk when Manuma appeared in the doorway. There was a silence between the two which to Mackintosh was endless. He seemed to read the thoughts which were in the Kanaka's mind. His heart beat violently. And then he felt as though something possessed him so that he acted under the compulsion of a foreign will. Himself did not make the movements of his body, but a power that was strange to him. His throat was suddenly dry, and he put his hand to it mechanically in order to help his speech. He was impelled to avoid Manuma's eyes.

"Just wait here," he said, his voice sounding as though someone had seized him by the windpipe, "and I'll fetch you something from the dispensary."

He got up. Was it his fancy that he staggered a little? Manuma stood silently, and though he kept his eyes averted, Mackintosh knew that he was looking dully out of the door. It was this other person that possessed him, that drove him out of the room, but it was himself that took a handful of muddled papers and threw them on the revolver in order to hide it from view. He went to the dispensary. He got a pill and poured out some blue draught into a small bottle, and then came out into the compound. He did not want to go back into his own bungalow, so he called to Manuma.

"Come here."

He gave him the drugs and instructions how to take them. He did not know what it was that made it impossible for him to look at the Kanaka. While he was speaking to him he kept his eyes on his shoulder. Manuma took the medicine and slunk out of the gate.

Mackintosh went into the dining-room and turned over once more the old newspapers. But he could not read them. The house was very still. Walker was upstairs in his room asleep, the Chinese cook was busy in the kitchen, the two policemen were out fishing. The silence that seemed to brood over the house was unearthly, and there hammered in Mackintosh's head the question whether the revolver still lay where he had placed it. He could not bring himself to look. The uncertainty was horrible, but the certainty would be more horrible still. He sweated. At last he could stand the silence no longer, and he made up his mind to go down the road to the trader's, a man named Jervis, who had a store about a mile away. He was a half-caste, but even that amount of white blood made him possible to talk to. He wanted to get away from his bungalow, with the desk littered with untidy papers, and underneath them something, or nothing. He walked along the road. As he passed the fine hut of a chief a greeting was called out to him. Then he came to the store. Behind the counter sat the trader's daughter, a swarthy broad-featured girl in a pink blouse and a white drill skirt. Jervis hoped he would marry her. He had money, and he had told Mackintosh that his daughter's husband would be well-to-do. She flushed a little when she saw Mackintosh.

"Father's just unpacking some cases that have come in this morning. I'll tell him you're here."

He sat down and the girl went out behind the shop. In a moment her mother waddled in, a huge old woman, a chiefess, who owned much land in her own right; and gave him her hand. Her monstrous obesity was an offence, but she managed to convey an impression of dignity. She was cordial without obsequiousness; affable, but conscious of her station.

"You're quite a stranger, Mr. Mackintosh. Teresa was saying only this morning: `Why, we never see Mr. Mackintosh now.'"

He shuddered a little as he thought of himself as that old native's son-in-law. It was notorious that she ruled her husband, notwithstanding his white blood, with a firm hand. Hers was the authority and hers the business head. She might be no more than Mrs. Jervis to the white people, but her father had been a chief of the blood royal, and his father and his father's father had ruled as kings. The trader came in, small beside his imposing wife, a dark man with a black beard going grey, in ducks, with handsome eyes and flashing teeth. He was very British, and his conversation was slangy, but you felt he spoke English as a foreign tongue; with his family he used the language of his native mother. He was a servile man, cringing and obsequious.

"Ah, Mr. Mackintosh, this is a joyful surprise. Get the whisky, Teresa; Mr. Mackintosh will have a gargle with us."

He gave all the latest news of Apia, watching his guest's eyes the while, so that he might know the welcome thing to say.

"And how is Walker? We've not seen him just lately. Mrs. Jervis is going to send him a sucking-pig one day this week."

"I saw him riding home this morning," said Teresa.

"Here's how," said Jervis, holding up his whisky.

Mackintosh drank. The two women sat and looked at him, Mrs. Jervis in her black Mother Hubbard, placid and haughty, and Teresa, anxious to smile whenever she caught his eye, while the trader gossiped insufferably.

"They were saying in Apia it was about time Walker retired. He ain't so young as he was. Things have changed since he first come to the islands and he ain't changed with them."

"He'll go too far," said the old chiefess. "The natives aren't satisfied."

"That was a good joke about the road," laughed the trader. "When I told them about it in Apia they fair split their sides with laughing. Good old Walker."

Mackintosh looked at him savagely. What did he mean by talking of him in that fashion? To a half-caste trader he was Mr. Walker. It was on his tongue to utter a harsh rebuke for the impertinence. He did not know what held him back.

"When he goes I hope you'll take his place, Mr. Mackintosh," said Jervis. "We all like you on the island. You understand the natives. They're educated now, they must be treated differently to the old days. It wants an educated man to be administrator now. Walker was only a trader same as I am."

Teresa's eyes glistened.

"When the time comes if there's anything anyone can do here, you bet your bottom dollar we'll do it. I'd get all the chiefs to go over to Apia and make a petition."

Mackintosh felt horribly sick. It had not struck him that if anything happened to Walker it might be he who would succeed him. It was true that no one in his official position knew the island so well. He got up suddenly and scarcely taking his leave walked back to the compound. And now he went straight to his room. He took a quick look at his desk. He rummaged among the papers.

The revolver was not there.

His heart thumped violently against his ribs. He looked for the revolver everywhere. He hunted in the chairs and in the drawers. He looked desperately, and all the time he knew he would not find it. Suddenly he heard Walker's gruff, hearty voice.

"What the devil are you up to, Mac?"

He started. Walker was standing in the doorway and instinctively he turned round to hide what lay upon his desk.

"Tidying up?" quizzed Walker. "I've told 'em to put the grey in the trap. I'm going down to Tafoni to bathe. You'd better come along."

"All right," said Mackintosh.

So long as he was with Walker nothing could happen.

The place they were bound for was about three miles away and there was a fresh-water pool, separated by a thin barrier of rock from the sea, which the administrator had blasted out for the natives to bathe in. He had done this at spots round the island, wherever there was a spring; and the fresh water, compared with the sticky warmth of the sea, was cool and invigorating. They drove along the silent grassy road, splashing now and then through fords, where the sea had forced its way in, past a couple of native villages, the bell-shaped huts spaced out roomily and the white chapel in the middle, and at the third village they got out of the trap, tied up the horse, and walked down to the pool. They were accompanied by four or five girls and a dozen children. Soon they were all splashing about, shouting and laughing, while Walker, in a *lava-lava*, swam to and fro like an unwiedly porpoise. He made lewd jokes with the girls, and they amused themselves by diving under him and wriggling away when he tried to catch them. When he was tired he lay down on a rock, while the girls and children surrounded him; it was a happy family; and the old man, huge, with his crescent of white hair and his shining bald crown, looked like some old sea god. Once Mackintosh caught a queer soft look in his eyes.

"They're dear children," he said. "They look upon me as their father."

And then without a pause he turned to one of the girls and made an obscene remark which sent them all into fits of laughter. Mackintosh started to dress. With his thin legs and thin arms he made a grotesque figure, a sinister Don Quixote, and Walker began to make coarse jokes about him. They were acknowledged with little smothered laughs. Mackintosh struggled with his shirt. He knew he looked absurd, but he hated being laughed at. He stood silent and glowering.

"If you want to get back in time for dinner you ought to come soon."

"You're not a bad fellow, Mac. Only you're a fool. When you're do-ing one thing you always want to do another. That's not the way to live."

But all the same he raised himself slowly to his feet and began to put on his clothes. They sauntered back to the village, drank a bowl of kava with the chief, and then, after a joyful farewell from all the lazy villagers, drove home.

After dinner, according to his habit, Walker, lighting his cigar, pre-pared to go for a stroll. Mackintosh was suddenly seized with fear.

"Don't you think it's rather unwise to go out at night by yourself just now?"

Walker stared at him with his round blue eyes.

"What the devil do you mean?"

"Remember the knife the other night. You've got those fellows' backs up."

"Pooh! They wouldn't dare."

"Someone dared before."

"That was only a bluff. They wouldn't hurt me. They look upon me as a father. They know that whatever I do is for their own good."

Mackintosh watched him with contempt in his heart. The man's self-complacency outraged him, and yet something, he knew not what, made him insist.

"Remember what happened this morning. It wouldn't hurt you to stay at home just to-night. I'll play piquet with you."

"I'll play piquet with you when I come back. The Kanaka isn't born yet who can make me alter my plans."

"You'd better let me come with you."

"You stay where you are."

Mackintosh shrugged his shoulders. He had given the man full warning. If he did not heed it that was his own lookout. Walker put on his hat and went out. Mackintosh began to read; but then he thought of something; perhaps it would be as well to have his own whereabouts quite clear. He crossed over to the kitchen and, inventing some pretext, talked for a few minutes with the cook. Then he got out the gramphone and put a record on it, but while it ground out its melancholy tune, some comic song of a London music-hall, his ear was strained for a sound away there in the night. At his elbow the record reeled out its loudness, the words were raucous, but notwithstanding he seemed to be surrounded by an unearthly silence. He heard the dull roar of the breakers against the reef. He heard the breeze sigh, far up, in the leaves of the coconut trees. How long would it be? It was awful.

He heard a hoarse laugh.

"Wonders will never cease. It's not often you play yourself a tune, Mac."

Walker stood at the window, red-faced, bluff and jovial.

"Well, you see I'm alive and kicking. What were you playing for?"

Walker came in.

"Nerves a bit dicky, eh? Playing a tune to keep your pecker up?"

"I was playing your requiem."

"What the devil's that?"

"Alf o' bitter an' a pint of stout."

"A rattling good song too. I don't mind how often I hear it. Now I'm ready to take your money off you at piquet."

They played and Walker bullied his way to victory, bluffing his opponent, chaffing him, jeering at his mistakes, up to every dodge, browbeating him, exulting. Presently Mackintosh recovered his coolness, and standing outside himself, as it were, he was able to take a detached pleasure in watching the overbearing old man and in his own cold reserve. Somewhere Manuma sat quietly and awaited his opportunity.

Walker won game after game and pocketed his winnings at the end of the evening in high good humour.

"You'll have to grow a little bit older before you stand much chance against me, Mac. The fact is I have a natural gift for cards."

"I don't know that there's much gift about it when I happen to deal you fourteen aces."

"Good cards come to good players," retorted Walker. "I'd have won if I'd had your hands."

He went on to tell long stories of the various occasions on which he had played cards with notorious sharpers and to their consternation had taken all their money from them. He boasted. He praised himself. And Mackintosh listened with absorption. He wanted now to feed his hatred;

and everything Walker said, every gesture, made him more detestable. At last Walker got up.

"Well, I'm going to turn in," he said with a loud yawn. "I've got a long day to-morrow."

"What are you going to do?"

"I'm driving over to the other side of the island. I'll start at five, but I don't expect I shall get back to dinner till late."

They generally dined at seven.

"We'd better make it half-past seven then."

"I guess it would be as well."

Mackintosh watched him knock the ashes out of his pipe.

His vitality was rude and exuberant. It was strange to think that death hung over him. A faint smile flickered in Mackintosh's cold, gloomy eyes.

"Would you like me to come with you?"

"What in God's name should I want that for? I'm using the mare and she'll have enough to do to carry me; she don't want to drag you over thirty miles of road."

"Perhaps you don't quite realize what the feeling is at Matautu. I think it would be safer if I came with you."

Walker burst into contemptuous laughter.

"You'd be a fine lot of use in a scrap. I'm not a great hand at getting the wind up."

Now the smile passed from Mackintosh's eyes to his lips. It distorted them painfully.

"*Quem deus vult perdere prius dementat.*"

"What the hell is that?" said Walker.

"Latin," answered Mackintosh as he went out.

And now he chuckled. His mood had changed. He had done all he could and the matter was in the hands of fate. He slept more soundly than he had done for weeks. When he awoke next morning he went out. After a good night he found a pleasant exhilaration in the freshness of the early air. The sea was a more vivid blue, the sky more brilliant, than on most days, the trade wind was fresh, and there was a ripple on the lagoon as the breeze brushed over it like velvet brushed the wrong way. He felt himself stronger and younger. He entered upon the day's work with

zest. After luncheon he slept again, and as evening drew on he had the
bay saddled and sauntered through the bush. He seemed to see it all with
new eyes. He felt more normal. The extraordinary thing was that he was
able to put Walker out of his mind altogether. So far as he was concerned he might never have existed.

He returned late, hot after his ride, and bathed again. Then he sat
on the verandah, smoking his pipe, and looked at the day declining over
the lagoon. In the sunset the lagoon, rosy and purple and green, was very
beautiful. He felt at peace with the world and with himself. When the
cook came out to say that dinner was ready and to ask whether he should
wait, Mackintosh smiled at him with friendly eyes. He looked at his
watch.

"It's half-past seven. Better not wait. One can't tell when the boss'll
be back."

The boy nodded, and in a moment Mackintosh saw him carry
across the yard a bowl of steaming soup. He got up lazily, went into the
dining-room, and ate his dinner. Had it happened? The uncertainty was
amusing and Mackintosh chuckled in the silence. The food did not seem
so monotonous as usual, and even though there was Hamburger steak,
the cook's invariable dish when his poor invention failed him, it tasted
by some miracle succulent and spiced. After dinner he strolled over lazily
to his bungalow to get a book. He liked the intense stillness, and now
that the night had fallen the stars were blazing in the sky. He shouted for
a lamp and in a moment the Chink pattered over on his bare feet, piercing the darkness with a ray of light. He put the lamp on the desk and
noiselessly slipped out of the room. Mackintosh stood rooted to the
floor, for there, half hidden by untidy papers, was his revolver. His heart
throbbed painfully, and he broke into a sweat. It was done then.

He took up the revolver with a shaking hand. Four of the chambers
were empty. He paused a moment and looked suspiciously out into the
night, but there was no one there. He quickly slipped four cartridges into
the empty chambers and locked the revolver in his drawer.

He sat down to wait.

An hour passed, a second hour passed. There was nothing. He sat at
his desk as though he were writing, but he neither wrote nor read. He
merely listened. He strained his ears for a sound travelling from a far dis-

tance. At last he heard hesitating footsteps and knew it was the Chinese cook.

"Ah-Sung," he called.

The boy came to the door.

"Boss velly late," he said. "Dinner no good."

Mackintosh stared at him, wondering whether he knew what had happened, and whether, when he knew, he would realize on what terms he and Walker had been. He went about his work, sleek, silent, and smiling, and who could tell his thoughts?

"I expect he's had dinner on the way, but you must keep the soup hot at all events."

The words were hardly out of his mouth when the silence was suddenly broken into by a confusion, cries, and a rapid patter of naked feet. A number of natives ran into the compound, men and women and children; they crowded round Mackintosh and they all talked at once. They were unintelligible. They were excited and frightened and some of them were crying. Mackintosh pushed his way through them and went to the gateway. Though he had scarcely understood what they said he knew quite well what had happened. And as he reached the gate the dog-cart arrived. The old mare was being led by a tall Kanaka, and in the dog-cart crouched two men, trying to hold Walker up. A little crowd of natives surrounded it.

The mare was led into the yard and the natives surged in after it. Mackintosh shouted to them to stand back and the two policemen, sprang suddenly from God knows where, pushed them violently aside. By now he had managed to understand that some lads who had been fishing, on their way back to their village had come across the cart on the home side of the ford. The mare was nuzzling about the herbage and in the darkness they could just see the great white bulk of the old man sunk between the seat and the dashboard. At first they thought he was drunk and they peered in, grinning, but then they heard him groan, and guessed that something was amiss. They ran to the village and called for help. It was when they returned, accompanied by half a hundred people, that they discovered Walker had been shot.

With a sudden thrill of horror Mackintosh asked himself whether he was already dead. The first thing at all events was to get him out of the cart, and that, owing to Walker's corpulence, was a difficult job. It took four strong men to lift him. They jolted him and he uttered a dull groan. He was still alive. At last they carried him into the house, up the stairs, and placed him on his bed. Then Mackintosh was able to see him, for in the yard, lit only by half a dozen hurricane lamps, everything had been obscured. Walker's white ducks were stained with blood, and the men who had carried him wiped their hands, red and sticky, on their lava-lavas. Mackintosh held up the lamp. He had not expected the old man to be so pale. His eyes were closed. He was breathing still, his pulse could be just felt, but it was obvious that he was dying. Mackintosh had not bargained for the shock of horror that convulsed him. He saw that the native clerk was there, and in a voice hoarse with fear told him to go into the dispensary and get what was necessary for a hypodermic injection. One of the policemen had brought up the whisky, and Mackintosh forced a little into the old man's mouth. The room was crowded with natives. They sat about the floor, speechless now and terrified, and every now and then one wailed aloud. It was very hot, but Mackintosh felt cold, his hands and his feet were like ice, and he had to make a violent effort not to tremble in all his limbs. He did not know what to do. He did not know if Walker was bleeding still, and if he was, how he could stop the bleeding.

The clerk brought the hypodermic needle.

"You give it to him," said Mackintosh. "You're more used to that sort of thing than I am."

His head ached horribly. It felt as though all sorts of little savage things were beating inside it, trying to get out. They watched for the effect of the injection. Presently Walker opened his eyes slowly. He did not seem to know where he was.

"Keep quiet," said Mackintosh. "You're at home. You're quite safe."

Walker's lips outlined a shadowy smile.

"They've got me," he whispered.

"I'll get Jervis to send his motor-boat to Apia at once. We'll get a doctor out by to-morrow afternoon."

There was a long pause before the old man answered,

"I shall be dead by then."

A ghastly expression passed over Mackintosh's pale face.

He forced himself to laugh.

"What rot! You keep quiet and you'll be as right as rain."

"Give me a drink," said Walker. "A stiff one."

With shaking hand Mackintosh poured out whisky and water, half and half, and held the glass while Walker drank greedily. It seemed to restore him. He gave a long sigh and a little colour came into his great fleshy face. Mackintosh felt extraordinarily helpless. He stood and stared at the old man.

"If you'll tell me what to do I'll do it," he said.

"There's nothing to do. Just leave me alone. I'm done for."

He looked dreadfully pitiful as he lay on the great bed, a huge, bloated, old man; but so wan, so weak, it was heartrending. As he rested, his mind seemed to grow clearer.

"You were right, Mac," he said presently. "You warned me."

"I wish to God I'd come with you."

"You're a good chap, Mac, only you don't drink."

There was another long silence, and it was clear that Walker was sinking. There was an internal hemorrhage and even Mackintosh in his ignorance could not fail to see that his chief had but an hour or two to live. He stood by the side of the bed stock still. For half an hour perhaps Walker lay with his eyes closed, then he opened them.

"They'll give you my job," he said, slowly. "Last time I was in Apia I told them you were all right. Finish my road. I want to think that'll be done. All round the island."

"I don't want your job. You'll get all right."

Walker shook his head wearily.

"I've had my day. Treat them fairly, that's the great thing. They're children. You must always remember that. You must be firm with them, but you must be kind. And you must be just. I've never made a bob out of them. I haven't saved a hundred pounds in twenty years. The road's the great thing. Get the road finished."

Something very like a sob was wrung from Mackintosh.

"You're a good fellow, Mac. I always liked you."

He closed his eyes, and Mackintosh thought that he would never open them again. His mouth was so dry that he had to get himself something to drink. The Chinese cook silently put a chair for him. He sat down by the side of the bed and waited. He did not know how long a time passed. The night was endless. Suddenly one of the men sitting there broke into uncontrollable sobbing, loudly, like a child, and Mackintosh grew aware that the room was crowded by this time with natives. They sat all over the floor on their haunches, men and women, staring at the bed.

"What are all these people doing here?" said Mackintosh. "They've got no right. Turn them out, turn them out, all of them."

His words seemed to rouse Walker, for he opened his eyes once more, and now they were all misty. He wanted to speak, but he was so weak that Mackintosh had to strain his ears to catch what he said.

"Let them stay. They're my children. They ought to be here."

Mackintosh turned to the natives.

"Stay where you are. He wants you. But be silent."

A faint smile came over the old man's white face.

"Come nearer," he said.

Mackintosh bent over him. His eyes were closed and the words he said were like a wind sighing through the fronds of the coconut trees.

"Give me another drink. I've got something to say."

This time Mackintosh gave him his whisky neat. Walker collected his strength in a final effort of will.

"Don't make a fuss about this. In 'ninety-five when there were troubles white men were killed, and the fleet came and shelled the villages. A lot of people were killed who'd had nothing to do with it. They're damned fools at Apia. If they make a fuss they'll only punish the wrong people. I don't want anyone punished."

He paused for a while to rest.

"You must say it was an accident. No one's to blame. Promise me that."

"I'll do anything you like," whispered Mackintosh.

"Good chap. One of the best. They're children. I'm their father. A father don't let his children get into trouble if he can help it."

A ghost of a chuckle came out of his throat. It was astonishingly weird and ghastly.

"You're a religious chap, Mac. What's that about forgiving them? You know."

For a while Mackintosh did not answer. His lips trembled.

"Forgive them, for they know not what they do?"

"That's right. Forgive them. I've loved them, you know, always loved them."

He sighed. His lips faintly moved, and now Mackintosh had to put his ears quite close to them in order to hear.

"Hold my hand," he said.

Mackintosh gave a gasp. His heart seemed wrenched. He took the old man's hand, so cold and weak, a coarse, rough hand, and held it in his own. And thus he sat until he nearly started out of his seat, for the silence was suddenly broken by a long rattle. It was terrible and unearthly. Walker was dead. Then the natives broke out with loud cries. The tears ran down their faces, and they beat their breasts.

Mackintosh disengaged his hand from the dead man's, and staggering like one drunk with sleep he went out of the room. He went to the locked drawer in his writing-desk and took out the revolver. He walked down to the sea and walked into the lagoon; he waded out cautiously, so that he should not trip against a coral rock, till the water came to his arm-pits. Then he put a bullet through his head.

An hour later half a dozen slim brown sharks were splashing and struggling at the spot where he fell.

"The Pool" (1921)

When I was introduced to Lawson by Chaplin, the owner of the Hotel Metropole at Apia, I paid no particular attention to him. We were sitting in the lounge over an early cocktail and I was listening with amusement to the gossip of the island.

Chaplin entertained me. He was by profession a mining engineer and perhaps it was characteristic of him that he had settled in a place where his professional attainments were of no possible value. It was, however, generally reported that he was an extremely clever mining engineer. He was a small man, neither fat nor thin, with black hair, scanty on the crown, turning grey, and a small, untidy moustache; his face, partly from the sun and partly from liquor, was very red. He was but a figurehead, for the hotel, though so grandly named, was but a frame building of two storeys, managed by his wife, a tall, gaunt Australian of five and forty, with an imposing presence and a determined air. The little man, excitable and often tipsy, was terrified of her, and the stranger soon heard of domestic quarrels in which she used her fist and her foot in order to keep him in subjection. She had been known after a night of drunkenness to confine him for twenty-four hours to his own room, and then he could be seen, afraid to leave his prison, talking somewhat pathetically from his verandah to people in the street below.

He was a character, and his reminiscences of a varied life, whether true or not, made him worth listening to, so that when Lawson strolled in I was inclined to resent the interruption. Although not midday, it was clear that he had had enough to drink, and it was without enthusiasm that I yielded to his persistence and accepted his offer of another cocktail. I knew already that Chaplin's head was weak. The next round which in common politeness I should be forced to order would be enough to make him lively, and then Mrs. Chaplin would give me black looks.

Nor was there anything attractive in Lawson's appearance. He was a little thin man, with a long, sallow face and a narrow, weak chin, a prominent nose, large and bony, and great shaggy black eyebrows. They gave him a peculiar look. His eyes, very large and very dark, were magnificent. He was jolly, but his jollity did not seem to me sincere; it was on the surface, a mask which he wore to deceive the world, and I suspected that it concealed a mean nature. He was plainly anxious to be thought a "good sport" and he was hail-fellow-well-met; but, I do not know why, I felt that he was cunning and shifty. He talked a great deal in a raucous voice, and he and Chaplin capped one another's stories of beanos which had become legendary, stories of "wet" nights at the English Club, of shooting expeditions where an incredible amount of whisky had been consumed, and of jaunts to Sydney of which their pride was that they could remember nothing from the time they landed till the time they sailed. A pair of drunken swine. But even in their intoxication, for by now after four cocktails each, neither was sober, there was a great difference between Chaplin, rough and vulgar, and Lawson: Lawson might be drunk, but he was certainly a gentleman.

At last he got out of his chair, a little unsteadily.

"Well, I'll be getting along home," he said. "See you before dinner."

"Missus all right?" said Chaplin.

"Yes."

"He went out. There was a peculiar note in the monosyllable of his answer which made me look up.

"Good chap," said Chaplin flatly, as Lawson went out of the door into the sunshine. "One of the best. Pity he drinks."

This from Chaplin was an observation not without humour.

"And when he's drunk he wants to fight people."

"Is he often drunk?"

"Dead drunk, three or four days a week. It's the island done it, and Ethel."

"Who's Ethel?"

"Ethel's his wife. Married a half-caste. Old Brevald's daughter. Took her away from here. Only thing to do. But she couldn't stand it, and now they're back again. He'll hang himself one of these days, if he don't drink himself to death before. Good chap, Nasty when he's drunk."

Chaplin belched loudly.

"I'll go and put my head under the shower. I oughtn't to have had that last cocktail. It's always the last one that does you in."

He looked uncertainly at the staircase as he made up his mind to go to the cubby hole in which was the shower, and then with unnatural seriousness got up.

"Pay you to cultivate Lawson," he said. "A well read chap. You'd be surprised when he's sober. Clever too. Worth talking to."

Chaplin had told me the whole story in these few speeches.

When I came in towards evening from a ride along the seashore Lawson was again in the hotel. He was heavily sunk in one of the cane chairs in the lounge and he looked at me with glassy eyes. It was plain that he had been drinking all the afternoon. He was torpid, and the look on his face was sullen and vindictive. His glance rested on me for a moment, but I could see that he did not recognize me. Two or three other men were sitting there, shaking dice, and they took no notice of him. His condition was evidently too usual to attract attention. I sat down and began to play.

"You're a damned sociable lot," said Lawson suddenly.

He got out of his chair and waddled with bent knees towards the door. I do not know whether the spectacle was more ridiculous than revolting. When he had gone one of the men sniggered.

"Lawson's fairly soused to-day," he said.

"If I couldn't carry my liquor better than that," said another, "I'd climb on the waggon and stay there."

Who would have thought that this wretched object was in his way a romantic figure or that his life had in it those elements of pity and terror which the theorist tells us are necessary to achieve the effect of tragedy?

I did not see him again for two or three days.

I was sitting one evening on the first floor of the hotel on a verandah that overlooked the street when Lawson came up and sank into a chair beside me. He was quite sober. He made a casual remark and then, when I had replied somewhat indifferently, added with a laugh which had in it an apologetic tone:

"I was devilish soused the other day."

I did not answer. There was really nothing to say. I pulled away at my pipe in the vain hope of keeping the mosquitoes away, and looked at the natives going home from their work. They walked with long steps, slowly, with care and dignity, and the soft patter of their naked feet was strange to hear. Their dark hair, curling or straight, was often white with lime, and then they had a look of extraordinary distinction. They were tall and finely built. Then a gang of Solomon Islanders, indentured labourers, passed by, singing; they were shorter and slighter than the Samoans, coal black, with great heads of fuzzy hair dyed red. Now and then a white man drove past in his buggy or rode into the hotel yard. In the lagoon two or three schooners reflected their grace in the tranquil water.

"I don't know what there is to do in a place like this except to get soused," said Lawson at last.

"Don't you like Samoa?" I asked casually, for something to say.

"It's pretty, isn't it?"

The word he chose seemed so inadequate to describe the unimaginable beauty of the island, that I smiled, and smiling I turned to look at him. I was startled by the expression in those fine sombre eyes of his, an expression of intolerable anguish; they betrayed a tragic depth of emotion of which I should never have thought him capable. But the expression passed away and he smiled. His smile was simple and a little native. It changed his face so that I wavered in my first feeling of aversion from him.

"I was all over the place when I first came out," he said.

He was silent for a moment.

"I went away for good about three years ago, but I came back." He hesitated. "My wife wanted to come back. She was born here, you know."

"Oh, yes."

He was silent again, and then hazarded a remark about Robert Louis Stevenson. He asked me if I had been up to Vailima. For some reason he was making an effort to be agreeable to me. He began to talk of Stevenson's books, and presently the conversation drifted to London.

"I suppose Covent Garden's still going strong," he said. "I think I miss the opera as much as anything here. Have you seen *Tristan and Isolde?*"

He asked me the question as though the answer were really important to him, and when I said, a little casually, I daresay, that I had, he seemed pleased. He began to speak of Wagner, not as a musician, but as the plain man who received from him an emotional satisfaction that he could not analyze.

"I suppose Bayreuth was the place to go really," he said. "I never had the money, worse luck. But of couse one might do worse than Covent Garden, all the lights and the women dressed up to the nines, and the music. The first act of the *Walkure's* all right, isn't it? And the end of *Tristan*. Golly!"

His eyes were flashing now and his face was lit up so that he hardly seemed the same man. There was a flush on his sallow, thin cheeks, and I forgot that his voice was harsh and unpleasant. There was even a certain charm about him.

"By George, I'd like to be in London to-night. Do you know the Pall Mall restaurant? I used to go there a lot. Piccadilly Circus with the shops all lit up, and the crowd. I think it's stunning to stand there and watch the buses and taxis streaming along as though they'd never stop. And I like the Strand too. What are those lines about God and Charing Cross?"

I was taken aback.

"Thompson's, d'you mean?" I asked.

I quoted them.

" *And when so sad, thou canst not sadder,*
   Cry, and upon thy so sore loss
   Shall shine the traffic of Jacob's ladder
   Pitched between Heaven and Charing Cross."

He gave a faint sigh.

"I've read *The Hound of Heaven*. It's a bit of all right."

"It's generally thought so," I murmured.

"You don't meet anybody here who's read anything. They think it's swank."

There was a wistful look on his face, and I thought I divined the feeling that made him come to me. I was a link with the world he regretted and a life that he would know no more. Because not so very long before I had been in the London which he loved, he looked upon me with awe and envy. He had not spoken for five minutes perhaps when he broke out with words that startled me by their intensity.

"I'm fed up," he said. "I'm fed up."

"Then why don't you clear out?" I asked.

His face grew sullen.

"My lungs are a bit dicky. I couldn't stand an English winter now."

At that moment another man joined us on the verandah and Lawson sank into a moody silence.

"It's about time for a drain," said the newcomer. "Who'll have a drop of Scotch with me? Lawson?"

Lawson seemed to arise from a distant world. He got up.

"Let's go down to the bar," he said.

When he left me I remained with a more kindly feeling towards him than I should have expected. He puzzled and interested me. And a few days later I met his wife. I knew they had been married for five or six years, and I was surprised to see that she was still extremely young. When he married her she could not have been more than sixteen. She was adorably pretty. She was no darker than a Spaniard, small and very beautifully made, with tiny hands and feet, and a slight, lithe figure. Her features were lovely; but I think what struck me most was the delicacy of her appearance; the half-caste as a rule have a certain coarseness, they seem a little roughly formed, but she had an exquisite daintiness which took your breath away. There was something extremely civilized about her, so that it surprised you to see her in those surroundings, and you thought of those famous beauties who had set all the world talking at the Court of the Emperor Napoleon III. Though she wore but a muslin frock and a straw hat she wore them with an elegance that suggested the woman of fashion. She must have been ravishing when Lawson first saw her.

He had but lately come out from England to manage the local branch of an English bank, and, reaching Samoa at the beginning of the dry season, he had taken a room at the hotel. He quickly made the acquaintance of all and sundry. The life of the island is pleasant and easy. He enjoyed the long idle talks in the lounge of the hotel and the gay evenings at the English Club when a group of fellows would play pool. He liked Apia straggling along the edge of the lagoon, with its stores and bungalows, and its native village. Then there were week-ends when he would ride over to the house of one planter or another and spend a couple of nights on the hills. He had never before known freedom or leisure. And he was intoxicated by the sunshine. When he rode through the bush his head reeled a little at the beauty that surrounded him. The country was indescribably fertile. In parts the forest was still virgin, a tangle of strange trees, luxuriant undergrowth, and vine; it gave an impression that was mysterious and troubling.

But the spot that entranced him was a pool a mile or two away from Apia to which in the evenings he often went to bathe. There was a little river that bubbled over the rocks in a swift stream, and then, after forming the deep pool, ran on, shallow and crystalline, past a ford made by great stones where the natives came sometimes to bathe or to wash their clothes. The coconut trees, with their frivolous elegance, grew thickly on the banks, all clad with trailing plants, and they were reflected in the green water. It was just such a scene as you might see in Devonshire among the hills, and yet with a difference, for it had a tropical richness, a passion, a scented languor which seemed to melt the heart. The water was fresh, but not cold; and it was delicious after the heat of the day. To bathe there refreshed not only the body but the soul.

At the hour when Lawson went, there was not a soul and he lingered for a long time, now floating idly in the water, now drying himself in the evening sun, enjoying the solitude and the friendly silence. He did not regret London then, nor the life that he had abandoned, for life as it was seemed complete and exquisite.

It was here that he first saw Ethel.

Occupied till late by letters which had to be finished for the monthly sailing of the boat next day, he rode down one evening to the pool when the light was almost failing. He tied up his horse and sauntered to the bank. A girl was sitting there. She glanced round as he came and noiselessly slid into the water. She vanished like a naiad startled by the approach of a mortal. He was surprised and amused. He wondered where she had hidden herself. He swam downstream and presently saw her sitting on a rock. She looked at him with uncurious eyes. He called out a greeting in Samoan.

"*Talofa.*"

She answered him, suddenly smiling, and then let herself into the water again. She swam easily and her hair spread out behind her. He watched her cross the pool and climb out on the bank. Like all the natives she bathed in a Mother Hubbard, and the water had made it cling to her slight body. She wrung out her hair, and as she stood there, unconcerned, she looked more than ever like a wild creature of the water or the woods. He saw now that she was half-caste. He swam towards her and, getting out, addressed her in English.

"You're having a late swim."

She shook back her hair and then let it spread over her shoulders in luxuriant curls.

"I like it when I'm alone," she said.

"So do I."

She laughed with the childlike frankness of the native. She slipped a dry Mother Hubbard over her head and, letting down the wet one, stepped out of it. She wrung it out and was ready to go. She paused a moment irresolutely and then sauntered off. The night fell suddenly.

Lawson went back to the hotel and, describing her to the men who were in the lounge shaking dice for drinks, soon discovered who she was. Her father was a Norwegian called Brevald who was often to be seen in the bar of the Hotel Metropole drinking rum and water. He was a little old man, knotted and gnarled like an ancient tree, who had come out to the islands forty years before as mate of a sailing vessel. He had been a blacksmith, a trader, a planter, and at one time fairly well-to-do; but, ruined by the great hurricane of the nineties, he had now nothing to live on but a small plantation of coconut trees. He had had four native wives and, as he told you with a cracked chuckle, more children than he could count. But some had died and some had gone out into the world, so that now the only one left at home was Ethel.

"She's a peach," said Nelson, the supercargo of the *Moana*.

"I've given her the glad eye once or twice, but I guess there's nothing doing."

"Old Brevald's not that sort of a fool, sonny," put in another, a man called Miller. "He wants a son-in-law who's prepared to keep him in comfort for the rest of his life."

It was distasteful to Lawson that they should speak of the girl in that fashion. He made a remark about the departing mail and so distracted their attention. But next evening he went again to the pool. Ethel was there; and the mystery of the sunset, the deep silence of the water, the lithe grace of the coconut trees, added to her beauty, giving it a profundity, a magic, which stirred the heart to unknown emotions. For some reason that time he had the whim not to speak to her. She took no notice of him. She did not even glance in his direction. She swam about the green pool. She dived, she rested on the bank, as though she were quite alone: he had a queer feeling that he was invisible. Scraps of poetry, half forgotten, floated across his memory, and vague recollections of the Greece he had negligently studied in his school days. When she had changed her wet clothes for dry ones and sauntered away he found a scarlet hibiscus where she had been. It was a flower that she had worn in her hair when she came to bathe and, having taken it out on getting into the water, had forgotten or not cared to put in again. He took it in his hands and looked at it with a singular emotion. He had an instinct to keep it, but his sentimentality irritated him, and he flung it away. It gave him quite a little pang to see it float down the stream.

He wondered what strangeness it was in her nature that urged her to go down to this hidden pool when there was no likelihood that anyone should be there. The natives of the islands are devoted to the water. They bathe, somewhere or other, every day, once always, and often twice; but they bathe in bands, laughing and joyous, a whole family together; and you often saw a group of girls, dappled by the sun shining through the trees, with the half-castes among them, splashing about the shallows of the stream. It looked as though there were in this pool some secret which attracted Ethel against her will.

Now the night had fallen, mysterious and silent, and he let himself down in the water softly, in order to make no sound, and swam lazily in the warm darkness. The water seemed fragrant still from her slender body. He rode back to the town under the starry sky. He felt at peace with the world.

Now he went every evening to the pool and every evening he saw Ethel. Presently he overcame her timidity. She became playful and friendly. They sat together on the rocks above the pool, where the water ran fast, and they lay side by side on the ledge that overlooked it, watching the gathering dusk envelop it with mystery. It was inevitable that their meetings should become known—in the South Seas everyone seems to know everyone's business—and he was subjected to much rude chaff by the men at the hotel. He smiled and let them talk. It was not even worth while to deny their coarse suggestions. His feelings were absolutely pure. He loved Ethel as a poet might love the moon. He thought of her not as a woman but as something not of this earth. She was the spirit of the pool.

One day at the hotel, passing through the bar, he saw that old Brevald, as ever in his shabby blue overalls, was standing there. Because he was Ethel's father he had a desire to speak to him, so he went in, nodded and, ordering his own drink, casually turned and invited the old man to have one with him. They chatted for a few minutes of local affairs, and Lawson was uneasily conscious that the Norwegian was scrutinizing him with sly blue eyes. His manner was not agreeable. It was sycophantic, and yet behind the cringing air of an old man who had been worsted in his struggle with fate was a shadow of old truculence. Lawson remembered that he had once been captain of a schooner engaged in the slave trade, a blackbirder they call it in the Pacific, and he had a large hernia in the chest which was the result of a wound received in a scrap with Solomon Islanders. The bell rang for luncheon.

"Well, I must be off," said Lawson.

"Why don't you come along to my place one time?" said Brevald, in his wheezy voice. "It's not very grand, but you'll be welcome. You know Ethel."

"I'll come with pleasure."

"Sunday afternoon's the best time."

Brevald's bungalow, shabby and bedraggled, stood among the co-conut trees of the plantation, a little away from the main road that ran up to Vailima. Immediately around it grew huge plantains. With their tattered leaves they had the tragic beauty of a lovely woman in rags. Everything was slovenly and neglected. Little black pigs, thin and high-backed, rooted about, and chickens clucked noisily as they picked at the refuse scattered here and there. Three or four natives were lounging about the verandah. When Lawson asked for Brevald the old man's cracked voice called out to him, and he found him in the sitting-room smoking an old briar pipe.

"Sit down and make yerself at home," he said. "Ethel's just titivating."

She came in. She wore a blouse and skirt and her hair was done in the European fashion. Although she had not the wild, timid grace of the girl who came down every evening to the pool, she seemed now more usual and consequently more approachable. She shook hands with Lawson. It was the first time he had touched her hand.

"I hope you'll have a cup of tea with us," she said.

He knew she had been at a mission school, and he was amused, and at the same time touched, by the company manners she was putting on for his benefit. Tea was already set out on the table and in a minute old Brevald's fourth wife brought in the tea-pot. She was a handsome native, no longer very young, and she spoke but a few words of English. She smiled and smiled. Tea was rather a solemn meal, with a great deal of bread and butter and a variety of very sweet cakes, and the conversation was formal. Then a wrinkled old woman came in softly.

"That's Ethel's granny," said old Brevald, noisily spitting on the floor.

She sat on the edge of a chair, uncomfortably, so that you saw it was unusual for her and she would have been more at ease on the ground, and remained silently staring at Lawson with fixed, shining eyes. In the kitchen behind the bungalow someone began to play the concertina and two or three voices were raised in a hymn. But they sang for the pleasure of the sounds rather than from piety.

When Lawson walked back to the hotel he was strangely happy. He was touched by the higgledy-piggledy in which those people lived; and in the smiling good-nature of Mrs. Brevald, in the little Norwegian's fantastic career, and in the shining mysterious eyes of the old grandmother, he found something unusual and fascinating. It was a more natural life than any he had known, it was nearer to the friendly, fertile earth; civilization repelled him at the moment, and by mere contact with these creatures of a more primitive nature he felt a greater freedom.

He saw himself rid of the hotel which already was beginning to irk him, settled in a little bungalow of his own, trim and white, in front of the sea so that he had before his eyes always the multicoloured variety of the lagoon. He loved the beautiful island. London and England meant nothing to him any more, he was content to spend the rest of his days in that forgotten spot, rich in the best of the world's goods, love and happiness. He made up his mind that whatever the obstacles nothing should prevent him from marrying Ethel.

But there were no obstacles. He was always welcome at the Brevalds' house. The old man was ingratiating and Mrs. Brevald smiled without ceasing. He had brief glimpses of natives who seemed somehow to belong to the establishment, and once he found a tall youth in a *lava-lava*, his body tattooed, his hair white with lime, sitting with Brevald, and was told he was Mrs. Brevald's brother's son; but for the most part they kept out of his way. Ethel was delightful with him. The light in her eyes when she saw him filled him with ecstasy. She was charming and naïve. He listened enraptured when she told him of the mission school at which she was educated, and of the sisters. He went with her to the cinema which was given once a fortnight and danced with her at the dance which followed it. They came from all parts of the island for this, since gaieties are few in Upolu; and you saw there all the society of the place, the white ladies keeping a good deal to themselves, the half-castes very elegant in American clothes, the natives, strings of dark girls in white Mother Hubbards and young men in unaccustomed ducks and white shoes. It was all very smart and gay. Ethel was pleased to show her friends the white admirer who did not leave her side. The rumour was soon spread that he meant to marry her and her friends looked at her with envy. It was a great thing for a half-caste to get a white man to marry her, even the less regular relation was better than nothing, but one could never tell what it would lead to; and Lawson's position as manager of the bank made him one of the catches of the island. If he had not been so absorbed in Ethel he would have noticed that many eyes were fixed on him curiously, and he would have seen the glances of the white ladies and noticed how they put their heads together and gossiped.

Afterwards, when the men who lived at the hotel were having a whisky before turning in, Nelson burst out with:

"Say, they say Lawson's going to marry that girl."

"He's a damned fool then," said Miller.

Miller was a German-American who had changed his name from Mueller, a big man, fat and bald-headed, with a round, clean-shaven face. He wore large gold-rimmed spectacles, which gave him a benign look, and his ducks were always clean and white. He was a heavy drinker, invariably ready to stay up all night with the "boys," but he never got drunk; he was jolly and affable, but very shrewd. Nothing interfered with his business; he represented a firm in San Francisco, jobbers of the goods sold in the islands, calico, machinery and what not; and his good-fellowship was part of his stock-in-trade.

"He don't know what he's up against," said Nelson. "Someone ought to put him wise."

"If you'll take my advice you won't interfere in what don't concern you," said Miller. "When a man's made up his mind to make a fool of himself, there's nothing like letting him."

"I'm all for having a good time with the girls out here, but when it comes to marrying them—this child ain't taking any, I'll tell the world."

Chaplin was there, and now he had his say.

"I've seen a lot of fellows do it, and it's no good."

"You ought to have a talk with him, Chaplin," said Nelson.

"You know him better than anyone else does."

"My advice to Chaplin is to leave it alone," said Miller.

Even in those days Lawson was not popular and really no one took enough interest in him to bother. Mrs. Chaplin talked it over with two or three of the white ladies, but they contented themselves with saying that it was a pity; and when he told her definitely that he was going to be married it seemed too late to do anything.

For a year Lawson was happy. He took a bungalow at the point of the bay round which Apia is built, on the borders of a native village. It nestled charmingly among the coconut trees and faced the passionate blue of the Pacific. Ethel was lovely as she went about the little house, lithe and graceful like some young animal of the woods, and she was gay. They laughed a great deal. They talked nonsense. Sometimes one or two of the men at the hotel would come over and spend the evening, and often on a Sunday they would go for a day to some planter who had married a native; now and then one or other of the half-caste traders who had a store in Apia would give a party and they went to it. The half-castes treated Lawson quite differently now. His marriage had made him one of themselves and they called him Bertie. They put their arms through his and smacked him on the back. He liked to see Ethel at these gatherings. Her eyes shone and she laughed. It did him good to see her radiant happiness. Sometimes Ethel's relations would come to the bungalow, old Brevald of course, and her mother, but cousins too, vague native women in Mother Hubbards and men and boys in *lava-lavas*, with their hair dyed red and their bodies elaborately tattooed. He would find them sitting there when he got back from the bank. He laughed indulgently.

"Don't let them eat us out of hearth and home," he said.

"They're my own family. I can't help doing something for them when they ask me."

He knew that when a white man marries a native or a half-caste he must expect her relations to look upon him as a gold mine. He took Ethel's face in his hands and kissed her red lips. Perhaps he could not expect her to understand that the salary which had amply sufficed for a bachelor must be managed with some care when it had to support a wife and a house. Then Ethel was delivered of a son.

It was when Lawson first held the child in his arms that a sudden pang shot through his heart. He had not expected it to be so dark. After all it had but a fourth part of native blood, and there was no reason really why it should not look just like an English baby; but, huddled together in his arms, sallow, its head covered already with black hair, with huge black eyes, it might have been a native child. Since his marriage he had been ignored by the white ladies of the colony. When he came across men in whose houses he had been accustomed to dine as a bachelor, they were a little self-conscious with him; and they sought to cover their embarrassment by an exaggerated cordiality.

"Mrs. Lawson well?" they would say. "You're a lucky fellow. Damned pretty girl."

But if they were with their wives and met him and Ethel they would feel it awkward when their wives gave Ethel a patronizing nod. Lawson had laughed.

"They're as dull as ditchwater, the whole gang of them," he said. "It's not going to disturb my night's rest if they don't ask me to their dirty parties."

But now it irked him a little.

The little dark baby screwed up its face. That was his son. He thought of the half-caste children in Apia. They had an unhealthy look, sallow and pale, and they were odiously precocious. He had seen them on the boat going to school in New Zealand, and a school had to be chosen which took children with native blood in them; they were huddled together, brazen and yet timid, with traits which set them apart strangely from white people. They spoke the native language among themselves. And when they grew up the men accepted smaller salaries because of their native blood; girls might marry a white man, but boys had no chance; they must marry a half-caste like themselves or a native. Lawson made up his mind passionately that he would take his son away from the humiliation of such a life. At whatever cost he must get back to Europe. And when he went in to see Ethel, frail and lovely in her bed, surrounded by native women, his determination was strengthened. If he took her away among his own people she would belong more completely to him. He loved her so passionately, he wanted her to be one soul and one body with him; and he was conscious that here, with those deep roots attaching her to the native life, she would always keep something from him.

He went to work quietly, urged by an obscure instinct of secrecy, and wrote to a cousin who was partner in a shipping firm in Aberdeen, saying that his health (on account of which like so many more he had come out to the islands) was so much better, there seemed no reason why he should not return to Europe. He asked him to use what influence he could to get him a job, no matter how poorly paid, on Deeside, where the climate was particularly suitable to such as suffered from diseases of the lungs. It takes five or six weeks for letters to get from Aberdeen to Samoa, and several had to be exchanged. He had plenty of time to prepare Ethel. She was as delighted as a child. He was amused to see how she boasted to her friends that she was going to England; it was a step up for her; she would be quite English there; and she was excited at the interest the approaching departure gave her. When at length a cable came offering him a post in a bank in Kincardineshire she was beside herself with joy.

When, their long journey over, they were settled in the little Scots town with its granite houses Lawson realized how much it meant to him to live once more among his own people. He looked back on the three years he had spent in Apia as exile, and returned to the life that seemed the only normal one with a sigh of relief. It was good to play golf once more, and to fish—to fish properly, that was poor fun in the Pacific when you just threw in your line and pulled out one big sluggish fish after another from the crowded sea—and it was good to see a paper every day with that day's news, and to meet men and women of your own sort, people you could talk to; and it was good to eat meat that was not frozen and to drink milk that was not canned. They were thrown upon their own resources much more than in the Pacific, and he was glad to have Ethel exclusively to himself. After two years of marriage he loved her more devotedly than ever, he could hardly bear her out of his sight, and the need in him grew urgent for a more intimate communion between them. But it was strange that after the first excitement of arrival she seemed to take less interest in the new life than he had expected. She did not accustom herself to her surroundings. She was a little lethargic. As the fine autumn darkened into winter she complained of the cold. She lay half the morning in bed and the rest of the day on a sofa, reading novels sometimes, but more often doing nothing. She looked pinched.

"Never mind, darling," he said. "You'll get used to it very soon. And wait till the summer comes. It can be almost as hot as in Apia."

He felt better and stronger than he had done for years.

The carelessness with which she managed her house had not mattered in Samoa, but here it was out of place. When anyone came he did not want the place to look untidy; and, laughing, chaffing Ethel a little, he set about putting things in order. Ethel watched him indolently. She spent long hours playing with her son. She talked to him in the baby language of her own country. To distract her, Lawson bestirred himself to make friends among the neighbours, and now and then they went to little parties where the ladies sang drawing-room ballads and the men beamed in silent good nature. Ethel was shy. She seemed to sit apart. Sometimes Lawson, seized with a sudden anxiety, would ask her if she was happy.

"Yes, I'm quite happy," she answered.

But her eyes were veiled by some thought he could not guess. She seemed to withdraw into herself so that he was conscious that he knew no more of her than when he had first seen her bathing in the pool. He had an uneasy feeling that she was concealing something from him, and because he adored her it tortured him.

"You don't regret Apia, do you?" he asked her once.

"Oh, no—I think it's very nice here."

An obscure misgiving drove him to make disparaging remarks about the island and the people there. She smiled and did not answer. Very rarely she received a bundle of letters from Samoa and then she went about for a day or two with a set, pale face.

"Nothing would induce me ever to go back there," he said once. "It's no place for a white man."

But he grew conscious that sometimes, when he was away, Ethel cried. In Apia she had been talkative, chatting volubly about all the little details of their common life, the gossip of the place; but now she gradually became silent, and, though he increased his efforts to amuse her, she remained listless. It seemed to him that her recollections of the old life were drawing her away from him, and he was madly jealous of the island and of the sea, of Brevald, and all the dark-skinned people whom he remembered now with horror. When she spoke of Samoa he was bitter and satirical. One evening late in the spring when the birch trees were bursting into leaf, coming home from a round of golf, he found her not as usual lying on the sofa, but at the window, standing. She had evidently been waiting for his return. She addressed him the moment he came into the room. To his amazement she spoke in Samoan.

"I can't stand it. I can't live here any more. I hate it. I hate it."

"For God's sake speak in a civilized language," he said irritably.

She went up to him and clasped her arms around his body awkwardly, with a gesture that had in it something barbaric.

"Let's go away from here. Let's go back to Samoa. If you make me stay here I shall die. I want to go home."

Her passion broke suddenly and she burst into tears. His anger vanished and he drew her down on his knees. He explained to her that it was impossible for him to throw up his job, which after all meant his bread and butter. His place in Apia was long since filled. He had nothing to go back to there. He tried to put it to her reasonably, the inconveniences of life there, the humiliation to which they must be exposed, and the bitterness it must cause their son.

"Scotland's wonderful for education and that sort of thing. Schools are good and cheap, and he can go to the University at Aberdeen. I'll make a real Scot of him."

They had called him Andrew. Lawson wanted him to become a doctor. He would marry a white woman.

"I'm not ashamed of being half native," Ethel said sullenly.

"Of course not, darling. There's nothing to be ashamed of."

With her soft cheek against his he felt incredibly weak.

"You don't know how much I love you," he said. "I'd give anything in the world to be able to tell you what I've got in my heart."

He sought her lips.

The summer came. The highland valley was green and fragrant, and the hills were gay with the heather. One sunny day followed another in that sheltered spot, and the shade of the birch trees was grateful after the glare of the high road. Ethel spoke no more of Samoa and Lawson grew less nervous. He thought that she was resigned to her surroundings, and he felt that his love for her was so passionate that it could leave no room in her heart for any longing. One day the local doctor stopped him in the street.

"I say, Lawson, your missus ought to be careful how she bathes in our highland streams. It's not like the Pacific, you know."

Lawson was surprised, and had not the presence of mind to conceal the fact.

"I didn't know she was bathing."

The doctor laughed.

"A good many people have seen her. It makes them talk a bit, you know, because it seems a rum place to choose, the pool up above the bridge, and bathing isn't allowed there, but there's no harm in that. I don't know how she can stand the water."

Lawson knew the pool the doctor spoke of, and suddenly it occurred to him that in a way it was just like that pool at Upolu where Ethel had been in the habit of bathing every evening. A clear highland stream ran down a sinuous course, rocky, splashing gaily, and then formed a deep, smooth pool, with a little sandy beach. Trees overshadowed it thickly, not coconut trees, but beeches, and the sun played fitfully through the leaves on the sparkling water. It gave him a shock. With his imagination he saw Ethel go there every day and undress on the bank and slip into the water, cold, colder than that of the pool she loved at home, and for a moment regain the feeling of the past. He saw her once more as the strange, wild spirit of the stream, and it seemed to him fantastically that the running water called her. That afternoon he went along to the river. He made his way cautiously among the trees and the grassy path deadened the sound of his steps. Presently he came to a spot from which he could see the pool. Ethel was sitting on the bank, looking down at the water. She sat quite still. It seemed as though the water drew her irresistibly. He wondered what strange thoughts wandered through her head. At last she got up, and for a minute or two she was hidden from his gaze; then he saw her again, wearing a Mother Hubbard, and with her little bare feet she stepped delicately over the mossy bank. She came to the water's edge, and softly, without a splash, let herself down. She swam about quietly, and there was something not quite of a human being in the way she swam. He did not know why it affected him so queerly. He waited till she clambered out. She stood for a moment with the wet folds of her dress clinging to her body, so that its shape was outlined, and then, passing her hands slowly over her breasts, gave a little sigh of delight. Then she disappeared. Lawson turned away and walked back to the village. He had a bitter pain in his heart, for he knew that she was still a stranger to him and his hungry love was destined ever to remain unsatisfied.

He did not make any mention of what he had seen. He ignored the incident completely, but he looked at her curiously, trying to divine what was in her mind. He redoubled the tenderness with which he used her. He sought to make her forget the deep longing of her soul by the passion of his love.

Then one day, when he came home, he was astonished to find her not in the house.

"Where's Mrs. Lawson?" he asked the maid.

"She went into Aberdeen, Sir, with the baby," the maid answered, a little surprised at the question. "She said she would not be back till the last train."

"Oh, all right."

He was vexed that Ethel had said nothing to him about the excursion, but he was not disturbed, since of late she had been in now and again to Aberdeen, and he was glad that she should look at the shops and perhaps visit a cinema. He went to meet the last train, but when she did not come he grew suddenly frightened. He went up to the bedroom and saw at once that her toilet things were no longer in their place. He opened the wardrobe and the drawers. They were half empty. She had bolted.

He was seized with a passion of anger. It was too late that night to telephone to Aberdeen and make enquiries, but he knew already all that his enquiries might have taught him. With fiendish cunning she had chosen a time when they were making up their periodical accounts at the bank and there was no chance that he could follow her. He was imprisoned by his work. He took up a paper and saw that there was a boat sailing for Australia next morning. She must be now well on the way to London. He could not prevent the sobs that were wrung painfully from him.

"I've done everything in the world for her," he cried, "and she had the heart to treat me like this. How cruel, how monstrously cruel!"

After two days of misery he received a letter from her. It was written in her school-girl hand. She had always written with difficulty:

Dear Bertie:
I couldn't stand it any more. I'm going back home. Good-bye. Ethel.

She did not say a single word of regret. She did not even ask him to come too. Lawson was prostrated. He found out where the ship made its first stop and, though he knew very well she would not come, sent a cable beseeching her to return. He waited with pitiful anxiety. He wanted her to send him just one word of love; she did not even answer. He passed through one violent phase after another. At one moment he told himself that he was well rid of her, and at the next that he would force her to return by withholding money. He was lonely and wretched. He wanted his boy and he wanted her. He knew that, whatever he pretended to himself, there was only one thing to do and that was to follow her. He could never live without her now. All his plans for the future were like a house of cards and he scattered them with angry impatience. He did not care whether he threw away his chances for the future, for nothing in the world mattered but that he should get Ethel back again. As soon as he could he went into Aberdeen and told the manager of his bank that he meant to leave at once. The manager remonstrated. The short notice was inconvenient. Lawson would not listen to reason. He was determined to be free before the next boat sailed; and it was not until he was on board of her, having sold everything he possessed, that in some measure he regained his calm. Till then to those who had come in contact with him he seemed hardly sane. His last action in England was to cable to Ethel at Apia that he was joining her.

He sent another cable from Sydney, and when at last with the dawn his boat crossed the bar at Apia and he saw once more the white houses straggling along the bay he felt an immense relief. The doctor came on board and the agent. They were both old acquaintances and he felt kindly towards their familiar faces. He had a drink or two with them for old times' sake, and also because he was desperately nervous. He was not sure if Ethel would be glad to see him. When he got into the launch and approached the wharf he scanned anxiously the little crowd that waited. She was not there and his heart sank, but then he saw Brevald, in his old blue clothes, and his heart warmed towards him.

"Where's Ethel?" he said, as he jumped on shore.

"She's down at the bungalow. She's living with us."

Lawson was dismayed, but he put on a jovial air.

"Well, have you got room for me? I daresay it'll take a week or two to fix ourselves up."

"Oh, yes, I guess we can make room for you."

After passing through the custom-house they went to the hotel and there Lawson was greeted by several of his old friends. There were a good many rounds of drinks before it seemed possible to get away and when they did go out at last to Brevald's house they were both rather gay. He clasped Ethel in his arms. He had forgotten all his bitter thoughts in the joy of beholding her once more. His mother-in-law was pleased to see him, and so was the old, wrinkled beldame, her mother; natives and half-castes came in, and they all sat round, beaming on him. Brevald had a bottle of whisky and everyone who came was given a nip. Lawson sat with his little dark-skinned boy on his knees, they had taken his English clothes off him and he was stark, with Ethel by his side in a Mother Hubbard. He felt like a returning prodigal. In the afternoon he went down to the hotel again and when he got back he was more than gay, he was drunk. Ethel and her mother knew that white men got drunk now and then, it was what you expected of them, and they laughed good-naturedly as they helped him to bed.

But in a day or two he set about looking for a job. He knew that he could not hope for such a position as that which he had thrown away to go to England; but with his training he could not fail to be useful to one of the trading firms, and perhaps in the end he would not lose by the change.

"After all, you can't make money in a bank," he said. "Trade's the thing."

He had hopes that he would soon make himself so indispensable that he would get someone to take him into partnership, and there was no reason why in a few years he should not be a rich man.

"As soon as I'm fixed up we'll find ourselves a shack," he told Ethel. "We can't go on living here."

Brevald's bungalow was so small that they were all piled on one another, and there was no chance of ever being alone. There was neither peace nor privacy.

"Well, there's no hurry. We shall be all right here till we find just what we want."

It took him a week to get settled and then he entered the firm of a man called Bain. But when he talked to Ethel about moving she said she wanted to stay where she was till her baby was born, for she was expecting another child. Lawson tried to argue with her.

"If you don't like it," she said, "go and live at the hotel."

He grew suddenly pale.

"Ethel, how can you suggest that!"

She shrugged her shoulders.

"What's the good of having a house of our own when we can live here?"

He yielded.

When Lawson, after his work, went back to the bungalow he found it crowded with natives. They lay about smoking, sleeping, drinking kava; and they talked incessantly. The place was grubby and untidy. His child crawled about, playing with native children, and it heard nothing spoken but Samoan. He fell into the habit of dropping into the hotel on his way home to have a few cocktails, for he could only face the evening and the crowd of friendly natives when he was fortified with liquor. And all the time, though he loved her more passionately than ever, he felt that Ethel was slipping away from him. When the baby was born he suggested that they should get into a house of their own, but Ethel refused. Her stay in Scotland seemed to have thrown her back on her own people, now that she was once more among them, with a passionate zest, and she turned to her native ways with abandon. Lawson began to drink more. Every Saturday night he went to the English Club and got blind drunk.

He had the peculiarity that as he grew drunk he grew quarrelsome and once he had a violent dispute with Bain, his employer. Bain dismissed him, and he had to look out for another job. He was idle for two or three weeks and during these, sooner than sit in the bungalow, he lounged about in the hotel or at the English Club, and drank. It was more out of pity than anything else that Miller, the German-American, took him into his office; but he was a business man, and though Lawson's financial skill made him valuable, the circumstances were such that he could hardly refuse a smaller salary than he had had before, and Miller did not hesitate to offer it to him. Ethel and Brevald blamed him for taking it, since Pedersen, the half-caste, offered him more. But he resented bitterly the thought of being under the orders of a half-caste. When Ethel nagged him he burst out furiously:

"I'll see myself dead before I work for a nigger."

"You may have to," she said.

And in six months he found himself forced to this final humiliation. The passion for liquor had been gaining on him, he was often heavy with drink, and he did his work badly. Miller warned him once or twice and Lawson was not the man to accept remonstrance easily. One day in the midst of an altercation he put on his hat and walked out. But by now his reputation was well known and he could find no one to engage him. For a while he idled, and then he had an attack of *delirium tremens*. When he recovered, shameful and weak, he could no longer resist the constant pressure, and he went to Pedersen and asked him for a job. Pedersen was glad to have a white man in his store and Lawson's skill at figures made him useful.

From that time his degeneration was rapid. The white people gave him the cold shoulder. They were only prevented from cutting him completely by disdainful pity and by a certain dread of his angry violence when he was drunk. He became extremely susceptible and was always on the lookout for affront.

He lived entirely among the natives and half-castes, but he had no longer the prestige of the white man. They felt his loathing for them and they resented his attitude of superiority. He was one of themselves now and they did not see why he should put on airs. Brevald, who had been ingratiating and obsequious, now treated him with contempt. Ethel had made a bad bargain. There were disgraceful scenes and once or twice the two men came to blows. When there was a quarrel Ethel took the part of her family. They found he was better drunk than sober, for when he was drunk he would lie on the bed or on the floor, sleeping heavily.

Then he became aware that something was being hidden from him.

When he got back to the bungalow for the wretched, half-native supper which was his evening meal, often Ethel was not in. If he asked where she was Brevald told him she had gone to spend the evening with one or other of her friends. Once he followed her to the house Brevald had mentioned and found she was not there. On her return he asked where she had been and she told him her father had made a mistake; she had been to so-and-so's. But he knew that she was lying. She was in her best clothes; her eyes were shining, and she looked lovely.

"Don't try any monkey tricks on me, my girl," he said, "or I'll break every bone in your body."

"You drunken beast," she said, scornfully.

He fancied that Mrs. Brevald and the old grandmother looked at him maliciously and he ascribed Brevald's good-humour with him, so unusual those days, to his satisfaction at having something up his sleeve against his son-in-law. And then, his suspicions aroused, he imagined that the white men gave him curious glances. When he came into the lounge of the hotel the sudden silence which fell upon the company convinced him that he had been the subject of the conversation. Something was going on and everyone knew it but himself. He was seized with furious jealousy. He believed that Ethel was carrying on with one of the white men, and he looked at one after the other with scrutinizing eyes; but there was nothing to give him even a hint. He was helpless. Because he could find no one on whom definitely to fix his suspicions, he went about like a raving maniac, looking for someone on whom to vent his wrath. Chance caused him in the end to hit upon the man who of all others least deserved to suffer from his violence. One afternoon, when he was sitting in the hotel by himself, moodily, Chaplin came in and sat down beside him. Perhaps Chaplin was the only man on the island who had any sympathy for him. They ordered drinks and chatted a few minutes about the races that were shortly to be run. Then Chaplain said:

"I guess we shall all have to fork out money for new dresses."

Lawson sniggered. Since Mrs. Chaplin held the purse-strings, if she wanted a new frock for the occasion she would certainly not ask her husband for the money.

"How is your missus?" asked Chaplin, desiring to be friendly.

"What the hell's that got to do with you?" said Lawson, knitting his dark brows.

"I was only asking a civil question."

"Well, keep your civil questions to yourself."

Chaplin was not a patient man; his long residence in the tropics, the whisky bottle, and his domestic affairs had given him a temper hardly more under control than Lawson's.

"Look here, my boy, when you're in my hotel you behave like a gentleman or you'll find yourself in the street before you can say knife."

Lawson's lowering face grew dark and red.

"Let me just tell you once for all and you can pass it on to the others," he said, panting with rage. "If any of you fellows come messing round with my wife he'd better look out."

"Who do you think wants to mess around with your wife?"

"I'm not such a fool as you think. I can see a stone wall in front of me as well as most men, and I warn you straight, that's all. I'm not going to put up with any hanky-panky, not on your life."

"Look here, you'd better clear out of here, and come back when you're sober."

"I shall clear out when I choose and not a minute before," said Lawson.

It was an unfortunate boast, for Chaplin in the course of his experience as a hotel-keeper had acquired a peculiar skill in dealing with gentlemen whose room he preferred to their company, and the words were hardly out of Lawson's mouth before he found himself caught by the collar and arm and hustled not without force into the street. He stumbled down the steps into the blinding glare of the sun.

It was in consequence of this that he had his first violent scene with Ethel. Smarting with humiliation and unwilling to go back to the hotel, he went home that afternoon earlier than usual. He found Ethel dressing to go out. As a rule she lay about in a Mother Hubbard, barefoot, with a flower in her dark hair; but now, in white silk stockings and high-heeled shoes, she was doing up a pink muslin dress which was the newest she had.

"You're making yourself very smart," he said. "Where are you going?"

"I'm going to the Crossleys'."

"I'll come with you."

"Why?" she asked coolly.

"I don't want you to gad about by yourself all the time."

"You're not asked."

"I don't care a damn about that. You're not going without me."

"You'd better lie down till I'm ready."

She thought he was drunk and if he once settled himself on the bed would quickly drop off to sleep. He sat down on a chair and began to smoke a cigarette. She watched him with increasing irritation. When she was ready he got up. It happened by an unusual chance that there was no one in the bungalow. Brevald was working on the plantation and his wife had gone into Apia. Ethel faced him.

"I'm not going with you. You're drunk."

"That's a lie. You're not going without me."

She shrugged her shoulders and tried to pass him, but he caught her by the arm and held her.

"Let me go, you devil," she said, breaking into Samoan.

"Why do you want to go without me? Haven't I told you I'm not going to put up with any monkey tricks?"

She clenched her fist and hit him in the face. He lost all control of himself. All his love, all his hatred, welled up in him and he was beside himself.

"I'll teach you," he shouted. "I'll teach you."

He seized a riding-whip which happened to be under his hand, and struck her with it. She screamed, and the scream maddened him so that he went on striking her, again and again. Her shrieks rang through the bungalow and he cursed her as he hit. Then he flung her on the bed. She lay there sobbing with pain and terror. He threw the whip away from him and rushed out of the room. Ethel heard him go and she stopped crying. She looked round cautiously, then she raised herself. She was sore, but she had not been badly hurt, and she looked at her dress to see if it was damaged. The native women are not unused to blows. What he had done did not outrage her. When she looked at herself in the glass and arranged her hair, her eyes were shining. There was a strange look in them. Perhaps then she was nearer loving him than she had ever been before.

But Lawson, driven forth blindly, stumbled through the plantation and suddenly exhausted, weak as a child, flung himself on the ground at the foot of a tree. He was miserable and ashamed. He thought of Ethel, and in the yielding tenderness of his love all his bones seemed to grow soft within him. He thought of the past, and of his hopes, and he was aghast at what he had done. He wanted her more than ever. He wanted to take her in his arms. He must go to her at once. He got up. He was so weak that he staggered as he walked. He went into the house and she was sitting in their cramped bedroom in front of her looking-glass.

"Oh, Ethel, forgive me. I'm so awfully ashamed of myself. I didn't know what I was doing."

He fell on his knees before her and timidly stroked the skirt of her dress.

"I can't bear to think of what I did. It's awful. I think I was mad. There's no one in the world I love as I love you. I'd do anything to save you from pain and I've hurt you. I can never forgive myself, but for God's sake say you forgive me."

He heard her shrieks still. It was unendurable. She looked at him silently. He tried to take her hands and the tears streamed from his eyes. In his humiliation he hid his face in her lap and his frail body shook with sobs. An expression of utter contempt came over her face. She had the native woman's disdain of a man who abased himself before a woman. A weak creature! And for a moment she had been on the point of thinking there was something in him. He grovelled at her feet like a cur. She gave him a little scornful kick.

"Get out," she said. "I hate you."

He tried to hold her, but she pushed him aside. She stood up. She began to take off her dress. She kicked off her shoes and slid the stockings off her feet, then she slipped on her old Mother Hubbard.

"Where are you going?"

"What's that got to do with you? I'm going down to the pool."

"Let me come too," he said.

He asked as though he were a child.

"Can't you even leave me that?"

He hid his face in his hands, crying miserably, while she, her eyes hard and cold, stepped past him and went out.

From that time she entirely despised him; and though, herded together in the small bungalow, Lawson and Ethel with her two children, Brevald, his wife and her mother, and the vague relations and hangers-on who were always in and about, they had to live cheek by jowl, Lawson, ceasing to be of any account, was hardly noticed. He left in the morning after breakfast, and came back only to have supper. He gave up the struggle, and when for want of money he could not go to the English Club he spent the evening playing hearts with old Brevald and the natives. Except when he was drunk he was cowed and listless. Ethel treated him like a dog. She submitted at times to his fits of wild passion, and she was frightened by the gusts of hatred with which they were followed;

but when, afterwards, he was cringing and lachrymose she had such a contempt for him that she could have spat in his face. Sometimes he was violent, but now she was prepared for him, and when he hit her she kicked and scratched and bit. They had horrible battles in which he had not always the best of it. Very soon it was known all over Apia that they got on badly. There was little sympathy for Lawson, and at the hotel the general surprise was that old Brevald did not kick him out of the place.

"Brevald's a pretty ugly customer," said one of the men. "I shouldn't be surprised if he put a bullet into Lawson's carcass one of these days."

Ethel still went in the evenings to bathe in the silent pool. It seemed to have an attraction for her that was not quite human, just that attraction you might imagine that a mermaid who had won a soul would have for the cool salt waves of the sea; and sometimes Lawson went also. I do not know what urged him to go, for Ethel was obviously irritated by his presence; perhaps it was because in that spot he hoped to regain the clean rapture which had filled his heart when first he saw her; perhaps only, with the madness of those who love them that love them not, from the feeling that his obstinacy could force love. One day he strolled down there with a feeling that was rare with him now. He felt suddenly at peace with the world. The evening was drawing in and the dusk seemed to cling to the leaves of the coconut trees like a little thin cloud. A faint breeze stirred them noiselessly. A crescent moon hung just over their tops. He made his way to the bank. He saw Ethel in the water floating on her back. Her hair streamed out all round her, and she was holding in her hand a large hibiscus. He stopped a moment to admire her; she was like Ophelia.

"Hulloa, Ethel," he cried joyfully.

She made a sudden movement and dropped the red flower. It floated idly away. She swam a stroke or two till she knew there was ground within her depth and then stood up.

"Go away," she said. "Go away."

He laughed.

"Don't be selfish. There's plenty of room for both of us."

"Why can't you leave me alone? I want to be by myself."

"Hang it all, I want to bathe," he answered, good-humouredly.

"Go down to the bridge. I don't want you here."

"I'm sorry for that," he said, smiling still.

He was not in the least angry, and he hardly noticed that she was in a passion. He began to take off his coat.

"Go away," she shrieked. "I won't have you here. Can't you even leave me this? Go away."

"Don't be silly, darling."

She bent down and picked up a sharp stone and flung it quickly at him. He had no time to duck. It hit him on the temple. With a cry he put his hand to his head and when he took it away it was wet with blood. Ethel stood still, panting with rage. He turned very pale, and without a word, taking up his coat, went away. Ethel let herself fall back into the water and the stream carried her slowly down to the ford.

The stone had made a jagged wound and for some days Lawson went about with a bandaged head. He had invented a likely story to account for the accident when the fellows at the club asked him about it, but he had no occasion to use it. No one referred to the matter. He saw them cast surreptitious glances at his head, but not a word was said. The silence could only mean that they knew how he came by his wound. He was certain now that Ethel had a lover, and they all knew who it was. But there was not the smallest indication to guide him. He never saw Ethel with anyone; no one showed a wish to be with her, or treated him in a manner that seemed strange. Wild rage seized him, and having no one to vent it on he drank more and more heavily. A little while before I came to the island he had had another attack of *delirium tremens*.

I met Ethel at the house of a man called Caster, who lived two or three miles from Apia with a native wife. I had been playing tennis with him and when we were tired he suggested a cup of tea. We went into the house and in the untidy living-room found Ethel chatting with Mrs. Caster.

"Hulloa, Ethel," he said, "I didn't know you were here."

I could not help looking at her with curiosity. I tried to see what there was in her to have excited in Lawson such a devastating passion. But who can explain these things? It was true that she was lovely; she reminded one of the red hibiscus, the common flower of the hedgerow in Samoa, with its grace and its languor and its passion; but what surprised me most, taking into consideration the story I knew even then a good deal of, was her freshness and simplicity. She was quiet and a little shy. There was nothing coarse or loud about her; she had not the exuberance common to the half-caste; and it was almost impossible to believe that she could be the virago that the horrible scenes between husband and wife, which were now common knowledge, indicated. In her pretty pink frock and high-heeled shoes she looked quite European. You could hardly have guessed at that dark background of native life in which she felt herself so much more at home. I did not imagine that she was at all intelligent, and I should not have been surprised if a man, after living with her for some time, had found the passion which had drawn him to her sink into boredom. It suggested itself to me that in her elusiveness, like a thought that presents itself to consciousness and vanishes before it can be captured by words, lay her peculiar charm; but perhaps that was merely fancy, and if I had known nothing about her I should have seen in her only a pretty little half-caste like another.

She talked to me of the various things which they talk of to the stranger in Samoa, of the journey, and whether I had slid down the water rock at Papaseea, and if I meant to stay in a native village. She talked to me of Scotland, and perhaps I noticed in her a tendency to enlarge on the sumptuousness of her establishment there. She asked me naïvely if I knew Mrs. This and Mrs. That, with whom she had been acquainted when she lived in the north.

Then Miller, the fat German-American, came in. He shook hands all round very cordially and sat down, asking in his loud, cheerful voice for a whisky and soda. He was very fat and he sweated profusely. He took off his gold-rimmed spectacles and wiped them; you saw then that his little eyes, benevolent behind the large round glasses, were shrewd and cunning; the party had seen somewhat dull till he came, but he was a good story-teller and a jovial fellow. Soon he had the two women, Ethel and my friend's wife, laughing delightedly at his sallies. He had a reputation on the island of a lady's man, and you could see how this fat, gross fellow, old and ugly, had yet the possibility of fascination. His humour was on a level with the understanding of his company, an affair of vitality and assurance, and his Western accent gave a peculiar point to what he said. At last he turned to me:

"Well, if we want to get back for dinner we'd better be getting. I'll take you along in my machine if you like."

I thanked him and got up. He shook hands with the others, went out of the room, massive and strong in his walk, and climbed into his car.

"Pretty little thing, Lawson's wife," I said, as we drove along.

"Too bad the way he treats her. Knocks her about. Gets my dander up when I hear of a man hitting a woman."

We went on a little. Then he said:

"He was a darned fool to marry her. I said so at the time. If he hadn't, he'd have had the whip hand over her. He's yaller, that's what he is, yaller."

The year was drawing to its end and the time approached when I was to leave Samoa. My boat was scheduled to sail for Sydney on the fourth of January. Christmas Day had been celebrated at the hotel with suitable ceremonies, but it was looked upon as no more than a rehearsal for New Year, and the men who were accustomed to foregather in the lounge determined on New Year's Eve to make a night of it. There was an uproarious dinner, after which the party sauntered down to the English Club, a simple little frame house, to play pool. There was a great deal of talking, laughing, and betting, but some very poor play, except on the part of Miller, who had drunk as much as any of them, all far younger than he, but had kept unimpaired the keenness of his eye and the sureness of his hand. He pocketed the young men's money with humour and urbanity. After an hour of this I grew tired and went out. I crossed the road and came on to the beach. Three coconut trees grew there, like three moon maidens waiting for their lovers to ride out of the sea, and I sat at the foot of one of them, watching the lagoon and the nightly assemblage of the stars.

I do not know where Lawson had been during the evening, but between ten and eleven he came along to the club. He shambled down the dusty, empty road, feeling dull and bored, and when he reached the club, before going into the billiard-room, went into the bar to have a drink by himself. He had a shyness now about joining the company of white men when there were a lot of them together and needed a stiff dose of whisky to give him confidence. He was standing with the glass in his hand when Miller came in to him. He was in his shirt sleeves and still held his cue. He gave the bartender a glance.

"Get out, Jack," he said.

The bartender, a native in a white jacket and a red *lava-lava*, without a word slid out of the small room.

"Look here, I've been wanting to have a few words with you, Lawson," said the big American.

"Well, that's one of the few things you can have free, gratis, and for nothing on this damned island."

Miller fixed his gold spectacles more firmly on his nose and held Lawson with his cold determined eyes.

"See here, young fellow, I understand you've been knocking Mrs. Lawson about again. I'm not going to stand for that. If you don't stop it right now I'll break every bone of your dirty little body."

Then Lawson knew what he had been trying to find out so long. It was Miller. The appearance of the man, fat, bald-headed, with his round bare face and double chin and the gold spectacles, his age, his benign, shrewd look, like that of a renegade priest, and the thought of Ethel, so slim and virginal, filled him with a sudden horror. Whatever his faults Lawson was no coward, and without a word he hit out violently at Miller. Miller quickly warded the blow with the hand that held the cue, and then with a great swing of his right arm brought his fist down on Lawson's ear. Lawson was four inches shorter than the American and he was slightly built, frail and weakened not only by illness and the enervating tropics, but by drink. He fell like a log and lay half dazed at the foot of the bar. Miller took off his spectacles and wiped them with his handkerchief.

"I guess you know what to expect now. You've had your warning and you'd better take it."

He took up his cue and went back into the billiard-room. There was so much noise there that no one knew what had happened. Lawson picked himself up. He put his hand to his ear, which was singing still. Then he slunk out of the club.

I saw a man cross the road, a patch of white against the darkness of the night, but did not know who it was. He came down to the beach, passed me sitting at the foot of the tree, and looked down. I saw then that it was Lawson, but since he was doubtless drunk, did not speak. He went on, walked irresolutely two or three steps, and turned back. He came up to me and bending down stared in my face.

"I thought it was you," he said.

He sat down and took out his pipe.

"It was hot and noisy in the club," I volunteered.

"Why are you sitting here?"

"I was waiting about for the midnight mass at the Cathedral."

"If you like I'll come with you."

Lawson was quite sober. We sat for a while smoking in silence. Now and then in the lagoon was the splash of some big fish, and a little way out towards the opening in the reef was the light of a schooner.

"You're sailing next week, aren't you?" he said.

"Yes."

"It would be jolly to go home once more. But I could never stand it now. The cold, you know."

"It's odd to think that in England now they're shivering round the fire," I said.

There was not even a breath of wind. The balminess of the night was like a spell. I wore nothing but a thin shirt and a suit of ducks. I enjoyed the exquisite languor of the night, and stretched my limbs voluptuously.

"This isn't the sort of New Year's Eve that persuades one to make good resolutions for the future," I smiled.

He made no answer, but I do not know what train of thought my casual remark had suggested in him, for presently he began to speak. He spoke in a low voice, without any expression, but his accents were educated, and it was a relief to hear him after the twang and the vulgar intonations which for some time had wounded my ears.

"I've made an awful hash of things. That's obvious, isn't it? I'm right down at the bottom of the pit and there's no getting out for me. '*Black as the pit from pole to pole.*'" I felt him smile as he made the quotation. "And the strange thing is that I don't see how I went wrong."

I held my breath, for to me there is nothing more awe-inspiring than when a man discovers to you the nakedness of his soul. Then you see that no one is so trivial or debased but that in him is a spark of something to excite compassion.

"It wouldn't be so rotten if I could see that it was all my own fault. It's true I drink, but I shouldn't have taken to that if things had gone differently. I wasn't really fond of liquor. I suppose I ought not to have married Ethel. If I'd kept her it would be all right. But I did love her so."

His voice faltered.

"She's not a bad lot, you know, not really. It's just rotten luck. We might have been as happy as lords. When she bolted I suppose I ought to have let her go, but I couldn't do that—I was dead stuck on her then; and there was the kid."

"Are you fond of the kid?" I asked.

"I was. There are two, you know. But they don't mean so much to me now. You'd take them for natives anywhere. I have to talk to them in Samoan."

"Is it too late for you to start fresh? Couldn't you make a dash for it and leave the place?"

"I haven't the strength. I'm done for."

"Are you still in love with your wife?"

"Not now. Not now." He repeated the two words with a kind of horror in his voice. "I haven't even got that now. I'm down and out."

The bells of the Cathedral were ringing.

"If you really want to come to the midnight mass we'd better go along," I said. "Come on."

We got up and walked along the road. The Cathedral, all white, stood facing the sea not without impressiveness, and beside it the Protestant chapels had the look of meeting-houses. In the road were two or three cars, and a great number of traps, and traps were put up against the walls at the side. People had come from all parts of the island for the service, and through the great open doors we saw that the place was crowded. The high altar was all ablaze with light. There were a few whites and a good many half-castes, but the great majority were natives. All the men wore trousers, for the Church has decided that the *lava-lava* is indecent. We found chairs at the back, near the open door, and sat down. Presently, following Lawson's eyes, I saw Ethel come in with a party of half-castes. They were all very much dressed up, the men in high, stiff collars and shiny boots, the women in large, gay hats. Ethel nodded and smiled to her friends as she passed up the aisle. The service began.

When it was over Lawson and I stood on one side for awhile to watch the crowd stream out, then he held out his hand.

"Good-night," he said. "I hope you'll have a pleasant journey home."

"Oh, but I shall see you before I go."

He sniggered.

"The question is if you'll see me drunk or sober."

He turned and left me. I had a recollection of those very large black eyes, shining wildly under the shaggy brows. I paused irresolutely. I did not feel sleepy and I thought I would at all events go along to the club for an hour before turning in. When I got there I found the billiard-room empty, but half-a-dozen men were sitting round a table in the lounge, playing poker. Miller looked up as I came in

"Sit down and take a hand," he said.

"All right."

I bought some chips and began to play. Of course it is the most fascinating game in the world and my hour lengthened out to two, and then to three. The native bartender, cheery and wide-awake notwithstanding the time, was at our elbow to supply us with drinks and from somewhere or other he produced a ham and a loaf of bread. We played on. Most of the party had drunk more than was good for them and the play was high and reckless. I played modestly, neither wishing to win nor anxious to lose, but I watched Miller with a fascinated interest. He drank glass for glass with the rest of the company, but remained cool and level-headed. His pile of chips increased in size and he had a neat little paper in front of him on which he had marked various sums lent to players in distress. He beamed amiably at the young men whose money he was taking. He kept up interminably his stream of jest and anecdote, but he never missed a draw, he never let an expression of the face pass him. At last the dawn crept into the windows, gently, with a sort of deprecating shyness, as though it had no business there, and then it was day.

"Well," said Miller, "I reckon we've seen the old year out in style. Now let's have a round of jackpots and me for my mosquito net. I'm fifty, remember, I can't keep these late hours."

The morning was beautiful and fresh when we stood on the verandah, and the lagoon was like a sheet of multicoloured glass. Someone suggested a dip before going to bed, but none cared to bathe in the lagoon, sticky and treacherous to the feet. Miller had his car at the door and he offered to take us down to the pool. We jumped in and drove along the deserted road. When we reached the pool it seemed as though the day had hardly risen there yet. Under the trees the water was all in shadow and the night had the effect of lurking still. We were in great spirits. We had no towels or any costume and in my prudence I wondered how we were going to dry ourselves. None of us had much on and it did not take us long to snatch off our clothes. Nelson, the little supercargo, was stripped first.

"I'm going down to the bottom," he said.

He dived and in a moment another man dived too, but shallow, and was out of the water before him. Then Nelson came up and scrambled to the side.

"I say, get me out," he said.

"What's up?"

Something was evidently the matter. His face was terrified. Two fellows gave him their hands and he slithered up.

"I say, there's a man down there."

"Don't be a fool. You're drunk."

"Well, if there isn't I'm in for D. T's. But I tell you there's a man down there. It just scared me out of my wits."

Miller looked at him for a moment. The little man was all white. He was actually trembling.

"Come on, Caster," said Miller to the big Australian, "we'd better go down and see."

"He was standing up," said Nelson, "all dressed. I saw him. He tried to catch hold of me."

"Hold your row," said Miller. "Are you ready?"

They dived in. We waited on the bank, silent. It really seemed as though they were under water longer than any men could breathe. Then Caster came up, and immediately after him, red in the face as though he were going to have a fit, Miller. They were pulling something behind them. Another man jumped in to help them, and the three together dragged their burden to the side. They shoved it up. Then we saw that it was Lawson, with a great stone tied up in his coat and bound to his feet.

"He was set on making a good job of it," said Miller, as he wiped the water from his short-sighted eyes.

"Rain" (1921)

It was nearly bed-time and when they awoke next morning land would be in sight. Dr. Macphail lit his pipe and, leaning over the rail, searched the heavens for the Southern Cross. After two years at the front and a wound that had taken longer to heal than it should, he was glad to settle down quietly at Apia for twelve months at least, and he felt already better for the jouney. Since some of the passengers were leaving the ship next day at Pago-Pago they had had a little dance that evening and in his ears hammered still the harsh notes of the mechanical piano. But the deck was quiet at last. A little way off he saw his wife in a long chair talking with the Davidsons, and he strolled over to her. When he sat down under the light and took off his hat you saw that he had very red hair, with a bald patch on the crown, and the red, freckled skin which accompanies red hair; he was a man of forty, thin, with a pinched face, precise and rather pedantic; and he spoke with a Scots accent in a very low, quiet voice.

Between the Macphails and the Davidsons, who were missionaries, there had arisen the intimacy of shipboard, which is due to propinquity rather than to any community of taste. Their chief tie was the disapproval they shared of the men who spent their days and nights in the smoking-room playing poker or bridge and drinking. Mrs. Macphail was not a little flattered to think that she and her husband were the only people on board with whom the Davidsons were willing to associate, and even the doctor, shy but no fool, half unconsciously acknowledged the compliment. It was only because he was of an argumentative mind that in their cabin at night he permitted himself to carp.

"Mrs. Davidson was saying she didn't know how they'd have got through the journey if it hadn't been for us," said Mrs. Macphail, as she neatly brushed out her transformation. "She said we were really the only people on the ship they cared to know."

"I shouldn't have thought a missionary was such a big bug that he could afford to put on frills."

"It's not frills. I quite understand what she means. It wouldn't have been very nice for the Davidsons to have to mix with all that rough lot in the smoking-room."

"The founder of their religion wasn't so exclusive," said Dr. Macphail with a chuckle.

"I've asked you over and over again not to joke about religion," answered his wife. "I shouldn't like to have a nature like yours, Alec. You never look for the best in people."

He gave her a sidelong glance with his pale, blue eyes, but did not reply. After many years of married life he had learned that it was more conducive to peace to leave his wife with the last word. He was undressed before she was, and climbing into the upper bunk he settled down to read himself to sleep.

When he came on deck next morning they were close to land. He looked at it with greedy eyes. There was a thin strip of silver beach rising quickly to hills covered to the top with luxuriant vegetation. The coconut trees, thick and green, came nearly to the water's edge, and among them you saw the grass houses of the Samoans; and here and there, gleaming white, a little church. Mrs. Davidson came and stood beside him. She was dressed in black and wore round her neck a gold chain, from which dangled a small cross. She was a little woman, with brown, dull hair very elaborately arranged, and she had prominent blue eyes behind invisible *pince-nez*. Her face was long, like a sheep's, but she gave no impression of foolishness, rather of extreme alertness; she had the quick movements of a bird. The most remarkable thing about her was her voice, high, metallic, and without inflection; it fell on the ear with a hard monotony, irritating to the nerves like the pitiless clamour of the pneumatic drill.

"This must seem like home to you," said Dr. Macphail, with his thin, difficult smile.

"Ours are low islands, you know, not like these. Coral. These are volcanic. We've got another ten days' journey to reach them."

"In these parts that's almost like being in the next street at home," said Dr. Macphail facetiously.

"Well, that's rather an exaggerated way of putting it, but one does look at distances differently in the South Seas. So far you're right."

Dr. Macphail sighed faintly.

"I'm glad we're not stationed here," she went on. "They say this is a terribly difficult place to work in. The steamers' touching makes the people unsettled; and then there's the naval station; that's bad for the natives. In our district we don't have difficulties like that to contend with. There are one or two traders, of course, but we take care to make them behave, and if they don't we make the place so hot for them they're glad to go."

Fixing the glasses on her nose she looked at the green island with a ruthless stare.

"It's almost a hopeless task for the missionaries here. I can never be sufficiently thankful to God that we are at least spared that."

Davidson's district consisted of a group of islands to the North of Samoa; they were widely separated and he had frequently to go long distances by canoe. At these times his wife remained at their headquarters and managed the mission. Dr. Macphail felt his heart sink when he considered the efficiency with which she certainly managed it. She spoke of the depravity of the natives in a voice which nothing could hush, but with a vehemently unctuous horror. Her sense of delicacy was singular. Early in their acquaintance she had said to him:

"You know, their marriage customs when we first settled in the islands were so shocking that I couldn't possibly describe them to you. But I'll tell Mrs. Macphail and she'll tell you."

Then he had seen his wife and Mrs. Davidson, their deckchairs close together, in earnest conversation for about two hours. As he walked past them backwards and forwards for the sake of exercise, he had heard Mrs. Davidson's agitated whisper, like the distant flow of a mountain torrent, and he saw by his wife's open mouth and pale face that she was enjoying an alarming experience. At night in their cabin she repeated to him with bated breath all she had heard.

"Well, what did I say to you?" cried Mrs. Davidson, exultant, next morning. "Did you ever hear anything more dreadful? You don't wonder that I couldn't tell you myself, do you? Even though you are a doctor."

Mrs. Davidson scanned his face. She had a dramatic eagerness to see that she had achieved the desired effect.

"Can you wonder that when we first went there our hearts sank? You'll hardly believe me when I tell you it was impossible to find a single good girl in any of the villages."

She used the word good in a severely technical manner.

"Mr. Davidson and I talked it over, and we made up our minds the first thing to do was to put down the dancing. The natives were crazy about dancing."

"I was not averse to it myself when I was a young man," said Dr. Macphail.

"I guessed as much when I heard you ask Mrs. Macphail to have a turn with you last night. I don't think there's any real harm if a man dances with his wife, but I was relieved that she wouldn't. Under the circumstances I thought it better that we should keep ourselves to ourselves."

"Under what circumstances?"

Mrs. Davidson gave him a quick look through her *pince-nez*, but did not answer his question.

"But among white people it's not quite the same," she went on, "though I must say I agree with Mr. Davidson, who says he can't understand how a husband can stand by and see his wife in another man's arms, and as far as I'm concerned I've never danced a step since I married. But the native dancing is quite another matter. It's not only immoral in itself, but it distinctly leads to immorality. However, I'm thankful to God that we stamped it out, and I don't think I'm wrong in saying that no one has danced in our district for eight years."

But now they came to the mouth of the harbour and Mrs. Macphail joined them. The ship turned sharply and steamed slowly in. It was a great land-locked harbour big enough to hold a fleet of battleships; and all around it rose, high and steep, the green hills. Near the entrance, getting such breeze as blew from the sea, stood the governor's house in a garden. The Stars and Stripes dangled languidly from a flagstaff. They passed two or three trim bungalows, and a tennis court, and then they came to the quay with its warehouses. Mrs. Davidson pointed out the schooner, moored two or three hundred yards from the side, which was to take them to Apia. There was a crowd of eager, noisy, and good-humoured natives come from all parts of the island, some from curiosity, others to barter with the travellers on their way to Sydney; and they brought pineapples and huge bunches of bananas, *tapa* cloths, necklaces of shells or sharks' teeth, *kava* bowls, and models of war canoes. American sailors, neat and trim, clean-shaven and frank of face, sauntered among them, and there was a little group of officials. While their luggage was being landed the

Macphails and Mrs. Davidson watched the crowd. Dr. Macphail looked at the yaws from which most of the children and the young boys seemed to suffer, disfiguring sores like torpid ulcers, and his professional eyes glistened when he saw for the first time in his experience cases of elephantiasis, men going about with a huge, heavy arm or dragging along a grossly disfigured leg. Men and women wore the *lava-lava*.

"It's a very indecent costume," said Mrs. Davidson. "Mr. Davidson thinks it should be prohibited by law. How can you expect people to be moral when they wear nothing but a strip of red cotton round their loins?"

"It's suitable enough to the climate," said the doctor, wiping the sweat off his head.

Now that they were on land the heat, though it was so early in the morning, was already oppressive. Closed in by its hills, not a breath of air came in to Pago-Pago.

"In our islands," Mrs. Davidson went on in her high-pitched tones, "we've practically eradicated the *lava-lava*. A few old men still continue to wear it, but that's all. The women have all taken to the Mother Hubbard, and the men wear trousers and singlets. At the very beginning of our stay Mr. Davidson said in one of his reports: the inhabitants of these islands will never be thoroughly Christianized till every boy of more than ten years is made to wear a pair of trousers."

But Mrs. Davidson had given two or three of her birdlike glances at heavy grey clouds that came floating over the mouth of the harbour. A few drops began to fall.

"We'd better take shelter," she said.

They made their way with all the crowd to a great shed of corrugated iron, and the rain began to fall in torrents. They stood there for some time and then were joined by Mr. Davidson. He had been polite enough to the Macphails during the journey, but he had not his wife's sociability, and had spent much of his time reading. He was a silent, rather sullen man, and you felt that his affability was a duty that he imposed upon himself Christianly; he was by nature reserved and even morose. His appearance was singular. He was very tall and thin, with long limbs loosely jointed; hollow cheeks and curiously high cheek-bones; he had so cadaverous an air that it surprised you to notice how full and sensual were his lips. He wore his hair very long. His dark eyes, set deep in their sockets, were large and tragic; and his hands with their big, long fingers, were finely shaped; they gave him a look of great strength. But the most striking thing about him was the feeling he gave you of suppressed fire. It was impressive and vaguely troubling. He was not a man with whom any intimacy was possible.

He brought now unwelcome news. There was an epidemic of measles, a serious and often fatal disease among the Kanakas, on the island, and a case had developed among the crew of the schooner which was to take them on their journey. The sick man had been brought ashore and put in hospital on the quarantine station, but telegraphic instructions had been sent from Apia to say that the schooner would not be allowed to enter the harbour till it was certain no other member of the crew was affected.

"It means we shall have to stay here for ten days at least."

"But I'm urgently needed at Apia," said Dr. Macphail.

"That can't be helped. If no more cases develop on board, the schooner will be allowed to sail with white passengers, but all native traffic is prohibited for three months."

"Is there a hotel here?" asked Mrs. Macphail.

Davidson gave a low chuckle.

"There's not."

"What shall we do then?"

"I've been talking to the governor. There's a trader along the front who has rooms that he rents, and my proposition is that as soon as the rain lets up we should go along there and see what we can do. Don't expect comfort. You've just got to be thankful if we get a bed to sleep on and a roof over our heads."

But the rain showed no sign of stopping, and at length with umbrellas and waterproofs they set out. There was no town, but merely a group of official buildings, a store or two, and at the back, among the coconut trees and plantains, a few native dwellings. The house they sought was about five minutes' walk from the wharf. It was a frame house of two storeys, with broad verandahs on both floors and a roof of corrugated iron. The owner was a half-caste named Horn, with a native wife surrounded by little brown children, and on the ground-floor he had a store where he sold canned goods and cottons. The rooms he showed them were almost bare of furniture. In the Macphails' there was nothing but a poor, worn bed with a ragged mosquito net, a rickety chair, and a washstand. They looked round with dismay. The rain poured down without ceasing.

"I'm not going to unpack more than we actually need," said Mrs. Macphail.

Mrs. Davidson came into the room as she was unlocking a portmanteau. She was very brisk and alert. The cheerless surroundings had no effect on her.

"If you'll take my advice you'll get a needle and cotton and start right in to mend the mosquito net," she said, "or you'll not be able to get a wink of sleep to-night."

"Will they be very bad?" asked Dr. Macphail.

"This is the season for them. When you're asked to a party at Government House at Apia you'll notice that all the ladies are given a pillow-slip to put their—their lower extremities in."

"I wish the rain would stop for a moment," said Mrs. Macphail. "I could try to make the place comfortable with more heart if the sun were shining."

"Oh, if you wait for that, you'll wait a long time. Pago-Pago is about the rainiest place in the Pacific. You see, the hills, and that bay, they attract the water, and one expects rain at this time of year anyway."

She looked from Macphail to his wife, standing helplessly in different parts of the room, like lost souls, and she pursed her lips. She saw that she must take them in hand. Feckless people like that made her impatient, but her hands itched to put everything in order which came so naturally to her.

"Here, you give me a needle and cotton and I'll mend that net of yours, while you go on with your unpacking. Dinner's at one. Dr. Macphail, you'd better go down to the wharf and see that your heavy luggage has been put in a dry place. You know what these natives are, they're quite capable of storing it where the rain will beat in on it all the time."

The doctor put on his waterproof again and went downstairs. At the door Mr. Horn was standing in conversation with the quartermaster of the ship they had just arrived in and a second class passenger whom Dr.

Macphail had seen several times on board. The quartermaster, a little, shrivelled man, extremely dirty, nodded to him as he passed.

"This is a bad job about the measles, doc," he said. "I see you've fixed yourself up already."

Dr. Macphail thought he was rather familiar, but he was a timid man and he did not take offence easily.

"Yes, we've got a room upstairs."

"Miss Thompson was sailing with you to Apia, so I've brought her along here."

The quartermaster pointed with his thumb to the woman standing by his side. She was twenty-seven perhaps, plump, and in a coarse fashion pretty. She wore a white dress and a large white hat. Her fat calves in white cotton stockings bulged over the tops of long white boots in glacé kid. She gave Macphail an ingratiating smile.

"The feller's tryin' to soak me a dollar and a half a day for the meanest sized room," she said in a hoarse voice.

"I tell you she's a friend of mine, Jo," said the quartermaster. "She can't pay more than a dollar, and you've sure got to take her for that."

The trader was fat and smooth and quietly smiling.

"Well, if you put it like that, Mr. Swan, I'll see what I can do about it. I'll talk to Mrs. Horn and if we think we can make a reduction we will."

"Don't try to pull that stuff with me," said Miss Thompson. "We'll settle this right now. You get a dollar a day for the room and not one bean more."

Dr. Macphail smiled. He admired the effrontery with which she bargained. He was the sort of man who always paid what he was asked. He preferred to be over-charged than to haggle. The trader sighed.

"Well, to oblige Mr. Swan I'll take it."

"That's the goods," said Miss Thompson. "Come right in and have a shot of hooch. I've got some real good rye in that grip if you'll bring it along, Mr. Swan. You come along too, doctor."

"Oh, I don't think I will, thank you," he answered. "I'm just going down to see that our luggage is all right."

He stepped out into the rain. It swept in from the opening of the harbour in sheets and the opposite shore was all blurred. He passed two or three natives clad in nothing but the *lava-lava*, with huge umbrellas over them. They walked finely, with leisurely movements, very upright; and they smiled and greeted him in a strange tongue as they went by.

It was nearly dinner-time when he got back, and their meal was laid in the trader's parlour. It was a room designed not to live in but for purposes of prestige, and it had a musty, melancholy air. A suite of stamped plush was arranged neatly round the walls, and from the middle of the ceiling, protected from the flies by yellow tissue paper, hung a gilt chandelier. Davidson did not come.

"I know he went to call on the governor," said Mrs. Davidson, "and I guess he's kept him to dinner."

A little native girl brought them a dish of Hamburger steak, and after a while the trader came up to see that they had everything they wanted.

"I see we have a fellow lodger, Mr. Horn," said Dr. Macphail.

"She's taken a room, that's all," answered the trader. "She's getting her own board."

He looked at the two ladies with an obsequious air.

"I put her downstairs so she shouldn't be in the way. She won't be any trouble to you."

"Is it someone who was on the boat?" asked Mrs. Macphail.

"Yes, ma'am, she was in the second cabin. She was going to Apia. She has a position as cashier waiting for her."

"Oh!"

When the trader was gone Macphail said:

"I shouldn't think she'd find it exactly cheerful having her meals in her room."

"If she was in the second cabin I guess she'd rather," answered Mrs. Davidson. "I don't exactly know who it can be."

"I happened to be there when the quartermaster brought her along. Her name's Thompson."

"It's not the woman who was dancing with the quartermaster last night?" asked Mrs. Davidson.

"That's who it must be," said Mrs. Macphail. "I wondered at the time what she was. She looked rather fast to me."

"Not good style at all," said Mrs. Davidson.

They began to talk of other things, and after dinner, tired with their early rise, they separated and slept. When they awoke, though the sky was still grey and the clouds hung low, it was not raining and they went for a walk on the high road which the Americans had built along the bay.

On their return they found that Davidson had just come in.

"We may be here for a fortnight," he said irritably. "I've argued it out with the governor, but he says there is nothing to be done."

"Mr. Davidson's just longing to get back to his work," said his wife, with an anxious glance at him.

"We've been away for a year," he said, walking up and down the verandah. "The mission has been in charge of native missionaries and I'm terribly nervous that they've let things slide. They're good men, I'm not saying a word against them, God-fearing, devout, and truly Christian men—their Christianity would put many so-called Christians at home to the blush—but they're pitifully lacking in energy. They can make a stand once, they can make a stand twice, but they can't make a stand all the time. If you leave a mission in charge of a native missionary, no matter how trustworthy he seems, in course of time you'll find he's let abuses creep in."

Mr. Davidson stood still. With his tall, spare form, and his great eyes flashing out of his pale face, he was an impressive figure. His sincerity was obvious in the fire of his gestures and in his deep, ringing voice.

"I expect to have my work cut out for me. I shall act and I shall act promptly. If the tree is rotten it shall be cut down and cast into the flames."

And in the evening after the high tea which was their last meal, while they sat in the stiff parlour, the ladies working and Dr. Macphail smoking his pipe, the missionary told them of his work in the islands.

"When we went there they had no sense of sin at all," he said. "They broke the commandments one after the other and never knew they were doing wrong. And I think that was the most difficult part of my work, to instil into the natives the sense of sin."

The Macphails knew already that Davidson had worked in the Solomons for five years before he met his wife. She had been a missionary in China, and they had become acquainted in Boston, where they were both spending part of their leave to attend a missionary congress. On their marriage they had been appointed to the islands in which they had laboured ever since.

In the course of all the conversations they had had with Mr. Davidson one thing had shone out clearly and that was the man's unflinching courage. He was a medical missionary, and he was liable to be called at any time to one or other of the islands in the group. Even the whaleboat is not so very safe a conveyance in the stormy Pacific of the wet season, but often he would be sent for in a canoe, and then the danger was great. In cases of illness or accident he never hesitated. A dozen times he had spent the whole night baling for his life, and more than once Mrs. Davidson had given him up for lost.

"I'd beg him not to go sometimes," she said, "or at least to wait till the weather was more settled, but he'd never listen. He's obstinate, and when he's once made up his mind, nothing can move him."

"How can I ask the natives to put their trust in the Lord if I am afraid to do so myself?" cried Davidson. "And I'm not, I'm not. They know that if they send for me in their trouble I'll come if it's humanly possible. And do you think the Lord is going to abandon me when I am on his business? The wind blows at his bidding and the waves toss and rage at his word."

Dr. Macphail was a timid man. He had never been able to get used to the hurtling of the shells over the trenches, and when he was operating in an advanced dressing-station the sweat poured from his brow and dimmed his spectacles in the effort he made to control his unsteady hand. He shuddered a little as he looked at the missionary.

"I wish I could say that I've never been afraid," he said.

"I wish you could say that you believed in God," retorted the other.

But for some reason, that evening the missionary's thoughts travelled back to the early days he and his wife had spent on the islands.

"Sometimes Mrs. Davidson and I would look at one another and the tears would stream down our cheeks. We worked without ceasing, day and night, and we seemed to make no progress. I don't know what I should have done without her then. When I felt my heart sink, when I was very near despair, she gave me courage and hope."

Mrs. Davidson looked down at her work, and a slight colour rose to her thin cheeks. Her hands trembled a little. She did not trust herself to speak.

"We had no one to help us. We were alone, thousands of miles from any of our own people, surrounded by darkness. When I was broken and weary she would put her work aside and take the Bible and read to me till peace came and settled upon me like sleep upon the eyelids of a child, and when at last she closed the book she'd say: 'We'll save them in spite of themselves.' And I felt strong again in the Lord, and I answered: 'Yes, with God's help I'll save them. I must save them.'"

He came over to the table and stood in front of it as though it were a lectern.

"You see, they were so naturally depraved that they couldn't be brought to see their wickedness. We had to make sins out of what they thought were natural actions. We had to make it a sin, not only to commit adultery and to lie and thieve, but to expose their bodies, and to dance and not to come to church. I made it a sin for a girl to show her bosom and a sin for a man not to wear trousers."

"How?" asked Dr. Macphail, not without surprise.

"I instituted fines. Obviously the only way to make people realize that an action is sinful is to punish them if they commit it. I fined them if they didn't come to church, and I fined them if they danced. I fined them if they were improperly dressed. I had a tariff, and every sin had to be paid for either in money or work. And at last I made them understand."

"But did they never refuse to pay?"

"How could they?" asked the missionary.

"It would be a brave man who tried to stand up against Mr. Davidson," said his wife, tightening her lips.

Dr. Macphail looked at Davidson with troubled eyes. What he heard shocked him, but he hesitated to express his disapproval.

"You must remember that in the last resort I could expel them from their church membership."

"Did they mind that?"

Davidson smiled a little and gently rubbed his hands.

"They couldn't sell their copra. When the men fished they got no share of the catch. It meant something very like starvation. Yes, they minded quite a lot."

"Tell him about Fred Ohlson," said Mrs. Davidson.

The missionary fixed his fiery eyes on Dr. Macphail.

"Fred Ohlson was a Danish trader who had been in the islands a good many years. He was a pretty rich man as traders go, and he wasn't very pleased when we came. You see, he'd had things very much his own way. He paid the natives what he liked for their copra, and he paid in goods and whiskey. He had a native wife, but he was flagrantly unfaithful to her. He was a drunkard. I gave him a chance to mend his ways, but he wouldn't take it. He laughed at me."

Davidson's voice fell to a deep bass as he said the last words, and he was silent for a minute or two. The silence was heavy with menace.

"In two years he was a ruined man. He'd lost everything he'd saved in a quarter of a century. I broke him, and at last he was forced to come to me like a beggar and beseech me to give him a passage back to Sydney."

"I wish you could have seen him when he came to see Mr. Davidson," said the missionary's wife. "He had been a fine, powerful man, with a lot of fat on him, and he had a great big voice, but now he was half the size, and he was shaking all over. He'd suddenly become an old man."

With abstracted gaze Davidson looked out into the night. The rain was falling again.

Suddenly from below came a sound, and Davidson turned and looked questioningly at his wife. It was the sound of a gramophone, harsh and loud, wheezing out a syncopated tune.

"What's that?" he asked.

Mrs. Davidson fixed her *pince-nez* more firmly on her nose.

"One of the second-class passengers has a room in the house. I guess it comes from there."

They listened in silence, and presently they heard the sound of dancing. Then the music stopped, and they heard the popping of corks and voices raised in animated conversation.

"I daresay she's giving a farewell party to her friends on board," said Dr. Macphail. "The ship sails at twelve, doesn't it?"

Davidson made no remark, but he looked at his watch.

"Are you ready?" he asked his wife.

She got up and folded her work.

"Yes, I guess I am," she answered.

"It's early to go to bed yet, isn't it?" said the doctor.

"We have a good deal of reading to do," explained Mrs. Davidson. "Wherever we are, we read a chapter of the Bible before retiring for the night and we study it with the commentaries, you know, and discuss it thoroughly. It's a wonderful training for the mind."

The two couples bade one another good-night. Dr. and Mrs. Macphail were left alone. For two or three minutes they did not speak.

"I think I'll go and fetch the cards," the doctor said at last.

Mrs. Macphail looked at him doubtfully. Her conversation with the Davidsons had left her a little uneasy, but she did not like to say that she thought they had better not play cards when the Davidsons might come in at any moment. Dr. Macphail brought them and she watched him, though with a vague sense of guilt, while he laid out his patience. Below the sound of revelry continued.

It was fine enough next day, and the Macphails, condemned to spend a fortnight of idleness at Pago-Pago, set about making the best of things. They went down to the quay and got out of their boxes a number of books. The doctor called on the chief surgeon of the naval hospital and went round the beds with him. They left cards on the governor. They passed Miss Thompson on the road. The doctor took off his hat, and she gave him a "Good morning, doc," in a loud, cheerful voice. She was dressed as on the day before, in a white frock, and her shiny white boots with their high heels, her fat legs bulging over the tops of them, were strange things on that exotic scene.

"I don't think she's very suitably dressed, I must say," said Mrs. Macphail. "She looks extremely common to me."

When they got back to their house, she was on the verandah playing with one of the trader's dark children.

"Say a word to her," Dr. Macphail whispered to his wife. "She's all alone here, and it seems rather unkind to ignore her."

Mrs. Macphail was shy, but she was in the habit of doing what her husband bade her.

"I think we're fellow lodgers here," she said, rather foolishly.

"Terrible, ain't it, bein' cooped up in a one-horse burg like this?" answered Miss Thompson. "And they tell me I'm lucky to have gotten a room. I don't see myself livin' in a native house, and that's what some have to do. I don't know why they don't have a hotel."

They exchanged a few more words. Miss Thompson, loudvoiced and garrulous, was evidently quite willing to gossip, but Mrs. Macphail had a poor stock of small talk and presently she said:

"Well, I think we must go upstairs."

In the evening when they sat down to their high-tea Davidson on coming in said:

"I see that woman downstairs has a couple of sailors sitting there. I wonder how she's gotten acquainted with them."

"She can't be very particular," said Mrs. Davidson.

They were all rather tired after the idle, aimless day.

"If there's going to be a fortnight of this I don't know what we shall feel like at the end of it," said Dr. Macphail.

"The only thing to do is to portion out the day to different activities," answered the missionary. "I shall set aside a certain number of hours to study and a certain number to exercise, rain or fine—in the wet season you can't afford to pay any attention to the rain—and a certain number to recreation."

Dr. Macphail looked at his companion with misgiving. Davidson's programme oppressed him. They were eating Hamburger steak again. It seemed the only dish the cook knew how to make. Then below the gramophone began. Davidson started nervously when he heard it, but said nothing. Men's voices floated up. Miss Thompson's guests were joining in a well-known song and presently they heard her voice too, hoarse and loud. There was a good deal of shouting and laughing. The four people upstairs, trying to make conversation, listened despite themselves to the clink of glasses and the scrape of chairs. More people had evidently come. Miss Thompson was giving a party.

"I wonder how she gets them all in," said Mrs. Macphail, suddenly breaking into a medical conversation between the missionary and her husband.

It showed whither her thoughts were wandering. The twitch of Davidson's face proved that, though he spoke of scientific things, his mind was busy in the same direction. Suddenly, while the doctor was giving some experience of practice on the Flanders front, rather prosily, he sprang to his feet with a cry.

"What's the matter, Alfred?" asked Mrs. Davidson.

"Of course! It never occurred to me. She's out of Iwelei."

"She can't be."

"She came on board at Honolulu. It's obvious. And she's carrying on her trade here. Here."

He uttered the last word with a passion of indignation.

"What's Iwelei?" asked Mrs. Macphail.

He turned his gloomy eyes on her and his voice trembled with horror.

"The plague spot of Honolulu. The Red Light district. It was a blot on our civilization."

Iwelei was on the edge of the city. You went down side streets by the harbour, in the darkness, across a rickety bridge, till you came to a deserted road, all ruts and holes, and then suddenly you came out into the light. There was parking room for motors on each side of the road, and there were saloons, tawdry and bright, each one noisy with its mechanical piano, and there were barbers' shops and tobacconists. There was a stir in the air and a sense of expectant gaiety. You turned down a narrow alley, either to the right or to the left, for the road divided Iwelei into two parts, and you found yourself in the district. There were rows of little bungalows, trim and neatly painted in green, and the pathway between them was broad and straight. It was laid out like a garden-city. In its respectable regularity, its order and spruceness, it gave an impression of sardonic horror; for never can the search for love have been so systematized and ordered. The pathways were lit by a rare lamp, but they would have been dark except for the lights that came from the open windows of the bungalows. Men wandered about, looking at the women who sat at their windows, reading or sewing, for the most part taking no notice of the passers-by; and like the women they were of all nationalities. There were Americans, sailors from the ships in port, enlisted men off the gunboats, sombrely drunk, and soldiers from the regiments, white and black, quartered on the island; there were Japanese. walking in twos and threes; Hawaiians, Chinese in long robes, and Filipios in preposterous hats. They were silent and as it were oppressed. Desire is sad.

"It was the most crying scandal of the Pacific," exclaimed Davidson vehemently. "The missionaries had been agitating against it for years, and at last the local press took it up. The police refused to stir. You know their argument. They say that vice is inevitable and consequently the best thing is to localize and control it. The truth is, they were paid. Paid. They were paid by the saloon-keepers, paid by the bullies, paid by the women themselves. At last they were forced to move."

"I read about it in the papers that came on board in Honolulu," said Dr. Macphail.

"Iwelei, with its sin and shame, ceased to exist on the very day we arrived. The whole population was brought before the justices. I don't know why I didn't understand at once what that woman was."

"Now you come to speak of it," said Mrs. Macphail, "I remember seeing her come on board only a few minutes before the boat sailed. I remember thinking at the time she was cutting it rather fine."

"How dare she come here!" cried Davidson indignantly. "I'm not going to allow it."

He strode towards the door.

"What are you going to do?" asked Macphail.

"What do you expect me to do? I'm going to stop it. I'm not going to have this house turned into—into . . ."

He sought for a word that should not offend the ladies' ears. His eyes were flashing and his pale face was paler still in his emotion.

"It sounds as though there were three or four men down there," said the doctor. "Don't you think it's rather rash to go in just now?"

The missionary gave him a contemptuous look and without a word flung out of the room.

"You know Mr. Davidson very little if you think the fear of personal danger can stop him in the performance of his duty," said his wife.

She sat with her hands nervously clasped, a spot of colour on her high cheek bones, listening to what was about to happen below. They all listened. They heard him clatter down the wooden stairs and throw open the door. The singing stopped suddenly, but the gramophone continued to bray out its vulgar tune. They heard Davidson's voice and then the noise of something heavy falling. The music stopped. He had hurled the gramophone on the floor. Then again they heard Davidson's voice, they could not make out the words, then Miss Thompson's, loud and shrill, then a confused clamour as though several people were shouting together at the top of their lungs. Mrs. Davidson gave a little gasp, and she clenched her hands more tightly. Dr. Macphail looked uncertainly from her to his wife. He did not want to go down, but he wondered if they expected him to. Then there was something that sounded like a scuffle. The noise now was more distinct. It might be that Davidson was being thrown out of the room. The door was slammed. There was a moment's silence and they heard Davidson come up the stairs again. He went to his room.

"I think I'll go to him," said Mrs. Davidson.

She got up and went out.

"If you want me, just call," said Mrs. Macphail, and then when the other was gone: "I hope he isn't hurt."

"Why couldn't he mind his own business?" said Dr. Macphail.

They sat in silence for a minute or two and then they both started, for the gramophone began to play once more, defiantly, and mocking voices shouted hoarsely the words of an obscene song.

Next day Mrs. Davidson was pale and tired. She complained of headache, and she looked old and wizened. She told Mrs. Macphail that the missionary had not slept at all; he had passed the night in a state of frightful agitation and at five had got up and gone out. A glass of beer had been thrown over him and his clothes were stained and stinking. But a sombre fire glowed in Mrs. Davidson's eyes when she spoke of Miss Thompson.

"She'll bitterly rue the day when she flouted Mr. Davidson," she said. "Mr. Davidson has a wonderful heart and no one who is in trouble has ever gone to him without being comforted, but he has no mercy for sin, and when his righteous wrath is excited he's terrible."

"Why, what will he do?" asked Mrs. Macphail.

"I don't know, but I wouldn't stand in that creature's shoes for anything in the world."

Mrs. Macphail shuddered. There was something positively alarming in the triumphant assurance of the little woman's manner. They were going out together that morning, and they went down the stairs side by side. Miss Thompson's door was open, and they saw her in a bedraggled dressing-gown, cooking something in a chafing-dish.

"Good morning," she called. "Is Mr. Davidson better this morning?"

They passed her in silence, with their noses in the air, as if she did not exist. They flushed, however, when she burst into a shout of derisive laughter. Mrs. Davidson turned on her suddenly.

"Don't you dare to speak to me," she screamed. "If you insult me I shall have you turned out of here."

"Say, did I ask Mr. Davidson to visit with me?"

"Don't answer her," whispered Mrs. Macphail hurriedly.

They walked on till they were out of earshot.

"She's brazen, brazen," burst from Mrs. Davidson.

Her anger almost suffocated her.

And on their way home they met her strolling towards the quay. She had all her finery on. Her great white hat with its vulgar, showy flowers was an affront. She called out cheerily to them as she went by, and a couple of American sailors who were standing there grinned as the ladies set their faces to an icy stare. They got in just before the rain began to fall again.

"I guess she'll get her fine clothes spoilt," said Mrs. Davidson with a bitter sneer.

Davidson did not come in till they were half way through dinner. He was wet through, but he would not change. He sat, morose and silent, refusing to eat more than a mouthful, and he stared at the slanting rain. When Mrs. Davidson told him of their two encounters with Miss Thompson he did not answer. His deepening frown alone showed that he had heard.

"Don't you think we ought to make Mr. Horn turn her out of here?" asked Mrs. Davidson. "We can't allow her to insult us."

"There doesn't seem to be any other place for her to go," said Macphail.

"She can live with one of the natives."

"In weather like this a native hut must be a rather uncomfortable place to live in."

"I lived in one for years," said the missionary.

When the little native girl brought in the fried bananas which formed the sweet they had every day, Davidson turned to her.

"Ask Miss Thompson when it would be convenient for me to see her," he said.

The girl nodded shyly and went out.

"What do you want to see her for, Alfred?" asked his wife.

"It's my duty to see her. I won't act till I've given her every chance."

"You don't know what she is. She'll insult you."

"Let her insult me. Let her spit on me. She has an immortal soul, and I must do all that is in my power to save it."

Mrs. Davidson's ears rang still with the harlot's mocking laughter.

"She's gone too far."

"Too far for the mercy of God?" His eyes lit up suddenly and his voice grew mellow and soft. "Never. The sinner may be deeper in sin than the depth of hell itself, but the love of the Lord Jesus can reach him still."

The girl came back with the message.

"Miss Thompson's compliments and as long as Rev. Davidson don't come in business hours she'll be glad to see him any time."

The party received it in stony silence, and Dr. Macphail quickly effaced from his lips the smile which had come upon them. He knew his wife would be vexed with him if he found Miss Thompson's effrontery amusing.

They finished the meal in silence. When it was over the two ladies got up and took their work, Mrs. Macphail was making another of the innumerable comforters which she had turned out since the beginning of the war, and the doctor lit his pipe. But Davidson remained in his chair and with abstracted eyes stared at the table. At last he got up and without a word went out of the room. They heard him go down and they heard Miss Thompson's defiant "Come in" when he knocked at the door. He remained with her for an hour. And Dr. Macphail watched the rain. It was beginning to get on his nerves. It was not like our soft English rain that drops gently on the earth; it was unmerciful and somehow terrible; you felt in it the malignancy of the primitive powers of nature. It did not pour, it flowed. It was like a deluge from heaven, and it rattled on the roof of corrugated iron with a steady persistence that was maddening. It seemed to have a fury of its own. And sometimes you felt that you must scream if it did not stop, and then suddenly you felt powerless, as though your bones had suddenly become soft; and you were miserable and hopeless.

Macphail turned his head when the missionary came back. The two women looked up.

"I've given her every chance. I have exhorted her to repent. She is an evil woman."

He paused, and Dr. Macphail saw his eyes darken and his pale face grow hard and stern.

"Now I shall take the whips with which the Lord Jesus drove the usurers and the money changers out of the Temple of the Most High."

He walked up and down the room. His mouth was close set, and his black brows were frowning.

"If she fled to the uttermost parts of the earth I should pursue her."

With a sudden movement he turned round and strode out of the room. They heard him go downstairs again.

"What is he going to do?" asked Mrs. Macphail.

"I don't know." Mrs. Davidson took off her *pince-nez* and wiped them. "When he is on the Lord's work I never ask him questions."

She sighed a little.

"What is the matter?"

"He'll wear himself out. He doesn't know what it is to spare himself."

Dr. Macphail learnt the first results of the missionary's activity from the half-caste trader in whose house they lodged. He stopped the doctor when he passed the store and came out to speak to him on the stoop. His fat face was worried.

"The Rev. Davidson has been at me for letting Miss Thompson have a room here," he said, "but I didn't know what she was when I rented it to her. When people come and ask if I can rent them a room all I want to know is if they've the money to pay for it. And she paid me for hers a week in advance."

Dr. Macphail did not want to commit himself.

"When all's said and done it's your house. We're very much obliged to you for taking us in at all."

Horn looked at him doubtfully. He was not certain yet how definitely Macphail stood on the missionary's side,

"The missionaries are in with one another," he said, hesitatingly. "If they get it in for a trader he may just as well shut up his store and quit."

"Did he want you to turn her out?"

"No, he said so long as she behaved herself he couldn't ask me to do that. He said he wanted to be just to me. I promised she shouldn't have no more visitors. I've just been and told her."

"How did she take it?"

"She gave me Hell."

The trader squirmed in his old ducks. He had found Miss Thompson a rough customer.

"Oh, well, I daresay she'll get out. I don't suppose she wants to stay here if she can't have anyone in."

"There's nowhere she can go, only a native house, and no native'll take her now, not now that the missionaries have got their knife in her."

Dr. Macphail looked at the falling rain.

"Well, I don't suppose it's any good waiting for it to clear up."

In the evening when they sat in the parlour Davidson talked to them of his early days at college. He had had no means and had worked his way through by doing odd jobs during the vacations. There was silence downstairs. Miss Thompson was sitting in her little room alone. But suddenly the gramophone began to play. She had set it on in defiance, to cheat her loneliness, but there was no one to sing, and it had a melancholy note. It was like a cry for help. Davidson took no notice. He was in the middle of a long anecdote and without change of expression went on. The gramophone continued. Miss Thompson put on one reel after another. It looked as though the silence of the night were getting on her nerves. It was breathless and sultry. When the Macphails went to bed they could not sleep. They lay side by side with their eyes wide open, listening to the cruel singing of the mosquitoes outside their curtain.

"What's that?" whispered Mrs. Macphail at last.

They heard a voice, Davidson's voice, through the wooden partition. It went on with a monotonous, earnest insistence. He was praying aloud. He was praying for the soul of Miss Thompson.

Two or three days went by. Now when they passed Miss Thompson on the road she did not greet them with ironic cordiality or smile; she passed with her nose in the air, a sulky look on her painted face, frowning, as though she did not see them. The trader told Macphail that she had tried to get lodging elsewhere, but had failed. In the evening she played through the various reels of her gramophone, but the pretence of mirth was obvious now. The ragtime had a cracked, heartbroken rhythm as though it were a one-step of despair. When she began to play on Sunday Davidson sent Horn to beg her to stop at once since it was the Lord's day. The reel was taken off and the house was silent except for the steady pattering of the rain on the iron roof.

"I think she's getting a bit worked up," said the trader next day to Macphail. "She don't know what Mr. Davidson's up to and it makes her scared."

Macphail had caught a glimpse of her that morning and it struck him that her arrogant expression had changed. There was in her face a hunted look. The half-caste gave him a sidelong glance.

"I suppose you don't know what Mr. Davidson is doing about it?" he hazarded.

"No, I don't."

It was singular that Horn should ask him that question, for he also had the idea that the missionary was mysteriously at work. He had an impression that he was weaving a net around the woman, carefully, systematically, and suddenly, when everything was ready, would pull the strings tight.

"He told me to tell her," said the trader, "that if at any time she wanted him she only had to send and he'd come."

"What did she say when told her that?"

"She didn't say nothing. I didn't stop. I just said what he said I was to and then I beat it. I thought she might be going to start weepin'."

"I have no doubt the loneliness is getting on her nerves," said the doctor. "And the rain—that's enough to make anyone jumpy," he continued irritably. "Doesn't it ever stop in this confounded place?"

"It goes on pretty steady in the rainy season. We have three hundred inches in the year. You see, it's the shape of the bay. It seems to attract the rain from all over the Pacific."

"Damn the shape of the said the doctor.

He scratched his mosquito bites. He felt very short-tempered. When the rain stopped and the sun shone, it was like a hothouse, seething, humid, sultry, breathless, and you had a strange feeling that everything was growing with a savage violence. The natives, blithe and childlike by reputation, seemed then, with their tattooing and their dyed hair, to have something sinister in their appearance; and when they pattered along at your heels with their naked feet you looked back instinctively. You felt they might at any moment come behind you swiftly and thrust a long knife between your shoulder blades. You could not tell what dark thoughts lurked behind their wide-set eyes. They had a little the look of ancient Egyptians painted on a temple wall, and there was about them the terror of what is immeasurably old.

The missionary came and went. He was busy, but the Macphails did not know what he was doing. Horn told the doctor that he saw the governor every day, and once Davidson mentioned him.

"He looks as if he had plenty of determination," he said, "but when you come down to brass tacks he has no backbone."

"I suppose that means he won't do exactly what you want," suggested the doctor facetiously.

The missionary did not smile.

"I want him to do what's right. It shouldn't be necessary to persuade a man to do that."

"But there may be differences of opinion about what is right."

"If a man had a gangrenous foot would you have patience with anyone who hesitated to amputate it?"

"Gangrene is a matter of fact."

"And Evil?"

What Davidson had done soon appeared. The four of them had just finished their midday meal, and they had not yet separated for the siesta which the heat imposed on the ladies and on the doctor. Davidson had little patience with the slouthful habit. The door was suddenly flung open and Miss Thompson came in. She looked round the room and then went up to Davidson.

"You low-down skunk, what have you been saying about me to the governor?"

She was spluttering with rage. There was a moment's pause. Then the missionary draw forward a chair.

"Won't you be seated, Miss Thompson? I've been hoping to have another talk with you."

"You poor low-life bastard."

She burst into a torrent of insult, foul and insolent. Davidson kept his grave eyes on her.

"I'm indifferent to the abuse you think fit to heap on me, Miss Thompson," he said, "but I must beg you to remember that ladies are present."

Tears by now were struggling with her anger. Her face was red and swollen as though she were choking.

"What has happened?" asked Dr. Macphail.

"A feller's just been in here and he says I gotter beat it on the next boat."

Was there a gleam in the missionary's eyes? His face remained impassive.

"You could hardly expect the governor to let you stay here under the circumstances."

"You done it," she shrieked. "You can't kid me. You done it."

"I don't want to deceive you. I urged the governor to take the only possible step consistent with his obligations."

"Why couldn't you leave me be? I wasn't doin' you no harm."

"You may be sure that if you had I should be the last man to resent it."

"Do you think I want to stay on in this poor imitation of a burg? I don't look no busher, do I?"

"In that case I don't see what cause of complaint you have," he answered.

She gave an inarticulate cry of rage and flung out of the room. There was a short silence.

"It's a relief to know that the governor has acted at last," said Davidson finally. "He's a weak man and he shilly-shallied. He said she was only here for a fortnight anyway, and if she went on to Apia that was under British jurisdiction and had nothing to do with him."

The missionary sprang to his feet and strode across the room.

"It's terrible the way the men who are in authority seek to evade their responsibility. They speak as though evil that was out of sight ceased to be evil. The very existence of that woman is a scandal and it does not help matters to shift it to another of the islands. In the end I had to speak straight from the shoulder."

Davidson's brow lowered, and he protruded his firm chin. He looked fierce and determined.

"What do you mean by that?"

"Our mission is not entirely without influence at Washington. I pointed out to the governor that it wouldn't do him any good if there was a complaint about the way he managed things here."

"When has she got to go?" asked the doctor, after a pause.

"The San Francisco boat is due here from Sydney next Tuesday. She's to sail on that."

That was in five days' time. It was next day, when he was coming back from the hospital where for want of something better to do Macphail spent most of his mornings, that the half-caste stopped him as he was going upstairs.

"Excuse me, Dr. Macphail, Miss Thompson's sick. Will you have a look at her?"

"Certainly."

Horn led him to her room. She was sitting in a chair idly, neither reading nor sewing, staring in front of her. She wore her white dress and the large hat with the flowers on it. Macphail noticed that her skin was yellow and muddy under her powder, and her eyes were heavy.

"I'm sorry to hear you're not well," he said.

"Oh, I ain't sick really. I just said that, because I just had to see you. I've got to clear on a boat that's going to 'Frisco."

She looked at him and he saw that her eyes were suddenly startled. She opened and clenched her hands spasmodically. The trader stood at the door, listening.

"So I understand," said the doctor.

She gave a little gulp.

"I guess it ain't very convenient for me to go to 'Frisco just now. I went to see the governor yesterday afternoon, but I couldn't get to him. I saw the secretary, and he told me I'd got to take that boat and that was all there was to it. I just had to see the governor, so I waited outside his house this morning, and when he come out I spoke to him. He didn't want to speak to me, I'll say, but I wouldn't let him shake me off, and at last he said he hadn't no objection to my staying here till the next boat to Sydney if the Rev. Davidson will stand for it."

She stopped and looked at Dr. Macphail anxiously.

"I don't know exactly what I can do," he said.

"Well, I thought maybe you wouldn't mind asking him. I swear to God I won't start anything here if he'll just only let me stay. I won't go out of the house if that'll suit him. It's no more'n a fortnight."

"I'll ask him."

"He won't stand for it," said Horn. "He'll have you out on Tuesday, so you may as well make up your mind to it."

"Tell him I can get work in Sydney, straight stuff, I mean. 'Tain't asking very much."

"I'll do what I can."

"And come and tell me right away, will you? I can't set down to a thing till I get the dope one way or the other."

It was not an errand that much pleased the doctor, and, characteristically perhaps, he went about it indirectly. He told his wife what Miss Thompson had said to him and asked her to speak to Mrs. Davidson. The missionary's attitude seemed rather arbitrary and it could do no harm if the girl were allowed to stay in Pago-Pago another fortnight. But he was not prepared for the result of his diplomacy. The missionary came to him straightway.

"Mrs. Davidson tells me that Thompson has been speaking to you."

Dr. Macphail, thus directly tackled, had the shy man's resentment at being forced out into the open. He felt his temper rising, and he flushed.

"I don't see that it can make any difference if she goes to Sydney rather than to San Francisco, and so long as she promises to behave while she's here it's dashed hard to persecute her."

The missionary fixed him with his stern eyes.

"Why is she unwilling to go back to San Francisco?"

"I didn't enquire," answered the doctor with some asperity. "And I think one does better to mind one's own business."

Perhaps it was not a very tactful answer.

"The governor has ordered her to be deported by the first boat that leaves the island. He's only done his duty and I will not interfere. Her presence is a peril here."

"I think you're very harsh and tyrannical."

The two ladies looked up at the doctor with some alarm, but they need not have feared a quarrel, for the missionary smiled gently.

"I'm terribly sorry you should think that of me, Dr. Macphail. Believe me, my heart bleeds for that unfortunate woman, but I'm only trying to do my duty."

The doctor made no answer. He looked out of the window sullenly. For once it was not raining and across the bay you saw nestling among the trees the huts of a native village.

"I think I'll take advantage of the rain stopping to go out," he said.

"Please don't bear me malice because I can't accede to your wish," said Davidson, with a melancholy smile. "I respect you very much, doctor, and I should be sorry if you thought ill of me."

"I have no doubt you have a sufficiently good opinion of yourself to bear mine with equanimity," he retorted.

"That's one on me," chuckled Davidson.

When Dr. Macphail, vexed with himself because he had been uncivil to no purpose, went downstairs, Miss Thompson was waiting for him with her door ajar.

"Well," she said, "have you spoken to him?"

"Yes, I'm sorry, he won't do anything," he answered, not looking at her in his embarrassment.

But then he gave her a quick glance, for a sob broke from her. He saw that her face was white with fear. It gave him a shock of dismay. And suddenly he had an idea.

"But don't give up hope yet. I think it's a shame the way they're treating you and I'm going to see the governor myself."

"Now?"

He nodded. Her face brightened.

"Say, that's real good of you. I'm sure he'll let me stay if you speak for me. I just won't do a thing I didn't ought all the time I'm here."

Dr. Macphail hardly knew why he had made up his mind to appeal to the governor. He was perfectly indifferent to Miss Thompson's affairs, but the missionary had irritated him, and with him temper was a smouldering thing. He found the governor at home. He was a large, handsome man, a sailor, with a grey toothbrush moustache; and he wore a spotless uniform of white drill.

"I've come to see you about a woman who's lodging in the same house as we are," he said. "Her name's Thompson."

"I guess I've heard nearly enough about her, Dr. Macphail," said the governor, smiling. "I've given her the order to get out next Tuesday and that's all I can do."

"I wanted to ask you if you couldn't stretch a point and let her stay here till the boat comes in from San Francisco so that she can go to Sydney. I will guarantee her good behaviour."

The governor continued to smile, but his eyes grew small and serious.

"I'd be very glad to oblige you, Dr. Macphail, but I've given the order and it must stand."

The doctor put the case as reasonably as he could, but now the governor ceased to smile at all. He listened sullenly, with averted gaze. Macphail saw that he was making no impression.

"I'm sorry to cause any lady inconvenience, but she'll have to sail on Tuesday and that's all there is to it."

"But what difference can it make?"

"Pardon me, doctor, but I don't feel called upon to explain my official actions except to the proper authorities."

Macphail looked at him shrewdly. He remembered Davidson's hint that he had used threats, and in the governor's attitude he read a singular embarrassment.

"Davidson's a damned busybody," he said hotly.

"Between ourselves, Dr. Macphail, I don't say that I have formed a very favourable opinion of Mr. Davidson, but I am bound to confess that he was within his rights in pointing out to me the danger that the presence of a woman of Miss Thompson's character was to a place like this where a number of enlisted men are stationed among a native population."

He got up and Dr. Macphail was obliged to do so too.

"I must ask you to excuse me. I have an engagement. Please give my respects to Mrs. Macphail."

The doctor left him crest-fallen. He knew that Miss Thompson would be waiting for him, and unwilling to tell her himself that he had failed, he went into the house by the back door and sneaked up the stairs as though he had something to hide.

At supper he was silent and ill-at-ease, but the missionary was jovial and animated. Dr. Macphail thought his eyes rested on him now and then with triumphant good-humour. It struck him suddenly that Davidson knew of his visit to the governor and of its ill success. But how on earth could he have heard of it? There was something sinister about the power of that man. After supper he saw Horn on the verandah and, as though to have a casual word with him, went out.

"She wants to know if you've seen the governor," the trader whispered.

"Yes. He wouldn't do anything. I'm awfully sorry, I can't do anything more."

"I knew he wouldn't. They daren't go against the missionaries."

"What are you talking about?" said Davidson affably, comming out to join them.

"I was just saying there was no chance of your getting over to Apia for at least another week," said the trader glibly.

He left them, and the two men returned into the parlour. Mr. Davidson devoted one hour after each meal to recreation. Presently a timid knock was heard at the door.

"Come in," said Mrs. Davidson, in her sharp voice.

The door was not opened. She got up and opened it. They saw Miss Thompson standing at the threshold. But the change in her appearance was extraordinary. This was no longer the flaunting hussy who had jeered at them in the road, but a broken, frightened woman. Her hair, as a rule so elaborately arranged, was tumbling untidily over her neck. She wore bedroom slippers and a skirt and blouse. They were unfresh and bedraggled. She stood at the door with the tears streaming down her face and did not dare to enter.

"What do you want?" said Mrs. Davidson harshly.

"May I speak to Mr. Davidson?" she said in a choking voice.

The missionary rose and went towards her.

"Come right in, Miss Thompson," he said in cordial tones. "What can I do for you?"

She entered the room.

"Say, I'm sorry for what I said to you the other day an' for—for everythin' else. I guess I was a bit lit up. I beg pardon."

"Oh, it was nothing. I guess my back's broad enough to bear a few hard words."

She stepped towards him with a movement that was horribly cringing.

"You've got me beat. I'm all in. You won't make me go back to 'Frisco?"

His genial manner vanished and his voice grew on a sudden hard and stern.

"Why don't you want to go back there?"

She cowered before him.

"I guess my people live there. I don't want them to see me like this. I'll go any where else you say."

"Why don't you want to go back to San Francisco?"

"I've told you."

He leaned forward, staring at her, and his great, shining eyes seemed to try to bore into her soul. He gave a sudden gasp.

"The penitentiary."

She screamed, and then she fell at his feet, clasping his legs.

"Don't send me back there. I swear to you before God I'll be a good woman. I'll give all this up."

She burst into a torrent of confused supplication and the tears coursed down her painted cheeks. He leaned over her and, lifting her face, forced her to look at him.

"Is that it, the penitentiary?"

"I beat it before they could get me," she gasped. "If the bulls grab me it's three years for mine."

He let go his hold of her and she fell in a heap on the floor, sobbing bitterly. Dr. Macphail stood up.

"This alters the whole thing," he said. "You can't make her go back when you know this. Give her another chance. She wants to turn over a new leaf."

"I'm going to give her the finest chance she's ever had. If she repents let her accept her punishment."

She misunderstood the words and looked up. There was a gleam of hope in her heavy eyes.

"You'll let me go?"

"No. You shall sail for San Francisco on Tuesday."

She gave a groan of horror and then burst into low, hoarse shrieks which sounded hardly human, and she beat her head passionately on the ground. Dr. Macphail sprang to her and lifted her up.

"Come on, you mustn't do that. You'd better go to your room and lie down. I'll get you something."

He raised her to her feet and partly dragging her, partly carrying her, got her downstairs. He was furious with Mrs. Davidson and with his wife because they made no effort to help. The half-caste was standing on the landing and with his assistance he managed to get her on the bed. She was moaning and crying. She was almost insensible. He gave her a hypodermic injection. He was hot and exhausted when he went upstairs again.

"I've got her to lie down."

The two women and Davidson were in the same positions as when he had left them. They could not have moved or spoken since he went.

"I was waiting for you," said Davidson, in a strange, distant voice. "I want you all to pray with me for the soul of our erring sister."

He took the Bible off a shelf, and sat down at the table at which they had supped. It had not been cleared, and he pushed the tea-pot out of the way. In a powerful voice, resonant and deep, he read to them the chapter in which is narrated the meeting of Jesus Christ with the woman taken in adultery.

"Now kneel with me and let us pray for the soul of our dear sister, Sadie Thompson."

He burst into a long, passionate prayer in which he implored God to have mercy on the sinful woman. Mrs. Macphail and Mrs. Davidson knelt with covered eyes. The doctor, taken by surprise, awkward and sheepish, knelt too. The missionary's prayer had a savage eloquence. He was extraordinarily moved, and as he spoke the tears ran down his cheeks. Outside, the pitiless rain fell, fell steadily, with a fierce malignity that was all too human.

At last he stopped. He paused for a moment and said: "We will now repeat the Lord's prayer."

They said it and then, following him, they rose from their knees. Mrs. Davidson's face was pale and restful. She was comforted and at peace, but the Macphails felt suddenly bashful. They did not know which way to look.

"I'll just go down and see how she is now," said Dr. Macphail.

When he knocked at her door it was opened for him by Horn. Miss Thompson was in a rocking-chair, sobbing quietly.

"What are you doing there?" exclaimed Macphail. "I told you to lie down."

"I can't lie down. I want to see Mr. Davidson."

"My poor child, what do you think is the good of it? You'll never move him."

"He said he'd come if I sent for him."

Macphail motioned to the trader.

"Go and fetch him."

He waited with her in silence while the trader went upstairs. Davidson came in.

"Excuse me for asking you to come here," she said, looking at him sombrely.

"I was expecting you to send for me. I knew the Lord would answer my prayer."

They stared at one another for a moment and then she looked away. She kept her eyes averted when she spoke.

"I've been a bad woman. I want to repent."

"Thank God! Thank God! He has heard our prayers."

He turned to the two men.

"Leave me alone with her. Tell Mrs. Davidson that our prayers have been answered."

They went out and closed the door behind them.

"Gee whizz," said the trader.

That night Dr. Macphail could not get to sleep till late, and when he heard the missionary come upstairs he looked at his watch. It was two o'clock. But even then he did not go to bed at once, for through the wooden partition that separated their rooms he heard him praying aloud, till he himself, exhausted, fell asleep.

When he saw him next morning he was surprised at his appearance. He was paler than ever, tired, but his eyes shone with an inhuman fire. It looked as though he were filled with an overwhelming joy.

"I want you to go down presently and see Sadie," he said. "I can't hope that her body is better, but her soul—her soul is transformed."

The doctor was feeling wan and nervous.

"You were with her very late last night," he said.

"Yes, she couldn't bear to have me leave her."

"You look as pleased as Punch," the doctor said irritably.

Davidson's eyes shone with ecstasy.

"A great mercy has been vouchsafed me. Last night I was privileged to bring a lost soul to the loving arms of Jesus."

Miss Thompson was again in the rocking-chair. The bed had not been made. The room was in disorder. She had not troubled to dress herself, but wore a dirty dressing-gown, and her hair was tied in a sluttish knot. She had given her face a dab with a wet towel, but it was all swollen and creased with crying. She looked a drab.

She raised her eyes dully when the doctor came in. She was cowed and broken.

"Where's Mr. Davidson?" she asked.

"He'll come presently if you want him," answered Macphail acidly. "I came here to see how you were."

"Oh, I guess I'm O. K. You needn't worry about that."

Have you had anything to eat?"

"Horn brought me some coffee."

She looked anxiously at the door.

"D'you think he'll come down soon? I feel as if it wasn't so terrible when he's with me."

"Are you still going on Tuesday?"

"Yes, he says I've got to go. Please tell him to come right along. You can't do me any good. He's the only one as can help me now."

"Very well," said Dr. Macphail.

During the next three days the missionary spent almost all his time with Sadie Thompson. He joined the others only to have his meals. Dr. Macphail noticed that he hardly ate.

"He's wearing himself out," said Mrs. Davidson pitifully. "He'll have a breakdown if he doesn't take care, but he won't spare himself."

She herself was white and pale. She told Mrs. Macphail that she had had no sleep. When the missionary came upstairs from Miss Thompson he prayed till he was exhausted, but even then he did not sleep for long. After an hour or two he got up and dressed himself, and went for a tramp along the bay. He had strange dreams.

"This morning he told me that he'd been dreaming about the mountains of Nebraska," said Mrs. Davidson.

"That's curious," said Dr. Macphail.

He remembered seeing them from the windows of the train when he crossed America. They were like huge mole-hills, rounded and smooth, and they rose from the plain abruptly. Dr. Macphail remembered how it struck him that they were like a woman's breasts.

Davidson's restlessness was intolerable even to himself. But he was buoyed up by a wonderful exhilaration. He was tearing out by the roots the last vestiges of sin that lurked in the hidden corners of that poor woman's heart. He read with her and prayed with her.

"It's wonderful," he said to them one day at supper. "It's a true re-birth. Her soul, which was black as night, is now pure and white like the new-fallen snow. I am humble and afraid. Her remorse for all her sins is beautiful. I am not worthy to touch the hem of her garment."

"Have you the heart to send her back to San Francisco?" said the doctor. "Three years in an American prison. I should have thought you might have saved her from that."

"Ah, but don't you see? It's necessary. Do you think my heart doesn't bleed for her? I love her as I love my wife and my sister. All the time that she is in prison I shall suffer all the pain that she suffers."

"Bunkum," cried the doctor impatiently.

"You don't understand because you're blind. She's sinned, and she must suffer. I know what she'll endure. She'll be starved and tortured and humiliated. I want her to accept the punishment of man as a sacrifice to God. I want her to accept it joyfully. She has an opportunity which is offered to very few of us. God is very good and very merciful."

Davidson's voice trembled with excitement. He could hardly articulate the words that tumbled passionately from his lips.

"All day I pray with her and when I leave her I pray again, I pray with all my might and main, so that Jesus may grant her this great mercy. I want to put in her heart the passionate desire to be punished so that at the end, even if I offered to let her go, she would refuse. I want her to feel that the bitter punishment of prison is the thank-offering that she places at the feet of our Blessed Lord, who gave his life for her."

The days passed slowly. The whole household, intent on the wretched, tortured woman downstairs, lived in a state of unnatural excitement. She was like a victim that was being prepared for the savage rites of a bloody idolatry. Her terror numbed her. She could not bear to let Davidson out of her sight; it was only when he was with her that she had courage, and she hung upon him with a slavish dependence. She cried a great deal, and she read the Bible, and prayed. Sometimes she was exhausted and apathetic. Then she did indeed look forward to her ordeal, for it seemed to offer an escape, direct and concrete, from the anguish she was enduring. She could not bear much longer the vague terrors which now assailed her. With her sins she had put aside all personal vanity, and she slopped about her room, unkempt and dishevelled, in her tawdry dressing gown. She had not taken off her night-dress for four days, nor put on stockings. Her room was littered and untidy. Meanwhile the rain fell with a cruel persistence. You felt that the heavens must at last be empty of water, but still it poured down, straight and heavy, with a maddening iteration, on the iron roof. Everything was damp and clammy. There was mildew on the walls and on the boots that stood on the floor. Through the sleepless nights the mosquitoes droned their angry chant.

"If it would only stop raining for a single day it wouldn't be so bad," said Dr. Macphail.

They all looked forward to the Tuesday when the boat for San Francisco was to arrive from Sydney. The strain was intolerable. So far as Dr. Macphail was concerned, his pity and his resentment were alike extinguished by his desire to be rid of the unfortunate woman. The inevitable must be accepted. He felt he would breathe more freely when the ship had sailed. Sadie Thompson was to be escorted on board by a clerk in the governor's office. This person called on the Monday evening and told Miss Thompson to be prepared at eleven in the morning. Davidson was with her.

"I'll see that everything is ready. I mean to come on board with her myself."

Miss Thompson did not speak.

When Dr. Macphail blew out his candle and crawled cautiously under his mosquito curtains, he gave a sigh of relief.

"Well, thank God that's over. By this time tomorrow she'll be gone."

"Mrs. Davidson will be glad too. She says he's wearing himself to a shadow," said Mrs. Macphail. "She's a different woman."

"Who?"

"Sadie. I should never have thought it possible. It makes one humble."

Dr. Macphail did not answer, and presently he fell asleep. He was tired out, and he slept more soundly than usual.

He was awakened in the morning by a hand placed on his arm, and, starting up, saw Horn by the side of his bed. The trader put his finger on his mouth to prevent any exclamation from Dr. Macphail and beckoned to him to come. As a rule he wore shabby ducks, but now he was barefoot and wore only the *lava-lava* of the natives. He looked suddenly savage, and Dr. Macphail, getting out of bed, saw that he was heavily tattooed. Horn made him a sign to come on to the verandah. Dr. Macphail got out of bed and follwed the trader out.

"Don't make a noise," he whispered. "You're wanted. Put on a coat and some shoes. Quick."

Dr. Macphail's first thought was that something had happened to Miss Thompson.

"What is it? Shall I bring my instruments?"

"Hurry, please, hurry."

Dr. Macphail crept back into the bedroom, put on a waterproof over his pyjamas, and a pair of rubber-soled shoes. He rejoined the trader, and together they tiptoed down the stairs. The door leading out to the road was open and at it were standing half a dozen natives.

"What is it?" repeated the doctor.

"Come along with me," said Horn.

He walked out and the doctor followed him. The natives came after them in a little bunch. They crossed the road and came on to the beach. The doctor saw a group of natives standing round some object at the water's edge. They hurried along, a couple of dozen yards perhaps, and the natives opened out as the doctor came up. The trader pushed him forwards. Then he saw, lying half in the water and half out, a dreadful object, the body of Davidson. Dr. Macphail bent down—he was not a man to lose his head in an emergency—and turned the body over. The throat was cut from ear to ear, and in the right hand was still the razor with which the deed was done.

"He's quite cold," said the doctor. "He must have been dead some time."

"One of the boys saw him lying there on his way to work just now and came and told me. Do you think he did it himself?"

"Yes. Someone ought to go for the police."

Horn said something in the native tongue, and two youths started off.

"We must leave him here till they come," said the doctor.

"They mustn't take him into my house. I won't have him in my house."

"You'll do what the authorities say," replied the doctor sharply. "In point of fact I expect they'll take him to the mortuary."

They stood waiting where they were. The trader took a cigarette from a fold in his *lava-lava* and gave one to Dr. Macphail. They smoked while they stared at the corpse. Dr. Macphail could not understand.

"Why do you think he did it?" asked Horn.

The doctor shrugged his shoulders. In a little while native police came along, under the charge of a marine, with a stretcher, and immediately afterwards a couple of naval officers and a naval doctor. They managed everything in a businesslike manner.

"What about the wife?" said one of the officers.

"Now that you've come I'll go back to the house and get some things on. I'll see that it's broken to her. She'd better not see him till he's been fixed up a little."

"I guess that's right," said the naval doctor.

When Dr. Macphail went back he found his wife nearly dressed.

"Mrs. Davidson's in a dreadful state about her husband," she said to him as soon as he appeared. "He hasn't been to bed all night. She heard him leave Miss Thompson's room at two, but he went out. If he's been walking about since then he'll be absolutely dead."

Dr. Macphail told her what had happened and asked her to break the news to Mrs. Davidson.

"But why did he do it?" she asked, horror-stricken.

"I don't know."

"But I can't. I can't."

"You must."

She gave him a frightened look and went out. He heard her go into Mrs. Davidson's room. He waited a minute to gather himself together and then began to shave and wash. When he was dressed he sat down on the bed and waited for his wife. At last she came.

"She wants to see him," she said.

"They've taken him to the mortuary. We'd better go down with her. How did she take it?"

"I think she's stunned. She didn't cry. But she's trembling like a leaf."

"We'd better go at once."

When they knocked at her door Mrs. Davidson came out. She was very pale, but dry-eyed. To the doctor she seemed unnaturally composed. No word was exchanged, and they set out in silence down the road. When they arrived at the mortuary Mrs. Davidson spoke.

"Let me go in and see him alone."

They stood aside. A native opened a door for her and closed it behind her. They sat down and waited. One or two white men came and talked to them in undertones. Dr. Macphail told them again what he knew of the tragedy. At last the door was quietly opened and Mrs. Davidson came out. Silence fell upon them.

"I'm ready to go back now," she said.

Her voice was hard and steady. Dr. Macphail could not understand the look in her eyes. Her pale face was very stern. They walked back slowly, never saying a word, and at last they came round the bend on the other side of which stood their house. Mrs. Davidson gave a gasp, and for a moment they stopped still. An incredible sound assaulted their ears. The gramophone which had been silent for so long was playing, playing ragtime loud and harsh.

"What's that?" cried Mrs. Macphail with horror.

"Let's go on," said Mrs. Davidson.

They walked up the steps and entered the hall. Miss Thompson was standing at her door, chatting with a sailor. A sudden change had taken place in her. She was no longer the cowed drudge of the last days. She was dressed in all her finery, in her white dress, with the high shiny boots over which her fat legs bulged in their cotton stockings; her hair was elaborately arranged; and she wore that enormous hat covered with gaudy flowers. Her face was painted, her eyebrows were boldly black, and her lips were scarlet. She held herself erect. She was the flaunting quean that they had known at first. As they came in she broke into a loud, jeering laugh; and then, when Mrs. Davidson involuntarily stopped, she collected the spittle in her mouth and spat. Mrs. Davidson cowered back, and two red spots rose suddenly to her cheeks. Then, covering her face with her hands, she broke away and ran quickly up the stairs. Dr. Macphail was outraged. He pushed past the woman into her room.

"What the devil are you doing?" he cried. "Stop that damned machine."

He went up to it and tore the record off. She turned on him.

"Say, doc, you can't do that stuff with me. What the hell are you doin' in my room?"

"What do you mean?" he cried. "What d'you mean?"

She gathered herself together. No one could describe the scorn of her expression or the contemptuous hatred she put into her answer.

"You men! You filthy, dirty pigs! You're all the same, all of you. Pigs! Pigs!"

Dr. Macphail gasped. He understood.

9

*

From *On a Chinese Screen*
(1922)

14
The Opium Den

On the stage it makes a very effective set. It is dimly lit. The room is low and squalid. In one corner a lamp burns mysteriously before a hideous image and incense fills the theatre with its exotic scent. A pig-tailed Chinaman wanders to and fro, aloof and saturnine, while on wretched pallets lie stupefied the victims of the drug. Now and then one of them breaks into frantic raving. There is a highly dramatic scene where some poor creature, unable to pay for the satisfaction of his craving, with prayers and curses begs the villainous proprietor for a pipe to still his anguish. I have read also in novels descriptions which made my blood run cold. And when I was taken to an opium den by a smooth-spoken Eurasian the narrow, winding stairway up which he led me prepared me sufficiently to receive the thrill I expected. I was introduced into a neat enough room, brightly lit, divided into cubicles the raised floor of which, covered with clean matting, formed a convenient couch. In one an elderly gentleman, with a grey head and very beautiful hands, was quietly reading a newspaper, with his long pipe by his side. In another two coolies were lying, with a pipe between them, which they alternately prepared and smoked. They were young men, of a hearty appearance, and they smiled at me in a friendly way. One of them offered me a smoke. In a third four men squatted over a chess-board, and a little further on a man was dandling a baby (the inscrutable Oriental has a passion for children) while the baby's mother, whom I took to be the landlord's wife, a plump, pleasant-faced woman, watched him with a broad smile on her lips. It was a cheerful spot, comfortable, home-like, and cosy. It reminded me somewhat of the little intimate beer-houses of Berlin where the tired working man could go in the evening and spend a peaceful hour. Fiction is stranger than fact.

23
God's Truth

Birch was the agent of the B. A. T. and he was stationed in a little town of the interior with streets which, after it had rained, were a foot deep in mud. Then you had to get right inside your cart to prevent yourself from being splashed from head to foot. The roadway, worn to pieces by the ceaseless traffic, was so full of holes that the breath was jolted out of your body as you jogged along at a foot pace. There were two or three streets of shops, but he knew by heart everything that was in them; and there were interminable winding alleys which presented a monotonous expanse of wall broken only by solid closed doors. These were the Chinese houses and they were as impenetrable to one of his colour as the life which surrounded him. He was very homesick. He had not spoken to a white man for three months.

His day's work was over. Since he had nothing else to do he went for the only walk there was. He went out of the city gate and strolled along the ragged road, with its deep ruts, into the country. The valley was bounded by wild, barren mountains and they seemed to shut him in. He felt immeasurably far away from civilisation. He knew he could not afford to surrender to that sense of utter loneliness which beset him, but it was more of an effort than usual to keep a stiff upper lip. He was very nearly at the end of his tether. Suddenly he saw a white man riding towards him on a pony. Behind came slowly a Chinese cart in which presumably were his belongings. Birch guessed at once that this was a missionary going down to one of the treaty-ports from his station further up country, and his heart leaped with joy. At last he would have some one to talk to. He hurried his steps. His lassitude left him. He was all alert. He was almost running when he came up to the rider.

The rider stopped and named a distant town.

"I am on my way down to take the train," he added.

"You'd better put up with me for the night. I haven't seen a white man for three months. There's lots of room at my place. B. A. T. you know."

"B. A. T.," said the rider. His face changed and his eyes, before friendly and smiling, grew hard. "I don't want to have anything to do with you."

He gave his pony a kick and started on, but Birch seized the bridle. He could not believe his ears.

"What do you mean?"

"I can't have anything to do with a man who trades in tobacco. Let go that bridle."

"But I've not spoken to a white man for three months."

"That's no business of mine. Let go that bridle."

He gave his pony another kick. His lips were obstinately set and he looked at Birch sternly. Then Birch lost his temper. He clung to the bridle as the pony moved on and began to curse the missionary. He hurled at him every term of abuse he could think of. He swore. He was horribly obscene. The missionary did not answer, but urged his pony on. Birch seized the missionary's leg and jerked it out of the stirrup; the missionary nearly fell off and he clung in a somewhat undignified fashion to the pony's mane. Then he half slipped, half tumbled to the ground. The cart had come up to them by now and stopped. The two Chinese who were sitting in it looked at the white men with indolent curiosity. The missionary was livid with rage.

"You've assaulted me. I'll have you fired for that."

"You can go to hell," said Birch. "I haven't seen a white man for three months and you won't even speak to me. Do you call yourself a Christian?"

"What is your name?"

"Birch is my name and be damned to you."

"I shall report you to your chief. Now stand back and let me get on my journey."

Birch clenched his hands.

"Get a move on or I'll break every bone in your body."

The missionary mounted, gave his pony a sharp cut with the whip, and cantered away. The Chinese cart lumbered slowly after. But when Birch was left alone his anger left him and a sob broke unwillingly from his lips. The barren mountains were less hard than the heart of man. He turned and walked slowly back to the little walled city.

38
The Philosopher

It was surprising to find so vast a city in a spot that seemed to me so remote. From its battlemented gate towards sunset you could see the snowy mountains of Tibet. It was so populous that you could walk at ease only on the walls and it took a rapid walker three hours to complete their circuit. There was no railway within a thousand miles and the river on which it stood was so shallow that only junks of light burden could safely navigate it. Five days in a sampan were needed to reach the Upper Yangtze. For an uneasy moment you asked yourself whether trains and steamships were as necessary to the conduct of life as we who use them every day consider; for here, a million persons throve, married, begat their kind, and died; here a million persons were busily occupied with commerce, art, and thought.

And here lived a philosopher of repute the desire to see whom had been to me one of the incentives of a somewhat arduous journey. He was the greatest authority in China on the Confucian learning. He was said to speak English and German with facility. He had been for many years secretary to one of the Empress Dowager's greatest viceroys, but he lived now in retirement. On certain days in the week, however, all through the year he opened his doors to such as sought after knowledge, and discoursed on the teaching of Confucius. He had a body of disciples, but it was small, since the students for the most part preferred to his modest dwelling and his severe exhortations the sumptuous buildings of the foreign university and the useful science of the barbarians: with him this was mentioned only to be scornfully dismissed. From all I heard of him I concluded that he was a man of character.

When I announced my wish to meet this distinguished person my host immediately offered to arrange a meeting; but the days passed and nothing happened. I made enquiries and my host shrugged his shoulders.

"I sent him a chit and told him to come along," he said. "I don't know why he hasn't turned up. He's a cross-grained old fellow."

I did not think it was proper to approach a philosopher in so cavalier a fashion and I was hardly surprised that he had ignored a summons such as this. I caused a letter to be sent asking in the politest terms I could devise whether he would allow me to call upon him and within two hours received an answer making an appointment for the following morning at ten o'clock.

I was carried in a chair. The way seemed interminable. I went through crowded streets and through streets deserted till I came at last to one, silent and empty, in which at a small door in a long white wall my bearers set down my chair. One of them knocked, and after a considerable time a judas was opened; dark eyes looked through; there was a brief colloquy; and finally I was admitted. A youth, pallid of face, wizened, and poorly dressed, motioned me to follow him. I did not know if he was a servant or a pupil of the great man. I passed through a shabby yard and was led into a long low room sparsely furnished with an American roll-top desk, a couple of black-wood chairs and two little Chinese tables. Against the walls were shelves on which were a great number of books: most of them, of course, were Chinese, but there were many, philosophical and scientific works, in English, French and German; and there were hundreds of unbound copies of learned reviews. Where books did not take up the wall space hung scrolls on which in various calligraphies were written, I suppose, Confucian quotations. There was no carpet on the floor. It was a cold, bare, and comfortless chamber. Its sombreness was relieved only by a yellow chrysanthemum which stood by itself on the desk in a long vase.

I waited for some time and the youth who had shown me in brought a pot of tea, two cups, and a tin of Virginian cigarettes. As he went out the philosopher entered. I hastened to express my sense of the honour he did me in allowing me to visit him. He waved me to a chair and poured out the tea.

"I am flattered that you wished to see me," he returned. "Your countrymen deal only with coolies and with compradores; they think every Chinese must be one or the other."

I ventured to protest. But I had not caught his point. He leaned back in his chair and looked at me with an expression of mockery.

"They think they have but to beckon and we must come."

I saw then that my friend's unfortunate communication still rankled. I did not quite know how to reply. I murmured something complimentary.

He was an old man, tall, with a thin grey queue, and bright large eyes under which were heavy bags. His teeth were broken and discoloured. He was exceedingly thin, and his hands, fine and small, were withered and claw-like. I had been told that he was an opium-smoker. He was very shabbily dressed in a black gown, a little black cap, both much the worse for wear, and dark grey trousers gartered at the ankle. He was watching. He did not quite know what attitude to take up, and he had the manner of a man who was on his guard. Of course the philosopher occupies a royal place among those who concern themselves with the things of the spirit and we have the authority of Benjamin Disraeli that royalty must be treated with abundant flattery. I seized my trowel. Presently I was conscious of a certain relaxation in his demeanour. He was like a man who was all set and rigid to have his photograph taken, but hearing the shutter click lets himself go and eases into his natural self. He showed me his books.

"I took the Ph. D. in Berlin, you know," he said. "And afterwards I studied for some time in Oxford. But the English, if you will allow me to say so, have no great aptitude for philosophy."

Though he put the remark apologetically it was evident that he was not displeased to say a slightly disagreeable thing.

"We have had philosophers who have not been without influence in the world of thought," I suggested.

"Hume and Berkeley? The philosophers who taught at Oxford when I was there were anxious not to offend their theological colleagues. They would not follow their thought to its logical consequences in case they should jeopardise their position in university society."

"Have you studied the modern developments of philosophy in America?" I asked.

"Are you speaking of Pragmatism? It is the last refuge of those who want to believe the incredible. I have more use for American petroleum than for American philosophy."

His judgments were tart. We sat down once more and drank another cup of tea. He began to talk with fluency. He spoke a somewhat formal but an idiomatic English. Now and then he helped himself out with a German phrase. So far as it was possible for a man of that stubborn character to be influenced he had been influenced by Germany. The method and the industry of the Germans had deeply impressed him and their philosophical acumen was patent to him when a laborious professor published in a learned magazine an essay on one of his own writings.

"I have written twenty books," he said. "And that is the only notice that has ever been taken of me in a European publication."

But his study of Western philosophy had only served in the end to satisfy him that wisdom after all was to be found within the limits of the Confucian canon. He accepted its philosophy with conviction. It answered the needs of his spirit with a completeness which made all foreign learning seem vain. I was interested in this because it bore out an opinion of mine that philosophy is an affair of character rather than of logic: the philosopher believes not according to evidence, but according to his own temperament; and his thinking merely serves to make reasonable what his instinct regards as true. If Confucianism gained so firm a hold on the Chinese it is because it explained and expressed them as no other system of thought could do.

My host lit a cigarette. His voice at first had been thin and tired, but as he grew interested in what he said it gained volume. He talked vehemently. There was in him none of the repose of the sage. He was a polemist and a fighter. He loathed the modern cry for individualism. For him society was the unit, and the family the foundation of society. He upheld the old China and the old school, monarchy, and the rigid canon of Confucius. He grew violent and bitter as he spoke of the students, fresh from foreign universities, who with sacrilegious hands tore down the oldest civilisation in the world.

"But you, do you know what you are doing?" he exclaimed. "What is the reason for which you deem yourselves our betters? Have you excelled us in arts or letters? Have our thinkers been less profound than yours? Has our civilisation been less elaborate, less complicated, less refined than yours? Why, when you lived in caves and clothed yourselves with skins we were a cultured people. Do you know that we tried an experiment which is unique in the history of the world? We sought to rule this great country not by force, but by wisdom. And for centuries we succeeded. Then why does the white man despise the yellow? Shall I tell you? Because he has invented the machine gun. That is your superiority. We are a defenceless horde and you can blow us into eternity. You have shattered the dream of our philosophers that the world could be governed by the power of law and order. And now you are teaching our young men your secret. You have thrust your hideous inventions upon us. Do you not know that we have a genius for mechanics? Do you not know that there are in this country four hundred millions of the most practical and industrious people in the world? Do you think it will take us long to learn? And what will become of your superiority when the yellow man can make as good guns as the white and fire them as straight? You have appealed to the machine gun and by the machine gun shall you be judged."

But at that moment we were interrupted. A little girl came softly in and nestled close up to the old gentleman. She stared at me with curious eyes. He told me that she was his youngest child. He put his arms round her and with a murmur of caressing words kissed her fondly. She wore a black coat and trousers that barely reached her ankles, and she had a long pig-tail hanging down her back. She was born on the day the revolution was brought to a successful issue by the abdication of the emperor.

"I thought she heralded the Spring of a new era," he said. "She was but the last flower of this great nation's Fall."

From a drawer in his roll-top desk he took a few cash, and handing them to her, sent her away.

"You see that I wear a queue," he said, taking it in his hands. "It is a symbol. I am the last representative of the old China."

He talked to me, more gently now, of how philosophers in long past days wandered from state to state with their disciples, teaching all who were worthy to learn. Kings called them to their councils and made them rulers of cities. His erudition was great and his eloquent phrases gave a multi-coloured vitality to the incidents he related to me of the history of his country. I could not help thinking him a somewhat pathetic figure. He felt in himself the capacity to administer the state, but there was no king to entrust him with office; he had vast stores of learning which he was eager to impart to the great band of students that his soul hankered after, and there came to listen but a few, wretched, half-starved, and obtuse provincials.

Once or twice discretion had made me suggest that I should take my leave, but he had been unwilling to let me go. Now at last I was obliged to. I rose. He held my hand.

"I should like to give you something as a recollection of your visit to the last philosopher in China, but I am a poor man and I do not know what I can give you that would be worthy of your acceptance."

I protested that the recollection of my visit was in itself a priceless gift. He smiled.

"Men have short memories in these degenerate days, and I should like to give you something more substantial. I would give you one of my books, but you cannot read Chinese."

He looked at me with an amicable perplexity. I had an inspiration.

"Give me a sample of your calligraphy," I said.

"Would you like that?" He smiled. "In my youth I was considered to wield the brush in a manner that was not entirely despicable."

He sat down at his desk, took a fair sheet of paper, and placed it before him. He poured a few drops of water on a stone, rubbed the ink stick in it, and took his brush. With a free movement of the arm he began to write. And as I watched him I remembered with not a little amusement something else which had been told me of him. It appeared that the old gentleman, whenever he could scrape a little money together, spent it wantonly in the streets inhabited by ladies to describe whom a euphemism is generally used. His eldest son, a person of standing in the city, was vexed and humiliated by the scandal of this behaviour; and only his strong sense of filial duty prevented him from reproaching the libertine with severity. I daresay that to a son such looseness would be disconcerting, but the student of human nature could look upon it with equanimity. Philosophers are apt to elaborate their theories in the study, forming conclusions upon life which they know only at second hand, and it has seemed to me often that their works would have a more definite significance if they had exposed themselves to the vicissitudes which befall the common run of men. I was prepared to regard the old gentleman's dalliance in hidden places with leniency. Perhaps he sought but to elucidate the most inscrutable of human illusions.

He finished. To dry the ink he scattered a little ash on the paper and rising handed it to me.

"What have you written?" I asked.

I thought there was a slightly malicious gleam in his eyes.

"I have ventured to offer you two little poems of my own."

"I did not know you were a poet."

"When China was still an uncivilised country," he retorted with sarcasm, "all educated men could write verse at least with elegance."

I took the paper and looked at the Chinese characters. They made an agreeable pattern upon it.

"Won't you also give me a translation?"

"*Tradutore—tradittore*," he answered. "You cannot expect me to betray myself. Ask one of your English friends. Those who know most about China know nothing, but you will at least find one who is competent to give you a rendering of a few rough and simple lines."

I bade him farewell, and with great politeness he showed me to my chair. When I had the opportunity I gave the poems to a sinologue of my acquaintance, and here is the version he made.[1]

I confess that, doubtless unreasonably, I was somewhat taken aback when I read it.

> *You loved me not: your voice was sweet;*
> *Your eyes were full of laughter; your hands were tender.*
> *And then you loved me: your voice was bitter;*
> *Your eyes were full of tears; your hands were cruel.*
> *Sad, sad that love should make you*
> *Unlovable.*

———

> *I craved the years would quickly pass*
> *That you might lose*
> *The brightness of your eyes, the peach-bloom of your skin,*
> *And all the cruel splendour of your youth.*

Then I alone would love you
And you at last would care.
The envious years have passed full soon
And you have lost
The brightness of your eyes, the peach-bloom of your skin,
And all the charming splendour of your youth.
Alas, I do not love you
And I care not if you care.

[1] I owe it to the kindness of my friend Mr. P. W. Davidson.

56
The Vice-Consul

His bearers set down his chair in the yamen and unfastened the apron which protected him from the pouring rain. He put out his head, like a bird looking out of its nest, and then his long thin body and finally his thin long legs. He stood for a moment as if he did not quite know what to do with himself. He was a very young man and his long limbs with their ungainliness somehow added to the callowness of his air. His round face (his head looked too small for the length of his body) with its fresh complexion was quite boyish, and his pleasant brown eyes were ingenuous and candid. The sense of importance which his official position gave him (it was not long since he had been no more than a student-interpreter) struggled with his native shyness. He gave his card to the judge's secretary and was led by him into an inner court and asked to sit down. It was cold and draughty and the vice-consul was glad of his heavy waterproof. A ragged attendant brought tea and cigarettes. The secretary, an emaciated youth in a very shabby black gown, had been a student at Harvard and was glad to show off his fluent English.

Then the judge came in, and the vice-consul stood up. The judge was a portly gentleman in heavily wadded clothes, with a large smiling face and gold-rimmed spectacles. They sat down and sipped their tea and smoked American cigarettes. They chatted affably. The judge spoke no English, but the vice-consul's Chinese was fresh in his mind and he could not help thinking that he acquitted himself creditably. Presently an attendant appeared and said a few words to the judge, and the judge very courteously asked the vice-consul if he was ready for the business which had brought him. The door into the outer court was thrown open and the judge, walking through, took his place on a large seat at a table that stood at the top of the steps. He did not smile now. He had assumed instinctively the gravity proper to his office and in his walk, notwithstanding his obesity, there was an impressive dignity. The vice-consul, obeying a polite gesture, took a seat by his side. The secretary stood at the end of the table. Then the outer gateway was flung wide (it seemed to the vice-consul that there was nothing so dramatic as the opening of a door) and quickly, with an odd sort of flurry, the criminal walked in. He walked to the centre of the courtyard and stood still, facing his judge. On each side of him walked a soldier in khaki. He was a young man and the vice-consul thought that he could be no older than himself. He wore only a pair of cotton trousers and a cotton singlet. They were faded but clean. He was bare-headed and bare-foot. He looked no different from any of the thousands of coolies in their monotonous blue that you passed every day in the crowded streets of the city. The judge and the criminal faced one another in silence. The vice-consul looked at the criminal's face, but then he looked down quickly: he did not want to see what was there to be seen so plainly. He felt suddenly embarrassed. And looking down he noticed how small the man's feet were, shapely and slender; his hands were tied behind his back. He was slightly built, of the middle height, a lissome creature that suggested the wild animal, and standing on those beautiful feet of his there was in his carriage a peculiar grace. But the vice-consul's eyes were drawn back unwillingly to the oval, smooth, and unlined face. It was livid. The vice-consul had often read of faces that were green with terror and he had thought it but a fanciful expression, and here he saw it. It startled him. It made him feel ashamed. And in the eyes too, eyes that did not slant as the Chinese eye is wrongly supposed always to do, but were straight, in the eyes that seemed unnaturally large and bright, fixed on those of the judge, was a terror that was horrible to see. But when the judge put him a question—trial and sentence were over and he had been brought there that morning only for purposes of identification—he answered in a loud plain voice, boldly. However his body might betray him he was still master of his will. The judge gave a brief order, and, flanked by his two soldiers, the man marched out. The judge and the vice-consul rose and walked to the gateway, where their chairs awaited them. Here stood the criminal with his guard. Notwithstanding his tied hands he smoked a cigarette. A little squad of soldiers had been sheltering themselves under the over-hanging roof, and on the appearance of the judge the officer in charge made them form up. The judge and the vice-consul settled themselves in their chairs. The officer gave an order and the squad stepped out. A cou-ple of yards behind them walked the criminal. Then came the judge in his chair and finally the vice-consul.

They went quickly through the busy streets and the shopkeepers gave the procession an incurious stare. The wind was cold and the rain fell steadily. The criminal in his cotton singlet must have been wet through. He walked with a firm step, his head held high, jauntily almost. It was some distance from the judge's yamen to the city wall and to cover it took them nearly half an hour. Then they came to the city gate and went through it. Four men in ragged blue—they looked like peasants—were standing against the wall by the side of a poor coffin, rough hewn and unpainted. The criminal gave it a glance as he passed by. The judge and the vice-consul dismounted from their chairs and the officer halted his soldiers. The rice fields began at the city wall. The criminal was led to a pathway between two patches and told to kneel down. But the offi-cer did not think the spot suitable. He told the man to rise. He walked a yard or two and knelt down again. A soldier was detached from the squad and took up his position behind the prisoner, three feet from him perhaps; he raised his gun; the officer gave the word of command; he fired. The criminal fell forward and he moved a little, convulsively. The officer went up to him, and seeing that he was not quite dead emptied two barrels of his revolver into the body. Then he formed up his soldiers once more. The judge gave the vice-consul a smile, but it was a grimace rather than a smile; it distorted painfully that fat good-humoured face.

They stepped into their chairs; but at the city gate their ways parted; the judge bowed the vice-consul a courteous farewell. The vice-consul was carried back towards the consulate through the streets, crowded and tortuous, where life was going on just as usual. And as he went along quickly, for the consular bearers were fine fellows, his mind distracted a little by their constant shouts to make way, he thought how terrible it was to make an end of life deliberately: it seemed an immense responsibility to destroy what was the result of innumerable generations. The human race has existed so long and each one of us is here as the result of an infinite series of miraculous events. But at the same time, puzzling him, he had a sense of the triviality of life. One more or less mattered so little. But just as he reached the consulate he looked at his watch, he had no idea it was so late, and he told the bearers to take him to the club. It was time for a cocktail and by heaven he could do with one. A dozen men were standing at the bar when he went in. They knew on what errand he had been that morning.

"Well," they said, "did you see the blighter shot?"

"You bet I did," he said, in a loud and casual voice.

"Everything go off all right?"

"He wriggled a bit." He turned to the bartender. "Same as usual, John."

BIBLIOGRAPHY

Behrman, S. N. "W. Somerset Maugham." *People in a Diary: A Memoir.* Boston: Little, Brown, 1972. Pp. 276–312.

Burgess, Anthony. Introduction to *Maugham's Malaysian Stories.* Hong Kong: Heinemann Asia, 1969. Pp. vi–xvii.

Calder, Robert. *W. Somerset Maugham and the Quest for Freedom.* Garden City, New York: Doubleday, 1973.

Calder, Robert. *Willie: The Life of W. Somerset Maugham.* New York: St. Martin's, 1989.

Connon, Bryan. *Somerset and the Maugham Dynasty.* London: Sinclair-Stevenson, 1997.

Coward, Noël L., *Diaries.* Ed. Graham Payn and Sheridan Morley. Boston: Little, Brown, 1982.

Curtis, Anthony. *The Pattern of Maugham.* London: Hamish Hamilton, 1974.

Curtis, Anthony. *Somerset Maugham.* New York: Macmillan, 1977.

Curtis, Anthony and John Whitehead, eds. *W. Somerset Maugham: The Critical Heritage.* London: Routledge & Kegan Paul, 1987.

Epstein, Joseph. "Is It All Right to Read Somerset Maugham?" *Partial Payments.* New York: Norton, 1989. Pp. 185–209.

Fleming, Ann. *Letters*. Ed. Mark Amory. London: Collins, 1985.

Greene, Graham. "Some Notes on Somerset Maugham." *Collected Essays.* New York: Viking, 1979. Pp. 197–205.

Isherwood, Christopher. *Diaries: Volume One, 1939–1960.* Ed. Katherine Bucknell. New York: HarperCollins, 1997.

Jeffreys-Jones, Rhodri, "Maugham in Russia." *American Espionage: From Secret Service to CIA.* New York: Free Press, 1977. Pp. 87–101, 233–235.

Kanin, Garson. *Remembering Mr. Maugham.* Foreword by Noël Coward. London: Hamish Hamilton, 1966.

King, Francis. *Yesterday Came Suddenly.* London: Constable, 1993.

Mander, Raymond and Joe Mitchenson. *Theatrical Companion to Maugham.* London: Rockliff, 1955.

Maugham, Frederic. "Early Days." *At the End of the Day.* Westport, Conn.: Heinemann, 1951. Pp. 3–21.

Maugham, Robin. *Somerset and All the Maughams.* 1966; London: Penguin, 1975.

Maugham, Robin. *Escape from the Shadows: An Autobiography.* New York: McGraw-Hill, 1972.

Maugham, Robin. *Conversations with Willie.* New York: Simon & Schuster, 1978.

Morgan, Ted. *Maugham.* New York: Simon & Schuster, 1980.

Pfeiffer, Karl. *W. Somerset Maugham: A Candid Portrait.* Introduction by Jerome Weidman. New York: Norton, 1959.

Powell, Anthony. "Somerset Maugham." *Under Review: Further Writings on Writers, 1946–1989.* Pp. 290–295.

Raphael, Frederic. *Somerset Maugham and His World.* New York: Scribners, 1976.

Rothschild, Loren and Deborah Whiteman, eds. *William Somerset Maugham: A Catalogue of the Loren and Frances Rothschild Collection.* Los Angeles: Heritage Book Shop, 2001.

Sotheby's. *Catalogue of the Collection of Impressionist and Modern Pictures Formed by W. Somerset Maugham.* London: Sotheby's, April 10, 1962.

Stott, Raymond Toole. *A Bibliography of the Works of W. Somerset Maugham.* Edmonton: University of Alberta Press, 1973.

Swan, Michael. "Conversations with Maugham." *Ilex and Olive: An Account of a Journey Through France and Italy.* London: Home & Van Thal, 1949. Pp. 67–76.

Vidal, Gore. "Maugham's Half & Half." *United States: Essays, 1952–1972.* New York: Random House, 1993. Pp. 228–250.

Waugh, Alec. "W. Somerset Maugham: RIP." *My Brother Evelyn and Other Profiles.* New York: Farrar, Straus & Giroux, 1990.

Wescott, Glenway. *Continual Lessons: The Journals of Glenway Wescott, 1937–1955.* Ed. Robert Phelps. New York: Farrar, Straus & Giroux, 1990.

Whitehead, John. *Maugham: A Reappraisal.* London: Vision, 1987.

Wilson, Angus. *Introduction to* A Maugham Twelve. London: Heinemann, 1966. Pp. vii–x.